GOLDEN FILLY

Books by
Lauraine Snelling

Golden Fill Collection One*
Golden Filly Collection Two*

Secret Refuge (3 in 1)

DAKOTA TREASURES
Ruby • *Pearl*
Opal • *Amethyst*

DAUGHTERS OF BLESSING
A Promise for Ellie • *Sophie's Dilemma*
A Touch of Grace • *Rebecca's Reward*

HOME TO BLESSING
A Measure of Mercy
No Distance Too Far

RED RIVER OF THE NORTH
An Untamed Land
A New Day Rising
A Land to Call Home
The Reaper's Song
Tender Mercies
Blessing in Disguise

RETURN TO RED RIVER
A Dream to Follow • *Believing the Dream*
More Than a Dream

*5 books in each volume

LAURAINE SNELLING

GOLDEN FILLY

COLLECTION 2

BETHANYHOUSE
PUBLISHERS

Golden Filly: Collection Two
Copyright © 1993, 1994, 1995
Lauraine Snelling

Previously published in five separate volumes:
  Shadow Over San Mateo Copyright © 1993
  Out of the Mist Copyright © 1993
  Second Wind Copyright © 1994
  Close Call Copyright © 1994
  The Winner's Circle Copyright © 1995

Cover design by Dan Pitts
Cover photography by Lauri Wade Higdon

Published by Bethany House Publishers
11400 Hampshire Avenue South
Bloomington, Minnesota 55438

Bethany House Publishers is a division of
Baker Publishing Group, Grand Rapids, Michigan.

Printed in the United States of America by
Bethany Press International, Bloomington, MN
November 2009, 2nd printing

ISBN 978-0-7642-0738-9

Library of Congress publication data is available for this title.

ABOUT THE AUTHOR

LAURAINE SNELLING is an award-winning author of over sixty books, fiction and nonfiction for adults and young adults. Her books have sold over two million copies. Besides writing books and articles, she teaches at writers' conferences across the country. She and her husband, Wayne, have two grown sons, a basset named Chewy, and a cockatiel watch bird named Bidley. They make their home in California.

EDITOR'S NOTE

Originally published in the early 1990s, these books reflect the cultural and social aspects of that time. In order to maintain the integrity of the story, we opted not to impose today's styles, technologies, laws, or other advancements upon the characters and events within. We believe the themes of love of God, love of family, and love of horses are timeless and can be enjoyed no matter the setting.

SHADOW OVER SAN MATEO

BOOK SIX

To Carolyne Mozel's
fifth and sixth grade class of 1992–1993.
What a super bunch of kids—top readers,
excellent writers, and just plain fun.

Chapter
01

Just get through the ceremonies. Get through the ceremonies. Tricia Evanston hung on to her brother's words as the waves of applause rolled from the stands and across the track infield. Trish and her Thoroughbred Spitfire had just won the famed Belmont Classic, the third diamond in the Triple Crown. Trish was the first woman jockey to win the honor.

But none of it mattered now. Not the trophies, not the applause, not the money. Unknown to her during the race, Trish's father had died at the hospital just before the race of her life began. When she didn't see him in the crowd, a nod from her brother confirmed her worst fears.

Just get through. Don't think. Don't feel. Get through.

Trish responded to the media as they clamored for her attention. She waved and smiled. And smiled some more. Her jaw felt like it would crack from the strain. Tears flowed freely down her cheeks.

She didn't dare look at her brother, David, and just leaned on the arm he had clamped around her. Spitfire stood at attention, ears forward, as the syndicate owners lined the shallow brick risers behind them. The blanket of white carnations covered the horse's withers and up onto his neck. When the cameras flashed again, he blew on Trish's neck, then nudged David.

Patrick O'Hern, their trainer and friend, clenched Spitfire's reins with one hand and Trish's shoulder with the other. "Easy, lass," he whispered.

Trish could hear him murmuring. She bit her lip until the sticky-sweet taste of blood nearly made her gag. Patrick's voice had that same soothing song her father's had; the song that calmed horses and riders—and now broke her heart.

Trish brought her mind back to the moment through sheer force of will. Now they would go up for the trophies. The biggest, shiniest engraved bowl was for the winner's owner—Hal Evanston. Only he wasn't there. He would never be there again. Trish clamped her teeth tighter.

"I'll take him now, lass." Patrick loosened Trish's fingers from Spitfire's reins. He handed her the racing saddle and nodded toward the scales. As the trainer led the colt away, David and Hal's long-time friend Adam Finley gripped Trish's arms and led her to the scale.

Trish weighed in and then strode between the two men up the broad brick steps to the podium. Hands reached out to shake hers. "Thank you . . . yes, thank you." The words came stilted, mechanical.

"And now, ladies and gentlemen, the moment we've been waiting for. . . ." Jim McKay, famous Thoroughbred-racing announcer, shook her hand. "Tricia Evanston, at sixteen, is not only the first female to win the Triple Crown, but the youngest ever to win it. You put on quite a show, young lady."

"Thank you" was all Trish could say.

"As you know, folks, this win is a family affair. Spitfire, bred and raised by Hal Evanston of Runnin' On Farm, is now the official winner of this year's Belmont Cup—" he paused for a moment "—accepted by his son, David Evanston." Trish could see the fleeting question on the man's face.

David stepped forward. "Thank you." He leaned into the microphone. "My father would be very proud of this honor. We all thank you." He raised the ornate silver Tiffany bowl in the air and smiled to the crowd.

Her teeth were clamped so tightly, it was almost impossible to smile, but Trish managed somehow. Just as McKay started to present her trophy, someone whispered in his ear.

Trish dashed the tears away. She *had* to be able to speak into the microphone—now!

"Ladies and gentlemen," McKay said, then paused. "I have an announcement to make." He paused again. A hush fell over the stands. "Ah-h-h . . ." He cleared his throat. The pain in his voice was obvious. "Fifteen minutes ago . . . about the time the horses broke from the gate . . . Hal Evanston died at the hospital. That is why . . . his son is here in his place to accept the trophy. Racing has lost a fine and generous man." He bowed his head, then looked to Trish and David. "Our hearts go out to you, Trish, David."

Sobs racked Trish's shoulders. She heard David blowing into his handkerchief. A baby wailed somewhere in the crowd. To honor Hal, the red-coated bugler stepped out onto the track and raised the long brass horn to his mouth. The clear notes of "Taps" lifted on the breeze and echoed across the infield to bounce back from the trees on the far side. The final notes seemed to hang on the air before fading away.

Trish stepped to the microphone. "We did it, Dad." Her voice broke. She took a deep breath. "You—we—we won—the Triple Crown. I love you." She waved to the crowd, which broke out in thunderous applause. With David at one side and Adam on the other, Trish turned and left the podium area. Security officers held back insensitive reporters as they shouted questions. Strobe lights flashed.

Trish concentrated on putting one foot in front of the other. *Down the stairs,* her mind prodded. *Follow the dirt back into the tunnel under the stands.* They turned left and exited through a door into the entrance area.

"There's a limo waiting outside," Trish heard someone say.

"Martha, you go with them, I'll take care of the questions," Adam said to his wife. He gave Trish and David a hug before he turned to the reporters.

Martha took his place, and with three men in front and more on each side, they passed through the crowd like the prow of a boat parting the sea; out the door and down the blue canopy-covered walk. Hanging baskets of geraniums passed in a pink blur.

Trish sank into the seat of the limo as though she were weighted down by the sorrow of the whole world. After the door slammed shut, she rubbed her face into David's shirt, and finally let the tears come. "He can't be gone, he can't." She thrashed from side to side, trying to wipe away the agony.

With her arms around her brother's chest, she could feel the heaving of his own sobs.

"I can't believe it either," David cried into her hair.

Martha Finley handed them each a tissue and rubbed Trish's back.

The limo slowed and stopped at the emergency entrance to the hospital.

Trish looked up. The windows blurred, and she wiped her eyes again. It was like looking through glass sheeted with rain. She leaned her head against the back of the seat and closed her eyes.

The man in the three-piece suit who had been sitting across from them passed her his handkerchief. Trish blew her nose and mopped her eyes—again. When she opened them, she saw her mother opening the side door.

"Oh, Mom!" Trish scrambled from the car and flung herself into Marge's arms. When David stepped out, the three clung together like lone survivors in a raging sea.

"I want to see Dad." Trish drew back. "I have to, Mom."

Marge nodded. With her arms around the waists of her children, she guided them to the second-floor room where Hal lay in the bed as if he were asleep. Trish had seen him like that many times before. Her mother had always said, "Go ahead, wake him. He wants you to." But this time, Trish knew there was no waking him.

She sank into a chair by the bed and picked up her father's hand. She smoothed the back of it with her fingertips. "He looks so peaceful." Trish caught her breath, as if waiting for him to breathe. She felt her mother's hand on her shoulder and leaned her cheek against it.

"He's even smiling—sort of." The quiet of the room seeped into Trish, surrounded her. She laid Hal's hand back on the white blanket. "I love you, Dad," she whispered. "I love you." Her tears fell unchecked and soaked the sheet. Somewhere in the depths of her mind and heart, Trish heard her father's voice again, just as she'd heard it at the track: *I have fought the good fight, Tee. I have won my race. I love you.* "Oh, Dad, I need you."

Trish felt as if she were swimming in her own tears. When she lifted her head, the heavy weight she'd felt in the limo washed over her again.

She tried to stand but her legs were like rubber. David caught her before she crumpled. Trish leaned against him and felt her mother support her other side. When Trish gained her footing, the three started toward the door. They turned together and with one voice said, "Good-bye."

In the hall, a woman waited with Martha Finley. She introduced herself. "I'm Chaplain Saunders. If you'd like, we can talk in the chapel. It's right this way."

Adam Finley met them halfway. He put his arm around Marge's shoulder. "Whatever we can do for you—"

Marge nodded. "We're going to the chapel now."

Trish's eyes and nose were still a fountain, but her mouth felt like a desert. She stopped for a drink of water.

The afternoon sun, streaming through a stained-glass window, bathed the chapel in soothing blues and greens. Trish still felt weak as she collapsed onto a padded chair. Martha Finley pressed a glass of water into her hand, and she smiled her thanks.

"N-now what?" Trish forced herself to straighten up in the chair and look at the chaplain.

"Your father's body will be taken to a funeral home and prepared for the flight to Portland. Someone will have to make the flight arrangements . . ."

"I will take care of that," Adam offered without hesitation.

"And you'll need to choose a casket . . ."

"I can help you with that," Martha volunteered.

Trish watched her mother collapse, weeping, into David's arms. No matter how much she wanted to, Trish didn't have the strength to reach them. She felt as if she were floating above them, watching all that went on. They couldn't be discussing her father, not *her* dad. Surely he was down at the barn, or at home, or—she felt a shudder that started at her toes and worked its way up to the top of her head. She huddled down in the chair, clamped her teeth again, this time to stop the shaking.

"Trish? Trish!" The voice seemed to come from far away.

She tried to take another sip of water, but the glass fell from her hands and bounced on the brown tweed carpet.

"Trish, put your head between your knees." She heard the voice and at the same time felt a hand pushing her head down. Then a blanket was gently wrapped around her shoulders.

All of a sudden Trish threw back the blanket and leaped to her feet. Marge started after her, but a nurse met Trish in the hall and after one look at her face steered her to a rest room. A cool hand supported Trish's head and a strong arm held her middle as she threw up into the toilet bowl.

When the worst was over the nurse handed her a wet washcloth. "Better now?" Trish nodded and wiped her face.

"I can't go back in there," she whispered. The tears started again.

"Come with me." Her arm around Trish's shoulders, the nurse gently led her to an empty room with an open window, and held her while she cried.

"It's not fair," Trish heard herself saying.

"No, dear, it's not." The nurse brushed the damp hair from Trish's cheek. "Your father was a fine man. And he was so proud of you."

"You knew him?"

"Oh yes. Hal was a favorite around here, even for the short time he was with us. You know, nurses really appreciate a patient who is grateful for their help." She smoothed Trish's hair again. "Why, his faith just lit up the room. We all felt it every time we walked in there."

Trish looked up to see tears glistening in the nurse's eyes. "Yeah, he was like that." Trish bit her lip and sniffed. "I didn't get to say good-bye—or anything." She dropped her forehead to the nurse's shoulder. "I didn't want my dad to die."

"I know. None of us did." The nurse reached over and pulled tissues from a box.

Trish felt hot, then cold. *God, how can I live without him?* she thought.

"Trish?" David came into the room. "We're ready to go now, okay?"

Trish nodded, and squeezed the nurse's hand. "Thanks" was all she could manage.

Marge was talking with a doctor when David and Trish returned to the chapel.

"I can give you some sleeping pills, tranquilizers," the doctor was saying. "It might make these next hours easier."

Trish shrugged and shook her head when the doctor looked at her. "They can't bring my father back."

"No, thank you," Marge said softly. "We'll be all right." She took the arms of her children and stepped into the hall.

Reporters were swarming around the door outside. "What will be done with Spitfire? Is he finished racing?"

Adam Finley spoke for the others. "Spitfire will be shipped to BlueMist Farms in Kentucky as soon as possible. That's all I can tell you now."

As that announcement crashed into her consciousness, Trish felt the last shred of hope being torn away.

Chapter
02

"Trish, you knew Spitfire was going to Kentucky," David whispered in her ear.

"I know." Trish climbed into the limo and huddled next to her mother. She wrapped both arms around herself to try to stop the shaking.

"Just a minute." Adam stepped back out of the car and spoke with one of the security officers. The man left and within a few minutes returned with several hospital blankets. Marge took them and gratefully wrapped two around her daughter.

A gray fog stole into Trish's head. As the warmth of the blankets and her mother's arms cradled her limp body, she felt herself floating again. When they reached the hotel, Trish barely felt the carpet beneath her feet as Adam Finley helped her to the room. Martha spoke softly while she helped her with her boots and silks.

Trish forced her eyes open when she heard her mother's voice. "Sleep, Tee. Jesus loves you, and so do I."

Trish barely nodded. "Me too, Mom." She wanted to ask a question but the fog hung too thick.

A raging thirst woke Trish hours later. When she tried to stand, the room whirled and she sat down again. She fumbled with the switch on the bedside lamp. The wings of the wood-carved eagle glistened in the soft light on her nightstand. The figure had been her gift to her father for Christmas, to remind him of the promise of the Father bearing him up on eagles' wings. The sight of it was too much, and Trish shoved it onto a shelf at the back of the closet.

Reaching the bathroom, she grabbed a bunch of toilet paper and wiped her eyes again and blew her nose. If only her father were asleep in the next room. Pretending didn't work.

She chug-a-lugged a glass of water, then refilled it to take with her.

Noticing a light coming from the living room, Trish opened the door. Martha Finley sat knitting in a wing chair, her feet propped up on a hassock. Adam was asleep on the sofa, snoring softly.

"Oh, Trish, can I get you anything? A glass of orange juice, or something to eat?" The lamp cast a halo around the older woman's white hair.

"Where's Mom?"

"She's sleeping, I think. So is David. We'll be going to our room in a bit. I just wanted to be here in case you needed anything."

"Thanks. I'm okay." Trish thought her own voice sounded like a frog. Back in her room, she switched off the light and was asleep almost before her head hit the pillow.

Trish felt herself smiling before she opened her eyes the next morning. How incredibly wonderful . . . She and Spitfire had won the Belmont Stakes, the final jewel in the Triple Crown! Then the awful reality struck . . . Her father was *dead*.

Trish rolled over and smothered her cries in the pillow. "It's not fair!" She punched the pillow with her fists. Would her broken heart ever mend?

This can't be real; it's like a nightmare. The words echoed through her mind. She squeezed her eyes shut. *If only it were just a bad dream.*

She sat bolt-upright in bed. *Dad always said God was his strength—our strength. But we prayed. Why didn't you answer, God?* She leaped from the bed and jerked on her clothes. She didn't want to think about it anymore.

"That's it! No more crying!" she ordered the swollen and blotchy face she saw in the bathroom mirror. She held a cold wet washcloth to her eyes for a minute, but it didn't help the puffy eyelids. She sniffed again and swallowed hard. "No more!"

By the time Trish had unbraided, brushed, and rebraided her dark wavy hair, she felt she had her armor in place. She squeezed toothpaste onto the brush and methodically brushed her teeth. Maybe doing all the routines would get her back on track, but when she looked in the mirror again she nearly lost it.

"Trish?" Her mother knocked on the bathroom door. "Are you all right?"

"Uh . . . yeah, I'm okay." She opened the bathroom door, but couldn't face her mother. "I gotta go, Mom. I need to feed Spitfire—work him and stuff, you know. See you later." She ducked her head and bolted for the door.

At the car, she dug in her pockets. No keys. She couldn't go back up there. Feeling the weight of the entire planet on her shoulders, she leaned her forehead on the rim of the car roof.

"I'll drive," David said from behind her. He nudged her over so he could insert the key in the lock.

Trish felt like shoving him back, but what good would it do? She stomped around to the passenger's side and climbed in.

"Quit acting like a spoiled brat," David said in his most reasonable big-brother tone.

Trish stared at him. *How could you . . . ?* She bit her lip and tried not to let the dam burst again. *What are we doing? We never act like this.*

"Look, I know you're mad at God . . . and all the world." David's voice cracked. "Well, so am I." Trish could hardly hear him. He took a deep breath. "Let's just get through this day, Trish. Can we do that?"

No tears! her mind screamed. "Whatever." She stared straight ahead and wished she didn't have to get through this day or any other day.

The guard at the gate nodded them through. His usual smiling face was somber. When David parked by their barn, he leaned his forehead on his crossed hands on the steering wheel. After a bit he straightened and turned toward Trish. His eyes filled with tears. "I just can't believe it. I can't believe he's gone."

Trish clamped down on her lip again. She gritted her teeth and swallowed hard. "Yeah, I know." She opened the car door and leaped out. When she tried to whistle to Spitfire nothing came. *You can't whistle when you're drowning in tears.* The little voice inside she called her nagger seemed to chuckle with glee. It always seemed happiest when she was in trouble.

As she entered the long green and white barn, a reporter peeled himself off the wall and approached her. "Can I ask you a few questions, Trish? I know this is a terrible time for you, so I'll keep it short."

Trish stared at him, shock paralyzing her vocal cords. Had he lost his mind? How could she talk to anyone now?

He took her silence for agreement. "Do you know when the funeral will be?" Trish shook her head. "What will you do with Spitfire?" Trish shook her head again and pushed past him. "Will he go directly to stud? How about the Breeder's Cup? You said once you'd like to race him there. . . ."

"Get on with you now." Patrick shook a gnarled fist in the man's face. "I already answered all your questions. You be leaving the kids alone."

"Just doing my job." The man touched a finger to his forehead in a salute. "Trish?" He raised his voice. "I want you to know how sorry I am. Please accept my condolences. Your father was one in a million. We'll all miss him. . . ."

Trish buried her face in Spitfire's mane. *Be polite.* Nagger seemed to perch right on her shoulder.

"Thank you." She heard David's voice outside the stall. "We'll let you know what's going to happen with Spitfire as soon as we know ourselves."

"Okay, lass, let's get the old man saddled here so you can walk him nice and easy. He's got an awful lot of pep for running a mile and a half yesterday." Patrick handed Trish the bridle, then spread the saddle cloth and settled the saddle in place.

Trish slipped the headstall over Spitfire's nose, then ears, then buckled the chin strap, all in one easy, fluid motion. She didn't need her mind in gear to perform these tasks. Spitfire blew gently in her face a strand of her bangs. She stared into his eyes. No mischief this morning, only a gentle caring.

Trish rubbed up behind the horse's ears and underneath the headstall. "You're such a good fella," she whispered.

"They sense things." Patrick checked the girth again. "I don't know how, but horses—most animals—seem to know when something bad has happened. He's trying to tell you how much he cares, how much he loves you."

Trish nodded, and raised her knee to be boosted into the saddle. She didn't dare look at Patrick; the kindness in his voice was enough. *You will not cry again!* she commanded herself.

David snapped the lead shank in place and handed Trish her helmet. "Come on, fella." He stopped at the end of the barn. "Would you rather just walk him around in the barn here? A couple of turns would loosen him up. That's why the aisles are so wide, you know."

"I know." Trish gathered up her reins. "But I think being outside will be better. Maybe the wind will blow away some of my fuzziness."

"Hey, wait up."

Trish turned to look over her shoulder. Red Holloran, the young jockey she'd dated in Kentucky, jogged up the sandy stretch. She would recognize his red hair anywhere. Had he been around yesterday after the race? Trish couldn't be sure. The evening was a blur in her mind.

"Hi." He reached up to clasp her hand. "You okay?"

Trish ducked her head in a kind of nod. *If okay means I'm here and riding, yes, it fits. But how will I ever be really okay again?*

"I'm so sorry, Tee."

Trish squeezed Red's hand. "Yeah, me too." She looked beyond Spitfire's twitching ears. Out there all the world seemed so normal. People were laughing, someone was singing, and the cicadas were warming up for their daily concert from the elm trees. Spitfire took a deep breath and exhaled noisily.

"I could work the filly for you, if you'd like."

"That's okay," David answered for Trish. "Why don't you walk over with us. Then we can come back for Sarah's Pride while Trish is walking Spitfire."

"Sure. Or does Patrick need some help?"

Trish felt a warm spot in her middle. Red really cared, she could tell. She squeezed his hand again. All the way out to the track, her hand stayed warm.

Spitfire jogged sideways as soon as David released the lead. Ears forward, neck arched, he danced in place, then set out at an easy extended walk. Trish let her feet dangle below the iron stirrups. It would be so easy to let her mind wander, but even in her fuzzy state she knew better. That's the way accidents happened.

Later Trish realized she had spoken with people and gone through all the proper motions, even talking with a reporter who evaded the barriers put up by Patrick, David, and Red. But life seemed to be happening at the end of a long tunnel or the small end of a telescope. If she kept it all far enough away, she didn't hurt so much.

The meeting with Spitfire's syndicate owners was held back at the hotel about noon. Trish nodded and answered in all the right places. When the Shipsons discussed the barn and accommodations for Spitfire at BlueMist Farms, Trish agreed that everything sounded great. When Adam Finley talked about the horse van he'd reserved for the trip back to Kentucky, Trish nodded again. A van was a van, and even though they'd had an accident with one coming up on the New Jersey Turnpike, it wouldn't happen again, she was sure.

But inside Trish screamed *No! Let me take him home. I want Spitfire at Runnin' On Farm where he belongs. I need him there. He needs me. No one else can even ride him! Please, please, let me . . .* But just like keeping Sarah's Pride under control, Trish rode herself with a tight rein.

Even when Adam talked about the flight arrangements to take the family and Hal's body back to Vancouver, Trish stared straight ahead. She clenched her teeth to shut off the voices in her head. *Just get through this. Just get through.* She repeated the phrase again and again until it assumed its own beat, like a bass drum in a parade. *Just get through.*

But when Martha Finley reached over and took her hand, Trish almost lost control. She could feel the tears burn behind her eyes. She sniffed and took her hand back. *Just get through.*

"Are you coming, Tee?" Her mother laid a hand on Trish's shoulder.

"Uh—where?" Trish tried to shut off the inner cadence so she could answer.

"To the funeral home. We're going to pick out the casket."

Trish forced her legs to lift her body off the chair. How long had she been sitting there? She looked around the room. "Where's everyone?"

"They left a bit ago. Do you want some lunch first?"

Trish shook her head. "No, let's get it over with."

"You don't have to go if you don't want to." Marge put both hands on Trish's shoulders.

Trish really looked at her mother. Marge seemed to have lost weight; her face was pale and drawn. There were deep creases from her nose to the sides of her mouth. Did they all look like that? "I'll go."

On the drive over, Trish pulled herself back to the small end of the telescope. The woman at the funeral home spoke so softly Trish could hardly hear her. *Oh well, do I really want to hear her?*

They entered a large room that displayed a wide variety of caskets—blue, gray, brown, wood tones, metallic, burnished. *Just get through.* Trish felt like heaving. They couldn't put her father in a box like this. Not her father. He was so alive and real.

He's not alive anymore. Trish dug her fingernails into her fists.

"Don't you have a simple wooden box?" Marge asked. "That's what Hal wanted."

"Are you sure?" David looked at his mother, confusion written on his face.

"Yes, he and I—uh—we discussed these things a long time ago. I have all his suggestions, requests. He wanted to make it as easy for us as possible."

"You know . . ." The woman paused. "Yes, we do have some wooden caskets." She led them to another part of the room. There were several of plain wood. One had a cross burned in the cover.

"I'll take that one," Marge said firmly. After writing the check, she thanked the woman for her help, and they stepped out into the entryway where Adam and Martha were waiting for them.

"They'll have everything ready and at JFK airport by twelve-thirty," Adam said. "I talked with the director while you were downstairs. He assured me that there would be no difficulties."

"Thank you." David nodded as he reached to shake Adam's hand. Instead, the older man drew the younger into a hug.

16

Just get through. Trish slipped behind her mother. She could manage as long as no one touched her.

That night Trish was already in bed when Marge came in to talk with her. She sat down on the edge of the bed. "Is there any way I can help you, Tee?"

Trish shook her head. At least when she was asleep, she didn't have to think.

Marge reached over and smoothed a lock of hair behind her daughter's ear. Trish flinched.

"It'll be easier for all of us if we help each other. You know your dad wanted it that way." Marge waited. The silence stretched, broken only by a car horn honking on the street. "I know you're trying to tough this out, but crying does make things easier."

Trish could hear the tears in her mother's voice. She didn't dare look, for fear her own would break through.

Marge reached for a tissue. "Where's the eagle?"

"I put it away."

"Where?"

"In the closet." Trish felt Marge get up from the bed, then heard the closet door slide open. The eagle was on the top shelf. She knew her mother had picked it up. If she let herself, Trish could picture the light glinting off the intricately carved wings, but she pushed the image from her mind.

Marge sighed.

As her mother reached the door, Trish turned over and asked the question that had been plaguing her. "How come he died—right then, I mean."

"It was a massive hemorrhage in his lungs. The doctors tried . . . nothing helped. We were on our way out the door—to come to the track. . . ." Marge paused and blew her nose. "Just like that, he was gone."

Trish didn't answer. She couldn't. One tear squeezed out from between her clenched eyelids and slipped down her cheek.

Chapter

03

Trish woke feeling as if the world were crumbling around her. Today they would fly back to Portland. Homecoming was supposed to be a celebration. She and her best friend since kindergarten, Rhonda Seabolt, had talked about a huge party. There wouldn't be one now.

Trish forced herself to get up. No matter what, Spitfire needed to be worked. *Why?* Her little voice spoke softly for a change. *He won't be running again.*

"Just because," Trish muttered as she crammed her feet into her boots. "And Sarah's Pride will be running again. She needs lots of work."

David met her at the door. "You all packed?"

Trish shook her head. "I suppose you are."

"Yeah, I couldn't sleep."

Trish looked closely at her brother's face. He had the same look she'd seen in her own mirror. While David tried to be strong for her, she knew he was hurting too.

At least the reporters had backed off. Trish found herself watching for them so she could run the other way. She also caught herself looking for a certain red-headed young man.

"Lookin' for anyone in particular?" Patrick grabbed for his hat as Spitfire tried to flip it off.

Trish could feel her neck get warm at Patrick's teasing. "Come on, horse, let's get going here. Quit goofing around."

Spitfire rubbed his forehead against Trish's chest, nearly knocking her over. When she ignored his plea he blew grain saliva in her face.

"Okay, okay. I get the hint." Trish scratched under his headstall and along the top of his neck under his mane. When she turned to a familiar voice at the door, the colt draped his head across her shoulder, his favorite position.

"You want me to work Sarah's Pride so you can get done quicker?" Red asked.

"No, that's okay." Trish could feel her face getting warm again. Would she *never* quit blushing when Red was around? "What I mean is—" She looked to David for help. He'd disappeared. She could hear him talking to the filly in the next stall. "I mean, ahhh . . . thanks. We'd appreciate that."

Red seemed to sense her unwillingness to talk as he rode beside her around the track. Sarah's Pride kept him pretty busy. She still fought her rider, always wanting to run when another horse came by.

"Keep your mind on what you're doing," Red ordered the fractious filly as he pulled her down to a walk again. "You just can't seem to understand *jog*, can you?" The horse shook its head.

Trish felt a small grin turn up the corners of her mouth. If only they could ride like this forever. Their return to the barn came much too quickly.

"I'll see you on Friday night then?" Trish studied her boot rather than look Patrick in the face.

"How about Saturday morning? You'll be gettin' in too late to make a stop by here."

"Yeah, I keep forgetting the time change." She drew circles in the sand with her boot. "Ahhh, take good care of him, okay?"

Patrick nodded. "You needn't worry. Red here will work the girl, and Spitfire and I can walk for miles round and round."

"Come on, Trish," David interrupted. "We gotta get going."

Trish rubbed Spitfire's nose one more time. "See ya, fella." The colt nickered as she followed David down the aisle. Red fell into step beside her. He took her hand and squeezed it.

Their footsteps lagged.

"I'll still be here when you get back, you know."

"Really? I thought maybe Patrick was making that up." Trish felt a little flutter of what could only be called joy. "I thought—I hoped—I, uh, thought I'd see you in Kentucky at least."

"I'm riding back in your van, if that's okay with you."

"Okay? That's great. But aren't you missing out on a lot of mounts?"

Red shrugged. "There'll be others. Being with you is more important right now."

Trish felt the now familiar burning behind her eyes. "Thanks." The word croaked around the lump stuck in her throat.

David already had the car running when they caught up to him.

"See you Saturday then?" Trish chewed her lip.

When Red put both arms around her, Trish leaned against him. "I wish I could help you, Tee." His breath stirred the wisps of hair around her ear.

Trish couldn't answer. The lump was still there. *What can I say, anyway? No one can help.* She wrapped both arms around his waist in answer. Her internal drum started thumping again. *Just get through.*

Red lifted her chin with one finger so his lips could find hers. The kiss was gentle, soft.

Trish pulled away. "Sorry." She swallowed other words she wanted to say. *Please understand.* How could she tell Red that she couldn't handle nice-and-gentle right now? Not and get through. Instead, she squeezed his hand and turned to fumble with the door handle of the car.

With one hand on her shoulder as if to hold her to him, Red opened the door with his right. Trish felt a second kiss on her ear as she slipped into the car.

"Take care now." Red gently closed the car door and thumped on the glass.

As they drove away, Trish forced herself not to look back. Even so, one tear sneaked by her control and slid down her cheek. She felt David's gaze when he stopped for a red light. But instead of answering his unspoken question, she huddled tighter in the corner. So many good-byes.

Trish worked her way back to the small end of the telescope as she packed her suitcase. When she cleaned off the closet shelf, she saw that the eagle was gone.

"Mom . . ." She started to ask what happened to it, but stopped herself. *Who cares? It's just a wooden bird.*

Trish slept most of the flight home, mumbling a refusal when the flight attendant asked her food preference. She vaguely heard her mother do the same. Thanks to a half-full flight, Trish was able to lie down.

"Approaching Portland International." The pilot's voice worked like an alarm.

Trish sat up, clutching the gray blanket around her shoulders. David had stretched out too, and was still asleep.

"Have we passed Mount Hood?" Trish asked. She felt too groggy to crawl over to the window seat to look out.

Marge raised her head from her hand and nodded. Trish could tell she'd been crying again. Pain for her mother briefly replaced her own. How would any of them manage without her father? She closed her mind against the thought of the days, months, and years ahead.

When the seat belt light went off, Trish pulled one bag from under the seat and waited for David to retrieve another from the overhead bins. Adam and Martha Finley led the way off the plane.

Staggering up the ramp, Trish caught a glimpse of Rhonda. Brad Williams, the other member of the four musketeers, was right behind her. *Their faces must mirror my own,* she thought. Sad, afraid to smile. For her it was the fear she'd never smile again.

"Oh, Trish," Rhonda whispered as she hugged her friend. "I can't believe this has really happened. Are you okay?" Rhonda wiped her tears away with the heels of her hands. "I can't seem to quit crying."

Trish just nodded as she felt her friends' arms wrap around her. Brad had included David in the community hug. *What's to say? What does okay mean anymore?* She felt the tears coming and pulled away. Closeness to anyone always brought the tears on. And if she started crying, she was afraid she'd never stop.

"Please, I . . ."

Rhonda studied Trish's face and nodded. They were the kind of friends who didn't need to finish sentences.

The pain hit Trish afresh. Theirs was like the relationship she'd had with her father. He'd been able to read her mind too. Was everything going to remind her of him? She felt as if she were running through a maze with no way out.

Brad slung Trish's pack over his shoulder and Rhonda picked up Trish's sports bag. She dropped it again to blow her nose.

"Come on," Brad said to Trish. "The van's in the short-term lot. David, if you want to head down for the rest of your luggage, we'll bring the van around. You coming, Tee?"

Trish turned to her mother and the Finleys. Marge nodded. "Adam, Martha, meet Brad Williams and Rhonda Seabolt. They're like our own kids." Turning to the young people, she said, "Kids, I know you've heard of the Finleys. They've helped us beyond measure."

Adam shook Brad's hand. "Glad to meet you. We'll pick up our car, then, and follow you."

Trish watched as if from the other end of her telescope. It all seemed so pointless. She followed her friends, not really joining in on the conversation but making the right responses. Still, the drive from the parking lot to the baggage claim was silent. Trish stared out the window. It had started to rain. *How appropriate.*

Trish kept her distance for the next two days. The funeral would be on Thursday. The only time it seemed bearable was when she was down at the barn. Her nearly year-old filly, Miss Tee, took some time to adjust to Trish's return.

"You've grown so much." Trish stroked the little filly's ears. "You're not really a baby anymore." She smoothed the golden mane that was turning from brush to full length. Miss Tee sniffed Trish's hair and nibbled at her fingers. Trish dug in her pocket for another carrot. "Here; all you want are treats. We're gonna have to start working with you pretty soon. Has Brad been leading you around?" The filly shook her head and sniffed for another carrot.

Trish rubbed the tender spot between the filly's ears. She leaned on the fence and watched four-month-old Double Diamond race across the field. At the filly's snort, Trish released the halter and smiled as her namesake dashed after the colt and kicked up her heels. They really looked good, both of them. It seemed as if she'd been away from home for years, not intermittent weeks. She'd been gone most of May and half of June.

When Trish wandered out in the field where the racing stock pastured, she nearly lost it with old gray Dan'l. He trotted up as soon as she whistled, nickering his welcome and rubbing his forehead on her chest. He'd been her track tutor for the last few years, hers and most of the young stock. They used the old race horse to help train the new racers. He always set a calm example on the three-quarter-mile track at the farm and in the starting gates.

Trish scratched his cheek and fed him another carrot. At least with the horses she didn't have to try to talk. Even with all the guests coming and going, the house seemed empty. If only she could pretend that her father was at the hospital as he'd been for those weeks last fall. But it was easier not to think about him at all. Not to look for him in the next stall. Not to remember his funny whistle as he worked with the horses. Not to—she fiercely shut her mind down again. It was like slamming a heavy truck door, one that had to stay shut.

Rhonda and Brad dropped by after school. Trish levered herself off her bed and dogtailed Rhonda back to the kitchen, where Martha Finley had baked chocolate chip cookies. The four teenagers took theirs back into the living room, where Adam had a fire going to chase the chill of a drizzly, windy afternoon.

"It's my California blood," he said, warming his backside in front of the blaze. "I don't do well in this dampness."

Trish crumbled her cookie and stared into the leaping flames. Talking took too much effort.

"We miss you at school," Rhonda ventured.

"Mmmm."

"*I* miss you."

Trish turned her head to look at Rhonda. "Me too."

"You coming back for finals?"

"I guess."

Brad and Rhonda left soon after that. They and their families would join everyone at church for the memorial service.

That evening, Trish heard her mother on the phone with her grandparents in Florida.

"Why don't you come out later this summer instead?" Marge said. "Then we can really have some time together. You know how I feel about traveling long distances to attend funerals."

Marge listened for a while. "But, Mother . . . No, please, stay there and come when Daddy is feeling better. Yes, I'll call you soon. No, I'm as good as can be expected, I guess. God will get me through this. I can sense Him taking care of all of us."

Trish snorted and shook her head. She wanted to shake her mother. God was taking care of them? Right!

Wednesday afternoon, Pastor Mort found Trish down in the barn cleaning tack. Everything had gotten dusty while they'd been gone, so she set to work. It helped when there was something to do. The only other way to forget was to sleep. Pastor Mort sat down beside her on a bale of straw.

Trish greeted him with a nod, and kept on rubbing the saddle seat. She scrubbed her rag in the can of saddle soap and began another circle.

"I'll get right to the point, Trish. It would help if you would talk about both your father *and* your feelings. Your mother says you've pretty much walled yourself away from everyone."

Trish didn't flinch, her eyes riveted on the saddle. Her hand trembled a bit as she turned the leather to work on the other side. The silence between the two deepened, stretching like a rubber band pulled taut and about to snap.

Then Pastor Mort picked up a rag and dipped it in the saddle soap. He started on the bridle on the floor between them, rubbing the leather in smooth strokes.

Trish looked at him in surprise.

He smiled. "I had horses when I was young. You never forget how to clean tack." The rubber band relaxed.

Trish felt her shoulders slump. She hadn't realized how tense she was. If he didn't leave soon . . . She bit her lip till the pain forced back the tears.

"Trish, I know how much you hurt inside. You and your dad had a really special relationship. Anyone could see that. And I know you must be so angry you want to tear things up." His voice floated through the telescope, encouraging Trish to close up the distance and talk with him.

"That's one of the problems with our society. We never allow people to grieve. I know you've all been grieving for a long time—a prolonged illness causes that in a family. Now you feel like God has let you down entirely; am I right?"

"He did!" The words exploded from the deep canyon of Trish's heart. She clamped her teeth on her lip, knowing if she said any more she'd fly apart into a million pieces and no one would ever be able to put her back together.

"It may seem that way, Trish. And I don't have any easy answers for you either. All I can say is that in spite of what we think and feel, God is in control. He loves us more than we can imagine, and promises to get us through times just like this."

Trish glared at the bald spot on the man's head as he bent over to smear more soap on his rag. *Another one of His promises? God doesn't live up to His promises,* she wanted to scream. "My dad said something like . . ." The pain tore into her subconscious mind and clamped off her words. She could not think about her dad, about all the things he had said and taught her.

She took a deep breath, but thought she would choke on the lump in her throat. "Whatever . . ." she croaked, and the fury she felt was stuffed down further than ever.

The next day, Trish awoke promising herself she would not cry at the funeral. That was after she'd punched and turned her damp pillow a few times. The tears she dammed up during the day spilled over at night.

She spent as much time as she dared down with the horses. David finally came and got her. "You're going to be late."

Trish glared at him. Swallowing her *Who cares?* she followed him back to the house. After jerking a brush through her hair and changing clothes, she joined her mother and the Finleys as they walked silently out to the waiting cars.

The silence enfolded Trish as she huddled in the backseat. *Sixteen-year-old kids shouldn't have to go to their father's funeral.*

25

Chapter
04

Nightmares are hobbyhorses compared to this.

Cars filled the church parking lot and down the streets. Trish watched people walk up the front steps of the church from the safety of her backseat. Her mother and David had already gone inside. *Come on, you can't just hide out here. You have to go in.* Her little nagger was beginning to sound desperate.

Trish bit at her lip again. Why did inflicting pain on herself seem to help? She rolled down the window to let in some fresh air. The glass had steamed up. Breathing in the cold, damp air didn't help. Nothing seemed to help.

Get out, you chicken! she told herself in no uncertain terms. *You managed to get to the hospital; you can walk yourself inside the church. You'll get through this. You have to.* The sight of David coming out the side door of the cedar-sided building and striding purposefully toward the car was all the force she needed.

She stepped out quickly, shut the car door behind her, and followed her brother inside. Organ music swelled and filled the church. It reminded

Trish of the family conference Pastor Mort had with them the night before. He said the service would be a celebration. Hal had wanted it that way.

In fact, Hal had planned the entire service—another reason Trish didn't want to be there. Her father had made a list of his favorite hymns and Bible verses. He'd asked that there be few flowers, preferring memorials to the jockey fund. He wanted everyone to remember and rejoice that he'd gone home. His race was finished.

But Trish couldn't rejoice. She stood behind her mother as Marge greeted the last of the families that had come to remember Hal.

Then she joined her family and the Finleys in the front pew. Rhonda was right behind her and squeezed Trish's shoulder. "You okay?" her eyes asked around the tears. Trish shook her head. She'd never be okay again.

That evening, Trish couldn't have told anyone about the funeral. She'd literally checked out. Her body was present, but not her mind. Her lip was raw and red, her head pounded, and her eyes burned from unshed tears. But she'd *gotten through.*

Long before dark, Marge offered Trish a pain pill and a sleeping pill. She took them without a second thought, and climbed into bed exhausted. Falling asleep was like tumbling down a long, dark tunnel. At the end she felt nothing.

Trish awoke early Friday morning. Her mouth felt like cotton balls and her head still pounded. Her eyes wouldn't focus. Everything looked about as blurry as she felt. She staggered to the bathroom, guzzled a glass of water, and stumbled back into bed—back down the tunnel to oblivion.

It seemed only moments later when she heard her mother calling her name, felt her mother's hand on her shoulder. "Trish, Trish. You need to get ready for your flight. The plane to New York leaves in an hour and a half. I let you sleep as long as I dared."

Trish rubbed the sleep from her eyes and pushed herself into a sitting position. She crossed her legs and held her head. It still throbbed, but not as bad as last night.

"Are you sure you're up to this?" Marge sat down on the edge of the bed and brushed a lock of hair from Trish's cheek. She tilted her daughter's chin with one finger so she could look into her eyes. "You know, you don't have to be superwoman. You could stay here and let David go."

Trish shook her head. "No. Every time they've tried moving Spitfire without me, there's trouble." She swallowed, but her throat was so dry it hurt. "Could you please get me a glass of water? I feel . . ." She shook her head. *Lousy, rotten, the pits*—none of those began to describe how she really felt. *Miserable, sick, lost.* The hole was too black and too deep to describe.

Marge patted Trish's knee. "I'll be right back."

Trish gulped the water down and asked for more. This time she forced herself out of bed and began pulling clothes out of the drawers to throw into her bag. She would only be gone three days—she didn't need much.

"You get a shower so you can navigate—I'll pack that." Marge handed her daughter the second glass of water. Trish sipped as she stared around the room. *Where are my boots?*

As she studied the room, her glance fell on the Bible verses pinned to the wall. Most of the three-by-five cards were in her father's handwriting. She looked away quickly. *Yeah, right.* The thoughts snarled like caged tigers in her mind. *Dad believed all those promises and what did it get him?* She kept her gaze straight ahead and stomped to the bathroom. The only way was to keep those thoughts at the other end of the telescope. She was getting pretty good at that.

But even the sound of the shower failed to drown out a voice that whispered, *He got heaven. That's the point.* Trish gritted her teeth. Back in her room, she ripped the cards off the wall and dumped them in the wastebasket, careful not to read any of the words.

"Be careful." Marge hugged her daughter just before she and Adam Finley boarded the plane at Portland International Airport.

Trish nodded. She forced herself to return the hug. That old burning started in the back of her throat. If only everyone would leave her alone. No talking, no touching. She made the mistake of looking into her mother's tear-filled eyes.

"I—" Trish swallowed—hard. She had to. The burning had turned to fire that made her eyes water. "We'll call you tonight. Now, don't worry. You know we'll be all right."

She heard her mother's "God keep you," then slammed the telescope to full length. *Sure, just like He kept Dad, right?* She snorted in disgust.

Adam wisely refrained from commenting on the thunderclouds that furrowed Trish's brow. He just handed their tickets to the young man at the gate and walked down the ramp beside her.

As soon as they were airborne, Trish flipped her seat back and curled under the blanket. This time the plane was full so she couldn't stretch out. It didn't matter. She slipped back into that blessed long black tunnel where pain and sorrow didn't exist.

Adam woke her when the plane began its approach to John F. Kennedy Airport on Long Island. *How come I always wake up with a raging thirst?* This time she'd have to wait until they landed before she could get a drink of water.

"You okay?" Adam asked.

Trish nodded. She snapped her seat upright at the request of the flight attendant. Getting oriented sounded simple, but her brain refused to function. She didn't just need a drink of water, she needed a bucket of water poured over her head.

By the time they arrived at the car rental office, Trish was getting impatient to see Spitfire. How could people be so slow? Getting a car in New York took longer than anywhere else she'd ever been. She took a long drink of the Diet Coke she'd bought at the first snack bar. Would the line *ever* move? She wasn't the only one getting frustrated. Two businessmen behind them expressed their sentiments in language that fit the situation.

When they finally got the car, the traffic on the beltway crawled along like a vast ribbon of parking lot. Trish slumped in her seat.

"It's too late to go to the track tonight." Adam glanced at his watch. "We'd be better off just checking in to the hotel and getting something to eat."

"I really wanted to see Spitfire first." Trish couldn't help voicing her desire.

"I know. We're still on Pacific time, but it's later here. Can you wait

29

till morning?" Trish nodded. Nothing ever seemed to go right anymore. "You hungry?"

"I don't think so." She did a body check. Food just didn't seem necessary.

"You didn't eat on the plane." Adam tapped his brakes again when the taillights in front of them flashed red.

"I know." *Will this drive never end?* Trish knew she was being rude, but she couldn't seem to think of anything to say. It was easier to retreat to the other end of her telescope.

By the time she fell onto her hotel bed, the pounding headache had returned. She dug in her case for some pain pills and slugged two of them down. The face in the mirror seemed to have lost all life and color. The circles under her eyes were getting blacker. She poured a glass of water to leave on the nightstand and flicked off the light. If only it were that easy to flick off all that had happened.

In the morning, Trish braided her hair and brushed her teeth without looking in the mirror. Who needed reminders of how bad she looked?

"The horse van will be ready at seven," Adam said when he knocked on her door. "I'm checking out now. I'll meet you downstairs."

"Okay." Trish finished stuffing her things into the bag and checked the bathroom again. She switched off the lights as she left the room.

The sun was just pinking the eastern sky as they approached gate six at Belmont Park. The guard waved them through when Adam flashed his identification. The huge elm trees were still the same. Early morning track sounds hadn't changed. Horses whinnied. Someone was whistling as he walked a horse across the road. Someone else laughed. Only Trish's world had changed. She clamped down on the thought. No, her father wouldn't be back. The old litany started again. *Just get through!*

She greeted Patrick and sidestepped the hug he offered. Hugs were off limits. Spitfire was nearly her undoing. His familiar nicker and bobbing black head revealed his joy at seeing her. Trish wrapped both arms around the horse's neck and buried her face in his mane. One tear forced its way through her clenched eyelids. She hung on for dear life.

Spitfire raised his head and nibbled on her braid. When that didn't get her attention, he blew in her ear. Trish reached up to scratch behind his ears and down his cheek. His silent whuffle thanked her.

"How you been?" Trish whispered in his ear. Spitfire nodded and nosed her pocket for his carrot. "You miss me?" The black colt nodded again and rubbed his forehead against her chest. "Hasn't Patrick been treating you right?" Spitfire snorted.

"Sounds to me like you two carry on a pretty good conversation."

Trish spun around at the sound of the familiar voice. "Red!" She flung herself into his arms before she had time to think. Red held her close and pressed a kiss on her hair.

"How you doin'?" His whisper brushed the wisps of hair around her ear.

Trish just shook her head. She knew she had to get away from him before the tears started, but for a moment longer she clung to his embrace. Reluctantly, she pushed back and ducked under Spitfire's neck. If she bit her lip hard enough the tears retreated. Forced back by sheer force of will, again. She was getting better at this.

"You want to take Sarah's Pride while I ride Spitfire? I'm sure she's ready for a run." She reached for the bridle Patrick handed to her. "How's she been doing?"

She could feel Red's stare boring holes into her back. How could she tell him that hugs and kind words were too much, even from him?

Trish felt as if she were caught in a time warp.

Red whistled a popular tune as he rode beside her out to the track. Both the horses picked up the pace as they neared the mile-and-a-half oval. Cicadas chirped their way into the morning chorus as the sun hit the elm trees. The fragrance of the air was a combination of horse, freshly mown grass, and summer.

Nothing had changed. If Trish closed her eyes and pretended . . . She shook her head. No pretending, even if it did feel good.

She studied the space between Spitfire's ears. Everything had changed. She and Spitfire had run their last race. She bit down hard on her lip.

"What is it?" Red asked.

"Ummm, I was just thinking of the Breeder's Cup in October. Do you think we could run in it?"

"We?"

"Spitfire and me."

Red shook his head. "I wouldn't count on it. He's too valuable for stud now. The syndicate would never agree."

"I always thought he would be my horse. I mean, I knew he was good, and winning the Kentucky Derby and then the Triple Crown was a dream come true, but I never thought—" She squeezed her knees and Spitfire broke into a slow gallop.

"Thought what?" Sarah's Pride kept pace, snorting and fighting the bit to go faster. She surged ahead until Red pulled her back down.

Trish focused on the horses in front of them.

"Thought what, Trish? What were you thinking?"

"I never thought I would have to give him up . . . have to live halfway across the country from him." She raised her voice to be heard above a horse grunting a hard gallop past them.

"You could always come and race in Kentucky."

"I thought about that." She pulled Spitfire back down to a walk. "But I have to finish high school first. My mom would never let me go now."

"Knock it off, horse." Red tightened his reins to keep the filly from chasing after another fast-working animal.

"You think she's ever gonna learn some manners?" Trish grabbed on to another topic. Racing and her mother were too close to home.

"Yeah, well, I tried. Now you get her. I'll watch for her name in the newspapers." Together they walked out the gate and down the narrow paved road to barn 12.

With Patrick and Adam helping, they quickly had both horses washed, walked, and ready to load. The van arrived promptly at seven, just as they were all returning from the track kitchen and breakfast. Both horses walked up into the van without even a snort of temper or fear, much to Trish's surprise. Maybe Sarah's Pride was learning something after all.

"Trish, you and Red ride in the van, and Patrick and I'll drive the car, okay?" Adam looked up in time to catch the grin on Red's face. "Any problem with that?"

Red shook his head. "Nope." He grabbed Trish's hand and raised it with his. "Those horses may need these hands. We gotta be prepared."

When Red didn't let go of her hand, Trish tried to pull it away without being too obvious, but Red turned toward the van with her in tow. "Y'all drive safely now, ya hear?" Red waved with his free hand before opening the cab door for Trish.

The cicadas turned up the volume of their good-bye chorus as the van pulled out onto the street and headed for the Cross Island Expressway. They were on their way south, to Spitfire's new home.

Trish pulled out her internal telescope and flipped to the large end. Maybe that way she could ignore the friendly conversation between Red and John Stokes, the van driver. And maybe if she concentrated hard enough she could sleep most of the trip. Maybe the moon was made of green cheese too.

Red was not easy to ignore.

Trish leaned her head back against the seat and instructed her muscles to relax. She concentrated on her hands, arms, legs, feet, willing each to relax.

Red told a joke and both men laughed. Trish felt herself smile. Red did tell a good story.

Back to relaxing. Trish felt warm and a bit floaty. Red's next story depended on his southern drawl for the punch line. He drew it out perfectly. A giggle started somewhere down about Trish's heels and bubbled its way up. She bit it back, but when Stokes came up with a topper she couldn't help it. The giggle escaped.

Red took her hand in his and stroked her fingers. She felt his smile and encouragement clear back down where that giggle had started. When she leaned back again, his arm cushioned her head.

His next joke was even more outrageous.

"You two trying to develop a comedy act or something?" she finally asked. "I think you could go on stage right now."

"Really?" Red drawled, wriggling his eyebrows like Groucho Marx.

Trish shook her head. "You're crazy, you know that?"

"Crazy about yoo-hoo-hoo-hoo," Red crooned. His eyebrows contorted again, and he let out a long yodel.

"I can't believe this." She stared from one to the other. "Did you two know each other before?"

"Before what?" Stokes raised his shoulders in a question.

"Before this trip!"

Red leaned forward to peer around Trish. "Do I know you, sir?"

"Beats me. Where'd you find her?"

34

"Hey, you're a poet!" They high-fived hands, nearly crushing Trish between them.

Trish groaned. "Hadn't you better think about driving?"

Stokes grinned at her, showing a chipped front tooth. Sandy hair curled from under his weathered and bent straw hat. "You doubtin' my driving?"

"No, it's just that—well—we had an accident on the way up this stretch of road and my dad . . ." The light went out again, and Trish bit down on her lip.

Nagger slipped in around her guard. *Here you are having a good time— laughing even—when you should be grieving for your father.* When she shuddered, Red's arm held her tighter. She couldn't look up to see the sympathy in his eyes. She just closed hers and prayed the miles would disappear. Maybe they should have flown the horses. But Spitfire hated loud noises, so her father had decided to truck him down.

Back to her father again. Everything always came back to him. Trish left off gnawing on her lip and attacked a torn cuticle on her left thumb.

When they stopped for lunch, they checked on the horses first. Spitfire nickered his welcome as soon as he heard Trish's voice. Sarah's Pride stamped her front foot and pawed at the rubber-coated flooring.

"You two behave now," Trish whispered as she gave Spitfire an extra scratching. He nudged her pocket, looking for the carrot she always carried. "Sorry, fella, I'm fresh out." She patted his rump on her way past. "You'll live without a treat this time." *That's something else to remember to tell the new groom. Always carry carrots.* Somehow the reminder didn't make her feel any better.

After pushing her lunch around on the plate so it looked like she'd eaten, Trish dug out her book bag before climbing back into the truck. But knowing she had to review for her finals and doing it were two different things. Her eyes kept drooping shut. An hour or so down the road and the book clunked to the floor.

Red drew her over to rest on his shoulder as he leaned back against the door.

Darkness had fallen long before the truck turned onto New Circle Road, the highway that encircled Lexington. Stokes followed the signs to Old Frankfort Pike, right in the heart of bluegrass country. Headlights flashed on both black and white board fences as the road narrowed.

The BlueMist Farms sign leaped into the headlight glare. White board fences lined both sides of the long curving drive. A magnificent white house in traditional southern plantation style graced a knoll off to their right. The road to the barns crossed a creek and passed a pond before ending in a graveled parking area.

Trish rubbed her eyes and stretched. While she'd only slept for a couple of hours, she felt as if they'd been in the truck for days. "What time is it?"

Red looked at his watch. "About ten-thirty. We made good time."

"Let's get them out and walk 'em around." Patrick stepped out of his car and arched his back. He and Stokes opened the doors to the van and slid out the ramp. The clanging of the metal sounded extra loud on the soft night air.

A pickup pulled into the paddock, its headlights trapping them in the intensity. As soon as the truck stopped, Donald Shipson stepped out and came forward to greet them. A short, wiry man, obviously an ex-jockey, joined him.

Trish tried to escape by ducking into the van, but Adam Finley took her arm and drew her back into the circle. She watched as Patrick and the new man slapped each other on the back.

"Can ya beat that?" Patrick beamed, his teeth gleaming in the car light. "Me old buddy, Timmy O'Ryan. Trish, meet the best man in the world to take care of Spitfire for you. Why, if I'da known . . ." He shook his head and slapped the man's back again.

Trish tried to swallow around the rock in her throat. Even she knew the name Timmy O'Ryan. While other kids collected baseball cards, Trish memorized racing times and the jockeys that set them. "I'm glad to meet you." Her voice came out strangled. "Ummm, excuse me, I need to see to Spitfire."

"Can I help you, miss?" Timmy O'Ryan spoke with the same soft lilt as Patrick. And he had the same steady, blue-eyed gaze. "Maybe he'll take to me better if you introduce us."

Trish nodded. Now she knew what a mouse caught in a trap must feel like.

Spitfire nickered his special welcome when Trish entered the van. He tossed his head, impatient to be free.

Timmy followed Trish as she patted her way up the horse's side to his head. "Hey, old fella, I have someone new for you to meet." She stroked the black's cheek and rubbed his ear.

Spitfire reached to sniff the hand the new man held out. He smelled the shirtsleeve and up to the porkpie hat, then down the other arm. Timmy stood perfectly still, but his voice seemed to whisper a love song as he and Spitfire became acquainted. At last he palmed a carrot and held it for the colt to munch.

"You've made a friend for life." Trish felt as if her forced smile would crack and her with it.

"Your father included suggestions like this in his letter of instructions. He wanted to make the transition as easy as possible."

Trish nodded. She turned to jerk the lead knot loose. "Come on, fella, back up."

Spitfire stopped in the doorway and trumpeted his arrival to any other horses who might be in the area. "Come on." Trish tugged on the lead. "You can quit showing off anytime."

Two answering whinnies came from the barn just past the gate. Spitfire raised his muzzle and sniffed the slight breeze to acquaint himself with the area. Then he followed Trish through the gate and around a second grassy paddock. Timmy loosely held the other lead and paced along with them.

"That's the stallion barn right over there." He pointed to a huge barn, shadowed now by the night. "He'll have his own paddock, and better care than most people give their kids. While I'm in charge of him, there'll be grooms helping me."

"He only lets me ride him."

"I understand. No one will ride him. We'll hand walk him or gallop him around the training track on a lead. You'll see, he'll get fat and sassy, but next spring when he goes to work, that'll change. I'll take care of him, miss. You needn't worry."

Trish felt like the horses must feel as Timmy's gentle voice soothed her fears. Spitfire even drooped on the lead between them. "Come on, fella, let's see what your new home looks like."

She knew her eyes were big as tennis balls as she stared around the softly lit interior of the stallion barn. *People don't live this good,* she thought as she took in the glistening woodwork, the shiny brass fittings, and the gleaming name plates on spacious stalls. "There's yours." She pointed Spitfire's head toward the large box stall with *Spitfire* lettered in brass on an oval blue sign. "I can't believe this."

Timmy stopped beside her. "You think he'll be comfortable here?" Trish could hear the teasing in his voice before she saw the light dancing in his eyes.

"Most people wouldn't believe horses could live like this."

Timmy nodded. "His stall opens onto his own private two-acre paddock. There're shade trees down on the lower corner, and deep grass."

Trish looked up to see a huge picture of a blood bay, about a quarter of life-size.

"That's Shenandoah, the first stud here, and grandaddy to three Derby winners and countless others who did their share of winning on tracks all around the country." O'Ryan walked forward and swung open the door to Spitfire's stall. "Come on, let's see how he likes it."

Spitfire inspected every corner of his new home before returning to Trish for an ear-scratching. He draped his head over her shoulder, as if moving into a new stall was boring.

Trish felt the now familiar boulder clog her throat. She wouldn't feel his head on her shoulder anymore, not after tomorrow morning. She blinked hard and rolled her eyes toward the ceiling. *No! You can't cry now!* She sniffed once and felt herself gaining some measure of control.

"See you in the morning," she whispered in her horse's twitching ear. "You be good now." She gave him a last pat and closed the lower part of the stall door behind her. Spitfire hung his head over the door and whuffled his soundless nicker. Trish brushed past Timmy O'Ryan and headed for the exit. She was nearly running by the time she caught up with Red, who was still walking Sarah's Pride.

"Whoa, you okay?" Red stopped Trish with a hand on her arm. The filly threw her head up and danced sideways at the interruption. "Easy now." His soft voice worked for both the filly and Trish.

"H-have they said where we'll keep her?" Trish stammered before she got her voice under control.

"Yeah, there're stalls over there." Red pointed to a low building on the other side of the graveled area. "John and Adam went into the stallion barn just as you came out. Come on, let's put this girl away."

Sarah's Pride inspected her new quarters just as Spitfire had. She drank out of the tub in the corner and nibbled at the hay in the mesh sling. Trish and Red leaned on the closed stall door, watching her.

"Spitfire's going to be fine here, you know," Red broke the silence.

"I know."

"You can come and see him—and me."

"I will." Trish took a deep breath and turned around to lean against the wall. She studied the faint outline of the cupola-crested stallion barn. "Sure different than home." Her voice faded away on the slight breeze. She heard a frog chirp in the distance; a bullfrog answered. Sarah's Pride dribbled water on Trish's shoulder and in her hair. "Thanks a heap." Trish brushed it off and gave the filly a cheek scratch.

She pushed herself away from the wall, and she and Red walked out to join the men clustered around the pickup.

"Tim, you show Patrick and Red where they'll be sleeping, and, Stokes is it?" The driver nodded. "And Adam and Trish'll come with me." Donald Shipson waved toward the house Trish had seen when they drove up. "Breakfast will be served on the veranda from six to nine. Just come and help yourself."

"See you in the morning," Red whispered for Trish's ears alone as he squeezed her hand.

Trish nodded, then followed John and Adam to the car. Too tired to even appreciate the grand staircase to the upper floor, or the bedroom filled with antique furniture, it was all Trish could do to say good-night to Mrs. Shipson without yawning. She fell down that long black tunnel she'd come to appreciate.

A rooster crowing woke her in the morning. She slipped from the lace-draped four-poster bed and went to stand in front of the open window. Sheer white curtains drifted over her bare feet in the slight breeze. The sun arced high enough to jewel the dew on the manicured lawns and paddocks. Newly mown grass perfumed the air. Someone whistled a friendly tune off to the side of the grand house, and downstairs a bass voice sang the words. She could see the roof of the stallion barn through the trees.

Trish turned from all the peace and beauty to dress. Today she had to leave Spitfire.

"I'll drive you over to the barn if you'd like," the silver-haired Mr. Shipson said after greeting her at the bottom of the stairs.

"I was hoping to ride him, ahhh—" Trish swallowed her lump. "Uhhh . . . before we leave, if that's okay?"

"Of course. Timmy will ride with you and show you the way to the track. I think you'll be pleased when you see everything in daylight."

"You have an awesome place here." They stopped between the two center pillars on the front porch. Trish looked up at her host. "I've only seen spreads like this in pictures."

"Thank you. My family's owned this land since before the war."

"The war?"

"The Civil War." His smile twinkled in his eyes. "We forget the rest of the world doesn't count time from the War Between the States. My great-great-grandaddy founded the stud here." He stepped down to the first stair. "I can't imagine living anywhere else."

Trish followed her host out to the pickup, surprised at how easy she felt with him. It was as if they'd known each other for a long time. She shook her head. And here she'd been all ready to dislike him—intensely. But she'd reminded herself that it wasn't his fault Spitfire was coming here and not back to Vancouver.

It was my father's fault, actually. He had started the syndication. Trish suddenly felt betrayed. Why had he done this to her? Her vision blurred so she could hardly see the sweeping drive, the stream, and the glass-like pond. She sank back into the seat.

"Trish? Are you all right?"

"Uh, yeah." She shook her head, trying to clear away the fog.

"I know leaving Spitfire here must be terrible for you. I wish there was some way I could help—"

You could let him go home with me. The words were so clear in her head Trish was afraid she'd shouted them.

"I want you to understand that you are welcome to visit here any time you'd like. If you want to come to Kentucky to race, I'll do whatever I can to help you. Spitfire is still your horse, you know."

Only part of him. Again Trish bit down on her tongue so as not to verbalize the words.

"Our home is yours. Both my wife and I would love having you here." Donald braked the truck and turned off the ignition. "I mean it, Trish; this isn't just southern hospitality talking."

"Thank you." Trish took a deep breath. "I'll remember that." She could feel her smile tremble at the edges. "Thanks."

Timmy and Patrick had Sarah's Pride and another horse saddled, and Patrick slipped a bridle over Spitfire's ears just as he whinnied his welcome to Trish.

"Right in my ear," Patrick grumbled. The next instant his hat went bowling across the floor. "Had to get one in, didn't you?"

Trish stooped down to pick up Patrick's stained and wrinkled fedora. "I keep telling you to watch it." She handed the hat back to Patrick, her grin securely in place. Spitfire's clowning made everything easier. "Had to get him, didn't you?" She rubbed under Spitfire's forelock and got a grainy lick for her efforts.

Red walked up with three helmets. He handed one to Trish and one to Timmy, then put on his own. "Hi, how d'ya like the summer morning? No other place like this on earth."

"You're prejudiced. You haven't seen a sunny morning in Washington yet." Trish walked between the two men, Spitfire tagging behind her.

Patrick gave her a leg up. "Now, don't be takin' too long," he said softly. "We need to be loading the girl here and heading for the airport."

"I know." The sun seemed to dim.

"This way," Timmy said from the back of his bay as he led the way through an open gate and between two white board fences. He pointed out the other four stallions and a field of mares and foals. While Red asked questions, Trish grew more quiet, savoring each moment. She listened with one ear, and planted each tree and fence post in her memory so she could visualize Spitfire being worked on this track. Spitfire's stall, his paddock, his barn, the smell of the grass, the song of the birds.

How could she leave him here? It was too much to ask.

Chapter
06

What was left of Trish's heart felt twisted and torn.

"Y'all come back now," Mrs. Shipson said, giving Trish a warm hug. "As Donald said, our home is yours—any time." She stepped back and shook hands with Patrick and Adam Finley. "Y'all take care now."

Trish waved as she stepped up into the truck. Her blurry vision made her stub her toe on the step.

Red caught her and helped her into the cab. "You okay?"

Trish just nodded. She fought the tears, teeth clamped so hard her jaw ached. As they drove down the fence-lined drive, she stared at the clock on the dashboard. Hands tucked under her arms, she shivered once. Red laid his arm across the back of the seat and massaged her neck.

All Trish could see on the back of her eyelids was Spitfire galloping across his new paddock. She could hear his whinny, feel his last whiskery whuffle. A lone tear squeezed past her iron control gate and meandered down her cheek.

Red brushed it away with one gentle finger.

"I meant it, Trish, about coming to California and racing for me this summer," Adam Finley said just before he boarded his plane in Lexington. "I know it's going to be rough for you in the days ahead, and new scenery might make your summer easier."

"I—I have to finish my finals, and then I promised my mom I'd take chemistry at Clark College. She'll never let me out of that."

"Well, just remember we have colleges in California too. I'm sure you could find a class in the evening." He reached as if to hug her then drew back. "I know how hard you are fighting this, Trish. Martha and I would love to be able to help you, and you would be helping us too. Your dad's passing has left a mighty big hole—in many lives."

"Ahhh . . ." Trish nodded instead of trying to finish her thought. "Thanks for all you've done for us." She looked up to see tears glistening in Adam's eyes.

"Crying isn't a sin, my dear." Finley sniffed and blinked a couple of times. "No matter how hard you fight it, letting the tears come will help you get better."

Trish shook her head. Her strangled "I can't" carried from over her shoulder as she headed for the exit.

She had her armor back in place by the time she joined Red and Patrick at the cargo dock.

Loading Sarah's Pride on the plane proved surprisingly easy. Patrick had come prepared with a tranquilizer shot, but the filly walked up the ramp with only a snort and a toss of her head. Once inside, she trembled and broke into a sweat while the men erected the stall around her, but she stood still. With Red doing the same on the other side of the horse, Trish rubbed the filly's neck and ears. At the same time she whispered her soothing monologue, the song she'd learned from her father.

"I'll call you soon." Red ducked under the horse's neck after she'd lipped a bit of hay from the sling. He put one arm around Trish and brushed a strand of hair off her cheek with his other hand.

"Okay." One word was all Trish could manage.

"You'll write or call? You can always get in touch with me through my mom and dad."

Trish nodded. Red raised her chin and brushed her lips with his. She

43

turned her head before he could kiss her again and shatter her control. Leaving hurt so bad. How much more could she stand?

Red squeezed her shoulder. "Take care." He levered himself over the stall.

Trish heard him say good-bye to Patrick. If she started to cry now, she knew she'd never be able to stop. *Just get through.* The inner order worked again.

The filly swung her rear end from side to side as the plane revved for takeoff. Patrick joined Trish in the box to try to keep the horse calm. Together they kept her from slipping as the plane floor slanted. When the plane leveled off, the horse quieted down. She sighed and dropped her head, as if all the tension had worn her out.

Trish stretched and wrapped both arms around her shoulders to pull the kinks out. She dropped her chin on her chest, then shrugged her shoulders to her ears.

"Ye did a good job, lass." Patrick walked around the filly, adjusting the travel sheet as he checked for any more sweating. He unbuckled the crimson blanket and pulled it off. "She needs a dry one after all that."

Trish handed him the extra sheet and helped buckle it.

"It'll get easier, lass, take my word for it."

Trish just shook her head.

"You want to go sit down for a while? I'll stay with the girl here."

"No. You do that." Trish dug a brush out of the tack bucket. "It helps me to keep busy." She flipped back the sheet over one front quarter and started brushing.

The remainder of the trip passed without incident. Trish spent part of the time studying, but failed to turn many pages. Her eyelids kept drooping.

David had the six-horse trailer ready and waiting when they landed at Portland International Airport. Unloading and reloading went without a hitch, and they were crossing the I-205 bridge within a few minutes. The overcast skies seemed to match Trish's overcast disposition.

She let Patrick tell about their trip to Kentucky and describe BlueMist Farms. She was back at the other end of the telescope, looking and listening from a great distance. It was easier that way.

David pointed out the sights to Patrick. Trish could feel her brother studying her between comments, but she shut her eyes and ignored him.

It wasn't so easy to ignore her mother. Marge met them when they drove down to the barns at Runnin' On Farm. She hugged her daughter once, then a second time before Trish could slip past.

Trish caught herself looking around for her father. Quickly she knelt to hug her dog, Caesar, and ruffle his pristine white ruff. The collie responded by quick-licking her cheek.

"I know, Tee." Marge stood beside Trish with her hands in the back pockets of her jeans. "I keep looking for him too."

A knife-sharp pain stabbed Trish. She felt as if her heart couldn't take any more blows. She knew if she said anything or looked at the pain in her mother's eyes, she'd crumble and lose the control she'd worked so hard to maintain.

Instead, she bit down on her lip and ducked her head as she followed David into the van to bring out Sarah's Pride. *Spitfire should be coming home too*. Where was the celebration? Who could celebrate? She stomped her rampaging feelings down into a steel box somewhere in her middle and bolted the lid.

"Easy now." David smoothed the filly's neck as he jerked loose the tie rope. "Welcome to your new home."

Welcome to nothing. Trish caught the words before she spoke them aloud. She could hear her mother and Patrick talking outside the van. She untied the opposite lead and kept pace as David led their new arrival out the door.

Sarah's Pride minced down the ramp and danced around in a circle, head up, surveying the area. She whinnied and pawed one front foot.

"Her stall is all ready," David said. "I figured we should keep her separated from the others for a while."

"You're right, boy." Patrick patted the horse's right shoulder. "Why don't you lead her around for a bit and let her work off some of her energy. We'll give her a real work tomorrow and see if we can't finish breaking some of her bad habits." He tipped his fedora back on his head. "She sure is a determined one."

"Well, stubborn fits right into this family," Marge said. "She ran well the last time she was out, though, didn't she?"

Trish felt her jaw drop in amazement. Since when had her mother cared anything about how a horse ran? She caught a grin that David tried to hide behind the filly's neck. What was going on here? Her brother trotted off with the horse in tow.

"Patrick, I think Hal told you that we'd ordered a mobile home for you." Marge leaned against the truck's front fender. "The people installing the septic tank will be here tomorrow. The power and phone will be in by the end of the week, and the trailer should be here Friday too. In the meantime, you can have David's room. He'll take the couch."

"No, no." Patrick shook his head. "Ye needn't be putting yourself out like that. I'll just fix a cot down here and . . ."

"No, Patrick. This is the way Hal would want it. We had planned to have everything ready before you arrived, but . . ." She raised her hands in a helpless shrug. "We'll make do until then. You're a member of our family, and while the kids used to have slumber parties down in the barn, you'll be much more comfortable up at the house."

Trish could hardly believe her ears. Who *was* this person who'd taken over her mother's body? And her mouth? Trish looked up in time to catch her mother wiping away a tear from the corner of her eye. Patrick looked misty-eyed too.

Trish dashed after David. "I'll see if he needs help." But David already had the filly loosed in her stall and was closing the lower half of the stall door.

"You know, I thought about bringing Dan'l up to keep her company, but Mom said to wait a couple of days. She's right, of course." David checked the latch and turned toward the house. "I've already done all the other chores."

"All right, what's going on here?" Trish kicked some gravel off to the side.

"What do you mean?"

"You know. Since when has Mom cared about what goes on down here?"

"Down here?" David picked up a stone and pegged it up the driveway.

"David!" Trish jerked on his arm.

"Okay, okay." He raised his hands in surrender. "We had a long talk,

Mom and I, and she said it was time she learned more about the horses and racing—since she doesn't want to sell the farm. . . ."

Trish breathed a deep sigh of relief.

"You thought she might, didn't you?"

"It crossed my mind." Trish shoved her fingers into her pockets.

"Well, she isn't. She said she and Dad had talked it all over. He told her to sell if she wanted to."

Trish felt a boot-kick in her gut. *Her father had said that?*

"But Mom says she wants to keep the farm; that with Patrick's experience, and maybe hiring some more help when I leave for school . . ."

She felt the kick again. "But I—you—but . . ." David couldn't leave too.

"I know." David stopped and picked up another piece of crushed rock. He ran his finger over the rough edges. "But Mom said . . ."

Trish felt an arrow of anger again, the sharp one that caused her to clench her teeth. Since when did her mother know all about what was best for everybody? That was her dad's job. She yanked her mind back to what David was saying.

"We had to pick up our lives and go on. My goal has always been to be a veterinarian, and now I want to specialize in equine medicine. You knew that."

Trish nodded. She kicked another rock and watched it bounce off into the grass. *Sure, pick up our lives and go on. He makes it sound so easy. As if the world hasn't totally fallen apart.*

"I know this is hard for you, Tee."

She shook her head. "Yeah." *You don't know the half of it, buddy-boy. What do you think you're doing, just making plans like . . . like . . .*

"Trish, Dad would want us to get on with our lives too—school, racing, all of it."

Trish flung away his arm when he reached out to touch her. "Easy for you to say. You just go away and step back into a life that didn't include us anyway. And Mom—she just acts like everything is fine. Well it's not. It'll never be fine again!" She felt like planting her fist in the middle of her brother's nose.

Caesar whimpered at Trish's harsh voice. He nudged her fist with his cold nose and whined again. When she ignored him, he tried a sharp bark.

Trish dropped to her knees and buried her face in the collie's heavy ruff. When David laid a hand on Trish's head, she shook it away. "Just leave me alone. Everyone, just leave me alone."

And that's what she felt like when she walked into the house. Alone. Her dad wasn't sitting in his recliner. He'd never sit in his chair again.

Chapter
07

Trish, I'm so glad you're here." Rhonda threw her arms around her friend.

"Yeah, me too." Trish stuffed her book bag into her locker. At least Prairie High hadn't changed in the month or so she'd been gone. Kids still bumped into each other in the halls, yelled across the commons, and rushed off to class when the bell rang. She kept expecting everything to be different, just because she was.

"Can I help you somehow?" Rhonda clutched her books to her chest.

Trish shook her head. She seemed to be doing a lot of that lately. "David says just to pick up our lives and go on. That's what Dad would want." She felt like slamming her locker door and running screaming down the hall. "So my dad died. So what's the big deal?" Trish lifted her chin in the air and glared at her friend.

"Tee, you know David didn't mean it like that," Rhonda scolded.

"We'd better get to class. I've got a final first period. I can't wait till this is over."

Others looked the other way when they caught Trish's eye. There would be no "welcome home" or congratulations this time.

Rhonda stopped Trish before she entered her first-period class. "They don't know what to say, Tee. None of us do."

"Yeah, congratulations doesn't fit, does it." Trish shifted her books to the other arm. "Forget it, Rhonda. Just ace your test."

Trish had a hard time focusing on the test paper in front of her. The words ran together. They carried no meaning. She glanced up at the clock. Fifteen minutes had passed; she'd written down one answer. Her jaw was beginning to ache from being clenched so tight, but Trish used the pain to help her focus. She *would not* fail these tests. She was tough—wasn't she?

Brad was waiting outside the school in his Mustang at the end of the day. Trish dropped like a stone onto the front seat.

"Pretty bad, huh?"

She exhaled and leaned her head back on the seat. "Worse."

"I'll bet they'd give you an extension if you asked." Brad tilted his seat forward so Rhonda could get in the back.

"Mrs. Olson told me she would. But I'd rather tough it out and get done."

"How's it feel to be done with high school?" Rhonda asked Brad, blowing upward to lift her bangs.

"Good. I just came back to gloat over you guys still struggling with finals. I also knew you wouldn't want to take the bus."

"Thanks," Trish said. "I don't think I could have handled the bus ride today. I was hoping to have my new convertible, but they aren't in yet."

"You think your mom will let you drive it to school?"

"I think she's going to have a cow every time I get in it."

"You want to study together? I can come over." Rhonda leaned her chin on the back of the front seat.

"No—I don't think so. I'm so tired; I'm going to bed. I'll probably study later." *If at all. Who cares, anyway?* Trish's thoughts seemed louder than her voice.

That evening her mom woke her to say Red was on the phone. Trish stumbled into the kitchen and sank down on the floor to lean against the oak cabinets, the phone clamped between her ear and her shoulder.

"How's my girl?" Red's voice sounded as if he were in the next room.

"Sleepy." Trish couldn't control a yawn. "I had two finals today; I have two tomorrow, and two on Wednesday. I'll be glad when they're over."

"I won today, and a place in the seventh. How about that for some good news?"

"Bet the winner's circle felt good." Trish yawned again. " 'Scuse me. I just can't wake up."

"I miss you."

Trish felt a little twinge of guilt. She hadn't even thought about Red since she left him at the airport. "Yeah, so how's it look for you? Lots of mounts?" She forced herself to stay with the conversation but couldn't think of anything to say. When the silence stretched for several seconds, she mumbled, "Well, I'll talk to you later; I need to hit the books." She hung up the phone as if it were a fifty-pound weight.

Man, he's gonna think you don't even like him, her nagger jumped right in. Trish had been able to shut him off lately, but even that was too much trouble tonight.

She sat down at her desk to study but found herself staring at the wall instead. Maybe if she propped herself against the headboard of her bed . . .

Her mother found her there, sound asleep, with her history book on the floor. Trish hadn't even heard it drop.

"How about crawling under the covers?" Marge smoothed wisps of hair back from Trish's cheek.

"I need to study." Trish stretched and yawned. "I'm just so tired."

"I know. Maybe you should take incompletes and—"

"No. I just want to get school over with. I didn't do so bad today, at least I don't think so." She swung her feet to the floor. "Maybe if I tank up on Diet Coke I can stay awake."

Trish fell asleep the next day during study hall.

"You want to run the track with me instead of lunch?" Trish asked Rhonda when they met at their lockers for break.

"Let's grab a sandwich and then I will. I'm starved. We'll have to run fast." Rhonda stuffed her money in her pocket and her books in her locker.

A brisk breeze scattered clouds across the sky and blew their hair in their eyes as Trish and Rhonda ran the cinder track behind the brick complex. They jogged the first lap, stretched some, and ran the second.

Rhonda puffed to a halt and grabbed her side. "Owww. We need to do this more often or not at all."

Trish sucked in huge gulps of air. "Want to go another?"

"You crazy?" Rhonda folded in half and wrapped her arms around her knees to stretch again. "If that didn't wake you up, nothing will. Besides"—she glanced at her watch—"we have ten minutes till the bell, and I'm spending mine eating."

Trish shivered as the breeze blew through her wet shirt.

"Here." Rhonda handed her a jacket. "We can walk and chew at the same time, or at least we used to be able to." She grabbed Trish when she tripped on a sprinkler head. "Ya gotta pay attention."

Those words haunted Trish all afternoon. Why couldn't she pay attention? Why did her mind seem to wander off all on its own? And she wasn't even thinking of anything, just wandering in a black fog. She felt better at the end of the day, however. She knew she'd aced the history test. All those hours of studying while she'd been traveling had paid off.

That evening she ran down the drive, up to Brad's, and back to their own barn to see Miss Tee. The filly snorted and dashed off to circle the pasture before coming to nibble her treat from Trish's hand.

"You sure are a beauty." Trish rubbed the filly's velvety cheek and inhaled the wonderful odor of horse.

"She has good speed for a baby." Patrick leaned on the fence beside her. "Good motion too. You can tell she loves to run; already makes sure she finishes first against Double D. 'Course he's a tad younger."

"She should be good. Her dam has thrown two colts. One Dad sold as a yearling—he's running at Longacres, won a couple; and the other went back to Minnesota, I think. Last I heard he was doing okay too. Dad said all our money went into stud fees the last couple of years. He knew it was necessary if we wanted to go someplace besides Portland Meadows."

"Well, looks to be paying off." Patrick tipped his hat back and scratched his head. "We got a lot of work to do, soon as you're done with school."

That night Trish turned her light off just after midnight. It looked like running was the answer—to staying awake, that is.

By Wednesday evening she felt brain-dead and ready to skip the last half day of school. But her finals and her junior year were finished.

"How does it feel to be a big senior?" Rhonda asked as she dug the last candy wrapper out of the back of her locker.

"I don't feel any different." Trish scraped at a piece of tape that had held the school calendar on the inside of her locker door. "Other than being totally beat."

"You want to go to a movie tonight? The four musketeers haven't done anything together for a long time." Rhonda slammed her locker shut and wiped her hands on the back of her jeans.

Trish shook her head.

"The mall?"

"I don't think so. Let's get outta here."

The sun hadn't broken through the overcast the next morning before Trish was galloping through the ground fog on Sarah's Pride. Patrick had decreed long gallops to build stamina for all three horses. Owner John Anderson decided to return Gatesby to Runnin' On Farm now that Patrick was the trainer, so Trish had the gelding and Firefly to work too. She could hear Patrick muttering as she walked the filly back to the barns.

David was trying hard to keep a straight face.

"Gatesby at it again?" she asked as she leaped to the ground.

"No manners. All we need is a cockeyed plug with a sense of humor. If I didn't know . . ." Patrick glared at Trish and then David. "And don't say I told you so either." He picked up his hat and beat it against his leg. "Fat and sassy, that's all he is. Well, son," he said, staring into the gelding's right eye, "you hear me now and listen up good. I won't tolerate that kind of nonsense."

Gatesby pulled his head as high as the tie rope permitted, and rolled his eyes till the whites showed.

Trish chuckled at the familiar sight. She looked around to share the joke with her father, and the moment popped like a shimmery soap bubble on a breeze. She lifted her knee for David to boost her up. The rock lodged back in her throat.

When she returned from the gallop, David and Patrick were discussing Longacres versus going to California to race with Adam Finley.

"Which would you rather do, lass?" Patrick asked as he tossed Trish aboard Firefly.

"Whatever."

"You must have an opinion."

Trish shook her head. "I don't really care."

That seemed to be her theme song. At least she heard herself saying it more than once a day. And she thought it a lot more often. Why should she care? Why bother?

On Friday the dealer called to say he had three red convertibles sitting on his lot waiting for them.

"What time would you like to pick them up?" the man asked.

"Would two be okay?" Trish said, after checking with David and her mother.

"You want to invite Brad and Rhonda to go along?" Marge asked when Trish hung up the phone.

"Is Patrick coming?" Trish drew circles in a puddle of water on the counter.

"That's up to you."

"Whatever . . ."

"No. *You* have to make a decision. We can turn this into a celebration like it should be or you can play 'whatever.' " Marge crossed her arms and leaned back against the kitchen counter. "It's up to you."

How can we celebrate when he's not here? Trish thought as she glared at her mother. She slapped her hand in the water, spraying it over the counter. "Fine. We'll invite everybody. Make it a big party. Winner of the Triple Crown—and it doesn't mean squat. Nothing means anything anymore, don't you know that?" Her voice rose to a shriek as she charged through the living room and down the hall to her bedroom. She slammed the door and threw herself across the bed, only to pound her fists on the floor.

"Sorry," she muttered an hour or so later when she came back to the kitchen.

"I know you are. It helps to get the anger out." Marge shut the oven after removing a sheet of chocolate chip cookies. Her eyes were red-rimmed like she'd been crying. She set the cookie tray on the counter and reached for a tissue to blow her nose. "It's easier if we help each other. So far you haven't let any of us close enough to help you." She dabbed at the corners of her eyes.

"I can't," Trish choked out. "I'd better call Rhonda and Brad. Where's Patrick?"

"Down watching them set up his new home. He's hoping to sleep there tonight."

Later, in the station wagon on the way into Vancouver, Rhonda asked, "What are you gonna do with the third car, give it to the church?"

Trish stared at Rhonda like she'd dropped her remaining marbles. "I wouldn't give God the time of day if He asked, let alone a car!"

"Trish!"

"Well, would you?" Trish slumped lower in her seat and chewed on her thumbnail.

"I thought maybe our youth group could get a used van with the money from the sale of the car. You'd said you might give it to the church."

"Yeah, well, God can buy a van for the church."

"Attitude . . ." Brad poked Trish in the ribs from the other side. "Your dad wouldn't be very happy to hear that."

Trish folded her arms across her chest and glared up at her friend. What right did he, or anyone for that matter, have to tell her what her father would want?

Her nagger got her attention. *You know your dad always gave of himself and what he had to help others.*

When they walked into the showroom, they were met by reporters and a television camera. Trish was surprised, and plastered a smile on her face.

"Yes, the second one goes to my brother David here. He earned it. . . . No, I don't know what to do with the third one. Guess I'll decide later."

"Where are you racing next?" a man asked around his camcorder.

Trish shook her head. "I—we're not sure yet."

"How'd you feel about leaving Spitfire in Kentucky?"

"I—I . . ." She shot a pleading look at Patrick and David.

David stepped forward. "Of course it was hard for Trish to leave her horse in Kentucky, but we know that's what's best for Spitfire."

"You still thinking of the Breeder's Cup?"

"No, that's out now." David took Trish by the arm. "How about letting us get our cars?"

Laughter rippled across the balloon-decked room. The camera held on Trish and David as they accepted the keys from the dealer, then followed them outside to the cars. Sunlight bounced off the windshield and sparkled on the cherry-red finish.

A reporter opened the door for Trish and winked at her as she slid onto the smooth black leather seat. "How's it feel?" he asked.

Trish placed both hands on the steering wheel. She adjusted the seat and turned the ignition key. "Fantastic." She smiled into the camera. "Come on, Rhonda. You get to ride first."

Rhonda slid in next to her. "Awesome." She stroked the gleaming dashboard. "Wow."

Trish waved at David and Brad in the next car. "See you guys."

"Drive carefully," Marge couldn't resist saying as they drove out onto the street.

Trish tooted the horn. "Shall we see how fast it'll go?"

"I wouldn't," Rhonda giggled. "Every cop in Clark County's gonna be watching for that hot young jockey with the red convertible."

"Where shall we go?"

"I don't know but don't look back, we're being followed."

"Meet you at the Burgerville in Orchards," Brad called as he and David pulled up alongside them.

"Yeah, we'll let *him* get the ticket." Trish hit the horn again, then stopped just as the light ahead turned red. A car full of boys behind them honked and waved. When Rhonda turned to look, they whistled and honked again.

"You know, this could get kinda fun." Rhonda settled back in her seat, grinning from ear to ear.

"What do you mean by that?"

"Well, I mean . . . we might meet some new guys. . . . Who knows?"

If only my dad were here, Trish swallowed the thought. *He'd be teasing Rhonda and me right now.* She drove into the restaurant parking lot. More guys were clustered around Brad and David's car.

"See?" Rhonda nodded at the scene. "Red convertibles *attract* guys."

Trish spotted a familiar station wagon on the other side of the parking lot and pulled in next to it. She didn't want the extra attention.

But she couldn't turn off the congratulations of the Prairie High students who were gathered inside. She glued her smile in place until she could hide behind a hot fudge sundae.

"What are you gonna name it?" Rhonda licked her spoon and stared at Trish's puzzled look. "The car, silly. You have to give it a name."

They hadn't come up with a good one by the time Trish dropped Rhonda off at home.

That evening Marge called a family meeting. "I think we need to lay some ground rules about the cars," she said as they gathered around the dining room table.

Trish tried to ignore the empty place where her father always sat. Patrick occupied the chair beside her. She listened with only half an ear, because she already knew what the rules would be. No picking up riders, no speeding, no crazy driving—as if Trish would do any of those things. She nodded in all the right places.

"Now, about the summer . . ." Marge folded her hands on the table in front of her. "What do you think of taking the summer off and not racing anywhere until Portland Meadows opens in the fall?"

Trish shrugged.

"Maybe my opinion's out of place," Patrick said carefully, "but it'd be a shame not to race those three. They'll be ready in a couple of weeks."

"Dad had planned on Longacres," David put in. "We could go up just for the races we enter."

"There's always California," Patrick spoke again, not sure of his place in the decision. "You know Adam wants Trish to come down there."

"Trish promised to take a class at Clark College this summer to make up chemistry," Marge spoke in her my-mind's-made-up tone.

Trish felt like an invisible child. Everyone seemed to be talking around her, as if they all knew what was best for her.

"Well, we could just ship the three horses to California, and let Adam take care of them." David rubbed the bridge of his nose. "That would make it easier for everyone."

Trish jerked alive. "*I* ride our horses." She stood up so fast her chair fell backward. "Where the horses go, I go." She stalked out of the room.

Chapter
08

Trish felt like kicking her bedroom door shut.

Her eyes burned. Her throat felt tight as if she were being strangled. When there was a knock at her door she muttered, "Leave me alone."

"Trish . . ." Marge tapped again, then opened the door.

"I said, leave me alone." Trish stared out the window, her knuckles white as they gripped the sill.

"I've tried that; it isn't working." Marge sat down on Trish's bed.

Silence hung in the room, like the oppression before a summer storm.

"Tee, I . . ."

"Don't call me that!" Trish whirled around. "That was Dad's name for me. And he's not here!"

"I know, Trish, but . . ."

"I can't stand it! You all talk as if nothing's happened. 'Trish is taking chemistry. We could ship the horses to California.' " Her voice rose as she spoke. "I can't take any more of this."

"It's not easy for any of us, Trish. You aren't the only one affected." Marge straightened up on the bed, trying to control her own emotions. "We're all doing the best we can with a situation none of us likes. Do you think your father *wanted* to die and leave us all?"

"Well, he did, didn't he?" Trish turned back to the window, unable to face the tears streaming down her mother's face. The desire to fling herself into her mother's arms was strong, but she hung on to the windowsill, unable to let down the floodgate of her own tears.

Finally Marge sighed and pulled a tissue from the nightstand. "Trish, I understand your anger, but you can't keep taking it out on the rest of us. We're trying to get through ourselves, and we want to help you."

"Don't."

Marge stood and joined her daughter at the window. "How about talking with Pastor Mort?"

Trish shook her head. "No way."

When Marge tried to give her a hug, Trish sidestepped so it turned into a pat on the shoulder.

"I need to go see how Miss Tee is."

The next morning, after long gallops on the three horses in training, plus a nip from Gatesby, Trish took a lead shank out to the pasture and waited for Miss Tee to meet her at the fence. The filly danced up and stopped just out of reach. She extended her muzzle in search of a treat, but leaped away when Trish reached for the halter.

"Great. This is turning into a perfect morning." Trish forced herself to stand perfectly still and wait for the filly to come to her; her patience lasting only long enough for Miss Tee to sniff her hand for the usual carrot.

"Sorry, you didn't earn one today." She snapped the lead shank in place and led the filly through the gate.

"Where you going?" David asked when Trish continued past the barns and toward the drive.

"Taking her for a long walk. She needs to learn some manners."

"Well, take her around the track then."

"David, quit the boss stuff. I know what I'm doing." She clucked to the filly and walked off. She could hear David muttering and complaining but chose to ignore both him and Patrick. "You're my horse, you'd think I could do what I want." Miss Tee bumped her head against Trish's shoulder as if begging for her treat. Trish gave her a small piece of carrot.

Her dog, Caesar, padded beside them as they alternately trotted and walked down the long gravel driveway. "Come on, Miss Tee," Trish encouraged the filly, "you have to do the same thing I do." She tugged on the lead shank to pick up the pace. Miss Tee pulled her head up and back, ears flat, each time the lead shank tightened over her nose. Trish patted her neck. "You're just making life miserable for yourself. *Go along with me; it's easier.*"

Trish turned forward and clucked with a tug again. They were nearly at the Runnin' On Farm sign; time to turn back. At the instant she turned, a rabbit dashed across the drive in front of them. Caesar exploded after the rabbit, his sharp bark cutting the air.

Miss Tee bolted. Her shoulder spun Trish around, sending her to her knees. The force ripped the lead shank from her hands, and the filly tore out onto the road, swerving just in time to avoid broadsiding an oncoming car.

The filly whinnied in fear, the lead shank slapping her on the side, and galloped up the road.

Trish felt as if she were watching a horror movie in slow motion. She leaped to her feet and dashed after the horse.

"Can we help you?" the driver of the car stopped to ask. "I thought we'd hit her for sure."

"If you could wait here . . . no, back there on the other side of our driveway, and stop any oncoming cars . . ." Trish pointed behind her.

"Okay." The man backed up.

Trish ran on ahead. She could see Miss Tee just over the rise, still running hard. A horn honked. Brakes squealed.

Trish poured on all the speed she had, terrified she'd find the filly crushed on the road ahead.

She topped the rise. A car was swerved sideways in the road, but the filly ran on.

Each breath burned her lungs as Trish sucked in great gulps of air, still pounding up the road. Then she heard a vehicle pulling up beside her.

"Trish, for pete's sake, get in!" David stopped the truck long enough for Trish to jump on the running board and hang on to the doorframe. "I told you—" David clipped off his words. "What happened?"

"A rabbit ran out and Caesar chased it. Miss Tee spooked. I'll never forgive myself if something happens to her."

Another car was stopped in the road ahead of them, the driver waving his arms to stop the rampaging horse. Miss Tee swerved to the side and galloped up the driveway to Brad's house.

"Thank you, thank you, thank you," Trish muttered, totally unaware that she was praying in spite of herself.

Brad had heard the commotion and swung open the gate to the corral by the barn. Miss Tee dodged away from his waving arms and into the corral.

Trish leaped to the ground as David slammed on the brakes.

"I'm going back to thank those people who helped us," David called as he backed out the driveway.

The filly stood spraddle-legged in the center of the dirt pen. Her head drooped, sides heaving as she struggled to catch her breath.

Trish and Brad slowly walked up to her on either side, both talking gently. Lather flecked both flanks and chest of the weary filly. Only her ears flicked back and forth to show she knew they were there. When Trish caught the lead shank under Miss Tee's chin, she trembled but stood still.

"I'll get another," Brad murmured when Trish had the horse secured. He returned in seconds with another shank to clip on.

All the while Trish crooned her song in the filly's twitching ears, scolding, but soothing. "You crazy horse, you've seen rabbits before. Boy, are we in for it now."

"What happened? How'd she get loose?" Brad stroked Miss Tee's sweaty neck.

"Don't ask." Trish shook her head. "Hang on tight, okay?" When

Brad had the strap secure, she squatted down to run her hands over the filly's legs, checking for any strains.

David joined them in the corral. "She okay?" At Trish's nod, he let out a breath.

Trish looked up. A thundercloud was perched on David's forehead; she knew lightning was about to strike.

"If you two lead her, I'll drive in front to protect you. I don't think we need to bring the trailer over."

"That okay with you?" Trish asked Brad.

"Sure."

Miss Tee released a huge sigh and nuzzled Trish's pocket for a carrot. While she munched the treat, she rubbed her forehead against Trish's shoulder.

The trek home passed without incident. Brad didn't let go until the filly was safely housed in one of the stalls.

"For crying out loud, Trish!" David slammed his fist against the wall. "You know better than that. I told you not to take her out. Where's your head? You could have gotten her killed; yourself too."

Patrick handed Trish a bucket of warm water. "Let's get her washed down and blanketed."

"She's not hurt," Trish snapped back. "And you don't have to tell me how stupid I was; I already know that."

Brad took the bucket from Trish, and he and Patrick each took a side of the filly and went to work.

"You don't know she's not hurt, and now she'll probably be scared to death of cars and everything else. She could be wind-broken for all we know."

"Quit yelling at me! You're not perfect either."

"You deserve to be yelled at. You were totally irresponsible. Dad woulda had your hide."

"If you two are going to fight, move it away from here," Patrick interrupted. "You're scaring her again."

"Fine." Trish spun on her heel and jogged up the rise to the house.

"We're not finished yet!" David called after her.

"Oh, yes we are." She pounded up the stairs and burst through the door.

"What happened?" Marge turned, her face in a frown.

"Ask David. He has all the answers." In her room, Trish pulled her suitcase off the closet shelf. She threw in jeans, T-shirts, and underwear. She was pulling blouses off hangers when her mother entered the room.

"Where are you going?"

"Kentucky." Trish rolled a sweat shirt and stuffed it in a corner of the case.

"What do you mean by that?"

"I mean I'm going to see Spitfire. The Shipsons invited me to come anytime, and I'm going."

"Trish, this is crazy." Marge stood between her daughter and the suitcase. "You're not going anywhere. That college class starts next week, and you've work to do here besides."

"Mother, listen to me. I cannot stay here another minute. I'm going stark-raving mad. Today I did something so stupid it almost cost us a horse. Everywhere I look I expect to see Dad, and he's not here. Right now, I wouldn't even want to see him."

"Well, you're *not* going to Kentucky. We can work this out."

"No." Trish shook her head. "I can't stand to stay here. Let me go see if Spitfire is all right."

"You don't have a ticket. It'll cost a fortune." Marge sank down on Trish's bed.

"You've forgotten, I have money now. More money than any girl needs." Trish dusted off her riding boots and added them to the bag.

"No. I just can't see it, Trish." Marge covered her face with her hands. "Not now, anyway."

"Running away? Great." David stood in the doorway.

"What's it to you? I'd think you'd be happy to have such a stupid person out of your way."

"Trish, David." Marge raised her voice.

"I'm going, and that's it!" Trish snapped the locks on the suitcase.

Marge rose to her feet. "Enough!" The word sliced the air.

Trish and David stared at their mother.

Marge took a deep breath. "Now . . ." She looked to Trish, then David. "I know you mean well, David, but you're not helping things right now. Let me deal with your sister."

"Right." David turned and retreated down the hall.

"Trish, I don't want you to go to Kentucky right now. Running away never solved anything."

You should know, Trish thought, glaring at her mother. *You checked out when things got too tough, remember?* But nothing came out of her mouth; she just gritted her teeth. Then, "Mom, I'll be back in time for school, I promise. Maybe this trip will help me. It can't hurt anything."

Marge pulled the desk chair out and sat with her arms resting on its back. She took a deep breath and sighed, watching Trish pace from the bed to the window.

Trish sank down on the end of the bed. "Mom, I feel like I'm going crazy. What am I going to do? What's happening to me? To us?" Her voice faded into a whisper.

Marge shook her head, then rested her chin on her rolled fists. "It's called grief, Trish. We all have to work through it." She looked out the window, seeming to study the leaves rustling in the slight breeze. Then she smiled at Trish, as if returning from a faraway place. "I know how much you love that horse. Maybe seeing him *would* help. But I have one condition—" she paused "—that you go see Pastor Mort first."

Trish fell back across the bed. "I can't, Mom. I just can't. Not now, anyway. I—I'll go when I get back." She chewed on her thumbnail. "Please don't make me go. Not now."

"What about Patrick's training schedule?"

"David can ride for the four, five days I'm gone."

Marge pushed her hair off her forehead. "You promise you'll see Pastor Mort when you get back?"

Trish nodded. "Yes. I will. I really will."

"Call the Shipsons, then, and ask if it's all right with them."

"Thanks, Mom!"

Chapter
09

Trish wondered if Spitfire would look different.

She stared out the plane window as the aircraft approached the Lexington airport. She still had a hard time believing she was in Kentucky. Only yesterday she'd had the incident with Miss Tee on the road. It seemed as if her telescope were playing tricks on her, putting home at the small end, far away.

She'd called Rhonda last night to say she was leaving for a few days. It was strange, but she hadn't told her best friend about the fight, if you could call it that, with her mother and her brother. Was she losing contact with Rhonda too?

Mrs. Shipson had promised to meet the plane, even seemed offended when Trish talked about renting a car.

Trish chewed on her knuckle. She hadn't called Red. Did she want to see him too? Why were there so many questions buzzing around in her head? She wished things could go back to the way they used to be.

Bernice Shipson, silver-haired and stylish as ever, greeted Trish with a quick hug. Her soft accent was musical and friendly. "Do you have other luggage to pick up?"

"Yes, I couldn't fit it all into my carry-on." Trish dug out her tickets to show the baggage claim. "I really appreciate your letting me come on such short notice."

"We meant it when we said you are welcome anytime, Trish. I found myself feeling a little jealous when Martha Finley talked about you going to California. We haven't had young people in our home for a long while."

"I don't remember hearing you speak of children." Trish switched her bag from one shoulder to the other.

"No, our only son was killed in Vietnam," Mrs. Shipson said softly.

"Oh . . . I—I'm so sorry," Trish stammered. "I didn't know."

"Not many people do. It was a long time ago. The pain has eased considerably . . ." She smiled at Trish. "That's why I can tell you with all honesty that you will get through this time of grief for your father. Right now it hurts so badly you don't know how you'll ever make it, but God lives up to His promises. Someday the pain will be bittersweet—blended with all the good memories."

It was hard for Trish to hear this. *Wasn't it God who had let her father die?*

As if reading her mind, Mrs. Shipson laid her hand on Trish's arm. "Right now you are so angry with God, you're certain you'll never have anything to do with Him again."

Trish stared at her. "You felt that way too?"

The woman nodded.

"What did you do?"

"I decided to trust God—and rest. There was nothing else I could do."

A hurrying traveler bumped into Trish and apologized.

"We'll talk again, if you like. I just wanted you to know that I understand what you're feeling. And I'm glad Donald and I could be here for you." She smiled through misty eyes. "Now, let's get your things. A certain black horse will be thrilled to see you."

As they were loading Trish's bags in the trunk, Trish said, "Mrs. Shipson . . ."

"Please call me Bernice."

"Bernice, thank you."

Conversation flowed between them all the way to BlueMist Farms as though they were old friends. Bernice pointed out the sights and shared bits of local folklore.

Trish felt as if she were in a whole new world. Even the soft leather seat of the Cadillac they were riding in seemed to wrap comfort around her. And the gentle, cool air blowing through the air vents refreshed her. *If only Dad were here, it would be perfect* flitted through her mind. *If only there were no more if only's.* She tried to concentrate on the story Bernice was telling her.

They drove straight down to the stallion barn. Trish whistled her two-tone call to Spitfire as soon as she stepped out of the car. A sharp whinny and pounding hooves was her immediate answer. Inside the barn, Spitfire waited impatiently at the door of his stall. He nickered again and then again, as though he couldn't believe what he was seeing.

Trish leaned her forehead against his and rubbed both his satiny cheeks with trembling hands. "I've missed you so, fella; you just have no idea."

He bumped her gently with his nose and nuzzled her pocket. Trish pulled out a withered bit of carrot, but Spitfire didn't seem to mind. He munched once and blew in her face, ruffling her bangs. Trish rubbed his ears and smoothed his forelock.

"I think he missed you as much as you missed him." Bernice stood back to let the two of them talk.

"I see you made it, lass." Timmy O'Ryan sounded so much like Patrick that Trish did a double take. "Like I told you on the phone, he was off his feed for a few days at first. Kind of moped around here, but I can see you're the medicine he needed."

"And you for me," Trish murmured into the colt's twitching ears. Spitfire shook his head. Her breath tickled. He draped his head over her shoulder, cocked a back foot, and sighed. His eyes closed in contentment as Trish kept stroking.

Timmy laughed, a low, musical chuckle. "What a baby he is. One of the grooms wouldn't believe this unless he saw it."

"Why, did something happen?"

"Spitfire was living up to his name one morning. Jumping around and backing his groom into a corner. Then he grabbed the guy's hat and threw it across the stall." The trainer rocked back on his heels. "You can be sure that Nick is real cautious around the big black now."

"Up to your old tricks, eh?" Trish jiggled Spitfire's halter to wake him up. "Hats are his favorite toy. I think he just likes to see how people react. Huh, fella?" Trish tickled the colt's whiskery upper lip.

Spitfire twitched it back and forth and licked her hand.

"Why don't you exercise him every morning while you're here," Timmy said, a grin creasing his leathery face.

"I'd love to." Trish smoothed one hand after the other down the black's long face.

"Dinner's waiting up at the house," Mrs. Shipson said, after checking her watch. "If you can bear to leave him, that is."

Trish gave Spitfire a last pat. "See you in the morning, fella." The colt nickered when she walked away, then let loose with a shrill whinny. "I'll be back." Trish waved from the door.

"There's no doubt he's your horse," Bernice said as she slid into the driver's side of the car.

"Yeah, I know."

At the house, Mrs. Shipson led Trish down the hall to the same lovely, antique-furnished room. "I've been calling this Trish's room ever since you were here," she said. The sheer curtains billowed in the evening breeze as she opened the door. "I hate to rush you, but dinner is ready to serve. Just wash and come down. You can put your things away later, if that's all right."

"Sure. I'll be right down."

The same friendly woman served dinner as before. "Now, y'all just eat up," she said with a broad smile. "There's nothing like my cookin' out your way." She set a platter of fried chicken right in front of Trish. "Now, that there's fried okra, in case you ain't had that before." She pointed to a bowl of unfamiliar green vegetable. "And I 'spect you to have more'n one biscuit. We gotta spoil you right quick if you're gonna stay only a few days." Her laugh drifted back over her shoulder as she returned to the kitchen for more food.

Mr. Shipson said the blessing and then smiled at Trish. "Sarah's one of a kind. She and I grew up together. Her mother was our family cook before her. And you'd better eat her food or her feelings will be hurt. There's nothing she likes better than seeing people enjoy her cooking."

Trish took a piece of chicken and passed the platter to Bernice. "She made enough to feed ten teenagers."

"I know. She's always afraid someone will go away hungry."

Not much chance of that, Trish thought as she turned down a third helping. She felt she would burst.

"I thought we might go to Louisville tomorrow to attend the races," Bernice said, tucking her snowy-white napkin back into the silver napkin ring. "I've heard a certain red-headed jockey is riding tomorrow."

Trish could feel the heat of a blush rise to her cheeks. She grinned at the older woman. "I'd like that."

"Does he know you're here?"

Trish shook her head.

"Then we'll just surprise him, won't we?"

The ride around the track the next morning was a bit of heaven for Trish. She rode Spitfire around several times, and then Timmy beckoned her off to a utility track that led toward a grove of trees.

Trish inhaled deeply of the soft morning air. The sun just peeked over the tops of the lacy-leaved oak trees, gilding everything with a golden brush. Spitfire snorted and jigged sideways. The bit jangled as he tossed his head.

"They fox hunt through here in the fall," Timmy said as they jogged along. "You should come for that sometime. You know how to jump?"

"Not really, although I've tried it a couple of times. My best friend is the jumper in the bunch. She'd go crazy here."

"Bring her along. I'm sure we could find mounts for both of you. You're planning on coming for the Breeder's Cup anyway, aren't you?"

A thrill of excitement skittered up Trish's back. "Uh . . . I don't know yet." *Wouldn't that be something. But I'd have to be back in school in October.* It was an idea worth thinking about, anyway.

Driving into the parking lot at Churchill Downs the next afternoon brought back a rush of memories for Trish. But being a spectator instead of a jockey made it easier as she leaned on the outside of the fence to the paddocks.

"Hey, Red, good luck!" Trish called after him as he followed the others to the saddling paddock.

Red stopped so fast the jockey behind him bumped into him.

"Trish!" He stepped toward her, a grin splitting his face. He clasped her cheeks in both hands and planted a kiss right on her astonished mouth. "I can't believe you're here. Why didn't you call? I could have met your plane."

"I know. So, I surprised you." Trish wasn't sure if her cheeks were warm from a blush or from his hands.

"See you right after this race, okay?" Red waved at the official who motioned him to the saddling paddock. "Don't you leave, hear?" He blew her another kiss as he backpedaled to the paddock.

"I think that young man is very fond of you." Bernice chuckled softly. "His face just lit up when you called his name."

Trish fanned herself with the program. *Talk about faces lighting up.*

"Would you like something to drink before we head for our box?"

"Thank you. That would be nice."

After another delicious meal in the evening, Trish thought, *I could get used to this lifestyle. A private box at the track, someone to wait on me, make my bed. I get to play with Spitfire, and no mucking stalls.*

Up in her room, she leaned back against the stack of lace-trimmed pillows on her bed. *Yes, I could like this.* Home seemed very far away— like on another planet. Thoughts of Red pulled her ahead to the next afternoon. He planned to take her out to dinner and to a movie. Mrs. Shipson had winked and nodded her approval when she heard of the invitation.

After their ride the next morning, Spitfire nibbled Trish's braid as she brushed him. "Knock it off." Trish smacked him on the nose, then hugged him. "You big goof; when are you gonna grow up?" Spitfire snorted and shook his head.

"I think he understands every word you say," Donald Shipson said as he watched the girl and horse together.

"I was the first human to touch him." Trish brushed a bit of straw off the colt's ear. "We've been best buds ever since."

"Must be terribly hard for you at home, with both him and your father gone."

Trish nodded. "It is."

"Well, if you ever decide to come to Kentucky, you know where your home is." He pushed away from the stall door. "You about ready for breakfast?"

"You people eat like this all the time?"

"You have to learn to pick and choose—and not let Sarah railroad you. Also, I run from the big house to the barns rather than take a car. That helps."

Together, they jogged down the road and across the creek. Huge oak trees shaded the drive to the house and made the rise deceptive. Trish was puffing a bit when they stopped at the front porch.

The date with Red would live on in Trish's memory for a long time. He took her to a white-tablecloth restaurant, where she wished she'd had a nice dress to wear instead of just slacks and a blouse. She tried cajun food for the first time and nearly choked on the spicy blackened red fish.

Red handed her the bread basket. "Here. This works better than water." His eyes twinkled in the candlelight.

After the dessert, which the waiter brought flaming to their table, Red set a small box in front of Trish. "So you think of me often," he said softly.

"I already do." Trish fingered the gold cross he'd given her before. "I wear it all the time."

Her hand trembled as she opened the box. Inside lay a gold link bracelet with a delicate gold charm. It was a racing horse and jockey. "Oh, Red, it's beautiful!" She lifted it from the box and looked at it more closely. "Thank you," she said to his smiling face. It was all she could manage. The familiar lump had taken up its place in her throat.

Red put the bracelet on Trish's wrist and fastened the clasp and the safety chain. "Now you can think of me *more* often." He leaned forward and kissed her softly.

Before she knew it, Sunday arrived—time to go home. Red, the Shipsons, and Timmy O'Ryan waved her off at the airport. Trish could feel a smile deep inside as she sat on the plane waiting for takeoff. If this had been a true example of southern hospitality, she knew she liked it.

Her mood lasted until the plane landed in Portland. Marge and David were there to meet her, but she still looked for her father. All the pain came crashing down around her. He would never again be there to welcome her home.

Chapter
10

Anywhere is better than home, Trish thought.

She stared at the empty recliner by the fireplace. It was always the first place she looked when she came in the front door—as if the last weeks had been a bad dream.

The weight of her loss settled heavier on her shoulders with each step down the hall to her bedroom. She dropped her suitcase, threw herself across her bed, and drifted off into that no-man's-land between waking and sleeping.

Sometime later she jerked upright. "Dad?" She stared around the room, her gaze searching for the source of the voice. She was so certain she'd heard her father call her. But there was no one there. She could only hear the drone of the television from the living room.

She rubbed her eyes and shook her head. Was she really going crazy after all? When she flopped back against the pillows, scenes of Kentucky drifted through her mind. Spitfire, the dates with Red, BlueMist Farms and the wonderful people there. Why did the pain return when she came home?

"I can't stand this," she muttered as she pulled on her boots. She ran down the hall and out the front door, totally ignoring her mother's questioning voice.

"Where you going?" David asked as she stormed into the tack room. He dropped the bridle he'd been cleaning and rose to his feet. Patrick looked up from the records he'd been studying.

"Welcome home, lass." He shut the book. "Can we be helpin' you?"

"No." Trish reached for bridle and saddle. "I'm just going riding for a while on Dan'l. I won't be gone long."

"It's getting late to be out on the road."

"I know. I'll go back up the hill."

"You okay, Trish?" David sat back down.

"I guess." But she shook her head as she said it.

Dan'l seemed to enjoy the ride more than Trish did. He danced back into the stable area and tossed his head when she jumped to the ground. "Thanks, old man." Trish stripped off the tack and gave the aging gray Thoroughbred a halfhearted brushing before she released him back into pasture.

The lights from Patrick's mobile home brightened the road up to the house. "I should stop and see him," she told Caesar as they padded up the gentle rise. "Maybe tomorrow."

She stopped for a moment on the deck at the back of the house. Her mother's fuchsias and begonias spilled over their baskets in explosions of pinks and purples. Peeper frogs chorused from down by the drainage ditch. Trish and her father used to sit out here and watch the humming-birds drink at the purple and white fuchsia blossoms.

Memories everywhere.

She slid open the sliding glass door into the family room. The fish tank bubbled away in the corner, just like always.

"There's dinner in the oven," her mother called from the living room. Trish could hear the squeak of her mother's rocker. She must be knitting—like always.

"Thanks, anyway, I'm not hung—" Trish froze in the doorway. "What are you doing in Dad's chair?" Her voice cracked on the words.

David looked up from his place in the worn leather recliner. "What's with you?"

"That's Dad's chair. You have no right sitting there." She advanced on him like she would pull him bodily from the chair.

"Knock it off. I can sit here; Dad wouldn't mind." David raised his hands to keep her from pounding him.

"Trish, what is the matter with you?" Marge rose from her rocker.

"That's Dad chair!" Trish screamed. "Neither of you care!" She stormed from the room, but before she was out of earshot she heard David say, "You'd better do something about her, Mom, before she goes off the deep end."

Trish entered the sanctuary of her own room and wrapped both arms around herself to stop the shaking. Her throat and eyes burned. Was this what life would be like at home from now on? She bit her lip hard. *Who needs this?*

It sounded as if her mother were in the next county when she came into Trish's room sometime later. "Trish, we need to talk about this."

Trish buried her face deeper in the pillow and shook her head. "I can't," she mumbled. She fell back into that black hole where memories and bad feelings didn't exist.

She missed morning works the next day, and slept until her mother came in at ten. "You have to register today, Trish." The voice cut through Trish's fog like a drill sergeant's.

Trish rolled on her back and threw an arm over her face. "I have all day."

"No, you have an appointment with Pastor Mort at one. And you need to register first."

Trish threw back the covers and leaped to her feet. "I'm not talking to him today, Mom."

"Yes, you are," Marge said firmly. "You promised me you would when you got back from Kentucky, remember?"

"Fine. I need to go to the bathroom." She brushed past her mother and headed down the hall. Her head pounded like a herd of runaway ponies.

She drove into Vancouver with the top of the convertible down even though the skies were gray. Maybe a little rain on her head wouldn't hurt. *You gotta get hold of yourself,* she ordered. *You're acting crazy.*

She stopped at a stoplight. Then the sound of a horn behind her made her pop the clutch. The car stalled. Another horn blared while Trish restarted her car and eased through the signal. She'd zoned out again.

A light mist was falling as Trish turned into the parking lot of the administration building at Clark College. She pushed the button to raise the convertible top and waited till it snapped in place. Raindrops formed a trickle down the windshield. Even the sky was crying. She clamped down on the thought.

She finally pushed herself out of the car and headed for the double glass doors. She could see long tables set up for registration inside.

"Excuse me," someone behind her said.

Trish still had her hand on the door. She removed it and stepped aside. She couldn't make herself go in.

She arrived early at the church for her appointment. When she closed her eyes and rested her head against the neck rest in her car, she tried to picture Spitfire—and their rides in Kentucky. The picture wouldn't come. All she could see was the misery on her mother's face, and on David's when she yelled at him. What was she doing to them?

A tap on her window brought her back to the present with a start. "Oh—Pastor Mort."

"Sorry, Trish. I didn't mean to startle you. Would you like to come in now?"

Trish nodded and bit back the "Not really."

"That's some car you have there. We missed you. How was Kentucky?"

"Oh, it was . . . wonderful. Spitfire was as happy to see me as I was to see him. It's hard being so far apart." She walked through the door he held open for her. "Thanks."

"Can I get you a Coke or something?" Pastor Mort hung his coat on a rack by the door.

Trish shook her head. "No, thanks."

"Sit down, sit down. I know this is hard for you, Trish, but I'm glad to see you. It seems like you've been gone a long time." He took a chair opposite Trish, rather than behind his desk.

Trish crossed her arms over her chest and slid down a bit in her chair. "I really have nothing to say." She tried to sound casual, but realized she sounded rude.

"Your mother's concerned about you, Trish."

"Yeah, I know."

"Did you get registered at the college?"

Trish shook her head. "I couldn't."

"No room in the class?"

She shook her head again. "No, that wasn't it. I just couldn't do it."

"I see." He tapped a finger against his chin and leaned forward. "Trish, I want to help you, and I know I can, but you have to want help. I'm here for you anytime—day or night. I'll come to your house, if that would be easier for you." He waited for her response.

"I . . . ah—" Trish bit her bottom lip. "Okay, that would be easier." She stood and fled from the room before the pastor could say anything more.

I just had to get outta there, she thought on the drive home. *Maybe I need to get out of here!*

"So what time is your class?" Marge asked from her rocking chair when Trish came in.

"No class." Trish started down the hall to her room.

"You mean they were full already?"

Trish leaned her forehead on her crossed arms against the wall. "No, I mean I didn't register. Mom, I can't even think. I zone out, fall asleep. I just can't take chemistry now; I'd flunk for sure."

"Did you talk to Pastor Mort?"

"I saw him. We talked a little."

"Trish, you *will* see him again? You promised."

"Yes, Mother. I will see him again. He's going to come to the house."

"Okay. I've backed off long enough, and I feel it's time you get some help. You've been rude, and even cruel—to all of us. I won't tolerate it any longer. Your dad and I did not raise you to act like this."

"Mom—you think I *like* what's happened to us?" Trish hurled the words at her mother. "You can't just put a Band-Aid on it and expect everything to be all right. What can Pastor Mort do? What can anyone do? You . . . you just don't understand." She whirled in the hall and marched out the front door.

Jumping into her car, she jammed the key into the ignition and cranked it hard. The engine roared to life. She threw it into first, and gravel spun from the tires as she roared out the driveway.

After shifting into third out on the road, Trish floored it. The car leaped forward, picking up speed—forty, fifty, sixty. She cranked the wheel hard around the first curve.

Was she trying to outrun the voices screaming in her head? Seventy. Trish hit the brakes to make it around a ninety-degree bend. Her front wheels hit the shoulder but she jerked the car back on course.

For a few minutes she drove more cautiously, her heart pounding. She flicked on the radio to drown out her thoughts.

Radio blaring, she picked up speed again. The mist was coming steadily now, and she turned on the wipers.

Up into the Hockinson Hills, Trish followed the winding road. Driving like this was like racing a Thoroughbred, the car responsive to the wheel like a horse to the bit. She swung a hard left. The car skidded. Trish caught it and gritted her teeth until she straightened again.

Another hard right. She tapped the breaks. A hard left. Too soon! She slammed on her brakes and left the road, bumping over ruts and into a hayfield. Her head hit the roof. Slamming down again she bit her tongue.

The car stalled on a hay bale.

Trish leaned her head on the steering wheel. She felt like throwing up. Her hands shook so hard she could hardly turn off the ignition. She threw open the door in time to lose whatever was in her stomach.

Her dad was gone. Spitfire was gone. And now she'd wrecked her car. What else was left? Maybe she should have hit that tree.

Then it all would have been over.

Chapter
11

But it wasn't over.

Trish dug in her purse for a tissue and wiped her mouth. "Oh, for a drink of water," she whispered in the stillness. When she finally felt like her legs would hold her up, she opened the door and stepped out. Walking around the car, she checked for damage. The only problem she could see was a flat tire on the front passenger side.

She got back in and turned the key. The engine started immediately, and Trish levered the gearshift gently into reverse. Slowly, she eased out the clutch and backed the car off the hay bale.

"Too bad you weren't equipped with a phone too," she said, patting the dashboard. "I don't see a house anywhere." She'd shut the engine off again, and her voice seemed to echo in the quietness around her.

"Well, if anyone is going to change that tire, it's going to have to be me." At least she had the tools and knew how to use them. Somehow, though, she'd never quite planned on changing a tire in the rain, at dusk, and in a hayfield—on her new car.

What is your mother going to say now? her nagger piped up.

"Plenty, I suppose," Trish answered curtly.

When she got back on to the road she noticed the alignment was off; it was hard to steer and keep the car on the road. Trish felt like crawling into the house. There was no way to hide the fact that she'd had some trouble. She was soaked, and her clothes were dirty.

"What happened to you?" Marge gasped.

Trish tried to sound casual. "I missed a curve and ended up on a hay bale. A front tire went flat, so I changed it."

"Where were you?"

"Somewhere up in the Hockinson Hills."

"Tricia Evanston, you scared me half to death when you took off like you did. And look at you."

"Are you hurt, lass?" Trish could hear disappointment in Patrick's voice.

"Not really. Something's wrong with the car, though."

David shook his head. "Nice going, Trish."

"I think we need to talk." Trish sighed. "Let me go to the bathroom first and get cleaned up. I need something to drink too. My stomach hurts."

Marge followed her daughter to the bathroom. "Let me see your mouth. Is it bleeding?"

"I just bit my tongue." Trish stuck it out for inspection. She rinsed her mouth and wiped off her face. "Really, I'm okay. Just shook up." Her hands trembled as she dried them.

Marge pulled Trish into her arms. "Oh, Tee, if anything happened to you, I don't know what I'd do."

Trish leaned limply against her mother. She'd held the tears in so long they wouldn't come even when she wanted them to. Her throat and eyes burned as she and Marge walked back to the kitchen.

Trish slumped into her chair at the big oak table. Lifting her head to look at her mother took a major effort.

"I think you bent the tie rods in the front end of your car," David announced, washing his hands at the kitchen sink. "I couldn't see any leaking from the radiator or the oil pan, though. You'll have to take it in to the garage in the morning."

"I guessed that, David."

"I think you ruined the tire too."

81

"What did you want to talk about, Trish?" Marge asked, stopping David's recital of damages.

"I need to get back to racing." Trish looked at her mother imploringly. "I'll go crazy unless I get busy again. Everywhere I look I expect to see Dad—"

"Don't you think the rest of us feel the same way?" David asked accusingly. "You're not the only—"

"David . . ." Marge cut him off.

"I know." Trish ran her fingers along the edge of the table runner.

"What about the chemistry makeup?" Marge asked.

"Adam said there are several colleges near where I'd be staying in California. I can take classes at night, or hire a tutor if I have to. Mom, please let me go."

The silence at the table stretched into minutes. The fish tank bubbled in the corner; Caesar thumped his leg on the deck as he scratched for fleas.

Trish looked up to see her mother with her eyes closed, her hand propping up her forehead. Trish knew her mother was probably praying.

She didn't dare look at her brother. She knew she wouldn't get any sympathy from him.

Marge finally dropped her hand and looked at her daughter. "I have one condition and there will be no arguing it. If you want to go to California, you will have to talk with Pastor Mort first. No games."

Trish swallowed hard. "Okay. I can do that."

David shook his head, and Marge laid her hand on his arm to keep him from leaving the table.

"And you'll be back in time for school, whether the season is finished there or not. There will be no discussion about that either."

Trish nodded. School seemed a long way off.

Patrick had stepped into the room when Marge mentioned California. She asked him, "How quickly can you make the necessary arrangements?"

"A couple of days. The horses are ready any time. I'll call Adam and get a horse hauler." He looked to David. "Who do you generally use?"

"We borrowed Diego's van last winter. I could call him and see about using it again. He may have a horse or two he wants to send down there too."

"How many does the van hold?"

"Six, I think."

Trish thought she'd be relieved if her mother agreed to her wishes, but instead she felt drained. She pushed her chair back and stood up. "Thanks, Mom. We'll talk more tomorrow." She tried to catch David's eye but he wouldn't look at her.

Once in bed, her nagger began to taunt her. *You used to trust God and His promises . . . the verses that were on your wall. Your life would be a lot easier if . . .* Trish groaned and turned over, burying her head under the pillow.

After working the horses in the morning, Trish called the Chrysler dealership and made an appointment to bring in her car.

"Mom, would you follow me into the shop?" Trish asked after she'd hung up the phone.

"Sure." Marge leaned against the sink, sipping hot coffee. "What time?"

"Right away. I just need to change clothes."

Trish brushed her hair in front of the bathroom mirror. She didn't think she looked like herself. Even her hair was unmanageable. The charm from her new bracelet clinked against the edge of the sink when she leaned over to brush her teeth. "Whoa, I haven't called Red since I got back."

After her car was looked over, Trish sat in a state of shock. The estimate on the repairs read between $2,500 and $3,000. New bumper, repair tie rods, adjust alignment, replace dented oil pan—and that was only what could be readily seen. There could be more damage inside.

The only good news was that she should be able to pick the car up the next evening.

"Are you going to file an insurance claim?" her mother asked as they walked back to the family station wagon.

"I don't know. What do you think?" Trish rubbed her forehead with the tips of her fingers. She winced as she hit a tender spot. She must have banged her head on the steering wheel.

"It might be better to pay it off yourself, since the accident was your fault. That way it won't show up on your record. Your insurance rate could go up quite a bit at your age."

"I'll have to get money transferred from savings to checking, then. Can we stop by the bank?"

Marge nodded as she pulled out onto the street. "When will you see Pastor Mort?"

She'd decided to see him at his office. "I'm going in this afternoon at three. Can I borrow your car?" Trish hated to ask, but she had no choice.

Sitting in the pastor's office, Trish felt like a child being reprimanded in the principal's office at school.

"Who are you mad at, Trish?" Pastor Mort said gently after a few moments of general conversation.

Trish shrugged. "No one, I guess."

"Do you think that drive you took was because of anger?"

Trish tightened her jaw. "Maybe." If she didn't talk much, maybe this would be over sooner than she thought. At least she was doing what her mother had asked.

"I think you're mad at yourself."

Trish raised her eyebrows. "Maybe. I know driving like I did was stupid. I'll never do that again." Her voice became stronger. "Actually, I can't believe I did it. Three thousand dollars—maybe more."

"Do you think you could be mad at your dad for dying?"

"That too . . ." Her voice trailed off.

"How about God?"

Trish nodded. How did he know all this stuff? "My dad used to say that God heals. He had me memorize Bible verses about it." Trish shoved herself to her feet. "Yes, I'd say I was mad at God. He doesn't live up to His promises. . . ." Her voice broke. "I don't want to hear about God's promises ever again."

Pastor Mort just nodded.

Trish sat down again. "What's worse—my mother is taking over Dad's place! And my brother sits in Dad's chair. Patrick's doing his work down at the barns. No one seems to miss him except me. Why did he leave me?"

"I don't think your father wanted to leave you, Trish, and I understand how you feel."

"Do you?" Trish glared at him. "You talk about how God is so good. Well, I don't see Him that way." Trish held her head in her hands. She felt like a volcano about to erupt.

She pulled her legs up underneath her. "I'm sorry—"

"It's okay." Pastor Mort poured her a glass of water from the pitcher on his desk. "Is there anything else you want to say?"

"That's not enough?" She sipped the water.

"No, I think there's more."

Trish stared into her glass. "I guess I—uh—I feel so . . . guilty. Like it's my fault that Dad died. And that I shouldn't be mad like this. Sometimes I just want to die . . . it hurts so bad." She leaned her head against the back of the chair.

"Do you know anything about the grieving process, Trish?"

Trish shrugged. "I—I guess you're sad, and you cry a lot."

"Have you cried a lot?"

"At first I did. Mostly when I was alone. Now I can't. There aren't any more tears, I guess."

"You've locked them away, Trish. There are more tears, and you should let them come. Grief comes in stages. Denial, anger, fear, guilt—it's all normal. Every person that suffers a loss experiences these stages of grief—in different degrees, of course. Sometimes we go back and forth between emotions. It's okay to be angry at God, by the way. He loves you no matter what you think of Him."

Trish muttered into her glass, "If this is love, what is hate like?"

"God isn't punishing you or trying to hurt you, Trish. We can't always know *why* or understand what life throws at us. As long as we live on the earth there is going to be some pain, illness, death. God only promises to get us through it—if we trust Him. You have to deal with your feelings. They aren't good or bad, they're just there—a part of you. By trying to lock them up, not allowing yourself to cry, you get stuck in the rage. Tears are healing, Trish. They are not a sign of weakness."

"Do you think I drove off like I did because I was stuck in a rage?"

"What do you think?"

Trish nodded in spite of herself. "But nothing will bring my dad back. And I can't live without him."

"It may seem like that right now. But you have to give it some time. You can't be over your grief so quickly. You know your dad would want you to go on and enjoy your life. He did the best he could with his. I have a suggestion. How about writing a letter to God, telling Him exactly how you feel? Don't hold anything back; tell it like it is. And then write a letter to your father."

Trish stared at the pastor, as if he were a little wacky.

"Your dad found writing in his journal was a big help back in the early days of his illness, when he was angry and scared."

"He was angry and scared?"

"Yes, he was. He and I did a lot of talking when he was in the hospital that first time. He said journaling helped a lot. He could say what he felt without feeling like he was being judged."

"I don't see how writing can help."

"I agree it doesn't make much sense at first, but try it. It works. Will you try, Trish?"

"I—I'll see. Maybe I will."

"Let me know when you do, and what you think of it."

Trish stood to her feet. "Is that all?"

"I think that will do for now. Thanks for coming, Trish."

Why is he thanking me? "Thank you."

Once outside, Trish felt free as a swallow in the spring. Maybe it was just the fresh air. She remembered her father suggesting journaling to her. And whether she wanted to admit it or not, talking to Pastor Mort *did* make her feel better.

At home, David greeted her with, "Patrick thinks Miss Tee may have torn a ligament in her shoulder—because of that run on the road."

Chapter
12

Gatesby didn't want to leave home.

"Do you always have to be a jerk?" Trish muttered as she clamped her hands tighter on the lead shank. Her shoulder already ached from the force of the gelding's high jinks.

"Walk him around and we'll try again." Patrick planted both hands on his hips. "Sure and he can be an ornery beast."

"You got that right." David glared at his charge. "Okay, Trish, let's take him around again and then right up the ramp without slowing or stopping."

This time Gatesby walked in without a snort. David kept up his muttering while tying the horse in place. "Anderson didn't do us any favors when he brought you back."

Gatesby nosed David's gloved hand. "Knock it off."

"You really gotta watch him when he does that," Trish told Patrick. The bay swung his hindquarters and trapped David in the stall.

"Move over, you miserable hunk of horse," David ordered, slapping Gatesby's shoulder. The horse squeezed him tighter. "Trish!"

"It's good to know I'm needed," she said sweetly. "All right, Gatesby, get over." The gelding straightened out and peered over his shoulder. Trish slipped in beside him and fed him a carrot piece from her pocket. "You really are a pain, you know." She rubbed his forehead and smoothed the forelock in place. "Now, you behave yourself."

The two fillies walked in with no problems. The men closed the doors and they were ready to roll. David and Patrick would take turns driving the van, and Trish would follow in her car.

"Please be careful," Marge cautioned as she handed a small cooler to the men and another to Trish. "Call me as soon as you get there." She leaned in the window to kiss Trish on the cheek. "I'll be praying for you."

"Don't worry, Mom. Okay?"

"You know I don't worry anymore." A smile flitted across her face and disappeared. For a long time worrying had been a serious problem for Marge, but now it had become a family joke. "It's not easy letting my sixteen-year-old daughter go off like this, though."

"The Finleys are probably more protective than you are," Trish said. "I'll call often."

"Maybe even write?"

"Maybe." Trish waved as she followed the silver van down the driveway.

The trip was uneventful, but long, because they had decided to drive straight through. They pulled into the backside of Bay Meadows at ten in the evening. The guard at the gate gave them instructions to the Finleys' barn.

"Any trouble?" Adam asked as they stepped down from the cab.

"None." David arched his back and dug his fists into the tight muscles.

Trish got out and stretched too. She bent from side to side and rotated her shoulders, then stepped easily into Adam Finley's embrace. "It's good to see you. That was a long haul; I'll take the plane anytime."

"Glad you could come, Trish."

"How are you, Adam?" Patrick asked. "Your barn looks real good."

"I'm doing good, and thanks. The vet will be down here right away to check your horses in. I called him as soon as the gate let me know you were here. So—four new horses in my care. Sure you don't want to stay and help me out, Patrick?"

Patrick shook his head. "Sorry, too much to do up north."

"You miss the track?"

Trish had never really thought about the fact that Patrick might miss the track. She waited for his answer. What if Patrick didn't want to stay with them at Runnin' On Farm?

"Oh, some, yes. But it won't be long before Portland opens. Time flies awful fast when you're having fun." Patrick tipped his hat back on his head. "Gotta keep up with these young folks here."

Trish breathed a sigh of relief. They really did need Patrick now that Dad was gone.

It didn't take long for the vet to check the animals for signs of fever or other illness. As soon as he finished drawing blood samples, they led the horses into their new stalls.

"You'll have plenty to keep you busy here," Patrick said to Trish as they hooked the last gate. "You'll be switching mounts right quick in the mornings."

"At least I don't have to clean stalls." She smiled.

"Yeah, like you've been overworked in that department lately." The sarcasm in David's voice touched a nerve in Trish. Obviously, he still wasn't pleased about her leaving home for the summer.

She missed the easy teamwork with her brother. Was that gone for good too?

"I made reservations for you at a motel across the street," Adam said to the two men. "You can park the van in the lot and I'll give you a ride over. Trish, your room is ready at our condominium. Martha can't wait to see you."

"See you in the morning," Trish called as she waved good-night to David and Patrick.

Trish tried to memorize their route as she followed Adam to his home. He said they had a little condominium, but when he showed her the program numbers on the entry gate she began to wonder.

After winding up a narrow road, he parked in front of a three-level home, stair-stepped into the hill. Martha Finley stood waving from a huge bay window on the second floor. The cream stucco building with a

Spanish-tile roof made her think of the Finley ranch in the San Joaquin Valley.

Martha met them at the ornately carved oak door. Black wrought-iron railings flanked the stairs. "My dear, you have no idea how happy I am to see you!" She hugged Trish and ushered her into the tiled entry. Stairs led up and down to the other levels, and to the right Trish could see the lights of San Mateo with the black hole of San Francisco Bay beyond.

"Wow!" Trish walked across the plush cream carpet to stand in front of the window. She could see the blinking lights of two planes on their slanting approach to San Francisco International Airport. "What a view!"

"We like it." Martha stood beside her. "Being up high like this makes city living bearable. We'd both rather be at the ranch, but this is where the tracks are. If you look off to the left, you can see the San Francisco skyline. I hope you like it here."

"I'm sure I will. Thank you for having me."

"It's our pleasure, dear. Adam teases me about needing someone to fuss over. Come on, I'll show you to your room. It's upstairs; I thought you'd like the view." She pointed to pictures of their three sons and families as they climbed the stairs.

Trish's room faced south. Martha opened the teal-blue drapes to show her the private deck.

Trish dropped her bag on the pile carpet of blues and greens. "What a beautiful room, Martha."

"It did turn out rather nicely, didn't it?"

"Is it new?"

"Yes. This was one of the boys' rooms. When I thought you might be coming to visit us, I redecorated it. You have your own bathroom; there are fresh towels. Now, is there anything else you need out of your car tonight? Are you hungry or thirsty?"

Trish shook her head. "No, I have all I need. And thanks, I'm just fine."

"Good night then, Trish. We'll see you in the morning."

Trish sank down onto the queen-sized bed and stifled a huge yawn. Morning would be here soon. . . .

"Yes?" she answered a tap on the door.

"You can sleep in tomorrow if you'd like." It was Adam. "I know you're beat from that long trip."

"I'll be ready when you are. What time do you leave?"

"Four-thirty." He chuckled.

Trish glanced at the clock. It was midnight. "See you then."

Trish slept well and awoke surprisingly refreshed. Her car was blanketed in fog when she stepped into it. She was mounted on Firefly and out on the track just as a tinge of pink cracked the eastern sky. One of Finley's regular exercise riders rode beside her.

"This is the training track; they're working on the main track behind us." Sam clucked her horse into a trot.

Trish did the same. Firefly settled into her easy gait, alert to every sight and sound on the new track.

"How's it feel to be a Triple Crown winner?" Sam pulled her mount to a walk.

"I don't know. It's like it all happened a long time ago—to someone else." Trish smoothed the filly's mane to one side. "So much has gone on since then."

"Yeah, I heard about your dad. What a bummer." She looked over at Trish. "We were all real sorry to hear it."

"Thanks." Trish didn't know what else to say. "Ahhh . . . you been riding long?"

"This is my third year. Adam says he'll let me race this season. I had some mounts on the fair circuit last year. . . . Well, I gotta gallop once around." She waved to Trish. "See ya."

By the end of morning works, Trish had ridden her own three, Diego's one, and three for Adam. Gatesby had given her a real ride—even her arms felt sore.

"How's it feel to be back in harness?" Adam asked as they headed for the track kitchen.

"Sore." Trish rubbed her right shoulder. A gift from Gatesby.

"A love bite?" David tapped her on the same spot.

"Owww." Trish flinched away. "Knock it off, David."

Patrick held the door open for all of them.

After breakfast David and Patrick prepared to head back.

"Did you call Mom last night?" David asked Trish.

"No, I thought you were going to."

David glared at her. "You said you'd call. I heard you tell Mom you would. You'd better start taking some responsibility."

Stung by her brother's criticism, Trish felt hurt. She'd have to do better, she knew that. They walked to where they'd parked the silver-and-blue van the night before. "Drive safely now," Trish echoed her mother.

David swung up into the driver's seat. "You sound like Mom. Call her once in a while. She still worries even if she won't admit it."

"Yes, boss." Trish touched a finger to her forehead. She waved to Patrick. "You guys coming down for some of the races?"

"We'll see."

"Bring Mom . . ." Trish could hear a note of pleading in her voice. "To the winner's circle."

David tooted the horn as he turned the van around and drove out the entrance toward Highway 101.

Trish felt like another part of her was being torn away—piece by piece. Soon there wouldn't be anything left of her. She kicked the gravel with the toe of her boot, and headed back to the barns. She'd wanted to come to California, and now she was here. What next?

Back at the condo she moved the rest of her things into her room and got settled. The next afternoon, Martha insisted on driving Trish over to the nearby college to register for the chemistry class. She would have classes four evenings a week from six to nine. One of those nights was a lab.

Trish purchased her books in the bookstore and glanced through them on the way back to the Finleys'. "Yuck."

"Not your favorite class?"

"No. They let me drop it because of all the pressure of racing and training, and then my dad being sick. But I'll tell you, I wasn't getting it. David tried tutoring me, but I just don't like chemistry."

"Why are you taking it?"

"I promised my mom. It's one of the requirements for college." Trish shut the book and slipped it back into the plastic bag. "You know any good tutors?"

"Check with your teacher the night of your first class. Maybe he or she will know of a student from last semester."

Trish nodded. "Good idea. Thanks."

Class started the following Monday, and Trish found a tutor right away. Finding a regular time to meet wasn't as easy. They finally settled on Saturday night, because Bay Meadows had late racing on Fridays.

Training was hard enough, and then racing would begin. There were the morning works, time for meals, afternoon study, and classes in the evenings. Then it was to bed and up again to start over.

Trish's agent, Jonathan Smith, met her at the kitchen on the morning of opening day. "I have two mounts for you."

"Okay."

"Second and fourth. You need to be in the jockey room by noon." He went on to tell her about the trainers and the horses. "I have only one for you tomorrow, in the seventh."

Trish waited for the thrill of excitement to bubble up. There was nothing there. "Thanks," she managed. After draining her orange juice glass, she took her tray back to the window.

At the barn she was met by two people. One of them sported an expensive camera. She could recognize reporters a mile away by now.

"You have a couple of minutes?" The young woman swept a strand of long, dark hair behind her ear and offered her hand. "I'm Amanda Sutherlin from *San Mateo Express*, and this is Greg Barton, our photographer."

"Hi." Trish shook his hand too. "I'm in a bit of a hurry. What can I do for you?"

Amanda dug a notebook out of a cavernous black bag. "Just a few questions, if you don't mind."

Trish nodded.

"What brought you to Bay Meadows?"

"Adam Finley. He insisted this would be a good place for me this summer."

"Couldn't you race anywhere in the country after winning the Triple Crown?"

"Possibly. But we've had some personal problems."

"I know. I'm sorry." Amanda glanced down at her notes. "How has that . . . your father's death . . . affected your riding?"

"It hasn't, as far as I know." Trish looked around to see Adam standing beside her.

"Did you bring horses down here to race?"

All the usual questions were asked, and Trish answered as best she could, backed up by Adam. She wasn't sure which was better—to talk about her father, or not. Pastor Mort had said talking about him would make it easier. But it seemed as if it made everyone uncomfortable, and brought back the pain.

Trish mulled the question over in her mind on the way to the jockey dressing rooms near the grandstands. Tall palm trees enhanced the visitor's entrance to the track, but offered little shade. Buses were already delivering loads of senior citizens. The stands were filling up for opening-day ceremonies.

Trish settled into a chair with her chemistry book and notebook. So far she was keeping up, but much of what they'd covered she'd already had. Reviewing it made her realize how quickly she forgot the stuff.

She chewed on a pencil while working out the equations. The women's jockey room, while clean and freshly painted, had none of the amenities of the men's. And none of the bustle. Two other female jockeys sat talking in a corner. They'd greeted Trish when they came in and then left her to her homework.

When the second race was called, Trish put her books away and began her pre-race routine. She polished her boots, cleaned and waxed her layers of goggles. At least a dry track surface meant no mud. She did her normal stretching, then finally put on green silks with a yellow diamond pattern. She snapped the cover over her helmet and waited for the call to the weighing room.

When she stepped outside to walk to the scale, her butterflies came alive and flipped a couple of aerial loops and spins.

"One-o-one," the man running the scale intoned, then grinned at her. "Welcome to Bay Meadows, Trish. And good luck."

Back to the weight training, Trish thought, realizing she'd lost four pounds. She knew most of it was muscle. Where would she find the time to work out in the schedule she'd set for herself?

She followed the parade of jockeys through the side entrance of the grandstands and into the saddling paddock. The stands were full and spectators lined both sides of the walkway. It almost felt like home.

Restless feet and a slashing tail told Trish that her mount in position six was unhappy about something. The tall, rangy dark bay rolled his eyes when she entered the stall.

"This is his first out since he got cut up in a fall last winter," the trainer said. "Take him to the outside where he can run without being bumped around."

Trish nodded and lifted her knee for the mount. The horse laid his ears back when he felt her weight in the saddle.

He fought her all the way to the starting gates. It took three tries to get him in. Trish tried to settle him down and get him thinking about racing, but when the gates flew open he hung back. They were already a stride behind when he finally lunged through the gate.

Trish swung him to the outside, and by the end of the first turn she had the gelding running like he should. The field ran six lengths ahead of them. She went to the whip and brought him even with the next runner, then moved him up as they rounded the next curve. But no matter how much she used the whip, he quit on her down the stretch. They finished dead last.

The next race wasn't much better. They finished off the pace by four.

"Tough luck," Adam consoled Trish that night when she returned from her chemistry class.

"Yeah. I just couldn't get them to run. I don't know, I didn't—" She paused, trying to put words to her feelings. "I just didn't seem to communicate with them; not like usual."

She went to bed that night feeling depressed. Where had the fun of racing gone?

Chapter
13

Trish was boxed in again. She felt like screaming in frustration. Gatesby had broken well from the gate, but here they were on the final turn and she had nowhere to go. If she dropped back they'd be clipped by the horses behind.

Finally the horse on the outside dropped off the pace. Gatesby burst through the hole, but it was too late. They finished fourth.

"Sorry. That was hard to take," Adam commiserated as they walked the gelding back to the barns.

"I shouldn't have let it happen. I must have been asleep or something." Trish slapped her whip against her boot. "Good thing Anderson didn't come all the way from Portland to watch his horse." She patted the gelding's steamy neck. "You deserved better than that, fella."

"Well, you can't beat yourself up over it. Things will turn around. You're too good a jockey for them not to."

"I'm beginning to wonder."

That evening there was a letter from Red. Trish still hadn't answered the last two. She slumped down on the sofa so she could enjoy the night lights while she read. He'd won again. *Glad someone is winning.* And he missed her. She stared out the window, thinking, *Do I really miss him?* If you missed someone weren't they in your thoughts—at least part of the time? Her thoughts seemed to be in a turmoil. Or was she thinking at all?

She toyed with the idea as she climbed the stairs to her room. She found a note on her bed from Martha. *"Help yourself to whatever you'd like to eat. We've gone to a friend's for dinner."*

Trish smiled at the happy face drawn at the bottom of the page. If only she had more time to spend with Martha. They'd have to set a date and go out to lunch and do some shopping. Maybe get some school clothes.

She was too tired to go back downstairs for something to eat. Instead, she fell into bed and back to the blessed emptiness of sleep.

Trish only pulled a D on her first chemistry quiz. She felt as if she'd been kicked by a flying hoof. The rest of the lecture passed in a blur. *Throw if off,* she ordered herself. *You can't let this get you down.*

But it did. It was one more failure to pile on to a load that was getting too heavy to bear.

Her mount the next afternoon swung wide on the turns and finished fourth.

"If I could just have kept him running straight, we'd have been in the money." She slumped on a green wooden trunk in the office at the barns. "What is the matter with me?"

Adam looked up from his paper work. "I think you're trying too hard. You talked about going home for a couple of days. Maybe you should; it might help."

"I'd have to cancel a ride on Sunday. . . . Big deal, the owner would probably be glad to give it to someone who wins once in a while. What about the one for you on Saturday?"

"I'll get someone; don't worry."

"If I skip my lab on Thursday . . ." She shook her head. "No. I'll catch an early flight on Friday morning. Maybe David can pound some chemistry into my head on Saturday. If he'll even talk to me, that is."

"Trouble there too?" Adam leaned back in his green and gold director's chair.

"Yeah. I haven't been too faithful about writing and calling home." *You haven't been too faithful about anything,* her nagger jumped in.

Adam handed her a phone book. "Call the airline now. It'll make you feel better."

Thursday afternoon, Trish rode Bob Diego's gelding to a place. They missed the win by a photo finish.

"You can't complain about that," Adam said as he snapped a lead shank on the gray's halter. "You rode well and that was a tough field. Any horse could have been the winner."

"I shoulda gone to the whip sooner. He could have done it."

"Trish . . ."

"Well, I won with him before."

"That was Portland. The horses here are faster. He did very well."

Trish planned to study the next morning on the plane, but fell asleep. It was easier.

Trish saw Rhonda's beaming face before she saw her mother's as she walked up the ramp from the plane. From the looks of it, Rhonda was in her perpetual-motion mode. She threw her arms around Trish, backed off, then hugged her again.

"Wow! Look at your tan. You been laying out or what?"

"Just the arms and face. The rest of me's white as ever. I don't have any daylight hours to lay out, even though there's a deck right off my bedroom. I've only been on it once."

"My turn." Marge laughed as she reached in for a hug. "I can tell I won't get a word in edgewise this trip home. You have other luggage?"

"Nope, this is it." Trish picked up her sports bag again. "I travel light when I can."

"And you're only staying till Monday," Rhonda groaned. "Why is it my best friend is always in some other part of the country?"

"That's the price of fame." Marge led the way down the escalator and back up to the parking lot.

Trish stopped on the sidewalk to look at Mount Hood with its summer snow streaks. Mount St. Helens was just visible to the north. "No mountains in San Mateo. I feel like I'm really home."

"Maybe someday we'll go skiing again." Rhonda turned to Trish and grinned. "Then, maybe not. Wait till you see—"

Marge stopped at a black-cherry-colored minivan and inserted her key in the lock. "What do you think?" She smiled at Trish.

"What a beauty! You didn't tell me you bought a new car."

"I wanted to surprise you." Marge flipped the electric lock and opened the passenger doors. "Just toss your stuff in. You two can fight for the front seat."

"What'd you do with the wagon?" Trish gave Rhonda a playful shove toward the front.

"I traded it in. Your father and I had looked at this one before, and our mechanic said the wagon needed work, so . . ." She slammed her door shut. "Here we are."

Trish felt the old familiar pain at the mention of her father. When she walked into the house, it hit her like a load of rock, and she could hardly make it to her bedroom.

"Still hurts, huh?" Rhonda sat down on the edge of the bed and hugged a throw pillow to her chest.

Trish nodded. "Shows, huh? It's not so bad when I'm away from home. But when I come back, and he's not here—" She went to look out the window, her hands stuffed in the back pockets of her jeans. "I don't know, Rhonda. Sometimes I wonder if the pain will ever go away."

"Wish I could help, Trish."

"I don't think anyone can." She stood at the window, silent for a few moments. "Let's go see Miss Tee."

Caesar met them at the door, tail thumping, and yipping with excitement.

"Where were you? You missed the car coming in. Some watchdog you are." Trish bent over to tug on his fluffy mane and got a lightning-quick nose lick for her efforts. Then the dog put one white paw on Trish's knee to balance himself and pawed the air with the other. Trish pulled his ears and knelt down to hug him.

"No dogs at the Finleys' city home, though they have two Rottweilers on the ranch." Trish stopped to look over the farm. She could see the horses in their paddocks beyond the barns. Patrick's new mobile home looked settled in on the property. The base was covered with matching skirting, and there were newly planted shrubs and flowers to make it look homey.

The girls trotted on down the rise. Trish's whistle was answered by a whinny from the paddock. Old Dan'l hadn't forgotten her. But Spitfire's shrill response was as absent as Hal's voice.

Trish stopped in the tack room to grab a carrot out of the refrigerator, and broke it into pieces as she and Rhonda meandered past the stables and out the lane to the paddocks.

Miss Tee trotted up to the fence and stood still when Trish took hold of the halter. She munched her carrot and nosed Trish's hand for more. Double Diamond and his dam did the same.

"Where'd you learn those manners?" Trish rubbed the filly's ears and the crest of her mane. "You sure are getting to be a beauty."

"She always has been. Remember what a cutey she was when she'd peek around her mother with the mare's tail draped over her face?" Rhonda patted Double D. "This one's pretty good-looking too."

Dan'l nickered from the next paddock. The yearling and two mares joined him at the fence. *If only Spitfire were here.* Trish leaned her forehead against the filly's.

"There'll never be another horse like Spitfire." She shook her head.

"You two had a pretty special relationship. I think he could read your mind and you his."

"I know. You know what scares me?" The filly blew in her ear.

"What?"

"I can't read my horses anymore. It's like we're not even on the same wavelength. You know how my dad used to say I had a special gift?" She closed her eyes. "It's gone."

"Oh, Trish, I . . ." Rhonda patted Trish's shoulder.

"If I can't race, I don't know what I'll do. Life just isn't worth it."

"Tricia Marie Evanston, don't talk like that!" Rhonda's temper flared like her red hair. "Things'll get better again. I know they will."

Double Diamond raced off at the sound of the raised voice. Miss Tee pulled against Trish's restraining hand. Trish let her go. "I hope so." She wandered over to pat Dan'l. "I sure hope so. It can't get any worse."

"Welcome home, lass," Patrick called as they returned to the barn. "What do you think of the home stock?"

"They're looking good, Patrick. And so are you. Your house is beautiful. You've been working hard."

"Well, your mother's done a lot of it. She sure has a green thumb. What's this I hear about you losing your touch?"

"It's true. I can't bring in a winner for the life of me." Trish and Rhonda flopped on a hay bale in front of the tack room.

"And she says life isn't worth living."

"Blabbermouth." Trish elbowed her friend in the ribs.

"It'll get better, lass, it will." Patrick propped a leg on another bale and leaned his elbow on his knee. "What's that saying?" He wrinkled his brow. "It's always darkest before dawn?"

"Yeah, well, dawn better come pretty soon." Trish levered herself to her feet. "You need me in the morning?"

"Nope. You're on vacation; sleep in."

David was about as friendly as a porcupine at the dinner table that night. He only answered when spoken to.

"What's with him?" Trish questioned her mother as she helped clear the table.

"Why don't you ask him?" Marge rinsed plates in the sink and loaded them into the dishwasher.

The thought of getting into an argument with David was more than Trish could handle. So much for having a chemistry coach.

Her mother had turned down the sheets, and Trish's bed welcomed her. She watched the dancing tree branches make shadows on her wall before sleep claimed her.

"Okay, David, what is it?" she asked after breakfast the next morning.

David looked up from circling the rim of his coffee mug with a forefinger. "You really want to know?"

Trish nodded.

"Okay. You don't call. You don't write. If Mom didn't talk with Martha, we wouldn't know if you were dead or alive." David set his mug down hard. "Even Red's called here asking if you're all right. What are we supposed to tell him?"

Trish's sigh could be felt all the way to her toes. "I'm sorry." She sucked in her bottom lip. "What can I say? You're right."

"I hear Mom crying at night. Losing Dad was bad enough; she shouldn't have to cry about you too."

A gray cloud settled around Trish's shoulders and pressed her to her chair. "I'll do better. I promise."

David stared at her. "Is that all you've got to say?"

Trish nodded.

"I expected you to at least yell at me." A tiny grin lifted one corner of his mouth. "I had all kinds of answers ready."

Trish was speechless. She could hear her mother talking to Caesar out on the deck.

"The four musketeers are going for pizza and a movie this afternoon. How does that sound?"

Trish looked at her brother for the first time in a long time—really looked at him. The frown was gone from his forehead. Her brother, her friend, was back.

That afternoon at the Pizza Shack, Brad asked David, "When do you leave for Arizona?"

"End of August—assuming I'm accepted and all my records transfer."

"That will go fast."

"How come I . . ." Trish shut her mouth. If she'd called home more often, she'd have known.

"I can't wait. I'll have a year-round tan then, not just rusty like you Washingtonians."

"Yeah, big talk." Rhonda flicked soda at him with her straw. "You know for sure where you're going to school, Brad?"

"Mom says Clark, Dad says University of Washington, and my scholarship is for Washington State. I had thought David was going to be there and we could room together." He rested his chin on his hands. "I'm accepted at all three."

"Now the *big* question. What are you going to be when you grow up?" Rhonda teased.

Trish felt like a spectator watching a play from the last row of the balcony. The voices faded in and out, as with a faulty sound system.

"What are you going to do, Tee?"

Trish snapped to attention. "Who, me? Uh—join the foreign legion." Trish took a bite of pizza before looking up to get her friends' response.

"Funny." David shook his head.

"We're seniors this year." Rhonda jumped in to fill the silence. "We can do anything we want."

"Right." David and Brad spoke in the same breath.

Trish sat through the movie but couldn't have told anyone the plot. Rhonda stayed overnight with Trish, and though they usually didn't lack for things to talk about, Trish had to force herself to stay awake. She drifted off in the middle of a sentence.

In the morning, Marge insisted they all go to church together. Trish felt about as much like going to church as to the dentist. She was the last one out to the minivan and sat in the back. Rhonda turned to talk with her but Trish was not in the mood.

She managed to ignore the songs, the Scripture-reading, and the sermon, until Pastor Mort quoted Jesus: " 'In my Father's house are many mansions. . . . I go to prepare a place for you, that where I am, there you may be also.' "

Trish clamped her teeth on her bottom lip. Her father had quoted that verse many times. She glared at the pastor. Had he purposely used this Scripture—because he knew she would be there? Arms locked across her chest, Trish mulled the thought over, trying to put his voice in another dimension.

Rhonda poked her in the side. "You okay?" she whispered.

Trish shook her head.

The service closed with the hymn from Isaiah: "He will raise you up on eagle's wings. . . ." Trish tried to shut it out. When that didn't work, she walked out the door. It may have been her theme song at one time, but not anymore.

"Pastor Mort asked about you," Marge said when she got to the car. "He wondered why you left suddenly. Do you want to go back in and say hello? We'll wait."

Patrick nodded. "It might do you good, lass."

Trish erupted from the backseat. "How come everyone knows what's best for *me*?" Her voice broke as she climbed out of the van and slammed the door after her.

She met Pastor Mort as he was entering his study. "I—I'm sorry I left church like that. I just couldn't take any more." She slouched in a chair in his office.

"I thought so. You looked pretty uncomfortable." His smile was easy; his voice without condemnation. "Contrary to what you might have thought, I did *not* choose that Scripture passage. It was the assigned portion for today."

Trish had to grin. He'd read her perfectly.

"I know that was one of your father's favorite verses. He was looking forward to that mansion, you know." Pastor Mort waited for Trish to say something. He was good at waiting.

"I didn't want to come to church today . . ."

"I figured as much. How's the anger these days?"

Trish grinned again. "Better, I think. It's hard coming home, though. Everything comes back as soon as I walk in the door." She looked down at her hands. "I can't do anything right anymore either. I can't ride like I used to; can't win anything. And I nearly flunked my chemistry quiz— and I'd studied. All I want to do is *sleep*. I can't breathe; it's like the air is too heavy."

Pastor Mort nodded. "Depression can be a part of the grieving process. It happens when we turn our anger inward. Does that seem to fit?"

"Maybe."

"Have you read your father's journal?"

Trish shook her head.

"Have you started one of your own?"

"I—I just don't have time right now. I—" She looked up to study the man's face. "I'm scared. Really scared."

"Why is that?" His voice was soft, compassionate.

Trish sensed that he really cared. "I—I don't think life is worth living anymore."

"Too much effort?"

"Mmmm."

"May I pray with you, Trish?"

Trish shook her head.

"Well, if I can't pray with you now, I promise I will pray *for* you."

She nodded, holding back the tears.

"Try the journaling. I know it will help. I could find someone down there for you to talk to, if you'd like."

"I gotta go. They're waiting for me." Trish stood to her feet. "Thanks."

"It'll get better. Believe me." Pastor Mort stood with her. "I'll send you the name of someone in San Mateo."

The next morning Marge drove Trish to the airport. "What did you think of Miss Tee, Trish?"

"Patrick's been doing a good job with her."

"No . . . I have."

Trish stared at her mother. "You?"

"Yes. Surprised?"

"Surprised isn't the word; you don't even *like* horses."

Marge drove into the short-term parking lot and turned off the engine. "It's funny, isn't it. All the years your father worked with the horses, I was busy raising you kids. Now he's gone, and you and David . . ."

"But I'm coming back."

"I know that. But you'll start your senior year this fall. After graduation who knows where you'll be." Marge turned toward her daughter. "I needed something to do—something to really occupy my time—so I asked Patrick if I could help with the horses. It's been good. I feel closer to your dad down at the barns than anywhere. Maybe it's because he was so happy there." She continued as the tears ran down her cheeks. "I found that I'm good with the babies. Of course, I always have been good with babies. . . ."

"Oh, Mom, I'm really proud of you."

"Thanks, Tee. I figured it couldn't hurt to try. Selling out had crossed my mind. How are things going for you in California?"

It was the first chance all weekend that Trish had had to really talk to her mother. "Not too good. I've lost my touch—can't seem to get them into the money."

"I'm sorry to hear that." Marge laid a hand on Trish's shoulder.

"The sportswriters even talk about it in their articles. Pretty bad, huh?" She opened the car door. "We'd better go."

"I know. . . . Just remember that I love you—and miss you. The house is pretty empty."

Trish tried to smile around the quiver of her lips. "It won't be too long till I'm home."

Aboard the plane, Trish pondered her mother's words—"selling out." Would her mother ever really consider that? Was there anything she could do to stop it?

The next afternoon, Trish's mount stumbled coming out of the gate. The filly went to her knees, and Trish somersaulted over her head and thumped in the dirt.

Chapter
14

Trish took the roll on her shoulder.

Her mount lunged back up on her feet and galloped down the track after the receding field.

Trish continued the somersault roll to a sitting position and took a moment to get her bearings. She sat in the dirt of the track, breathing hard; coughing, and spitting some dirt from her mouth. After flexing her arms and legs to be sure everything was intact, she staggered to her feet, still a bit woozy from the force of the fall.

A track ambulance stopped beside her and the paramedics jumped out. "You okay?" one asked as he swung open the rear door and reached for his case.

"I'm fine. You don't need any of that stuff." Trish flinched when she moved her head. "I'm just shook up." She grimaced again when she touched her right shoulder.

"Bruised too, I'd guess." A young woman grasped Trish's right hand. "Squeeze." She watched Trish's flinching response. "You'd better have them look at that in First Aid. Come on, jump in. We'll take you over there."

Jumping was a bit beyond Trish's ability at that moment, but she climbed into the ambulance for the ride to the nurse's station in the same building as the jockey rooms.

By the time Trish sat down on a gurney in one of the curtained-off examining alcoves, her shoulder was throbbing. She rotated it carefully. It worked, but it hurt.

Waiting for the nurse, Trish laid back and closed her eyes.

"I think she's done for as far as racing is concerned." Trish tried to ignore the man's voice on the other side of the room, but he spoke too clearly. "Anyone could have won on Spitfire; he was that good."

"I don't know," the other voice responded. "She's won plenty of other races too."

"Yeah, *before* her father died. She's just a lucky kid who's run out of luck." His voice was a hoarse whisper, but Trish heard him with no trouble.

Does he think I'm deaf or something?

"No better than a green apprentice. It was all hype, nothing more."

Was it true? Is that what people were actually saying and thinking about her?

"So, how're you doing?" A gray-haired nurse with a warm smile swished back the curtain. "Heard you took quite a spill out there."

Trish nodded. "It's just my shoulder. A hot shower'll take care of the rest." The man's insensitive words pounded in her brain. While the nurse helped her remove her silks, she could feel the anger and hurt burning in her stomach and flaring up into her chest.

Trish winced when the woman moved the injured shoulder and gently but firmly felt for a break. "Just a bruise, I'm sure. You have any more mounts today?" Trish shook her head. "Good. Let's ice it and put it in a sling to take the pressure off. Knowing jockeys, though, you'll be up and riding again tomorrow."

Trish tried to smile, but it felt as if her face would crack with the effort. Was her gift with horses really gone? Buried with her father?

The nurse slapped a chemical ice bag to activate it. Trish turned onto her stomach, and the woman placed the bag high on Trish's shoulder blade, then pulled a sheet over her.

"Lie there with the ice for a bit, and I'll get you some aspirin. A nap wouldn't hurt either."

But sleep was out of the question. Trish had a hard time lying still. When she squirmed, the pack slipped. She slid it back in place again and took a deep breath to relax. The pack slipped again. Trish rolled over and swung her feet to the floor. *This is not working.*

She pulled her silk shirt around her shoulders and headed for the door. In the hall she ran into the nurse. She shook her head. "Why don't you go down to the whirlpool and then see the masseuse?"

"Yeah, thanks."

"And use the sling . . ."

Trish ignored the pain in her shoulder as she changed clothes in the women's jockey room. She jammed her things into her sports bag, her arm back in the sling, and hurried out the door. All the way around the south end of the track and into the parking lot, her shoulder throbbed and the anger churned in her stomach.

Slinging her bag into the backseat of her car, Trish slid into the driver's seat. She punched the button to put the top down and started her engine.

Each time she shifted, the pain in her arm reminded her of the pain in her heart, the pain in her mind. *How much more of this can I take?*

She stopped for the lights, northbound on Camino Real. She had no particular destination. The sign read "92 to Half Moon Bay." Trish took the cloverleaf and headed west, over the hills to the Pacific Ocean.

The winding road invoked speed. Trish shifted down on the upgrade and leaned on the accelerator. Wind blew her hair back and made her eyes water. She roared around one curve and hit the brakes. A truck and trailer rumbled up the grade in front of her.

You don't learn too fast, do you, her nagging voice shouted above the roar of the car's engine.

Trish backed off. All she needed right now was a traffic ticket or, worse, an accident. The truck ahead of her picked up speed after it crested the last hill. Trish could see the ocean in the distance. She followed the curving road down between bushy hills that finally opened onto a narrow valley, lined on both sides with Christmas tree farms. As the valley widened, she passed truck farming, a winery, and the houses and businesses of the town of Half Moon Bay. The road ended at a traffic light on Highway 1.

Waiting for the light, Trish debated. Left or right—where was the nearest beach? Because she was in the left-hand lane, she turned south when the light changed. She watched for beach access signs, but only saw more housing and planted fields of squash or pumpkin that reminded her of her mother's garden. There were huge green spiky plants that looked like thistles along the sides of the road.

Finally, she spotted a sign—Redondo Beach. It pointed to the right. She turned at the edge of a golf course and slowly followed a bumpy road between giant eucalyptus trees. She'd asked Adam about them one day. Today's heat caused their pungent aroma to drift on the breeze.

A poor excuse for a fence corralled a group of horses to her left. It was made of sticks, baling wire, bent or broken posts, and colored baling twine. Her father would have deplored a fence like that.

The road dead-ended in a parking area on a high bluff. Trish could see a beach off to the right and a few small buildings. To the left a sign read Strawberry Farm. There was a house with lots of windows overlooking the ocean. She got out of her car and shaded her eyes to look over the water. A freighter steamed north on the horizon. A couple of small fishing crafts bobbed on the swells closer in.

The surf roared below, while gulls rode the thermals and screeched overhead. *A peaceful scene,* Trish thought. *Where's the peace?* She reached for her bag in the backseat. Stuffing it into the trunk, Trish grabbed a blanket that was kept there for occasions such as this. When she pulled it out, she saw a box she didn't remember bringing.

She dropped the blanket and picked up the box. An envelope was taped to the top of it. There was a note inside, in her mother's handwriting.

> Dear Trish,
> *I hope you find this when you need it and are ready for it.*
> Love always, Mom

Trish's fingers trembled as she cut the tape that secured the lid with her car keys. She took a deep breath. *Do I really want to see what's in this box?*

She shook her head at the silly thought. What could possibly be in a box from her mother that she wouldn't want to see?

She lifted out the first item, wrapped in newspaper. "No!" She knew by the weight of it that she held the carved eagle she'd given her father for Christmas. Gently undoing the paper, she ran her hand along the delicately carved wings, then set it down, her jaw clenched against the memories. There were three books in the box also. On top was her father's journal, then the blank book he'd given her to write in, and finally, her own Bible.

Trish rubbed her aching shoulder and stared at the contents of the box as if they were a snake ready to strike.

She could hear Pastor Mort's voice in her head: *"Read your father's journal."*

"No. I can't handle this right now." She slammed the trunk lid shut and started down the steep embankment to the beach. A third of the way down, Trish stopped short. She'd forgotten her blanket.

She turned and wearily climbed back up the washed-out path. When she opened the trunk for the blanket, she impulsively grabbed the two journals with it and slammed the lid again.

After slipping and sliding her way to the hot sand, she walked up the beach a ways before dropping her stuff at the base of the cliff. She took off her tennis shoes and socks, rolled up the pant legs of her jeans, then jogged down to the surf.

"Yikes! I thought California water was warm." She backed up and let a dying wave wash over her feet. The backwash sucked the sand out from under her heels. As her feet adjusted to the frigid water, she followed the wave action out, tugging on her pants in an effort to keep them dry. When a wave slapped higher than she thought it would, she threw up her hands and waded farther. Next time she'd bring shorts and a swimsuit.

But even the crashing symphony of the surf couldn't drown out the conflicting voices in Trish's head. She rubbed her burning eyes, and pounded up the beach at the edge of the waves. It didn't help. Nothing helped.

Trish returned to the blanket and flipped it out. The journals tumbled into the sand. She picked up her father's journal and carefully brushed it off. A pen dropped loose when she opened the clasp.

She flopped back on the blanket and shielded her eyes with her arm. *Do I really want to read this?* She sat up again and opened the book to the first page.

Dear God . . . Right now I am so angry I can't even begin to describe it. Why are you doing this to me? Cancer! I thought you loved me, and now this. How can this be consistent with love?

Trish closed her eyes and rested her forehead on her bent knees. *He felt the same way I do!* She continued reading.

How can I love you and tell others about your love when you do this to me? Why didn't you just strike me dead and get it over with? Oh, God, why? Why?

Trish wanted to shout the same questions, but with the lump in her throat she could hardly whisper. "Why did you take my dad away? He was a good man." She sobbed as she dropped the journal beside her on the blanket. "Why?"

A seagull drifted overhead, screaming into the wind.

Trish searched the blanket for the pen. She picked up the blank journal and began to write. The words flowed out as fast as she could get them down. There was no "Dear God," only hurt and rage and despair.

After a while her hand cramped and her eyes burned. Her throat was so dry she could hardly swallow. The sun hovered over a bank of gray fog that shrouded the horizon, and a breeze whipped sand over the edge of the blanket. Trish shivered. She flipped back to the first pages again. *I wrote that?* She wanted to rip out the pages, but caught herself. She dropped the book and picked up her father's again.

But I know God is my strength and power. He makes my way perfect. That is my Bible promise for today. I will hang on to it. How will I get through this without you, my Father?

Trish slammed the book shut. She picked up her blanket and tucked the books into the folds. She had a chemistry class tonight.

Back in the car Trish slumped against the seat. She felt like a deflated balloon, but somehow rested too. She stared out at the fog creeping in to the shore, and watched a gull wheel and cry. He rose higher, then lower, basking in the flow of the wind current. Trish wished she could take life's ups and downs that effortlessly.

Chapter
15

When would she learn to study the right stuff?

Trish stared at the chemistry paper she'd just corrected. She'd missed four out of twelve this time—barely passing. Why was she wasting her time taking this stupid class? It wasn't as if she wanted to be a scientist or something. She bit down on her lip. Nothing was going right.

When Trish walked through the doorway to the Finleys' living room, she saw Martha reading in a chair by the window. The soft light seemed to surround her in a golden glow. A nature tape was playing, and the music was unbelievably peaceful. Martha looked up and smiled. "I'm glad you're home. How about something to eat?"

Trish dropped her bags on the stair. "I had some yogurt before class. I think I'm okay."

Martha rose to her feet. "Well, I'm hungry. How about a piece of homemade apple pie with ice cream? Adam says my pies would take a blue ribbon. I don't know about that, but I think they're pretty good."

"Okay." Trish felt lethargic. Maybe something to eat would help. She followed her hostess into the bright blue-and-white-tiled kitchen. "All right if I have some milk with it?"

"Of course, dear. Help yourself. I'll have coffee." Martha set two plates on the glass-topped table in the bay window, overlooking a flower-bordered patio.

"Hmmm, this *is* good," Trish said, tasting the pie. "You bake as good as my mom."

"That's some compliment; I've tasted her baking. Marge gave me her recipe for cinnamon rolls. I'll have to make them while you're here."

When they'd finished eating, Martha asked, "What's happened, Trish? You look unhappy."

Trish tried to brighten up. "Oh, nothing."

"You can't fool me, Trish. Something is wrong. You'll feel better if you tell me what's troubling you."

Trish sighed. "I—I barely passed another chemistry quiz." She rubbed her shoulder. "Did Adam tell you I took a dive at the track?"

Martha nodded. "Yes. When you didn't return to the barns, he said he checked First Aid. The nurse said you'd left in a hurry."

"I drove out to Redondo Beach."

"Oh? How bad is your shoulder?"

"It's just a bruise. I'm supposed to be wearing a sling, actually."

"Where is it?"

"In the car. I couldn't shift gears with it on."

"Trish, if I can help you in any way, I'd be grateful to do that. I know you miss your dad terribly, and you never talk about him. Someone told me something a long time ago that has stuck with me. 'A joy shared is doubled; a burden shared is cut in half.' Please let us help you."

Trish nodded. "Thanks. You always do." She shoved her chair back and picked up her plate and glass. "You know anything about chemistry?"

"I wish I did." Martha followed Trish to the sink. "Leave these till morning. How about if you and I go shopping Monday afternoon? I know you're needing school clothes, and I haven't shopped for something like that for years."

Trish looked at her in amazement. "I was going to ask you to go."

"See? Great minds . . ." Martha flipped off the light switch. "Hope tomorrow is better for you."

Martha's good wishes seemed to help. Morning works went better than usual. Sarah's Pride acted as if she finally believed Trish was in charge, and Gatesby slow-galloped without pounding her to pieces. By the time they were finished with the entire string, Trish caught herself whistling. It was a tune she'd heard someone else singing on the way to the track.

She still felt great when she joined Adam in the saddling paddock for the second race. She stroked Firefly's neck and smoothed the filly's forelock. "How about your first race in California? You ready to whip 'em?" The filly rubbed her forehead against Trish's chest.

"You know, I'd rather you come from behind," Adam was saying. "Hang off the pace about third or fourth until the stretch. She's got plenty of power. Make sure you don't get boxed in on the rail. That happens real easy in the number-two position."

Trish nodded. Maybe this would be her day. Maybe she'd finally find herself in the winner's circle.

A good crowd filled the stands for the mile-long Camino Real Derby. The big purse had drawn some horses up from Southern California. The parade to post increased Trish's feelings of both exhilaration and confidence. She patted the filly's neck.

"This is our day, girl; I can feel it."

Firefly stood quietly in the gate while the horses on both sides of her acted up. Number three had to be released and brought back in. At the bell, they broke clean. Firefly hit her stride immediately. So did the two on either side of her. Going into the first turn, the three were neck and neck. Halfway through the turn the horse on the outside bumped Firefly, who bumped the inside horse and sent it crashing into the rail.

Firefly kept her feet but lost ground. She straightened out on the stretch but couldn't seem to gain what she needed to be in competition. They finished fifth.

When Trish jumped to the ground, she saw blood running down the filly's rear leg. She'd been cut in the fray.

"That crazy jock on three," she muttered as she stroked the filly's neck. "He should be disqualified for riding carelessly like that. You're going to lodge a complaint, aren't you?" she asked Adam as soon as he'd inspected the wound.

"Yes, but it probably won't do much good. Three came in third."

"How bad is she?"

"I'll call the vet, just in case." Adam handed Trish her saddle. "See you back at the barn?"

Trish nodded. "If I'd just . . ."

"Trish, it wasn't your fault. You can't take responsibility for what every rider does." Firefly limped off behind him.

Trish didn't need her nagger. She scolded herself all the way to the barn, her anger rising with every negative thought. *Maybe everyone's right. Maybe I'm not any good anymore. I sure should have kept out of that mess. What a lousy ride.*

The vet had just finished checking Firefly's leg when Trish arrived. "How is she?"

"Not too bad. She's got plenty of heart to have finished with a cut like this. But it should heal clean." He turned to Adam. "Call me if there's any problem."

Trish went to the tack room and dug in the refrigerator for a carrot. Trish broke it in pieces and fed them to the filly one at a time, all the while telling her what a great horse she was. By sheer force of will, she kept her own anger at bay.

"See you tomorrow." She waved to Adam as she left the area.

"You okay?" he called.

Trish nodded and waved again. He couldn't see her tight jaw or burning eyes. She was not okay. Instead of going home, she took the road to Half Moon Bay.

Firefly was too good a horse to be messed up by an incompetent rider, Trish told herself. She kept up the internal harangue while swinging through the turns of Highway 92 to the ocean.

Arriving at Redondo Beach, Trish opened her trunk for her blanket and the journals. The box with the eagle inside had tipped over and the eagle was only partially wrapped. She pulled it out, securing it by the base. With one finger she followed the arch of the spread wing. She'd been so happy at the time to find the perfect gift for her father. Now he was gone—and his daughter couldn't even race anymore. *Why? . . . Why?*

Trish carelessly rewrapped the eagle and stuffed it into the box again, shoving the offending reminder as far back in the trunk as possible. She grabbed her books and blanket and a small cooler with drinks and an apple, and slipped and slid her way to the sand.

The sun played hide-and-seek between the high clouds as Trish hiked south from the trail. She threw her things on the sand, pulled off her shoes, and jogged to the water. The jog made her shoulder muscles scream with pain. The race and the fact that she hadn't been wearing a sling hadn't aided its healing. Trish kicked at the foam frosting left on the beach by the outgoing tide. She wished she could run forever, leaving the hurt and pain behind her, but she tired quickly and trudged back to the blanket.

All of a sudden her anger flared against her father. Before he could break his smoking habit, he had developed lung cancer. *What kind of father would smoke, when he knew it could make him sick?* She opened her father's journal again, and the first words she saw were from the Bible. She slammed it shut.

I'm no good. I can't ride, let alone win, and I can't even get a decent grade on a stupid chemistry quiz. She lay back on the blanket, exhausted, wishing the sky would come crashing down on top of her.

After a while, she sat up again and stared out over the surf. Way out there her problems would be over. . . . Trish rose to her feet and plodded to the edge of the water. A wave rolled in and rippled around her toes. She waded out to her knees.

I could just start swimming—straight out. Once through the surf, it would be so easy. She waded farther, oblivious to the depth. Waves broke and surged around her hips and waist. *Just keep on walking. Then start swimming. No more problems.*

Trish had no idea how long she stood watching the horizon, transfixed. When a gull shrieked overhead, she realized her feet were so cold she couldn't move them.

She watched the gull. *To have wings like that . . . to soar and ride on the wind. To look down from that height. Maybe then I'd see all that was happening—and understand.*

"God, if you care at all, help me," she spoke aloud. "I can't stand this anymore."

Her feet ached, but she turned and forced one foot ahead of the other until she reached the shore and her things.

She crumpled to the blanket and wrapped it around her feet, rubbing them briskly.

When she picked up her journal, it fell open near the back. The pages were filled with handwriting. *What's this? I only wrote that junk to God in the front of the book.*

Trish looked again. It was her father's handwriting!

Dear Trish,

It was almost as if she could hear his voice.

If you are reading this, I'm either in the hospital near the end, or I'm with my heavenly Father.

No! her mind screamed. *I want you here with me—I need you!* Tears squeezed out from under her clenched eyelids. Then the dam burst. Great racking sobs shook her body. She hadn't cried like this since her father's death.

I love you, Tee, with all my heart. I'm begging your forgiveness for my selfish habit that caused this whole thing. Knowing I must leave you and David and your mother breaks my heart. It's more than I can bear alone. I wanted to see you grow up; see what a wonderful young woman you would become. I wanted to be there for you when you needed me.

Oh, Dad . . . God, please . . . She couldn't see for the tears. She couldn't breathe for the sobs. She cried for all the times she hadn't . . . couldn't . . . wouldn't.

I know that you are a fine and gifted jockey, Tee. Don't let anyone convince you differently. Don't let the hard times get you down. There will be some, you know. Believe in yourself as I believe in you. And when you're hurting, call on your heavenly Father. He hears you, and He's there for you, no matter what happens. He is the only one who can get you through the troubles of life. He's gotten me through, even though I've failed Him so many times.

I know you will be angry. I know I was. But don't become bitter, Trish.

*Tell God just how you feel. Let it all out. You can't shock Him. He under-
stands you and knows you.*

*Always remember that I love you. I know where I'm going . . . to the
mansion He has prepared for me. Someday, I'll meet you there, Trish. Don't
ever give up.*

Your dad

Trish lay back on the blanket, relief washing over her like a wave.
High above, a gull floated on the rising thermals. Then a song, almost
audible, drifted on the wind and echoed through the sandstone cliffs
above her. "And He will raise you up on eagle's wings. . . . Bear you on
the breath of God . . ." The gull, dark against the sun, dipped and soared.
"And hold you in the palm of His hand."

Trish hummed the familiar melody, allowing the words to work
their healing. The tears flowed again, unchecked, and a smile tugged at
the corners of her mouth.

ACKNOWLEDGMENT

My thanks to Candy in the public relations department at Bay Meadows track in San Mateo, California, for the track tour and her wealth of information.

OUT OF THE MIST

BOOK SEVEN

To my dad,
Laurel,
who gave me my first horse,
a stubborn Shetland pony named Polly,
and who set me back on when I fell off.
Thanks for loving me,
even through those in-spite-of years.

Chapter

01

What do you do when you're only sixteen and your father has died? You've reached the pinnacle of success, winning the Triple Crown, about the highest honor in Thoroughbred horse racing. Where do you go but down?

Tricia Evanston tried to stop the questions from racing through her mind, but she didn't seem to have control over much of anything anymore. What did it all mean? Would she feel like the bottom of a manure pit for the rest of her life?

She rubbed the sand off her feet and drew them up to rest on the red plaid blanket she'd spread on the beach. After clamping her arms around her bent legs, she leaned her chin on her knees and stared out at the horizon. Only here at the beach did she seem to find any peace, any trace of the song.

Trish shifted her gaze to the seagulls wheeling and dipping on the air currents above her. They looked so free. Held up by the air. *Do seagulls cry?* she wondered. She hadn't cried since the day her father died a month ago—until yesterday—and now she couldn't seem to quit.

"Well, do you cry?" she shouted at one bird hovering so close she could see the black ring around his yellow beak. He shrieked back at her and let the wind carry him away. "You just wanted something to eat, you didn't want to talk. I don't want to talk either. Talking hurts. Crying hurts. Everything hurts."

She reached in her cooler for something to feed him but all she found was an orange. That was one good thing about living in California—the fresh oranges. She dug into the stem end with her thumbnail and pulled back the peel.

The gull returned, tracking her movements with a beady eye. When she tossed up a peeling, he snatched it up but dropped it immediately.

"You're smarter than I thought. I don't eat the peelings either." Trish chewed each juicy section, wiping her chin with the back of a tanned hand. She flipped a section up toward the gull. He dropped that too. "Don't like oranges, period, huh?" When she finished, she glared at her chemistry book and flopped back on the blanket.

Her outstretched hand grazed the journal her father had kept in the months before he died. When she turned her head, the carved wooden eagle she'd given him for their last Christmas together lay right in her line of vision.

Eagle's wings. The song from Isaiah 40 had been her theme song. Only yesterday had she finally heard it again, deep within the hidden places of her mind and heart. She listened intently. Against the thunder of the surf and shriek of the gulls, was it still there? Trickling through and dancing on the sunbeams?

She closed her eyes. *Please, let me hear it again,* her soul pleaded. I need the song. "Raise you up on eagle's wings . . ." It was so faint maybe she only imagined the words. "Bear you on the breath of God . . ." It flowed from within her now, growing stronger, like a stream rushing downhill. "And hold you in the palm of His hand."

Trish wrapped her hands around her shoulders. If she reached out with only a fingertip she would surely touch the *hand*, it felt so real. She waited, hoping for more of the song, but as it faded away, the peace remained.

When a cloud darkened the sun that slid on its downward trail, she took a deep breath, shivering slightly in the breeze. Could she hold on to this feeling on the way back to San Mateo and through the days ahead? Or was it only here at the beach it came to her?

Carefully, so as not to disturb her fragile feelings, Trish picked up her own just-begun journal along with her father's, wrapped them in a towel along with the eagle, and slipped them into her pack. Then folding the blanket and picking up the Swingline cooler, she slogged her way through the soft sand to the base of the eroded sandstone cliff.

The trail staggered its way up through the rocks, now hiding, then pitching vertically. It took sure feet and a gymnastic balance to make it to the parking lot with full hands. Trish stopped at the rim to catch her breath.

She listened. Yes, it was still there. Stowing her gear in the trunk, Trish dusted off her feet and slipped on her sandals. She glanced in the side mirror and despaired of ever getting a brush through her thick, wavy, midnight hair. That's what someone had called it once, the color of midnight. She liked the sound of that. Wearing her hair in a braid down her back was the only way to control it. Trish fluffed her bangs and covered her green eyes with dark glasses. Her nose looked about ready to peel—again. Would she ever learn to use sunscreen?

Trish unlocked the door of her red Chrysler convertible—the car presented her when her colt Spitfire won the Kentucky Derby—and slid behind the wheel. She listened intently. The song—yes, she could hear it.

She drove slowly out the bumpy road, past the towering eucalyptus trees, and turned left onto Highway 1. With each sweeping curve up the hill, leaving the town of Half Moon Bay behind, the song grew fainter. By the time she reached the College of San Mateo campus, located high on the hill overlooking San Francisco Bay, her song, like the beach, was only a memory.

Trish had come from her home in Vancouver, Washington, to stay with friends of the family, the Finleys, in hopes that the busyness at the track and a makeup chemistry course at the College of San Mateo would help get her mind off her father's death.

Welcome back to the real world—and a D in chemistry. Tonight was a lab, and that was always more interesting than the lecture—or the quizzes. As she and her partner, Kevin, lit up the Bunsen burner, Trish studied the experiment instructions.

While he added the first two elements, her mind flipped back to the beach. "And then what?" Kevin's sharp voice brought her back.

"Then heat until the color changes to . . ."

The compound fuzzed, smoked, and smelled atrocious.

"What are you trying to do—kill us both?" Kevin dropped the test tube in a deep sink, where it shattered.

"Clear the room, everyone," the teacher's assistant ordered, turning the fans on high.

When Trish finally quit coughing, along with everyone else, lab time was over and she was still further behind. An F sure wouldn't help her grade any.

It was a miracle she was able to reach the condominium with her eyes streaming like they were. She dragged herself up the stairs and, after closing her bedroom door, threw herself across the bed. She buried her face in a pillow to muffle the heart-wrenching sobs. Trying to pray only made her cry harder.

"Trish," Martha Finley, wife of breeder/trainer Adam Finley, and Trish's "other mother," poked her head in the doorway after knocking several times. Without another word, she crossed the room and, sitting down on the bed, gathered the sobbing girl into her arms. She murmured soothing sounds and stroked Trish's hair, allowing her to cry.

"I—I'm so tired—of cry—ing."

"I know. But tears are necessary when you've been wounded like you have. Only by crying and talking through your grief and confused feelings will you ever begin to heal."

"I want my d-a-d."

"I know you do, honey. I know."

When the sobs finally lessened, Martha handed Trish a tissue.

"Everything is such a mess. I can't think straight. I can't concentrate on anything. It's like I live in a big black fog." Trish reached for another tissue and Martha handed her the box.

"I just want to run away—and keep on running."

"But you'll take yourself with you," Martha answered wisely.

"That's the pits."

"Ummm."

Silence but for a hiccup and sniffs.

"Martha, I want my dad back." The tears flowed again. "I *need* my father."

Martha held Trish close, rocking back and forth and crooning the songs that mothers have used through the ages to comfort their children.

When Trish finally crawled between the covers, she felt like a wrung-out stable rag. Swollen-shut eyes, raw, burning nose, and a heart that weighed two tons didn't make her feel any better. While she feared another night of tossing and turning, sleep crept in before she could turn over even once.

The song—that was it. Trish opened her eyes to check the clock. Had the song come before she slept or just now as she awoke? It didn't matter. It had come—and not only at the beach.

She threw the covers back and leaped from the bed. This was sure to be a better day. The song had come. She flew into the bathroom and turned on the shower. As she stepped under the pelting water, she was humming.

Fog swirling about the streetlights and blanketing the ground made driving to the track an exercise in concentration. Trish squinted through the windshield, driving slow enough that she could stop before hitting anything—or anyone. Morning sounds at the track seemed muffled by the gray miasma.

She left her car in the parking lot and trotted through the gate, lifting a hand in greeting to the guard. She dodged to the side as a bug boy, the fringe of his leather chaps dangling in the breeze, sped past on his bicycle. A pony rider on a bay quarterhorse plodded past on his way to escort another high-strung Thoroughbred out to the track. Trish knew that watching her feet instead of the traffic around her could cause an injury, so she kept her head upright. This morning that wasn't difficult.

Gatesby tossed his head and whinnied a greeting as soon as she turned the corner into the Finley stalls. Firefly, in the stall next to him, added her welcome. Trish kept a careful eye on the gelding; she didn't feel like getting nipped today—or any day for that matter. Gatesby harbored the genes of a natural rowdy, not malicious, but a bite in fun hurt just as much as one in anger.

Trish scratched behind his ears, always keeping one hand on his halter. "You old goof-off. Been buggin' anyone yet today?"

"*Sí, el estúpido caballo me mordió,*" Juan, one of the grooms, told her. He pointed to a spot on his arm, shaking his head.

Firefly nickered again.

"Your turn, I know." Trish left the gelding and ducked her shoulder under the filly's chin. Standing like this, his head draped over Trish's shoulder, was Spitfire's favorite position. Trish swallowed a lump at the thought of her big black colt, now a stud at BlueMist Farms in Kentucky. Oh, how she missed him! But when a colt has won the Triple Crown, he goes into syndication and retires to stud. The money from that transaction would keep her family comfortable for years to come.

But that knowledge didn't make things easier for Trish. She gritted her teeth and, giving the filly one last scratch, moved on to the next stall.

Adam Finley and Carlos Montanya, the head groom, stood inside discussing the problems the colt was having as they wrapped his legs for the morning work.

"Who'm I doing first?" Trish asked after waiting for a pause in the conversation.

Adam turned, a smile creasing his apple cheeks. "Morning, Trish. Think we'll go with Diego's. Juan is saddling him now." Finley unhooked the canvas gate across the stall door and stepped outside. "How you doin' this morning?" He peered into her face and nodded. "Better, I can tell."

"Martha blabbed."

He nodded again. "Yes, and we're grateful."

"For what?"

"You." He reached inside the tack room and brought out her whip. "Be careful out there this morning. Everyone's kinda antsy."

How could such a simple comment, that the Finleys were grateful for her, make Trish want to bawl, she wondered. She raised her knee for the mount.

Two horses later, Adam's advice paid off. A horse galloping beside her spooked at something and leaped sideways, crashing into her mount's shoulder. Her horse stumbled badly and within a few paces pulled up limping. Trish dismounted and led him back to the barn.

"If I'd just paid closer attention," she grumbled to Adam when she reached the row of stalls.

"Lass, for crying out loud, you can't foresee everything. You kept him from a bad fall. Coulda done a lot more damage, and hurt yourself on top of it." He stripped the saddle off so the stable hands could wash the animal down and pack the injured leg in ice.

But the near-accident ruined the morning for Trish, knocking her right back into her pit of despair.

A black horse galloping by reminded her of Spitfire—the way he held his head, the way he begged for a run, his deep grunts when he ran hard. It seemed like months since she'd seen her horse. Would he still remember her?

Thoughts of Spitfire brought thoughts of home. How were the babies, Miss Tee and Double Diamond, coming along? How she needed a hug from her mother, and a good old bad time from her brother, David. She watched out for the other working horses and paid attention to her own mount, but one part of her mind visited Runnin' On Farm—and home. When could she go back?

I'll call as soon as I'm done with these beasts, she promised herself.

The rising sun had burned off all but stray wisps of the morning fog, which hid in the lowest places by the time the last horse was worked according to Adam's schedule.

"You got any mounts this afternoon?" Adam asked when Trish had dropped down into a faded-green director's chair. When she shook her head, he said, "Good. I'm taking you out for lunch." When she started to object, he raised a hand. "No, I know you have homework, and you'd probably rather head for the beach, but we need to talk." He looked up as Carlos stuck his head in the door with a question. After giving the needed answer, Adam turned back to Trish. "Someplace without so many interruptions." He grinned at her. "Besides, it's still overcast at the beach and will stay so all day."

Trish glanced at her watch. "Can I go home and change first?"

"If you want. I'll meet you at the Peking Gardens at noon."

When Trish entered her bedroom, the first thing she did was dial home. The phone rang and rang. "You'd think they'd have the answering machine on at least," she muttered as she dropped the receiver back in the cradle.

She tried her best friend, Rhonda. At least they had the answering machine on.

When she looked in the bathroom mirror, she saw that tiny spatters of mud had given her freckles. She washed them away and scrubbed her hands. The face in the mirror didn't smile back. A smile was too much effort.

She shucked off her clothes and tossed them into the hamper. Damp mornings messed up her jeans. Maybe she should wear chaps like some of the others. She looked in the mirror again. *Maybe I should just quit.*

The thought scared her. It was coming too frequently lately.

"All you need is one good win." She pointed her hairbrush at the grim face.

And that's about as likely as you acing a chem test, her little nagging voice rejoined. *You know, if you'd . . .*

Trish slammed the hairbrush down on the counter and left the room. All she needed was one more person telling her what to do, even if it was her own head.

Adam waited for her in a corner booth. While the restaurant had many patrons, the tables around them were empty for the moment. Trish slid into the red vinyl booth seat across from him. An icy Diet Coke stood in front of her.

"Thanks." She sipped and set the glass back down. A sigh escaped from deep within.

Adam reached across the table and covered her clenched hands with his own. "How can I help you, Tee?"

Tee, her father's pet name for her, did it. Trish covered her brimming eyes with her hands.

Would she ever stop crying?

Chapter

02

"Oh, lass, I'm so glad for you."

Trish heard the words, but they didn't make any sense. Here she couldn't seem to quit crying, and Adam said he was glad for her! Her thoughts tumbled over each other, shutting off the tears like a faucet.

She mopped her eyes with the napkin in front of her, then dug in her purse for a tissue. After blowing her nose and wiping her eyes again, she took a deep breath and blew it out. She stared at the face across from her.

"How come you and Martha both say you're happy to see me crying? Seems kinda mean to me." Trish sniffed, and sipped her Diet Coke.

"Well, Trish, these weeks since your father died, you've been all frozen up inside. And that's not healthy." He shook his head. "Not at all."

Without looking up, Trish said, "It didn't hurt as bad that way. Now I hurt all the time."

"Maybe, but the healing has begun. You have to let the feelings out, cry them out, express them, in order to deal with all that has happened."

"But my dad is still gone."

"I know. And nothing can bring him back. But you *will* be able to go on, and one day you'll look around you and life will be good again. Not the *same*, but good again."

Trish let the tears spill over and stream down her cheeks. When she could speak, she took courage and brought up the question that was scaring her: "Do you think I'll be any good as a jockey again?"

"Oh yes. You have been given a wondrous gift with horses, and that hasn't been taken from you. It may be put under wraps for a while, but it will come back."

"You really think so?"

"I don't just think, I *believe* so."

Trish kept his words in her mind as she drove back to the Finleys' condominium. The sun, now hot on her back as she climbed the stairs to the front door, begged her to come out and enjoy it. Once in her room, she changed into a lime green swimsuit and, picking up her homework, went out on the deck off her room for some serious studying. The words and symbols danced on the page in the bright sunlight, so she went back inside for her sunglasses.

Within a few minutes, she went back inside and down to the kitchen for a glass of iced tea. Next she needed a highlighter. By the time she finally got settled and tried to concentrate, the words swam before her eyes. She rolled over to her stomach and squinted against the glare. Within moments she lay fast asleep.

That evening Trish walked in the door of her chemistry class, homework unfinished, and suffering a headache that made her sick to her stomach. And if she had touched water to her skin, it would have sizzled. She sat straight up in the chair, without touching the back of the seat. Her clothing was painful enough.

How could you have done such a stupid thing? Her nagger was perched on her right shoulder, she was sure. *To fall asleep in the hot afternoon sun like that, when you've hardly been in the sun at all . . .*

Trish just groaned and rested her head in her hand.

The teacher walked to the front of the room and announced a quiz, worth ten points.

Trish covered her eyes with her hand and shuddered. She answered

12

only two of the ten questions, got up, and left. There was no point in staying. She could hardly spell her own name, let alone pay attention to a lecture she didn't understand in the best of times.

All the way home, she could think only of the beach. At least at the beach she felt closer to her father. And out there she could think; she could hear her song. *Tomorrow,* she promised herself. *As soon as you're done at the track tomorrow, you can go to the beach.* She flinched at the sting of her back. Tomorrow she'd keep a shirt on.

She hardly slept that night. Twice she got up and into the shower to cool the burning.

At three a.m. Martha knocked on the door, just after Trish had crawled back into bed. "Trish, what's wrong? Can I come in?"

"Sure. It's just my sunburn. I fell asleep on the deck this afternoon."

"Here, let me see."

Trish pulled up the back of her nightshirt.

"Oh, you poor dear." Martha gingerly touched one spot. "Hang on, I'll be right back." She returned in a few moments, carrying a bottle of green gel. "This will do the trick. Aloe vera, God's burn ointment. Only instead of just using pieces of the plant like we used to, you can buy it in a bottle now." She sat down on the bed by Trish and poured some into her hands. "Now, this will feel cool."

Trish flinched when the stuff touched her back, but she soon breathed a sigh of relief as the cooling strokes took away the pain.

"Now I think you'll sleep, my dear." Martha stood up and set the plastic bottle on the nightstand. "Put this on again when you wake up, and before you leave for the track, I'll cover your entire back with it."

"Thank you," Trish mumbled, already half asleep.

Gatesby was in rare form when Trish took him out on the track in the morning. He tossed his head and jigged sideways down the track. "Knock it off, you dunderhead." Trish tightened the reins as she scolded him. Gatesby half reared, ears flat against his head. Trish felt like clobbering him one, right between those flat ears. Instead, she pulled him to a stop and waited until he blew out a deep breath and settled his weight evenly on all four legs. When his ears pricked forward, she loosened the reins. "All right now, let's see if we can behave." Gatesby shook his head and set off at a smart walk as if he'd never acted up in his life.

By the time works were finished, Trish's sunburn cried for the soothing green gel. She trotted over to the women's rest room and pulled off her shirt.

"Whoa, that's a bad one." Another jockey turned to study Trish's flaming back. "Here, let me help you." She took the bottle and applied the gel.

"Thanks. It feels so much better when someone else puts it on."

"What'd you do? Fall asleep in the sun?"

Trish nodded. "Dumb, huh?"

"Yeah, well, we've all done it." She leaned closer to the mirror to study a spot on her chin. "You're Trish Evanston, aren't you?" Trish nodded. "You've won the biggies. We were all so excited when a woman won the Triple Crown. We were yellin' and screamin'. The guys thought we were crazy. That colt of yours, he's something else."

"Thanks." Trish leaned a hip against the counter. "What's your name?"

"Oh, sorry, I'm Mandy Smithson." She turned from the mirror. "I want you to know we all feel terrible about your dad." She shook her head. "Tough break."

Trish sniffed and blinked her eyes. "Thanks."

Mandy turned to face her. "Trish, I know how you feel. My mom died from cancer when I was thirteen. She'd been sick for a long time."

"Oh no. How awful for you."

"Yeah, it was. I never had much of a childhood. And then I kinda went off the deep end. Took me a long time to get back on track, so don't let that happen to you." She touched a finger to Trish's cheek where a tear had fallen. "Don't try to tough it out. I did, and it's not worth it."

"But I can't even ride decent anymore."

"You will. Just takes time, that's all." Mandy squeezed Trish's arm. "Hey, something else I learned. People don't know what to say to you so they look the other way. Makes you feel kinda like you're invisible."

Trish nodded again. "Uh-huh."

"So you smile first. Don't wait for them." She waved with one hand as she left the room. "See ya."

Trish blew her nose with paper from one of the stalls. After taking a deep breath, she left the room. *Invisible,* that's exactly what she felt like sometimes.

After a light lunch, Trish grabbed her bag and walked around the track to the jockey rooms just south of the grandstands. The white building gleamed in the sunlight. Tall palm trees rustled in the breeze in the front courtyard of Bay Meadows Racetrack, where busloads of retired spectators were already disembarking. It promised to be another perfect California day at the track, now that the fog had burned off.

Trish sighed. In spite of the weather, she hadn't had a perfect day here since she arrived. Today she had one mount and that was only because Adam still had faith in her. No one else seemed to want to hire her anymore. Well, after this race she would head for the beach. At least there she felt like there was *some* hope.

She couldn't keep her eyes open even though she sat in the most uncomfortable chair in the room. The conversation of the other women jockeys flowed around her while she tried to study. She scrunched farther down in the chair, flinched from her sunburn, got up, splashed water on her face—and still nodded off.

When someone touched her shoulder, she jerked awake.

"Time to suit up," the attendant said.

Trish checked her watch against the clock on the wall. "Thanks," she mumbled, still caught in the slog of sleep. At least she'd shined her boots and goggles earlier. She pulled on a white sleeveless turtleneck, then her white pants, and laced up the front closure. Boots next, and after grabbing her helmet, she made it to the silks keeper and then the scale, the last in line.

"I was beginning to wonder about you," Adam said with a smile when she met him at the stall in the saddling paddock under the grandstands. The layout of the paddock felt so much like the one at Portland Meadows, Trish caught herself looking over her shoulder for David.

At the "riders up" call, she stroked the filly's nose and ducked under the horse's neck to be tossed into the saddle.

"Now, let her get her stride good and keep her off the pace about

15

fourth or so. The track's good and fast and you've only six furlongs, so you need to make your move as you come out of the turn. Remember, this is only her third time out and she's not always quite sure what to do."

Trish nodded in all the right places. She swallowed hard to get her butterflies back down where they belonged. They seemed to be engaged in a somersault contest, at her expense.

"You okay now?" Adam looked up at her before backing the horse out of the stall.

Trish nodded and swallowed again. Down, butterflies, down!

The filly pricked her ears at the roar of the crowd as the field of ten trotted out on the track. When they lined up, waiting for the handlers to take each horse into its stall, the entry on her left reared and slashed out at the pony rider. Three men grabbed the animal and wrestled him under control before leading him into position four.

Trish walked her filly into their stall, crooning her song of comfort all the while.

The horse on their right walked in, and two more when number four reared again. The jockey scrambled off this time in case the animal went over backward. Again the handlers took the time to work the horse back into the stall and get the jockey remounted.

Trish felt the tension ripple up her back. The filly stamped her front feet and switched her tail. Trish stroked the dark brown neck where dots of moisture revealed the filly's agitation. "Easy, girl. Take it easy."

Silence. A brief, heart-thumping moment and the gates clanged open. They were off.

Number four broke, stumbled, and crashed into the filly as she barely cleared the gate. Trish fought to keep her horse on her feet, and miraculously they made it through. By the time they were running true, the field clustered in front of them and all Trish could see was a solid wall of moving rumps. She started to swing out around when a hole opened in front of her.

She drove the filly in and through the hole to be caught in a box. They were halfway through the turn before she could see another hole, and when they went for it, the filly gave her all. She dove through and headed for the three leaders two lengths in front.

Trish rode her hard, but at the half-mile pole the jockeys went to their whips and number two took off. Trish's filly passed the number three horse and crept up, nose to tail, nose to shoulder, nose to nose, straining for all she had. When the front runner passed the post, Trish and her filly were number two by only a whisker. It took the camera to declare the winner, but Trish knew it before the numbers flashed on the board.

"Good race, lass," Adam commented as he trotted out on the track to snap on a lead line.

"She shoulda had it. What a sweetheart to come back after a bum start like that. They shoulda scratched that stupid beast beside us. And then to let her get caught in a box like I did. Adam, I'm sorry."

"Trish, I said you did a good job." Adam clipped each word, enunciating clearly, as if she were hard of hearing.

Trish shook her head. "She should have won that. A good jockey woulda brought her in to win."

Adam let her rant on. At his "Don't be so hard on yourself," Trish just shook her head and, clamping her hands under her saddle, strode over to the scale.

At least now she could go to the beach.

She tossed her bag in the backseat and pushed the button to put the top down. Maybe the wind in her hair would blow away the cobwebs. "And maybe all it'll do is make your hair a rat's nest," she grumbled to the face in her mirror as she set her black plastic sunglasses in place.

A gray fog bank hovered just on the horizon, sending high spindrift clouds to tease the sun. The ride was quick and effortless, and Trish could feel herself unwind as she arrived at her favorite spot. An offshore breeze kicked up sand as she tried to lay out her blanket that billowed and flipped up at the corners. Once on the ground, she plunked her cooler in one corner, her schoolbag in another, and herself on the rest.

At least today she wouldn't be tempted to sunbathe and fall asleep. She pulled an orange out of the cooler and, after peeling it, ate the whole thing, ignoring the cries of the gull wheeling above her.

She dug her journal out of her bag and turned to the first blank page. She didn't have too many pages to turn, because writing in a journal like her father had done still wasn't a habit. She bit the end of her pen.

But once she began, the words seemed to flow out of a deep well of despair:

> *I feel like I'm being jerked around like a yo-yo. Yeah, and by a kid who doesn't know how to use the thing. One minute I'm rolling high and feeling like maybe I'll make it, and the next I'm bouncing on the floor and my string is all wrapped in knots around me.*
>
> *Everyone keeps telling me things will be better in time, but how much time? I miss you, Dad, I can't even begin to tell you how much. Why did you leave me? What kind of God takes a father from his kids? Why didn't you quit smoking years ago when we first asked you to?*

Trish gritted her teeth. She could feel the anger again, red hot and fiery, flaming in her stomach. The "whys" fueled it higher. She flung herself down on the blanket and clenched her arms around her middle. When she finally rolled over on her back, she winced in pain.

"Ahhh." She sat up and tried to arch her back away from her clothes. She tore into her bag. No green bottle. It was up in the car in her track bag. The pain eased when she turned her back to the breeze, but now her hair blew in her eyes.

She picked up the pen again, but the urge to write had flown away like the gull who'd screamed for her orange. She snorted. Yeah, even the gulls yelled at her. She swiped at her eyes again. Whatever happened to that iron will she had?

She couldn't lie on her back because it hurt. She couldn't lie on her stomach because, when the sun did come out, the heat hurt her back. She rolled on her side and pillowed her head on her book bag. At least her chemistry book was good for something!

She lay in that no-man's-land between waking and sleeping until the breeze blew more cold than cool. Struggling up the cliff helped wake her up, but when raindrops misted the windshield she put the top up.

The foggy mist hovered over the campus too when she arrived, so she pulled on her sweats and, because she was late, ended up in the back row. Keeping awake in class was hard in the best of times, and now certainly wasn't one of those times. She left for home at the break.

"Your mom called," Martha announced when Trish pushed open the door and stumbled in. "Said she'd gotten your message and was sorry the machine was off earlier. Was just a few minutes ago." She glanced up at the clock. "You're home early."

"I just couldn't stay awake. Tomorrow night I meet with my tutor. Maybe he can work a miracle." Trish went to the kitchen and poured herself a glass of ice water. "Good night."

Once in her own room, Trish dialed the phone and waited for an answer. At the same time, she kicked off her shoes and sweats. "Hi, Mom . . ." Trish got no further. At her mother's "hi," she lost it.

"Oh, Trish, I'm so glad you called." Her mother's words were separated by sniffs. When they'd both calmed down again, Trish could hear her mother's gentle words. "You're finally crying, Trish. Thank you, God, thank you."

Trish blew her nose and wiped her eyes. "Mom, I want to come home." She sniffled again and rolled her eyes toward the ceiling to control the tears. Sometimes the trick worked. She drew in a raggedy breath. "What's happening up there? How's Miss Tee?" The questions poured out.

Trish lay on the bed, feeling limp like the seaweed on the beach.

"David has some really great news," her mother was saying. "Here, I'll let him tell you."

"Hi, baby sister. How ya doing?"

"Not so good."

"I can tell."

"Well, how'd you like to have red, swollen eyes all the time? And the puffier my eyes are, the easier it is to fall asleep. That's the only thing I do well right now."

"How's the chemistry?"

"Don't ask." She grabbed another tissue and blew again. "So what's your news?"

"I've been accepted at the University of Arizona, pre–veterinary medicine. I'll be leaving the last week in August."

"Oh, David, n-o-o!"

Chapter
03

Come on, Trish. I'm not going to the ends of the earth. This won't be any different than when I went to Washington State."

"Yes, it will. You'll be farther away." Trish scrubbed her fingers through her hair.

"Not really. Now it'll be air time instead of drive time, so really I'll be closer."

Trish could tell her brother was forcing patience into his voice. Why couldn't she be happy for him? He was finally getting to do what he wanted to after taking a year off college to help at home.

"Hey, look who's been gone the last months."

"I know, David." Trish leaned against the pillows she'd stacked up behind her on the bed. "I guess . . ." She struggled to find the right words. "I guess I don't want any more change. So much has happened that sometimes I'm afraid my whole world is going to explode and fly away in a million pieces—and that I'll never be able to put it all back together again."

"Things will never be the same again, Tee. You can't expect that, and you've got to face it."

"I know."

A silence lengthened between them, but it was comforting, not awkward.

"So, how's your chemistry coming?"

"I *said* don't ask. Oh, David, how come I'm so stupid when it comes to chemistry? I study and think I have stuff memorized, and when I take the test my brain flies right out the window. The other day I nearly caused everyone to die of smoke inhalation."

"What happened?"

"I was reading the instructions for the experiment to my partner, and I accidentally gave part of the next one. The two didn't mix very well."

David swallowed a chuckle. "You have to pay close attention in the lab."

"Tell me about it. That's the problem, my attention span. It goes to sleep on me every chance it gets." She wiped her nose with a soggy tissue. "And takes my brain and body right along with it. I feel as if I could sleep for years."

"Sounds like you're depressed to me."

"Thank you, Dr. Evanston."

"No, I read some stuff on grieving that Mom gave me. It said depression happens a lot, and wanting to sleep all the time can be part of it."

"Mmmm." Trish pulled on her earlobe. When it hurt, she removed the gold post and laid it on the nightstand. "I gotta hit the books again, David."

"Hey, if you don't make it home before I leave, I'll stop by there on my way. You can show me this beach you keep running away to."

"Sure, sounds good. Good night, David. Say good night to Mom. And tell Rhonda and Brad I could use some mail. Or a phone call." She hung up. She was glad she'd called but she didn't feel as good as she'd expected. She picked up her book bag, and the chemistry book fell out on her chest. She felt like throwing it across the room, but managed to calmly open it to the assignment.

She fell asleep at some point and awoke with a terrible thirst. She stared groggily at the clock. *One-thirty.* She staggered to the bathroom, drank some water, and shed her clothes on the way back to her bed. When the alarm rang, Trish felt like pulling the covers over her head and pretending the world didn't exist. Instead, she slammed her fist on the snooze button and drifted off again.

The crowd screamed as she and Spitfire surged across the finish line, winning by two lengths. They did it; they won! She could hear his breathing, whistling like a freight train, his heart pounding against his ribs. The crowd screamed again as they trotted back to the winner's circle.

It wasn't the crowd screaming. Trish reached over and turned off the alarm. She rolled onto her back and closed her eyes again. At least in her dreams she was still a winner. And winning felt so good.

She pushed herself to a sitting position. Maybe she was jinxed without Spitfire! She shook her head. That was crazy. It wasn't as if the only time she won was when she was riding the big black colt, her best friend in all the world. But now Spitfire lived at BlueMist Farms in Kentucky and wasn't even hers any longer. At least not all hers.

She tugged on her clothes and headed for the track. That was part of the problem, wasn't it? She was so alone. Except for Mandy, the jockey she'd talked to maybe once, the only people she really talked to here were the Finleys and her tutor, Richard. And all he wanted to talk about was chemistry. Yuk!

You just have to make the effort. She wished her nagger had stayed at home in bed, asleep for about an eternity or so. *Besides, who'd want to be your friend? You're about as much fun as . . . as a chemistry quiz.* Trish slammed the door of her car and the one on her mind also. She did *not* need his advice right now, especially when all it did was make her feel worse. Even if he was right.

At least the horses were glad to see her. Even Gatesby seemed to want some extra loving. Trish scratched ears and cheeks down the line, inhaling the good, honest smell of horse. Even though she wasn't winning, this part of her world seemed right. The horses didn't care if she felt brain dead half the time. Firefly lipped a tendril of hair that framed Trish's face, just like Spitfire used to do, and whuffled in her face.

Trish wrapped her arms around Gatesby's neck and tried to picture Spitfire there instead. But he wouldn't come in. Was she even losing his memory?

The fogless morning felt good for a change as she worked the string of horses. She would walk some, breeze Firefly, and slow-gallop others, all the time following the conditioning program Adam had designed for the horses in his care.

"How'd she do?" Adam asked of a new mare that he'd started training.

"Kinda sluggish. Not what you'd think after all the time she's had off. I don't think she feels tip-top."

Adam nodded. "We'll check her temp. No limping on that right front?"

Trish shook her head. "Gracias," she said as Carlos gave her a leg up on Gatesby, her last mount for the morning. When the gelding didn't act up, she looked at Carlos with a question. He shrugged and shook his head, keeping a wary eye on the horse just the same.

"Okay, what's happening?" she asked after a rather dispirited trot around the oval track. She leaned forward and stroked the dark neck flecked with sweat. "You shouldn't have worked up a sweat. It's back to the barn with you, fella."

"We better check temps all around," Adam said to Carlos when Trish told him what she'd observed.

Trish held the horses' heads while Carlos and Adam checked temperatures. They drew blood on the mare, ready to send it out for diagnosis, when they saw the mare was running a fever.

"What could it be?" Trish asked when the third animal in a row showed a rise in body heat. She walked beside Adam back to the office.

"Who knows?" Adam dropped into his swivel chair and picked up the phone. He pushed the speed dial for the vet. "I think we've got trouble," he said after the greeting. "Anyone else running temps?" He rubbed the back of his neck with one hand. "Okay, see you in a couple of minutes."

"What did he say? Anyone else got trouble?" Trish dropped down to the lid on a green tack box.

Adam shook his head. "Not that he knows of. Carlos, disinfect all the buckets."

"Already doing that. No one was off their feed this morning. But now that mare has a runny nose." Carlos removed his hat to scratch his head.

"Well, she was clean when she came in here." Adam pulled out the record book. "Doc wouldn't have let anything by, and his inspection was only two days ago. She came in at night, right?"

Trish listened to the discussion with one ear while her memory flipped back to the siege of infection they'd had at Runnin' On Farm the fall before. The first time her father'd been in the hospital. She'd had some mighty sick horses. Her stomach turned queasy at the thought. Could *she* have brought back the virus from some other farm she rode for?

The pickup containing the portable veterinarian clinic pulled up at the barn, and the vet climbed out. "Well, let's see what's going on." He raised the door on the rear of the canopy and removed a stainless steel bucket with equipment in it.

Trish watched from the doorway as he checked over the bay mare. She looked droopy all right, and had a runny nose.

"Looks like we better vaccinate the entire string. I'll take that blood sample in, but I'm sure it's going to show herpes virus 1. You know the game plan, and I know you've vaccinated your horses regularly. Where'd this one come from?"

As the discussion continued, Trish stroked the mare's neck and rubbed her ears. "Poor old girl, sorry you caught this. But you keep the bug to yourself, you hear?"

"This should blow over in a week or so, but make sure she drinks plenty of water. If you hear any rales in her lungs or the coughing gets really bad, she could develop pneumonia. Keep me posted."

Trish followed him to the truck. "Ah—can I ask you a question?"

"Sure, shoot away." He slung the bucket back in the truck.

"Could I—ah—do you think I brought the virus back from another barn?"

"Naa, she was probably a latent carrier. Wouldn't be surprised if she had it a long time ago and all the stress of shipping and a new environment brought it on. You know Adam is really careful about his horses, but not everyone is as cautious as he is."

"Thanks." Trish felt like someone had just lifted a load from her shoulders and her stomach settled back down.

You're beginning to think everything is your fault, her nagger whispered in her ear. *That's not smart, you know.*

Later, as she walked up to the jockey room, Trish thought ahead to the afternoon program. For a change her agent had gotten her mounts for two other trainers. Neither were top horses, but that certainly wasn't surprising. If she could just get them to run.

By the time the third race was called, her resident troupe of butterflies flipped around on their warm-ups. She listened to the trainer's instructions carefully. The gelding did not like being boxed in, and they were in gate two.

Why didn't they put blinkers on him? Trish thought as they trotted past the stands. Then tight quarters wouldn't bother him so much.

"Ya gotta break fast," she told the twitching ears as the horse shifted from side to side in the gate. "Easy now, you know what's happening." The singsong was as much for her as the restless horse under her. "Come on, fella, I need this win even more than you do."

The gate, the horse, and Trish all exploded at the same instant. But it was like time stood still for just a fraction before the gelding caught the first stride. The first three animals surged stride for stride, but that pause gave number four the opportunity he needed. Going into the first turn he pounded directly in front of Trish.

Her mount shook his head, watching the horses on either side of him more than concentrating on the job he was set to do. Trish swung her whip back once and he leaped forward. But it was a fight all the way to the pole. And they were caught in the middle the entire distance, giving them a fourth.

The trainer looked at her with a blank face. *I told you so,* seemed to hover all around them. All he said was "Tough break."

Tough break, my eye, Trish scolded herself all the way back to the jockey room.

And the next race wasn't any better. This time she had the horse in front, just like the trainer told her to do, but he quit running with four lengths to go. They took a show.

"I'm sorry," she told the trainer. "He just quit."

"Yeah, well, that was his first time at a mile. Thought you had it there, though."

"Me too." As she walked back to the jockey's room, she felt the loneliness return. If only she had someone to talk to. She checked her watch.

Rhonda ought to be home now. She headed for the phone and dialed her friend's number.

Trish felt her heart leap when the familiar voice answered on the second ring.

"Hi." Trish cleared her throat. "It's me."

"Trish, I can't believe it. How are you? What's going on? David says you're not doing so well at the track. And how's the beach? You all tanned?"

Trish laughed at the rapid-fire stream of questions. Yup, this was Rhonda all right. Words running over each other. "How can I answer all that at the same time?"

"You can't. I'll make it easy. You won any races lately?"

"Thanks, friend. Get me right where it hurts. I haven't won since Belmont, so that answers another question. I'm not doing well, anywhere, anytime."

"Why don't you come home?"

"Why don't you come down here? We could go school shopping like we never dreamed."

"Oh, I can't. I've got jumping shows coming up the next two weekends. How about after that?"

Trish sighed. "That's so far away. I was hoping you could come now." She leaned against the wall, the phone clamped between her ear and shoulder.

"Sorry, Tee."

"I know. I'll call the travel agent and she'll send you the ticket."

"Hey, you heard from the sexiest jockey in the world?"

"Rhonda!"

"Well, Red Holloran is a hunk in my book."

"He is nice."

"Nice! Nice! Your dog is nice. A hot fudge sundae is yummy. Red is . . ."

"Rhonda, you nut." Trish giggled.

" . . . sweet, likes you a whole lot, rides like a dream, and kisses like a—"

"That's enough." Trish strangled on her laughter. "You didn't kiss him."

"No, but you did, and when you just so happened to mention it to your best friend in all the world, your eyes glazed over. That should tell you something."

"Spitfire's my best friend in all the world."

"Okay, your best *human* friend, then." They swapped chuckles over the line. "Now, back to my original question before you so rudely side-tracked me."

"All right. Yes! I got a card from him last week."

"Was it a mushy one?"

"You are the nosiest—"

"Best friend in all the world. Well?"

"No, it was funny. I need funny things in my life right now. That's why I called you, and now you say you can't come."

"I'll be there. You just keep those stores warmed up. We're going to do some serious shopping."

"See you in two weeks." Trish hung up the phone. Maybe she should call Rhonda every day. Maybe every hour.

Two weeks to wait. Ugh!

She checked her watch. Yes, time to stop by a card shop on her way home. Red was long overdue for an answer.

Reading the messages made her giggle out loud. She chose two funny ones for Red and then one for Rhonda. Writing them when she got home made her feel even better. How lucky she was to have such good friends in her life.

She thought a moment. Would Red be called a friend? Or a boyfriend? She fingered the cross on a chain around her neck. He'd given it to her to remember him by. She felt a shiver travel up her back. He really was a neat person. She touched her lips. The kisses had been nice. She giggled at the thought. Nice was not a good enough word. Rhonda was right.

That night she fell asleep in front of the television in the family room.

"Trish, it's two o'clock." Martha shook Trish's shoulder. "Come on, get up to bed."

Trish blinked her eyes and sat up, trying to clear the fog from her brain. The last she remembered was—she blinked again, she couldn't remember. "Uh, okay, thanks." She got up and stumbled up the stairs. She was asleep again before she pulled the covers up.

She was late for morning works.

"I'm sorry, guess I forgot to set my alarm." Trish slumped into the canvas chair.

Adam studied her face. "Looks to me like you shoulda slept about ten hours longer. But no matter, since three of the horses won't work this morning . . ."

Guilt made her bite her lip. She should've checked on the horses herself, at least the horses from Runnin' On Farm. "How's the mare?"

"About the same. We caught it in time, I think. We'll let Gatesby have a rest too, just in case. Firefly seems fine, just warm her up this morning. She's in the Camino Diablo, the stakes for this afternoon." He rose to his feet. "Carlos has her ready, if you are."

Trish nodded. As ready as she'd ever be. She and Firefly slow-trotted the oval of the smaller track that lay close to the freeway. Cars were already slowing down in the morning rush-hour commute. The brassy sun peeped above the hills on the eastern side of San Francisco Bay, promising another hot day.

The filly tracked all the sights, sounds, and smells of the morning bustle, her ears and nostrils in constant motion. Trish leaned forward and stroked the shiny red neck. "You're a beauty, you know that?" Firefly tossed her head and snorted.

Back at the barn when works were finished, Trish slumped back in her chair in the office. She crossed one booted foot over the other knee and picked off a piece of dried mud. A sigh escaped. She dropped her chin on her chest and rotated her head from side to side and back to front.

"Okay, what is it?"

"Huh?" She sat up straight.

"Something's on your mind." Adam leaned back in his chair, hands behind his head.

Trish ran her tongue over her lower lip. "Maybe—I—uh—I think you should put someone else up on Firefly today so she has a chance. She could win that—if . . ."

"If?"

Trish almost swallowed the words. "If I weren't riding her." The silence in the office was broken only by a huge fly buzzing at the window. "Adam, I can hardly even get 'em around the track. You could still get someone good, anyone would be better'n me."

When the silence stretched until Trish felt it quivering between them, she looked up to see Adam staring at her and shaking his head. "No, Trish. All you need is one good race and you'll be fine again. I think this afternoon will do it for you."

Trish pushed herself to her feet, shaking her head all the while. *I can't believe you did that,* she scolded herself on the way out to her car. *Maybe you should just chuck it all in and go home. Maybe you really are all washed up.* She leaned her forehead against the black cloth roof of her car. *Quitters never win and winners never quit.* How many times had her father said that through the years? If only he were here to say it now.

That afternoon Firefly pranced as if all the world applauded her personally. She trotted beside the pony rider, ears forward, neck arched, her coat almost the same crimson as that in Trish's silks. Crimson and gold, Runnin' On Farm colors and also those of Prairie High.

All ten entries walked into the gates without a problem. Trish gathered her reins and crouched forward, feeling Firefly settle on her haunches, ready for the gun.

The gates flew open. Firefly leaped forward. The horse on their right stumbled, crashed into Firefly, and hit the ground.

Chapter

04

Sheer willpower kept Firefly on her feet.

Trish wasn't sure whose willpower won as she clung to the filly's neck and held the reins firm. Another stride and the filly regained her balance. Two more strides and they were running straight. One more stride and Trish could feel a shudder in the right fore.

Firefly pulled up limping badly.

Trish vaulted to the ground. She ran a hand down the filly's leg, all the while murmuring the soothing sounds that calmed the horse. She could feel the swelling popping up right under her fingertips.

Slowly she led the limping filly out the gate and back to the barns. Adam caught up with her before she passed the first row of stalls.

"You should have . . ."

Adam held up a hand. "That could have happened to anybody."

Everything in Trish wanted to scream *I told you so!* She bit her tongue to keep the words back. Now her filly was injured and a strain like this could cause permanent damage. She thought of all the trouble they'd had with Spitfire's leg.

Her eyes felt scratchy along with her throat. After Carlos and Adam took over the care of the filly, she pulled a bottle of water out of the refrigerator and chug-a-lugged half of it. When would this cycle end?

Trish left the track and headed for the beach. While it was already late afternoon, she didn't have to meet her tutor until seven. Maybe, just maybe, she'd hear her song again and find the peace that went along with it. Traffic snaked to a crawl where Highway 92 crossed the Crystal Springs Reservoir and became a two-lane road. All the way up the winding, hilly road and down the ocean side to Half Moon Bay, the cars played either stop-and-go or slow-and-go.

Trish thrummed her fingers on the steering wheel. They were using up her time, her precious beach time. The sun hovered above the band of clouds hugging the horizon when she finally parked the car at Redondo Beach. She grabbed her blanket and pack from the trunk and slipped and slid down the rough trail.

Low tide exposed a wide expanse of beach as Trish trudged south toward her favorite spot. Since she and the gulls were the only visitors, she quickly spread her blanket and dropped into the middle of it.

Hugging her knees, she watched the gulls wheeling and dipping above her. Would her song come? She listened intently. The offshore breeze sent sand skittering before it and peppered the cliff behind her with its breath, loosening bits of rust and orange sandstone. It tugged on her hair, freeing tendrils from the braid down her back and blowing them into her eyes.

Impatiently she brushed them away. Where was her song? She tried humming a few bars but her throat closed.

Clutching her legs, Trish rocked forward and back, leaning her cheek on her jeans-clad knees. When she despaired of the song coming today, she hauled the journals out of her pack and, laying her father's beside her, dug out a pen and opened her own. The words poured out.

> *Why? Why is everything falling apart? I can't ride, I can't win, and most of all—I can't quit crying. This isn't fair! And when I'm not crying, I'm sleeping. Right now, I could lie down and in one minute be sound asleep. Maybe there's something terribly wrong with me. God, where are you? My dad always said you loved us no matter what. If this is what love is like, do me a favor. Go love someone else.*

Trish stared at what she'd written. After blowing her nose, she picked up the pen again. *I want to have faith like my dad did.* She thought a bit, chewing on the end of her pen. *I guess. Do I really? Or do I just want to run away from the pain? I hurt so bad. My head aches, my nose is all plugged, and I'm so tired.*

"Please, God. Help me." She closed the book. Did she hear it? The song? "Dear God, I need those eagle's wings so bad."

She laid her book down and picked up her father's. Flipping through its pages, she saw verse after verse. One stuck out because it was underlined and circled. *"Peace I leave with you; my peace I give you."*

Trish felt like tearing the page out and ripping it to shreds to let the wind blow it away. Peace, there was no peace. She ground her teeth together. Fury, red hot and snapping sparks, blurred her vision. Her father said God lived up to His promises. Then why, even here at the beach today, was there was no peace? No song. No nothing.

The seagull dipped low and screeched at her.

"Shut up, you—you stupid bird." She threw a handful of sand at him, and with one last keening cry he tipped his wings and drifted off.

Never had she felt so alone. She looked up and down the beach. Totally empty. "Father, Dad, Daddy, help me!" The scream tore from her raw throat.

She dropped her head on the leather-covered journal and waited for the burning tears to flood her eyes. But they didn't. The burn continued.

Dry-eyed, she traced the embossed design of the cross on the front of the journal. "Please, please," she whispered, "please help me."

The sun disappeared behind the two-toned gray band of clouds swelling on the horizon. The wind, cold now, tugged and pulled at the figure sprawled on the square of red plaid spread on the shifting sand.

Trish sat up. She picked up her journal and stuck the pen in the pages, then placed it and her father's journal back in her blue pack. The song hadn't come. She stood, shook out the blanket, and folded it up. If peace came, what would it feel like? What did Jesus mean by "His peace"? She dug the journal out of the bag again and opened it, searching for the right page.

There. *"Peace I leave with you; my peace I give you."* The words hadn't changed. She read them again. And then her father's words that followed:

Father, God, I need your peace so desperately. Sometimes I am so afraid, and then I am comforted by your words. Peace means to me, right now, that you are in control and you will never let me go. Your love, your grace, are eternal, forever, and that means right now. Thank you, my Lord and my God.

Trish shivered in the wind. Her dad had been afraid too. She closed the book, keeping one finger in the place. "Thank you."

The tune floated in on the wind and curled around her bleeding heart.

When she reached the top of the cliff, she turned and looked over the white frosted breakers that crashed on the sand. One last ray of sun beamed up and painted the underside of the cloud in molten fire.

Trish hummed the song under her breath as she placed her bag and blanket in the trunk and removed her purse and schoolbag. She'd have time to grab a hamburger in Half Moon Bay before driving the curving road back up to the school.

"You look like something the cat wouldn't even drag in," Richard, her tutor, said when she dropped into the chair beside him.

"Thanks a lot. I needed to hear that." Trish smoothed the windblown hair back from her face. "Driving a convertible messes my hair. So what!"

"Nah, not just that. Your eyes are all red; you look like you've been crying for a week. What happened, your boyfriend dump you?"

Trish stared at him. "Since when do you care? All you've ever talked about is chemistry."

"Trish, that's what you pay me for."

"Well, you're not doing a very good job." Trish leaned back against the seat and crossed her ankles.

"Hey, your grades aren't my fault. You just aren't concentrating. I've watched you, your mind is off someplace far away. I think I'm just wasting my time."

"Fine. Quit then." Trish bit the inside of her cheek.

"No, we need to get to the bottom of this. You want to tell me what's wrong?"

Trish stared at him, her mind at war behind her burning eyes. "Not really."

Richard stared at her.

Trish stared back at him. One fat tear slipped from under her control and meandered down her cheek.

She clenched her fingers into fists until she could feel the nails biting into the palms of her hands. She would not back down.

Richard leaned forward and pulled a handkerchief from his back pocket. With a gentle touch, he wiped the tear away.

Trish's lip quivered. Her nose ran, followed by the tears she'd tried so hard to hold back.

Richard handed her the handkerchief. "Here. While you wipe your face, I'm going out in the hall to get us a couple of sodas. You like Diet Coke, right?" Trish nodded. "And then we'll talk, okay?" Trish nodded again.

The drink felt heavenly, both slipping down her throat and as the can pressed against her swollen eyes. "Thank you." She swallowed several more times and put the can to her cheek.

"My dad died a couple months ago." She took another drink. "Do you know much about Thoroughbred horse racing?"

Richard shook his head.

"Well, I'm a jockey and . . ." Once having begun, Trish told the entire story, about their dream of winning with Spitfire, and about all the races they'd won. "And now I can't quit crying; I can't think; I can't do anything right anymore."

"Man, that's a bummer. No wonder you look sad, kinda spaced out all the time." Richard tugged at an earlobe that held a tiny diamond post. "Bummer."

"Yeah, you could call it that." Trish blew her nose again. "Sorry, I messed up your handkerchief. I'll take it home and wash it."

"No problem." Richard stared down at the chemistry books forgotten on the oak table in front of him. He looked up at her, seeming to stare through her eyes right into her brain. "I have something that can help you."

Trish stared back. "You do? Really?"

"Really." He dug in the pocket of his sweat shirt. "Here." He dropped four white capsules into her hand. "Uppers. They'll make you feel better. I promise."

Chapter
05

Don't worry, you can't get hooked on a couple of uppers."

Trish's fingers trembled. "I—I know that."

"Well, I just thought they might help—like give you some energy and make you think better, maybe win a race or two. You know, even the doctors give these out."

Trish nodded. "I know. He—the doctor offered me some right after my dad died. Said it would help make things easier."

"Did you try it?"

Trish shook her head.

Richard looked at her and rolled his eyes. "Why not?"

"My dad always said we should depend on God for help, not pills and—stuff."

"Didn't he take the medicines the doctors told him to?"

Trish felt like her head was tied to a string. Nod yes, shake no. Her hands wouldn't quit trembling.

"Well, think about it." He checked the clock on the wall. "We better get on the chemistry. I gotta be somewhere else in a while."

Trish shoved the pills in her pocket and opened her book. Maybe it was a good idea if those simple little white things could make her understand this stuff. But as Richard explained the formulas, her mind flitted off again. She fought to keep her eyes open. The warm room, full stomach, a droning voice—

"Trish, you're not paying attention!" Richard slammed his book shut.

Trish started. Her eyes flew open and her heart pounded. "You scared me."

He looked at her in disgust. "Take it from me, you *need* help." He pushed himself to his feet and gathered up his books. "And there's always more where those came from. All you have to do is ask."

Trish watched as he strode out the room, his blond ponytail curling down past his shoulders. He was trying to help, he really was. If only she could stay awake.

All you have to do is ask, kept ringing in her ears on the drive back to the condominium. That's what her father always said too. He quoted the verse all the time, "Ask and you shall receive." Just ask. She snorted. She was sure he didn't mean ask for drugs.

But she *had* asked. She'd begged and pleaded for God to make her father well again. And He had—or the medicines had—for a time. But then her father died. The tears that always hovered just behind her eyelids pooled and blurred her vision. She wiped them away with the back of her hand.

And she'd prayed to win races. She had. And not just she and Spitfire. She'd won on plenty of other horses too. Her father always said she had a gift for understanding horses and getting the best out of them. So—had God taken the gift away?

She parked in the driveway at the hillside condo. Did God give gifts and take them away? Did He just answer prayers when He felt like it?

Wait a minute! She thumped her fist on the steering wheel. *You said once you didn't believe in God anymore—remember? You said He wasn't real, but at the beach you were praying and begging again.*

The battle waged in her mind. One side yelled there was no God, and the other insisted God was her Father and loved her dearly. Trish dug her fingers into both sides of her scalp and rubbed until it hurt.

But who else can I turn to? What else is left? She pulled the pills from her pocket and stared at them in the light of the streetlamp. Would they *really* make her feel better? She stuffed them in her purse, grabbed her bags, and ran up the brick stairs.

She fell asleep after working only one chemistry problem. The thump of the book on the floor woke her so she could undress and crawl into bed. Another evening shot down. Would she never get this stuff?

The next morning, after working the horses that were healthy, Trish slumped into the chair in the office. She alternately sipped orange juice and munched a bagel. Adam and Carlos both favored coffee with their bagels, and Adam's was smeared liberally with cream cheese.

"You got any mounts in the next week or so?" Adam asked around a mouthful.

Trish shook her head. "Should bug my agent, but—I don't know—who'd want to hire me?"

Adam glared at her. "Well, there're lots of other jockeys who make up the races without winning."

"Yeah, right." She looked up in time to find Carlos glaring at her too, sparks seeming to fly from his dark eyes.

"I think you should go home for a few days, then." Adam set his coffee cup down and leaned forward. "If you leave today and come back Monday, you'll only miss one class."

"As if that makes any difference."

"Trish!"

"Okay, okay. I'm going. You want me to leave right now?"

Adam leaned back again with a grin on his face. "Martha will drive you to the airport. No sense paying for long-term parking if you don't have to."

"You had this all worked out, didn't you?" She stared from one smiling face to the other. "What about Firefly?"

"I think I can take care of her." It was the first time Trish had heard Carlos resort to sarcasm.

"I'm sorry, I didn't mean . . ."

"We know. Now get outta here."

Trish felt hope leap within her. Home—she was going home. She stopped at the first phone booth and called Runnin' On Farm. When the answering machine clicked on, she glanced at her watch. *Only eight-thirty.* She left a message. "I'm on my way home, first flight I can get. Call you as soon as I know. Oh, I hope you haven't gone for the day."

She called again from the house after making reservations. Same thing, just the answering machine.

A repeat at the airport.

"Don't worry, I'll keep trying," Martha assured her as they called the final boarding for Trish's flight. "You just have a good visit with your family. We'll miss you."

Trish returned Martha's hug and boarded the plane.

Halfway through the hour-and-a-half flight, something set her butterflies off. Her stomach felt like just before a major race. She thought about her time at home before coming to California. Eyes closed, she leaned her seat back and remembered. Would the pain be as bad? She thought of the accident she'd had with her new car and that last hurried trip to Kentucky. No matter what, her father would not be there.

She pinched the bridge of her nose with her fingers and swallowed the scratchy lump in her throat. She leaned back in the seat and closed her eyes. But at least she would see the rest of her family, and Rhonda and Brad. She turned and drew her feet up onto the seat. Good thing she had a seat by herself.

Eventually she opened her eyes and stared out the window. Mount Hood, its snow covering slashed by granite faces after the summer melt, loomed below them to the left. Mount St. Helens glowed faintly in the haze to the north.

How would she get to the farm if no one was home? *Take a taxi, silly,* she told herself. *Or you could rent a car.* She shuffled along with the rest of the deplaning passengers. As she strode through the doors at the top of the ramp, the first thing she saw was her mother's face. David stood just behind her.

Trish ran the last few yards and threw her arms around her mother. "You came! You came!"

"Oh, my dear Tee, you didn't give us much notice." Their tears ran together as mother and daughter clung to each other.

"I drove like a bat out of . . ." David sniffed along with the others.

Trish transferred her bear hug to her brother's neck. "I'm just so glad you're here. Feels like a year or two since I've been home."

"Well, not quite that long." David set her back on her feet. "You ever think of planning ahead?"

Trish shook her head. "Adam said I should take a break—Firefly nearly did—and get outta there. I didn't argue too much. Oh, I've been so homesick!" She hugged her mother again.

"You got any more than this?" When Trish shook her head, David and Marge picked up the bags, and with Trish in the middle, the three headed for the parking lot.

Trish caught up on all the latest news on the drive across the I-205 bridge and through the small town of Orchards on the way to Runnin' On Farm. Trish kept one eye on the scenery to see any changes, and her mind on the conversation.

"But wouldn't it have been easier to go back to WSU?" she asked at one point when David was telling her about Tucson.

"Yeah, but after Dad and I talked to the people in Kentucky about the equine program in Tucson, that's all I wanted to do. You have to admit I have some experience in doctoring horses by now."

"So much for the small animal practice you talked about, huh?"

"I think caring for horses is in my blood. Since I'm too big to ride and you'll want to do all the training eventually . . ."

"What about me?" Marge asked. "I'm getting better and better with the babies. You'll see, Tee."

"She is. Who'd ever dream that *our* mother would be down training Miss Tee and Double Diamond. And she's good."

"As you said, brother mine, must be in the blood." Trish turned to grin at her mother. "I'm really proud of you."

"Patrick's talking about attending some of the sales after you get back. Like the yearling sale down at Santa Anita this fall." Marge clasped her daughter's hand. "What do you think?"

"You want to expand?" Trish could feel her chin hit her chest.

"I'm thinking about it. We have a lot of talking to do."

Trish kept waiting for the pain to strike again. But it didn't. Maybe riding in the new van helped since her father had never been in it.

When they turned into the drive of Runnin' On Farm, Trish felt her heart leap. Caesar, the farm's sable collie, met them halfway up the drive, dancing and barking his greeting.

Everything looked the same as usual. Pink, purple, and white petunias lined the sidewalk up to the front door and drifted down the sides of the two tall clay pots flanking either side of the steps. Lush rosebushes fronted the house, covered in blossoms of pink, yellow, and deep red, with all the shades in between.

Caesar planted both front feet on Trish's shoulders as soon as she stepped out of the car. "Down, you goofy dog!" Trish grabbed his ruff with both hands, shaking and hugging him at the same time. "I think you missed me."

Caesar whimpered, and did his best to make sure Trish's face was cleaned of all traces of California.

"I want to go to the barns first, okay?"

"Why am I not surprised?" Marge locked arms with Trish. "Patrick is off looking at a mare we heard about. She's in foal to Seattle Slew also. You know how much your father thought of that stud."

Trish swallowed a gulp of surprise. Was this really *her* mother talking? "You might buy her?"

"We're thinking about it. We have a lot to talk about, things that need discussing if Runnin' On Farm is to be managed wisely."

David poked Trish in the ribs and gave her an I-told-you-so grin. Trish poked him back.

"Wow, look at Patrick's trailer . . ."

"Manufactured home," David drawled out his bit of information. "They don't call them trailers or mobile homes anymore."

"Whatever. Looks like it's been there forever."

"I think he loves flowers and landscaping as much as he does horses. Says he has to have something to keep him busy while half the string is in California." Marge stuck her hands in the back pockets of her jeans. "The whole place looks good, don't you think?"

"Yeah, you even painted the barns."

"I did that," David said. "Amazing what a little extra money can do, along with a lot of elbow grease. Brad helped me."

"And me." Marge grinned at her daughter. "I was the go-fer." She grabbed Trish's hand again. "Come on, see my babies."

Marge whistled as they rounded the long, low row of stalls and headed down the lane to the pastures. The mares had returned from breeding and now grazed peacefully in the deep rich grass. Marge whistled again and the two youngsters in a paddock of their own thundered up to the fence.

"Oh, they've grown! Just think, Miss Tee is almost a year old." The colt and filly pushed at each other to get to Marge's offered carrot bits. When Trish extended her hand, the filly snuffled and lipped her fingers. "Oh, you sweetie, you're just getting prettier and prettier. Look how red you are." Trish rubbed up the filly's cheek and behind her ears.

Marge entertained Double Diamond with the same kind of motions. Both the horses stood quietly, Miss Tee sniffing Trish's arm, shoulder, and hair.

"Mom, you've sure calmed them down." Trish kissed the filly on her soft nose. "See ya later, kid." The babies followed along the fence line as the three strolled to the next paddock, with the dog that never moved an inch from Trish's side.

"I enjoy the time with them. It's like I'm closer to Hal this way. It's funny, all those years I think I was a bit jealous of the time he spent with the horses and the way you kids idolized your father. And then I worried too, of course."

"About everything you could think of and then some," David said with a teasing grin.

Trish forced a smile on her face to match theirs. Her mother had changed so much; was she still the same person? "And you really don't worry anymore?"

"I save it for the seventh Tuesday of the month." Marge leaned her crossed arms on the mare's paddock fence. "But really, Tee, I try to turn everything over to God immediately. And when the worries come back, I give them up again. I win most of the time."

"Wow." Trish shook her head. She stared out at the mares. Old gray Dan'l grazed with them. She rolled her bottom lip tightly over her teeth to whistle for him, but the quivering in her chin flubbed the effort. She scrubbed the back of her hand across her mouth and tried again. This time the high-low-high tone reached the horses' ears.

While all the animals lifted their heads, the gray flung his up and stared toward the fence. Trish whistled again. Dan'l broke into a lope and charged to the fence, his mane and tail feathering in the breeze. He skidded to a halt, nickering and tossing his head. When he reached Trish, he nosed her face, blew, and whuffled all at the same time.

Trish buried her face in his mane. "Oh, Dan'l." The old gelding had been her confidant and comforter for years. As she hugged the horse, she could feel her mother's arm around her shoulder.

David handed her a handkerchief when she stepped back.

"Sorry." She blew her nose and mopped her eyes.

"No, don't be. I'm just so grateful you can cry now. That tough shield you put up kept us all apart. We couldn't help you." Marge turned and leaned against the fence. "Oh, Tee, I prayed so hard for this."

"Yeah, I think she even worried about you, in spite of her good intentions."

"Wash your mouth with soap." Marge lightly punched her son on the arm. "Although I have to admit, sometimes the line between praying and worrying is mighty narrow."

Dan'l leaned his head over Trish's shoulder, settling in for a good scratching. Trish obliged, murmuring love words to him every once in a while.

"Don't be afraid or ashamed of the tears, Trish. There's a verse in the Old Testament that talks about God saving our tears in a bottle. That's how important they are."

"Well, He better have a mighty big bottle, the way I've been blubbering." Trish gave Dan'l a last pat and pushed away from the fence. "Come on, I'm thirsty for a drink of real water. That stuff down there isn't fit for drinking." Dan'l nickered as they left. "Maybe I should take a jug back with me."

Patrick clamped his hand to his heart when he walked into the house that evening. "Lord love ye, lass, what a sight for these poor old eyes." Trish met him in the middle of the room and fell into his hug.

"Poor old eyes, my foot." She sniffed—again—and stepped back to study him. "Patrick, you look wonderful. I think living in the rainy state agrees with you."

"That it does, lass." He studied her back. "Wisht I could say the same for you."

42

"You don't like my California tan?" Trish put her fingertips to her cheeks.

"Nay, it's not the tan." He nodded, squinting his eyes and clicking his tongue. "But I think you'll be better now."

"Better than what?"

"Just better, is all."

The evening passed more easily than Trish had imagined. She caught herself laughing as David, the David she used to know and love, teased them all in turn. He kept digging at her when she tried to sidestep their questions, until she confessed all. Her loneliness, the constant falling asleep, the fears of never riding well again, never winning. She told them everything—except about the pills she still had in her purse.

Should she—could she—tell them that?

Chapter 06

They'd surely think California had turned her into a druggie.

Why hadn't she just flushed the stupid things so she wouldn't have to feel guilty about carrying them around? Maybe she'd do that later.

But she didn't do it before she crawled into bed, her own bed, in her own room. Her wandering gaze stopped at the empty bulletin board above her desk where she and her father had pinned up three-by-five cards with Bible verses on them.

Why had she ripped them down and dumped them in the trash?

She pressed her knuckle against her teeth, trying to remember which verses had been up there. A knock on the door broke her concentration.

"Trish." Her mother poked her head in. "Okay if I come in?"

"Sure." Trish shifted over in the bed so there was room for her mother to sit. "What's up?"

Marge sat down on the edge of the bed and turned so she could look at Trish. "I just want to tell you how happy I am to have you home. You have no idea how I've missed you."

"Yeah, I know. Only I think I didn't figure out what part of my problem was until last week. Then when I admitted I was homesick, I couldn't get it out of my mind."

"You know something else?"

"What?"

"You're *you* again, not that angry person who was ready to tear anybody and everybody limb from limb." Marge brushed a tendril of hair back from Trish's cheek.

"Was I that bad?"

"Uh-huh. I know you think I'm crazy, but when I see you cry . . ."

"You cry too."

"I know, but some of those are tears of gratitude. I think I'm walking by sight now, not just faith, faith that you're getting better."

Trish thought of the pills in her purse. "Mom, I . . ." A silence invaded the room.

"What?"

"Ah, nothing. Just sometimes I feel like a yo-yo, and whoever's pulling the string isn't very good at it."

Marge smiled. "That's a pretty good description."

The silence stretched again.

"Are you so tired all the time you can hardly stay awake?" Trish asked.

"I was. That's part of the grieving. Takes a lot of energy. I slept a lot. Prayed a lot. Cried a lot. No particular order." Marge clasped her hands around one raised knee. "And I talked with Pastor Mort. He gave me Bible verses that helped. You might want to try that while you're home."

"Maybe I will." A yawn cracked her jaw.

Marge copied the jaw cracking, then rose to her feet. She leaned over and kissed Trish on the cheek. "Good night, my dear. Always remember, God loves you and so do I."

Trish wrapped her arms around her mother's neck and clung. "Good night, Mom."

When Trish awoke in the morning, she lay in her bed looking around her room in the early light. Her clothes all hung neatly in the closet; the racing posters she'd collected were on the walls, the framed pictures of her and Spitfire in the winner's circles were there—it was her room. She stretched and yawned, then stretched her arms way over her head and twisted her body from side to side.

What was different? Besides being at home. She thought of the night she'd just slept through—no dreams, no nightmares, no lying awake thinking of failures. Just pure, peaceful rest. The verse flashed through her mind. "Peace I leave with you, my peace I give unto you." Was this what it meant?

She lay there, savoring the thought. She'd prayed for peace, hadn't she? Or had she just begged for help? Was God really answering her prayers?

She threw the covers back and went to stand at the window. Sunshine, no clouds—in Vancouver, Washington? God must indeed be welcoming her home. All the pastures were green, not brown like the hillsides of California. She inhaled. The rosebushes under her window welcomed her with their fragrance.

Patrick's whistled tune floated up on the breeze. She could hear her mother singing in the kitchen. Caesar barked at something off in the woods. All the sounds of home. Trish felt like a grin all over.

She glanced at the clock. *Six-thirty*. She'd really slept in. After pulling on jeans and a T-shirt, she grabbed her boots, stopped in the bathroom to brush her teeth and hair, and trotted into the kitchen.

"Thought maybe you'd sleep in." Marge turned from the sink. "Breakfast will be ready about eight."

Trish looked at the dough spread on the counter. "Cinnamon rolls?" Marge nodded. "Wow!" Trish gave her mother a two-armed hug and started from the room. She turned and backpedaled. "Hey, I've turned into a bagel connoisseur. We'll have some when you come down to California." She slid open the sliding glass door to the deck and plunked herself down on one of the cedar benches while she pulled on her boots.

All the fuchsia baskets dripped with flowers in shades of purple, pink, white, and red. She sat perfectly still as a hummingbird clicked his way past and dined on the hanging blossoms. Her father had loved the hummingbirds. Trish felt a catch in her throat. So often they'd sat together just like this to watch the flying jewels sipping at their flowers.

She had the distinct impression that if she could turn quickly enough, she would see him—her father smiling at her and walking beside her. The feeling persisted down at the barns when she checked each stall, and in the tack room where they'd so often cleaned gear. Patrick sat there now, right outside the door, soaping a bridle.

"Top o' the morning, lass. You wouldn't be looking for a mount now, would you?" He laid the bridle in his lap. "Dan'l would love a lap or two around the track, if you've a mind."

"Thanks, but not today. I'm on vacation, remember?"

"That you are." He watched as she inspected the office.

If she closed her eyes, she could see her father sitting in his chair. She opened them quickly. He was gone. She waited, waited for the crashing pain to leap through her again. Instead, she heard a tuneless whistle—or did she?

Caesar caught up with her when she visited the foaling stall. She scratched his ears while she waited in the empty box stall. Less than a year ago, on her birthday, they'd come home from dinner out and found Miss Tee's dam in hard labor.

Trish wandered down the lane to the paddocks. Miss Tee and Double Diamond rushed up to see her, and Dan'l nickered for his turn to be scratched.

"Thank you, Father, thank you." She rested her forehead against Dan'l's warm neck. What words could she say? None were enough.

When she turned for the house, she waited a moment. Such a strange feeling, but such a good one. A metallic blue Mustang was parked in the drive. When she opened the front door, she could hear Brad and Rhonda bantering in the dining room.

Trish paused for another moment. Her father's recliner looked like he'd just left it to go into another room. His Bible lay open on the lamp-stand beside it.

"I thought you had a show this weekend." Trish rounded the corner and attacked her two friends.

"I do, I do." Rhonda spun around and grabbed Trish around the waist. "We leave in an hour, but I couldn't turn down your mom's cinnamon rolls. Oh, Trish, I'm so glad you're here!"

"Even though you won't be." She turned to hug Brad, the tall fourth of their four musketeers. The four young people had been best friends since grade school. "Seems like forever since I've seen you guys."

"Well, we haven't been anywhere. How ya doing, kid?" Brad swung her off her feet. When he set her down, he cupped her face in his hands. "You're better." It was a statement, not a question.

How could they all tell? Was she wearing a sign or something?

"Come and eat!" Marge set a platter of scrambled eggs with bacon on one end of the table and one of cinnamon rolls at the other. "David, you say grace." They all slid into their seats, Patrick where Hal used to sit, and held hands while David said the blessing.

When Trish looked up, a tiny barb of resentment for Patrick usurping her father's chair dug at the edge of her mind. She cringed when she remembered the blow-up not so long ago. No, she told herself, no more. Again, there was that feeling that if she turned quickly enough she would see her father smiling and nodding at her. The peace stayed with her.

Trish took her first bite of homemade cinnamon roll and rolled her eyes in ecstasy. "Mom, no one bakes like you do. You should open a shop and sell these. You'd make a million in California."

"As if I had any desire to move to California. Here, Brad, have some more. I know you have a big day ahead of you." Marge passed the plate of rolls again.

"Why, what's happening today?" Trish asked after a bite of scrambled eggs.

"Brad has a job," Rhonda answered.

"Yeah, they laid me off at Runnin' On Farm." Brad waved his fork in the air. "So I had to go to work for my dad during the week. I run the stop-and-go signs on his road repair jobs, and on Saturdays I work at the cinema over at the mall. I get to see all the movies for free."

"Two jobs?"

"Yeah, college costs money."

"I thought you were going to Clark, and you got a scholarship."

"I did and I am, but WSU is expensive so I'm saving ahead." He reached for another cinnamon roll. "Trish is right, Mrs. E, you oughta go into business."

Marge shook her head, her smile the kind that mothers give their hare-brained kids' ideas. "I have a business already. Remember, you worked

48

for us. And will again when the racing string comes home, if you can fit us into your busy schedule."

"Hey, that's right. And this way you can make cinnamon rolls just for us."

"And chocolate chip cookies and peanut butter cookies," Trish and Rhonda said together.

"And I'll be so far away, no one will bake for me." David adopted a soulful look.

"Yeah, right!" Trish sent him a pretend glare. "Like you never got any care packages when you were at WSU."

"Oh, that's right." He raised one finger in the air. "But I had to fight for my rights. Whenever a box came from home, every guy on my floor dropped in to visit. Had to hide the goodies under my bed."

"Phew! Along with all the dirty socks and sweaty underwear. Yuk!"

"Okay, okay," Marge said, laughing along with them. "I promise to bake—when I have time."

"You didn't want cookies anyway." Trish got her last dig in. She looked over at Patrick and caught the telltale sheen in his eyes. He smiled back at her and winked. Was he a mind-reader like her father?

The day flew by like the view from a car traveling sixty miles an hour. Trish watched her mother work both Miss Tee and Double Diamond on the lunge line.

"You've taught them good manners," she said as she helped her mother brush the filly down. "This baby seems so willing to learn, she'll be easy to train."

"Yes, I think so. And does she ever love to run." Marge stopped her brushing. "You remember how much your father loved to work with the babies? He always said that was the fun part of training Thoroughbreds."

"I know. He'd be so proud of you, Mom."

"I know he is. Trish, I don't think heaven is some faraway place. I think he knows what's going on and—well, sometimes he seems so close."

"I've felt it at home this time too. Like if I look around quick enough, he'll be there." Trish rolled her lips together. "Mom, I'm so glad to be home."

They finished the filly and started on the colt. Trish tickled the colt's nose so he twitched his whiskers. "You think Dad could be a guardian angel?"

"If there is any way to be one, I'm sure he would be."

That evening the Evanstons and Patrick adjourned to the living room after a steak dinner broiled to perfection on the barbecue and devoured out on the deck.

"That was so good, Mom. And, David, you're a super chef, almost as good as Dad. I haven't had home-cooked food since the last time I was here."

"Don't you eat with Adam and Martha?" Marge settled into her rocking chair.

"I'm never there at mealtime. Leave before breakfast, lunch at the track, and then grab something quick before class." Trish shrugged. "It's not their fault. Martha sometimes has a plate saved for me, but I hate to put her out. They're so good to me anyway."

"I know. That makes having you down there easier for me." Marge leaned back in her chair. "How about we bring Trish up to date on the stuff we've been talking about. We're going to have to make some decisions soon."

"What stuff?"

Marge gave Patrick the nod. "You tell her."

"We've been looking for some more horses, like the mare I saw yesterday. I think we should buy her. I saw her filly from last year. Looks real good. In fact, we could probably get the filly too. Anson pretty much wants to sell out. What with Longacres closing and the trouble at Portland Meadows, he says he'd just as soon get out now."

"What trouble at the Meadows?" Trish interrupted as soon as he paused.

"You know, more of the same. One day the place is up for sale and the next they're closing down." David shook his head in disgust. "Why they can't manage that place better, I'll never know."

Trish poked him in the ribs. "Maybe we oughta buy the track."

Marge rubbed her chin with one finger. "I've thought about it."

"What!" Trish and David stared at their mother and then each other.

"Your mother has some good ideas," Patrick said. "You know she's been the business manager for your father all these years with such a tight budget, now she—you all have to think and invest wisely."

"Maybe I should be taking a business course instead of chemistry." Trish slumped back, one ankle crossed over the other knee. She thought of the incredible amount of money sitting in her bank account. She hadn't thought about investing it. She didn't even have time to spend much of it.

"What if Adam and I see a good claimer? Should I go for it?" She looked from Patrick to her mother and back again. "Sarah's Pride was a good deal."

"We'll think about it. We'll probably go to the yearling sales this year too."

Trish went to bed that night in a total state of shock. Her mother was not only not thinking of selling the farm, but she planned to expand. She stared at the pictures of the winner's circles. *Oh, Dad, if only you were here to enjoy all this. You worked so hard for it, and now that your dream has come true, you're missing out.*

Trish woke in the morning to gray skies, but the gray couldn't dim the wonder she felt. Another night without nightmares. She thought back to the discussion the night before. How exciting! She threw back the covers and bounded out of bed.

"Think I'll take Dan'l for a ride," she said as she entered the kitchen.

"I think that'll be fine after church." Her mother set her coffee cup down on the counter. "You going down to help the guys with chores?"

Trish nodded. "I'd really like to go riding."

"I know. How long since you've been to church?"

"Ahh . . ." Trish leaned over to pull on her right boot.

"Since the last time you were home?" Marge picked up her cup and studied her daughter over the rim.

"Ummm . . ." She pulled on her left boot.

"Martha and Adam don't go to church?"

"Depends on the schedule at the track." *You could have gone if you wanted to,* her nagger whispered. *How many races have you had on Sundays anyway?* "Don't worry, Mom. I'll be ready on time." Trish gave up gracefully. Much as she didn't really want to go to church, she didn't want to cause a fracas with her mother either.

But she had a bad feeling on the drive to their church in Orchards. And it didn't get any better when they parked in the parking lot. *I think I'll just stay here,* she wanted to cry out as they all got out of the car.

David waited at the open van door after Marge stepped down. "You gonna wait all day?" He peered in at his sister.

Trish chewed on her cuticle. She took a deep breath and let it out. Even so, her knees turned to mush when her feet met the ground.

Patrick took her arm and tucked it in his. "You'll be fine, lass," he whispered in her ear.

Trish stared straight ahead. She walked up the six outside steps and through the door. She shook hands with the greeters, hoping they didn't feel her shaking.

When she sat down in the pew, she kept her gaze glued on her hands, clenched together in her lap. The tears prickled at the first hymn. She bit them back, her teeth grinding together in the effort.

If she didn't look at Pastor Mort, she could handle it. She tried to block out the words he read from the Bible. She used to be so good at blocking things out. She tried to think of racing Spitfire, of the feel of him thundering for the finish.

That was worse.

She tried to make her mind blank. Utter failure.

Pastor Mort entered the pulpit. He waited for the last feet to stop shuffling, the last cough and rustle.

Trish scrunched her eyes closed.

"Grace and peace from God our Father and the Lord Jesus Christ." The voice rolled over the congregation and invaded Trish's heart. The dammed-up tears choked her. Trish pushed herself to her feet and strode down the aisle.

Chapter 07

God, I can't do this!

"Can I get you something?" An usher touched Trish on the shoulder as she stood at the back of the church.

"No, no thank you." Trish blew her nose in a soggy tissue. "I'll be fine." *No you won't.* Her nagger even came to church with her. *Unless you give it up, you'll never be fine again.* Trish hiccuped on a sob.

"Here." The man handed her his handkerchief.

When Trish's brain reformed after mushing during the tears, she thought back to what her nagger had said. *Give what up?* She sank down on a chair and took a shaky breath. She'd wait for her family here.

Pastor Mort closed his sermon with the benediction. "The Lord bless you and keep you . . ." The words bathed Trish's wounded feelings in the balm of love. " . . . and give you His peace."

That's what it was. The feeling was back again. Trish sighed in relief.

The guitars played the opening chords of the closing hymn. At the sound of her theme song, Trish fled from the church before she broke down completely. The congregation's singing followed her out the door. "And He will raise you up on eagle's wings. . . ."

She huddled on the backseat of the van, her knees drawn up to her chest, her hands over her face. The tears poured through her fingers and soaked her hair. Finally, after what seemed eons, she pushed herself upright. She slumped against the seat, too drained to sit up. Lifting her hands to push her hair back took all her energy.

A red and black handkerchief, big enough to be a bandanna, appeared from her right. She turned enough to see Patrick sitting on the step, extending the cloth.

She took it and blew her nose for the millionth time. Her nose was raw, her throat was raw, and her feelings the most raw of all.

When she put the handkerchief down, he handed her a cup of water.

"Should I pour this over my head or down my throat?"

"Whichever. Looks to me like you're wet enough already." A smile wreathed his face, telling her without a word that he understood, and that he appreciated her attempt at humor. "Aye, lass, when ye can laugh at yerself, ye be on the way."

"On the way to what?" Trish sniff-sniffed on a breath.

"To learning to deal with the blows life gives ye. Yer takin' this one young-like, but now I know you'll be makin' it."

Trish finished the water in the cup. "What makes you so sure?"

"I just know, lass, I just know. Must be that faith that Pastor Mort talked about today."

"But, Patrick, the last couple of days, I thought this was all over. I felt good again for the first time in—in, I don't know how long. And then to fall apart like this . . ."

"But don't you see, the falling apart, as you call it, is part of the giving up." His waving hands punctuated his words.

"But, Patrick, you keep saying give it up . . . but I don't know what I'm supposed to give up." She strangled the handkerchief.

"The wall, lass, that tough spirit so full of anger no one could come near you."

"What I want to give up is the black hole I live in all the time." The words faded away to a whisper.

"You will."

David and Marge joined Patrick at the side of the minivan. When Trish opened her eyes again, most of the other cars had left the parking lot. She looked back to the church entry. Pastor Mort had only one more family to greet.

Trish drew a staggery breath again. She sniffed and wiped her nose. "Think I'll go see Pastor Mort. Is that okay? You guys in a hurry?"

Marge smiled through the tears that brightened her eyes. "No, Tee, take your time."

Pastor Mort, the sun glistening on the bald top of his head, was just turning to go back into the church when Trish called to him. The smile on his face set her lip quivering again.

"Ah, Trish, I'm so glad to see you." He met her at the bottom of the steps.

When she took his extended hand, he pulled her into a hug, then leaned back to study her face. "I could tell how hard it was for you to sit there, even as long as you did."

Tears pooled in her eyes again. How could there be any tears left in her body? "How come church is so hard? I get so tired of crying."

"Yes, I know." He sat down on the step and tugged on her hand to join him. "So many people tell me that. I guess it's because we're more vulnerable in God's house. I think He uses that time to draw us closer to himself so He can take the pain away."

"But it only hurts more."

"No, you only feel it more. And the more you let the feelings out, the easier it will get. Besides, what better place to fall apart than with all these people who love you and want to help any way they can? You gave them a chance to pray for you, to reach out in love. And near as I can figure, that's what being part of the family of God is all about."

Trish leaned her chin on her hand on her bent knees. "I tried not to come today."

"I'm not surprised, but I'm sure glad you're here."

"You *really* think I'm better?" The thought of the pills in her purse flashed through her mind.

"Yes, I do."

"Do you believe in angels?"

"Of course."

"My mom and I wondered if Dad could be an angel."

"I don't know the answer to that, Trish. But I do know that if there were any way possible for him to help you, he would."

"He's all better now, isn't he?" She rolled her lips to keep from crying out loud.

"Yes, Trish, he is."

When she looked up, Pastor Mort was wiping away tears too. Trish held up Patrick's soaked handkerchief. "I think I should buy shares in Kleenex."

"Oh, Trish." Pastor Mort laughed. He blew his nose and chuckled again. "Yes, my dear, you're definitely better."

"Well, I hope you're right." She rose to her feet and extended her hand. "Thanks. See you next time I'm home."

"Bless you, child." He squeezed her hand, then held her in a firm embrace.

When they got home, Trish felt like someone had pulled the plug and let out all the bath water. *Drained* was the only word that applied. She sat down on her bed to remove her shoes. She eyed the pillow. Maybe if she lay down for just a minute she'd feel like going in to help her mother make Sunday dinner. Then maybe David would help her with her chemistry.

Her mother shook her two hours later. "Come on, Trish, dinner's ready."

"Okay, be there in a minute."

David shook her fifteen minutes later. She hadn't even heard him come into her room.

"Okay, okay." She pushed her hair back from her face. "What's wrong?"

"Trish, time to eat. Mom came and called you fifteen minutes ago."

"Nah." She swung her feet off the bed and sat up. Her gaze focused on the clock. "Why'd you guys let me sleep so long?"

David thumped her on top of her head. "Just come and eat."

When she shuffled out to the table, she saw Brad in his usual place. "Hi, sleepyhead."

"Hi." Trish blinked once and then again. She just couldn't wake up. " 'Scuse me a moment. I need a cold-water treatment." When she returned after dousing her face in cold water, she could at least see straight. "Now, what all did I miss out on?"

David bowed his head. "Father, we thank you for this food, for our family and friends, and we ask you to help Trish work through this bad time. Amen."

Trish had a hard time swallowing. Here was David praying for her too. And saying grace just like her father used to.

"You do that good, Davey boy, just like Dad."

"Thanks, he taught us well."

Marge watched her daughter; two little worry lines creased the space between her eyebrows. "Trish, is this typical, falling asleep like that?"

"No, not quite the same. This time was like someone hit me over the head. Usually I just nod off. My brain turns to dandelion fluff and blows away." She glanced from face to face around the table. "Hey, that's a joke, guys. I'm tired a lot, can't concentrate, that's all."

"Okay, but it might be a good idea to see a doctor and get checked out. Maybe you're anemic or something."

"M-o-m." Trish felt the hairs on the back of her neck rise. This felt too much like the times when Marge drove everyone nuts with her worrying. Back when they had a hard time getting along. Were those times returning?

Marge raised her hands in a gesture of surrender. "Don't panic, I'm not worrying. It's just that sometimes parents have to insist on what they think is right—and this is one of those times."

"But I leave tomorrow afternoon."

"There are no doctors in California?"

Trish looked up at her mother with a lopsided grin and a shake of the head. "I'll ask Martha for the name of one."

"Good idea, Trish," Patrick said from his end of the table.

"Whew! Glad that's over." David nudged Brad, who also wore a look of relief. "No World War Three this time," he added under his breath.

"David?" Trish asked so sweetly that bees would think it was honey. "How about if I just pour this glass of water on your head now?"

"Whoa . . . we better watch out!" David and Brad swapped big-brother smirks.

The glow in her middle reminded Trish that this was the kind of stuff she missed the most.

"How's the chemistry coming?" David asked that evening after chores.

"You don't really want to know." Trish stared glumly at the book on her lap.

"Have you prayed about it?"

She shot him a look of surprise. "You sound just like Dad."

"I'll take that as a compliment, even though right now I don't think you meant it that way. But he was right. Ask for help. Ask God to make this stuff clear to you. If He could create the world, what's a little chemistry?"

"If He created it, He understands it," Trish muttered. "It's getting it through my thick head that's the problem."

"True. But I thought you got a tutor."

"I did. Richard keeps trying, but he says I just don't concentrate enough. Seems to be the story of my life lately." Trish chose not to mention the earring, the ponytail, and the pills. Instead she told her brother about the hours she'd spent studying and the crummy test and quiz scores she'd gotten.

"David, I just don't like chemistry," she whispered so her mother wouldn't hear.

"So *pass* it and be done with it," he hissed back.

"I need a B on the final to pull a C. You know what that's going to do to my grade average?"

"So—when all else fails, *pray*. What have you got to lose?"

Trish dug her elbow into his rib cage. "Thank you so very much."

But when she went to bed that night, Trish knelt on her rug and rested her head on her clasped hands. "God, I don't know where else to turn. As David says, you're it. Your Word says I should ask and receive. I'm asking—for help with my chemistry, and for—to keep me awake when

I need to study." She thought for a moment. "And please get me out of the pit I've been in. Amen."

She climbed into bed. "And thank you for bringing me home."

Early the next morning, Trish, David, Marge, and Patrick drove north in the minivan.

Trish yawned in the backseat. "So much for sleeping in. You really think these horses are worth buying, huh, Patrick?"

"That I do, lass."

"Patrick's looked a lot around Portland and southern Washington," Marge said. "Your dad always said Patrick had an eye for a good horse, like a man for a pretty woman." Marge copied Trish's yawn. "Excuse me. Now look what you've started."

Patrick handed a sheaf of papers to Trish. "Look at these and see what you think."

Trish flipped through copies of registration papers, bloodlines, and racing statistics. "Which ones are you thinking of?"

"That mare in foal to Slew, the yearling colt, and possibly one of the fillies. Depends on how much your mom wants to spend."

"That would give us three to train this fall. But where would we race them if Portland Meadows doesn't open?"

"California, I suppose." Marge took the pages about the mare. "We thought about talking to Adam if we need to. He could race them down south if we have any good enough."

"They just better get the Meadows running." Trish deciphered blood-lines while she kept track of the conversation. How strange to be having this kind of discussion with her mother.

They left the I-5 freeway at Chehalis, heading west through dairy country. Acres of white board fences bounding knee-deep pastures announced the horse farm before the sign at the driveway.

"Is the farm for sale too?" Trish asked. "This is beautiful." Babies kicked up their heels in a pasture to their right and a couple of yearlings raced along the fence beside them. Up ahead, on a slight rise, the house reminded Trish of those in Kentucky—white, tall pillars in front, and an air of history.

The barns even sported cupolas like many of those in Kentucky. "Why are they selling their horses?"

"Anson Danielson is getting up in years, and with Seattle closing and the trouble at Portland, he feels it's time to retire. They have no living children to take over, so they're selling. Patrick got wind of it, and because he knew Mr. Danielson years ago, called him. You know the rest."

"Aren't they having a dispersal sale?"

"Not if they can get decent prices without it." David glanced at Trish in the rearview mirror. "His wife has been sick and he doesn't want all the hassle."

Dad should be here doing this, Trish thought as Patrick greeted the man. She sighed and followed the others. The horses were all that Patrick had said.

Trish walked around the mare, checking confirmation as her father had taught her. She tickled the little filly's nose and felt down her legs. Her dad said it was hard to tell anything at this age, but the filly had the look of a winner. The way she carried her head, you could tell she liked to show off. She had both the body and the bloodlines for speed.

But there was something about the colt. What would her dad have said? This just wasn't fair. He should be here. He worked all his life for this dream, and now he was gone. Trish tried to think what he would say and do. First, her father would be happy, with the day and the trip and the horses. He had liked nothing better than visiting horse farms.

She squinted her eyes to think better. Then he would have studied the horses. Really looked them over.

She leaned her chin on her fists on the top of the board fence. While she watched the horses grazing in the field, she could almost feel her dad standing beside her. What was it about the colt?

"So, what do you think?" Marge leaned on the fence beside her daughter.

"Whatever."

"No, this has to be a family decision. If you have doubts, say so."

"I wish Dad were here," Trish whispered.

"Yeah, me too."

They watched the grazing animals a while longer before Marge turned and propped her elbows on the fence. "Okay now?"

Trish nodded. "Better." And surprisingly, she was.

"We better get a move on or you'll be late for your flight. We don't have to make a decision today. I just thought you might like to see them first."

"But if we don't, someone else could outbid us?"

"There's that."

"Then I'd say yes on the mare and filly, and I don't know on the colt. Something about him bothers me. I tried to figure out what Dad would have said but I'm not sure."

Patrick and David joined them at the fence. "You're right, lass, about the colt. It's in the way he moves. No sense in buying a future problem."

"But he could outgrow it?" David asked.

"Maybe."

"Then we agree? The mare and filly?" Marge looked to each of them in turn. At their nods, she dug in her purse and pulled out her checkbook. "I think your dad would be proud of us right now."

Trish gulped as her mother signed the check and handed it to Mr. Danielson. They now owned two new horses. Amazing what money could do. She dozed off on the way home in spite of the discussion about transporting and training the new additions.

They got home just in time for her to grab her things and load the van.

"Now, you're stopping to see me on your way to Tucson," she made David promise. "And, Patrick, you and Mom are coming down to see Firefly run. Maybe we'll have a horse or two for you to look at by then."

"Aye, lass. That we will," Patrick agreed. "Say hello to Adam for me."

Trish hugged each of them, and slid into the front seat of the minivan. "You guys take care now."

David slammed the door shut. "Remember what I said."

"Yeah, sure."

"I mean it."

Trish waved as Marge turned the van in the graveled drive. Caesar yipped beside them halfway down to the county road. Trish stared out the window.

When the van turned out onto the blacktop, Trish took in a deep breath and let it out. "Mom, I meant it about you and Patrick coming to see us run. Maybe that'll be the boost I need."

"All right. Call me with the date and times. I should have been down before now, but there's been so much to do. And I hated to leave home."

"Great." Trish settled back in her seat. Another idea niggled at the corner of her mind. She chewed on her cuticle. "You been talking with the Shipsons?"

"Some, why?"

The idea burst forth like a Fourth of July rocket. "We could go to Kentucky—you and me. On Labor Day weekend. Mrs. Shipson said to come anytime. Please, Mom, please!"

"I don't know, Tee. If we come to your race—then we have to ship the horses home again—and get you ready for school—and . . ."

"We've never had a trip together, just you and me." Trish turned so she could watch her mother's face. "Please."

"Let me think about it." Marge flashed Trish a smile. "But I don't see why not."

"Yes!" Trish settled back in her seat. Who would have believed she and her mother would plan a trip together—to a horse farm, no less. Things certainly were changing.

Trish caught herself still humming the next morning at the Finleys when she got out of bed at the first ring of the alarm. When she looked in the mirror on the drive to the track, she saw a smile on her face.

Her "Good morning" to Adam and Carlos carried a lilt. She neatly sidestepped Gatesby when he attempted a love bite, and spent a few minutes comforting Firefly for not being ready for a morning work yet.

When she trotted Gatesby out, they entered the smaller track because morning works were about finished. Trish had left her jacket back at the office, the sun being quite warm after peeling away the early fog.

The gelding fought her all around the track. He wanted to run, and Adam had decreed a trot. Trish felt like lead weights were draped over her arms. As they rounded the far turn, the screech of brakes shattered the commuting hum on the freeway. The crash of colliding cars echoed over the track.

Gatesby whirled, and before she realized what was happening, Trish catapulted over his shoulder and thumped onto the dirt. She watched Gatesby finally take his run around the track alone.

"Stupid—good-for-nothing—" Trish called him every name she could think of. When she could breathe evenly, she got to her feet and dusted herself off.

"You okay?" one of the officials stopped to ask while the others chased after her horse.

"Yeah, I'm fine. Thanks." Trish watched Gatesby lead the riders around the track again. Finally one grabbed a rein and pulled him to a stop.

"You want a ride back?" The man leaned forward to give her a hand up. Trish nodded and swung up behind him.

"Looks like a real bad accident out there."

"I know. And I should know better than to take my mind off my mount even a moment. My horse was asking for trouble."

"And you got it. Happens to the best of us." He dropped her at the gate where the other official held Gatesby in tow.

"Thanks." Trish took the reins and led the sweaty horse back to the stable. She spent the time explaining to him exactly how he should have behaved, in no uncertain terms.

It's your fault. Her nagger leaped into the fray. *If you'd been paying better attention . . .* Trish wished she'd landed on her resident critic.

Gatesby rubbed his forehead against her shoulder. He knew better than to act up now.

"What happened?" Adam strode toward her as soon as he saw her walking. "Are you all right?"

"Yeah, I think my pride hurts worse than my posterior. There was a major crash out on the freeway. I looked over, and my friend here dumped me. I know better than that. What's the matter with me?"

"Trish, Trish . . ."

"I can't even stay on a horse for a trot around the track, let alone win anything."

"Trish!"

"What?" She finally looked up, caught by the command in his voice.

"That could've happened to anybody. It's no big deal; no one was hurt. . . ."

"But they could have been. Gatesby could have been injured. . . ."

"But he wasn't. Just be grateful no one was hurt." With that, Adam left her to her thoughts.

Trish drew circles in the dirt with the toe of her boot. She tried to recapture the peace of the morning by remembering how good the weekend at home had been. Instead, she felt like she was falling into the black pit again.

You had such a good time, even without your dad there, her nagger reminded her. Trish felt like a hand was clenching her heart—and twisting it. How could she be happy without her father there? How could any of them go on like they were? Why had she invited her mother to go to Kentucky with her—it should have been her dad. Her breath was coming in short gasps. Her heart pounded like Gatesby's must have after his run.

She leaned against the office wall, struggling to get her breath. The war in her head—it was too much. Her eyes filled. She grabbed her purse from the cabinet and dug for a tissue. Four white pills lay in the bottom of the tan leather envelope bag.

"They'll make you feel better." She could almost hear Richard's voice in her ear.

Anything to feel better. Trish clenched a pill in her hand and strode to the water fountain. She turned the crank with one hand and watched the water arc in the sunlight. She placed the pill on her tongue and leaned forward.

Chapter

08

Sorry."

The bump made her snort water. She coughed. Pill and water spewed across the gravel. Trish choked and gagged a second more.

"Really, I'm sorry."

She turned and flung her arms around the young boy beside her. "No, thank you!" She patted his cheek and beamed into his dark brown eyes. "Thank you."

Trish stepped back while the boy got a drink. He kept watching over his shoulder, as if worried what she might do next.

Trish took a drink—a long drink of plain, cold water. That had been a close call. She glanced over her shoulder. The boy walked backward, keeping a wary eye on her.

That afternoon she brought one of Adam's horses in for a place in the first race of the program.

"I don't want to hear it," Adam ordered before she could even say a word. "That was better than I expected him to do."

"But I . . ."

He held up a hand to stop her. "No. Just be glad for a place."

Trish thought about his words on the way out to the beach. "Just be glad." Why was it so hard to be glad anymore? She thought of the weekend at home. They'd laughed and had a good time. If only her father were around to enjoy it too.

After settling all her gear on the sand at the beach, Trish drew her father's journal out first. When she read his words, she could almost hear his voice saying them to her. She opened to the first page. In bold letters, he had written: *To God be the glory. Amen. Hal Evanston.*

She traced the letters with a fingertip. That was her dad all right— giving God the glory no matter what. She flipped the pages, reading snatches here and there. He too had pleaded *why*? One page was blurred with a water spot. Had his tears fallen like hers?

She continued reading.

Even your Son cried, "My God, my God, why hast thou forsaken me?" Father, I feel so alone. The pain—knowing I brought this on myself. I did this to my family, who are more dear to me than life itself. I did it. How will they ever forgive me?

Trish buried her face in her hands. "Oh, Dad." When she could see clearly again, she returned to the same page.

But, Father, I know one thing for sure. You are in control and you love my family even more than I do. You only are worthy of praise. My Lord and my God.

Trish shut the book. How could he do that? How?

She flipped it open again, farther back. Again, the words of praise. She flipped the pages. It was on each one. One time it was underlined and written over so the stark words leaped off the page: *I WILL PRAISE THE LORD!* Another: *GOD IS MY STRENGTH!*

Trish stuffed the book back into her bag and staggered to her feet. She ran down to the water and let the cold surf bathe her feet. Then, turning to the left, she trotted down the beach, her feet leaving deep imprints in the packed wet sand. When she reached the rocks blocking her way, she turned and started back, running until a pain pierced her side and her lungs burned for air.

She dropped back on her blanket, gasping, with sweat pouring from her face. She fished a Diet Coke out of her cooler and popped the top. As her breathing steadied and her heart rate returned to normal, Trish made a decision. She held the cool can to her cheeks for a minute longer before pulling her own journal out of the bag.

On the flyleaf she wrote, *I WILL PRAISE THE LORD!* She turned to the first blank page and began writing as fast as her pen would allow.

> *If my father could live a life of praise when he was dying of cancer, I will do so too. I will give God the glory. I will ask for help. I will. Beginning right now.*

She dated it and signed her name.

Then in bold, underlined, and with the letters blackened by repeated over-strokes, she wrote, *GOD IS MY STRENGTH!*

Trish flopped back on the blanket, drained as if she'd run a marathon. On the wings of the gull, the sigh of the wind, the swish of the blowing sand, she heard her song. Trish sang the words to the chorus between huffs on the upward path. She sang it again while she wrapped the journals and the eagle carefully and put them back into the backpack. She hummed the tune on the drive up the winding road.

"Take out paper. This is your last quiz for the quarter." The instructor stood in front of the room with a smile on his face. Was this supposed to be good news?

Trish muttered her verse as she opened her notebook. "God is my strength. God is my strength." She threw in an "I will praise the Lord" as the teacher wrote the problems on the board.

She took a deep breath and focused on the first question.

"Just dissect each equation," Richard's voice floated in her mind. *"And concentrate."*

She could hear David repeating over and over. *"Concentrate, Tee. Concentrate. Focus on what you're doing. You can do this."* He might as well have been sitting right beside her.

When she started to panic, Trish brought her mind back with her verses. After correcting the quiz, Trish felt like shouting. She'd only missed two. A record!

The high stayed with her all the way home. She danced up the steps and through the door. Yes! She'd only missed two. Yes! She could do it!

"You look like you've got good news." Martha looked up from her needlepoint.

"I only missed two problems on the last quiz of the quarter!" Trish's feet tapped out a dance step.

"Wonderful! Oh, there's a letter here for you." Martha pointed to the hall table. "From Kentucky."

Trish danced back to the entry. She picked up the envelope. Red's handwriting sent a warm squiggle down to her middle. She slit open the envelope. The card showed a kitten hanging desperately from a branch with outstretched claws. Inside, the words "Hang in there" made Trish smile.

Dear Trish,

Thanks for your card. I am now sure you didn't fall off the face of the earth. I hit the winner's circle twice yesterday. Can you believe that? Of course, two days before that I got dumped on my butt. No injuries, unless you count the ones to my pride. I think of you every day. I wish California and Kentucky weren't so far apart. Good thing prayers can cross mountains because I'm praying you are better and that I'll see you again—soon.

Love, Red

To Trish, the *soon* leaped out in big letters. *So do I,* she thought. *You're like Rhonda; you make me laugh.* She thanked Martha Finley for the mail and skipped up the stairs to her room.

But all the next week, Trish felt at the mercy of the yo-yo kid. She'd be going along just fine, even remembering to give God the glory, and then something would trigger the sadness. It might be a word, the way someone walked, a repeat of a past event, and she'd fall down again. The pain would come crashing back, bringing tears and droopy spirits.

She forced herself to keep her mind on the horse she was riding and the others around her, but when she was driving the car, her mind could freewheel.

"I even cry in the shower." She tried to joke about it to Martha when she went home for lunch on Monday.

"I know. The tears catch you when you think everything is okay. When I lost my mother, doing dishes was hard for me. Me and the tap water, we'd flow together."

"Did they—the tears—ever go away?" Trish folded and creased her napkin with shaky fingers.

"Not completely. Sometimes, all these years later, I think of something my mother and I could have done together and the tears come. But as time passed, the crying didn't hurt as bad and didn't last as long. And the bouts were much farther apart."

"People keep telling me time will make things easier, but . . ." Trish crumpled the napkin, then flattened it again.

"The passage of time helps, but I believe God brings the real deep-down healing."

"Mom says I need to see a doctor because I want to sleep all the time. You know anyone?" Trish made a face. "I hate to go to a doctor, especially a new one. Maybe I could wait until I go home."

Martha pushed back from the oak and glass table. She fetched a card from the file by the phone. "Here. I think you'll like her."

"Thanks, I guess."

"Something else . . . I tried to find two things I could be thankful for every day. Of course, that was after I got over being mad at God for taking my mother."

Trish felt her mouth drop open. "You were mad too?"

"Everyone is. That's part of grieving."

Trish traced the outline of the pink flowers on her plate with the tines of her fork. "I think—" She closed her eyes to concentrate. "I think that part, being so mad all the time, is getting better."

"I think so too."

The talk helped—for a day or two.

Talking to the doctor helped too. When Trish told her all that had gone on, the woman said, "Of course you're tired all the time. That's one way the body tries to heal itself. You need to get extra rest and eat properly."

"But that's when the nightmares come back." Trish studied the knuckles on her right hand, then looked up at the doctor. "I see my dad as he was the—the last—" Tears swamped her words. "The last time I saw him. He . . ."

The doctor let her patient cry, handing over tissues as needed. When Trish sat, calm and spent, the doctor asked. "How did he look?"

"Like he was asleep, only I could tell he—he wasn't there anymore."

"Did he look in pain?" Trish shook her head. "Was it awful to look at him?"

Trish peered through her tears. "No, it wasn't bad. I just wanted him to come back so bad . . . I want my father back."

"I know, Trish. But death doesn't have to be a nightmare. You know he would have stayed with you if he could, but his body couldn't handle any more."

Trish studied the doctor's kind face. "I know, but I still miss him so."

"Yes, and that will always be. But nightmares scare us because we see things we don't understand. Death is a natural part of living."

"But aren't you supposed to die when you're old?"

"Usually, but life isn't always as we think it should be, and death often comes before we're ready for it. I could recommend a group for you if you'd like. There's a counselor and other young people like you, who've lost a parent or someone close to them."

Trish shook her head. "I won't be here that long."

"Okay. How about if I write a name and phone number on this pad and you call them if you want to? In the meantime, let's give you a once over, even though I'm almost certain there's nothing wrong with your body."

"Yeah, it's all in my head." Trish blew her nose again.

"And your heart. It takes a while for a broken heart to heal."

"I'll call you if anything shows up in the blood work," the doctor said after the tests were finished. "In the meantime, rest when you can, eat right, and think about calling that group."

"Thanks." Trish left the office feeling lighter again.

That night on the phone, when she told her mother about the doctor's suggestion, Marge said, "Groups like that do help. I go to one every Thursday."

"You do?"

Trish fell asleep that night after reading her Bible and slept through the night.

After works the next morning, Trish and Adam sat in the office munching their favorite breakfast, bagels and cream cheese.

"Hey, I like this one." Trish held up her bagel, spread with walnut-raisin-cinnamon cream cheese. "What other kind did you get?"

Adam picked up the container and read the label. "Spinach/garlic. You'll know you're an adult when you like this one."

"Hah! Carlos, which do you like best?"

"All of them. You riding this afternoon?"

Trish nodded. "Two mounts. I'm coming up in the world." She licked the cheese from her fingers. "I've been meaning to ask you guys . . . Mom and Patrick said we should keep our eyes open for a good claimer."

"How much do they want to go?" Adam crossed his feet on his desk.

"I don't know. But if I buy part of it, I'd rather have a filly."

"Is Patrick going to train for anyone else?"

"I think so. At least for the owners we had before. With David going off to school, we'll have to hire help."

"There's a gelding running on Saturday that might be one to look at." Carlos leaned against the doorframe. "I'd buy him myself if I had the money. Just coming back from a quarter crack in the off-rear hoof. Hasn't been handled right either, far as I can tell."

Trish shrugged. "So much for my idea of a filly. How much is the claim?"

"Thirteen thousand. I'll find out when he's working tomorrow."

"Okay. I'll call Mom tonight. We can look at his papers today, can't we?"

At their nods, Trish stood up. "I better get going. I'll come by after the fourth."

Mounted in the saddling paddock a couple of hours later, Trish felt the stirrings of excitement. Her butterflies must have sensed it too, for they started their pre-race warm-ups. Trish listened carefully to the trainer's instructions. Her butterflies proceeded to aerial flits and flutters.

The gelding she rode trotted docilely beside the pony rider. The trainer had said this old boy needed waking up. Trish tightened the reins and squeezed her heels into his sides. The gelding pricked his ears and danced sideways.

Trish kept tuning him up, right into the starting gates. When the gun went off, so did the gelding. He lit out for the turn as if there were tin cans on his tail. She let him run, pacing the horses on either side. They were three across coming out of the turn. The gelding ran easily, and with two furlongs to go Trish made her move.

One swing of her whip and he stretched out. Another and he took the lead. "Go for it, you wonderful beast!" Trish urged him on, the finish pole thundering closer. A nose crept up on her right side. Even with her boot, the shoulder, the neck.

She went to the whip and the two dueled the final strides. But it was number three to win by a nose, giving her a place.

Trish vaulted to the ground. The black clouds took up their positions on her shoulders—again.

"Good race, young lady. He ran better for you than he has for anyone. When I told you to wake him up, you did a fine job."

"Thank you. Sorry it wasn't the win." The simple words didn't begin to communicate Trish's feeling of regret. He should have won.

The black cloud hung close when Trish mounted again. The filly, entered in her first race, exhibited little to no confidence as she tentatively did what Trish asked. She tiptoed into the starting gate. The gun and the gate startled her so she broke off-balanced. It took till half the backstretch for her to gain her stride.

"Come on, baby," Trish crooned instead of yelling. The filly opened up and headed for the pack surging in front of her. She swung wide to pass the clustered horses and, coming out of the turn, seemed to realize what she was supposed to do. But too many seconds were wasted in learning and she tied for fourth.

Trish bit her lip to be polite to the trainer. He congratulated her for the fine riding job. *If you'd finished training that horse, she might have won.* Trish roped the words before they left her mouth and corralled them in her mind.

And you should have ridden her this morning so you'd have known how to handle her, the nagger added to the shouting match already going on.

"Yeah, I know." Trish slapped her whip against her boots. If only she could go to the beach, but it was too late in the day. She had lab tonight and somehow had to find time to make up a couple of labs that she'd missed.

Or, messed up on, the voice reminded her.

On the way to inspect the gelding, Adam and Carlos took one look at her face and refrained from commenting—on the races, the weather, or even the horse.

"I don't really like him," Trish muttered as they walked back to the barn.

"I'm not surprised," Adam answered.

Trish ignored his tone. To question him would be too much trouble. Right now, anything was too much trouble. It took all her energy to drive to the college.

At least she didn't burn the place down. But driving home, she could barely keep her eyes open.

You said you'd give God the glory, the voice in her head gloated.

"Oh, shut up!" She fell across her bed exhausted.

Chapter 09

Rhonda, over here!"

"Trish, I made it, I really made it!" Rhonda, her crop of carrot-colored hair flying as she zigzagged between the crowd, waved her hand, and jumped to see over the shoulder of a woman in front of her. "Excuse me. . . . Excuse me." Finally, she dropped her bag and collapsed into Trish's arms.

A woman in a tailored business suit glared at them both. "Teenagers . . ." she muttered as she passed them.

The two girls looked at each other, at the woman's broad-shouldered back, and burst out laughing.

The giggles overwhelmed them again as they held each other at arm's length. They sank into two chairs until they could catch their breath.

"Welcome to California!" Trish tried to adopt a straight face—and failed.

"So how much can we cram into three days?" Rhonda picked up her bag and pulled Trish to her feet.

"I thought we'd go to the beach today. I have two mounts tomorrow—

Gatesby is one—and then I took Sunday off. We can shop or sightsee or . . ."

"Yes!"

"Yes what?"

"All of the above!" Rhonda dropped her bag again and whirled Trish around in a circle. "I want a drop-dead outfit for the first day of school. Something so different, no one at home will have anything like it. Just think, we're seniors this year!"

"Excuse us . . ." An elderly couple waited for the girls to stop blocking the aisle.

"We're going shop-ping!" Rhonda flung an irresistible grin at them.

"Have fun, dear." The white-haired woman smiled back.

"We will!"

Rhonda talked nonstop all the way to Half Moon Bay and out to Redondo Beach. "Wow, this is super!" She raised up in the seat to look over the windshield. The beach curved from the space-station-looking government buildings on the north to the Strawberry Ranch promontory on the south. White frosted breakers curled onto the golden sand, rolling in from the blue-green ocean.

"No surfers. I thought California beaches had surfers."

"There are some at the jetty; that's a couple of miles up the road. We can go there if you'd rather."

"How about later?"

"Sure."

"So this is where you come all the time." Rhonda sat back down and opened the car door.

"Yep." Trish got out and went around to open the trunk. "I brought the blanket and cooler. There's no place to change if you want to put your suit on. The water's so cold here I don't really swim, so shorts are usually fine."

"Okay." Rhonda stuffed her bag into the trunk. "I'm ready."

They slid and slithered their way to the warm, dry sand, then trudged south to Trish's favorite place. Even her gull hovered nearby, circling and dipping in the hopes the girls had treats. Together they spread the blanket and plopped down.

"No wonder you like it here." Rhonda lay spread-eagle on the blanket. "There's hardly anyone else around."

"More today than usual." Trish nodded at a woman with three school-age boys playing in the waves with their black lab. A couple shared a blanket, absorbing the rays. "You want a pop?" At Rhonda's nod, Trish opened the cooler and pulled out two Diet Cokes.

As they popped the tops and poured the cold liquid down their throats, they both sighed.

"So, how are things *really* going?" Rhonda brushed her hair back from her face with one hand and tilted her pop can with the other.

"Up and down. I think I'm a yo-yo sometimes and don't know who is jerking the string."

"I'd hoped things would be better by now."

"So did I." Trish crossed her legs and pushed to a stand. "Come on, let's go walk in the water and I'll fill you in on all the gory details."

"Can we leave your stuff?"

"I always do. So far nothing's been stolen. I think the stories you hear of everything being lifted are totally exaggerated." She walked toward the waves, dragging her bare feet in the loose sand.

"Yikes! This is as cold as Washington coast water. I thought California water was warmer."

"Told you so. That's farther south. Here, you wear a wet suit or freeze."

They stayed in the shallows where the waves rolled and receded, sometimes splashing their knees but mostly just swooshing at their ankles.

"So, how's your riding coming?"

"Don't ask."

"Hey, this is me, Rhonda, your best friend, remember? To me you tell all."

Trish conceded and told her about the poor showings at the track, her difficulty with chemistry classes, how she fell asleep all the time, the pit that seemed to yawn at her feet. She told about the Finleys, how good they were to her, how she overheard some guys say she was all washed up, and how she missed Spitfire. And finally, she mentioned the journals, the song, and missing her dad. She didn't mention the pills.

"Pretty bad, huh?"

"A doctor I saw, because Mom insisted, said I maybe should join a group she knew of for kids who've had someone near to them die."

"You gonna go?"

"No. I leave for home in a couple of weeks. Things were better when I was home." Trish stopped and tossed water with one foot, staring out at the horizon.

"Bet you could find a group like that at home. I'd go with you if that would help."

"Thanks." Trish stuck her hands in the back pockets of her cut-offs. "One day I thought about walking out into the surf and not stopping, but that was quite a while ago."

"Trish, no!"

"Don't freak. I won't. My dad's journals have helped a lot. Did I tell you he wrote me a letter in the blank book he left for me? He hoped I'd start a journal too."

Rhonda shook her head. "We haven't had much time to talk lately, if you recall. What did he say?"

"You can read it if you like. It always makes me cry. Of course, everything makes me cry nowadays."

"Remember, we used to laugh until we cried."

"Yeah, a lifetime ago." They returned to the blanket and two more cans of Coke. The wind picked up from out at sea and raised goose bumps on their arms as they sat watching the sun sink into the clouds layered on the horizon.

"Let's go," Trish said suddenly. "I know a great mini-mall with bargain stores calling our names. Tomorrow, after the races, I thought we could drive out to the Stanford Mall. It's something else."

"Stanford . . . as in Stanford University?"

"Sure. Palo Alto isn't far from here."

"You mean, like maybe we could drive around the campus? I would love to go to school there."

"Yeah, right. What independently wealthy relative is bank-rolling your education?"

"It's pretty tough, huh?"

"Uh-huh, and you have to be a near genius to get accepted there."

"So far I have a four-point average."

"Good for you. Here, which do you want to carry, the cooler or the blanket? This hill could get you in shape for a marathon."

They spent the hours till closing trying on tons of clothes. While the number of packages they toted grew with each store, they still hadn't found *the* outfit—for either of them.

"Tomorrow! If we can't find what we want at Stanford Mall, it hasn't been made yet." Trish slammed the trunk shut on their latest buys.

"Are the mall prices as bad out there as the school prices?"

"Don't worry about it. I'm buying."

"You idiot." Rhonda thumped Trish on the shoulder. "You can't do that. You already bought my plane ticket."

"Rhonda, think it through. I have more money than you and I can picture, so if I want to spend some on my best friend, I will. You'd do the same, wouldn't you?"

"What did we use to say? 'All for one and one for all.' You, me, David, and Brad. Remember?"

"Yeah, back in the good old days . . . before my dad . . ." Trish choked on the words. She turned the ignition and her car roared to life. "You can sleep in, you know. I'll go over for morning works, then come back for you before the race. Or Martha said she could bring you over."

"They sure are nice, the Finleys." The two girls were sprawled on Trish's bed after visiting downstairs for a while. "I can get up with you. I haven't been at a track so early since last summer, I guess."

"Okay, but bring a book along or something. You can't go up in the jockey room with me, so you'll have quite a wait until the afternoon program starts."

"Fine, you know me. I always have a book or two along." She indicated her bag, the corners of books poking out the canvas fabric.

"Or you could stay here and catch some rays out on the deck."

"The sun doesn't shine at the track?"

"Most people don't walk around at Bay Meadows in a swimsuit, you nut."

Trish fell asleep with a smile curving her lips. Her last thought winged heavenward. *Thank you, God, for Rhonda.*

"Hey, I think she remembers me," Rhonda exclaimed as Firefly greeted her with a whicker in the morning.

"She should. You helped train her." Trish rubbed behind the filly's ears and down her neck. "And of course, you remember Gatesby."

"How could I forget?" Rhonda held on to the gelding's halter as she stroked his neck. "Still up to your old tricks, I hear." Gatesby twitched his upper lip to the side, as if reaching for her hand. "Oh, no you don't!"

"You never give up, do you, fella." Trish slipped the bit in his mouth and the headstall over his ears. "Now we just warm up so you can save all your energy for this afternoon." She led him out so Carlos could cinch the saddle.

Adam handed her a helmet. "Now watch him. He's primed, fit to bust."

Trish touched her whip to her helmet. "Yes, sir. He's not gonna dump me again. I still have a bruise from the last one."

"What happened?" Rhonda looked up at Trish seated on the rangy gelding.

"Ask Adam. He loves to tell tales on me." Trish nudged her mount forward. "See you soon."

Gatesby was indeed ready to run. He snorted and danced to the side, but when Trish lightly thwacked him with the whip, he jumped forward, then settled down.

Anytime he started to jig, Trish pulled him back to a flat-footed walk. About halfway around the track, she let him extend to a gentle jog, as long as he behaved. Even Gatesby realized she meant business after she thwacked him the second time.

They returned to the barn with both of them tuned up for the coming race.

Trish walked Firefly around the entire track for the first time since the filly had strained her leg. After hassling with Gatesby, the filly was pure joy.

"Come on back to the track with me," Adam said after Trish finished with a couple more horses. "I want to show you something."

Trish looked at Rhonda and shrugged. They walked with Adam out to the platform overlooking the smaller track.

"See that chestnut on the far side, the one with blinkers?"

"Sure." Trish took the binoculars he offered and studied the horse trotting nearer the freeway. "What about him?"

"Tell me what you see."

"Filly? Colt? What is it?"

"Gelding. Three-year-old."

"I don't know. He moves well, kinda leggy and rangy like Gatesby; too far to see his eyes, and with the blinkers you can't really tell about his head. Looks to be in pretty good condition. Why?"

"That's the claimer you said you didn't like."

"Oh." Trish handed back the binoculars. "Maybe we—I should look again, huh?"

"I talked to Patrick and your mother about him; faxed them the information. They said if we think so, that's good enough for them."

Trish watched the horse carefully as he galloped by them. What hadn't she liked about him? She thought back. She hadn't liked much of anything right then. *You'd have turned down Spitfire that day,* her nagger whispered in her ear.

"You really think he would pay off for us?"

"With an old pro like Patrick training him, I think you'd see some real wins with him." Adam turned back to the barns. "You want me to start the paper work?"

Trish nodded. "I guess."

Gatesby was raring to go when Trish mounted him in the saddling paddock. He pranced and danced his way past the stands and out to the starting gates. Trish felt him quiver as the last gate slammed shut. A moment of hushed silence and they were racing. Gatesby surged from stall number four and headed for the first turn in the mile-long race. Into the backstretch, Trish held him three paces off the leader and right even with two others. Around the far turn, and the horse on their right made his move.

The jockeys went to the whip. Trish gave Gatesby more rein and crouched tighter into his neck. Gatesby lengthened out, left the one he paced behind, and passed the second-place horse. Trish swung her whip once and the gelding laid back his ears. They edged up on the front runner, each stride bringing them closer to the lead.

The other jockey whipped his horse again. Gatesby drove for the finish line. The two dueled, neck and neck.

Trish asked Gatesby for more. He gave it, and the other horse matched him. Thundering down the track, locked together, they crossed the finish line.

Trish had no idea who won. She rose in her stirrups and let Gatesby slow of his own accord. *Photo finish* was flashing on the scoreboard when she trotted back to the front of the winner's circle. She walked him in a tight circle, her mind pleading, *Let us win, let us win.*

Number five flashed on the scoreboard as the announcer boomed the same over the loudspeaker. Number four to place. She clamped her teeth on her bottom lip to stop the trembling. They didn't win. He should have won.

"You rode a fine race, girl." Adam held the bridle while she slipped to the ground. "Now, you have nothing to feel bad about. You—he—you both did your best, hear me?"

Trish unhooked her saddle and slung it over one arm. "Yeah, sure." She strode off to the scale.

As soon as she could get away, Trish and Rhonda walked back to the car. "See, I told you," Trish said. I can't win anymore. What do I think I'm doing out there?" She slammed the palm of her hand against the steering wheel of her car. "A *real* jockey would have brought Gatesby in first."

"Trish."

"It's not fair to a good horse . . . to put me up on him."

"Trish." Rhonda raised her voice.

"This was his last race down here and he shoulda won it."

"Trish!" Rhonda pounded her hand on the dashboard.

"What? I'm not deaf. I heard you."

"Coulda fooled me. You quit tearing yourself down like that. That race could have gone either way and you know it."

"All I know is that I didn't win." Trish drove toward the condominium. "I need to shower and change clothes before we go."

"Go where?"

"To the Stanford Mall, remember?" Her tone cut the air like a whip.

"We don't have to go."

"No, no, I want to. Maybe it'll make me feel better."

Trish tried to drive out the drummers in her head with the shower spray but it didn't help much. And when she saw another card from Red on the hall table as she left, she felt lower. The pit yawned before her.

Shopping with Rhonda seemed to drag her back from the edge. They tried on clunky jewelry, funky hats, and outrageous boots. They cruised the aisles of Saks, I. Magnin, and Macy's.

They both bought shoes at Nordstrom.

"Look." Rhonda grabbed Trish's arm and pointed at a window across the courtyard. "That's it."

They walked into the store. Half an hour later, each was richer by one brocade vest, a long-sleeved silk shirt in hues to match the vest, a blue denim skirt, and wide belt with silver conch buckle. While their outfits matched in style, the colors fit each girl.

"Will your boots go with this?" Trish asked as they left the store.

Rhonda crinkled her face. "They should."

"Want new ones?"

"Trish, no. This is enough."

"No it isn't. Come on." When they left the boot store, they each had new boots and leather purses to match.

"Are you hungry?" Trish asked.

"More thirsty."

"Come on." They tucked their packages under the table in a sidewalk cafe and ordered iced tea while they studied the menus.

After the waitress brought their drinks and took their orders, Rhonda leaned her elbows on the table and looked directly at her friend. "Trish, I can't believe we just did that . . . you did that."

"What?" Trish took a long swig of her drink.

"Bought all that stuff." Rhonda toyed with her straw.

"Listen, my friend. Remember all the time you spent helping David and me in the last year?"

"Yeah, but your dad paid me for that."

"He could never pay you enough. You helped keep me . . ." Trish sniffed and took another drink of tea. "You helped me feel better today too."

Rhonda blinked a couple of times and sniffed also. "Okay. Thank you."

They both blew their noses in the paper napkins and asked for replacements when the waitress returned with their croissant sandwiches.

On Sunday they crammed three days' sightseeing into one. They hung from the sides of the cable car past Chinatown, up Knob Hill, then down the hills again to the turntable between Fisherman's Wharf and Ghirardelli Square.

"Come on, we have to share a sundae at Ghirardelli. Besides, there're neat shops there." Trish started up the sidewalk lined with vendors of T-shirts, sweat shirts, jewelry, and artwork of every kind. "Come on, we'll never see it all if you insist on looking at every pair of earrings here." Trish dragged Rhonda, protesting, onward.

They placed their order at the counter of the world-famous ice cream and candy shop in Ghirardelli Square, then walked through the display showing how cocoa turned from beans, that looked like coffee beans, into real chocolate.

"Creamy, dark chocolate." Rhonda drooled at the sight of the rich brown river streaming between two stones.

"Let's find a table before you faint." Trish grabbed her friend's arm. "I should have known better than to bring a chocoholic like you in here." She plunked their packages down at a round table and went up to get their order when the young man behind the counter called their number.

"I can't believe that," Rhonda whispered, her eyes as big as her mouth. The scoops of ice cream, hot fudge, and whipped cream dripped over the sides of the tulip glass and down onto the plate.

"Eat fast before it melts." Trish dug in with a long-handled spoon. "Ummm." She let the ice cream slip down her throat and licked the fudge from the back of the spoon.

"Good thing we didn't order two."

Afterward, they laughed at the antics of the street clowns and mimes, accepting funny balloon hats from one clown. They bought San Francisco sweat shirts and watched the sun go down over the Golden Gate Bridge from the deck above the sea lions on Pier 39.

"There's another neat chocolate store here," Trish said as they turned away from the barking sea lions spread over the boat docks below.

"Oh-h." Rhonda groaned. "I'm still full from the sourdough bread and shrimp cocktails. And our sundae."

"You don't have to eat any, just look. Everything in the store is made of chocolate."

Rhonda bought chocolate cable cars to take home for souvenirs. She handed Trish a piece of fudge as they strolled the wooden pier.

Back home that night, they showed Martha all their purchases from the past two days.

"You about bought out the town." Martha fingered the brocade stitching on the vests. "These are beautiful. You'll knock 'em dead when you walk into school wearing these outfits."

"I've never had a silk shirt before." Rhonda held her cream-colored one up in front of her.

"You think I have?" Trish hung her things in the closet. She stroked the sleeve of her flaming-rust shirt. "But doesn't it feel heavenly?"

"Did you bring an extra suitcase?" Martha asked, looking at all the things Rhonda needed to pack.

"Just this." Rhonda held up her sports bag. "And it was full when I came."

"No sweat. We'll buy you a new one in the morning." Trish yawned and went into the bathroom to brush her teeth. "Just stack the stuff on the floor so we can get in bed."

Rhonda lay out on the deck, sunning, when Trish returned from the track in the morning. Trish changed into her swimsuit, and after pulling up another lounger, flopped down on her stomach.

"Feeling better?" Rhonda asked.

"Better than what?"

"I can tell you're trying to be up 'cause I'm here. So, buddy, what's buggin' you?" Rhonda turned onto her stomach.

"I haven't won a race since Belmont; I lost again Saturday, my chemistry final is coming up, and I feel like some stupid moron who can't think. That enough?"

"I guess."

"And on top of that, you're leaving today." Trish could see the pit reaching up to suck her in.

"But you said things are better than they were."

"Yeah, they are. While I check out mentally, I don't feel like checking out permanently."

"Oh, Tee, I just wish I could help somehow." Rhonda reached across the space between them and patted Trish's elbow.

"Me too."

Silence and sun lay across the deck for a time before Rhonda raised her head. "Whatever did you do with the third convertible you won?"

"It's still at the dealer. I told him I'd get back to him. I guess I will—sometime.

"Have you decided what you're going to do with it?"

"Just sell it, I guess."

"Mmmm. I liked your original idea of giving it to the youth group at church."

Trish blew out the breath she'd been holding. "Hardly."

Rhonda held up her hands. "Just a thought."

After she waved good-bye and Rhonda walked down the ramp to the plane, Trish felt like the pit was engulfing her again. She went through the motions of completing a makeup lab before class and listening to the instructor cover as much material as possible before the final. She couldn't decide which was worse, the dry burning behind her eyes or when they ran with tears. Either way, she ended up with a headache.

Back in her bedroom, she paced the floor, fighting to keep awake. If only she could crawl into bed and sleep, sleep away the pain, the confusion.

She forced her eyes back to the notes she'd made in class. The words turned into squiggles that danced on the page. Her gaze fell on her purse.

Richard had said the pills would help her think better. They'd give her some energy. Better than caffeine, he'd said. Just one pill; what could be wrong with taking one simple little pill? People took them all the time.

Trish picked up her purse. She dug around. Panic dried her mouth. Where were they? Finally she felt them, down at the very bottom, a baggie with the three little white pills.

She strode into the bathroom and ran a glassful of water. She put a pill on her tongue and stared at the face in the mirror.

Chapter
10

There was no one to bump her this time. . . . She raised the glass to her lips and filled her mouth with water. . . . No one to tell her no.

Trish gagged and leaned over the toilet. She spit out the pill and water and gagged again.

The black pit grew before her eyes. She ran back into the bedroom and grabbed the remaining pills. The face she glimpsed in the mirror looked like it had seen a ghost. She flung the remaining pills into the toilet and flushed it.

Trish staggered back into the bedroom and sank down on the edge of the bed. Oh, to lay her head down on the pillow and forget this had ever happened. She clamped her hands to her head and rocked back and forth.

God, what do I do? Help me! The cry swirled down into the blackness engulfing her.

And He will raise you up . . .

She gulped for air.

. . . on eagle's wings . . .

Where was it coming from? *I will praise the Lord. I WILL praise the*

Lord. God is my strength, my very present help in times of trouble. I can do all things through Christ who strengthens me. The verses scrolled through her mind. She could see the wall above her desk at home as if she were standing right in front of it. The wall with cards written by both her and her father. The wall of Bible verses she had memorized. *For God so loved the world, loved Trish . . .*

She grabbed the box of tissues and ripped out a handful. The tears flowed. The verses sang. Her heart settled back in her chest and resumed its steady beat. She mopped her eyes again and again. *Let not your heart be troubled . . .* That one sure fit.

A troubled heart. She sniffed and mopped.

When the tears finally dried up, she went into the bathroom and soaked a washcloth in cold water. She could almost hear it sizzle as she buried her face in it. "Thank you. Thank you." She let her shoulders droop and her head fall forward. She inhaled, a breath that went clear to her toenails. And when she released it, she felt her body relax. Another breath seemed to inhale the peace she could feel seeping into the room.

Peace floated around the room like tendrils of golden-hued clouds, kissed by the rising sun.

Trish propped her back against the headboard of the bed and her chemistry book on her lap. "Please, Father, help me read and understand what I am studying. Help me to stay awake and think clearly. I can't do this on my own. I can't seem to do much of anything right—on my own. Thank you for helping me."

Three hours of sleep wasn't enough. Trish tried rubbing the grit from her eyes but resorted to a wet washcloth instead. If only she had time for a shower—a cold one.

Remnants of the nightmare tugged at her memory. Had it been as bad as usual? She wasn't sure. If only she could wake up enough to change it like the doctor had suggested. But the end would always be the same. Her father was gone.

Dawn cracked the sky over the eastern hills as she mounted her third horse for Adam.

"Better now?" Adam patted her knee after boosting her aboard.

Trish nodded. The man could read her like a book. Did she wear her thoughts on her face like an open page, or was he just a good reader?

He walked beside her out to the track. "Trot her once around, then breeze her for four furlongs. I'll be clocking you, so let her go at the half-mile pole."

"Okay." Trish nudged the mare into a slow trot. The horse, long used to the routine, trotted around the outside of the track. But when Trish turned her and eased toward the rail, she perked up.

Trish could feel her mount pulling at the bit. She snapped her goggles over her eyes. She let the mare extend to an even gallop and, at the pole, let her out. The mare hit her running pace in three strides. With Trish encouraging her, the old girl flattened out, reaching for top speed. The finish pole flashed by and Trish rose in her stirrups to bring the mare back down to a gallop.

Trish and her mount hugged the rail to pass a horse galloping in front of them. Just as they pulled even, the other horse stumbled and started falling.

The mare swerved to miss the falling horse but kept to her feet, thanks to Trish's firm hands and the rail they grazed on the left. Trish's ankle took the brunt of the force.

She pulled the mare to a walk and glanced back to check on the other horse. He was limping off the track. The jockey shrugged an apology.

Trish rubbed her ankle through her boot. What a stupid thing to have happen. When would she learn to pay better attention? She checked the mare's shoulder. Part of her hide was burned bare. But she wasn't limping, seemed no worse for the near miss.

"You're okay?" Adam asked when he met her at the exit.

"Yeah, but . . ."

"I don't want to hear it." He raised his hands. "You did a good job in a tight situation and everyone came out all right."

"But . . ."

"Trish, you can't take responsibility for the whole world. Accidents happen; that's life." He examined the graze on the mare's shoulder.

"I feel like I'm an accident waiting to happen."

Adam glared up at her. He shook his head and strode off to the barns.

At the barns he said, "You might want to thank God you weren't hurt. I do." He boosted her up on Gatesby. "Give him a couple of laps nice and easy."

Trish finished her morning rides without much feeling. She felt guilty that Adam had to scold her like he did. She dragged her feet into the office and sat down on the edge of her chair. "Adam . . ." She had to clear her throat. "I—I'm sorry. I just want to be the best, or even good again, and everything seems to go against that." She looked up to see him nodding at her. "I'm up when everything's okay and down when it isn't."

"I've noticed. But you've got to take it as it comes and just do the best you can."

"My father kept on praising the Lord all through his cancer. I want to do that too, but it doesn't come easy for me."

"Your dad was a lot older than you, Trish. Learning to thank God for everything takes time and practice. It's a lot like a mother teaching her child to say thank-you. She has to remind him over and over—and over. God isn't going to smack you because you forget sometimes. He loves you too much."

"I smack myself often enough."

"And is it doing any good?"

Trish shrugged. "Maybe one of these days I'll remember."

"And in the meantime, you feel terrible."

Trish leaned back in her chair. "How come you got so smart?"

"See this white hair?" Adam pointed to the fringe around his balding head. "I earned every one of them—mostly the hard way."

That night when Trish returned from class, in which she'd stayed alert for a change, Martha told her that David had called.

"Thanks." Trish ran up the stairs and dumped her stuff on the floor by the bed. She dialed the number, then pulled off her boots while it rang.

Marge answered. "Good evening, Runnin' On Farm."

"Hi, Mom, it's me."

"Hi, Tee. We're getting him all packed."

"What do you mean?"

"David's leaving for Tucson tomorrow so he has time to stop and see you. Martha said they had plenty of room for him there. You'll see him some time late in the day."

"Whew, you guys don't waste any time, do you?"

"Not much." There was an awkward silence.

"Mom, are you okay?"

Trish heard a faint sniff. "I will be. It's just that this house will be awfully empty till you come home."

"Why don't you come with him?" Trish lay back on her pillows.

"I wish I could, but I've still too much to do with all the paper work and stuff. I'm not even sure I can make it down to watch you race."

"M-o-m!"

"I know. But even though your father had his will in order and a lot of other stuff, there's still too much to do."

Trish gripped the phone till her knuckles whitened. "You have to come, Mom. I'm counting on you to help me win."

"No, Trish. You count on God and yourself for that, not me. Is there anything you want David to bring?"

"Just you."

"Rhonda came over and showed me what you bought. Her new outfit is beautiful."

"Isn't it? I have one too. Oh, I almost forgot, we've started the paper work on the claimer. He looks good. I wanted a filly but Carlos found this gelding. He said he'd buy it himself if he had the money."

"Good. The mare and filly come tomorrow. Sure will be busy when you're all home again."

"Well, I gotta get to sleep. See you in a couple of days."

"Trish. . . . Good night, Tee."

So David would arrive tomorrow. Would he want to go sightseeing too? Trish brought out her journal, propped herself up against the headboard, and began writing. She managed only two sentences before her eyes closed. The book thumping to the floor woke her enough to turn out the light and set the alarm.

"Okay, just walk her around the short track nice and easy. The swelling is gone, and if it stays down she should be okay for Sunday." Adam stroked Firefly's shoulder after boosting Trish into the saddle. "We'll need to clock her day after tomorrow, so we're cutting it pretty close."

. "I'd rather scratch her than take a chance on a long-term injury." Trish smoothed a stubborn strand of the filly's mane to the right side.

"I agree, but this is the last good race for her this season and I hate to miss it unless we're forced to." He stepped back. "Have a good one."

Trish brought Diego's horse in for a show that afternoon. The horse that won ran all the others right into the ground and then left them lengths behind. Even Trish couldn't fault herself for not winning that one.

"You have nothing to say?" Adam cocked one eyebrow at her.

"Yeah, you think they want to sell that horse?" Trish looked over at the winner's circle, where the colt, jockey, and entourage posed for pictures. "He was moving."

Trish lost the next one. Ended up next to last. The horse broke badly, swung wide on the turns, and ran out of steam down the stretch.

"I rode better than that as an apprentice," she muttered, following the other jockeys back to the jockey room.

She gathered up her gear and headed around the track to the barn. Maybe David would get here before she had to leave for school. But probably not. She checked her watch. She needed to go early to finish making up two more labs. At least on Friday all she had was a lab. Richard had canceled their last tutoring session. Maybe she could get David to coach her.

When she got in her car, her gaze automatically fell on the Post-it Note on her dashboard. She'd written it as a reminder. Big letters. PTL. Praise the Lord. Sure, praise the Lord for losing a race. How about for riding a dud of a horse? It would be easy to praise the Lord if she owned the horse who won the first race.

She could thank Him that no one got hurt today. And that David was coming. There, those were her two things for the day. "And please help me finish these experiments fast. And right."

The wind felt wonderful in her hair and even the traffic moved smoothly as she drove to school.

When she got home that night, David sat in the living room visiting with the Finleys.

"You made it okay." Trish crossed the room to give her brother a hug. Strange, they never used to hug, but now it seemed natural—and necessary.

"That's a *long* drive." David rubbed the small of his back with doubled . fists.

"That's why I like flying."

"There's iced tea in the fridge if you want," Martha said.

When Trish returned from the kitchen, she smacked her lips. "This is really good. You did something new."

"Added a bag of mint tea to the regular sun tea."

"I like it."

"What's sun tea?" David asked. He took another swallow from his sweating glass.

"You put the tea bags in cold water in a jug and set it out in the sun for the day."

"One of the good things about California sun." Trish chose to sit on the floor between David and the Finleys. "But the oranges alone are worth living here."

"There are some of those on the kitchen table, if you like." Martha turned to David. "Trish found out that oranges that never saw the light of a cooler are a whole different fruit."

"Like, are they ever. 'Course you'll have them in Arizona too." She took another swallow of tea. "Still, I wish you weren't going."

"You want me around to do your chemistry." He patted her on the head.

"You want to? I just happen to have some here." Trish leaned forward like she was going to get it right then.

"No, no, baby sister, you do your own homework."

"Rats." Trish finished her tea and checked the grandfather clock on the far wall. "Speaking of which, I need to go do some and hit the sack. We working people have to get up early."

"Call me when you get up. I'll be ready when you are." David leaned back on the sofa. He covered a yawn with his hand. "If you think driving down here in one day isn't work, you're crazier than I thought."

"Thank you." Trish smiled at the Finleys and rolled her eyes.

They both smiled at her antics. "'Night, Trish."

Having David at the barns in the morning felt like old home week. When he boosted her into the saddle on Gatesby, he stood by her knee, smiling up at her.

Trish caught the flick of Gatesby's ears. Before she could do any more than open her mouth, the gelding clamped a bit of David's shirt in his teeth and yanked.

"Ouch." Gatesby obviously got more than cloth. "You idiot horse." David rubbed his upper arm. "Why we keep you around . . ." He glared up at Trish, who had collapsed on Gatesby's neck with laughter.

"You should s-s-see your f-face." She broke up again.

Adam and Carlos tried for all their worth to keep straight faces, but Trish's laughter tickled them into joining. Trish tried to straighten up, but when she looked over their heads, Juan was leaning against the barn, his shoulders shaking, his hands clasped over his mouth.

"Go ahead. All of you. Laugh it up." David clamped a hand on the reins right under Gatesby's chin and raised the other hand as if to strike. Gatesby lifted his head away and rolled his eyes. He knew how to play the game.

"It's so good to be the butt of the joke my first morning. . . ."

"The bite." Trish cracked up again at her own cleverness.

"Huh?"

"Not the butt, the bite of the joke." She spoke slowly as though he didn't understand the language.

David made as if to grab her, but when he dropped the reins, Gatesby reached around and David grabbed the reins again.

"Hah, think I'll go work off some of his energy. When we get back, maybe David'll be in a better mood," Trish said for Gatesby's benefit.

"Give her a real ride, you old nag," David muttered to the horse. Gatesby tossed his head as much as the hand on his reins would allow.

Trish heard herself humming as they trotted out on the track. That *had* been fun. She stroked Gatesby's neck and patted his shoulder. "We should put you in a circus act," she told him. "Gatesby, the fastest-running clown on earth." Her horse jigged sideways. He seemed to enjoy the fun as much as she did.

But the fun in the morning had no bearing on the racing in the afternoon. Trish had two mounts and neither one of them made it into the money. The first one quit running in the stretch and no amount of the whip made any difference.

Trish hated to use her whip at all, let alone enough to get the horse to try harder. He just didn't have it in him.

The second one, in the third, kept pulling away from any horse that came up on his right side. And since they had the rail, that meant every horse in the field. "You might want to put blinkers on him," she mentioned to the trainer after dismounting. "Is he that shy all the time?"

"Nah, only since he took a bad bump. You're probably right." The trainer led the horse away.

Trish couldn't believe she'd offered her opinion. Only disgust had made her do it. She tried not to yell at herself, but discouragement won out. By the time she got back to the barn, she was down again.

"You want to watch the rest of the program or go to the beach?" she offered David the choice.

"The beach." He turned to Adam. "Unless we should go see that gelding now."

"Tomorrow will be fine. You two have a good time."

She drove all the way without a word. She could feel David glancing at her, waiting for a response to his comments, but she focused only on the road. She parked in her usual place, with the Pacific stretching before them. A fishing boat, dark against the gray swells, chugged north to the man-made harbor.

"So this is where you've been coming. I can see why."

"David, I'm thinking of quitting racing." There, the words were out.

Chapter
11

That's the stupidest idea I ever heard."

"You saw that race. It was typical, just the way my season is going."

"Trish, every athlete, every jockey, has a down time."

"I hardly get any mounts, other than ours and Adam's."

"There are more jockeys here; the track is bigger, and so is the money. Besides that, you're not the darling here you were at home."

"I'm not a winner here either." She clamped her lips shut, then turned her head. "So you're saying my wins were because of Dad and Spitfire?"

"No, that's not what I meant. Quit twisting my words around."

"So?" She crossed her arms across her chest.

"So what?" David looked at her, confusion written all over his face.

"So, what did you mean—about me being the darling at home."

"Well." David clicked his teeth together and pursed his lips. "At home you were known before you apprenticed. Everyone liked you, and Dad had both a good name and lots of friends. And then you had that gift . . ."

"*Had* is the right word."

"Shut up and let me finish this. You have a gift of understanding horses and getting them to perform at their best for you."

"Had, David, *had*. It's not happening anymore." Trish twisted to open her car door.

David grabbed her arm. "No. Let's get this out in the open and talk about it." As she started to pull away, he tightened his hold. "Now. You want to make Dad a liar?"

"That's a low blow if I ever heard one."

"He believed in you. I believe in you, and so does Mom. You've lost your confidence, that's all."

"David, I have tried. I do everything I can and still nothing works out right. Maybe I can come back to racing later, but for now, if I don't win a race, especially the one with Firefly before I have to leave for home, I'm quitting." She shoved open her door. "You coming down to the beach or not?"

She grabbed her bag, cooler, and blanket out of the trunk and headed for the trail.

David took the cooler from her as soon as he caught up. He followed her down the trail and out to her favorite spot.

Trish dumped the gear, removed her shoes, and scuffed through the dry, loose sand down to the wet, where foamy waves scalloped an edge. She hunched her shoulders against both the inward and outward chill and watched the waves curl around her feet. The sand being sucked away from under her felt about as secure as the world she'd been living in lately.

"I can see why you like it here." David stopped beside her.

Trish raised her face to the sun. "Dad wrote about peace in his journal, and this is the place where I seem to find it best."

"Mom said she gave you his journal and the carved eagle."

"Yeah." Trish turned and started walking in the ankle-deep water. "Don't you miss him so much you want to—to . . ." She kept her gaze on the foamy water curling about her feet.

"To scream? To cry? Bash my hand against a wall?" David snorted. "Sure I have. I've done it all. And then I felt better—for a while." He turned his fist over so she could see a fading scar line. "That's what I got for it." He traced the line with a fingertip. "But you have to go on, Tee. Dad would want that."

"Have you read his journal?"

"No." David shook his head. "You had it down here."

"It's back on the blanket in my bag." She turned and started back.

"Come on. We have a little bit of time before I have to leave. Chemistry calls, you know."

Back at the blanket, Trish pulled the leather-covered journal with the cross tooled on the front from her bag and handed it to her brother. "Here." She then lifted two sodas from the cooler and gave him one of those too.

While he paged through their father's journal, she wrote in her own. After a few pages, David pushed himself to his feet. "I'll be back."

She could hear his voice choking up. But David, being David, didn't like others to see him cry. Arms wrapped around her raised knees and chin on one, she watched him walk toward the surf.

Maybe not winning is God's way of telling me to get out of racing, she wrote in her journal, as David fought his private battle on the water's edge. *While I can't see quitting forever, maybe I'm supposed to spend all my time being a senior this year, getting the good grades Mom was after me for all last year. Dad, I sure wish you were here to give me your good advice. I have said I will praise the Lord, but that's so hard when things aren't going the way you want them to.* When she rubbed the moisture from her eyes, she rubbed sand into them. Now her nose really dripped.

She tucked the journal away and rummaged for a tissue. She blew, blinked, and lying back, kept her eyes closed to let the tearing wash away the grit. She heard David's scuffling feet and then felt him drop to the blanket beside her.

"You okay?" he asked.

"Just some sand in my eyes. How about you?"

"I'll live." He tapped her arm with the corner of the journal. "I have something to ask you."

"Okay." She shielded her eyes with her arm.

"Will you please think this idea of yours through? Don't make any decisions about what you will or won't do until you talk with Mom."

"David."

"No, listen to me. You've seen how Mom is working with the babies and taking an active part in the farm. She thinks Dad would want it that way."

"David, she's the one who didn't want me to race, remember? The track was too dangerous for her little girl. . . . Maybe she'll be happy if I quit."

"All I'm asking is that you keep an open mind."

"Look who's talking. Do you think you can just tell me what to do?" She sat up and turned to him.

"I'm not telling you what to do—I'm asking." David spoke softly, gently. "I'm just asking."

Trish glared at him, trying to stare him down. But the look on his face forced her to swallow her words. "All right," she whispered. She put the books back in their bag and the empty cans in the cooler. "We better get going. I have a final on Monday."

The instructor spent the class time reviewing for the final. Trish listened with total attention and took careful notes so she'd know what best to review. For a change she didn't feel like falling asleep. Maybe it was an adrenaline high clicking in early. At least she didn't have any mounts the next day, and could spend the afternoon studying.

"Here." She handed David the periodic table of elements and their symbols when she got back to the car after class. "You can quiz me on them on the way home." She turned the key in the ignition. "Did you eat already?"

"Yeah. I called Mom too."

"Wonderful."

"How'd your class go?"

Trish only shrugged. When she realized David couldn't see her response in the dark car, she said, "The teacher spent the time reviewing. The final is on Monday. Right now I just want to get it over with. If I never see another chemistry book, it'll be too soon." She turned the car into the parking lot of a take-out Chinese restaurant. "You want anything more?"

"You know I can always eat Chinese. Just get plenty and I'll eat part of yours."

Trish muttered under her breath and got out of the car. She placed the order and paced the room. *What'd he have to call home about, and get Mom all worried before she needs to be? Not that she needs to worry about this anyway. After all, racing or not is my decision.*

"Your order is ready." The soft-spoken woman behind the counter smiled as she placed the styrofoam containers on the stainless steel surface.

"Thanks." Trish paid and walked out. *Runnin' On Farm could hire jockeys just like the other owners did. Couldn't they?*

If they could, why did the thought of someone else riding her horses give her a pain in the heart region? Would this be one part of her father's dream that fell apart?

She handed the containers in to David. As she plopped onto the seat, she spoke through gritted teeth. "You didn't have to tell Mom." They ate their dinner in silence.

Trish had just gotten to her room back at the Finleys' when the phone rang.

"It's for you, Trish," Martha called up the stairs.

Trish picked up the receiver. "Hello." At the sound of her mother's voice, she sat down on the bed. "Hi, Mom."

"My flight comes in at seven on Saturday. Can you pick me up?"

"Sure." Trish felt her heart beat faster. Her mother was coming to see the race!

"I thought we'd go out for dinner, so think of someplace nice."

"Okay."

"So how are you doing?" Her mother's gentle question ignited the burning in Trish's eyes.

"Ummm." Trish looked up through her bangs. "I guess David told you what I've decided. And the cruddy way I rode today—I don't know. Sometimes it all seems more than I can handle."

"Ah, Tee, that's the point. You don't have to handle it, at least not all by yourself."

"Yeah, I know, but the doin' is the hard part." Trish sniffed. "Mom, I just can't stand losing all the time."

"Well, we'll talk more when I get there. The gelding runs Saturday?"

"Right. In the fifth race. I have a mount in the fourth."

"Give it all you've got. I'll see you Saturday night."

Trish tried studying for a while, but when her eyes kept drifting closed, she got up and went downstairs. David lay on the sofa watching television, with Martha working her needlepoint under the lamp. Adam had already gone to bed. Trish wished she could.

"How about helping me for a while?" She poked a finger into David's shoulder. "You don't need to see the end of this program anyhow."

He turned into a sitting position. "Didn't your mother ever teach you to say please?"

"She tried, brother dear, she tried. Come on, David, please. I can't stay awake, and you explain this stuff so it makes sense."

"Oh, all right." He rose to his feet. "Good night, Martha. Thanks for the pie."

"Pie? You ate Chinese just before we got home!"

"Have to keep up my strength." He followed her up the stairs.

"Let's go through this thing first." She handed him a copy of the periodic table. "Give me the element and I'll give you the symbol."

"Iron."

"Capitol F, small e."

"Aluminum."

"Capitol A, small l." They continued on through the entire table, with David asking for weights and definitions at times.

Trish paced around the room, her brow furrowed in concentration.

"I'd say you have those down pretty good. How about a list of terms."

She handed him a sheaf of papers stapled together.

"Okay." He glanced down the page. "Stoichiometry."

Trish groaned. "The determination of the atomic weights of elements, the proportions in which they combine and . . ." She scrunched up her face. "And . . ." She gave David a pleading look.

" . . . and the weight relations in any chemical reactions."

Trish repeated the entire definition twice more. "Next."

"Avogadro's Law."

"Oh, I hate this one. Avogadro's Law is the theory that equal volumes of all gases . . ." She shook her head and started again. "Something about molecules and weights."

"Come on Trish, think."

"Avogadro's Law: Equal volumes of all gases under identical conditions of temperature and pressures contain equal numbers of molecules."

"Yes!"

When Trish fell into bed an hour later, her head was full and her heart running over. If only she'd had David around all summer.

Friday morning fog gave David a taste of summer on the San Francisco Peninsula. "I'm freezing," he said as he huddled into his jacket. "Turn on the heat."

"I don't suppose you want the top down."

He gave her a dirty look. "The sun's not even up yet."

"You could have stayed at home in bed."

"And miss this? You outta your mind?"

Everyone seemed in good humor that morning, even Gatesby. He galloped the track in an even gait, not pulling against the bit more than once or twice. Trish patted his neck as she came through the exit.

"What a good fella. I was beginning to think you had it in for me." He shook his head and walked back to the barn. He didn't even shy when another horse dumped its rider and tore off down the road.

After dismounting, Trish stood right in front of the horse, took both sides of the snaffle bit in her hands, and looked him straight on. "You up to no good or don't you feel all right?"

Gatesby blew at her and tried to rub his forehead on her chest.

"Watch him, Juan. He's behaving himself."

Firefly trotted the track like the perfect lady she was. While Trish concentrated, to detect any limping on that foreleg, the filly trotted on with a strong, even beat. Trish felt a load release from her shoulders. She wasn't aware she'd been worrying about the filly.

But you said you'd quit if she doesn't win, her nagger whispered. *Your dad always said winners never quit and quitters never win. That'll make you a quitter.*

As the sun burned away the fog, Trish felt her own black cloud rolling in. *Do I really want to quit? Maybe I could call it taking a break. What's the word—a sabbatical? One year off.*

She worked the rest of the Finley string with the argument jumping back into her mind every time she dismounted.

"You sure got awful quiet," David said as he boosted her up for the last time. "You all right?"

Trish shook her head. "No, but I will be." *One of these days—or years.*

If you quit, it'll be like starting all over when you go back, the nagger threw in.

"Give it a rest!" Trish gritted her teeth. Her horse flicked his ears back and forth and broke his even gait. "No, no, not you, easy now." The animal relaxed again at Trish's soothing voice.

After works, Trish joined David, Carlos, and Adam in the office. The box of bagels and two kinds of cream cheese lay open on the desk.

Trish unfolded her chair and, after smearing spinach and garlic cream cheese on a sesame-seed bagel, sat down. She crossed one ankle over her other knee to help form a table.

"Well, what do you think of bagels?" she asked David, who had his mouth full.

"He hates them; he's only on his fourth half." Adam pushed the box closer to David.

David swallowed, and after a sip of coffee, could talk. "Who's counting?"

Trish concentrated on her breakfast. Biting a bagel just the right way took plenty of thought and planning. She tried to ignore the voices in her head. She tried to ignore the voices of the men in the office. She tried to ignore the pain in her heart. She failed on all counts.

You said you'd praise the Lord too. Remember? She jumped to her feet and threw the uneaten third of her bagel in the trash. She left the office without a word.

David found her a while later, sitting in her car, chemistry book propped against the steering wheel, sound asleep. "Trish." He shook her shoulder. "Trish, come on. Wake up."

Trish stretched her neck and rotated her head from shoulder to shoulder. She yawned fit to bust her jaw. When she blinked her eyes for the fourth time, they finally focused. "What do you want?" Her voice came out flat and dark, just like her feelings.

"You said you wanted to come along when we went to see the gelding."

"The gelding?" While her eyes might have been functioning, her brain stayed stuck in the sleep mode.

"The claimer. We have to make a decision." His voice came across so big-brother patient she nearly gagged.

Instead she yawned. This time she heard it crack.

"Well, if you're not interested, we'll go without you. But since you'll be the one training and racing him, I'd think you'd like to be there."

"I might not be the one racing him, you know."

"Ah, Trish. I don't want to hear any more about your quitting."

Trish pushed open her car door. Going with them was better than staying alone.

"I like him," David whispered in Trish's ear as they watched a woman walk the gelding around in the deep sand circle to cool him down.

"I'd rather have a filly."

"Geldings usually make more money in the long run."

"He seems even tempered. We've watched him galloping. And the stats don't lie." Trish turned back with the others.

"Why do you think he hasn't done better?" David asked as they walked back to their own office.

"He's coming back from a quarter crack on the off rear that ended his two-year-old season. I think he's a late bloomer too. He still hasn't finished growing and the owner got too ambitious in the races they entered him in. A lot of things can happen, you know." Adam seemed to be thinking out loud.

"He'll do good this year," Carlos added.

Yeah, if we get him. Trish kicked a rock ahead of her. *The way things are going, I'll probably jinx that too.*

"So you want to do it?" Adam sat back down at his desk.

David looked over at Trish. At her nod, he dug his billfold out of his back pocket and took out a check. "Mom signed this. We just have to fill in the amount."

Trish left for the jockey room. She was riding in the first race.

"How's it going?" Mandy asked as Trish walked into the locker-lined room. The wall-mounted television was on, as usual, showing past races until the day's program started.

Trish shrugged. "Still up and down, I guess. I got to go home for a few days and that helped. And then my best friend came down to shop and sightsee. Now, that was fun."

"Good. How's the racing?"

"No wins."

"Me either. I think some of those big guys got a scam going. They just take turns, if ya know what I mean." Mandy leaned back in her chair. " 'Course, now, if I won once in a while, I probably wouldn't feel this way."

"How long you been racing?"

"Four years. Started out on the fair circuit and last year moved up to the big time at Bay Meadows. I'll try my luck at Golden Gate Fields this year too."

"You ever think of quitting?"

"You kidding? About every time I get tossed. One time I was laid up for a month; thought about it lots then. But I make a decent living and I'm doing what I like best." She took a brush out of her bag and started brushing her hair. "Besides, I don't have training for anything else."

"Did you go to college?"

Mandy shook her head. "College? Honey, I never made it through high school. Finally went back and got my GED. I wasn't kidding when I said I went downhill for a time. A hard time."

She turned and leaned her hip against the counter. "You hang in there, kid." She waved her hairbrush for emphasis. "You've been at the top. You'll get there again."

"Wish I could be so sure."

And Trish felt even more unsure after the first race. She and her mount started out well. The trainer said the colt liked to be in front so Trish got him out and kept him there. But the pace was fast and the colt gave up when another horse caught up with him.

While the trainer was happy with a show, Trish wasn't. "You did a fine job with him," the young man said. He led his horse away and Trish followed the other jockeys back under the stands and out to the jockey rooms. At least now she could head for the beach.

When David suggested driving into San Francisco, Trish shook her head. "I've gotta study. I was hoping you'd help me again. We could go to the beach." She smacked herself on the forehead. "Ah, no. I've got one more lab to make up. This afternoon's it. You could help me do my lab!"

"Right. Think I'll go into the city while you're at school. I'll help you again tonight when I get back."

"Oh, David." The cloud that hid her sun looked like rain.

Chapter
12

Who screamed?

Trish blinked. She'd been sound asleep, but someone had screamed. She listened, every nerve ending taut. Was it someone in the house?

Nothing. She cleared her throat; it was hot and raw. Was it she who had screamed? When she thought about it, the screaming had been going on for a long time—or so it seemed.

She swallowed again. Water . . . a glass of water would help. She raised her head and checked out the corners of the room, all the places she could see, anyway, in the light that filtered through the eucalyptus branches outside the deck.

The glow from the streetlights flickered. It must be blowing out there. Had the scream come from outside?

For a moment she wished she had closed the drapes. But there was nothing to be seen. She sat up and swung her feet to the floor. It must have been her. Had she screamed out loud? Had anyone heard her?

Surely they would come if they had. She tiptoed into the bathroom and filled a glass with water. After the first few swallows she could slow down and sip it.

She rubbed her throat. It hurt.

When she crawled back in bed, she was afraid to close her eyes. It *had* been a dream. She had been screaming in the dream, but about what?

When she closed her eyes to remember, the scene flashed right back. Spitfire ran away from her. The more she called him, the faster he ran away. All the other horses too. Firefly, Gatesby, Sarah's Pride, even Miss Tee and Double Diamond. All of them were running away.

She caught her breath. Dan'l, old gray Dan'l. She wanted to call to him but he was running after the others.

N-o-o! She sat bolt upright in bed. Tears streamed down her face. She turned on the light and reached for a tissue. What did it all mean?

When her heart finally resumed its normal beat, she lay back down. A long time ago she'd learned to say the name of Jesus over and over when she had a nightmare.

"Jesus. Jesus. Jesus." She let her eyes drift closed. *Jesus, Jesus, Jesus.* She could feel her muscles relax. First in her neck and shoulders, then down her arms. She inhaled and held the breath. *Jesus, Jesus, Jesus.* When she let the breath out, she felt like she was sinking into the mattress.

Thank you, Father. I was so scared. Thank you for being right here with me. Amen.

Trish struggled up out of sleep again, but this time she knew the sound. Her alarm. She reached over and hit the snooze button.

She still felt like a field of fourteen Thoroughbreds had used her body for a track when the alarm buzzed again. If she didn't get going now, she wouldn't get a shower, and if she didn't get a shower, she wouldn't make it to the track. She dragged her loudly protesting body out of bed and, after turning on the shower, stood under the pounding water until she could think.

What had the dream meant? In the Bible God used dreams to tell people things. Was He doing that now with her?

She thought back to the night before. David had helped her with her chemistry again. She'd fallen asleep asking God to help her make a decision. That was it. To quit or not to quit.

Her head ached. Along with most of the rest of her body.

She didn't feel a whole lot better by the time she arrived at the track but at least she was moving.

Dense fog muffled the morning sounds of the track. The cold mist only added to Trish's feeling of confusion.

"Let's wait a bit before we take the first one out," Adam said when she joined him and David at the stalls.

"Yeah, I love this sunny California," David said, shivering beside them. He'd brought his own car today in case he decided to do something different. "This is colder than winter at home."

"If we were across the bay, on the other side of the hills, there'd be no fog at all." Adam stuck his hands in his pockets. "Clear as a bell with the sun pinking the sky behind Mount Diablo."

"You're kidding. Let's go there."

"No racetrack out there either." Trish tucked her chin down into her jacket collar.

"Coffee's hot. Come on." Adam led the way back to the office.

Trish accepted a mug and wrapped both her hands around it. While she didn't much care for coffee, it was good for warming hands. She added a spoonful of sugar and two of mocha-flavored creamer. The closer it came to hot chocolate, the better she liked it.

But the hot drink didn't help much out on the track. Dawn lightened the sky so that the fog floated more dingy white than gray. The jingle of gear, people's voices, and horses snorting still sounded hollow.

The wind sneaked around Trish's neck and up her cuffs, any place it could get in to chill her body. She poured herself a second cup of coffee between mounts. And this was August.

But by the time they were finished, the sun shone bright and the track slipped back into its usual cheery morning atmosphere. All except for Trish. She listened to the others discuss the training schedule and how the horses had done.

Adam and Carlos debated the relative merits of one race over another for one of the horses. David cleaned up the last of the bagels.

Trish was just leaving to go to the car to pick up her chemistry books when her agent called. Adam handed her the phone.

"I wanted to make sure you heard that the horse you were riding this afternoon was scratched," he said.

"Great." Trish couldn't keep the disgust out of her voice.

"Sorry. Talk to you later."

Trish hung up the phone and, at the question on David's face, told him what had happened.

"I could spend the afternoon at the beach if we didn't have that gelding running."

"You don't have to stay."

"Or we could go into San Francisco."

"You have to study. Remember?"

"Yeah, I know. You want to help me?"

"For a while. Then I need to go shopping. You and Rhonda aren't the only ones who need school clothes."

"You'll live in shorts most of the year. I heard it can get pretty hot there." Trish got herself a bottle of water out of the fridge. "You want to study here or at the condo?"

That afternoon Trish returned to the track in time for the fifth race. She walked with Adam and David over to the grandstands, where they all leaned on the rail.

The sun beat down hot on their heads and shoulders.

"Hard to believe the chill of the fog this morning, and hot like this now," David commented after wiping the sweat off his face for the second time.

"The paper said it was 115 in Phoenix yesterday." Adam wiped his forehead too.

David groaned. "And Tucson is farther south. Thank God for air conditioning."

Trish listened to their conversation with only half an ear. When the bugle called for parade to post, she watched for number four. Gimmeyourheart trotted out on the track.

"I hate his name," she muttered as the gelding crossed in front of them.

"You don't have to like it. They call him Sam for short," David reminded her. "Just hope he wins so we start recouping our investment."

"If you want him to win, I better leave."

"Trish." David poked her with his elbow.

Trish gave him an I-told-you-so look when Gimmeyourheart came in sixth. "Well, Carlos, I sure hope you're right about what that beast can become. Looks to me like he needs a long vacation." *Kinda like me.* The thought galloped through her mind.

"You wait." Carlos turned from the rail with the rest of them. "When you ride him tomorrow, you'll see what I'm talking about."

Trish could see the fog rolling over the tops of the coastal hills as they left the track. The fog was coming back over the land and into her heart.

You better get a smile on your face before your mother sees you, her nagger whispered. Trish slammed the door on her mind at the same time she slammed the door of her car.

She felt the good old tears congregating as soon as she saw her mother's face in the crowd. And when Marge's eyes held the same telltale sheen, Trish gave up. They held each other close and then wiped their eyes at the same time.

"Come on, you two crybabies. I'm starved." David took his mother's bag and nodded toward the exit.

But when Trish looked up at him, she caught him blinking too.

"You look all grown up in that outfit," Marge said as they crossed the skywalk to the short-term parking lot. "It's beautiful."

"Thanks." Trish glanced down at the rust silk blouse. "I love the feel of silk. Now I know why people rave about it all the time."

"Yeah, but the dry-cleaning bills are atrocious."

"No, this is washable. The tag says so. Rhonda and I wouldn't have gotten them otherwise. You should stay long enough so we can go shopping."

Marge looked to David walking beside her. "Is this *our* Trish, or did you bring a substitute?"

"Mother." Trish squeezed her mom's arm. "Even I can grow up. And besides, the Stanford Mall is something else."

Trish pointed out landmarks as they drove to a restaurant high on the hill overlooking the entire bay. So far the clouds remained to the west, so they enjoyed the lights coming on around the bay. The San Mateo bridge arched high on the west side and then down to water level, crossing the bay like a belt with a fancy buckle.

"Okay, what's happening?" Marge asked after they'd enjoyed their dinner and conversation.

"Trish still says if she loses tomorrow, she's quitting."

"Thank you, David." She wanted to kick him in the shins.

"Want to talk about it?" Marge asked gently.

Trish shook her head but the words came anyway. "I just can't stand losing all the time. I've been wondering if this is God's way of telling me to quit; maybe only a year, but for now. I hate the word quit. I could think of it as time off."

"I've been praying about this too." Marge patted Trish's hand. "I remember your dad saying how he always felt you had a gift for animals, especially horses. He really believed that you had all the attributes of a top-notch jockey. Sometimes I thought it was just a dream of his, but when you did so well I began to believe him." She traced around the top of her water glass. "And now I believe you are a good jockey going through a terrible time. But more than a jockey, you are my daughter. And you are becoming an adult." She reached out to clasp Trish's hand. "All I know for certain is that that will never change. You must make the decision. I won't make it for you. But whatever you decide, we'll live with it."

"All these races that I've prayed to win, and now what?"

"Would you trade a minute of it?" When Trish shook her head, Marge smiled. "How about we share a dessert?" The waiter returned to fill the coffee cups and Trish's iced tea. At their nods, she asked the waiter to bring the dessert tray.

"Let's get two," David said when he saw the fancy desserts.

They settled on a tart with raspberries and kiwi fruit on top and cheesecake with fresh strawberries. Trish looked longingly at the mud pie but gave it up. The piece was so huge it could have been a whole meal.

As they each took bites from both desserts, Trish brought up her dream from the night before. "It was so strange; all the horses kept running away from me. Even Spitfire. I cried and cried for him to come back but it was like he couldn't."

Marge leaned on her elbows on the table. "Sounds to me like it has something to do with racing. How did you feel?"

"Afraid. Mad. Like crying. I was crying in the dream." Trish nibbled on one of the raspberries. "It was like they were all mad at me."

"Sure." David snorted. "'Cause you'd quit racing."

"But I haven't quit yet."

"But you might. Who knows. It was just a dream anyway."

"You can pray for an answer to the dream too, you know," Marge said. "Oh, and by the way, I almost forgot. I have something for you." Trish waited while her mother dug in her purse. "Here." Marge handed Trish an envelope.

Trish opened it and drew out a packet of three-by-five cards. The top was in her father's handwriting. She flipped through them, the tears blurring her eyes. Some were in her handwriting. All of them were Bible verses, the verses that had covered her wall. The verses she had thrown in the trash.

"Oh, Mom." She threw her arms around her mother. "How come you're so smart? I felt terrible about throwing them away."

"I knew you would—someday. When I was dumping the trash, I found them. If you didn't want them, I did."

That night, kneeling beside her bed, Trish changed her prayer. Up to then it had always been, "God, what do I do?" Now she prayed, "Father, not my will but yours. Whatever you want me to do, that's what I want."

Just before she fell asleep, she was sure she heard her nagger give a deep sigh. Was it approval?

She awoke to butterflies but they calmed down during morning works. She and Firefly trotted around the track like this wasn't a big day, just an ordinary one.

When Trish began her warm-up routine before the race, the butterflies flipped cartwheels along with her hamstring stretches. They fluttered up into her throat when she laid her head on her knees. But they were flying in formation when she stood beside David and Adam in the saddling paddock.

"Riders up," the announcer called over the loudspeaker.

Trish blinked her eyes as David boosted her into the saddle. Firefly snorted and pawed one front hoof. The sights and sounds around them receded like the fog in the morning. Trish looked from David to her mother to Adam. They all seemed to shimmer in a sea of peace, surrounded by a halo of light in the shadowed stalls.

The bugle notes echoed from outside. The parade to post. Would this be her last one?

Your will, Father, your will.

Her mother's smile said I love you. Words weren't necessary.

"You can do it, Tee." David gripped her knee. He too was saying I love you in the best way he knew how.

"Just do your best." Adam backed the filly up and led her out to the pony rider.

Trish could hear the announcer introducing the horses as they trotted into the sunshine from under the stands. The roar of the crowd set Firefly to dancing.

"You love it, don't ya, girl?" Trish waved to the stands and stroked the filly's arched neck. She felt like laughing out loud. What an incredibly wonderful, beautiful day! A song from Bible camp ran through her mind: *Rise and shine, and give God the glory, glory. . . .* The tune made her want to sing and dance.

The filly did it for her. They entered the starting gate, all seven horses without a slip-up. Trish and Firefly settled for the break.

The gates flew open and they were off. The field bunched together and didn't start stringing out until the first turn. Firefly ran easily with two other horses, Trish letting one set the pace with Firefly hanging to the right and just off the pace. Going down the backstretch, the three ran four lengths in front of the rest of the field.

Trish crooned her love song into the filly's ears as they went into the far turn. Soon it would be time to make their move. The horse behind them pulled even as they came out of the turn. The jockey in front went to the whip.

"Now! Let's go, Firefly." The filly lengthened out. She gained on the front-runner, stride by stride. The horse on her right dropped off. With a furlong to go, they ran neck and neck.

"Come on, girl, you can do it." Trish willed the filly forward. She could see the finish line. "Come on."

Firefly stretched again. Her hooves and heart thundered together. She inched in front. By a nose, by a neck. They won by a length.

"Thank you, Father!" Trish yelled to the heavens, her whip raised in salute.

She pulled the filly down to a gallop, then a lope, and turned back to the front of the grandstands. To the winner's circle.

"You did it, girl. I knew you had it in you." She stroked the filly's neck.

David got to her first. He thumped on her knee, failing miserably at racing decorum. He led them through the fence and over to the raisers.

Marge and Adam met them in the winner's circle. Trish sniffed back her tears until she saw her mother's face, wet with joy.

"Good ride, my dear." Adam looked up at her and nodded. They lined up around Firefly and posed for the official pictures. The camera flashed. Trish leaped to the ground and more cameras flashed. Trish stepped on the scale, all the while her heart singing, *Give God the glory, glory.*

"You sure got your answer," David said as they walked Trish back to the jockey room for her things.

"Yep, that I did."

As she came out, a reporter stopped her. "Got a minute, Trish?"

Trish looked at him in surprise. "Sure, why?"

"This is your first win since the Belmont, right?" Trish nodded. "I've been following your career," the young man said. "Think we'll head this 'The Comeback Kid.' You've had a hard time and I want you to know I've been rooting for you."

Trish swallowed her state of shock and answered a few more questions.

"Is that right about a possible endorsement for Chrysler?"

"What?" Trish blinked at the question. "Where'd you hear that?"

"I have my sources." His grin said he wouldn't tell her.

"Well, it's news to me."

"Here's my card. When you know more, would you give me a call?"

Trish shrugged. "Sure, I guess."

"Endorsement!" David choked on the word.

"Yeah, right. He's got his wires crossed, that's all. Can we get something to drink? I'm dying."

That night in bed, Trish thought back to the winner's circle. It was like she was standing off to the side so she could see everyone there. David held the reins, standing in front of Firefly's shoulder. Adam, Martha, and Carlos stood behind on the raisers. Just in front of the filly's head stood her mother, and behind her shoulder, a man with a smile to dim the noon sun.

She could finally picture her father with the family. And what better place than in the winner's circle?

Monday evening David drove Trish to the College of San Mateo. "Now, I'll be sitting out here praying for you. Tee, you're going to do fine. Just remember to ask for help; pray your way through this."

"But I need a B to get a C out of the class." Trish clamped her lips on her moan. *I've got to pray my way through this.* She squared her shoulders and marched into the classroom.

An hour and a half later she returned to the car, sank into the seat, and closed her eyes.

"Rough?"

"Yeah." Sprinklers sang on the lawn. Trish sniffed. They'd mowed the grass recently. She took in a deep breath. "Davey, my boy, there were only two questions I had no idea about. And only a few I had to guess on. I *think* I did it."

"Mom's waiting at the Finleys'. They think we should go for hot fudge sundaes. What do you think?"

"Yes!" She turned the ignition. "Yes! Yes! Yes!"

That night Trish and Marge sat out on the deck before going to bed. "I am so proud of you," Marge said after letting the night silence steal over them.

"Me too." Trish looked up at the stars over the eucalyptus trees. "You know what?"

"What?"

"I think I learned something."

"Only one thing?" Marge chuckled. "What is it?"

"I think when things get tough, all you can do is grab God's hand and slog through."

"True, that's the best way."

"And if you slog long enough, you'll come out of the mist . . ." She paused. "And into the sunlight."

"Ah, Tee, you are wise beyond your years."

The breeze set the leaves above them to whispering.

"I have something for you to take to Pastor Mort."

"What?"

"A letter, and the title to the other convertible. He can use the money from it however he wants, but it's to be a memorial to Dad. That okay?"

"Trish, that's more than okay. You truly are your father's daughter."

Trish was sure she heard a chuckling on the breeze.

I'd like to thank all those kids who read my books and beg for more. Writers need readers. We're all in this together. That's part of being in the family of God. Hoorah!

SECOND WIND

BOOK EIGHT

To my mother.
Cheerleader, friend,
confidante,
and my shining example of
love in action.

Chapter
01

Why is it when everything finally starts going great again, something changes? Tricia Evanston chewed on the question as she settled into her favorite green canvas director's chair in Adam Finley's office at Bay Meadows Racetrack. She heaved a sigh of relief. Morning works had gone smoothly—for a change. But something wasn't right. Like a hunter sniffing the air, she could sense it.

Her brother David entered, rubbing his shoulder. "That horse should be sent to the glue factory."

Trish tucked her chin to hide the smile she couldn't resist. Gatesby was up to his old tricks. David had forgotten to duck.

"He's just playing." She toyed with the end of her dark, thick braid to keep from chuckling at the disgust on her brother's face.

"Yeah, well tell him to go play somewhere else, with someone else."

"Now, be honest. Think how much you'll miss him." She waved a hand to encompass the early morning track activity. "And all the rest of this when you're stuck in a library studying your brains out." Trish leaned back in her chair, one booted ankle crossed over the opposite knee. "Think of all the chemistry and yucky stuff you have to do."

"You forget. I like chemistry, not like someone else we all know and love." David tapped on the toe of her dusty boot.

"Here, you two. Have a bagel. We bought extra this morning in honor of David's last day." Owner/trainer Adam Finley opened the cardboard box and pulled the lids off the plastic containers of cream cheese. "I bought some of each so you children wouldn't have to fight for your favorites."

"Children! I like that." Trish bounded to her feet and tried to muscle David away from the box. "I want the raisin bagel with raisin-walnut cream cheese."

David grabbed her choice and held it up in the air. "What'll you give me?"

"A sock in the gut, you goof." Trish drew back her fist.

"Children, children, I thought we settled this long ago." Marge Evanston sailed through the door, shaking her head and grinning at the same time. "You'd think they'd act more grown-up by now, wouldn't you?" She winked at Adam, who watched the mock fight with a twinkle in his blue eyes.

"And you thought we invited you here for a serious meeting, right?" Adam smiled his welcome and rose to offer Marge his chair.

"Right. Trish, David gets to choose first. He probably won't be able to find bagels in Tucson, not that he'll have any time to look." Marge snagged a plain bagel out of the box and applied the vegetable cheese spread to the circular bread.

"He always gets to choose first, just 'cause he's bigger." Trish retrieved her bagel from her brother's grasp and handed him the one she knew he liked best. Licking cream cheese from her fingers, she pulled an orange juice from the refrigerator in the corner and leaped for her chair before David could steal it.

"You two sure are . . ."

"Full of the dickens?" Trish tried to look innocent.

"Better than what I was thinking." Marge slapped David's fingers away from her cup of coffee. "Thanks, Adam." She acknowledged the poured coffee. "Have they been like this every morning?"

"Naw. I think that finally winning a race has gone to Trish's head.

And David? Well, you know what happens when you get on the wrong side of Gatesby."

Marge groaned. "The wrong side or any side. Did his teeth break the skin this time?"

David shook his head, his mouth too full of bagel to answer.

Trish swallowed. "What do you mean, gone to my head? I was fine till he showed up." She licked more cheese from her fingers and eyeballed her brother. The glow inside her had nothing to do with the spices in the cream cheese. Yes, she had won yesterday. She and Firefly. Finally. But today the good feeling came just because her family was together.

If only—she clamped a lid on the thought. *If only* usually triggered memories of her father, who'd died just as she and Spitfire won the Belmont, and thus the Triple Crown, in June. Now at the end of August she could sometimes think of him without crying. She rolled her eyes upward and sniffed quickly. She didn't want to make the others feel sad today. David would leave in the morning for Tucson, Arizona, for his second year of college.

"Okay, let's get down to business." Adam pushed papers aside to set his coffee mug on the scarred wooden desk.

Trish blinked one more time. She'd won—barely.

She cocked her ankle over her knee again and locked her hands behind her head. Wouldn't it be something if they let her take Spitfire out of retirement and train him for the Breeder's Cup? Oh, to race the big, black colt again at Churchill Downs! She could feel the wind on her face . . . hear the crowd. She brought her attention back to the present with a thump.

"What do you mean, something funny's going on at Portland Meadows? I thought the season was a go . . . starting in September like always."

Marge shook her head. "I didn't want to have to tell you this until we got home, but there have been rumors."

"What kind of rumors?" Trish leaned her elbows on her denim-clad knees.

"Like the track won't open, for one thing." David wiped his mouth with a napkin. "But, you know, we've heard that before."

"So, what's new?" Trish stared from her mother to her brother and over to Adam.

"Some say it's just bad management, but . . ." Marge twisted her wedding ring on her finger.

"But . . . ?" Trish felt as if the starting gun was about to go off and her mount wasn't ready.

"But I don't know." Marge lifted a troubled gaze to her daughter. "I have a funny feeling, but I haven't had time to follow through on anything."

"What does Patrick think?" Since her father had hired the old jockey as trainer, Trish had grown to trust the Irishman's opinion.

Marge looked to David, as if seeking help.

"He thinks we should leave these horses down here until things are straightened out. Maybe ship some others down if we have to." David combed restless fingers through his dark, curly hair.

"But how could I ride then and still go to school?" Trish clamped her teeth against the rush of dread. They couldn't close The Meadows. They just couldn't. Not now when she'd finally won again and decided God wanted her to keep racing.

"That's why I haven't said anything. You know what your father always said about borrowing trouble. You could fly down here on the weekends, I guess." Marge shrugged. "There are no easy answers, Tee."

"But is the Thoroughbred Association doing anything about the situation?"

Marge shrugged again. "As I said, I haven't had time to follow any of this to the source."

Trish could tell her mother was feeling a bit pushed about the entire situation. What a bummer. Here she was, just beginning her senior year at Prairie High School. She couldn't miss a lot of classes this year. It was too important. Besides, she and her forever-friend, Rhonda, had so many plans.

"There's nothing you can do about it now," David said just before he stuffed the last of his bagel in his mouth. "We need to talk about the Breeder's Cup."

"Aye, that we do." Adam brushed a hand over his shiny dome, fringed by a fluff of white hair. "I plan on taking two horses to run that weekend, and I think Firefly has as good a chance as any in the Down's Handicap on Saturday. She ran well yesterday, and both Carlos and I think she's just coming into her own. I'd be glad to take her with us about ten days ahead, and Trish can fly in on that Thursday or Friday before."

"Who would you get to work them for you?" Trish hated the idea of someone else riding her horses in the morning. She should be the one doing that. She sneaked a peek at her mother.

"Don't even think it." Marge didn't crack a smile.

Trish shrugged. "As Dad always said, 'It doesn't hurt to dream.' " She turned to Adam. "Wouldn't it be something if we could run Spitfire in the Breeder's Cup? That was another of Dad's dreams, you know, having an entry in the Breeder's Cup."

"Sorry, Trish, you know our syndicate would never go along with that. Spitfire's too valuable at stud to risk an injury. Just think, maybe in three years you'll be running one of his sons at Churchill Downs."

Trish cupped her hands around her elbows. "Won't that be something?" She gave a wriggle of anticipation. "What if one of his colts, or even a filly, won the Triple Crown? I can just see it now."

David snapped his fingers in front of her eyes. "Calling Trish . . . come in, Trish. We're talking about right now. You can dream about another Triple Crown on your own time."

"Oh." She flashed her brother a brilliant grin. "Okay, okay, back to the present. You already know I would love to take Firefly to Kentucky." She turned to Adam.

"How about asking Red to ride for you? I'm sure he'll be riding there then." Trish felt a tingle race around her middle and gallop out to her fingers. Red Holloran had to be the nicest—no, not a good enough word—the sexiest, that's what Rhonda called him, sweetest, most fun. . . . She clamped off the words. Face it, she *really* liked that certain redheaded jockey. Just think, if she could spend two weeks back there . . . Her mind took off again.

"What about keeping the rest of our horses down here until we know what's happening up in Portland?" Marge asked. "Patrick suggested you might race the others too if Portland Meadows doesn't open."

Trish reentered reality with a thump. She carefully hid her thoughts behind a nod and a smile. If nobody else in their family was going to fix things at Portland Meadows, she'd look into it. There had to be a way to have racing in Portland this winter.

"That's decided then." Adam started writing on a pad on his desk. "I'll be sending my entries in today. You better do the same. I have extra forms here if you'd like." He dug in the file cabinet to his left and pulled out a file folder.

With the forms filled out, Marge rose to her feet. "Thanks, Adam, for all the care you've given us. You have no idea how much your friendship and advice, let alone keeping Trish down here, has meant." She extended her hand, but instead of shaking it, Adam pulled her into a hug.

"You've become like family to us, my dear. We couldn't have done any differently." His voice cracked on the words.

Trish felt that old familiar lump take up residence in her throat again. It threatened to choke her when she recognized the sheen of tears in her mother's eyes. She hugged her knees to her chest. Outside, down the line of green-painted stalls, a horse whinnied. Another answered.

"Thank you." Marge stepped back and drew a tissue from the pocket of her tan slacks. After blowing her nose, she tucked the tissue back and picked up her purse. "Martha and I are going to church. Anyone care to join us?"

"I'll go." David made a bank shot into the trash with his napkin and stood up.

"Tee?"

"I need to be back by noon. I ride in the fifth and seventh today."

"Good. Then we'll be able to worship together for a change." Marge turned to Adam. "You coming?"

"I'm right ahead of you." He stepped outside and told Carlos, the head groom, he'd be leaving.

When they all walked back to the parking lot, Trish shoved her hands in the back pockets of her jeans. After today, it would be just she and her mother. She cut off the sad thoughts and nudged David with her hip. Teasing him always made her feel better.

"We need to call the Shipsons to ask if we can come," she said to her mother as they reached the cars.

"Later—after church."

Trish forced her mind to concentrate on the service. Her thoughts kept skipping ahead to the visit with Spitfire. Every time she left him, she was afraid he would forget her.

Marge handed Trish the hymnbook as they rose to their feet. The look she gave her daughter left no doubt that she knew where Trish's mind roamed.

The young pastor stepped into the pulpit and looked over the congregation. His gaze seemed to stop at Trish, as if speaking right to her. "Let not your heart be troubled. . . . In my Father's house are many mansions; if it were not so, I would have told you." He closed the Bible and leaned forward.

Trish gritted her teeth and kept her eyes on the speaker. That had been one of her father's favorite passages. He often spoke of his Father's mansions. But when she tried to picture him there, she always felt the tears.

"What a comfort," the pastor said, "to know we will see our loved ones again. They are there waiting for us. Cheering us on. You know that chorus the children sing? 'Heaven is a wonderful place.' What a promise Jesus gave us!"

Marge slipped her hand into Trish's. She took David's on the other side and squeezed. Shoulder to shoulder, the three of them faced forward, still a family in spite of their loss.

Trish looked up to see the sun streaming through the stained-glass window of the shepherd with a lamb. The beams of light glinted off the gold cross on the altar, as if to restate the promise. When the organ music rose in the final hymn, Trish felt as if she'd truly been in a holy place. Her heart swelled along with the song. "Thank you, Father," Trish whispered under the strains of music. "I needed this."

That afternoon at the track Trish continued to feel the peace she'd found in church. While the colt under her danced and pranced his way to the starting gate, she entertained him with her song. The horse flicked his ears and snorted but walked flat-footed into the gate. Trish settled herself and him, a smile on her face and the song still singing in her heart.

The gate flew open. The gray colt broke. Trish exploded along with him and drove him toward the turn. With only six furlongs, they had no time to fool around.

The colt lengthened his stride. Neck and neck with a horse on their right, they left the field behind and headed for the finish line. Stride for stride the two dueled down the stretch. The other rider went to the whip. Trish leaned forward and sang into her mount's ears, "Go, fella, you can do it. Come on now, baby."

The colt lengthened his stride again. He pulled forward by a head, a neck, and then the contender disappeared behind them. Trish and her mount surged across the finish line two lengths in the lead. Trish let him slow down, her jubilation punctuated with a "Thank you, God!" at the top of her lungs.

Back at the Finleys' condo that evening, Trish called the Shipsons in Kentucky. When they learned of Trish's plan, they responded with delight. Trish hung up the phone and turned to Marge. "They can't wait until we get there. Mrs. Shipson—Bernice—is thrilled you are coming along." Trish danced a step and shuffle in delight. They were going to see Spitfire. "I better send Red a letter to let him know."

"Too late." David lay back on the couch. He stretched his arms above his head. "He'll be too busy to see you anyway." He ducked when Trish thumped him with the pillow. "Mother, call off your kid," David laughed.

"Guess I'll call him then." Trish flipped through her address book for the Holloran number and headed for the bedroom to make the call in private. After her conversation, she returned to the living room. "He's racing at Keeneland, his mother said. She'll let him know I called."

"Did you ask how he's doing? Racewise, that is," Marge asked from her place in the corner of the eight-foot couch.

"Better than me, that's for sure. Guess he's been in the money most of the summer. Mrs. Holloran says they haven't seen much of him at all."

"Will he be riding at Louisville?" Adam asked.

"I guess." Trish refused to look at her brother when she heard his snort. She could feel the warmth begin at her collarbone and work its way upward. David could always make her blush about Red. "You leaving before works or after?" She felt like bopping him with the pillow again. A couple of times, just to let him know how much she cared.

"About the time you do. That's a long haul to Tucson." David stretched again and rose to his feet. "The car's all packed." He crossed the room to Margaret Finley's rocker. "Thank you for all you've done for me. After staying with you, I know why Trish calls this her second home."

Margaret set her needlepoint on the floor and stood to give him a hug. "You come back anytime. The farm is even closer to you than this, so if you need a weekend away from school, just let us know." She stood on tiptoe to kiss his cheek. "I'll bake an apple pie just for you."

"See you in the morning, son." Adam waved from his laid-back recliner. "Just remember, if you ever need a job, there's always an opening with me."

"We have first dibs on him." Marge uncurled her legs and stood. "See you all in the morning. Come on, you two. I'll tuck you in."

The three followed one another up the stairs.

Trish told David good-night at the door and preceded her mother into the bedroom they shared. "You want to go shopping in the morning after works at the track? Tomorrow's my day off."

"Is this my Trish inviting her mother to go shopping?" Marge raised her eyebrows in mock surprise.

"Rhonda and I had a blast. We could too."

"I know. We will. And if we keep busy enough, maybe I'll be able to not think about David and his trek for a few minutes."

"Bad, huh?" Trish sank down on the edge of the bed. "Me too. I keep hoping things will go back to normal, but I can't find normal anymore."

Chapter

02

Surely it was the fog making her eyes water.

David hugged his mother one last time, and then Trish. "Take care of yourself, twerp." He tapped the end of her nose and grinned—a jaunty grin that didn't quite make it to his eyes. "Bye all." He waved and slid behind the wheel of his car, which matched Trish's red LeBaron convertible.

Trish heard Marge sniff as the red taillights disappeared in the fog. *Please take good care of him, God,* Trish prayed as she blew her nose. *And us. Our family just keeps getting smaller.*

Adam laid a hand on her shoulder and squeezed. He too seemed to be suffering from early foggy morning nose dripping. Trish revised her prayer. Maybe their family was really getting bigger.

"You could go back to bed for a few hours," she told her mother as she and Adam prepared to leave for the track. "One of us needs plenty of sleep before we attack those stores."

Marge wiped her eyes and shivered in the chill. "Think I will. Unless I could do something for you at the track."

Trish caught her jaw before it bounced on her chest. Was this really *her* mother talking? "Thanks, but you sleep. See you around ten or so."

Trish checked the clock on the dashboard as she turned the ignition. Ten to five. They were running late. She followed Adam's taillights down the hill and past the guarded entry to the condominium complex. Once on El Camino Real, the golden light from the fog-piercing streetlamps shone on the early commuters.

Trish let her mind fly north to Portland and the problems at Portland Meadows. Somebody had to do something, but what? And who? Was there really something going on that shouldn't be?

She tucked those thoughts away when she parked her car in the parking lot and got out to walk with Adam to the stalls. If she allowed her mind to really wander, it would head back home for a few more snoozes.

The morning passed without a hitch. Gatesby even acted like a gentleman, rubbing his forehead against her chest rather than sneaking in a nip or three. Trish followed Adam's instructions and warmed up Sarah's Pride before letting her out at the half-mile pole to breeze her. She mentally ticked off the seconds as the poles blurred by and pulled the excited filly down again at the mile. They trotted back to the exit gate, the filly pulling at the bit all the while.

"You've come a long way, girl," Trish sang to the twitching ears as the filly kept track of everything going on around her. "You behave real well now. Wait till Patrick sees you." Sarah's Pride snorted and tossed her head, sending bits of foamy spit flying into Trish's face.

Trish wiped off a glob with a gloved hand and settled back into the saddle as Adam fell into step with them.

"Well, what do you think?" His blue eyes twinkled when he looked up at the girl on the horse.

"Fourteen and seven tenths." Trish named the time she estimated they'd used.

Adam shook his head. "You amaze me. For one so young . . ." He held up the stopwatch. "You were only five tenths of a second off. That's about your best time." He patted the filly on the shoulder. "And you did right well, young lady. Nice to see you mind your manners."

"You've a stakes race for her this time, right?" Trish kept a firm hand on the reins. She wanted no surprises this morning.

"Umm-humm." Adam nodded and smiled greetings to everyone who walked past. Whether he admitted it or not, he was a popular person, not to mention a respected trainer at Bay Meadows. "I thought she was ready, and this breeze proves me right. She's well conditioned, and I think we've broken her bad habits. We'll see if Patrick knows his stuff, won't we?"

Patrick O'Hern, the ex-jockey/trainer her father had hired and who was now helping Runnin' On Farm build a larger string, had recommended they put an offer on Sarah's Pride in a claiming race at Pimlico. He saw the potential, and her father had agreed.

"She's lookin' good," Carlos, the head groom, said when Trish jumped to the ground. "Your agent came by . . . said for you to call him."

"Gracias, Carlos." Trish ducked under the filly's neck and headed for the office. She only had Gimmeyourheart to work and she'd be finished. Hopefully her agent had plenty of mounts for her this week.

She felt like spinning round and round, like a top flashing reds and golds in its humming dance. Friday evening they'd be flying to Kentucky to see Spitfire.

Her imaginary top wobbled and toppled over. After Friday she wouldn't be racing for—for who knew how long. Here she'd been nearly ready to quit, and now the thought of it made her throat tighten. Would she ever understand herself?

She finished marking the four mounts her agent had for her in her calendar and stuffed it back into her pack. That gave her nine mounts in four days. Things were looking up.

After riding Gimmeyourheart, Trish forced him to walk back to the stables. "He acts like he has no idea what he's supposed to do out there," she said as she kicked her right foot out of the irons and slid to the ground. "No wonder he didn't do well."

"Maybe he was just testing you." Carlos stripped off the saddle and cloth while Juan, Trish's favorite stableboy, prepared a soapy, warm water bucket. "What about that hoof?"

"Feels like he favors it. You sure it's all healed?"

"Maybe we should send him out to the farm and let him loose for a while. Since you don't know whether Portland will start or not in a couple of months, let's give him another rest." Adam checked each hoof and felt for any heat in the fetlocks. "Seems fine, but . . ." He shook his head. "You watch . . . when he comes back, he'll be a sizzler."

Trish hoped the doubt didn't show on her face.

When she got back in her car, the first thing she saw was PTL! written in huge letters on a Post-it she'd stuck to her dash earlier. Praise the Lord. She'd promised to do just that—in everything—as the Bible said and her father had done. Her nagger seemed to stretch and uncurl on her shoulder to chuckle in her ear. *What's it been? Two days? Three? And no praise. I told you you couldn't do it. Or wouldn't.*

Trish wished she could brush him away like a pesky fly. She studied the slip of pink paper. Good reminder. She turned the ignition and put the car into gear. "I will praise the Lord. Thank you for the sunshine." That one was easy. "Thank you for taking care of David as he travels." That one was hard. "I praise you for helping me win again." Super easy.

Streets and stores, cars and pedestrians, flashed past in her peripheral vision as she struggled to find ten things to be grateful for. She had only promised to do three a day, but she had several days to make up for. "Thank you, Jesus, that Mom is here and we are going shopping." Easy. She pushed her black sunglasses up on her nose with one finger. Portland. How could she praise God for the mess in Portland? She tried the words out several ways. Nothing felt right. She sucked in a deep breath as if she were preparing to dive. "Thank you that you know what is happening up there and you can . . ." She paused. Yes, God *could* take care of things. But would He?

She saluted the guard at the gate to the condominiums and drove on up the hill. Marge waved at her from the front door. Trish grabbed her bag and leaped up the steps. *Thank you for my mother.* That was certainly a lot easier now than it used to be.

Marge was as totally overwhelmed by the Stanford Mall as Trish and Rhonda had been.

"You ever think that you can afford to buy from any of these stores now?" Trish asked as they looked from Neiman Marcus to I. Magnin and over to Saks.

Marge turned, shaking her head as she answered. "But why would I want to? I don't really *need* anything."

"I know. But you could if you wanted to." Trish took her mother by the arm. "I guess it's just that all these years you've made do, bought stuff for us kids when we needed it and not something you needed because we couldn't afford both. Now I want to buy *you* something for a change. I can afford it."

"So can I."

"Too bad. It's not the same. You want to hit the fancy stores or see where Rhonda and I found our cool outfits?"

Marge squeezed Trish's hand against her side. "Both."

By three o'clock the number of packages had grown to fill all four of their arms. "You know that phrase 'Shop till you drop'?" Marge set her shopping bags down on the sidewalk.

Trish nodded as she followed her mother's actions.

"I dropped . . . about an hour ago." Marge shrugged her shoulders and rubbed her hand where the bags' skinny handles had dug a groove. "And I'm starved."

"Me too. Let's take this stuff to the car, and then I know of a super-good deli. Their dessert tray is to die for."

"Sounds good to me." They wended their way across the palm-tree-studded parking lot to the red convertible. Marge helped Trish put the packages in the trunk and then sank down on the car seat. "How come shopping makes me more tired than cleaning house all day, even doing the windows?"

"Yeah, I'd rather muck stalls for four hours." Trish leaned against the front fender. She clasped her hands above her head and twisted from side to side. "That rust suit and hat will be a standout in the winner's circle at Churchill Downs. You're movie-star material in it." Trish turned to look—really look—at her mother. "You know, Mom, if you wanted to, you could—"

Marge held up a hand. "Don't say it. I am not going to color my hair or fuss with my makeup or wear the latest style. That's just not me."

"That rust suit is pretty stylish." Trish rolled her lips to keep from laughing. "Come on, Mom, ya gotta go with the flow."

Marge heaved herself to her feet. "Just flow me to food before I flow right down the drain from hunger." She stopped when they started back across the asphalt. "You think maybe I better take that suit along so we can find some shoes to match?"

Trish locked her arm in her mother's. "It's right here in the bag." She swung the shopping bag she carried in her other hand. "And you need boots too."

"We're going to have to buy another suitcase for me to take all this home," Marge pretended to grumble.

"That's okay. I know where the luggage store is. I had to find one for Rhonda, remember?"

Later that night, after showing all their treasures to Margaret, Trish and her mother sat out on the deck watching the moon come up over the Eastbay hills. The evening breeze rustled in the palm fronds as birds twerped and tweeted in the branches, settling in for the night.

Trish lifted her face to catch the scent of jasmine drifting from the ground cover on the hill beyond them.

"You have time to take me to the airport on Wednesday?" Marge lay back on the green and white padded chaise lounge. "Oh, this smells so good."

"Wednesday. Why don't you just fly out of here with me on Friday? There's no sense making two flights if you don't have to."

"But I have so much to do at home."

"It'll wait. Besides, Patrick can handle everything with the horses. Consider this your vacation." Trish closed her eyes and breathed in deeply. When a yawn caught her unaware, she patted her mouth and yawned again.

"Sounds like you're about ready for bed."

"I know. So what do you think?"

"I'm too comfortable to think. I'll play Scarlett O'Hara and think about it tomorrow." Marge stretched full length, like a kitten awaking from a deep sleep. "I'll stay. Now that I even have clothes to wear, who needs to go home?"

"Great!" Trish swung her feet to the deck. "If you want my car in the morning to go shopping . . ."

Marge groaned.

" . . . or anything, I can ride with Adam." Trish stood up. "And if you stay out here much longer, the mosquitoes will get you." She slapped at one on her arm. "Good night."

Finding three things to be thankful for was easy when Trish said her prayers: shopping, the peaceful look on her mother's face, and the call from David saying he'd made it safely. "Thank you that I get to see Spitfire on Friday." She paused. "And you are taking care of the mess in Portland, aren't you? Amen." She heard her mother return from the bathroom. "Night, Mom."

"Night, Trish." Marge stopped at her daughter's bed and bent down for a good-night kiss. "God loves you and so do I."

Trish felt the immediate rush of tears to the back of her eyes. Her father had always said that to her along with a good-night hug. "Me too." She swallowed the quiver in her voice and turned on her side. Margaret Finley had said the tears came unbidden for years after losing someone you love. And for Trish it had been only months. But at least they stopped now and the pain was more like an ache.

The week flew by with Trish winning one race, placing in two, coming up with a show, and at least getting paid for running the others around the track. The day she won she found tons to be grateful for . . . and the others? Well, as the psalmist David said, praise sometimes was a sacrifice.

Thursday night Trish closed her Bible after reading a couple of psalms where David moaned and groaned. But he always praised God somewhere in them. She hadn't been in the top four in either race. Moaning looked good.

But her heart felt overflowing with praises. Tomorrow she would see Spitfire.

In the morning Gatesby nearly left her a painful reminder to pay attention, but his teeth closed only on her shirt. "Whew. That was close." Trish jerked on his halter and shook her finger at him. "You want to be sent home, you dopey horse? I thought you were my friend."

"He's laughing at you," Juan said, his Mexican accent more pronounced around his giggle.

"I know. And you are too because this time you weren't the target." Trish tried to glare at him, but her mouth wouldn't stay straight. The corners kept tipping up in a grin.

"Sí." Juan rubbed his shoulder. "From yesterday."

Trish kept her eyes and ears open wide for the rest of the morning. She sure didn't need any accidents to mess up this day. Their flight left at one. She said good-bye to all the horses, with a special reminder to Firefly to keep improving. Her big chance was coming up in October.

"I'll see you all next Friday night." She paused in the door to the office. "You want anything from Kentucky?"

"Get outta here." Adam shooed her out the door. "And you be nice to that certain redheaded jockey. He might not know how to handle a California girl."

Trish felt the blush start flaming on her neck and explode to her cheekbones. She shook her head as she jogged out to the parking lot. Would she be a blusher for the rest of her natural life? The wind in her face felt especially good while she drove back to the condo.

Trish stared out the window of the 727, the words "California girl" stuck on continuous replay in her mind. She leaned her head back against the seat, listening to the roar of the plane's engines, and tried to relax. Had she changed this summer? Would Red still like her as much as he said in the cards he wrote? Would she still like him?

Chapter

03

Dark had overrun dusk by the time they landed in Lexington.

Donald and Bernice Shipson met them with hugs and laughter when they came off the plane.

"He's fine," Donald Shipson answered Trish's question before she could ask it. "I'd have brought him along if there were any way possible." He took Marge's carry-on bag and led them off to the baggage claim.

The drive to BlueMist Farms seemed like a transcontinental trip. Trish could feel her foot pressing against the floorboard as if she could make the car go faster by sheer willpower. They drove directly to the parking area near the stallion barn. A mercury light cast a blue-white sheen on the crushed gravel, but it was no rival for the moon riding high in the sky. The cupolaed stallion barn threw its own hulking shadow. A carriage lamp glowed golden against the white barn wall.

"Do you think he'll remember me?" Trish voiced the doubt that had crept in when she wasn't looking.

"The horse that tips all but Runnin' On Farm hats? You watch. He'll be as excited as you are." The tall, elegantly slim horse owner shook his head. "That is one smart stud we have there. He figured out how to open his stall one day. Followed Timmy right out the door. So now we put a horse-proof fastener on it."

Trish felt like skipping and twirling down the wide path. Not too long now till she saw Spitfire. As they neared the barn, Trish whistled the high-low tone with which she always called her horses. She waited for only a breath before she heard a stallion's penetrating whistle followed by Spitfire's whinny. She would recognize it anywhere. He called again. She could hear him banging a hoof against the stall wall.

"I think your friend is calling you." Donald Shipson beckoned toward the barn door. "Come on, I'll turn on the lights."

Trish whistled again as she reached the door, this time softly. Spitfire's nicker brought tears to her eyes. It felt like years since she'd seen him, even though it had been less than two months.

Spitfire blinked in the sudden light, but he tossed his head and nickered again as if Trish couldn't get there quickly enough. His nostrils quivered in a soundless love call. Trish buried her face in his thick, coarse mane and hung on, letting her tears wet the shiny black coat.

Spitfire heaved a sigh as if he too had come home. He rested his head on her shoulder and closed his eyes when her fingers found all his favorite scratching places. Trish stroked his ears and down his cheek. After her tears dried, she turned around so she could really look at him. "How ya doin', big guy?" Spitfire raised his nose so she would scratch under his chin. Trish tickled his whiskers and giggled when he whiskered her hand.

"I don't even have a carrot for you." She stroked her hands down his face and rubbed up around his ears.

Spitfire leaned against her and closed his eyes again.

"Not keeping you up too late, am I?" Trish used her fingertips to tickle his whiskery upper lip. Spitfire licked her hand and whuffled at the familiar scent. When Trish raised her head, she caught the gleam of tears in her mother's eyes.

"Guess he remembers me, huh?" Trish swallowed the last of her own tears and hugged her horse again. "Tomorrow we'll go for a ride, okay?" But when she stepped away, he nickered and pawed the straw in his huge box stall.

"You may have to spend the night down here," Bernice Shipson said with a smile. "And here I have your room all ready for you."

Trish stepped back and let Spitfire rub his forehead on her chest. "Now you go back to sleep and I'll see you in the morning." She shoved his head away. "Go on now, you heard me." Spitfire tossed his head, his forelock swinging in the motion. But this time when she moved away, he just stood there, dark eyes alert, nostrils quivering.

"It's okay. I'll be here to feed you in the morning." Trish backed away. Spitfire pawed once, then stood perfectly still, the tips of his ears nearly touching as he watched Trish leave. He whinnied again after they closed the door, and then silence.

"Seems he knows every word you say." Donald Shipson shook his head. "You two are some pair."

"My dad always said Spitfire and I were soul mates from when he was foaled. We just understand each other." Trish took her place in the backseat of the car. *Thank you, God.* Her prayer wafted silently upward. She'd mentioned her father without tearing up. That had to be a first.

Trish fell asleep counting her blessings. Today had been easy to find three things—last count she remembered was eleven. But then, who was counting?

Early morning in Kentucky fell soft on her skin as Trish jogged down to the stallion barn. A bright red cardinal serenaded her from a stately elm tree, then flitted across the sloping drive and sang the chorus to his mate. The rising sun cast glittering diamonds on the grass bent with dew. Off in a manicured paddock, two babies kicked up their heels and raced the fence line. Trish inhaled a breath of pure joy. While later in the day it would be hot and muggy, right now felt soft like thistledown.

She heard a stallion trumpet, but it wasn't Spitfire's voice.

Someone whistled a happy tune from the barn ahead of her. Trish stopped and threw her three-tone whistle into the air, a gift to the horse she came to visit.

Spitfire answered immediately. A full-blown whinny, not just a nicker. He whinnied again and Trish heard a hoof bang the wooden wall.

"Easy now, me boyo, easy." A man's voice, with the words sounding more like "aisey," told Trish that Timmy O'Ryan, Spitfire's personal groom, was already in attendance.

Trish strode through the open door, bits of carrots she'd begged from the kitchen stuffed in her pockets. Spitfire, his entire being concentrated on the door, tossed his head and nickered again. With his head out the stall, he pushed against the blue webbing gate as if to lunge out to her.

"Morning, Trish. Donald said you'd be down early." Timmy left off brushing the glossy black coat and joined Spitfire at the gate.

"Hi, Timmy. Morning, Spitfire." Trish smoothed the black forelock and rubbed the colt's cheek.

"Himself here's been awaitin' for you. I went ahead and fed him since I knew you'd want to ride."

"Thanks. How ya doin', fella?" Trish held out two carrot pieces. Spitfire snuffled her hair and blew in her face before lipping the carrots. As he crunched, he rested his forehead against her chest so she could reach his ears easily.

"You big baby." Trish rubbed all his favorite places while she talked. "Been a while since anyone's been on your back. You gonna behave yourself?" Spitfire nuzzled her pocket for another carrot.

"I'll get him saddled and then bring around a mount." Timmy pushed his porkpie hat back on his head. "He sure is happy to see you."

"I'll saddle him, if you don't mind."

"Not at all." The slim man, garbed all in tan but for shiny black boots, crossed to the tack room and returned with an English saddle, pad, and bridle. "You don't need a racing saddle on him now, or would you rather have one?"

"No, that's fine." Trish took the saddle from him and set it over the half door of the stall. "Come on, fella, let's get ready to see the country."

While Trish set the saddle in place and hooked the girth, Spitfire watched her over his shoulder, as if not wanting her out of his sight. When she led him outside, he sighed and nuzzled her shoulder.

"You be careful now . . . no nipping." Trish let him droop his head over her shoulder while they waited for Timmy to join them. She stroked his nose, all the while murmuring the singsong she'd trained him with. Love words with their own special meaning. The colt's eyes drooped and his chin sank lower.

"Hard to believe he's that same ball of fire that won the Triple Crown." The groom led his mount up and stopped to give Trish a boost into the saddle. Then he swung aboard his horse and led the way down a lane between two black board fences that stretched over the gently rolling hills.

When they returned, Donald Shipson met them in the exercise ring off to the side of the two-story barn. "Breakfast's ready, Trish, so how about letting Timmy cool him out and brush him down? We're running today at Keeneland and thought maybe you and your mother would like to join us. Bernice says not to tell you our surprise."

Trish swung to the ground and let Spitfire rub his forehead against her shoulder. She had planned on spending more time with her horse, grooming and bathing him. She glanced up in time to see a wink flash between the two men. Something was up, all right.

She gave Spitfire the last carrot from her pocket and scratched between his ears while he munched. "See you later, fella. You be good now." Trish smoothed his forelock and handed Timmy the reins. "See you later too."

Spitfire nickered as she climbed in the pickup with Mr. Shipson. When Trish waved, he raised his head and sent his shrill whinny floating after her.

"What surprise?" Trish turned to the man driving.

"I promised not to tell." Shipson looked as innocent as a kid with his hand in the cookie jar.

"Not fair."

"I know, but it sure is fun." His soft Kentucky drawl floated on the air.

"What races are you in?"

"Second and seventh. There's a three-year-old filly I think you should look at while we're there. Almost claimed her myself, but right now I don't need any new animals. Patrick asked me to keep my eyes open." Shipson parked the pickup in front of the pillared plantation house. "Sure hope you're hungry. Sarah outdid herself she was so glad to hear you were coming. Said she'd get you convinced southern cooking has no equal, one way or another."

Trish groaned. "If I ate all she wanted me to, I'd weigh enough for

24

SECOND WIND ☊ Chapter 03

two jockeys." Together they climbed the three broad stairs to the double
doors with a stained-glass fanlight above them.

Trish discovered the surprise when she joined the Shipsons in the
saddling paddock for the second race. As the jockeys paraded down from
the jockey room, Red Holloran stopped at stall number three.

Trish felt her stomach catch on her kneecaps going down and plunk
about on her ankles. Yep, she still liked him. Her stomach didn't travel
so far for *any* guy—just this one.

The grin that split his freckled face and the powerful arms that
wrapped her in a hug told her the answer to her other question. Yep, he
still liked her. When he let her loose, her face matched his hair. She could
feel the heat, like a sunburn.

"You didn't know, did you?" Red asked as he kept her hand clasped
in his.

"No, I wondered why there was no message at the Shipsons'. Then
I was afraid you hadn't heard I was coming." Trish wished sheer mind
control could cut the flaming in her cheeks. That and the current that
sizzled up her arm.

"Riders up." The call echoed from the loudspeakers in the center of
the paddock.

Red let go of her hand. "You'll still be here when I'm done?"

Trish nodded. "How many mounts do you have today?"

"Four; two for BlueMist." Red accepted the mount from Donald Shipson. "Pray me a win." He touched his whip to his helmet and away they
went, Shipson leading until they picked up their pony rider.

When all eight entries filed out the tunnel, the group made their way
to the owner's box. "He's not only an excellent jockey but a fine young
man." Donald Shipson mounted the stairs beside Trish.

"Does he ride much for you?"

"Whenever I can get him. He's gotten pretty popular in the last few
months. Good hand with the horses and developing real skill in bringing a horse out of the pack. I think he'll become one of the greats if he
goes on like he has."

Trish thought about her last two months of not winning. Her father
had said much the same about her and look what happened.

She watched across the infield to where the horses were

25

entering the gates. As the shot fired, she sent her prayer for Red's safety heavenward.

It seemed so strange to be in the grandstand instead of down along the fence or, even better, mounted on one of the straining horses rounding the turn and making their first drive past the stands.

"He's right where I wanted him," Shipson said, his eyes fixed on the surging field. "Let that number one wear himself out with too fast a pace." He raised his binoculars as they moved into the backstretch.

Trish wished she'd brought some. It was easy to lose a bright red gelding in the midst of three others. And at that distance, the blue and white silks of BlueMist disappeared also.

Coming out of the turn, the blue and white silks on a bright red gelding pulled away from the two on either side, and with each stride the horse increased his lead. Red won by six lengths.

Trish heard herself screaming encouragement as the winner crossed the line and raised his whip in victory. She hugged her mother and danced in place until they paraded down to the winner's circle. This time, instead of standing in front of the horse, she joined the others on the risers behind. The camera flashed, the horse was led away, and she thumped Red on the arm as he accepted congratulations from the Shipsons.

"Thanks for the prayers," he whispered in her ear, all the while smiling and graciously acknowledging the good wishes from others around him.

"I only prayed for your safety, not a win." Trish smiled along with him.

"Thanks anyway. I'll see you after the seventh. Pray for more wins." He squeezed her hand and left to return to the jockey room.

He won again on Shipson's horse in the seventh, the largest race of the day. This time the excitement in the winner's circle crackled like an electric wire. Red had come from behind after a bad bump and won by only a nose.

Trish's heart still hammered after the near miss. She could tell that her *thank you, God* had been heartily joined with those of the Shipsons and her mother. Now she knew what it felt like to be helpless in the stands when someone you cared about fought their way around the track.

"Thanks again." Red pulled a red rose from the bouquet he held and handed it to her. "You prayed the best way."

Trish held the bloodred blossom to her nose. The sweet fragrance overlaid the smell of horse and sweat and fear. "You're welcome." She pushed the words past the lump in her throat.

"You'll join us for dinner, won't you, son?" Donald Shipson asked.

"Be glad to, sir," Red answered. "Is it all right if Trish rides with me?" At Marge's nod, he turned back to Trish. "I'll meet you right here then?"

"How about down at barn fourteen? I want them to see that filly of Orson's. She was scratched from the fifth today, but at least they can look at her."

"Fine. See you. Oh, and I rode that filly once. She's got heart but not enough condition." He waved again and trotted off to the jockey room.

Talk at the supper table revolved around the races of the day and then to the gray filly.

"I don't know," Marge answered. "If Portland Meadows doesn't open this fall, I guess we're shipping ours down to Adam Finley. I hate to take on another new horse when we're in such a state of confusion."

"What have you heard about the situation there?" Shipson wiped his mouth with a snowy napkin. "Any change?"

Marge shook her head. "No one seems to know anything for sure."

"Rumor has it that The Meadows is already closed." Red leaned forward. "I hate to see another track go down."

"What about me? I'll have to commute to California to ride." Trish carefully refrained from looking at her mother. How would they ever run their horses only on the weekends when she could fly down there? "It just isn't fair."

Since when is life fair? her nagger whispered in her ear as if he'd been waiting for a chance to dig in his claws.

Chapter
04

The rest of the weekend passed in a blur. Before Trish knew it, she was back on the plane, heading for Vancouver. School would begin in the morning.

She leaned back against the headrest and let her mind play with the scenes of the weekend. Red Holloran nearly nosed Spitfire out for first place. She'd see both of them again in October, less than a month away. And this Friday she would fly down to San Francisco to race on Saturday and drive back to Vancouver on Sunday.

"You're awfully quiet." Marge put down her magazine and turned to look at her daughter.

"Just thinking. I'm going to be really busy, aren't I?"

Marge smiled and nodded. "Seems that way to me."

Trish rubbed the bridge of her nose, unconsciously mimicking David's action when he was thinking. "You thought any more about Portland Meadows?"

"Sort of. I figured we'd get this weekend out of the way first and then tackle the next item on the agenda." Marge accepted a glass of soda from the flight attendant and passed Trish her standard Diet Coke. "It's like I keep hoping the situation will resolve itself if I look the other way." She shook her head. "But that is rarely the case."

"We had a super weekend, though." Trish sipped her drink. "I'm really glad you came along."

"Thanks." Marge patted Trish's cocked knee. "Back to Portland Meadows. I'd just as soon you didn't get involved in the situation there, whatever the situation is."

"Are you telling me I can't talk to the other owners?" Trish felt a niggle of resentment settle around her chest.

"No, I'm giving you my opinion. I'd like you to have a sane and normal senior year with time to take part in all the activities."

"Thanks, Mom." Trish sipped her drink again. That had been close. She knew she'd want to make sure something was done about racing at PM. At least they weren't going to start out fighting about something so important as that. The thought of other jockeys riding their horses bothered her more than she wanted to admit. That was her job. But she sure couldn't do it if all the horses were based in California.

Dad, what would you do in this situation? Trish closed her eyes and leaned her seat back. If she sat real quiet, she could almost feel him sitting right beside her. He'd be reading the latest *Blood Horse Journal* or one of his "good books," as he called authors like Norman Vincent Peale.

He always said you could find your answers in the Scriptures if you looked hard enough. Trish rubbed her tongue on the back of her teeth. Where would she find a reference for horse racing?

Immediately a verse leaped into her mind. "Do unto others as you would have them do unto you." The golden rule. She wrinkled her eyebrows. What did that have to do with racing?

Their meal arrived and Trish poured dressing on her salad in an unconscious gesture. "Do unto others." It seemed as if they were being done unto and not in a good way. She ate her meal, all the while mulling over the verse. Another came into her mind. This one she could picture on her wall of three-by-five cards, all verses printed either by her or her father. "I can do all things through Christ who strengthens me." Now *that* one made more sense.

After giving her empty tray to the flight attendant, Trish flipped back the armrest and curled up in the double seat for a nap. She was just about

out when she felt her mother spread one of the airline blankets over her. "Thanks, Mom," Trish mumbled.

When Trish and her mother walked off the plane, Patrick waited there to meet them. Trish nearly walked on by because the retired jockey stood behind a man tall enough to play professional basketball.

"You're going to have to stand in front of guys like that," Trish teased after they swapped hugs and started down the long walk to the baggage claim. "Or you'll get lost."

Patrick gave her a poke with his elbow. "And let's be lookin' at who's talking. He'd be taller'n you and Spitfire put together. Speaking of which, how's our son doin'?"

"Great." Trish turned with a grin. "And yes, you were right."

"And what might that be about?"

"He didn't forget me."

"I told you, that horse has a memory like an elephant. And he'll never be forgettin' ye. Yer the most important person in his life."

"I still wish we could race him again." Trish sighed.

"Give it up, lass. We'll bring on a young'un to do it again." Patrick stood back to let Trish and Marge onto the escalator in front of him.

"What's happening at The Meadows?" Marge asked in an undertone because Trish stood three steps down in front of her.

"The Thoroughbred Association has called a meeting for Tuesday night. The city council is supposed to make a decision at their meeting on Thursday." Patrick tried to speak softly enough for Trish to miss it.

"But that's tomorrow night." Trish stepped to the side at the bottom of the escalator.

"I know." Marge and Patrick exchanged a look that told Trish they'd rather not discuss this now.

Fine, Trish thought. *I can play that game too. But tomorrow night Runnin' On Farm will be well represented at the meeting.* "They've started our luggage carousel" was all she said as she walked through the turnstile to stand by the moving luggage line.

On the way home, the three caught up on all the news of Runnin' On Farm. The new mare and filly they'd purchased from the breeder in Chehalis were settling in well. Miss Tee and Double Diamond had grown an inch a night, or so it seemed.

"We'll be working with the yearling Calloway's Joker soon as you get out to the barn. I'm too heavy for him and a'course Brad makes me look like a midget."

"Brad's already started school?" Trish leaned between the two front seats of the minivan.

"Nope. Later than you. But he's sure been a help these last couple of weeks. That boy's awful good with horses."

"He should be. Brad Williams nearly grew up at our place. He and David . . ." Marge shook her head. "And Trish and Rhonda. What those four couldn't think of."

"Come on, Mom, we weren't *that* bad."

"You won't believe the mountains of cookies I used to bake. Hal teased me about becoming a professional baker."

"You still could. Like Brad said, you make the best cinnamon rolls around." Trish leaned her elbows on her knees and her chin on the palms of her hands. "You think David likes the cooking at the dorm?"

"I doubt it. All college students complain about the food. There's a rule somewhere that says they have to." Marge turned in her seat. "We'll call him when we get home and let him know we got through the weekend all right."

Dusk colored the farm amethyst and faded the edges as they turned into the long, graveled driveway. The farm and family collie, Caesar, leaped and yipped beside the slow-moving van, doing his best to welcome them home.

The cedar-sided house lay to the right. Flower skirts of red and gold and pink flaunted their bursts of blooms before fall dimmed their glory. One last ray of golden sun reflected off the picture window, brassy and brilliant in the dusk.

Off to the left and down a bit lay the barns with the horse paddocks out behind. Patrick's mobile home, surrounded by another flower display, nestled against the rise as if it had lived there forever.

Trish felt a lump in her throat. Was coming home always the best part of a trip? It felt like she'd been gone for months, years maybe, instead of weeks.

Her father would be down at the paddocks, checking on the horses for the final time of the day. She sighed and blinked against the moisture that stung her eyelids. If only that were true. How much she had to tell him. She rolled her lips together and pulled open the sliding door. But now she had to keep on keeping on. He wasn't here and he wouldn't be.

Caesar planted both his front feet on her knee before she could slide out. The fastest tongue in the West caught her chin and the tip of her nose before she dug her fingers into his blazing white ruff and let him lick away the tears too. "You silly old dog." Trish shook her hands and Caesar grinned his doggie grin. "You missed me, huh?" Caesar dropped to all fours, yipped and ran around in a circle, scrabbling dirt into the air.

"I think he's glad to see you." Marge retrieved her purse from the van and chuckled at the dog's antics. "If you hurry, you can check on the horses before absolute dark."

Trish waved at her mom and trotted down the rise, her three-tone whistle calling both the dog and the horses. A whinny answered her and then another. Caesar ran in front of her, turned to bark, then dashed off again.

Trish dropped to a walk when she rounded the long, low stable and started down the lane between the board-fenced paddocks. Another whinny floated up to her on the evening breeze. Old, gray Dan'l, their now-retired-from-racing Thoroughbred and her riding teacher, was welcoming her home. The second whinny had the young sound of Miss Tee or Double Diamond. Who had whistled like she did so they recognized it?

Ahead in the dimness, she could faintly see a gray horse standing with his head over the fence. He whinnied again. Trish ran down the lane, stopping just in time to walk up to the aging animal. "Hello, old man. How ya doin'?" Dan'l whuffled, his nostrils fluttering in a soundless nicker. He sniffed her hand, her arm, and up to her cheek, then nosed at her pocket where she usually kept the carrots.

"None today, fella. I haven't even been in the house yet." She rubbed his ears and down his cheek. "You're lookin' good for such an old son." Dan'l nodded and blew in her face. He licked her cheek and hung his head low so she could rub the crest of his mane and between his ears. When he sighed, it was as if she'd never been away. Trish patted him again, then worked her way down the row of horse heads bobbing at the fence line.

Miss Tee and Double Diamond stood back a ways and reached out to sniff her proffered hand. The new filly hung back even further. "Scaredy cats," Trish murmured, all the while keeping her hand palm down so they could sniff comfortably. "You'll have to learn to trust me again, you know. Mom's spoiled you, I bet."

Caesar shoved his nose into her hand and whined. The peeper frogs sang their nightly three-part chorus down by the swamp. Up above, three stars ran interference for the heavenly host to come as the sky deepened from cobalt to black.

Trish gave Dan'l an extra hug and strode back up the lane. Time to call Rhonda and plan their big entrance in the morning. And time to read the clippings Patrick had been saving about the mess at Portland Meadows.

"Patrick carried your luggage to your room," Marge said when Trish opened the sliding glass door from the deck behind the house. "We're going to have coffee in about five minutes if you want to join us."

"Okay. How about if I call Rhonda first?"

"You think you can talk for only five minutes?"

"Prob'ly not. But I can always call her back." Trish glanced into the living room at her father's recliner. So often he'd sat there reading his Bible or resting after he got so sick. A circle of light from the lamp beside it fell on the worn cushions. Even his patchwork quilt lay folded across the back. His worn black Bible occupied its usual place on the end table.

Trish walked quickly down the hall. She *would not* cry.

Her room wore the look of perfection only possible when she lived elsewhere. No jeans, sweat shirts, boots, or even tissues out of place. Everything dusted, the crimson and gold throw pillow not thrown but centered against the other pillows. She raised her gaze to the blank wall above her desk. The first thing she'd do when she got back from California on Sunday would be to pin all the cards with Bible verses back in place. Her mother had saved them from the trash.

Trish ignored the yawn that attacked her from the sight of the pillows and marched back down the hall to the kitchen. She might still be on Kentucky time, but now she had to function on Washington time, and here it was only eight o'clock. Time to call Rhonda. And later, Brad.

"Hi, Rhonda, it's me." Trish sank to the floor and propped her back against the corner of the door and the kitchen cabinets. "So, how's everything for the morning?" After telling Rhonda as much as possible about the Kentucky trip, Trish waved a hand at her mother. "I gotta go. Mom's dishing up peach pie and ice cream. You and Brad should be here. So I'll pick you up about twenty to eight, okay?" Trish hung up the phone and pushed herself to her feet. "Rhonda said to tell you hi and she's glad we're home."

"Here, you take the tray. We're going to eat in the living room for a change." Marge picked up the coffee carafe and followed Trish into the living room.

Patrick sat in the corner of the sofa, reading *Blood Horse* in the lamplight. He put the magazine down and smiled up at Trish. "Sure and it's good to have ye home, lass." He took the plate of dessert and set it down on the end table. "It's been lonely here, even though Brad came to help me. I got real spoiled having a family around all the time."

Marge handed him a coffee mug. "You need to be spoiled after all those years alone. Besides, you're making it easier for Trish and me too. This house seems mighty big for two women."

"Maybe we could bring Caesar in?" Trish grinned around the spoon she licked.

"And maybe not." Marge shook her head. "Some people will try anything. Finish your dessert, child. It's time for you to be in bed since you have school tomorrow."

Trish licked her ice cream from the spoon again. "You haven't gotten to say something like that for a long time." She turned to Patrick. "Used to be her famous last words every night." Trish caught herself in a big yawn. "And tonight you're right. Patrick, Mom said you'd been keeping the articles on The Meadows."

"Aye. But they're down at my house. I'll bring them up tomorrow. We'll work horses and I'll catch you up on the training we're doing after school."

"Good." Trish stretched and yawned again. "Night." She swallowed another yawn and, after kissing her mother good-night, ambled down the hall to her room.

While her bags needed unpacking, her mother had been kind enough to hang up the garment bag containing the new outfit for school. Trish unzipped the bag and drew out the hangers holding her new skirt, vest, and rust-colored silk blouse. The silver-toed western boots that finished off the outfit nestled in their wrapping in the stuffed bag on the floor. She hung the outfit on the door to let it shake out and undressed for bed.

After she crawled under the covers she heard Patrick leave and her mother's steps coming down the hall. Marge tapped on the half-open door and leaned her head in.

"You sleeping yet?"

"Nope." Trish patted the side of the bed. "Here."

Marge sat as invited and drew one knee up on the bed. She studied her daughter, a half smile playing across her face. "You have no idea how wonderful it is to see you here in your own bed again."

Trish wriggled and smiled back. "Maybe not, but I know how good it feels."

"There's a song, goes . . . something . . . something, you and me against the world." Marge sang a snatch of the tune. "That's kind of the way I feel right now." She clasped her hands around her knee and rocked back on her spine. "But let me tell you, I'm not ready for the empty-nest syndrome. Half a nest is better than no nest at all."

Trish turned on her side and reached out with one hand to stroke her mother's hands. "So I'm half a nest, am I?"

"We've got a lot ahead of us, Tee." Marge's voice wavered.

"Sometimes it scares me. I mean, like this is my last year in high school. And I want to do so many things in the racing world too. How am I gonna do it all?"

"Well, one thing I've been learning is that I have to make choices. So I pray and ask God to help me make the right choices. Then I do what seems best. Remember what your father always said: 'The right choice always follows God's principles, and then you pray for God to close the doors He doesn't want you to go through.' " She paused and wiped away a tear that trickled down her cheek. "It helps to talk about him, you know."

"I think I finally can." Trish sniffed and reached for a tissue. "I still feel like a yo-yo sometimes. And I never know when it will happen."

"Me too. But thank God we've got each other." Marge leaned forward and kissed Trish on the cheek. "Good night, Tee. You and Rhonda will knock 'em dead tomorrow."

After saying her prayers with lots of things to be thankful for, Trish snuggled down under the covers. What a day this had been!

The alarm rang after Trish had already headed for the bathroom. The *beep, beep, beep* met her when she returned. She thumped it off and dressed quickly. When she stood in front of the full-length mirror, she couldn't keep from smiling. Who was that person?

Marge walked up behind her. "Wow. You're all grown up. Trish, you look beautiful." She stroked the waves of glossy, midnight hair that swung just past Trish's shoulders. "I haven't seen you with your hair down for so long; I forgot how rich it is." She touched the dangly turquoise-and-bead earrings. "The whole outfit fits together so perfectly." She gave Trish a quick hug. "Breakfast's ready. I had cinnamon rolls in the freezer, so you get the royal send-off."

"What, no bagels?" Trish slipped an arm through her mother's. "Lead me to 'em."

A few minutes later Trish stepped out into the sunshine. "You sure you don't need your car today?"

"Nope. I'm home to stay. I'll drive you if I need it any other day this week or use the pickup." Marge stood in the door and waved. "Of course, you could take the bus."

Trish flipped a grin and a wave over her shoulder. She was spoiled, she knew it. The last three years, first David, then Brad drove. And this year she would have her own car when she brought it back from California.

She waved again as she drove down the driveway. Her senior year was about to begin.

She picked up Rhonda, who wore her wild red hair confined in a braid and finished with a broad ribbon. Their outfits matched except for Rhonda's turquoise blouse and darker denim skirt.

"Welcome home and don't we look like something out of a magazine ad? My mom can't get over the difference." She swung up in the van and dumped her purse and book bag on the floor. "I don't think I'm ready to dress like this all the time, though. Takes too much time."

"Me too. Bad as polishing boots and goggles before a race." Trish checked both ways before pulling out on the road. "Hey, you want to fly to California on Friday? That way I'll have someone to ride back with me."

"I'll ask. Sounds like fun."

A few minutes later, Trish chewed her bottom lip while she drove up and down the lot at the high school, looking for a place to park. Last year had been a rough one. What did this year hold?

Football quarterback Doug Ramstead waved her into a parking place beside his shiny black pickup with red flames painted on the side. "Good to see ya, Trish, Rhonda." He clapped a hand to his forehead. "Oh, wow! You two are . . ." A wolf whistle came from another car.

Rhonda and Trish grinned at each other as they strolled across the parking lot. Yep, that was the reaction they wanted.

"Maybe he still likes you." Rhonda nudged Trish and glanced toward the blond, biceps-bulging football star. "He did last year."

Chapter
05

I think this is gonna be a fun year." Rhonda slid into the seat next to Trish. Fourth-period government was the only class they had together.

"What makes you think that?" Trish dug in her purse for a lipstick. She ducked her head to peek into the narrow mirror attached to the lipstick tube. After applying a coat of cranberry lip gloss, she rolled her lips together and put everything back in her purse. She straightened just as the teacher, Ms. Wainwright, entered the room.

"She's new," Rhonda whispered. "She's the drama coach too."

"I know, I have her for speech seventh period," Trish answered.

The final bell rang. Trish caught a movement out of her eye. She turned her head to see Doug Ramstead take the seat on her other side. He grinned at her and waved at Rhonda.

"From now on, you will all be in your seats by the final bell." The teacher stood in front of the class, looking more like one of the students than a faculty member. Her wavy blond hair, caught up in combs on the sides, tumbled below her shoulders. Wire-rimmed glasses failed to hide the twinkle in her blue eyes, even though her words sounded stern.

Trish heard a faint whistle from somewhere behind her. He was right. Their new teacher could make plenty of money modeling in her spare time.

"As you can see on the board, my name is Carolyn Wainwright, and due to the school policies, you'll be wise to call me Ms. Wainwright. You may have heard, I am also the new drama coach, and I'll see some of you in speech this afternoon.

"Now, I know you all groan at the thought of a semester on how our country is governed, but I guarantee you'll understand the process better by the time we're finished. As our preamble says, this is government 'of the people, by the people, and for the people.' Since many of you will be eligible to vote in the next election, we'll start with local government and politics. By the way, there'll be ways to earn extra points for outside activities."

Trish listened carefully. The teacher's enthusiasm overrode even the rumbling of a hungry stomach. Trish rubbed her midsection and hoped no one could hear the noise.

"Me too," Doug Ramstead whispered.

Trish could feel the heat begin at the base of her neck. Rhonda giggled on the other side of her. Trish shot a glare at her friend and tried to ignore the blush she knew stained her cheeks by now. She felt like using the papers in her notebook to fan her flaming face.

When the bell rang, she joined the rush for the door.

"What a babe."

Trish heard two guys talking behind her.

"Yeah, and to think she's a teacher. What a waste."

Trish glanced at Rhonda, and the two rolled their eyes upward in the age-old feminine sign of disgust for crude comments. Especially such comments from those of the male gender.

"So, how's our world-class jockey doing?" Doug Ramstead inserted himself between them with an arm about each of their waists. "You two starting a new rage at good old Prairie?"

"Meaning?" Rhonda shifted her books to her other arm.

"Such hot threads." He grinned at Trish. "Being a world-class jockey must be paying off."

"Thanks, I think," Trish answered.

"How about eating lunch at my table?"

"Your table!" Rhonda pulled open the door, only to have him reach over her and hold the door for both of them. "Who died and made you king?"

"He thinks being the big QB gives him special rights. Like there's a table in there labeled *football stars*." Trish turned to leave her stuff in her locker.

"I'll save your places," Doug said over his shoulder.

"Did that all just happen or have I been caught in a dream warp?" Rhonda leaned against the closed locker next to them and fanned her face.

"You nut. He's just Doug, same as he's always been."

"Yeah, a flirt, gorgeous, *the* quarterback of Prairie High, and he liked our outfits."

"Who wouldn't?" The girl with the locker next to them interrupted. "Where'd you find clothes like that?"

"California." Rhonda assumed a model's languid pose against the lockers. She ruined it with a giggle.

"You still racing?" the girl asked Trish.

"Yeah, but now only on weekends. Depends on when Portland Meadows opens." The three made their way toward the lunchroom.

"You sure did well. I kept reading about you and Spitfire winning the Triple Crown. That was really something." She tucked her long straight hair behind her right ear.

"Thanks. Seems like it all happened so long ago."

"Over here." Doug Ramstead waved from the table Brad, Rhonda, and Trish had always sat at.

Trish and Rhonda exchanged glances. Rhonda shrugged and raised her eyebrows. "This is gonna be fun," she whispered as together they carried their trays with salad, milk, and rolls across the room, dodging bodies and trays as they went.

"Sit here." Doug patted the seats beside him on his left. "I beat off those meatheads for you."

By the time they finished lunch, Trish felt like she'd returned to a world she'd nearly forgotten. It seemed as if her life at the track and her life at home were in two different galaxies, at least a time warp apart.

"I think he likes you," Rhonda said just before they separated to go to their classes.

"Right. He invited us both, remember?"

"Yeah, but he *likes* you."

"And I like a jockey."

"Who's in Kentucky."

"Rhonda, go to class." Trish stepped into her classroom just as the bell rang.

By the end of the day, she felt like if she had to sit still one more minute, she would fly into bitty pieces. What a difference between tracktime and schooltime. During the last minutes before the bell rang, she pictured what she would be doing at the track. Most likely waiting in the jockey room or riding in a race, the horse driving for the finish line.

Her mind flashed to Kentucky. *Wonder what it would take to bring Red out to the tracks on the West Coast?* she thought. What if she could see him more often? Her middle turned to mush.

The bell rang, sending her dream into a billion splinters.

She caught the end of the teacher's statement. Something about bringing gear for the weight-training class.

She stopped one of the other students. "What did he say at the end?"

"Bring your gear tomorrow."

"I know, but what gear specifically?"

The boy looked at her like she'd slipped a cog somewhere. "Like gloves, sweats or shorts, you know." He stared at her a moment more. "Say, you're Trish, the jockey, aren't you? How come you need weight training? Don't you get enough of a workout at the track?"

Trish fell into step beside him. "Nope, not right now. Especially not since Portland Meadows might not be opening."

"What are you going to do?"

Trish shrugged. "Beats me. There's a meeting tonight about it."

"Well, good luck." He paused before turning off to his locker. "See you tomorrow?"

Trish nodded. "All ready for a workout." After dropping off her books at her locker, Trish headed for the van. The boy's question drummed in her ears. What *was* she going to do?

Her nagger uncurled from his prolonged nap and whispered in her ear, *Nothing, if your mother can help it. And remember, you don't want to get on her bad side again. This new peace between the two of you has been pretty nice.*

Trish answered a couple of greetings as she crossed the parking lot, but she didn't slow her step. She and Patrick had plenty of work to do. And today she would see her long-time friend Brad Williams. No, Clark College hadn't started yet. Funny, she didn't know his schedule either. She had lots of catching up to do.

Rhonda waited for her beside the maroon minivan. A guy tall enough to make her look short leaned against the van door, occupying all the redhead's attention.

Trish stopped a bit away. Rhonda sure was getting the looks today. Who was this guy? Certainly a new man on campus. And one who looked like he'd already made himself at home.

"Hi." Trish unlocked her door and threw her book bag on the floor between the seats. She hit the automatic unlock button on the door so Rhonda could get in.

"See ya." Rhonda followed Trish's actions and slid into the seat. "Cool dude, huh?" She waved just before slamming the door.

"Who is he?" Trish put the key in the ignition.

"Jason Wollensvaldt. Our exchange student from Germany. Would you believe I met him in German class?" Rhonda's words tripped over themselves in her rush to give Trish the news.

"Why's he taking German if he's from there?" Trish followed the line of vehicles out the side gate of the parking lot onto 117th Avenue.

"Telling us about life in Germany. He's planning to play basketball."

"I'm sure by tomorrow you'll know his life history."

"Maybe. He said he was going to call me this evening."

"Fast work, Seabolt." Trish shook her head. "Hope he likes horses."

Even the van seemed to take a deep breath to recover from Rhonda's nonstop enthusiasm after she had made her exit. Trish waved in return and sucked in the silence. Rhonda thought school would be fantastic this year. Trish wasn't ready to concede fantastic, but things were looking mighty good. Doug Ramstead seemed determined to spend more time with them. Or was it her? She mentally shrugged. Didn't hurt to be invited to sit at the same lunch table as the most popular guy at Prairie High.

The baby blue Mustang occupied its normal place in the driveway.

Brad would be either down helping Patrick or in the kitchen making sure the latest batch of cookies didn't go to waste.

Trish stepped out of the van with ladylike precision, simply because with a long, straight skirt, jumping wasn't possible. She leaned forward to accept a doggie kiss, and after ruffling Caesar's ears, entered the front door.

Chocolate-chip-cookie perfume greeted her nose even before the sound of voices announced her mother's whereabouts. Trish dropped her bag on the counter, picked up two cookies, still warm from the oven, and ambled into the dining room where Brad, Patrick, and Marge sat around the table.

"Look at you." Brad accompanied his comment with a wolf whistle, a difficult accomplishment with a mouthful of cookie.

"Thanks, I guess." Trish patted his head as she walked by him to her place at the end of the table. "Hi, Patrick."

"How was school?" Marge handed around a napkin.

"You should ask Rhonda. I think she's in love."

"Already?" Marge leaned back in her chair. "Other than that, how was your day?"

"I think this'll be a good year. New drama coach. I have her for American government and speech. She says we each need a special project. Plus a term paper, plus a couple of shorter papers." She copied her mother's laid-back pose. "Nothing much to keep me busy."

Brad leaned over and snitched the cookie she'd laid on the table. "Be glad you're not in college yet. They think term paper means once a week." Trish groaned along with him and made a grab for her cookie. "Hey, pig face, that's mine."

"Now children, there's plenty more where that came from."

Brad grinned around a mouthful of crunch. "David told me to keep you on your toes while he was gone. Afraid you'd get soft or something without a big brother to keep you in line."

Trish snorted in mock disgust. "Dream on."

"Well, how about the two of you joining me at the stables before you come to blows." Patrick pushed his chair back and picked up his battered fedora. "Thanks for the coffee." He stopped at the sliding glass door. "You coming down too, Marge? We need to be showin' these young hotshots how much you've done with the babies."

Marge nodded. "I have to return a phone call, so Trish and I'll be down in a few minutes."

"Who was on the phone?" Trish asked after changing her clothes.

"Bob Diablo. Reminding us about the meeting tonight. Said to tell you 'buenos dias' and he's glad you're home again."

"So we're all going?" Trish shoved Caesar with her knee so he could tear around and bark at her. His tongue lolled to one side in a doggie grin of delight.

"Unless you have homework."

"Right."

After galloping the three horses Patrick was training for outside owners, Trish leaned on the paddock fence and watched her mother lunge Miss Tee. The filly half reared and struck out at an imaginary foe with her front legs. At a twitch of the line, she settled back to a spirited trot, her lengthening brush of a mane bouncing in the breeze.

"Hard to believe she's really a year old." Trish rested her elbows on the fence.

"We'll start with a saddle and pad soon. The gelding Feelin' Free is ready for breaking." Patrick watched the action with a smile on his face. "Your mother has come a long way."

"Yep. Makes me jealous that Miss Tee knows her better than me."

"True, for now. But that'll change when you start riding her." Patrick turned to look directly at Trish. "Caring for the babies filled a big hole in your mother's life. She gets terrible lonesome sometimes."

"She tell you that?" Trish turned her head to look at him with surprise.

Patrick shook his head. "Didn't need to."

Trish studied her mother. Graying hair feathered back on the sides, and one lock flopping down on her forehead, Marge looked years younger than forty. Her full mouth curved in a smile as the filly shook her head. Booted feet spread to brace against any coltish behavior, and her plaid shirt rolled up to the elbows, Trish's mother looked totally relaxed and competent.

Why, she's beautiful, Trish thought. *And she's having a great time.* Trish shook her head. All those years when Hal had been alive, Marge had never worked with the horses. In fact, Trish thought her mother hated or at least disliked the animals. Maybe this was another of those things she'd have to rethink. Could they work together?

That night the three of them rode to the racetrack in the minivan. Trish sat in the back, thinking about the meeting ahead. This was another first for her: The first TBA—Thoroughbred Association—meeting without her father. He'd been president of the organization several times through the years.

With a rush the tears stung the backs of her eyelids and clogged her nose. Trish sniffed and dug in her purse for a tissue. Before she could roll her eyes in evasive action, the drops trickled down her cheeks. She blew her nose and mopped her face.

Marge reached back with one hand and patted her daughter's knee.

Trish sniffed again. When she took a deep breath, it was as if a storm had crackled with heat lightning and then blown over after smattering the earth with only a drop or two. "Whew." She let her air out on a sigh. With one finger she wiped beneath her eyes to keep her mascara from smudging. At least she wouldn't go into the meeting looking like a raccoon.

It seemed like years since she'd been at Portland Meadows. The lighted horses that usually raced across the front of the dark green building were only dim outlines. Vehicles filled the parking slots closest to the building. It didn't look to be a large crowd.

Trish walked through the glass doors along with her mother and Patrick. Her father should be here. He'd know what to do. She swallowed the thought and clamped her jaw against the quiver she could feel returning.

"Good to see you Trish," someone called from the group of men congregating in the corner. "Welcome home," another voice added.

"Thanks." Trish tossed the word in that direction along with an almost smile.

"You all think you could get in here so we can start this meeting?" Bob Diego poked his head out of the door. "Buenos dias, amiga." His dark eyes crinkled at the corners when he saw Trish. Even his mustache smiled. "Welcome home."

Trish stilled the quiver enough to return his greeting. As the members filed into the room, she started toward a chair at the back.

"Mind if I sit here?" A man wearing a brown leather bomber jacket pointed at the chair beside her.

Trish looked up into smiling hazel eyes. "No, I guess not."

"My name is Curt Donovan. I'm from *The Oregonian*." He took off his jacket and hung it over the back of the tan folding chair.

"I'm Trish Evanston."

"I know. I've been writing about you for months. Not often a reporter gets to be in on history." He sat down on the chair and turned to watch her.

"History?" Trish felt like she was reacting in slow motion.

"You set records. First woman to win the Derby. First woman to win the Triple Crown. Congratulations."

"Oh, that." Trish blinked. It seemed like that had all happened in another lifetime. "Umm, thanks." She dug deep for her manners, aware that her mother sat on her right.

A gavel rapped from the podium. "Let's call this meeting to order."

Trish thought a moment and then asked the questions that had been plaguing her. She spoke in an undertone so as not to disrupt the meeting. "Curt?"

"What?" He leaned close to hear her.

She turned her head, keeping one eye on the speaker. "Do you think . . ." She stopped to listen as Bob Diego called for a report from the secretary. "Have you heard anything, you know, illegal or something going on here at the track?"

Marge put a finger up to her lips and shook her head. Trish leaned close to hear Curt's answer.

"No, have you?"

Trish nodded and watched her mother out of the corner of her eye. "Sort of."

"We'll talk later."

Trish could feel her mother's frown clear down to her bones.

Chapter
06

I thought I asked you to stay out of that." Marge laid her purse on the counter with extreme care.

Trish walked to the sink and filled a glass of water at the tap. "I just asked if he'd heard anything."

"And then you agreed to talk with him further." Marge crossed her arms across her chest. "Trish, I just don't want you to get involved."

"Mother, we are involved whether we want to be or not. If that track doesn't open, where will we race? I race." Trish put her hand to her chest. She fought against the catch in her voice. "You know how much I hate to have someone else ride our horses. That's my job."

"I know how . . ." Marge shook her head. "No, I don't know exactly how you feel, but I think I understand." She held up a hand to ward off Trish's protests. "I know you want to ride, especially after almost quitting, but things aren't the same as they used to be. No one else could ride Spitfire. You had to be there. But now others can ride for us, and if we have to, that's what we'll do."

Trish felt an angry fist grab her gut and twist. She stared at the square set of her mother's chin, then clamped her arms across her belly to halt the twisting. "Why are you being so unreasonable?" She fought to keep her voice from rising to a screech. If only she could scream and yell. "I don't want someone else to ride our horses."

Go ahead, act like a little kid again and then she'll really think you're ready to be treated like an adult. Trish's nagger was only voicing the words she'd been burying.

Marge turned and leaned her weight on her rigid arms, staring out the window at the mercury-lighted yard. "I think I'm being very reasonable. All I'm asking is that you stay out of the controversy—if there really is one—at Portland Meadows."

"But somebody has to be involved."

"Somebody is. You heard them vote to ask for an extension before the city council votes. Bob Diego will take the petition to the council tomorrow night."

"Sure, after they argued back and forth. They're scared to do anything. You'd think they want the track to close. What a bunch a . . ." She sucked in a deep breath and adopted a more controlled tone. "All I want is to be able go to the meetings and see what happens. That isn't too much to ask."

"Trish, we'll talk about this later." Bright red stained Marge's cheeks, and her voice snicked each word like a scalpel.

Trish stared at her mother. Angry words threatened to pour past her clenched teeth, but instead of spitting them out, she turned and stormed down the hall to her room. This was such a stupid fight. She grabbed the edge of the door, ready to slam it closed, but stopped. The click sounded even louder than her pounding heart.

All the things she wished she'd said thundered through her mind as she undressed for bed. She threw her jeans in the corner and flung her shirt over the back of the chair. Why bother to put things away? Just because her mother liked a clean room. She barely resisted kicking the chair leg when she nudged it with her stockinged toe.

"If you really cared about my riding, you'd let me go," she muttered to herself as she pulled her nightshirt over her head. "You never wanted me to ride anyway." The box of tissues fell to the floor when she snapped off the lamp on her bedstand. The name she called it wouldn't fit in Sunday school.

When Trish curled up under the covers, she shivered in her fight against the tears. Here she'd been home only a few days, and she and her mother were already fighting. *It's not fair. She just doesn't understand.*

Yeah, sure, you think you're so grown-up, and here you are fighting again. Thought you promised not to lose your temper anymore. The voices raged inside her head.

If Mom only cared enough about me and the horses. She doesn't understand. What if I have to quit riding. I can't stand all this. I hate being mad.

She turned over and fumbled on the floor for the tissue box. After blowing her nose—again—she flopped back on the bed and let the tears trickle down into her ears. The yawning pit reached up with tentacle arms to suck her down in.

At the thought of saying her prayers, she blew her nose again and turned over. Sure, ask God for help. How could she when she knew He'd expect her to go and tell her mother how sorry she was. Sorry was right. What a sorry mess.

The nightmares returned with a vengeance. Trish awoke sometime in the night with her heart pounding like she'd run two miles. A weight seemed to sit on her chest, threatening to cut off the air she gulped as if it were nearly gone.

When she tried to picture Jesus in her mind, all she could see was her mother's eyes. Sad eyes with a hint of a tear at the corners. Angry eyes too, with sparks that flashed when the two of them got into it.

Trish scrubbed her hands across her own eyes. She had promised herself to never fight with her mother again. They didn't need it, either of them. A sense of desolation settled over Trish's bed, pushing her heart down through her ribs and into the bedsprings. It lay there, heavy and thick, clogging her throat and burning her eyes.

When she finally fell asleep again, it was to toss and turn, trying to throw off the suffocating blanket.

When she awoke, she knew she should go ask her mother's forgiveness. It was the only thing to do. But when she entered the kitchen ready for school, the emptiness echoed around her. The full coffeepot told her that Marge had been there. Trish walked back through the living room and checked her mother's bedroom. Empty. In the living room, she stopped to stare at her father's recliner. If only he were here, life would be so different.

Back in the kitchen, Trish looked out the window. The van stood dripping in the misting rain. So her mother hadn't left the farm anyway.

Trish sucked in a deep breath that only went as far as the top of her lungs. The weight wouldn't let it go any further. So her mother was down at the barn. She probably had plenty to do down there. So what?

After fixing herself a slice of peanut butter toast and pouring a glass of milk, Trish meandered back to her bedroom, munching as she went. If only she could talk with her mother the way she had with her father. He understood. And he wasn't a worrywart. She shook her head and blinked her eyes. If she started crying now, her mascara would run and she'd have to do her makeup all over again.

She grabbed her book bag and purse, retrieved the empty glass from her desk, and headed for the front door. The urge to throw the glass into the sink surprisingly changed into rinsing it out and sticking it in the dishwasher. At least she couldn't be accused of leaving the kitchen in a mess.

She headed out the door for the van. If only she had her own car, then she wouldn't have to use her mother's. She tossed her bags in the center and buckled her seat belt. What a lousy, rotten day this looked to be. And all because her mother lived at the height of unreasonableness. If she'd dared, she'd have spun gravel on the way out.

She turned into Rhonda's driveway. Maybe she should go live with the Finleys. They seemed to know what a kid needed.

"Hi." Rhonda leaped into the van, shaking her head to keep the raindrops from sinking into her fly-away mass of carrot waves and curls. She took one look at Trish's face. "Uh-oh. What's wrong now?"

"You don't want to know." Trish put the van in motion before Rhonda finished settling into the seat.

"Probably not, but tell me anyway. That way I know when to duck."

"Yeah, well." Trish clamped her teeth on her lower lip. If she talked about it anymore, she'd cry. And she was *not* going to cry over a fight with her mother or anything else.

After the silence lengthened, Rhonda turned to her friend. "Let me guess then. You had a fight with your mom."

Trish shot her a surprised glance. "How'd you figure that out?"

"Easy. No one else to fight with at your house, and you're wearing your don't-mess-with-me look."

Trish muttered something under her breath.

"Well?"

"Well what?" Trish waited for traffic to pass and turned into the Prairie High parking lot.

"What happened?" Rhonda enunciated carefully as if Trish were hard of hearing.

"She's telling me not to get involved with this mess at Portland Meadows."

"So."

"So what?"

"So, are you involved? And what does she mean?"

Trish parked the van by the back fence. "You know we went to the TBA meeting last night." Rhonda nodded. "I met a reporter there, Curt Donovan, from *The Oregonian*, and he got all interested when I asked him if he'd heard about anything wrong going on over there. Said he'd call me."

"Is he cute?"

"Rhonda Seabolt, for pete's sake, you got guys on the mind all the time?"

Rhonda rolled her eyes and shook her head. "No, dummy, but face it, if you're gonna be working with this Curt guy, you'll have more fun if he's cute."

Trish shoved her door open. "Forget it." She grabbed her gear and stepped down, locking the doors in the same motion.

Rhonda fell into step beside her as they crossed the parking lot, trying to dodge between the raindrops. "Face it, now you're not so bummed out about your mom, are you?"

Trish just glared at her. Bummed out fit the bill, all right.

The drippy rain hadn't let up and neither had her mood by the time Trish returned home that afternoon. Sure she'd laughed and joked with the guys at the lunch table, but she could have been someone else for all she cared. She let Rhonda talk nonstop all the way home about Jason, the exchange student. That way she didn't have to answer any questions.

The truck was gone when she got home—and so was her mother.

After changing into her work clothes, Trish grabbed an apple from the bowl on the table and walked past the bubbling fish tank and into the living room. As if drawn by a magnet, she sank into the comforting arms of her father's recliner. When she closed her eyes and tipped her head against the cushiony back, thoughts chased each other through her mind. She needed to talk to her mother—that was a sure thing. She wished she could talk with her dad—that was impossible. And talking to God—why bother?

If she opened her eyes, Trish knew she would see that old black pit yawning before her.

You'd think you'd have learned all this by now. Her nagger took this moment to come out of hiding. *You know we've been over and over this.* Trish laid her arm across her eyes.

Yeah. She thought she'd learned the lessons too. But it was so hard to praise God when things were in such a mess again.

"And I had such good intentions." She opened her eyes and let her gaze drift around the room. . . . The fieldstone fireplace where they'd toasted marshmallows and burned hot dogs. Her mother's rocking chair. Trish's gaze skittered past that item. Her father's Bible on the end table beside the chair.

It was as if he could come back at any moment; everything was waiting for him. She closed her eyes again. *She* was waiting for him. Before the burning could swell into tears, she pushed herself to her feet and headed for the barn. At least down there she wouldn't have time to think.

"Hi, Patrick, sorry I'm late." Trish pasted an almost smile on her face. It was the best she could do. And she didn't look the trainer in the eye.

"Not to worry." Patrick brought out the saddle and settled it just behind the gelding's withers.

"Where's Brad?" Trish fetched her helmet from the tack room.

"Had some errands to run before work today. He should be along any minute." Patrick checked the girth and cupped his hands to give her a leg up. "You want to tell me what's wrong now or later?"

Trish paused with her knee in the air. "How'd you know?" Patrick just shook his head and tossed her into the saddle. Trish stared down at the top of his grungy fedora. "Mom and I had a big fight."

Patrick nodded his head. "Sure and she's hurtin' too."

"She tell you?"

This time the old trainer shook his head. He looked up at Trish, laying his hand on her knee. "No. Just these old eyes see more'n I want them to sometimes."

"She said I had to stay out of the mess at The Meadows." Trish stroked her mount's black mane and down his shoulder.

"And yer sure there's something wrong there, then?"

"I don't know. What do you think? What have you heard?"

"I think you should walk this son once around and then gallop him nice and easy for another two." He took hold of the reins and turned the bay gelding toward the fenced oval. "Be watchin' him for any weakness in that right fore."

Trish started to say something but thought the better of it and nudged her mount forward instead.

"So what do you think I should do?" Trish asked when they'd finished the schedule Patrick had set. Brad had left for the day and no lights showed at the house yet.

"I think you know what to do. Your mother has good reasons for what she asks. The two of you will work something out."

Trish shut the tack room door and shoved home the latch. "What have you heard?"

Patrick shook his head. "I'm thinkin' I shouldn't be tellin' you this, but I know you'll hear it somewhere. A couple of bug boys were laughing about how Smithson, the assistant manager, must have won the lottery or something."

"The lottery?"

"He's driving a brand-new, loaded Corvette XR1. Cherry red."

"Smithson?"

"Now, it may be that his uncle died and left him money . . ."

"Or he's in debt to his armpits."

"So I'm just a'tellin' you what I heard."

"Thanks, Patrick." Trish whistled for Caesar and trotted past Patrick's mobile home up to the house. She had homework to do, and maybe she'd put dinner in the oven.

"How come a house can feel and even smell empty?" she asked Caesar after sliding open the glass door to the deck. "Yes, you can come in." A quick yip and a doggie grin was her thanks.

Trish turned on the lights, retrieved a frozen casserole from the freezer out in the garage, and slid it into the heating oven. The collie padded behind her down the hall to her room and curled up on the rug by her bed. She was on the second chapter in her American government book when she heard the truck return.

Trish's gaze locked on a card on the wall. "I can do all things through Christ who strengthens me." That one was in her handwriting. She muttered the verse for a second time before shoving the chair back. This wouldn't be easy.

"Mom, I'm sorry—"

"Tee, we have to talk." Their words mishmashed together into cords that drew the two of them into each other's arms.

Marge brushed Trish's bangs to the side and kissed her daughter's forehead. "I think I let the worries get to me again. I keep telling myself you're about grown-up, but something in me doesn't believe it."

"Where were you?"

"At my grief group, and then I stopped to talk with Pastor Mort. He said to remind you that the one for teens meets on Mondays at the Methodist church right after school."

Trish let that pass. "I hate fighting. Please forgive me?" She leaned her cheek against her mother's chest. Somehow the words weren't as hard to say as she'd feared.

"Of course." Marge leaned her cheek against her daughter's thick hair. She sniffed and dug in her pocket for a tissue. After blowing her nose, she sniffed again, this time in appreciation. "You started dinner. And here I was trying to figure out what we'd eat." She hugged Trish one last time. "How soon till it's ready?"

After dinner, Marge lit a fire in the fireplace and settled into her chair with her knitting. Trish brought her books in and curled up in her father's chair. Music drifted from the stereo, playing a countermelody to the snapping and hissing of the burning wood.

"We need to lay some ground rules for this year," Marge said when Trish closed her books.

"Okay." Trish felt a tug of resentment but reined it down.

"School has to be your first priority, and good grades are—"

"Mom, I'll maintain a B or better, I promise."

"Thank you. I want you to be able to choose any college you want, and grades count." Marge leaned forward. "And no more than one road trip a month." The words fell into a shocked silence.

"But, but what if The Meadows doesn't open? I can't—I need—M-o-t-h-e-r." Trish put all her pleading into that one word.

"We'll just have to deal with that when and if the time comes. Dad always said to take one day at a time, and that's what we'll do."

Trish leaned back in her chair. One road trip a month. Why, the trip to Kentucky would take care of October. And she was heading for San Francisco on Friday. So much for September. She raised her hands and then dropped them in her lap.

They *had* to get racing back at The Meadows. They just had to.

The ringing phone brought her to her feet. "I'll get it."

"Trish, I've decided to let you attend the city council meeting with me tomorrow night." Her mother tossed the comment at Trish as she passed.

Trish nearly lost her voice to the shock. "R-Runnin' On Farm," she stammered into the kitchen phone.

"Can I speak with Trish Evanston, please?" a strong male voice said in her ear.

"Speaking." The voice sounded familiar.

"Hi, this is Curt Donovan, the reporter from *The Oregonian*. You remember me?"

"Sure." Trish propped the phone between her shoulder and ear. "How can I help you?"

"I think I have some information you might be interested in."

Trish sank down to her corner, propped in the V of the cabinet and wall. "Really?"

Chapter
07

an I meet with you after school tomorrow?"

Trish fumbled for an answer. "Ummm, I really don't have time. I start working with our horses here as soon as I get home from school."

"I could come there."

Trish thought hard. What if he had something important to ask her? Shouldn't she tell him what Patrick had said? He needed all the available information to conduct a decent investigation. "Just a minute, okay? I'll be right back."

She crossed her legs and rose to her feet. Placing the phone carefully on the counter, she walked back into the living room. "Mom?" Marge raised her head from counting stitches. "That's Curt Donovan on the phone. He'd like to come talk with me tomorrow after school."

"About Portland Meadows?"

Trish shrugged. "I guess." What else would he want to see her for? She kept her pose relaxed, nonchalant, like this didn't really mean much to her. Inside she was screaming *please, please!*

Marge laid her knitting in her lap. "If he comes, I want to be there, along with Patrick. And I need your promise that if I tell you to back out down the road, you'll do it without an argument."

Trish sucked in her breath. That was a tall order. "You mean . . ."

"I mean that Runnin' On Farm will do all we can to make sure there's racing at Portland Meadows this year, but we will do this together." She stared at her daughter, as if assessing Trish's honor. A hint of a smile tugged at the corners of her mouth. "After all, three heads are better than one." She picked up her knitting again. "And besides that, he's too old for you."

Trish felt the heat flame her cheeks. "Mother!" She fled to the kitchen, chased by her mother's chuckle.

After making the arrangements with Curt, she hung up the phone and ambled back into the living room. She shook her head at the question in her mother's eyebrows and settled back to finish her homework. Stranger things had happened, but at that moment, she was hard pressed to think of any.

Crossing the parking lot after school the next day, Rhonda pleaded for the chance to join the discussion.

"Oh, Rhonda. You just want to see what Curt looks like." Trish threw up her hands. "If I didn't know you better, I'd think guys took over your brain this summer."

"What's wrong with that? We're seniors, remember? We should have some guys in our lives. You have Red."

"Yeah, two thousand miles away." Trish flinched at the pang of guilt. She hadn't written to him since she'd come home. And she hadn't thanked the Shipsons yet either.

"Well, you could have Doug too, if you'd open your eyes."

"Rhonda Seabolt, you're the most . . ." Trish spluttered. She couldn't think of a name bad enough. At least not one that she would use on such a long-time friend and cohort.

Rhonda slammed the car door and pulled out her seat belt. "So, can I come?"

"Whatever." Trish started the car and joined the line of vehicles snaking out the back gate. "But if you . . ."

Rhonda raised one hand in pledge. "I'll keep a lid on this mouth of mine, I promise. Best friend's honor."

Trish carefully kept her gaze away from Rhonda after she'd introduced them. She knew she'd see that I-told-you-so expression. Curt Donovan wasn't just cute; he was good-looking. Dark blond hair, square jaw, and hazel eyes that lighted with laughter. All six feet of him announced an athletic past, if not present.

She would not look at Rhonda.

"So let me tell you what I've learned so far." Curt's deep voice brought her back to the moment. He raised his hands and shrugged. "Nothing."

Trish felt her stomach bounce down about her knees. She glanced at her mother, who raised an eyebrow. Patrick tipped his hat back and leaned against the board fence.

"Tell him what you heard." Trish nodded toward the trainer.

"Well, it ain't much. Just that Smithson, the assistant manager, is drivin' a fancy new Corvette."

"Really." Curt jotted something on his note pad.

"He drove a dented, chugging, rusted pickup before that," Trish added.

Curt raised an eyebrow. "Anything else?"

All three of them shook their heads.

"Except Mom's bad feeling."

Curt looked at Marge, who shook her head. "I have no basis for it in fact. Just that sometimes I have a feeling about things, and Hal always said to go with my gut."

Curt jotted down something else and stuck his paper back in his pocket. "Well, this gives me something to go on. Maybe I'll spend some time on the backside and keep my ears open. You hear anything else, you let me know, okay?"

"Will you be at the city council meeting tomorrow night?" Marge asked.

"Of course. I'll see you all then?" His question was for everyone, but his eyes asked Trish. At her nod, he smiled, said good-bye to them all, and strode back to his car. He waved just before climbing into the well-used compact.

"I think I'll go to the meeting too." Rhonda sighed.

"You nut." Trish gave her an elbow in the direction of her ribs. "Come on, you can ride Patrick's filly. I'll take the gelding."

When she got back to the house after chores were finished, a letter from Red lay on the oak table in the entry. "Fiddle." Trish slit the envelope and read the funny card as she walked down the hall. How come he always managed to write before she did? He must have mailed it from the airport just after they left.

Before she could get involved in anything else, she sat at her desk and wrote letters to both Red and the Shipsons. Thank you seemed such weak words for all the charming couple had done for her and her mother.

Trish sealed the envelopes and took them down the hall with her. "You got any stamps?" She paused at the doorway of the kitchen to inhale. "What smells so good?"

Marge turned from checking something in the oven. "Sure. Stamps are in the desk like always, and roast beef. How about mashed potatoes?"

"Great." Trish retrieved the stamps. After sticking them in place, she left the envelopes on the entry table so they'd get mailed. "Mom, I've been thinking."

"I'm glad."

"No, I mean really." Trish leaned a hip against the counter. "What could we send to the Shipsons as a thank-you gift? A card just doesn't seem enough."

"You're right." Marge poured herself a cup of coffee. "How about flowers?" Trish wrinkled her nose. "Candy." A shake of the head. "How about we give it some thought?"

"Okay." Trish rubbed a finger across her chin. It felt like a zit was starting. She headed for the bathroom and some medication. She stared at the face in the mirror, making faces to check her skin. Sure enough, another one by her nose. Must be close to that time of the month. Maybe that's why she'd been feeling like falling into the yawning pit.

She made another face at the girl in the mirror and flicked out the light. She had a speech to prepare for next week. What could she talk about?

Something you're grateful for. For a change her nagger tried to be helpful.

She was still thinking about it when she climbed into bed that night. One thing she was grateful for—no chemistry this year. Another thing, tonight she could say her prayers. Somehow when she was angry, like at her mother, praying didn't seem to work. *Maybe because you don't pray then.* Her nagger honed in like a laser.

She remembered to ask for forgiveness along with the praises. The "please helps" included Portland Meadows. "Please, God, let the track open again. If there is a mess there, please clean it up. And take care of David. The house sure seems lonesome without him." Her last thought was that she should have sent him a card by now too. So much to do.

She ignored Rhonda's teasing looks all the next day. But it wasn't hard. Her friend really had a friend, of the male variety. The tall exchange student sat at their table for lunch and hung out at their locker to walk Rhonda to class when he could.

"Is it okay?" Rhonda asked in an undertone after Jason invited her to go with him for a milkshake after school.

"Sure." Trish shoved the books she'd need into her bag and slammed their locker. "Have fun." But the drive home seemed long and lonely. Was this to be another change in her life? The thought didn't help lighten her mood any.

Patrick had Dan'l saddled when Trish got down to the barn. "What's happening?" Trish took a last bite from her apple and fed the core to Dan'l. The old gray Thoroughbred crunched the treat, then nosed her pockets in the hopes of more. Trish scratched his favorite spot, right behind his ears, and stroked down his cheek while waiting for an answer.

"Thought we'd give these two a taste of real racing, even though they haven't learned the gate yet." Patrick led out the filly, and Brad brought the gelding. "You take her there and Brad, you on the boy." Patrick gave the instructions after mounting Dan'l.

Trish and Brad exchanged grins. "Kinda like old times." Brad settled his mount down to a flat-footed walk. The gelding obeyed for only an instant before he sidestepped and jigged in place.

"Think you can handle him?" Trish stroked the docile filly's neck.

"Who'd you think's been working this joker while you were gone?" Brad tightened his reins again.

Trish massaged the inside of her cheek with her tongue. "Shame you didn't teach him better manners then." She heard Patrick's chuckle just behind her. Dan'l snorted and pranced up alongside her left. "Hey, old man, you're looking mighty fine."

"Thank you." Patrick tipped his hat with his whip.

"I meant the horse." Trish grinned to let him know she was teasing.

"Sure and ye'll be hurtin' an old man's feelin's."

"Right." Trish nudged her mount into a trot. "Once around and then let them out at the quarter pole, right, Patrick?" At his grunt, she let the filly extend her trot.

The sun in her face, the breeze ruffling her bangs even under the helmet, the grunt of good horseflesh, and time with her friends. What more could she ask for, Trish thought. She smashed the lid on the thought of her father riding Dan'l instead of Patrick.

When they neared the quarter pole, they broke into an easy gallop, lining three abreast and, at Patrick's signal, let the excited horses out.

Trish, on the rail, crouched over the filly's withers, the horse's mane whipping her chin. "Come on, girl, we gotta do this fast. You can't let those other two past."

The filly lengthened her stride, running flat out and low to the ground. Her heavy grunts rang like music in Trish's ears.

Dan'l, in the middle, dropped back so the filly and gelding ran neck and neck. Inch by inch the filly pulled ahead. "We did it!" Trish stood in her stirrups and eased the filly back to a slow gallop. "We won! Good girl."

"Just because you weigh so much less." Brad kept pace with his mount. "This poor fella had to carry too much weight."

"Excuses, excuses." Trish flipped her goggles up and after sitting back in the saddle, patted the filly's dark neck. "Face it, girls are just better than guys, right girl?" The filly snorted and tossed her head.

Brad snorted too, but the sound carried a different meaning.

"Isn't that right, Patrick?" Trish threw a grin at the trainer when he trotted up to join them.

"Don't answer," Brad said. "She'll get the big head if you agree. Besides, we all know that men are better. That's why God created Adam first."

"Naa, He got it right on the second time. Practice makes perfect, you know."

By this time they were back at the barn.

"Children, children. You'll never solve that old quibble, so let it be." Marge stood with her hands on her hips, laughing up at them. "Sorry, Patrick. I tried to teach them correct biblical principles."

"You did fine with me, Mrs. E. Just that girl-child you messed up with." Brad ducked behind his horse when Trish faked a punch at him.

"How about if we all go out to dinner before the meeting?" Marge held the filly's reins while Trish stripped the saddle off. "You can eat with us and then go home if you'd rather not go to the council meeting, Brad."

"You think I'd miss that? No way." Brad brought buckets out with him so they could wash the horses down.

"How about pizza?" Trish heard Patrick's groan. "All right then, Mexican." A groan this time from Marge.

"Patrick likes good old American best." Brad cross-tied his horse and started sponging him down. "And not hamburgers."

"Steak it is." Marge picked up a sponge and started on the filly. "If we hurry, we'll get there before the crowd."

Between them, they had all three animals washed, scraped, and on the hot-walker in record time.

"You're getting pretty good at this horse stuff," Trish said as she and her mother walked up the rise to the house.

"Strange, isn't it? All those years I missed out on."

"You been riding yet?"

"Tee, give me a break. Training, washing, the business end—all that's in. Riding is definitely out. *You* can be queen of the saddle."

"You might really enjoy it. You know Dan'l could use more exercise." Trish shoved open the sliding door off the deck.

"Fine. We'll put him on the walker more often."

It is strange, Trish thought as she changed clothes. *Mom used to be almost afraid of the horses, and now look at her.* But when the picture of her father riding Dan'l galloped into her mind, she blacked it out immediately. Would she ever be able to think of him without crying?

Curt Donovan met them on the front steps of the city hall building. "He didn't win the lottery," he said after greeting them all and being introduced to Brad.

"No rich uncle either?" Marge asked.

"No time to check that, but I'd sure like to see his bank account."

"Can you do that?" Trish turned in surprise.

"Not legally. We'd need a subpoena. But I can find out if he paid cash."

"How?" Trish let the others go through the door ahead of her.

"I have a friend at the dealership where he bought the car."

"How'd you know . . ."

"Checked the license plate, dummy," Brad chimed in. At Trish's questioning look, he shook his head. "You know, they all have their signs on either the plates or the surrounding frame."

"Oh." Trish shrugged. "That must be a guy thing, knowing stuff like that."

Brad shook his head again. "We've been having this discussion," he answered in response to Curt's questioning look.

"That's going to stop now. They've already started the meeting." Marge led the way through the door. They joined Bob Diego and several other Thoroughbred breeders and trainers in the back rows.

After discussion raged on several other issues, the mayor finally announced the agenda item for Portland Meadows.

The topic had no more been introduced when one of the council members raised his hand. "I move we close the Portland Meadows Racetrack, effective immediately."

Trish felt her jaw sag. Surely she hadn't heard him right!

Chapter
08

Don't panic. That's how the process starts," Curt whispered.

Trish let her breath out again, unaware she'd been holding it. "Good."

"Is there any discussion?" Mayor Bonnie Muldoon asked, then nodded at the presenting council member. "John."

The man shuffled some papers in front of him. "You all know that the track has been a problem for years, both financially and socially." He continued on with his comments, all in the negative. The five minutes seemed to stretch for an hour.

Trish felt like jumping to her feet and yelling back. Marge put her hand on her daughter's arm. Wasn't anyone going to speak for the track?

The man droned on. "And so you see, closing the track will not only cease to be a drain on city resources, we will be able to dispense with both a criminal and social problem with the transients out there."

Trish shut her mouth with a snap. What in the world was the idiot talking about? She turned to make a comment to her mother but again felt a restraining hand on her arm.

"We'll talk later," Marge whispered.

A current phrase flashed through Trish's mind: "Never let 'em see you sweat." She pasted herself to the back of the seat and forced her face to hide her thoughts, not telegraph them. Only by crossing her arms over her chest could she subdue the shaking.

Would no one defend horse racing in Portland?

Another council member raised his hand to talk. "Now I think we are getting the cart before the horse here," he said. "We race both Thoroughbreds and quarter horses out there at the track, and I think we need to hear from some of those folks."

Trish breathed a sigh of relief.

Before the mayor could recognize Bob Diego, the man who spoke earlier began talking again. Trish read his nameplate: John Reimer.

"Why doesn't he be quiet?" Trish muttered under her breath.

She stared at the man talking. His dark three-piece suit stuck out from the other casual attire like a black sheep in a light flock. As she listened, his arguments made sense if one didn't know about life at the track and the people there. It made her want to gag.

Curt sat beside her, taking notes.

"Thank you, John," the mayor interrupted. "Mr. Diego, you wanted the floor?"

"Madam Mayor, I have here a petition from the Thoroughbred Association, asking for a delay in making the decision, called a continuance, I believe." Tall, dark, and with a commanding air, Diego spoke with a slight Spanish accent, his words carrying the same air of confidence he projected.

Trish felt like clapping. Talk about a good presentation; Diego had it.

The mayor looked down at her calendar. "Agreed. We will bring this issue to a vote in three weeks. That will give you time to present any reasons for not closing the track." Diego nodded.

"But, Mayor, I showed you all we need to know." Reimer leaned forward. "There's no need for a continuance. I—"

The mayor slammed her gavel. "Next order of business."

When Trish looked back at Reimer, the daggers in his gaze pinned her to the seat. Chills snaked up her spine and out to her fingertips. The man was furious. But when she glanced to her mother and then back to the front, a mask had fallen in place . . . just like the daggers had never been there.

When the mayor announced an intermission, the TBA group gathered in the hall.

"So what happens now?" Marge asked the question Trish had on the tip of her tongue.

"Now we hire a lawyer and start preparing affidavits of fiscal and social responsibility." Bob Diego tapped the papers he carried against his other hand. "We have to convince them that keeping the track open is a sound business plan and good for the city of Portland. Not just for us."

"Mr. Diego, you heard Reimer's accusations about the problems at the track. What do you have to say?" Curt Donovan asked.

"I hate to hear anyone calling our people transients. They work too hard for that." A murmur of agreement ran through the group. "And his hinting at mafia or underworld connections, those innuendoes go along with all the racetracks, and it's just not true. At least not here."

"But there have been money problems out there?"

"They've had a hard time finding a good management company."

"Excuse me," Trish muttered to her mother. Without waiting for an answer, she strode after Mr. Reimer. This time her "excuse me" rang more loudly.

The man stopped and turned. "Yes?"

Trish hadn't realized how big he was until she stood toe to toe with him. "What is it you really have against Portland Meadows?" She forced her voice to remain calm.

"You heard me in the council room." As if playing to an audience, his voice expanded. "I pledged my support for a cleaner city, one without the riffraff around the track."

Trish narrowed her eyes. "I'm at the track a lot. Am I riffraff?"

"Now see here, young lady."

"The name's Trish Evanston. And without Portland Meadows I wouldn't have won the Triple Crown this year. I think you need to do some more research. Now, if you'll excuse me, I hate to take up any more of your valuable time." Trish spun on her heel and returned to her group.

"Bravo, Trish." Curt silently clapped his hands.

"You shouldn'ta done that." Patrick shook his head, his eyes sad.

Trish was sure if she turned around, she'd see the daggers again. With her back to the man, she could feel them. She didn't dare look at her mother.

By the time they walked out to the van, Trish felt as if she'd been riding a monster roller coaster—for an hour.

"But what can *we* do?" Trish slammed the van door after her.

"Attend the TBA meeting on Sunday." Marge turned the ignition. "And keep our mouths shut in public, at least until we know more."

Patrick buckled his seat belt. "What kind of business does that Reimer have?"

"He's a lawyer," Brad answered. "I asked one of the other council members."

"Figures." Trish rested her elbows on her knees. "I didn't like him much."

"Now that's an understatement if I ever heard one." Marge followed the arrows out to the I-5 freeway.

"What time is your flight tomorrow?" Brad asked.

"Seven, why?"

"I can take you over, if you want. Maybe Rhonda'd like to come too."

"I wish one of you would fly down with me so I wouldn't have to drive home alone."

"Sorry, gotta work for my dad tomorrow."

"Yeah, and Rhonda has a show tomorrow and Sunday. One of these days I'm going to get to watch her jump again." Trish hid a yawn behind one hand. "How about you, Patrick? You want a quick trip to sunny California? My treat."

"Don't do me no favors." Patrick tapped her knee with his hat. "Besides, I'm busy."

"You can take some time off, you know. Mother isn't that bad a slave driver."

"Thanks for the vote of confidence. Besides, Patrick and I have something to do tomorrow."

"What?"

"There's a garden show at Washington Park. We have tickets."

"Oh." That's all Trish could think to say.

"And there's the TBA meeting on Sunday. You *do* want someone from Runnin' On there, don't you?" What could Trish say?

Getting off the plane the next evening in California was like stepping into another world. Margaret greeted her with open arms.

"Oh, I've missed you so. Adam and I just rattle around in the condo without you there." She kept an arm about Trish's shoulders. "And how is your mother?"

Trish talked nonstop all the way home, bringing her "other" mother up-to-date on their adventures.

"And Spitfire remembered you?" Margaret asked questions whenever Trish took a breath.

"Boy, did he. I hated leaving him again." Trish patted away a yawn. "How's Adam?"

"You'll see in a minute. He said he'd wait up for us."

Walking into the condo felt about as comfortable as walking into her home in Vancouver. Trish set down her bag and gave Adam a hug.

"So, you're in trouble already, I hear?" Adam kept his hands on her upper arms and studied her face.

"What?"

"Trouble—can't keep you out of it, no matter how hard we all try."

Trish looked at Margaret, question marks all over her face.

"Don't tease her, dear. Can't you tell she has no idea what you're talking about?"

Trish felt like she'd just come in on a movie halfway through.

Adam dropped his hands and fished in his shirt pocket. He pulled out a folded paper and handed it to her.

"Patrick faxed this to me. I thought you'd already seen it."

Trish read the article through. "Well, I have to say he did a good job."

"You know this Donovan fellow?"

"Yep. He's nice. Told him all our suspicions about the track." She glanced back at the article. Third paragraph from the bottom talked about her confronting Reimer. She shrugged with a grin. "What can I say? The guy bugs me."

"He sounds like one of the movers and shakers."

"Yeah, the way he talked about the people at The Meadows, I wanted to move and shake *him*. According to Reimer, everyone out there is either a low-life transient or part of the mafia."

"So, from what the article says, TBA has three weeks to prove The Meadows is financially sound and should be supported?"

"Right." Trish shook her head. "Big order. 'Cause it's not, and we don't know why."

Before going to bed, Trish called home to let her mother know she'd arrived safely. Funny, how it seemed she lived in two separate worlds, one in Washington and the other here in California. Was she ready to be a truly professional jockey and travel all over the country, following the racing seasons? Maybe jetting around to ride certain horses? She snorted at her wonderings.

Not to worry. No one would fly her anywhere to ride with her lousy win record.

Trish shivered in the predawn chill. Trees and lampposts appeared to float on low-lying fog, the same fog that distorted both human and animal sounds, giving the track a spectral air.

"This would be fine for Halloween." Trish tried to bury her head in her jacket collar.

"Look at you, two weeks off and you've turned into a wimp."

"It's supposed to be warm in California, don't ya know?" When they rounded the corner to approach the Finley stalls, Firefly nickered immediately.

"See, she missed you." Adam waved at the bright sorrel filly. In the stall next to her, Gatesby hung his head over the gate and, trailing a mouthful of hay, tossed his head and nickered. "So did he."

"All he missed was my shoulder. Cut it out, you goof." Trish hung on to the gelding's halter to keep him from landing his famous nonverbal hello. She moved down the line, stroking and greeting each of the horses. Even their new addition, Gimmeyourheart, accepted her caresses.

When she reached the office, Adam handed her a whip and helmet. "Get up there and go to work and you'll warm up all right." Trish tucked the grip of the whip into her back pocket and raised her knee for the mount. "Just loosen him up. You're in the third with this old boy." Adam patted the gelding's neck. "Not been much for the winner's circle, but he's usually in the money. You two pushed the winner across the line last time."

"Yeah, maybe if we hadn't pushed so hard, we'da won." Trish tucked her gloved hands under her knees. "Hey, fella, at least you're warm." When Adam shook his head and *tsk*ed, Trish took up the reins and headed for the track.

In spite of her grousing, being back in the saddle felt mighty good. Bay Meadows felt more like home now than Portland Meadows. Fog and chill at both places. She smiled at the thought. But here the sun would be out soon, and the bustle told everyone there was racing ahead. Would that happen in Portland?

She forced her mind back to concentrate on the horse under her and those moving at paces from walk to breeze to flat-out. Her mount jigged sideways as they trotted counterclockwise around the outer edge of the track.

"Hey, Trish, welcome back!" One of the women jockeys waved when they met and passed. Another jockey saluted her with a whip to his helmet. When Trish dismounted back at the barn, Juan's grin stretched across his face and back again.

Carlos boosted her aboard her next mount. "Good to have you back." Since he was never one to waste words, his greeting made her feel even more a part of the family.

"Gatesby been behavin' himself?" Trish asked.

"Right." Since Carlos's black eyebrows met his equally dark and shiny hair, the one word made up for many.

"You think he could make it at Golden Gate?"

"Possibly. If we don't knock him in the head first."

Trish's grin drew an answering one. "Don't eat all the bagels before I get done."

With works finished, Trish, Adam, and Carlos relaxed in the office around the coffeepot and bagel box. "So, according to that article, something smells rotten in Portland." Carlos wiped the cream cheese off his mustache.

"Could be. Curt Donovan—he wrote that article—says he'll do some snooping. Who knows what good he can do, but let me tell you, that Reimer ticked me off from his first words."

"He's a lawyer, right?" Trish nodded. "Then who's he representing?" Adam sipped from his chipped "lucky mug."

Trish thought a moment. "He never said. He's a council member, though."

"Could be a conflict of interests there if he's tied up with anyone."

"Meaning?" Trish stopped chewing and stared at him.

"Well, he's supposed to look out for the good of the city, not any special interests, like TBA or . . ."

"He's not looking out for TBA, that's for sure."

"I know, that's just an example. Ya gotta keep an open mind."

"My mother wants me to keep my mind out of it, along with any other part of me that might get involved." Trish swigged her orange juice.

"She's right." Adam got up to pour himself another cup of coffee. "Anything going on here that I need to know about?" This question he directed at Carlos. "Good, then I have a meeting to attend. See you later."

Later for Trish was in the saddling paddock, preparing for the third race. "Now you just relax," Adam reminded her. "You both know what to do so give it your best."

Trish followed the pony rider out into bright sunlight. The clamor of the crowd, the blue of the sky, and the snapping flags over the infield combined to put her on top of the world. They paraded around the track and then back past the grandstand with Trish stiff-legged, high above the gelding's withers. He entered gate three like the pro he was and with no further ado, they were off.

Trish crouched tight against his mane, singing her song to his twitching ears. When she asked for more coming out of the second turn, he lengthened out and pounded after the two front-runners. Like an out-of-control express train, he bore down on and passed the horse running second. Stride by stride he ate up the length between them and the front-runner.

Trish could hear the crowd roaring. The two white pillars loomed ahead. Her mount grunted with each stride. Neck out, ears forward, he drew even, neck and neck. Nose to nose. And he was past. One length, two. He charged across the finish line like he won every race.

"Yahoo!" Trish pumped the air with the whip in her fist. "Thank you, God. What a way to start the day."

She tried to smile professionally for the picture but couldn't suppress the beaming. Winning felt so good.

"That's my girl." Adam and Martha flanked her, with Carlos holding the gelding's bridle. "See you again in the seventh."

Trish hustled back to change silks for her mount in the fourth. The trainer counseled her about keeping the filly back until the stretch because she had a tendency to run herself out too soon. This would be her first time at a mile.

Trish nodded and stroked the gray neck. Again the crowd greeted the post parade with a roar. The filly acted as if the show was all for her benefit and walked into the gate like a pro.

A horse two down had to be gated twice, but then they were off. The poles whipped by. The filly decided to let Trish be the boss after the first turn and settled down to run. Which she did. She ran the others right into the dirt and won going away by four lengths.

Two wins in one day. This felt like old times at The Meadows back up in Portland, where Trish had won nearly half of her races.

After the ceremonies, Trish stopped her walk back to the jockey room when she heard a voice call her. She looked around to find the reporter who'd dubbed her "The Comeback Kid."

"Lookin' good there, Trish. How does it feel to be back in the winner's circle?"

"Good. Awesome good."

"Heard you were in Kentucky. You going to ride in the Breeder's Cup?"

"Who knows. I'm just glad to be riding today."

"You heard any more from Chrysler?"

"Nope, I think your sources are all wet. They use models in ads like that, not a kid like me." She waved a thanks at congratulations from someone in the crowd.

"I'll be the first to say I told you so. And good luck on the rest of your rides today. Sorry you're leaving California."

Trish looked after his retreating figure. How'd he know so much about her? And who were those sources of his? She shook hands with a young girl who offered her program for an autograph. After signing it, Trish answered what had become a pretty standard question: "No, I don't get to race Spitfire again. And yes, you can try to be a jockey when you get older. Start by learning all you can about horses and riding right now."

By the time she got up to the jockey room, she needed a drink, and water wasn't enough. She headed for the pop machine, quarters in hand. She could hear a Diet Coke calling her name.

Her third mount quit running two furlongs from the finish line. It was all she could do to keep him going until the end.

Adam winked at her from his place by the fence. He met her by the walkway to the jockey rooms. "You think we should've put a claimer on that one?" Her snort made him laugh.

Her agent called to her before she went in. "Hey, Trish, I got a new one for you in the eighth, that okay?"

"Sure. How come?"

"Jockey came up sick. Think he has the Heidelberg flu."

Trish rolled her tongue across her teeth. The Heidelberg flu meant the jockey suffered from a hangover. She felt no sympathy at all for him.

"Glad to. I'm riding for Adam in the seventh. That makes five mounts today. Super!"

"Might as well go out with a bang." He shook her hand. "If I don't see you again before you leave, have a good trip. And I sure hope they race in Portland this year."

"Thanks. Me too."

Trish brought Adam's other horse in for a show. It was the filly's first stakes race, and Adam thumped her on the knee with joy. "You did good, kid."

And Trish agreed. She'd pulled the filly out of a tight spot and felt grateful for the placing.

She mounted a rangy gelding for her final race. He met her with ears back and shook his head when the trainer secured the blinkers in place.

"Maybe we should scratch him," the trainer said in an undertone.

"Naw, he'll be fine," the owner insisted. "He just got up on the wrong side of the bed this morning." When the trainer tried to say something else, the burly owner cut him off.

Trish felt guilty for eavesdropping. But at this point, she wished the trainer had more guts.

The horse argued with the pony rider and half reared when the gatekeepers tried to lead him into slot five. Trish felt alarm leap from bone to bone up her spine.

"Come on, knothead." She forced the soothing tone into her voice. The horse shook his head. His back arched beneath her.

"Watch him." The gate assistant's warning was lost in the animal's shrill whinny.

Chapter 09

He's going over!"

Trish heard the warning as she felt the animal rise beneath her. As he went up, she pushed herself up and out of the irons. She threw herself at the round iron bars separating each horse. Anything to keep from being crushed against the rear gate by the brute she rode.

Pain shot through her left shoulder when she smacked against the rail. Hands grabbed her and hauled her up before she fell below the gelding's slashing feet.

It all happened so fast her heartbeat didn't catch up until she had her feet on the ground outside the gate.

Two of the keepers hung on to the horse where he stood shaking. "Got more than you bargained for, you old . . ." He called the horse a name not nearly bad enough in Trish's mind.

Like the horse, she couldn't stop shaking. Her left arm hung useless at her side. It felt like she'd struck her crazy bone, only instead of just the elbow, her arm screamed from shoulder to wrist. What would her mother say to this?

"You okay?" one of the men asked.

"All but my arm." Her teeth chattered between the words.

"Right. Let's get you outta here." He waved to the official. The gun sounded and the remaining field burst from the gates.

"I'm so sorry," the trainer apologized when he retrieved his horse. "I shoulda just did what I thought best."

Trish nodded. Her knees felt like cooked spaghetti, and they weren't the part of her that hurt.

"How about a hand getting over to first aid?" one of the gate men asked.

Trish nodded. Her chattering teeth let her know she was going into shock, so a warm arm to lean on sounded good. Adam met her at the fence.

"Thanks, I'll take her now." He wrapped an arm about Trish's waist and let her lean against him. "You want Carlos to carry you?"

Trish shook her head. "I can walk." She clutched her injured arm with the other, cradling it so the jolting didn't hurt so much.

"You think it's broken?" Adam pushed open the door to the first aid.

"Uh—uh." The thought of a broken arm sent her heart into overdrive.

"Let's have a look at that." The staff nurse sat Trish down in a chair and after closing the white curtain, unfastened her silks. The woman kept up a soothing monologue, not unlike Trish's own for spooky horses, while she examined the arm and shoulder.

"Good news. It's just dislocated. We can fix that in a jiffy." She stepped back to study Trish's face. "Now, we can give you something for the pain first, but I'll tell you, the sooner we put it back where it belongs, the less inflammation we'll have. You tough enough for that?"

Trish nodded and bit her bottom lip. "Just do it."

"Would you rather wait for a doctor?"

"No."

The nurse called the masseur in to help. She explained what they had to do. "Now, you yell if you need to. We don't need any heroes here, okay?" Trish nodded again. Together they applied the right pressures and, on three, snapped the shoulder joint back in place.

"Ahhh!" Trish heard the grind and snap. Before she could say any-more, she could already feel the relief.

"We did it. Good job, Trish. You're a real trooper."

Trish panted out a "thank you." She accepted a glass of water along with a couple of pain killers. When she could breathe again, she forced a smile to her mouth. Licking her lips helped too.

"Okay, let's ice that sucker and then you can go home to bed. You don't have any mounts tomorrow, do you?"

"No, I'm driving to Vancouver early in the morning." Trish winced again when the nurse laid the blue plastic ice packets over the wet wash-cloths against her skin.

"You're what?" The nurse talked as she wrapped towels around the injury. Trish repeated herself. "That's what I thought you said. You get up here and lie down for a bit." She helped Trish climb up on a gurney and lie back. "Can't someone drive for you?" Trish shook her head. "Then wait a couple of days or fly."

"I wish." Trish closed her eyes. "I'll be fine. You said this was simple."

"True, but I didn't say it wouldn't hurt."

If only I'd left well enough alone, Trish thought as she lay staring at the ceiling. *One more mount. I had to take one more mount.*

"Can I see her for a moment?" she heard Adam ask the nurse.

When she agreed, he pulled the curtain back enough to enter and leaned over the gurney. "How ya doing?"

Trish could feel her eyes fill at the concern in his voice. "Thank God it's not broken," she managed.

"What a bummer. They shoulda scratched that beast. Hank knows better than that."

"He tried. The owner wouldn't buy it." Trish turned her head so she could see him when he sat down in the chair by her bed.

Adam shook his head. "So now what are you going to do?"

Trish raised an eyebrow in question.

"About going home tomorrow."

"Drive. Why?" When she recognized the stubborn look on his face, she added. "I'll be fine, really I will. If I need to stop, I can do that.

Adam, it was just dislocated. I'll wear the sling, and my shifting arm isn't injured."

"I'll drive you." He crossed his arms over his chest.

"No." She almost controlled the wince when she shook her head.

"Then Martha will. Or you'll fly."

"I have to get my car home." Trish blinked her eyes against the sleepiness caused by the pain pills. The warmth started at her feet and flowed upward. If she could just sleep awhile—

"Okay, Missy, let's get that sling in place and let you go home before this man paces a groove in my floor here." The nurse's voice called Trish back from the floating land of comfort.

Sitting up snapped her fully awake. "Ow."

"I know." The nurse adjusted the blue canvas sling and eased Trish's silks back in place, tucking the empty sleeve inside. She handed Trish two bottles with pills in them. "Now, you take these to keep the swelling down, and these will help the pain."

"Will they make me sleepy?"

"Most likely."

"Thank you." Trish stuffed the two small containers in her pocket. While she felt a bit woozy when she stood up, she ignored the feeling and nodded when Adam asked if she was ready. He had her bag from the jockey room in his hand. Trish thanked the nurse again and followed Adam out the door.

The sun setting behind the western hills told her how much time had passed since the accident. Trish got in the car carefully. She'd hoped to go out to the beach tonight. That's where she heard her song best, the one about eagle's wings. Boy, did she need eagle's wings right now.

That's where she'd finally found peace again, and now she wouldn't even get to say good-bye. She leaned her head back against the headrest of the car seat. It would be so easy to blubber right now. She sniffed against the moisture pooling at the back of her nose and eyes.

But if she cried now, Adam would never let her drive tomorrow.

When Trish forced her bruised body out of bed in the morning, a knock on her door announced Martha.

"How're you feeling?" She didn't wait for Trish's answer, and instead handed her the blue ice packs. "Now, you let this ice for a bit while I finish your packing for you. Then Adam will help load the car, and you and I'll be off."

"Martha, I'll be fine. You don't need to do this."

The older woman planted both fists on her rounded hips and stared at Trish, eyes narrowed. "If you think I'd let you go off by yourself injured like this . . ." She shook her head and turned back to the closet. "Why, your mother would kill me."

Not really, Trish thought, flexing her fingers. *She's going to want to kill me!* She knew she should have called home last night but—she rubbed her forehead with the uninjured hand. But she hadn't had the strength to argue and she *was* going to have her car at home.

"Don't even think about arguing with me." Margaret looked up from folding and packing Trish's things. "You know I'm right, and since your mother isn't going to be pleased about another injury, at least she'll applaud your good sense in allowing help."

What could Trish say? "Thank you" were the only words that came to mind.

She slept most of the eleven-hour trip home, waking only for food and rest stops.

"Those muscle relaxers appear to work pretty well," Martha said at one point when Trish rebuckled her seat belt.

At least it doesn't hurt as much this way, Trish thought as she dozed back to sleep again. Fighting to stay awake had already proven a wasted effort.

She woke up enough to direct Martha once they reached the southern edge of Portland. It didn't take long to get through the city and cross the Columbia River to Vancouver. Each mile closer to home brought increased alertness. Her heart picked up speed when they turned into the drive at Runnin' On Farm.

Caesar did his best to announce to the entire world that Trish was home again. Marge came out the front door as Trish stepped from the car. They met at the gate.

"How bad is it?" Marge checked her daughter over, looking for visible injuries.

"Just a dislocated shoulder. Margaret drove me up."

"Thank God." She squeezed Trish's good hand and walked on out to the car. "How good to see you. And thank you for caring for my kid there." The two women swapped hugs and retrieved the suitcases from the trunk and backseat. Burdened down, they made their way to the house.

Trish held the door for them. "At least I can do this one-handed." Her feeble attempt at a joke fell flat.

Marge set the things down and turned to her daughter. "Has it been X-rayed?" Trish shook her head. "Then I think our next order of business is to visit the emergency room and take care of that."

"Mother, the nurse said . . ."

"You haven't seen a doctor either?" At the look on Trish's face, Marge walked to her bedroom and returned carrying her purse. "Martha, if you'd like to kick back and relax for a while . . ."

"No, I'll go along. We can use the time to visit."

Trish didn't dare say I told you so on the drive home again, but she sure wanted to. The doctor said exactly the same things the nurse had and approved the pills Trish was taking. Said she'd feel lots better in a day or two and the more she iced it, the better.

She didn't argue either in the morning when her mother prepared to drive her to school. The tight-lipped look her mother wore when helping Trish dress was enough to keep any thinking person silent, let alone a daughter who already felt guilty as charged.

"I'm sorry, Mom," Trish muttered. "It wasn't my fault."

"Tee, I know that. I'm not angry at you." Marge turned the ignition.

"Coulda fooled me." Trish buckled her seat belt with one hand. Having an injured arm wasn't easy, but she would not ask for help again.

Marge leaned her head on her hands. "It's just when something like this happens, I realize all over again what a dangerous sport you're—we're—in. You could be critically injured—or killed so easily."

Trish rolled her upper lip between her teeth. "But, you promised not to worry anymore."

"Yeah, well, the promise was easy. Livin' it ain't." She shot her daughter a watery grin. "It's only through the grace of God I keep my sanity at all. So . . ." She took a deep breath and let it out. "Thank God for His grace that can keep even a dyed-in-the-wool worrier like me under control. Times like this send me back to 'I can do all things through Christ who strengthens me.' "

Trish thought about her mother's words later that day when her arm got bumped in the crush of students hurrying to class.

In government class, the teacher announced that all of them would be involved in class projects. "We'll divide into groups of three or four, and each team will come up with its own idea and plan. The goal is to understand more about how our democratic system functions."

Trish and Rhonda looked at each other across the aisle. How could they get on the same team?

"Now, we could number off, but since we're learning about the democratic process, I will entertain ideas from the floor."

Trish and Rhonda stared at each other, raised eyebrows matching. The classroom had never been so silent.

"You mean about how we should choose teams?" The hesitant question came from the other side of the room.

"That's correct."

"Each of us choose two partners," someone then responded.

"What if someone is left out?" Ms. Wainwright shot back.

"Take the first three in a row . . ." Groans from around the room.

"Go alphabetically." More groans.

"Vote." A hush waited for the teacher's response.

"Now how would you work that out?" Added groans. The suggester shrugged.

"We could elect a committee to divide the class into groups."

Ms. Wainwright wrote their suggestions on the board as they came up. "Remember how we talked about democracy being a slow process?" She read each suggestion again. "All of these take time."

"You could assign the groups."

"True. That form of government is called a . . ." She waited for responses.

"Dictatorship."

"Monarchy." Trish glared at someone behind her who hissed at her answer.

"True, if I were the queen," Ms. Wainright said with a smile. "We're going to vote on which method to use, so raise your hands for the one you like best. Just remember, when we're finished, everyone must be on a team."

The class selected personal choice so Rhonda, Trish, and Doug formed a group. "We gotta make sure everyone's on a team." Trish checked over her shoulder to see if anyone appeared left out.

"Is everyone finished?" the teacher asked. At their nods, she shook her head. "Did you include those who are absent?"

"Who's not here?"

"We only have two," someone else said. "They can be on our team."

"Good. Now, what have you learned from this?"

"Democracy can be a pain in the . . ." one of the guys muttered.

The teacher laughed along with the class. "True. Any kind of government can. What else?"

"It takes time and cooperation," Rhonda answered.

"Good." After waiting for more answers, Ms. Wainright finished. "Government is a method of solving problems, hopefully for the good of the greatest number of people."

"Yeah, and if you're absent, you don't have no say."

Again, the chuckles rippled around the room. "So true. So voting is a must." She started two sheets of paper down the outside aisles. "Now sign up together when the paper comes to you. Then you have five minutes to talk about your project." She raised her hand for silence. "Deadline for the topic is Friday."

"Don't we get to vote on that?"

She shook her head, laughing along with the rest.

"She's cool," Rhonda said as they left the classroom at the bell.

"Yeah, but what are we gonna do?" Doug walked beside Trish.

"Got me. Guess we could attend a trial or something." The three looked at each other and shrugged.

"How about stringing up a certain pain-in-the-neck lawyer?" Trish tossed her books in her locker. She grinned at the rolled-eye looks from her friends. "Just a thought."

When she got home from school, there was a message from Curt to call him back.

"Hi, this is Trish Evanston." She polished the apple she'd retrieved from the refrigerator.

"Guess what? Your suspicions were right on. Smithson, the assistant manager, has put two rather large deposits into his savings account in the last six months. And one in his checking. These are besides his regular paychecks."

"How'd you . . ."

"Don't ask. Let's just say I owe a computer friend of mine a favor."

"The deposits could be legal."

"Sure. But at least if we need them, the police will have some place to start."

"Whoa, this gets scary." Trish turned and, leaning her elbows on the counter, stared out the window. "Now what?"

"You suppose you could ask some questions over at the track? Just if anyone's noticed anything unusual. They'll talk with you since they all know you. Better not to have a stranger like me butting in."

"I guess." Trish munched her apple after she hung up the phone. As he'd said, at least they had a place to start. And all she'd be doing is talking with her friends at the track. Surely her mother couldn't yell at her for that.

Trish wasn't exactly thrilled about the topic idea her team turned in on Friday, but they hadn't thought up anything better. They would contact their local legislator and ask how they could help with her campaign. They'd probably end up stuffing envelopes.

But Saturday morning she headed to Portland Meadows. When her mother had asked why, Trish just said she'd like to see how things were going there.

That wasn't a lie. That's what she told her nagger when he started grousing.

Since many of the local trainers used the barns and track on a regular basis (not everyone had their own track like Runnin' On Farm), Trish felt right at home in the bustle. She answered all the greetings and stopped to visit with some on her way to the Diego stalls.

"Trish." Bob Diego leaped to his feet when she thumped on the desk where he sat going over training charts. "Good to see you. You bringing your horses in?"

"No, just came to . . ."

"I know, you need some extra money, so you'll ride for me in the mornings."

Trish shook her head and laughed.

"Okay, then how about I buy you a cup of coffee?" Bob closed the book on his desk and slipped it into the drawer. "Or breakfast." He checked his watch. "Mine's long overdue."

They discussed the goings-on at the track on their way to the kitchen, and after getting their food, Trish brought up the council meeting. In an undertone, she told Diego of the money in the assistant manager's account.

"How'd you find that out?" Diego asked after chewing a mouthful of pancakes.

"Don't ask, as the man told me."

The trainer shook his head. "You better stay out of this, young lady, or your mother'll—"

"I know. I'm being careful. Just told him I'd ask around. See what the scuttlebutt is here."

After they finished eating, Diego pushed back his chair. "I better get back. Some of us have to work for a living."

Trish grinned up at him. "You could ride in the Triple Crown too."

"Cheeky kid." Diego knuckled her cheek. "You be careful."

Trish caught the gaze of a couple of jockeys at another table. Beyond them sat a table of owners/breeders. Trish noticed a new man talking with the owners she'd ridden for. Who was he, she wondered.

"Hey, come on over." Genie Stokes waved. "Haven't seen you in a coon's age."

Trish visited with them for a while, and soon others came by. But no one had heard anything for sure. Just made jokes about the new Corvette and grumbled about the possibility of the track not opening. Some thought they'd head for California maybe; others mentioned the South. None of them had met the new man.

Trish felt the weight of everybody's depression by the time she left the track. *Someone* had to do *something*; that was clear.

When she got home, she heard her mother blowing her nose in the kitchen. Marge hastily wiped away telltale tears as Trish walked into the room.

"What's wrong?" Trish felt that much-too-familiar clutch in her heart region.

"Nothing." Marge drew another tissue from her pocket and blew her nose again. "Just all of a sudden this house seemed so empty I wanted to scream." She tried to blink back the tears, but one escaped and rolled down her cheek. "Some days I miss your dad so much I . . ." She shook her head and squeezed her lips together. "I don't know . . . it'll go away again." With shaking fingers, she scrubbed at the tears that continued to fall.

Trish put her arms around her mother's waist and held on. She understood . . . oh, how she understood! They remained in each other's arms for a while before Trish leaned back.

"How about we bake some cookies for David?" Trish suggested. "I'll call Rhonda and Brad. Maybe they'd like to help. The house won't be so empty if we have a party."

Marge nodded and mopped her face again. "Let me get myself together first."

"They can." Trish hung up the phone and turned with a grin. "Said they'd be here in half an hour."

"You're pretty special, you know that, Tee?" Marge brushed back a lock of hair that refused to stay confined in Trish's braid.

"Thanks."

By the time they finished, the box for David contained chocolate chip, peanut butter, and oatmeal cookies, plus brownies. All the cookie jars bulged, and more containers made it to the freezer.

After helping Patrick, Brad went out for pizza, and the party continued, including the trainer.

When Trish fell into bed that night, she hugged herself and couldn't quit smiling. What fun they'd had. Like old times, even without David and their father. Her thank-you's to God were the music she slipped into sleep by.

She was totally unprepared for what happened in church the next morning. Pastor Mort read her letter, deeding the third red convertible to the congregation.

"The church council has voted to use the money from the sale of the car to begin a fund for a fifteen-passenger van to be used by all the organizations here at church." He smiled at Trish. "But especially for the youth groups."

Someone stood in the back of the church. "Why don't we change the idea from a van to a full-sized bus? Seems that would be much more practical."

"I'll pledge a thousand dollars." Trish had no idea who volunteered that amount, but within five minutes, thousands more had been pledged. She gripped her mother's hand.

"Guess that makes it all legal, then." Pastor Mort winked at Trish. "The council will appoint a committee to find us a bus."

Pastor Ron, the youth pastor, rose to his feet. "I think we should name our bus *Hal*, in memory of Hal Evanston and in thanks to his daughter, Trish."

That did it. Trish fought down the urge to flee and instead let the tears flow. After all, if even a pastor can cry from the steps of the altar, why should the congregation do less? And from the sniffs she heard, there weren't many dry eyes in the entire place.

Marge tugged on her hand so that together they got to their feet and turned to face their church family. "Thank you." What other words were necessary?

Amidst all the community hugs and happy discussion, Trish felt like pulling a "Rhonda" and spinning in place as her friend still sometimes did when the excitement grew too great.

"You didn't tell me," Rhonda whispered when they had a moment.

"Didn't think it would be a big deal," Trish whispered back.

"Right! With Pastor Mort in on it, anything can be a big deal."

Trish returned a watery grin. "But who knew all the others would jump in like that?"

"God?"

The glow stayed with her through the night and all day at school.

When she walked in the door at home, her mother handed her an envelope. Trish's name and address were typed on it. There was no return address.

Trish looked at her mother, shrugged, and slit open the envelope. The message leaped out at her. Letters cut from newspapers and magazines spelled out "Keep your nose out of other people's business. Stay away from Portland Meadows!"

Chapter
10

She felt like she'd been slugged in the gut.

"Trish, what is it? You're white as a sheet." Trish handed her mother the piece of paper. "Oh, my . . ." Marge stared at her daughter and then read the letter again. "That's it! You are *not* to talk to anyone again. Who did you talk to? What'd you do?" Her voice rose with each word.

"Mom, Mom. I didn't do anything. I didn't say anything to anyone."

"Then why this letter?" She flicked the paper with the backs of her fingers.

"I don't know." Trish swallowed the thought of *All I did was ask a few questions, get people talking to me. Someone sure told the wrong party.* Her mind cataloged all the people she'd talked to at the track. Which one of them was the snitch?

The phone rang. Trish answered it and only muttered answers before hanging up.

"Curt is calling the cops. He got one just like this."

"Oh, wonderful! They'll be shooting at you next." Marge rubbed her forehead with her fingertips.

"This isn't television, for Pete's sake. No one's gonna hurt anyone."

"Famous last words."

"Mom, you're worrying again."

"With just cause."

"I gotta get down to work the horses." Trish laid the letter on the counter. "Don't worry, Mom. It'll be okay."

But Trish wasn't so sure of that when the white Portland Police cruiser pulled up to the front gate. She dismounted from her last mount of the afternoon and strode quickly up the rise. Marge was already inviting the two officers inside by the time Trish made it to the house.

"Tricia Evanston?" The man's broad shoulders made his six-foot frame seem even taller. He would have no trouble commanding respect anywhere, as far as Trish could figure, and his deep voice only added to the illusion of power. He dwarfed the woman beside him. He extended a hand that could have doubled for a baseball mitt, but when he shook Trish's hand, gentleness passed through the contact.

When Trish nodded, he continued. "I'm Officer Don Parks, and this is my partner, Sheila Dunning. We've been assigned to look into this case after Curt Donovan called the station."

"You've already talked with Curt?" Trish kept her voice from squeaking by sheer act of will. Why did meeting these officers make her want to hide under the bed? She hadn't done anything wrong.

"Yes, and we have his letter to run through some tests. Do you mind if we sit down?" He indicated the living room.

"Oh, I'm sorry," Marge said. "What happened to my manners? Can I get you a cup of coffee? Cookies?"

Trish could tell her mother had an attack of nerves also. And she really hadn't done anything wrong.

"Now, may we see your letter?" Officer Dunning spoke in a musical voice. Her smile set Trish as much at ease as Parks' power made her shake.

Trish held out the letter. "It came in the mail today. Here's the envelope too." She watched as the man took the letter by the upper corner and held it out so both officers could study it at the same time.

"Looks like a match." Parks pinned Trish with laser-blue eyes. "You have an idea who would send something like this?"

Trish shook her head. "Nor why, either."

"Why don't you tell me what you know about the events at Portland Meadows, including the city council meeting."

Trish did as asked. While she talked, her mother brought in a tray with coffee mugs and cookies. The officers listened intently, writing on small notebooks but not asking questions until she finished.

Trish really felt she was finished by the time they stood up an hour later and thanked her and her mother for their time. As they left, the man turned to her.

"Watching you win the Triple Crown was some experience. You look so small and vulnerable up on that black colt of yours. My daughter talks nonstop of racing Thoroughbreds someday ever since she saw you."

"Your daughter will be over six feet tall by the time she's twelve." Sheila winked at Trish. "Becky, his daughter, is a doll, but she's been the tallest in her class since kindergarten."

"Yeah, well, anyway, congratulations. You did a fine job."

"Thank you. Bring Becky by at the track sometime—that is, if we ever get to race there."

"I will, and if you think of anything else, here's my card. Call me."

"Okay. Will you let me know if you find anything in the letter?" Trish couldn't believe she asked the question. It's just that her curiosity got ahold of her. She saw the frown that creased her mother's forehead.

"We'll see." The two left. Trish watched them walk back to their patrol car, then she turned again to her mother.

"I know, I'll stay out of it. I will." But she couldn't get the words "I promise" past the idea stage. Surely this was all over now.

The next day in government class, Ms. Wainwright opened a discussion about ways the people can influence government. They talked about voting and how important it was for eighteen-year-olds to voice their opinion too.

"How else?" The teacher nodded to a hand raised in back.

"You can attend meetings in your community and say what you think, like at the school board."

"Good. I see several teams have decided to use that for their project." She glanced down the list in a file folder.

Trish raised her hand. When the teacher acknowledged her, she began. "We have a problem at the racetrack, and it involves the Portland city council." Trish continued on with the story, bringing the class up-to-date, including the visit from the police officers.

"So, what'd they find on the letter?" one of the students asked.

Trish shrugged. "I don't know. But I feel so—so helpless. You know—who listens to kids, anyway?"

"Someone must have for you to get a warning like that." Ms. Wainwright turned and began writing on the chalkboard. "Okay, class, this is what I want you to do. Turn to page 126 of your textbook. This section talks about petitions and referendums. When you are finished reading, raise your hand."

The silence after everyone found the place deepened. Trish did as she was instructed, at the same time wondering what this had to do with her problem at Portland Meadows. As she read, she grew more excited.

"That's it!" Rhonda fairly jumped in her seat. "We could get up petitions to keep the city from closing down The Meadows." She poked Trish in the side.

Trish nodded without looking up and waved Rhonda's hand away. Could she and Rhonda and Doug take *this* on as a project instead?

As soon as all hands were raised, the teacher moved back to the front of her desk and leaned against it.

"Are there any questions?"

"Could kids do this? Do you have to live in Portland? How long do we have? What do we do first?" The questions ricocheted from the walls.

"What do you think?" The teacher returned to the chalkboard. "Okay, let's lay out a plan. Step one."

"Get more information about petitions." Doug winked at Trish.

"How?"

Some volunteered to do research in the school library; someone else's team said they'd hit the Fort Vancouver Public Library; Doug said Rhonda, Trish, and he would go to City Hall in Portland and ask there.

"We will?" Rhonda shot him a questioning glance.

"Good! Day after tomorrow we'll all bring in what we've found." The bell rang before the teacher could finish her instructions. No one moved. "And then we'll set up a real plan of action. Let's just call this the Prairie Political Action Committee . . . PAC in political jargon. Class dismissed."

"How can you go to Portland?" Rhonda asked as the three of them left the classroom. "You've got football practice."

Doug smacked his palm against his forehead. "I got so excited in there I forgot. Guess that means you two have to go. Think you can handle it?"

"My mother's going to kill me."

"No she won't. Tell her this is a class assignment. If she's not happy about it, she can call and talk to Ms. Wainwright." Doug raised his eyebrows and shrugged. "That's all you have to do."

"You know, for a dumb jock, you make an awful lot of sense." Trish looked up at the guy walking beside her.

"Look who's calling who a dumb jock. At least my opponents don't try to mash me against steel bars or . . ."

"I get the picture." Trish held up a hand. "How about if I call Curt and have him get us all the information he can from the newspaper? The city offices probably close by five, so we better hustle. No hanging out with what's-his-name after school today, Rhonda, okay? See you guys." Trish grabbed her gym bag and headed for weight training. That should get her mind off "The Mess," as she was beginning to refer to it.

All the way to Portland the two girls discussed the situation and the petitions. And they always came back to "why?" Why would anyone cause problems there?

"My dad says it probably has something to do with drugs." Rhonda sipped her Diet Coke.

"Your dad thinks everything has to do with drugs." Trish braked for the car that slowed in front of them. I-5 was already slowing with pre-rush-hour traffic.

"I know, but he also said that's a prime piece of real estate, and with all the development going up around there—"

"Yeah, Patrick mentioned that too. But why would a developer send a stupid letter like I got?"

"Beats me. Jason said he wanted to help with the petitions too."

"He just wants to be wherever you are."

"No, really. Said he'd learn more about the American political system this way."

"Gimme a break."

By the time they left the courthouse, they carried bags of stuff. A booklet about drafting a petition seemed the most valuable. The people they'd talked with appeared really pleased that a group of kids was taking an interest in local government.

"Just make sure you follow all the guidelines, honey," one woman reminded them. "If it's not done exactly right, all your efforts will be wasted."

A man had volunteered to come talk to their class about running for public office. Everyone wished them well.

"They were all so helpful," Rhonda said for the third time when they got back in the car.

"Yes, Rhonda. And now, do we ever have plenty of homework to do! And I have horses to work. You want to help?"

"Sure. I don't have any shows for another month or so. George can go one day without working." Her Thoroughbred Arab gelding's name was really Akbar Sadat, but they'd called him George ever since Rhonda had bought him four years earlier as a two-year-old.

Curt Donovan's tiny white car was parked by the front gate when they turned into Runnin' On Farm. They found him inside, munching cookies and visiting with Marge.

"I have a packet of stuff for you," he said after greeting them both. "I hit the paper archives. Amazing the stuff you can find down there."

"Yeah, and look what we got at the courthouse." Trish dumped their armloads on the table. "And I have horses to work, so let me change and I'll be right back." She didn't look at her mother. She could feel the frown all the way down the hall.

Curt strolled down to the barns with them. "I seem to be hitting a dead end with my investigations. Without a court order, I can't find out where Smithson got his money. When I tried to talk with him, he hung up, and ever since then he's been out whenever I call or go by."

"Maybe he left the country," Rhonda said.

"No, his Corvette is parked in its usual place. What a fool if that money was a bribe!"

"What are the police doing?"

"Nothing that I can tell. Letters like that are pretty small stuff compared to all the cases they try to solve." Trish and Rhonda groaned in unison.

"Yeah, somebody has to get killed before the cops take any action." Rhonda was being her dramatic self.

"They did come talk to me—and they seemed to care."

"Caring isn't the problem. Lack of time, money, and personnel are the issues. Thanks to city budget cuts, the police department has been taking it in the neck." Curt greeted Patrick and Brad, who already had three horses saddled.

"We'll be about an hour." Trish raised her knee for a leg up.

"I better get going. See you." Curt turned and strode back up the rise to his car.

"I think he likes you."

"Rhonda!"

Brad just shook his head as they trotted the horses out to the track. "Patrick wanted to work the gates today."

"I know, but we had to do our school assignment first." Rhonda could sound real self-righteous when she tried.

Later that evening Trish had just finished her zoology assignment when her mother knocked on her bedroom door. "Can I come in?"

"Sure." Trish stretched her arms above her head and yawned. "You don't happen to have a Diet Coke with you, do you?"

Marge shook her head. "I'll be right back." She returned in a couple of minutes, a glass filled with ice and Diet Coke in her hand. "Here you go."

"Thanks. That was really nice of you." Trish sipped and rotated her shoulders. She waited for what she knew was coming.

Marge sat down on the bed. "I asked you not to get involved with the investigation."

"I know and I'm not."

"Then what about all this?" Marge waved a hand over the papers stacked on Trish's bed.

"That's an assignment for my government class. We're studying local government and how ordinary people can influence those in office." Trish parroted her teacher's words. "You can check with Ms. Wainwright if you like."

"And the situation at The Meadows has nothing to do with this?"

What could Trish say? She gathered her thoughts before answering. The truth was always best, her father always said.

"I brought up The Meadows because she was talking about ordinary people influencing government, like I said. I just thought we'd kick it around a bit, but she got all excited and pretty soon everyone was volunteering to do the research, and Doug said our team would pick up stuff at the courthouse, and so here I am."

Marge nodded, one fingertip on her chin. "You know, Tee, I just don't want you to get hurt."

"How could I get hurt? I'm just studying government." She didn't say, "You worry too much," even though she wanted to. Sometimes keeping your mouth shut was smarter than spouting off.

By the time Trish read all the stuff they'd collected, she felt like her head was stuffed. You didn't just walk in and come out ten minutes later with a petition in hand and start collecting signatures. She glanced at the clock. Five to midnight. And she hadn't yet written the paper due in English. Here school hadn't been going two weeks and she was already behind.

She drew her notebook out and started writing. Two pages taking the pro side of an issue. "Should Horse Racing Continue at Portland Meadows?" Easy topic. She sure knew plenty about it.

She closed her books at twelve-thirty and climbed into bed. At least she didn't have to be up at four to work horses at the track before school. That would have gone on the . . . She fell asleep before she could finish the thought.

Her class spent the next three days working on their petition. On Monday they car-pooled over to the courthouse and submitted their final forms. The clerk looked them over, read their application, assigned it a number, and typed in the required information. When they left they had the original ready to make copies.

Curt and another reporter, along with a photographer, met them on the courthouse steps. After asking questions, they lined the class up and, with Ms. Wainwright standing to the side, took pictures.

"Now, where are you going to collect signatures?" Curt asked.

"At a couple of malls and several grocery stores. We have to make copies first, so that won't start until tomorrow."

"Some of us are going to go house to house," one of the boys said. "We're working in teams of three so we'll be plenty safe."

"Since it's Saturday, we can work all day," Rhonda added.

All the student teams had their assignments, along with clipboards, extra copies of the petition, and plenty of pens, by the time they left school late that afternoon.

Trish, Doug, and Rhonda had volunteered to work at Clackamas Town Center to the southeast of Portland. "That way we can go shopping afterward," Rhonda whispered. Trish just shook her head. Shopping and guys had gone to her friend's head.

They had their spiels down pat the next morning when the four of them—Jason came along like he promised—arrived at the huge mall.

"Now remember, qualify them first. Ask if they are registered voters 'cause otherwise their signature won't count." Trish opened her trunk to remove their box of supplies.

By the end of their two-hour stint, Trish felt as if her tongue would stick to the roof of her mouth, it was so dry. Her shoulders ached, her feet hurt, and her friends suffered the same.

"I'm starved." Rhonda sank down on a bench overlooking the central courtyard. "Let's head for the food."

"We have to wait for Jennifer and her team. They'll be here any minute. Just keep at this till they come." Trish pushed herself to her feet. "Come on, not much longer." She walked over to a woman coming in the door. "Please, ma'am, we have a petition here to keep Portland Meadows Racetrack open. Are you a registered voter?" When the woman nodded, Trish extended the clipboard. "Would you be willing to sign here?"

Trish saw the other team push open the doors. Help had arrived.

The story and pictures hit the front page of *The Oregonian*'s Sunday edition. The class stood grinning on the courthouse steps, and the article said, "More pictures and story inside." There was a close-up of Rhonda with her clipboard and someone signing it. Trish was quoted several times. An accompanying article by Curt Donovan detailed the situation at The Meadows.

"At least my picture isn't in it." Trish broke the uncomfortable silence as she and her mother drove to church.

"Oh, no? Second from the right, first row. You and all your class-mates." Marge clenched her hands on the steering wheel. "Couldn't you at least have stood behind somebody?"

At school the next day, the fourth-period American government class rated hero status. Copies of the articles wore out from being passed hand to hand.

"Cool. Awesome. Good picture. Bad picture." The raves depended on who was speaking.

"I'm really proud of all of you," their teacher said. "So far we have collected five thousand signatures. And we have a week to go."

Different kids shared their experiences as signature gatherers. Most of the comments from the people they'd talked to had been favorable.

Trish came out of weight-training class feeling high both physically and mentally. What a day this had been!

She waved good-bye to Doug on his way to football practice and crossed the parking lot to her car. A crowd of students surrounded it.

They parted like the Red Sea, all voices silent as Trish approached.

Big block letters scratched in the sides of her car read, "Stay out of PM or ELSE!"

Trish thought she would throw up.

Chapter

11

G o tell Mr. Adams."

Trish heard the voice as if from a long tube. Her car, her beautiful car. She knelt beside the door and traced the hateful words with a shaking finger. Why would anyone do such a thing?

"Trish." Rhonda knelt beside her. "Maybe you shouldn't touch it—there might be evidence, you know."

Trish snatched her hand back. "What have I done to make someone do this?" She could feel the tears running down her face but did nothing to stop them.

"Okay, let's move back. Come on, kids. Let me through." Mr. Adams' voice preceded his arrival.

Trish rose to her feet, feeling as if she were pushing the entire county up with her. She read the words again and walked around the car, seeing the entire damage for the first time. The same words were scrawled on the passenger side and a tic-tac-toe game covered the trunk.

"Are you all right, Trish?" the principal asked when he joined her.

Trish shook her head. "Umm, my car." She wiped her cheeks with her fingertips.

"But you weren't hurt?"

"It was like that when we got here. We saw it first. Trish didn't get here till a minute ago." One of the guys who answered was parked right next to the red convertible.

"I had Mrs. Olson call the police. They'll be here soon." Mr. Adams raised his voice from talking with Trish. "The rest of you go on home now, unless any of you saw strangers in the parking lot."

The crowd broke up. Trish could hear their conversations, but she didn't respond. She clamped her arms across her chest to still the shaking. Inside, the old rage sputtered and sparked.

The police cut their siren when they reached the drive to Prairie High School. Their flashing light-bar helped clear the way for them to park next to Trish's damaged car.

The two male officers introduced themselves before one began questioning those still around, while the other studied the damage. But no one had seen anything. No one had heard anything unusual.

"Do you patrol the parking lot?" one officer asked Mr. Adams.

"Not really, but there are always people coming and going. Surely someone would have seen strangers out here."

"Could this be the prank of a student? Anyone have any grudges?" He asked this last question of Trish, who shook her head.

"It's like that letter she got," Rhonda said. "Tell them, Trish."

After she told her story, she looked up to see the officer studying her. "You sure have ticked someone off. Any idea who?"

"The only one I know might be involved is Smithson, the assistant manager at the track. The Portland police are investigating him for problems at Portland Meadows."

"Do you know who's in charge of that investigation?"

Trish dug in her purse for the officer's business card and gave it to the sheriff deputy. He copied the information into his notebook and handed back the card.

"If there's no more, can I go home now?"

"Do you have a ride?" The officer snapped his notebook shut and stuck it back in the khaki shirt pocket.

"My car . . ."

"We'll need to tow it in and go over it for fingerprints. Though I'm not sure what good it will do, not if all those kids touched it."

"When can I have it back?"

"Depends."

"I'll go call my mom." Rhonda turned and headed back inside.

Trish swallowed hard to trap the screams she felt in her throat. She sucked in a deep breath and looked across the parking lot to the fir trees on the other side of the road. "Depends on what?"

"Look, miss, if this car is involved in a felony of any kind, we have to impound it for evidence. From what you say, a felony may have been committed at the track. And it's under investigation, so we would be remiss in not impounding evidence."

The guy talked like he'd just memorized the textbook. Trish recrossed her arms over her chest and gritted her teeth.

They were going to take her car.

"Look, it's still locked." She pointed in the window. "And they didn't touch anything in there. Can I please open the door and get my stuff out?" If she spoke precisely enough, maybe she could keep the tears at bay. Why, oh why, did she have to cry when she was so furious she could have chewed the man up and spit him out?

"Give me your keys and I'll open it for you. Then just touch your jacket and bag. They may have forced the lock, put something inside, and locked it up again."

Trish looked to the side and down to the ground. If he didn't start talking like a human being she might flip out.

"Easy, Trish, he's just doing his job." Mr. Adams laid a firm hand on her shoulder.

Trish wasn't sure if it was to help her control herself or to offer comfort. But whichever, it helped. She took in another deep breath and handed the deputy the keys.

"My mom's coming right away," Rhonda panted after dashing across the parking lot.

Trish could feel the anger bubbling and snorting down in her midsection. All the way home, she answered questions in monosyllables while she tried to figure it out. Why her? Why her car?

"Well, at least it's better damaging the car than you, Trish," Mrs. Seabolt said, her voice calming and so very reasonable.

"Yeah." Trish agreed in voice, but her insides would have no part of it. *Of course it is. But why damage anything? What's going on over there that's so important—maybe someone is running drugs like Rhonda said.*

Marge was working on the farm books at the rolltop desk in the living room when Trish slammed in the door. "What happened, Tee? You're so late." She finished her entry before raising her head.

At the look on her daughter's face, she shoved the rolling chair back and leaped to her feet, catching Trish in her arms.

The fury let loose in tears.

Marge looked across her sobbing daughter's head to meet the matching blue eyes of Rhonda and Dot Seabolt. "Trish's car was keyed. The police are impounding it." Rhonda patted Trish's heaving shoulder.

"Keyed?"

"Someone scratched it up."

"Actually, the message was . . ."

"The message?" Marge interrupted. "What in the world is going on here?"

"It said 'Stay out of PM or ELSE!' on both sides and a tic-tac-toe game scrawled on the trunk."

"Oh my! Are you all right?" Marge stepped back to study her daughter.

"Yes! Mother, it's my c-a-r!"

"Cars can be replaced. Daughters can't." Marge clutched Trish to her chest but let her go when Trish jerked back.

"How can you be so calm? I—my car—" Trish sucked in a breath that finally made it past the boulders blocking her throat. "They won't give me my car back for months."

"So you can drive the van. I'll use the pickup." Marge handed her daughter a tissue. Her clipped words said she wasn't as calm as she acted.

"You want me to come back and help with the horses?" Rhonda asked.

"I guess. With my luck, I'll probably get dumped and break a leg."

"Trish!" Marge's order cut through Trish's self-pity. "We'll hear no talk like that!"

Trish started to say something but clamped her mouth shut instead.

"Now, where is that card Officer Parks gave you?"

"In my purse, why?"

"To let them know what happened. It's time for someone to get serious about this—now!"

Trish dug in her purse and handed her mother the business card.

"I take it we're not going out to collect petition signatures tonight?" Rhonda asked.

"No, you're not, at least Trish isn't." Marge's tone brooked no argument. When Trish started to sputter, one look did her in.

"But *I* am."

"Me too." Dot added her vote. "And tomorrow during the day, I'm available too."

"There's a TBA meeting tonight." Trish hesitated to remind her mother.

"Fine. You go take care of the horses—I've already worked with the babies—and I'll meet you there. I'll pick you up, Dot, in say . . ." Marge checked her watch, "half an hour."

"I'll be ready in fifteen minutes." Dot took her daughter by the arm. "I'll bring Rhonda back with me."

Trish and Rhonda looked at each other, their total shock evident in wide eyes and shut mouths.

"Oh, and call Curt. Ask him for the DA's number. Tell him about the meeting and that I want a few minutes to talk with him." Trish did as she was told.

Later that evening after the meeting, Trish wanted to rehash the events with her mother, but Marge said she had letters to write. Trish worked on her zoology and then ambled into the kitchen for a drink and an apple. Just then the phone rang.

"David!" Trish's squeal brought Marge on the line too. After they exchanged greetings David said, "Thanks for the goodies. I still have some hidden in a box under my bed."

"Under your bed, yuk. Along with all the dirty socks and . . ."

"Listen, bird brain, I'll have you know we vacuumed just last—uh, last week."

"Okay, children," Marge interrupted their banter, "knock it off. Tell him what's gone on here, Tee, and I'll add what you miss."

"Maybe I better come home," David said when they'd brought him up-to-date.

"What good would that do?" Marge asked. "We'll handle it. You are going to Kentucky, though, aren't you?"

"I guess. I haven't really given it a lot of thought. How many horses are you taking?"

"Only Firefly." Trish hugged the phone to her ear. This was the first time her mother talked about Kentucky like it was a for-sure thing. Even though they'd paid the earlier racing fees, they still could back out. "Adam's taking two others, running one in the Breeder's Cup."

"He gonna have Red ride for him?" David's chuckle echoed over the line. "How is he anyway?"

"Fine, last I heard."

"I can't believe they keyed your car." David returned to the earlier discussion.

"Me either. Take care of yourself, brother. You're the only one I've got."

"I'm not the one in trouble. You ever thought of keeping your mouth shut?" He groaned. "Don't answer that. Love you guys."

Trish took her treats and returned to her bedroom, resolved to read a chapter in English and write to Red. By the time she finished the letter, her eyes refused to focus. She signed it "Thinking of you" and "Yours, Trish." She thought about signing "Love, Trish," but she couldn't.

Did she love him? What did love really mean? Sure she felt all warm and melty inside when he held her hand. And yes, the kisses were nice. No, nice was far too . . . too . . . nice a word. She *liked* kissing Red and being kissed back. But was this love? More than love between two friends? *Real* love?

She clicked off the desk lamp and got ready for bed. After crawling under the covers, she took her Bible from the bedside table and flipped it open to her verse for the night. She chuckled when she read the first part. "Count it all joy, my brethren, when you meet various trials. . . ." Guess you could call what she'd been going through "trials."

But the "count it all joy" . . . now that was the sticky part.

You haven't even been giving God the glory like you promised, her nagger whispered in her ear. *Let alone counting it joy. What happened to giving thanks for all things?*

Trish nodded. He was right. She finished reading the verse. "For you know that the testing of your faith produces steadfastness. And let steadfastness have its full effect, that you might be perfect and complete, lacking in nothing."

Now, perfect and complete, that sounded pretty good. She closed the book and put it away. "God, how am I supposed to do all this? And you know, it doesn't really make a lot of sense."

She waited, as if hoping for a mighty voice to explain all these goings-on. Outside, the branches of the tree scraped against the house in the night breeze. Beside her bed, the clock ticked as the number panels fell to the next minute.

"What am I supposed to do? What's going to happen?" She sighed. What a mystery. She clutched the blanket under her chin. What was happening was she was changing from girl-super-jockey to girl-sleuth, and she'd never read a mystery in her life.

She lay in the quiet. *So I just give thanks and count it all joy—right?* Her song trickled through her mind. She hummed along with it. How easy to picture eagle's wings and soaring over the earth. She snuggled deeper. And those large, warm hands holding her. She fell asleep with a smile on her face and a matching one in her heart.

"Curt's story hit the front page." Marge handed the paper across the table. "He writes well."

Trish studied the story of the TBA meeting and the continuing investigation. "At least he didn't quote me this time," she said after finishing the bottom few paragraphs about the students gathering petition signatures. "Mom?"

"Ummm?"

"You remember that new man at the meeting last night?"

"Sure, why?" Marge lowered her paper.

"He looks so familiar, like I've seen him before, but I can't remember when." Trish rubbed her forehead with the fingertips of both hands.

"His name was—ah—Highstreet, Kendal Highstreet. He's a businessman up from California, thinking of buying a farm up here since land prices are so outrageous in California. He wants to breed and race Thoroughbreds."

"That's it. I saw him at the track kitchen the morning I went over there. He was sitting with . . ." Trish scrunched her eyes closed, trying to see the picture again. "With a couple of owners and Ward Turner, the track manager."

"So?"

Trish shrugged. "I don't know. Just seemed important somehow." She carefully brushed toast crumbs into her palm and dusted them off over the plate. "You doing anything special today?"

"I'll let you know more when I do." Marge disappeared behind her paper again.

Trish drained the last of her milk and got to her feet. Her mother's curious response bugged her all the way to Rhonda's.

"You thought anything about your birthday yet?" Rhonda asked. "It's only two days away."

"I'm not having a birthday this year."

"Trish, why that's the stupidest thing I ever heard."

Trish rolled her eyes and sniffed. Good thing they were stopped at a stop sign. How could her mood change so fast? Raindrops splattered on the windshield. How fitting. Tears both outside and in. And here she'd promised herself no more crying. Especially after the storms of yesterday.

"You need to pay better attention, lass," Patrick reminded her when she brought the bay gelding back to the stables that afternoon. "He nearly dumped you out there."

"I know." Trish patted the deep red neck and jumped to the ground. Sure she knew enough to pay attention. And her inattention nearly cost her. Blowing leaves were enough to spook any horse, but a good rider would have anticipated his reaction—been prepared.

She was reminded again when they worked each of the horses through the starting gates. Old gray Dan'l acted as instructor and tranquilizer, pacing through the gate without the flicker of an ear. But one of the fillies didn't care for the tight squeeze and bolted—or rather tried to. Trish caught her in time.

"Tomorrow we'll close the front gate and let them stand there." Patrick slipped the saddle off the filly. "You two wash this one down and I'll take care of Dan'l. Oh, Brad, Marge said to remind you about supper tonight."

"You mean dinner?" Brad winked at Trish. Patrick still couldn't get used to calling the evening meal dinner.

"Whatever. Just get busy, you two, or we'll eat without you." Patrick went back to his brushing of the gray gelding.

Trish and Brad could hear him muttering about "smart aleck kids," but they knew he was teasing. She wondered sometimes if he didn't say some things just to get a rise out of them.

They'd finished dinner before Marge brought up the reason for the family meeting. Trish scraped the plates, stacked them, and carried them in to the sink. On her return, she brought the coffeepot and poured three cups. She only felt like drinking coffee in the morning and then at the track.

"I was hoping you could go to Kentucky with us," she was saying to Brad. "With all you've done, I thought you might like a trip."

"Would I! Old David will be there too?" At Marge's nod, he said, "Good."

"Adam called today and asked if we'd decided yet when or if we were bringing the horses back up. Or if we were bringing others down. Either way, he has to arrange for stalls, so he needs to know. I told him what's happened here and that we still don't know if The Meadows will open or not."

"When does he have to know?" Patrick pulled on one earlobe, a sure sign that he was thinking.

"Soon. Also he wants to schedule races for those down there if they are going to stay."

Trish could feel the slow burn starting again. "Well, why not leave them there? I haven't raced for so long, I've probably forgotten how." She shoved her chair back and stood up. "I have homework to do. Whatever you decide is fine with me."

Liar! That seemed to be one of her nagger's favorite names for her. He repeated it as she strode down the hall.

The argument the next night had been raging for hours. At least it seemed so to Trish. Except *she* was the only one raging. Her mother sat calmly in her chair, knitting.

"How about if we go out to dinner, like we always have?"

"Mother, I don't want to go out to dinner. It won't be like it's always been because Dad and David aren't here."

"Choose something else then."

"That's the point. I am choosing. It's my choice and I choose to do nothing."

"We could get pizza with Brad and Rhonda—invite Patrick. I bet he hasn't had birthday cake for years. Rent a movie."

"You don't get it, do you? We're—I'm skipping my birthday this year." She started to leave the room. "The rest of you can go do whatever you want."

It was the worst birthday of her life.

Chapter 12

"Trish, you're going to be late for school."

"No, I won't. I'm not going." Trish pulled the covers over her aching head and burrowed down into that cocoon of gray where pain didn't hurt so bad and the crack in her heart didn't show.

"Are you running a fever?" Marge sat down on the bed and felt Trish's forehead. "Sore throat?"

Trish wished she could lie. "I hurt all over but it's not a cold." A tear squeezed from under her clenched eyelid.

"The old black pit?"

Trish nodded. "Maybe if I sleep more today, I'll feel like going tomorrow."

"You know you're letting people down?"

Trish nodded.

"Yourself most of all."

Who cares? Trish wanted to scream. *Who gives a flying fig? Just get off my case!* But she didn't. Screaming was far too much trouble. Took far too much energy. When she sensed her nagger *tsk*ing on her shoulder, she snatched a tissue from the box and tried to blow him away. Her head hurt. Maybe she *was* coming down with a cold after all.

"Trish, I know how you feel. When your dad's and my anniversary rolled around, I felt like crawling in a hole and pulling it in after me too. The grief group helped me through a real rough time. I know the one for teens could help you."

"I'll think about it, okay?" Her tone said *Just leave me alone*.

Marge remained sitting silently on the bed for a time, then stood with a sigh. "Hiding out isn't the best way to handle this, Tee. Trust me, I know."

You sure do, Trish thought. *You checked out for days.*

And what good did it do? Her nagger chimed in. *You know better than this. What happened to all that joy and giving God the glory?* Sticking her fingers in her ears didn't help.

Trish tried to go back to sleep, but by now she was wide awake. Even deep breathing to relax failed to bring oblivion. Finally she threw back the covers and headed for the shower. So she missed first period. She'd make it on time for second.

"You look awful," Rhonda said when they met at the locker before lunch.

"Thanks."

"Your mom said you were hiding out."

"Yeah, well, she's a big help."

"Trish, the grief group meets this afternoon. I know things are rough for you right now, but this could help. I'll go with you."

Trish shoved her books in her locker and almost climbed in after them. With her face hidden in the locker, she gave up. "All right, I'll go." She jerked upright and glared at Rhonda. "But that doesn't mean I'll say anything." She slammed the metal door. "And then both you and my mother can get off my back!"

Rhonda didn't say anything through lunch, and the others at the table saw the scowl on Trish's face and left her alone.

When he got up to leave, Doug Ramstead laid a hand on her shoulder. "It'll get better," he whispered in her ear.

Trish pushed to her feet and fled the room.

The group met at the local Methodist church. Trish parked in the graveled parking lot and ordered her fingers to unclench from around the steering wheel. They were as reluctant as the rest of her. When she finally slammed the van door, Rhonda came around the vehicle, put an arm around her friend's shoulders, and squeezed. Together they walked up the four stairs to the front of the cedar-sided building. A sign with an arrow pointed to a comfortably furnished room with bookshelves along one wall and a fireplace on another. Extra chairs joined the sofas and easy chairs in a circle. Half of them held teens of varying ages.

A young woman stood and extended her hand. "Hi, I'm Jessica Walden, the facilitator for this bunch. Welcome."

Trish put on her company manners and introduced both herself and Rhonda. "My mom thinks this group will help me and Rhonda—" She didn't say "dragged me here," but anyone of sensitivity could hear it.

"Came along for moral support." Rhonda beamed as if she'd just won a jumping trophy.

"You don't have to talk if you don't want to, Trish," Jessica said. "And you can call me Jessie. I even answer to 'hey you' on occasion. We'll have everyone introduce themselves when we start. If you want something to drink first, there's sodas in the fridge or ice water."

Trish declined even though her mouth felt stuffed with cotton balls. The butterflies trapped in her stomach flipped and flopped, seeking release.

When the kids started introducing themselves, Trish almost ran again. But when her turn came, she lifted her chin, gave her name, and finished with, "My father died of cancer in June."

She listened to the others share their feelings and fears, all the while fighting back her own tears. When someone started to cry, Jessie passed the tissue box, and the two on either side of the girl patted her shoulders or rubbed her back.

I'm not gonna talk. I'm not gonna talk. Trish repeated the words like a rap song. She went into a state of shock when her mouth said, "I just had a birthday and my father wasn't here for it."

"Your first holiday?" someone asked.

Trish nodded.

"That's always the worst. Christmas will be really rough too," someone else chimed in.

"This group helped me get through those first 'happy' occasions." The girl on Trish's left looked at her with caring deep in her brown eyes. "Happy they weren't. But I got through, and now the depression doesn't hit me so hard."

"You were depressed?"

The girl nodded. "We all have been, one time or another or all the time."

"Whatever fits," someone else added.

"We learn here to take it one day at a time," Jessie said. "And that there are others who've been there who can be there for us now."

"Sometimes I get so mad I—" Trish swallowed hard.

"Yep . . . yeah . . . me too . . . sure . . . right on." The voices echoed around the circle.

Trish leaned back in her chair. "So what do you do?"

"Talk it out. Run. Cry till it's over. Pray. Call one of my friends here." Again the answers came from around the circle.

"Just don't stuff it," Jessie said.

"Or try to tough it out." The girl next to Trish patted her arm. "Talk. Call me." She wrote her phone number on a piece of paper and handed it to Trish. "My name's Angela."

Trish left the room feeling two tons lighter than when she went in. "You don't have to go with me next week," she told Rhonda as they walked back to the van. "Thanks for coming today. And making me come."

"I didn't *make* you."

"Wanna bet?" Now she owed just about everyone in her life an apology.

The next day in government class, Ms. Wainwright made a major announcement. "We did it! You did it. You collected more than five thousand signatures over the necessary number. The county clerk figured that even with all the mistakes and people signing twice, we're well over our goal."

The class broke into cheers.

"So, Trish, the results will be presented to the city council at their next meeting. Why don't you come up and tell us what has been happening at Portland Meadows lately?"

Trish got to her feet, her butterflies suddenly doing their flip-flop routine. When she turned to face the class, she remembered why she'd rather race. *There* she didn't have to say anything.

"All the Thoroughbred and quarter-horse owners and trainers are going ahead with training as if the track will open on time. The program for the season is all planned, so we've been paying pre-race fees just like we always do.

"Some of the trainers are at the track, but we still have our horses at home since we have a half-mile training track there. Four of our best horses are still down in California, where I raced this summer."

"Where's Spitfire?" someone asked.

"Back in Kentucky at BlueMist Farms, where he will stand at stud this winter. I went back to visit him over Labor Day weekend."

"What if our petitions don't work and the track never opens?" a boy asked from a seat by the windows.

Trish took a moment to answer. *That* had been the big question on her mind for forever, it seemed. "Some of the trainers are talking about racing in other parts of the country. Lots of the smaller stable owners will probably sell out or send their horses to trainers elsewhere. That costs a lot, so unless you have a really good horse, you wouldn't do that."

"What happened about your car?"

"Got me."

Mutual groans came from the back. Everyone knew about her bright red convertible, now impounded. When she saw no more hands, Trish started back to her seat. She paused and then said, "All of us at the track want to thank you for what you did. They were pretty impressed that you took the time to collect signatures. Thanks."

"Aw, Ms. Wainwright made us do it. No big deal."

Trish returned to her seat under cover of the laughter that broke out.

"You'll keep us posted then, Trish?" the teacher asked.

Trish just wished she had more to tell them. Who *was* responsible for the troubles at Portland Meadows? What was happening with the police investigation? How come she hadn't heard from Curt lately? She returned to reality in time to hear the assignment. "Describe your experiences collecting signatures and what you learned."

What had she learned? The whole thing wasn't over yet.

When she got home a message lay on the counter for her to call Curt. Trish dialed the Portland number and tucked the phone onto her shoulder while she flipped through the stack of mail. A card from Red. This was certainly her day. A picture of Garfield clutching his chest made her smile. The inside read, "I'm dying to hear from you." Trish giggled. At least she'd written him a letter, so they'd crossed in the mail.

Curt's voice interrupted her thoughts. "Trish, they indicted Smithson. He's in jail right now, and from what I heard, singing like a canary."

"Yes!" Trish pumped the air with a closed fist. "So now what's going to happen?"

"Hopefully they'll snag whoever's behind all this and Portland Meadows can get on with business. I'll let you know as soon as I hear any more."

Trish hung up and danced all the way down the hall. Surely now the council would see the truth and reopen the track. She changed clothes and, after grabbing an apple, jogged down to the barns, Caesar barking and leaping beside her.

"That's wonderful," Marge said, never taking her eyes from Miss Tee working on the lunge line. The filly tossed her head and nickered when she saw Trish. Maybe all those carrot pieces were finally paying off. "Okay, girl, we'll quit for today." Marge looped the line over her arm and drew the filly in. "Good job, little one. Isn't she getting prettier all the time?"

Trish agreed. The young horse was filling out, and she carried her head with the same style Spitfire did. Even though she'd be racing a year late because of her late birth, she had all the earmarks of a winner. Trish rubbed the filly's ears and the tiny white star set smack in the middle of the broad forehead.

"I can't wait to train you," she murmured, scratching all the while. "Wait till you see that crowd and hear them cheering for you. You're gonna love it." The filly nibbled Trish's fingers and nosed her pocket for the treat that usually hid there. "Sorry, kid. I haven't filled my pockets yet." The two of them led the filly back to the stall and cross-tied her there for a good brushing.

"Maybe we'll be able to call Adam and tell him to ship our horses home at the same time as he leaves for Kentucky. I sure would love to ride Sarah's Pride in the Hal Evanston Handicap." Trish opened the office refrigerator and dug in the carrot sack. She used the knife on the table and cut the carrots into thick slices.

"That's a mile, you know, lass." Patrick sat in the old-fashioned wooden office chair at the desk. "We'll have to ask Adam if she's ready for that." He tipped his stained fedora back on his head. "Or you could run Firefly, rather than shipping her to Kentucky."

"Fat chance. She's going to win with the big guys." Trish munched one of the carrot slices herself. "Hi, Brad. You hear the news?"

"Hi, all." Brad greeted them, then answered Trish. "No, what?"

Trish brought him up-to-date. "So we can start racing soon. Won't that be great?" Trish ignored the air of caution she could feel coming from both her mother and Patrick. They *were* going to start running soon. They had to.

When they got back up to the house, the message light was blinking on the answering machine. Curt's voice sounded like he was scraping bottom. "Smithson fingered Turner. Says he was behind it all, so really, things are in a worse mess than ever."

Trish felt her heart drop down around her ankles. *God, when are you going to straighten all this out?* Her groan of misery sounded more like an accusation than a prayer of praise, her nagger leaped to remind her. She could actually see the pit yawning before her when she lay down on the bed in her room, the back of her hand hiding eyes dry and gritty with unshed tears.

"I just can't believe Ward Turner would do such a thing," Trish said that night at the dinner table. "He loves horse racing with a passion."

"True." Marge spread ketchup on her hamburger and added lettuce. "But you never know what some people will do when a great deal of money is involved."

"But Curt never said there'd been money in Turner's bank account."

"Maybe he didn't look there. The Corvette is what made everyone suspicious of Smithson."

"Yeah, right." Trish nibbled on a potato chip, her mind whirling. "Smithson is out of jail now too, Curt said." She leaned back in her chair. "Think I'll go over to The Meadows tomorrow after school."

"What for?" Marge's "mother" tone took over.

"I don't know. Maybe just being there will give me some ideas. Besides, being there sometimes helps me feel closer to Dad."

"Then I'll go with you. We can both use some of your dad's wisdom right about now."

What could Trish say?

"Maybe I'll leave school early so we won't be so late working the horses here."

"Maybe not." Marge now *wore* her "mother" look, along with the sound of her voice.

Trish had a hard time with her homework that evening. Her gaze kept returning to the verses posted on the wall above her desk. One in particular seemed to stand out. "If any of you lacks wisdom, let him ask God, who gives to all men generously and without reproaching and it will be given him." Trish substituted her name for "all men," putting herself into the scripture like her father had taught her.

"If I, Trish, lack wisdom, I will ask God who gives to Trish generously and without reproaching, and the wisdom will be given to me." She cupped her chin in her hands and propped her elbows on the desk. "So, God, I'm asking for wisdom. I sure want to know what to do."

A song from Bible camp tiptoed into her mind. "Give God the glory, glory. Rise and shine and give God the glory, glory . . . children of the Lord."

Trish shook her head. That didn't seem to be doing anything. She'd better get back to her homework. There was to be a quiz in zoology in the morning. She hummed along with the song while she studied the list of Latin names. How come zoology was fun and chemistry had been such a bear? She shrugged off the question. She still hated even the thought of chemistry.

The next afternoon when Trish and her mother drove into the parking lot in front of The Meadows, a bright red Corvette occupied one of the reserve parking places near the entrance. Next to it sat a silver BMW.

"Looks like Smithson is back at work," Trish commented. "You'da thought they'd have fired him."

"Maybe he's cleaning out his office." Marge turned to study the cars. "That's an out-of-state license on the gray car. Must have bucks to be driving that beauty."

They parked the minivan on the south side of the weathering grandstand and entered by the gate the golfers used. All of the golfers were gone for the day, so the nine-hole golf course laid out in the infield appeared nearly as desolate as the rest of the track in the gray of an overcast day. The triangular flags at the holes snapped in the breeze and made Trish shiver.

Off to the left and above them, the sheet of windows overlooked the track, metallic-gray like the clouds scudding above them.

Trish shivered again. "Wish I'd worn a warmer jacket."

"It is chilly. See over there to the curve. That's where you went down that day. I thought sure you were dead."

"Have you heard about the Snyder family, how they're doing?"

"I think she went back to live near her parents, someplace in the Midwest sticks in my mind. Come to think of it, we got a beautiful card from her after your father's death. She said she sure knew how we felt." Marge leaned on the fence rail. "I don't know if death coming instantly like that or prolonged like Hal's is easier."

"They're both awful." Trish turned from studying the infield and looked up at the grandstand behind them. "Seems almost spooky here. The whole thing needs repainting, and they haven't even washed the windows yet. It's as if they don't really plan on racing here this year at all." She heard a horse whinny from the barns on the east side of the track. At least something was alive around here.

"You suppose the rest rooms are open? I need to use one." Marge turned back to the grandstand.

"Sure. We'll go up through the tunnel and use the one in the women's dressing room." Trish, hands in her windbreaker pockets, led the way up the tunnel to the circular saddling paddock. The gate from the paddock squawked in the silence, echoing in the cavernous room.

The door to the women's dressing room was locked. "We'll go to the public rooms up near the lobby. They'll be open for the office workers." She felt like tiptoeing, the smish of her tennis shoes sounding an intrusion. Why hadn't anyone turned on the lights?

When they reached the door, Marge pushed it open and disappeared inside. Trish started to follow her, but angry voices made her pause. She held the door so it shut without a sound.

Light from the huge windows in the entrance left shadows in the vaulted lobby. Trish halted her silent passage just where the hall opened into the foyer. The voice came from the offices to her left.

"But I need more money!"

A chair screeched back.

"I paid you. It's not my fault you were so stupid to buy a flashy car."

"Yeah, well I gotta get outta here. They'll figure out that Turner didn't do anything and come back to me. If you don't pony up, I'll be forced to tell 'em everything I know."

Trish knew who whined. Smithson, the assistant manager. But who was the other? She forced herself to stay glued to the wall. If she moved they might see her.

"You stupid . . ." A stream of names, including a few Trish hadn't heard before, made her glad her mother wasn't there.

"All I need is a hundred thou. You won't miss it when you get this place, and it would set me up for life in Mexico. Help me out this time and I swear you'll never hear from me again."

"There's nothing that can tie you back to me."

"I'll tell them everything, I swear I will."

"Put that phone down, you imbecile." Where had Trish heard that voice?

"What are you doing with that gun?"

Chapter

13

Trish darted back down the hallway.

"What's the rush?" Marge caught her as the two of them nearly collided. Trish shook her head and put a finger over her lips to signify silence. When she located the phone on the wall, her hands were shaking so badly she could hardly dial 9-1-1.

"Speak up, please," the woman on the line said clearly.

"I can't," Trish whispered as distinctly as she could. "Please, there's a man waving a gun in the lobby at Portland Meadows. I'm not sure if the front doors are open or not, but I think so."

"We'll be right there. Can you get out of the building without being seen?"

"I think so. Please hurry. And get a message to Officer Parks about this if you can."

Marge grabbed Trish's arm and pulled. Trish dropped the receiver in the hook, and they ran on their tiptoes back to the saddling paddock. When the gate screeched again, they heard a man yell, "Who's there? Stop or I'll shoot!"

They ran as fast as they could, down the tunnel, out the gate, and into the car. Trish jammed the key into the ignition and, when the engine roared to life, threw the car into reverse and spun in a tight curve. She slammed her foot to the floor and headed for the exit.

Halfway across the parking lot, a red Corvette swerved across in front of her. Trish cranked the wheel to the right only to be confronted by the broad side of a silver BMW. They were trapped. The sight of a gun sticking out of the BMW's window kept her from reversing out of there.

She looked at her mother. Marge's lips moved. Trish knew she was praying. All Trish could say was "Help, God! Help!"

"Get out of the car." The man in the BMW eased his door open, so his voice carried well.

Trish fought the panic rising in her throat. What could they do? She looked to her mother.

"Just do as he says," Marge answered softly. "Somehow God will protect us."

Trish reached for the door handle.

Flashing red and blue lights at every exit announced the arrival of the police. Before the two in the other cars could even start their engines, they were surrounded.

"Get out of your car with your hands on your head." An officer with a bullhorn gave the instructions.

"Thank you, God. Thank you, thank you," Trish and Marge murmured together, the only words they could think of.

"Trish, are you all right?" Officer Parks reached the van.

She nodded and slowly opened the door. When she stepped out, her knees buckled. The man's quick action kept her from hitting the ground.

"Sorry."

"Shock does that to you. What about you, Mrs. Evanston? You okay?"

Marge laughed a shaky laugh. "Think I'll just stay right here if that's okay with you."

"Fine, ma'am. We'll get these two taken care of and then we'll come for your statement." He gave Trish a hand as she climbed back into the minivan. "Take some deep breaths and let yourself relax. You did one fine job, young lady."

By the time they'd given their information to the officers, Trish and Marge wore matching looks of exhaustion.

"I'll bring these statements by tomorrow for you to sign," Officer Parks said. "Trish, do you think you can drive, or would you rather one of us drove you home? We can do that."

"I think I'm okay now. I'm not shaking anymore. I'm mad. Clear through."

"Not a good time to drive either. How about you, ma'am?"

"We'll be fine. I need to stop and call Patrick, our trainer, and let him know we're all right. He'll be sending a rescue squad out any time now."

"If you're sure?"

"See you tomorrow." Trish turned the ignition and pressed the electronic button to roll up the windows. She very carefully put the van in gear and eased out of the parking lot. By the time she reached the on ramp to I-5, she felt almost normal.

Curt was parked in their drive when they arrived. He'd heard about the arrest on the police scanner.

Brad and Patrick met them at the front door, so the five of them gathered around the table where Trish could tell her story. When she finished, Patrick shook his head.

"Lord love ye, lass. What'll it be takin' to keep ye out of trouble?"

Trish looked at her mother, and both of them broke into giggles. One by one the others chimed in.

When they all wiped their eyes, Marge pushed herself to her feet. "I'm calling for pizza—delivered. How hungry are all of you?" She looked from Brad to Curt and shook her head. "Silly question. How about a supreme and a Canadian bacon with pineapple, both large?" At their nods, she went to the phone. She called from the counter by the door. "Trish, you got any coupons?"

Trish sighed. Everything was back to normal. She looked around the room and from face to face of the three men talking, discussing what might happen next at Portland Meadows. Normal sounded heavenly. "I don't think so."

When the doorbell rang a few minutes later, Trish assumed it was the pizza delivery. Instead a television reporter with a cameraman introduced herself. The pizza truck arrived just as the television people left.

"You're going to be famous over this one," Curt warned after gobbling his pizza and calling in his story. "Bet this hits the front page."

He was right. It hit the front page and the Associated Press wire. When Trish arrived home from a school that buzzed with excitement, the reporter who called her "The Comeback Kid" had called. Trish answered his questions and hung up just in time for the two reporters from the local papers who'd shown up that morning after she left for school.

The afternoon paper carried banner headlines. "Portland Meadows to Open in Two Weeks." Her picture topped another article about the arrest the night before. "Local Girl Solves Track Mystery" read the headline on that one.

"Thank you, God" seemed so inadequate, but that's all Trish could say.

The next two weeks passed in a whirl of activity. Adam Finley hired a van to bring the horses up from California and flew Firefly back to Kentucky. They moved the horses to the track and prepared for opening day. Sarah's Pride and Gatesby were both to run that day, the filly in the Hal Evanston Memorial Handicap like they'd planned. Half the student body from Prairie High promised to be there to cheer them on. Red called, several times, just to make sure Trish was really all right and then to ask how she was holding up as a celebrity.

Trish rose early to exercise the horses at the track before leaving for school, and by Friday, the lack of sleep and strain of all the excitement gave her a colossal headache.

"Just go to bed." Marge turned back the covers. "After this weekend, we'll have Genie ride for us in the morning."

Trish didn't even argue. Her mother was right. No matter how hard it was to admit, she didn't want to live on this schedule for the next six months.

Saturday morning dawned with a heavy cloud cover and a fifty-fifty chance of rain. Trish sniffed the wind as she trotted Sarah's Pride out on the track to loosen her up. "Please, God, here I am asking for something again, but could you possibly let the sun come out for the races this afternoon? A fast, dry track would be such a great way to start the season."

A light mist shrouded a sun circle while she finished her duties and headed for the track kitchen. She could hardly get through the line for her food, so many people stopped to talk with her. Trainers, bug boys, grooms, owners, everyone commenting on the investigation and how grateful they were the track had opened.

The hubbub sounded more like a party than a normal track morning.

Trish sat with Bob Diego and put her plates out on the table so he could put her tray back. "He sure suckered me in," Diego said when he sat back down. "Here I was introducing the crook around and trying to make him feel welcome. I even took him out to see a ranch I know that's for sale." He shook his head. "How could I be so stupid?"

"Well, he scared me out of a year's growth," Trish grinned at her friend. "Let me tell you, a gun looks different when it's pointed at you than it does on TV. I was so glad to see those patrol cars I nearly cried."

"I thought that attorney was part of this, the way he acted at the council meetings."

"Patrick calls him a do-gooder who just believed the wrong man. Strange that a lawyer got sucked in like that. I thought they knew everything."

"They just think so. His ears must be burning; he's been talked about enough." Diego held up his cup for the waitress to refill it. "Sorry you're not riding for me in the handicap, but I guess it is important for you to ride your own horses. I'll let Genie Stokes give you a run for your money."

Trish finished the last bite of her toast. "That's okay. With your other one, I have six mounts today anyway." She waved Patrick over to take her chair. "I gotta get going. See you in the paddock."

By the time the call came for the jockeys to parade to the saddling paddock for the eighth race, Trish had won two, had a place and a show, and still had the ninth to go. Wearing the crimson and gold silks of Runnin' On Farm, Trish fell in behind the others. She weighed in, thanked the official for his good wishes, and tried to swallow the butterflies doing their grandstand performance in her middle.

Why was this race scarier than the others? After all, she'd walked this path four times already today. She smiled at the crowd and waved to a group of crimson-and-gold-garbed students hanging on the rail.

"Tri-cia, Tri-cia, Tri-cia." They turned her name into a two-syllable chant.

David boosted her aboard and patted her knee. "Give it all you got, kid. Sure good to see you up on one of ours."

"Thanks, David. I'm so glad you could make it home for this."

"You'll be knowin' what to do." Patrick looked up at her, a sheen of moisture in his eyes. "Do this one for your dad."

Trish swallowed and tried to smile at her mother, but she could feel the wobbles at the edge of her mouth.

"God keep you" was all Marge could say.

Sarah's Pride minced out of the tunnel and tossed her head when the sun hit her. Trish blinked in the brightness. God had answered another prayer. While much of the day the sun played hide-and-seek with the clouds, now it shone on a dry, fast track.

"Your favorite kind, huh, girl?" Trish patted the sorrel neck and smoothed the filly's slightly darker mane to the left side. Off to the east, Mount Hood waited patiently for its yearly snow cover.

The Prairie students continued their chant.

When they cantered back past the grandstands, Trish raised her whip in acknowledgment. She couldn't quit grinning. But she didn't try very hard.

The filly walked into the number-three slot as if she owned it. Trish focused on the spot between the filly's ears and settled into her saddle. The shot! The flag was up and they were off.

Sarah's Pride broke clean and settled into her stride. Trish took her favorite position slightly off the pace and running easily. She didn't want the filly tired before the final stretch.

With a dry track and all fresh horses, the pace was fast, the seconds ticking past. Coming out of the turn, Trish felt someone coming up on the outside. With three in front of her, she made her move. Stride for stride, the outside horse paced her.

They passed the third runner and then the second.

The other riders went to their whips. Neck and neck, three abreast, they thundered for the finish line.

"Now, girl." Trish swung her whip just once. Sarah's Pride leaped forward, nose straight out. One stride, three, and they crossed the line.

Trish grinned at the rider on her right. Genie Stokes grinned back. Neither of them knew who won. Nor did anyone else.

"And that's a photo finish, ladies and gentlemen," the announcer intoned. "We'll have the results for you shortly. Rarely do you see three so close. Numbers three, five, and seven."

Trish cantered on around the track and walked toward the winner's circle. Gold and bronze chrysanthemums bordered the boxed-in area.

David reached her as number three flashed on the scoreboard to win. "You didn't have to cut it quite so close." He grinned up at her.

"Keeps you on your toes that way, Davey boy." Trish tapped him on the head with her whip. She raised a hand at the chanting that swelled rather than diminished from her friends at Prairie High.

In the winner's circle, the announcer presented her with the ornate silver cup Runnin' On Farm had donated as a permanent trophy for the race.

"It's only fitting, ladies and gentlemen, that the winner today should be Trish Evanston, daughter of the man we honor. While we didn't plan it this way, it couldn't have worked out better."

The three Evanstons accepted the trophy together. Trish took the mike in her hands and stopped to look out at the crowd. "We nearly didn't have racing here anymore, but justice won out. We've been given a second chance, a second wind, and I—we—thank God for the opportunity. May Portland Meadows continue to provide you racing fans with the sport of kings, and we'll give the only King that counts all the glory. Thank you." She handed the mike back.

Arm in arm, Trish, David, and their mother walked out of the winner's circle and into the circle of all their friends and fans. *What a start to a new year,* Trish thought. *Today really is a second wind.*

CLOSE CALL

BOOK NINE

To Elaine Aspelund
who shared her near-death experience
with me and who has been sharing
the special love, joy, and peace she found
with those around her
all her life.

Chapter 01

Winning races is better than . . . than . . . Trish Evanston struggled to think of anything better. Hot fudge sundaes . . . Miss Tee, the filly born on Trish's sixteenth birthday . . . riding her Thoroughbred, Triple-Crown-winning colt, Spitfire—well that rated number one. No contest there. She waved again at the racing fans who'd packed Portland Meadows Racetrack for the opening program.

A solid block of teenagers wearing crimson and gold, the colors of both Prairie High School and Runnin' On Farm, whistled and shouted back at her. Even her government teacher, Ms. Wainwright, whooped and hollered with the best of them.

On the edge of the winner's circle, Trish accepted the congratulations from the fans pressing in around her. "Well, winning the Hal Evanston Memorial Cup is not quite as big as winning the Triple Crown, but it's right up there." She grinned at the woman who asked the question. "Thanks for coming and for supporting racing in Portland."

Someone else handed her a program. "For my daughter, Becky. She's a real big fan of yours."

"Tell her hello for me." Trish signed the program and handed it back to the man.

"She wanted me to tell you how sorry she is your father died." The look on his face conveyed his own sorrow.

"Thank you. That means a lot." Trish shook his hand. "It really does."

"Trish!"

She looked up to see Doug Ramstead, all-American guy and Prairie High's quarterback, waiting his turn.

"Hi, Doug. I could hear you whistling above everybody."

He lifted her clear off the ground with a breath-snatching hug. "You were great, little one. I'm so proud of you." He set her back down and tapped the tip of her nose with his forefinger. "Now you just get the next two, okay?"

"I'll do my best." Trish watched the Big Man on Campus of Prairie High make his way through the crowd. No wonder half the girls were in love with him. He was just as nice as he was good-looking.

"Your father sure would be proud of you, Tee. I know, because I sure am." Trish's mother, Marge Evanston, put an arm around her daughter's shoulder.

"Thanks, Mom." Trish blinked a couple of times. So did Marge.

It was one of *those* moments—when her father seemed so close that she knew if she turned quickly enough, she'd see him standing right behind her, his face split by a smile to dim the sun. Hal Evanston had loved racing, but he'd loved his Lord even more—and was never afraid of telling the world so.

Trish vowed to always follow his example.

She followed the others out of the bronze and gold chrysanthemum-bordered winner's circle only to be confronted by a cluster of reporters, already shouting questions. She answered as best she could. "Yes, God willing, I'll be riding in the Breeder's Cup. Our filly Firefly will run in the Oaks the day before. No, I'm fine after all that mess over The Meadows. After all, they never shot at me."

She tried to edge her way toward the jockey room, but the reporters refused to budge. "Yeah, I miss my dad every day, but especially at times like this." She kept the thought *dumb question* from showing on her face. Finally she threw her hands in the air. "Hey, I've got another race to ride. How about we meet after I'm done and I'll answer any questions you have?"

They grumbled but good-naturedly backed away.

David walked beside her, back up the tunnel to the saddling paddock, and opened the gate so she could cross to the jockey rooms.

"Thanks, David. I thought you'd headed for the barn."

"Patrick and Brad can take care of that end. I just wanted to make sure you were all right."

Trish stopped and looked up at him. "Huh?"

"Well, with what's gone on and all—" He stopped and took a deep breath. "I worry about you, you know."

"Hey." Trish patted his chest. "That's Mom's job. She'd be the first to tell you."

David nodded, a rueful grin tugging at the corners of his wide mouth. "She gave up worrying, remember? I guess I just realized this world is full of kooks and I don't want them hurting my sister."

"It's over, David. And we're no worse for wear."

"Really?"

She could feel the depths of his caring clear to the center of her heart. "Really. God says He'll take care of us and He did." She started up the hall to the silks room, then stopped and turned. "It's over, brother of mine. All but the court stuff."

David nodded, but she could see the concern still reflected in his dark eyes.

He settled his Runnin' On Farm cap more firmly on his head and, with a flick-of-the-wrist wave, trotted off to the backside.

Trish headed once more to pick up Anderson's silks. How good David's caring felt! She was lucky to have a big brother like him.

"Some ride!" Genie Stokes raised her hand for a high five. "Couldn't happen to a nicer person."

"Thanks. You didn't do so bad yourself. You ever seen a three-way photo finish before?"

Genie shook her head. "But then I haven't been in the winner's circle as much as you. I think that filly of yours just reached farther with her chin. Gotta get Patrick to teach me how to get my mounts to do that."

"Right. He keeps a secret book of tricks that he shares only with his friends." Trish pulled her helmet off and shook out her dark, shoulder-length hair while dropping the helmet on the bench and plunking down beside it. She waved and acknowledged the comments of the other women jockeys. Drawing in a deep breath of the steamy, liniment-scented air, she dropped her head forward and rotated her neck, then shoulders.

"Takes some reconditioning, doesn't it?" Genie sank down beside Trish after pulling her own silks over her head. She massaged her temples and up into her hair with her fingertips. "Man, no matter how much I work out, nothing is the same as riding in the races."

"I know."

A squall from the black box-speaker up in the corner cut into the locker-room buzz.

"We better get moving." Trish hung her silks on a hook and dragged the Anderson pink and gray colors over her head. "If I sit here much longer, I'll tighten up."

"Go ahead, see if I mind." Genie walked over to the long mirror and winked at Trish. "More for me that way."

"You want Gatesby?" Trish joined her at the counter, one eyebrow raised.

Genie shook her head. "He's still up to his old tricks, isn't he?"

"Let's just say I've learned to duck fast."

But Gatesby seemed on his best behavior when she joined Patrick, David, and owner John Anderson in the saddling paddock. The bay gelding stood calmly while Patrick tightened the racing saddle one last time. After Gatesby rubbed his forehead on her silks, the horse blew gently and tipped his head slightly for her to scratch his other ear.

When Trish looked at Patrick with a question, he just shrugged and shook his head. "He's feelin' up to snuff, waren't he, David?"

"Don't trust him for a minute." David glared at the animal in question. "He's just setting you up."

John Anderson conveniently stayed out of tooth range.

But when David gave Trish a leg up, the gelding pricked his ears and tossed his head. After pawing with one front hoof, he lifted his nose, snorting drops of moisture right in David's face.

"I know this horse hates me." David wiped his face with his sleeve. "Get him outta here, Tee."

The parade to post bugled across the grassy infield and echoed in the tunnel.

"Right." Trish chuckled again while Patrick led them out to the pony rider.

"Bless ye, lass." Patrick handed the lead to the pony rider and grinned up at her before stepping aside.

"Thanks." Trish patted Gatesby's deep red neck and would have leaned forward to hug him if they'd been at home. Even loving Gatesby was easy right now.

In fact, with the students chanting along the walkway, a race to run, and the light making her blink when they cleared the tunnel, loving the entire world was easy. As number one, they led the parade past the grandstands and back again.

"See over there, fella?" Trish murmured in her horse-calming sing-song. "Your owner is here to watch you for a change. You gotta do good for him." Gatesby danced from one side to the other, tugging against the lead. He snorted with each stride when they broke into a canter, strutting his stuff for the crowd.

Trish rose in her stirrups, glorying in the wind against her face and the powerful animal beneath her. "Yeah, this is your day, fella. I can just feel it."

Gatesby argued with the handlers for a moment when they started to lead him into the number one slot, pulling against the lead and swinging his rump to the side.

"Easy, easy," Trish sang to the twitching ears. "Watch him!"

The assistant clamped his hand down hard right under Gatesby's chin.

"Did he get you?"

The man gave her a rueful grin, rubbing his shoulder with his free hand. Having had his say, Gatesby walked into the stall as if he'd never dreamed of causing a ruckus.

"You rotten horse, you." Trish couldn't keep the chuckle out of her voice. "You just have to show off, don't you?"

Gatesby tossed his head and turned to look at the horse in the stall on his right.

"You should warn those guys about him," Genie Stokes said over the noise of horses and humans.

"Yeah, make him wear a name tag that says 'I bite.' " Trish patted Gatesby's neck one last time and settled herself for the break. The number seven horse had to be brought in a second time, giving Gatesby a few added seconds to settle down. He took in a deep breath, just like Trish, and let it all out.

"Okay!" the call came. A brief silence. Trish relaxed her clenched fists. The shot! The gates sprung open and with a mighty thrust they broke free.

Gatesby never liked being on the rail, so Trish let him set the pace as they thundered into the first turn. Halfway through, the horse running shoulder to shoulder with them crowded the turn and, in the instant between one breath and the next, slammed Gatesby against the rail.

Trish fought to keep his head up and at the same time remain in the saddle. With things happening too fast to think, only reflex actions saved her from catapulting over the rail.

At the same time all her senses were tuned to the horse beneath her, checking to see if he was injured. But Gatesby pulled against the reins, gaining his rhythm again and extending his stride.

The field now ran a furlong ahead of them.

Trish settled back to ride. Had the bump been intentional?

Gatesby stretched out, each stride carrying them closer to the solid wall of rumps in front of them. By halfway up the backstretch, the wall disappeared as tired horses fell back, giving Gatesby room to maneuver. He surged past the laggers as if they were pulled to a stop. Around the far turn he gained on two more.

Trish rode tight on his withers, head tucked, making herself as small as possible. Down the stretch he paced the second-place horse and drove past it.

"Give it all ya got, fella," Trish crooned in his ear. "You can do it, come on." Gatesby thundered on, stretched out so far he seemed to float above the ground. Nose to rump, even with the stirrup. The finish line loomed ahead.

Genie Stokes laid on the whip. Her horse surged—and faltered. Neck and neck. Over the line.

Trish had no idea who won. "What a run, Gatesby! You did fantastic!" She looked over at Genie, who kept pace with her as they slowed their mounts down. Both girls shrugged and swapped grins.

The second photo finish of the day and the two jockeys had been contestants in the earlier one.

"I don't know how you did it," Genie said as they walked their horses in circles in front of the grandstand. "How far back did you fall?"

"I'm just grateful we didn't go down. That was a close one. I wonder if we should turn in a grievance." She flexed her fingers to help stop the quivering that stretched from her hands to her shoulders.

"Did you see what happened?"

"Not really."

Trish looked over the spectators at the fence to see her mother's frown. David and Patrick were striding across the track toward her. When she circled again, she looked at the scoreboard, recently painted for the new season and still flashing "photo finish."

She waved her whip at the Prairie students and patted Gatesby's sweaty neck one more time.

"And the winner of the ninth race today is number one, Gatesby, ridden by Trish Evanston, owned by John Anderson, and trained by Patrick O'Hern."

"Congratulations." Genie vaulted to the ground. "You earned that one."

"You okay, lass?" Patrick and Marge wore matching concerned looks. At Trish's nod, the old trainer took the reins and led Gatesby through the gate into the winner's circle.

"Fine job, Trish." John Anderson reached up to shake Trish's hand. At the same moment, Gatesby reached over and, before even Patrick realized what was happening, nipped his owner's shoulder. The camera caught the gelding's "who, me?" expression for all time.

"You . . . you . . ." Anderson sputtered, rubbing his shoulder and trying to shake hands with well-wishers at the same time.

Trish looked over at David, tried to catch her giggle, and failed miserably. She vaulted to the ground and hid her grin while unsaddling.

9

"Go ahead, all of you, laugh and get it over with." Anderson's blue eyes danced along with theirs. "If that's what I pay for a winner, I'll do it gladly. But Patrick, isn't there some way you can break him of it?"

"Did he really hurt you?" Trish stepped back off the scales and turned to the others.

"No, mostly jacket." Anderson shook his head. "It's just the principle of the thing."

Trish looked across the track to where David led the bay back to the barn. "I never knew he could run like that. I think the bump made him mad."

"Well, don't make a habit of it. I don't think my heart can stand it." Anderson turned to shake hands with someone else before saying, "Thanks, Trish. You did one fine job there."

"Welcome."

"Thank God you're all right," Marge muttered only for Trish's ears. "I'll meet you after you're dressed again. We're invited out for dinner."

"Okay. Yeah, I'm coming." She waved again at the group of students and let herself be captured by the waiting reporters.

By the time she'd showered and dressed, the crowd had gone home and only jockeys and clean-up crews called their good-nights in the cavernous building. Trish shivered as sound echoed. Such a short time ago she'd heard gun shots in this same hall. She walked out of the tunnel and crossed the infield to the backside.

Dusk softened the angles and muted the sounds of the track. Off in the distance a train rumbled by, its whistle warning drivers to beware. The sound echoed lonely in the letdown of the day.

Trish felt as if someone had pulled her plug and all her energy gurgled out like bath water down the drain. From watching where her feet stepped, she lifted her gaze to Mount Hood, off to the east. Setting sun brushed the tip of it pink and painted mauve shadows down the mountain's flanks.

A horse whinnied. Two others answered.

"Thank you, Father." She ordered her feet to move again.

When she rounded the corner to the Runnin' On Farm stalls, an excited chorus greeted her. A group of Prairie students had remained behind to congratulate her.

"That was some ride." Doug Ramstead picked her up in a bear hug and swung her around. He planted a kiss on her cheek before setting her back down.

Trish felt instant heat stain her neck and face. She glanced over to see David and Brad with duplicate eyebrows asking questions.

"Th-thanks." When she tried to step back, Doug kept one arm around her waist.

"Isn't she something?" Doug asked to no one in particular. "Man, I'd rather be sacked on a football field any day of the week than have some horse run into me."

Trish answered questions and teased her friends back. "Thanks for coming, guys. You all made this day really cool for me."

When they turned to leave, Doug dropped another kiss on her cheek. "See ya Monday, Tee." He strode off with the others, leaving Trish looking after him, shaking her head.

"See, I told you he likes you," Rhonda Seabolt whispered after calling a last good-bye to their friends.

Trish glanced up at her redheaded best friend in all the world. "Gimme a break. He treats all the girls like that."

"Oh, really?" Rhonda must have practiced eyebrow raising along with Brad and David.

"Rhonda, see that bucket of ice-cold water over there?" Trish pointed to a black rubber bucket by the stall. "How'd you like to wear it?" She heard two identical snickers behind her. "Or you guys either."

Trish sank down in a canvas chair in the tack room office. "Patrick, make them quit picking on me." She got to her feet again and opened the refrigerator door. "We got any Diet Coke in here or did those clowns drink it all?" She turned, popping the top on a soda can at the same time. "I'm starved. When do we eat?"

"Dinner's at the Red Lion." David leaned against the doorframe. "Mom's already gone on with Bob Diego. We said we'd come as soon as we could. You ready?"

Trish caught herself in a mighty yawn. "I'd rather stop for pizza and go on home."

"Tough, kid." Tall, lean Brad Williams put an arm around her shoulders and guided her outside. "The price celebrities pay."

Trish punched him in the ribs with her elbow. "Knock it off or I'll sic Gatesby on you."

"Just so it isn't Doug the mighty Ramstead." Brad sidestepped her second punch.

Together the four Musketeers—as Marge had called them for years—and Patrick strode out to the parking lot.

Trish could hear the Thoroughbred Association board members and the others in the ballroom before walking through the doorway. But if she'd hoped to sneak in unnoticed, she'd hoped in vain. Bob Diego whistled for silence as soon as he saw her. Everyone broke into applause when they turned at his bidding.

Instant sunburn—so hot the heat would scorch her fingers if she touched her face. Trish wisely kept her hands out to shake those of the people around her. By the time they made it to the front of the room, she must have said "thank you" a hundred times.

"And now that we're all here, take your places and let's eat."

Trish looked longingly at the round table where her family settled into their seats. Instead she took the place Diego indicated at the head table by his side. What in the world was she doing up there? When she looked over at her mother, Marge just smiled back and sketched a nod.

David shrugged. Patrick raised his eyebrows and shook his head. Rhonda winked and blew her a kiss.

Trish rolled her eyes and concentrated on the salad in front of her. The question of why she was where she was hovered in the back of her mind through the prime rib and into the cheesecake.

"Can I get you anything else?" Diego asked. When Trish shook her head, he rose to his feet and clanked a knife against a water glass to call the group to attention.

When the hubbub quieted, he began. "This has been a momentous day for Portland Meadows and for all of us. I'm reminded of a verse I once heard: 'And a little child shall lead them.' Now, I'm not calling this young lady by my side a child, but when the rest of us were wringing our hands and being taken in by a master con artist, she and her friends went out and did something to change the situation."

Applause broke out and gained momentum. A burning face seemed to be the order of the night. At his request, Trish rose to her feet.

"We have here, Trish, a check made out to your school, Prairie High, in appreciation for what all the students there did for us. Would you be willing to give our gift to them for us?"

Trish automatically took the envelope and shook his hand. "I-I . . ." She cleared her throat and started again. "Thank you, I had no idea. . . ."

"We can't begin to thank you all, but maybe this will help." Bob started the applause and everyone joined him. People pushed back their chairs and stood, their clapping hands drowning out even the thundering of her heart.

Trish felt a tap on her shoulder. She turned. A waiter handed her another envelope and left. Trish looked up at Diego, who stared back with a shake of his head.

"I'll gladly take this money to Prairie on Monday morning, and thanks again." Trish waved one more time at a whistle from the back of the room and stepped away from the podium. After a sip of water while Bob added his closing remarks, she dug under the envelope flap and slit it open. When she opened the square sheet of paper, cut-out block letters seemed to leap off the page. "I'LL GET YOU."

Chapter
02

Feeling gut-punched was becoming a habit.

"Trish, what is it?" Bob Diego grabbed her arm when he felt her sway.

Trish handed him the sheet of paper. Her hand was shaking so violently she dropped it. Instead of reaching for the floating paper, she watched it flutter to the floor at her feet.

Diego knelt to pick it up. When he stood, the thundercloud furrowing his brow told Trish he'd read it. It didn't take long. The words were simple. "I'll get you."

Who, why? The words pounded through Trish's mind like horses going for the finish line. *I thought this was all over!* Trish gripped the back of her chair. Like fireworks exploding in the night, pure fury erupted from somewhere inside her. It steeled her knees and straightened her spine.

No one was going to make her live in fear again!

Jaw tight, Trish looked across the space to the table where her family waited. Marge half rose from the chair but sank down again at Trish's minuscule shake of the head.

"It seems we have a bit of a damper on our festivities." Bob Diego took the mike again. He shifted his gaze to Trish's face, as if asking permission to continue.

She nodded.

"If any of you know about this note or where it might have come from, we'd appreciate your sharing that information." He waved the paper in front of him. "Someone still seems to have it in for Trish. This one says 'I'll get you.' I think it's up to all of us to help any way we can in the investigation."

Trish moved closer to the podium. When Diego paused, she reached for the black mike. The steel in her spine had worked its way clear to her fingertips, and steel never trembles.

"As my dad would say, 'We're just giving God another chance to prove His power.' Whoever wrote this—this . . ." She snorted and shook her head. "He's sick, that's all. And evil. I think we all need to pray for God's protection—for me, for us, and for racing at Portland Meadows—so that we can have a clean sport." She could feel her words gaining strength. "And now we'll let the police deal with this. I don't know about you, but I have work to do in the morning. Thanks."

A nervous chuckle flitted around the room, then changed to applause. But when Trish looked at her mother, Marge wasn't clapping. Her hands were clenched together on the tabletop. Her bottom lip clamped between her teeth. Trish recognized the I-will-not-cry expression.

The group had just broken up, with many coming up to wish Trish the best, when Officer Parks strode in the door. The waiter trotted along beside him.

"I'm sorry, miss," the white-shirted man said. "If I'da known what it was, I would never have given it to you."

"Who gave the envelope to you?" Parks removed his notebook while asking the question.

"One of the girls from the front desk. She just said there was a message for Trish Evanston. We do things like this all the time."

"I understand. Do you know the girl's name who gave you the envelope?"

The waiter smoothed a hand over his balding head. "Not really. I only work here for banquets, part time, you know. I don't know very many of the regular staff."

"We'll take care of that later." Parks turned to Trish. "Sorry to meet again like this. I thought we had this problem solved."

Trish raised her eyebrows. "So did I." She could feel her mother standing at her side. "I'm afraid we left fingerprints on the paper."

"Yeah, well, we know yours by now."

"I'll bet that makes my mother real happy." Trish couldn't believe she'd said that. Here she was making a joke when she'd just gotten another threatening letter.

Officer Parks chuckled obligingly. The approval that beamed from his eyes congratulated Trish on handling the situation.

She hoped with grace. She felt her mother's hand resting on her shoulder. They'd been through a shooting together—surely they could handle a measly letter.

She could feel David fuming on her other side. He kept clenching and unclenching his fists. "I could kill him . . ." she heard him mutter under his breath.

She shot him a look meant to caution him, but the fire in his eyes never dimmed.

After all the questions had been asked, most of which had no really helpful answers, they all walked out to the van together. Officer Parks pulled his squad car over, insisting on escorting them all home.

"What a day." Rhonda sighed, then yawned.

"Been enough excitement for you?" Brad opened the van door for them.

"I think so, even for me." Rhonda climbed into the backseat. "You okay, David?"

Without answering, David spun gravel turning onto the frontage road for Janzen Beach Shopping Center. He let up on the accelerator at a look from his mother, but even though he leaned back, his shoulder propped against the window, and he drove straight-armed, not with his usual relaxed ease.

Stumbling at first, the conversation again picked up and eddied around the driver, who continued to ignore even direct questions.

"You going to give that check to Mr. Patterson on Monday or what?"

"Guess so. That was pretty neat, them voting money for Prairie." Trish glared at the back of her brother's head. "Don't you think so, big bro?" She looked at Rhonda and shook her head over her brother's obstinacy. "David, for pete's sake, it's not as if he shot at me or something."

"Let him alone, Tee." The tone of Marge's voice brooked no argument.

Trish looked over her shoulder at Rhonda and Brad. They shrugged along with her.

Patrick sat rubbing his chin with work-worn fingers. "Give him some time, lass," he murmured for her ears alone. "He wasn't here for the last ones."

Trish sighed. Patrick was right. While she'd felt fury burn through her at first, the flames had died away until only ashes remained. She couldn't—wouldn't stay mad like that. She'd have to let God take care of this again. He had before.

"That cute reporter, Curt Donovan, was taking notes like crazy," Rhonda said around a huge yawn, obviously changing the subject.

"Rhonda Louise Seabolt . . ." Trish whipped around to shut her up but threw up her hands instead.

"Well, he is, and if I had a guy cute as that looking at me like he looks at you . . ."

Trish groaned. "Can't you think of anything besides guys?"

"Sure I can, you dope, but I think David almost smiled."

The words hissed in Trish's ear quite effectively set Trish to sputtering. "Say good-night, Rhonda."

"Good night, all. See you in church tomorrow, or is it today?"

When they finally drove into Runnin' On Farm after dropping Brad off too, the area in front of the house looked like a parking lot—a full parking lot.

"What is going on?" Marge leaned back against the seat.

"Oh, no, reporters. See? That's the Channel 3 van." Trish pointed at a white minivan with a big orange 3 on the side. "How'd they hear about this already?"

"Curt." David made the name sound like a curse.

"No, he wouldn't do this to us." But it didn't matter how they heard. Questions and microphones, along with camcorders and eye-blinding strobe lights, met them as they stepped from the van. Before Trish had a chance to answer, Officer Parks pushed his way to the front and took Trish and Marge by the arms.

"I need to talk with these people first," he said to the crowd. "So you can wait around or come back in the morning, which would be much more polite."

"Right," a sarcastic voice came from the crowd. A rumble of chuckles agreed. "Just doing our job," said another. At every "How do you feel?" and "What will you do?" Trish just shook her head. The temptation to yell, "How do you think I feel when I get threatening letters? Like inviting the jerk out for ice cream?!"

Officer Parks pushed Marge and Trish through the crowd till they reached the steps. Trish stopped and turned while Marge unlocked the door. "Look, I'm tired. This has been a pretty big day. I'm mad clear through that—that *jerk* is starting up again, or whoever is. And I don't know any more than that. So you might as well head home. Good night." She obeyed the tugging on her arm and followed Marge, Officer Parks, David, and Patrick into the house.

They heard doors slamming and car engines revving almost immediately afterward.

"There go the vultures." Parks unbuttoned his coat and drew out his little black notebook. "Trish, you handled them very well. Guess I really don't have to run interference for you."

"Well, I'm glad you did." Marge hung up her coat. "We'd still be out there if you hadn't. Now, how about I make some coffee?"

"Just a minute, Mrs. Evanston, if you would. I have something to tell you."

Marge turned back and crossed her arms across her chest, as if afraid of what she was going to hear. Unconsciously, Trish did the same.

"I'm afraid it's bad news. Kendall Highstreet was released on bail this afternoon."

"The developer who wanted to get Portland Meadows real cheap?" David leaned forward, his teeth snapping together like a shot. "He's crooked as they come. Doesn't attempted murder count for more than a few weeks in jail?"

"It will when he comes to trial, but for right now, the judge agreed to bail."

Trish felt the embers leap to life. So much for letting God handle all this.

"Now, I need all of you to go over this evening again—try to think of anything you might have missed. How could an outsider have known where you would be meeting? How about if you make that coffee and we'll all sit down and rehash this?"

Marge nodded. "Hot chocolate anyone? I can make that too."

This time it was Trish's turn to nod. When she started to follow her mother, Officer Parks shook his head. "I need to talk to you first."

While Marge served the hot drinks, they went over every detail together. But try as they might, nothing new came up. All anyone needed to do to learn about the dinner was to stand near some of the owners and eavesdrop.

"Plenty of people were talkin' about it." Patrick set his cup back on the coffee table. "Both by the track and at the barns. I heard 'em meself."

They all looked up when car lights flashed through the big square-paned living room window.

"That's probably Officer Jones now." Parks closed his notebook. "I requested protection for you, Trish. I—after the last scene, well, I don't think we can be too careful. She'll be here through the night, most likely turn into your shadow." He turned to look at Marge. "Would it be okay if she slept here on your sofa?"

"I—I guess so." Marge stood to answer the doorbell.

Trish glanced at David sitting in her father's recliner. The light from the lamp glinted on dark curls that had repeatedly been tangled by David's fingers. The set of his jaw said it all. "She can have my bed. I'll take the sofa."

"But, David . . ." Trish didn't get any further. The look he sent her could have sizzled a steak.

Chapter
03

She's a cop? Trish blinked a second time.

Long blond hair, blue eyes fringed with impossibly long lashes, a cheerleader's smile, Officer Jones would fit in any high school in America. "Hi, my name's Amy, like short for Amanda." She looked like a Barbie doll next to Officer Parks.

Trish looked over at her brother. He had the sad appearance of a knocked-down bowling pin. The force of impact had slammed his chin to his chest.

"I'm Trish and this . . ." She swallowed a chuckle. "This is my big brother, David." She waited for him to respond, blink, answer something. "David?" Trish glanced at her mother in time to catch an infinitesimal shrug.

"I'm Marge Evanston and this is our trainer, Patrick O'Hern."

Trish watched David out of the corner of her eye. He sure got over mad quick. Now instead of the open-hanging-mouth look, he wore the famous Evanston smile, guaranteed to win votes. Or break hearts, as Rhonda had so often told him.

Amy smiled back at him, or rather up at him when he rose to his feet.

"I hear you're going to Tucson this year. I have a brother who got his degree at the University of Arizona last year. How do you like it there?"

"F-fine." David swallowed, his Adam's apple dipping below the collar of his shirt.

Trish hugged her arms across her chest. If only Rhonda were here to see this.

"Think I'll be going now . . . let you all get acquainted." Parks brought Trish back to the real issue at hand. Amy wasn't just a friend dropping by. She was a police officer, here to guard Trish from some jerk who hated her.

Trish felt the shudders start at her feet and work their way up. Why? Who? *Why?* She stood and crossed the room, her legs feeling stiff, as if she'd locked her knees to keep upright.

"Now, if you think of anything else, you call me." Parks looked from Trish to her mother. "And, Trish, go on about your daily life as normally as possible. Let Amy do the worrying for you. That's what we pay her for."

"Right. You'll let me know if you learn anything new, won't you?"

"Much as I can. Good night now."

"I'll be goin' too. See you in the morning." Patrick followed the tall police officer out the door.

Marge closed the door behind them and leaned her forehead against the wooden frame for only a moment before turning and beginning to gather the coffee things together.

"Where's David?" Trish asked, setting the mugs on the tray.

"He said something about getting his sleeping bag. I have my things with me. I don't want to put any of you out." Amy might look like a teenager and sound like one when she wanted to, but the tone now was all adult. "I'm not here as a guest."

Marge nodded, a polite smile barely lifting the corners of her mouth. "Let him fuss a bit. It'll take his mind off all this."

The two shared a woman-to-woman look that Trish recognized only because she and Rhonda used the same frequency. What fun the two of them could have over David being star struck by Amy! If only she weren't here for such a serious reason.

Trish sighed. She ran the tip of her tongue over her bottom lip. Oh, great . . . a cold sore popping out. She could feel the tender spot. By tomorrow it would probably cover half her lip. She headed for the bathroom to put salve on it.

The face in the mirror looked as if it had seen a ghost. She smeared on the cream and waited for the bite of it to penetrate her skin. In the meantime she smoothed skin cleanser over her eyes and face. The water running to get warm drowned out any sounds from the living room. In here it was easy to pretend this was an ordinary night. Racing during the day. Out for dinner. Company afterward. They'd done this plenty of times. She splashed her face with hot water, then cold.

But they hadn't had a police officer sleeping down the hall before. Would normal, whatever that was, ever return?

Trish followed the sounds of activity down the hall to David's room. The shock stopped her in the doorway. David was changing the sheets on his bed. Trish stifled the grin that threatened to crack her face and strolled over to the bed to help tuck in the blanket ends.

"Don't say a word." David flipped the navy bedspread in place and tossed her a pillow along with its case. "Just put that on while I dump the rest of this in the laundry."

"Yes, sir." Trish did as asked and folded the spread over the wrinkle-free pillow. *So David isn't immune to a pretty face after all.* She shook her head at her thoughts. He'd talked about a girl at WSU last fall, but that seemed three lifetimes ago. And who knew if he was seeing anyone in Tucson?

He returned with a set of matching towels and laid them across the foot of his bed. "Thanks, twerp." He dug his sleeping bag off the shelf of his closet and turned to leave. "You coming or what?"

The tip of her tongue found the blossoming cold sore again, but this time instead of feeling as if some unknown something was picking on her, she giggled when she followed him down the hall. David could get flustered too; the red on the back of his neck told her so.

"Don't even say a word." She caught his muttered command just before they entered the living room.

Keeping quiet was hard. Thoughts of all the times he'd hassled her about Red fed the desire to get even. But she managed. The conversation between the four of them seemed easy, as if Amy had been a guest before, or a friend they hadn't seen for a long time.

"Trish, if you hear or sense anything out of the ordinary, you tell me—immediately, okay?" Amy told her when they finally turned off the lights and headed down the hallway.

"I will." Trish stopped at David's door and pointed to the softly lit room. "You'll sleep here. My room is right across the hall. I need to be at the track to work horses at five, so it'll be a short night."

"Just wake me when you get up. What's your schedule for the rest of the day?"

"To church, back to the track, home again, and homework." Trish paused a moment. "Oh yeah, and sometime in there we take David back to the airport."

"If I can get you anything, please tell me." Marge joined her daughter in the doorway. "I-I'm—we're grateful you're here."

"Thanks, Mrs. Evanston . . ."

"Marge."

"Okay, Marge. I'll try to stay out of your way as much as possible."

"Good night then. Oh, and remember, we have an early warning system in place already here."

"The collie?"

"His name is Caesar and he barks at anything unusual. Good night then." Marge started to shut the door behind her as she left.

"Please leave that open so I can hear easily."

"Oh, I didn't think." Marge pushed the door open again.

Trish shivered at Amy's quiet command. As long as they were all talking, any danger seemed to fade away. Surely no one would bother her here at home. The guy wasn't that crazy, was he? She hung up her clothes when she took them off and slipped into her Mickey Mouse nightshirt. All the while her body accomplished her nightly ritual, her mind followed the twists and turns of trying to unravel this latest attack.

By the time she crawled under the covers, shudders racked her body from hair to toe. She reached up to turn off the lamp but pulled her arm back under the covers. Maybe she'd revert to her little kid days and sleep with the light on.

"Trish, you sleeping yet?"

"Sure, Mom, can't you tell?"

Marge entered the circle of lamplight and sat down on the edge of Trish's bed. "How are you *really* feeling?"

"Scared. Mad. Tired of it all."

Marge nodded. "Me too." She ran her fingers through the feathered sides of her graying hair. "I wish I could lock you up in a box so no one could get to you."

"Great. I've always wanted to live in a box." Trish rolled onto her back and laced her fingers behind her head. "I can't believe Highstreet is really so stupid."

"No one ever said criminals were smart."

"They shoulda just kept him in jail."

"That's one of the problems with our legal system—everyone has rights."

Trish glanced up to see a smidgen of a grin tugging at the corners of her mother's mouth. "I get to learn all about that in government, right?"

Marge nodded. "Back to the fear—you want to pray with me about that?"

Trish shook her head. While her own prayer life was improving, she still suffered when asked to pray with someone else, even her mother.

"You used to say your prayers with me."

Trish's gaze leaped from examining the cuticle on her left thumb to her mother's face. *Dad used to read my mind like that. Now can you?* She studied her mother's expression. "Is mind reading something all parents can do, or just you and Dad?"

Marge smiled gently and patted Trish's clasped hands. "I'm praying for your safety and protection—God's promised special protection to widows and orphans."

"Thanks, but I'm not an orphan."

"Half a one . . . whatever. I claim all the love and protection I can." Marge paused; her gaze dropped to her hands before she looked back to Trish. "You need to pray for whoever is writing those notes. You can't let anger and bitterness come back into your heart."

Trish shook her head slowly from side to side. "I don't think so." But "pray for your enemies" leaped into her mind as she flatly denied her mother's wishes. And that wasn't even one of her memory verses. How did God do that?

She could feel the thoughts chasing each other around the corners of her mind. *Gotcha, didn't she?* Her nagger seemed to chuckle.

Marge rose to her feet and bent down to give Trish a hug. "Think about it." She kissed her daughter's cheek. "And always remember that God loves you and so do I."

Trish wiped away the tears that sprang to her eyes at her mother's words. Her father had always said good-night the same way. She listened to the sounds her mother made getting ready for bed. Water running, the toilet flushing, the bed creaking—all audible because the bedroom doors were open. She reached up and shut off her light.

While the house quieted, other noises magnified: the scrape of a branch against her window, a dog—other than Caesar—barking somewhere, the shifting of a truck. Trish tried to swallow her stomach back down where it belonged. This was as bad as waiting for a stubborn horse to enter the starting gate for the third time.

She knew that sound was the tree outside; she'd heard it for years. Branch shadows ghost-danced on her wall, lit by the mercury light in the circular drive around. She scrunched her eyes shut, clamped her hands together, and tried to pray. When she pulled the covers over her head, all she could hear was her breathing—which grew more rapid until she flung the covers back, leaped from the bed, and stormed over to the window.

After checking the lock and drawing the lined drapes, she turned to a pitch-dark room. She could never remember drawing the drapes before. Within two strides, she slammed her little toe on the bed leg. Hopping on one foot so she could massage the two littlest toes on the other, she banged her knee on the footboard.

The sounds she muttered had no exact words, but if they had, they wouldn't have been the kind her mother liked to hear.

"Trish, are you all right?" Amy asked from the doorway. At least as far as Trish could tell, it was the general direction of the doorway. By now her eyes had adjusted to the darkness, so she reached for the lamp, knocking off the shade in the process.

Another mutter. "I'm fine. Just got banged up trying to close the drapes." She blinked against the light from the lamp.

"What's going on?" David loomed over Amy's back.

"Trish?"

"Come on in, Mom. Everyone else is here." Trish rubbed her sore toes with one hand and combed back her hair with the other. "I was just closing the curtains to keep out the sounds and I banged into the bed. I'm not used to it being so dark in here."

"What did you hear?" Amy leaned her hip against Trish's desk.

"The tree scraping on the window, a car . . ." Trish listed the sounds. "Guess I'm just spooky tonight."

"Yeah, something like the rest of us." David imitated Trish's act of pushing hair back with his fingers. A dark curl dropped back over his forehead as if it belonged there.

Marge returned from looking out the window. "Your foot okay?"

"It will be. Sorry to cause such a hassle." Trish pushed her hair back again. By the time they all left, she felt like hiding her head under her pillow. Maybe if she'd done that in the first place, this sideshow wouldn't have happened.

After turning out the light again, she snuggled down under her covers. *God, this is crazy. I've never been scared here at home before, at least not like this. If you've got extra angels up there who need a job, could you just put 'em around the house?* Her mother's suggestion to pray for the developer slipped into her mind. The thought brought a blaze of anger instead. *How can he do such a thing? And if it isn't him, then who?* Her mind took off with a will of its own.

Trish jerked it back. *Please help me do my best tomorrow. Amen.* She turned over and settled herself on her other side. *Three praises. I forgot the praises.*

When are you gonna learn? Her nagger sounded like he was shaking his head.

Thank you for the wins today, for the money for Prairie from the TBA, for having David home . . . She rubbed the cold sore with her tongue. *For healing my lip in advance . . .* She felt herself smiling. *And for all my friends.* She sighed at the memory of crimson and gold going crazy at the track. *Amen.*

This time when she took a deep breath, she could feel the tension drain out of her body and leave a puddle of warmth behind. *Thank you again, Father.*

By the time Trish had worked all of the racing string in the morning, she'd gotten over watching over her shoulder and checking to see if anyone she didn't know was hanging around. Amy seemed right at home. She and Patrick watched the works from the raised and covered viewing stand by the gate leading onto the track from the backside. He'd volunteered to explain things to her so she could have a better idea how to watch Trish.

At first Trish caught herself paying more attention to the pair, but by the second horse, she forgot about that too and just did her job. Besides, she was freezing. The rising sun had faded the eastern sky to gray with a thin stripe of gold between the overcast and the horizon. But the breeze making fog tendrils dance blew right through her, making even her bones shiver.

"You've turned into a California girl for sure," David teased when Trish wiped her dripping nose on a tissue pulled from a box in the office.

"Yeah, you get out there where the wind hits you and we'll see who's used to warmer weather." She tucked her gloved hands under her armpits and stamped her feet. "I'm going to buy some of those socks with warmers in them and dig out my long johns."

"Well, you've only one after this, and I promise to turn the heater in the truck up full blast." He boosted her into the saddle of the gelding Patrick was training for another owner. "I'm not sure what Patrick wants done here, so you better ask him. You gonna ride the mounts you have for this afternoon?"

Trish shook her head. "Not and make it to church." She checked her watch. "We better hurry." She tapped her brother on top of the head with her whip. "You want me to say anything to Amy for you?"

"Get outta here."

Trish sniffed again. If only her nose would quit dripping. She felt the hackles rise on the back of her neck. Who was that man walking down the aisle to Diego's barns? "This has got to stop!" At the tone of her voice, the gelding jigged to the side.

Trish patted the horse's neck and crooned an apology to the high-stepping animal. "Not your fault, fella. You just do what you know is right. We'll go around nice and easy to loosen you up, then a breeze for the clockers." Trish raised her hand to Patrick and shivered again as the wind hit her. "Maybe we should all move to California."

Brad arrived just when Trish brought the gelding back to the barn. "Sorry I'm late. My alarm didn't go off." He stopped and shot Trish a questioning look when he saw Patrick and Amy walking back to the stalls.

"That's Amy Jones," Trish said after vaulting to the ground. "Because of the note last night, Parks brought me a guard."

"Well, she could guard me any day."

"You and David. She's really a nice person."

"I bet."

"Brad Williamson, you're as bad as your friend over there. Now, I gotta get home and get warmed up. How about you finish grooming this guy?"

When Amy and Patrick joined them, Brad nudged Trish until she relented and introduced him. Had everyone gone girl or boy crazy but her?

"I don't know about you guys, but I need to get something to eat and get ready for church. David, you coming or what?"

Back at the truck, Trish swallowed a snort. David opened the door for them. Trish stepped back to let Amy sit in the middle and caught a nod of approval from her non-smiling brother.

"No, I'll take the window . . . lets me see better." Amy ushered Trish in first.

Trish shrugged when David shot her a glare as he started the engine. She adjusted the heater controls and soon a blast of hot air could be felt into her boots.

"I forgot how cold it can be out there."

"Yeah, well we froze in the fog at Bay Meadows, even if it was California."

"But it always burned off there. I think I'm beginning to like it down south." Trish rubbed her hands together.

"I've only been south twice. Once for my brother's graduation"—Amy pulled the cap off her head and let her blond hair swing down around her shoulders—"and once to Disneyland. My fiancé says maybe we'll go there on our honeymoon."

Trish could feel David deflate. Wait till she saw Brad again.

Cinnamon roll perfume met them at the door when they pulled off their boots at the jack and entered the dining room.

"Thought you could eat in shifts while taking turns for the shower." Marge set a plate of bacon on the table. "Amy, would you like coffee or hot chocolate?"

"Coffee, please."

Trish heard them visiting when she headed for the shower. She'd have to wear her hair in a braid today, no time to wash and dry it.

Everything was fine until Pastor Mort started the prayers after the sermon. Trish had no trouble with him praying for safety for her and the family, but when he began praying for the person causing the harassment, she wanted to plug her ears. He didn't say anything like "God, get the man" or "Help the police capture him."

Instead he said, "Father, bring this person to a knowledge of you and your will for his life that he may know your love and forgiveness."

Trish felt like gagging.

Chapter
04

When a flute began to play the opening bars for her song, she breathed a sigh of relief. Right now she really needed those eagle's wings to lift her up and the hand of God to hold her. She shared her songbook with Amy and sang with all her heart.

"I love that song," Amy said after the service was over.

"Me too. It's kinda become my theme song. When I'm really down, it helps pick me up."

"I can see why."

"Come on, David, I need to get back to the track," Trish muttered. But getting out of church quickly might take one of God's miracles. By the time her mother had introduced Amy to a dozen people and others had extended their assurance of praying for the family, time had sprouted wings.

"Can I help?" Rhonda whispered from right behind Trish's shoulder.

"You could yell fire!"

"Nope, I thought more along the lines of sneaking you out the back, but then your bodyguard might think you'd been snatched."

"Rhonda, you've been watching too many movies. Amy is *not* my bodyguard."

"She's not your long-lost cousin either. Wish I hadn't let you take me home first last night. I missed out on all the excitement."

"Right. You can have all this excitement. I need to get to the track and soon. My first mount is in the second race."

Trish smiled when someone else said something to her, but she could feel her mask beginning to crack.

Amy caught Trish's look and nodded. Suddenly they were outside the church and on their way to the car.

"Hey, you're good," Trish and Rhonda said at the same time.

Amy grinned at them. "You should have said something sooner. One of the first things we learned at the Academy was crowd control."

"And you never offended anyone." Trish shook her head. "I should have you teach me some tricks."

"Sure 'nough." Amy climbed into the backseat of the van last and smiled at David when he slammed the door.

Trish watched Amy watch the surrounding area. While carrying on a conversation, Amy still scoped out the parking lot, the cars, and the people getting into them. If this was one of God's answers to prayer, Trish decided, it was one of those easy to be thankful for.

By the time Trish arrived at the track, she had to head directly to the jockey room.

"Will my being there cause a problem for you?" Amy asked halfway across the infield. "I could wait outside, kind of mingle with the crowd."

"No, you're short enough that you could be a visiting jockey."

"Great! What I know about riding could fit on the point of a pencil. Just say I'm your cousin visiting—like we have been. The less lies we tell, the less chance there is of getting messed up. Now, have you noticed anyone unusual?"

Trish grinned at her companion. "Look around you. Is there anyone here *not* unusual?"

Just then one of the bug boys walked by and grinned. *"Buenos días."* He wore fringed leather chaps and a purple helmet, and sported a handlebar mustache under a nose that looked as if it had met one too many fists.

Amy returned the smile. "I mean anyone you don't know. There is definitely a collection of characters here."

"Yeah, this is really my extended family. Dad started bringing me here when I was about ten. I always wanted to race."

"And now you're doing it. You're lucky."

A few early fans leaned on the rails; others studied their racing programs. When Trish looked up to the glass-fronted stands, reflecting the gray clouds, she felt a chill snake up her spine. Someone could be watching her and she wouldn't even know it. She responded to a "Hi, Trish" and a "Good luck, little lady," but the arm at her elbow didn't allow for stopping to visit. For the first time, Trish felt stomach-relaxing relief at the thought of her escort.

The other jockeys greeted Amy when Trish introduced her, and then continued their business of preparing for the upcoming races.

As Trish went about her routine, she nearly forgot Amy was there; the woman blended into the woodwork, almost. Trish polished her boots and applied wax to all five pairs of her goggles, stacking them on the front of her helmet and snapping them in place. She'd use one till it was dirty, then bring down the next pair. The muddier the track, the more goggles used per race.

After the first race had been called, Trish moved to the floor for her stretches. Extenders, twists, straddles, all used different muscles and stretched joints. The more limber she was the less chance of injury. Her father had drilled her well.

She'd just pulled a white long-sleeved turtleneck over her head when Genie Stokes returned from running in the first race.

"How'd you do?" Trish asked, popping her head out of the shirt like its namesake.

"Don't ask." Genie sank down on the bench beside Amy. "That filly acted like she'd never seen a racetrack before, let alone the starting gate." She shook her head. "And I know she has because I've been riding her for training."

Trish finished lacing her white pants and sat down to pull on her boots. "Well, starting tomorrow, Patrick wants you to ride for us in the morning."

"I know. Maybe he'll teach me more about handling youngsters like that one."

"Was it her first race—a maiden, right?" Amy asked.

"It was her first, but maiden means any horse that hasn't won a race yet, not just their first." Genie stepped to the mirror and wiped a smear of dirt off her cheek.

"Oh. And here I thought I was being pretty smart."

"Well, if you're around us for any length of time, you'll learn plenty. Most of us don't know anything but horse talk."

The squawk box announced riders for the second race to the scales, so Amy and Trish followed another jockey out the door. *Much as I like you,* Trish thought, *I hope you're not my shadow long enough to learn all about racing.*

"Sure wish I could keep you home away from all these crowds," Amy muttered when they joined the parade of jockeys out to the spoke-wheel-shaped saddling paddock. Spectators lined the rails, some leaning over with programs to be autographed. Others hollered their greetings and encouragement.

To Trish, the scene felt familiar and comfortable—a far cry from San Mateo, where, as a loser, she'd had few fans. Maybe being a big frog in a little pond wasn't such a bad thing after all.

She blocked out thoughts of everything but the coming race when she joined Bob Diego in stall three. "Bob, I'd like you to meet my cousin, Amy Jones. She's visiting here from Spokane."

"I'm glad to meet you."

Trish met his gaze without flinching, hoping he'd pick up on what Amy's job really was. No one brought their cousin into the saddling paddock unless that "cousin" owned the horse.

Diego studied the petite blonde for a moment, before his gaze shifted back to Trish, crinkles tightening the corner of his dark eyes. "I'm *very* glad you brought Amy along, *mi amiga.* Family is so important, is it not?"

Trish nodded, grateful for his understanding. She stepped to the gelding's head and let him sniff her arm before rubbing his cheeks and up behind his ears. "How ya doin', fella? Long time no see." She had ridden him the year before, once into the winner's circle. "Think we can get in line for the camera again?"

"He should do well. He's in top condition and rarin' to go."

The call came for riders up, so Trish gave the dark bay one last pat and turned for a leg up. Diego checked the cinch again and looked up at Trish. "You've a big field, and with a mile to go, he'll need a kick left for the stretch. He likes being in the lead, but the last time he set too fast a pace and came in with a fourth."

"I'll watch him." Trish smoothed the black mane to the right and gave the gelding a final scratch when Diego backed the animal out of the stall. She nodded at the greeting from the pony rider and waved when someone called her name. How could she ever have thought about giving up racing? Her butterflies gave a leap just to remind her they still resided in her midsection, the crowd roared when the horses trotted onto the track, and the horse beneath her jigged a response to the excitement. Yeah, this was what she was born for.

When they cantered back past the grandstands, the starting gates were wheeled into position behind them. The roar of the crowd drowned out the tractor noise, but Trish concentrated only on the grunts of the animal beneath her as he tugged against the bit, wanting to catch up with the two ahead. As Diego had said, his horse was primed and ready.

When Trish looked ahead she could see the number one horse giving both the jockey and the pony rider a bad time. The gray gelding swung his rump to the side and jerked against the lead tie.

"Sure glad we're not next to him," she sang to her mount. "But let him use all his energy now. We have a race to win." Her horse snorted and tossed his head, as if in agreement.

Behind the gates, number one continued to act up. He refused to enter the stall, sitting back on his haunches when the handlers tried to lead him in. Trish trotted her mount around in a tight circle, keeping him active so he'd be ready. After the second refusal to the gate, number one struck out with his front feet.

Send him back to the barns, Trish felt like telling them. *We don't need trouble out here.* She could feel her horse begin to tense in response. "Easy, fella. His bad manners have nothing to do with you."

The gate assistants motioned the remaining horses into the stalls. One by one they entered and settled. This time number one walked in as if he'd never hesitated. The gates clanged shut. The pause.

Trish forgot about the gating problem, focusing all her attention on the horse she rode. She could feel him settle and gather his weight on his haunches.

The shot, the gates clanged open, and they were off.

The field remained bunched going into the first turn, and then both the leaders and trailers emerged. Trish kept her mount running easily, one off from the leader and abreast with another. He didn't fight for the lead as Diego had warned, instead seeming content to let Trish do her job.

The three leaders held their position down the backstretch and going into the far turn, but the pace was fast. Trish hung above her horse's withers, aware of a horse coming up on the outside but not ready to move yet. Going into the stretch, the lead horse slowed and the rider went to the whip.

Trish loosened the reins. "Okay, fella, now." The gelding spurted forward. With each step he left his running mate behind and gained on the front-runner. He stretched out again and flew past the leader as if he'd been shot from a cannon. Trish let him go, glorying in the speed and power beneath her. No one was coming even close behind them. When they drove across the finish line, her mount was still gaining speed.

"That was some race," Bob Diego greeted her back in front of the winner's circle. "You played him just right."

"I don't think he even needed a jockey. He knew what to do. I just went along for the ride."

"Well, it was certainly a good ride. Thank you, mi amiga. You can ride my horses anytime."

After posing for the pictures, Trish weighed in and headed for the jockey room. Amy picked her up at the fence and paced the dirt track with her.

"Was that as much fun to ride as it was to watch?"

"More. That old boy could have gone farther and faster if I'd let him. The long rest hasn't hurt him any."

"I might turn into a racing fan by the time this assignment is over." Amy held the gate for her. "You should hear all the good things the crowd says about you. Except of course for those rooting for another horse."

"Naturally." Having Amy shadowing her again brought back the fears Trish had managed to forget on her circles around the track.

Trish picked up her silks for the next race and entered the jockey room. Racing in two, three, and four didn't leave her much time to relax, but then she didn't have to worry about cooling off too much either.

The overcast deteriorated to mist by the time she trotted her next mount onto the track. Trish hunched her shoulders to keep warmer, wishing she'd switched to her warmer turtleneck. The newly risen wind tugged at neck and sleeves, sending the cold deep into her skin.

By the time all seven horses were in their gates, the mist had turned to drops. When Trish lowered her goggles into place, she felt grateful for the remaining pairs. Shame the glasses didn't have wipers.

The filly she rode broke clean and surged forward with her running mates. Down the backstretch they galloped, shifting positions when first one then another took the lead. Into the turn Trish and another ran stride for stride. Out of the turn the front-runner slowed, then surged again at the whip.

The other jockey went for the whip. Trish loosened the reins, but when her mount failed to respond, she smacked the filly with a right-handed stroke and then another.

But the spurt of speed wasn't enough. They came in with a show by only a nose.

"Sorry, girl. That was my fault." She stood in her stirrups to bring the filly back down. *You shoulda gone to the whip sooner,* she scolded herself. *Not all horses are voice-trained like yours are, and you know it.* After adding a couple of choice names to the roster, she apologized to the trainer as well.

The woman shook her head. "I thought you brought her in real well. That's the best she's ever done. You can ride for me anytime."

But the vote of confidence failed to override the berating Trish was still giving herself when Amy fell in with her. As Amy opened the gate, Trish felt the hairs on the back of her neck tingle. She stopped and looked around, seeking a strange face or something out of the ordinary, like Amy had told her to look for.

"What is it?" Amy had placed herself in front of Trish nearly before Trish stopped.

"I don't know. Maybe just the rain making my back chilled." Trish turned at the tug on her elbow and continued up the hall to the jockey room. "I didn't see or hear anything—just all of a sudden, I had the creeps."

"Glad to hear you have those senses. Makes my job easier." Amy hustled her from the silks room to the jockey room. "Next time, don't stop. You set yourself up as a target that way."

Trish felt as spooky as her horse for the next race. Rain falling steadily served to curb the audience excitement, and the snap and whoompf of an opening umbrella made her horse snort and leap to the side.

Her heart started pounding before the umbrella finished stretching. She ordered her hands to relax, loosening one finger at a time. The urge to look over her shoulder struck so powerfully she almost grabbed her chin to keep her concentration to the front.

You're nuts to react like this. She took up the inner scolding again. *Your job is to ride this horse, right now, to the best of your ability. Not look over your shoulder because you've got a bad case of the spooks.*

The horses entered their gates willingly as if they all understood that the faster they got this over with, the faster they could get out of the rain. The shot, the gates swung open, and Trish forgot all but the horse beneath her and those around her. In the number four slot, they broke in the middle of the pack. The eight animals bunched around the turn, and being right in the middle, Trish had no place to go. Not without bumping someone else.

She ignored the urge to scream her frustration at the heavens. Would someone get moving and get out of her way? But when the chance came, the filly took too long to move and the hole closed. Down the stretch when the horses strung out, Trish, even going to a steady whip, could move her no farther than fourth.

Start in the middle and end in the middle. If Trish had given herself a tongue-lashing before, it was only a practice run. Now she flayed herself with both anger and purpose. She'd done a terrible job with this horse. *All because you can't keep your mind on what you're doing! If you can't do better than this, stay home.*

Patrick just shook his head when she made that same statement back at the barns. "Ye know, lass, you can't blame yourself for everything. Those things just happen."

Trish shot him a look guaranteed to fry eggs.

David's comment earned an identical look.

"Trish thought she sensed something wrong back there," Amy said.

Trish felt like throttling her bodyguard.

David grabbed Trish's arm and brought her to a stop. "What did you see?"

"Nothing, big brother." Trish put all the sarcasm she could muster into her voice. "It was nothing at all."

"That's it, I'm staying home." David dropped her arm and headed back to the office. "Mom can cancel my flight."

"Yeah, right. As if you could protect me or something." Trish strode up the walk. "Let's just get home. I'm freezing."

By the time they crossed the I-5 bridge over the Columbia River, neither Trish nor David were speaking, especially not to each other.

"Have you any idea what gave you the feeling of being watched?" Amy finally broke the silence.

Trish shook her head. "I've tried to figure it out, but nothing. Maybe I'm just being paranoid or something."

"Gut feelings are pretty important. I'm just glad you're not racing for the next two days. Maybe we'll have a breakthrough by then and you won't have to worry anymore."

"I wish." The shiver that shimmied up Trish's back had nothing to do with the dampness of the day.

"But, Mom, you've always said an extra pair of eyes or hands or whatever makes for light work. In this case, the more of us to watch out for Trish the better. If I miss a few classes, it's no big deal."

"It *is* a big deal, but you don't have to worry about it, because you'll be there." Marge planted her hands on her hips and the set of her chin warned everyone not to argue with her.

"Mother, be reasonable. You and Trish could be in real danger—at least Trish is. They keyed her car and shot at her, remember?"

"Oh, I remember all right. I was there. But you can't guard your sister and neither can I. Amy is doing her best, and the rest we have to trust to God."

"He didn't seem to do so well last time," David muttered under his breath.

Trish leaned her hips against the counter, sipping a cup of hot chocolate. One eyebrow raised at David's comment. But she kept her mouth shut—with difficulty. *Let them battle it out for a change,* she thought. *They don't pay much attention to what I say anyway.*

Amy entered the kitchen and joined Trish against the counter. "Would you like the latest bulletin?" she asked when a silence lasted more than a second or two. When the two turned to face her, she included Trish in her smile.

"Parks says Highstreet has a solid alibi, so that, at least temporarily, leaves him out of the picture. Parks wondered if there was anyone you might have offended at the track, Trish, that could do a copycat crime? Since this was so well publicized, thanks to our esteemed press corps, things like that happen more than you know."

Trish looked to both Marge and David and then shook her head. "I've been gone so much, and then helping to solve the problem out at the track, that I've hardly even seen anyone, let alone ticked them off."

"Could anyone be jealous?"

"Course, she won the Triple Crown, didn't she?" David crossed both his arms over his chest and his ankles as he leaned back against the counter. "And she drives a flashy red convertible, travels around the country, gets her name in all the papers, has the money to buy what she wants. I'm sure there's no one the least bit jealous."

"David."

"Gets shot at, becomes a heroine . . ."

"We know all those things, David." Amy's quiet voice stopped his tirade like his mother's hadn't been able.

"Then why don't you do something about it?"

"We are."

"They are." Marge added.

"I'll get it." Trish pushed herself upright and crossed to the ringing phone. "Runnin' On Farm. Trish speaking."

"I can tell."

"Who is this?"

"Don't you wish you knew."

Chapter
05

Trish's hand shook so hard she dropped the phone.

"Dial tone," Amy said after grabbing the receiver. "What did he say?"

"I—I didn't hear all of it." Trish wrapped her arms around her middle to keep from shattering into small pieces. "To—to watch out."

David slammed his hand down on the counter. "And you think I'm leaving here? No way!"

"Okay, let's all calm down." Amy raised her hands for silence. "From now on, Trish, you don't answer the phone. I will. We'll put a tap on it so maybe we can get him that way. David, I know you mean well and I appreciate what you're trying to do. But right now, we're going to try to go on with life as usual. Please, let your mother take you to your plane as you planned."

"The best thing you can do is pray for all of us." Marge placed her hands on her son's shoulders and stared deep into his eyes.

"Doesn't seem to do much good. Look at all that has happened."

"But, David, no one's been hurt."

"What about Trish's car?"

"As I said, no one's been hurt. God is doing His job; now let's all of us do ours."

"And mine is going back to school." David sighed and shook his head. "This is against my better judgment."

"I know. And I appreciate that."

Trish watched the interchange between the two people she loved most on this earth and marveled at the way they understood each other. *Dad and I were like that,* she thought. *I miss that. Dad, I miss you. What would you do with all this stuff that is going on?*

David gathered his things as his mother requested and brought his bags to the door. "You be careful, Tee. Whoever this guy is, you can't count on him to make sense."

"I know, and you take care of yourself." Trish fought back the burning behind her eyes, and she wrapped both arms around her brother. "I miss you when you're gone. Now that you've been home again, I figured out how much."

"I'll see you in Kentucky in less than two weeks, then it'll be Christmas before you know it."

"Thanks. With all I have to do, that doesn't sound too comforting."

As soon as Marge and David left, Amy got on the phone to order a tap and bring Parks up-to-date on the latest development.

Trish wandered back to her bedroom to change clothes and head for the barn. She whistled for Caesar and pounded down the cedar deck stairs fully expecting the collie to bound into view. She whistled again. No yipping, cavorting bundle of energy danced around her legs and tried to lick her nose.

Fear niggled at her mind.

Must be a female in heat somewhere around here. She forced herself to think of reasons for his absence. *Or he's off chasing rabbits or . . .* She couldn't keep the thoughts going. Caesar *never* left the farm when they weren't home. He took his guard-dog duties as seriously as did the Secret Service around the president.

Trish whistled again. "Caesar! Hey, fella! Caesar!"

The horses whinnied from down in the paddocks. A crow cawed from up in a fir tree. But no sable collie with a snowy white ruff whimpered an apology for being late.

41

Trish debated. Should she tell Amy that Caesar was missing? Or should she just get the chores done so she could go look for him? *God, help me.* She shot her arrow prayer heavenward and trotted down to the barns. Tonight she would put all the horses in their stalls and feed them there.

"You guys seen Caesar?" she asked the nickering babies. Miss Tee and Double Diamond greeted her with tossing heads and quivering nostrils. They lipped their carrots and nuzzled her shoulder as if she were a long-lost friend. "Don't care for the yucky weather, huh?" Trish snapped the lead shanks onto their halters and trotted the young horses up to the barn.

Where was Caesar? Fear dried her mouth so her whistles lost their soar.

Old gray Dan'l, the gelding who'd helped train her in the fine arts of Thoroughbred racing, whinnied repeatedly, as if afraid she might forget him. Trish trotted back down the lane and stopped at his paddock. "Hey, easy on the fence." She pushed him back while hugging his gray neck at the same time. "Come on, let's get you up to the barn. You seen Caesar?"

Dan'l munched his carrot without answering her.

By the time she'd fed everybody, dusk faded into darkness. The drifting mist caught rainbows in the area lit by the mercury yard lamp. She trotted up the front walk and entered through the front door.

Amy was still on the phone.

"Caesar's missing." Trish grabbed the truck keys off the pegboard by the phone and headed for the door again.

"Hang on, Trish. I'll come with you." Amy finished her conversation and hung up. "Is this unusual?"

"He never leaves, especially when we're not home." Trish waited by the door for Amy to get her coat.

Car lights from Patrick's new half-ton pickup met them back in the drive. He stopped at Trish's wave.

"Caesar's missing. Thought I'd check the road just in case." The thought of her beloved collie lying in a ditch made her want to heave.

"You looked through the barns?"

"Not really. Fed the horses though and everyone's in."

"I'll search down there."

Half an hour later, Trish turned the truck back into the lane at Runnin' On Farm. She'd call Rhonda and Brad to ask for their help too.

"This would be so much easier in the daylight." She banged her fist against the steering wheel. "Where could he be?"

"Wish I knew." Amy opened her door. "Wish I knew."

"No one would hurt a dog, would they?" Trish finally voiced the thought that had been flitting around in her head.

"I hope not."

The answer didn't sound convincing.

Trish spent the next half hour calling some of the neighbors to ask if they'd seen the dog. The phone rang and rang at Rhonda's. Brad answered on the second ring.

"Sure I'll help call," he said. "Want me to go out with you again?"

"Not right now. How about asking if anyone has a dog in heat? That's the only thing I can think of that would get him to leave."

"Sure will. Have you walked down by the creek and way out in the pastures?"

"Not really. He just never answered, so I figured he wasn't there."

"I'll be over after I make these calls. You got a good flashlight?"

Trish hung up and leaned against the counter, staring out into the night without really seeing it. Where could he be?

She walked over to the refrigerator and took out a Diet Coke. "You want something to drink or anything?" The guilties grabbed her. Some kind of hostess she was.

Amy looked up from the notes she was writing. "No thanks—and, Trish, you don't have to play the good hostess with me. I'm a member of the family, remember? I can help myself."

Trish nodded. Where could Caesar be? She sipped her drink and went to stand at the sliding glass door. When she flipped on the light switch, her mother's baskets of pink and purple fuschias sparkled with droplets of mist. Soon they would be put to sleep for the winter before the frost killed them.

Trish shuddered at the thought of being put to sleep. She slid open the door and stepped out on the deck, staying under the overhang of the house to keep dry.

Country silence filled the crisp, damp air. Listening hard, she caught the tinkle of runoff in the downspouts. A breeze sent droplets cascading from the fir trees and plopping on the ground.

Trish held her breath. What had she heard?

"Caesar?" She waited again. Had it been a whine?

She whistled, three tones pleading for an answer. She held her breath, concentrating everything she had on listening.

The sound came again, weak, distant, sad.

Trish flung open the door and grabbed the high-powered battery light from its nest plugged into the wall. "Amy, I think I heard something." Out the door, down the steps, and around the deck, quartering the ground with the intensive beam, Trish searched each shadow and cranny.

Down on her hands and knees she flashed the light underneath the deck. "Caesar? That you, fella?"

A faint whimper seemed to come from the back corner.

"You hear that?" Trish asked as Amy crouched down beside her. The sound came again.

"Yes. Can we get under there?" Amy leaped to her feet. "I've got another flashlight in the car. And a tarp to pull him out on."

"Go tell Patrick. He might be able to help us."

As soon as Amy left, Trish concentrated again on the sounds from under the deck. A whimper came in response to her gentle, "Caesar? You under there? What's happened to you?"

She edged underneath, digging in with her elbows to pull herself forward. When she tried to use her knees, she bumped her butt on the cedar joist above her. "Ouch." She flashed the light again but still couldn't see her dog.

Laying her cheek flat on the cold, damp ground, she scanned the beam under the low-lying joists. One red eye reflected back at her. "Good dog, Caesar. I'm coming." Caesar huddled three joists over.

Trish back-crawled as fast as she could, paying no attention to bumps and muddy spots.

"You found him?" Amy met her as Trish stood upright again.

"Yes, he's back in the corner." Trish dropped to her knees again at the right joist. "There's no room for two to work under there. I'll go back with the tarp, roll him onto it, and then pull it out, I guess."

"We'll use this rope to help pull. You think he'll let you handle him?"

Trish paused for only a moment. "Of course. He's my dog."

"Ye found him then, lass?" Patrick joined them.

"Uh-huh. Pray for us, Patrick." Trish shoved the tarp under the wooden frame and crawled after it. "I'm coming, old man. Hang on."

"Here, I can help you from this side." Amy elbowed into the adjoining crawl space, pushing her light ahead of her, just like Trish. Matching grunts marked their progress as they dug in their elbows and pulled themselves forward. "Ugh, I hate spider webs."

The smell of wet earth filled Trish's nostrils and clogged her throat. Her jerking light reflected off the beams above her and glistened on the wet slime covering the bare ground. No eyes reflected back from the dog she knew lay ahead.

"Caesar, fella, you okay?"

Only the panting of her partner broke the stillness. "Can you see him?" Amy's voice seemed almost in her ear.

"Not yet. Never realized how big this deck really is."

"Or how hard belly crawling under this decking would be."

"There he is." Trish dug and pulled faster, almost crawling over the tarp in her eagerness. The muddy form ahead of her never moved. "Caesar?"

She swallowed the bite of fear stinging her throat and causing tears to blur her vision. "Caesar, please fella, hang in there. We're coming for you." She shoved the tarp next to him and inched across it to lay her hand over his ribs.

She clamped her teeth on her bottom lip. *God please*. His matted fur lay still. She pressed harder. There under her fingers a faint heartbeat. "He's alive—barely."

"Okay, can you see any blood?"

Trish flashed the light over the inert dog. "No. Just dirt, like he's crawled a long way."

With trembling fingers she spread the tarp, accepting the help Amy provided from under the cedar joist. "Ouch." She only acknowledged the bang on her head with the word while she slid her fingers under Caesar's shoulders.

"I've got his hindquarters. Now on three, we'll pull him onto the tarp." Amy reached as far as her shoulders. "This would be a good time to have basketball-player arms." She clenched the matted fur. "Okay— one, two, three."

Together they heaved. Trish banged her head against the cedar boards above her and ended up with her nose buried in Caesar's muddy shoulder. He didn't move. She scrunched backward. "Okay, you ready? We'll go again. One, two, three."

Caesar lay on his side on the tarp. Trish laid her face against his muzzle while she caught her breath. A warm tongue flicked the side of her cheek.

"He's alive. Come on, Patrick, pull." Trish scrambled backward as fast as her knees and elbows permitted, trying to keep ahead of the sliding tarp.

"I've got your flashlight." Once out Amy pushed herself into a kneeling position at the same moment as Trish. "How is he?"

"He can't lift his head but he licked my cheek. We call him the fastest tongue in the West." Trish grabbed the corners of the tarp. "Come on, let's get him to the truck."

"Marge has the van running. She already called the vet." Patrick hefted along with the two women and together they lugged the heavy body around the house and up to the open back doors of the van.

"Dr. Bradshaw will meet us at the office." Marge gave Trish a boost so she could follow the dog into the van. "Amy, you coming?"

"I'll ride back here with Trish." Amy clambered onto the carpet. Patrick slammed the doors at the same time Marge closed hers, and she immediately set the van in motion.

"Can you feel any broken bones or anything?" Amy joined Trish in probing the dog's legs and spine.

"No. This doesn't make sense. He was fine this morning, so unless he was hit on the road . . ."

Amy smoothed her fingers over the dog's grimacing lips, revealing teeth in pale gums. "See the way his head is pulled back?"

"Then what could it be?" Trish wiped her drippy nose on her sleeve. "Come on, fella, hang in there." She grabbed the carpeted wheel well for support as her mother swung around a corner.

"Trish, could he have eaten anything—anything that—"

"Like what? He got into a salmon years ago and nearly died from salmon poisoning—" Trish bit off her sentence. "Poisoning. Do you think he's been poisoned? Who would poison a dog like Caesar?"

"Could he have gotten into something for coyotes or some such?"

"No one poisons coyotes around here." She could feel the fear clamping off her wind, raising her voice to a shriek.

"We're here, Tee. There's Dr. Bradshaw."

Trish had the back doors open even before the van came to a complete stop. She and Amy leaped to the ground at the same instant and turned to lift the muddy blue tarp, easing the dog over the bumper.

"Right through here." Bradshaw held open the door to his surgery.

Trish blinked against the glare when they sidestepped through the doorway and down the hall, the heavy-laden tarp slung between them.

"Up on the table." He took one corner of the tarp and Marge another. "On three—one, two, three." Together they laid the limp form on the stainless steel examining table. The overhead light glared down, highlighting each clump of mud-clotted fur. Eyes closed, his breathing so shallow it failed to lift his ribs, Caesar lay unconscious.

Trish gently stroked his muzzle, whispering encouragement. She watched the vet apply the stethoscope to the once snowy chest. He moved it under the front leg.

"He's still alive, but barely. From the looks of him, I'd say poison. Let's get an IV started and then I'll draw some blood. See if we can figure out what they used."

Trish held the leg as the vet clipped the hair and swabbed a pink patch. While her body did what he requested, her mind bombarded the gates of heaven for her dog.

An hour later Caesar opened his eyes and whimpered deep in his throat. Trish heard him only because she stood crouched over the table by his head. The tip of his tail whisked an inch on the metal surface.

"Easy, old man," she whispered around the knot in her throat. "You're gonna make it; you gotta." She smoothed the short hairs back in front of his ears.

"We'll put him back in a kennel now," the vet said while applying the stethoscope again. "He sounds stronger. The next twenty-four hours will tell the tale."

"Can't we take him home? I'll watch him real careful." Trish kept her eyes on the collie. She knew if she looked up at the vet, she'd cry.

"Trish, you know he's better off here in case he needs emergency procedures." Dr. Bradshaw laid a hand on her shoulder. "I promise to take good care of him."

"I—I know." She stroked the top of Caesar's head, doing her best to tell her dog how much she loved him in the language he knew best. "You don't think someone poisoned him deliberately"—she raised her gaze to meet the doctor's and swallowed—"do you?"

Chapter
06

Dr. Bradshaw nodded his head. "I'm afraid I do."

"Maybe he got into some rat poisoning . . . or . . . or coyote bait, or . . ." Trish couldn't think of anything else.

"But you say he never leaves the farm. Have you put out any such substances?"

Trish shook her head.

"Then I imagine it was doctored meat left where he would find it. He didn't eat very much or he'd have been dead for sure."

"But—but why? Why a dog? He never hurt anybody!" Trish tore her gaze from the vet's and swung around to find Amy studying her, compassion evident in her blue eyes.

"Parks will come by in the morning for a statement. I think—I'm afraid this was a warning." Amy shook her head. "And maybe this was accidental. As soon as the lab analyzes the bloodwork we'll know what we're up against. At this point we have to cover all the possibilities. My job is to keep you safe, Trish." She turned back to the vet. "Will there be someone here all night?"

The doctor nodded.

"Good then, let's move him and we'll head home."

Together they hoisted the tarp and, with Marge carrying the intravenous bag, transported Caesar back to the kennels. Dr. Bradshaw transferred the dog to the wire cage, laying him on some shredded newspaper. He hung the IV pouch on the door and stepped back so Trish could tell Caesar good-night.

Trish bit her lip to keep the tears from taking over. "You do what he says now, you hear, old boy?" Caesar sighed but didn't open his eyes. "I'll see you tomorrow." She dropped a kiss on his muzzle and stepped back so the vet could close the cage.

"You'll call us if . . ." She couldn't say the words. He *had* to get better.

"Of course. But I think we're on the right track."

Trish dashed the backs of her fingers across her eyes. "Thanks."

By the time she fell into bed hours later, they'd discussed the situation until her mind felt like a tangled skein of yarn. She thumped her pillow and flipped over on her other side. If only she could flip a switch and turn off her mind like she did the lamp.

The old rabbit race persisted around the tracks in her head. If God loved them, why didn't He protect them better? But if God wasn't protecting them, maybe someone in the family would have been hurt! Could God keep the animals safe? If He hadn't been, Caesar would probably be dead by now. She ended up by ordering her rabbits back to their burrows and focused on her three things to be thankful for. Number one: Caesar was still alive and improving. She thought about the word *improving.* Was he? And wasn't this one of those times like her father said, when you thanked God for the outcome in advance, going on faith that He was making it so? She sucked in a deep breath and let it all out, clear to the bottom of her lungs. The warmth seeping into her body felt like a warm bath but without the wet.

Number two was easy. Thanks for Amy. And for winning at the track, for a safe flight for David, for his coming home for the weekend. . . . Trish drifted off on her litany of praise.

First thing in the morning she called the vet. When he said Caesar was much stronger, she jigged in place to let some of the joy escape before she bounced on the ceiling like a runaway balloon. After sharing her news with Marge and Amy, she danced down the hall to take her shower. Caesar was mending. Now all was right with her world.

The phone rang just before Trish opened the door to leave for school. She reached for it but stopped when Amy grabbed it first and frowned at her. "Oops," she grimaced and flinched. She always answered the phone. How would she remember not to?

"Runnin' On Farm." Amy waited, poised with pencil in hand. "Of course. I'll get her for you." She covered the receiver with her hand. "Wait to answer until I pick up the other line, okay?"

Trish nodded and reached for the phone. The wink Amy gave her pushed her curiosity button to full alert. When she heard the click on the line, she said, "Hi, this is Trish."

"Trish, this is Sandra Cameron from the Public Relations Department of Chrysler Corporation in Detroit. How are you today?"

"Fine." Trish's curiosity button turned neon.

"I'm sure you're curious as to why I'm calling."

"Ah, yes." What an understatement.

"Mainly I'd like to set up an interview with you. We could bounce some ideas around. Would that be possible?"

"Sure." The neon button turned into a flashing strobe light.

"How about tomorrow? I can hop a plane and be there about eleven."

"I have school." Trish felt her tongue stumbling over her teeth. What was going on?

"I think this is important enough you'll want to miss a couple of hours. Please make sure your mother can be there also. Will this be all right?"

Trish mumbled an assent and then gave directions from the airport before gaining the courage to ask, "What's this all about?"

"I'd really rather wait until we can talk face-to-face. I'll see you tomorrow about eleven. Oh, and here's my number in case there's a problem."

When Trish hung up the phone she understood what being run over by a steamroller felt like. What in the world was going on? She stared out the window down toward the barns. A thought teased the back of her mind but refused to be identified.

"You really don't know what that's about?" Amy asked from the front door.

51

"Not a bit." Trish headed down the hall and knocked on the bathroom door, where she could hear the shower running, before sticking her head inside the steamy room. "I'm outta here. Oh, and, Mom, you gonna be home tomorrow about eleven?"

"I think so, why?"

"A Sandra Cameron called from the Chrysler Corporation—wants to meet with us."

The shower stopped. Marge peeked out the shower door. "What?"

"Gotta go. Love you." Trish shut the door on her mother's "Tricia Marie Evanston!"

"You know anything about that?" Amy asked when they drove down the lane.

"Not really." Trish shrugged. "Guess we'll find out tomorrow." What was it she couldn't remember?

When they picked up Rhonda they brought her up to speed on all the excitement.

"I'm so glad Caesar's better. I prayed for him all night."

"All night?" Trish glanced in the rearview mirror to check out her friend's face.

"Well, every time I woke up. Seemed like all night. So you see this Detroit lady tomorrow?"

"Yeah . . . wish I knew what it was about. The suspense is killing me."

"It's about the advertising campaign, you know, the one that reporter down in San Mateo told you about. They want you to—"

"That's it! The thing I've been trying to remember." Trish thumped her hand on the steering wheel. "How do you think he knew about this? That was weeks ago." None of them came up with any answers, just more questions, by the time they arrived at Prairie High School.

Trish dropped her things off at her locker and stopped at the front desk just as the second bell rang. "I need to talk to Mrs. Olson," she told the student working the counter. "She's my advisor," she whispered to Amy.

"You better ask for the principal too," Amy replied. "I need to talk with both of them."

By the time the meeting was over, Trish remembered how little kids felt when grown-ups talked about them as if they weren't there. They could at least have asked her opinion rather than planning her life for her.

"Sorry about that," Amy said as they headed for first period. "It just seemed to work faster if I handled it." Trish muttered her agreement. "But from now on, I'm just your favorite cousin from Spokane, right?"

"Right."

"I forgot to tell them about the gift money from TBA." Trish smacked her forehead with the heel of her hand. "Now I'll have to stay after school to catch them."

"Would now be better?"

"No, we're late enough for class as it is." Trish didn't need her nagger to call her names. She was doing a good enough job of that all on her lonesome. She retrieved her things from her locker and headed for class.

The boys at their lunch table reacted to Amy with the same drop-the-jaw expression David and Brad had adopted. Trish and Rhonda swapped their *oh brother* looks and kept from giggling by sheer willpower.

"Should I tell them the bad news—that she's engaged?" Trish whispered behind her hand.

Rhonda shook her head. "Naw, let them suffer later. Serves 'em right." She glared at Jason Wollensvaldt, a foreign exchange student from Germany and her somewhat boyfriend, who looked as star struck as the rest.

Mrs. Olson and Mr. Patterson, the principal, kept Trish waiting for an extra fifteen minutes after school before they could see her. Counting the seconds as the clock ticked them off did nothing to calm her twitching fingers. If only she had the vet's number with her. But by the time she decided to head for the pay phone with a phone book, they beckoned her into the office.

Trish laid the check on the desk in front of the man whose shoulders were as broad as his forehead was bare. He tipped his head to peer through horn-rimmed bifocals. "What in the world?" He looked at Trish, question marks all over his face, while handing the paper to Mrs. Olson.

Mrs. Olson read it and grinned. "Okay, Trish, come clean. What's going on here?"

Trish sat forward on the edge of her seat. "Like it?"

"Of course." Patterson leaned back, his hands clasped behind his head. "But what did we do to deserve a thousand dollars?"

"It's in thanks for the work Prairie kids did to collect signatures. I was going to give it to you this morning but I forgot."

"Well." Mrs. Olson picked up the check and studied it again. "Did they make any recommendations for how we use it?" Trish shook her head. Mrs. Olson shifted her gaze to the principal. "Then I think the government class that started all this should vote on how it's put to use. Agreed?"

Mr. Patterson massaged the shiny front part of his scalp with beefy hands. "Don't see why not. That should be another good lesson in government by the people. What do you think, Trish?"

"You mean it?" She could feel a grin cracking her cheekbones.

"Yes, and I think you should be the one to tell them."

"Really?" She caught herself just before sliding off the chair. "Even Ms. Wainwright?" At their nods, she slapped the arms of the chair. "All right!" Trish jumped to her feet. "I'll tell them in class tomorrow. What a blast that'll be!" She headed for the door, only pausing to beckon, "Come on, Amy, we've got stuff to do."

Trish opened the glass-windowed door. "Oh no! I won't be here tomorrow." She spun back around. "That woman from Chrysler is coming."

"Then you'll have to tell them Wednesday." Mrs. Olson rose to her feet. "You can handle the secret for one more day, can't you?"

"I guess." Trish rolled her eyes and shrugged. "But it won't be easy."

"Good things never are." Mrs. Olson patted Trish's shoulder. "We'll get a thank-you letter off immediately. Pick up the check to show the class after lunch on Wednesday, all right?"

Trish nodded again. "Thanks." And out the door they went.

As soon as Trish walked in the front door back at Runnin' On Farm, she called the vet. "Caesar's been drinking water on his own," she announced. "Vet says he maybe can come home tomorrow if he continues like this." She executed a jig step to the refrigerator. "Amy, you want something to drink?"

The warm glow stayed in her middle while she changed clothes and headed for the barns. Patrick would be at the track feeding the racing string, and someone had to take care of the home stock. Amy carried her can of soda with her.

Trish breathed both a sigh and a prayer of relief that night when she snuggled down under the covers. They hadn't heard a peep from the stalker. That was the good news. The bad news? She couldn't get him out of her mind. Where—and how would he strike next?

She woke in the morning feeling like her nagger had been going at her all night—with his foot to the floorboards. Here she was beginning to think he'd moved on to pester someone else. The vacation had been grand.

She rubbed her eyes with both hands, then dragged the same through her tangled hair. Even the sheet and blankets were wrapped around her legs as if they'd been the opposing side in a free-for-all. She lay still a moment trying to remember what she'd been dreaming about. Nothing. Just this heavy feeling in the pit of her stomach and a pounding headache.

Caesar! She jerked her feet from the binding covers and sprinted down the hall. Good thing they had the veterinarian's number on speed dial. She punched 4 and drummed her fingers on the counter, waiting for an answer. When she looked at the clock, it registered only six-thirty.

"Come on, be there."

The answering machine kicked in. Trish groaned and dropped the receiver in the hook, fishing for the phone book under the counter with her other hand. His home number was listed in their file at the front of the book. She dialed again.

When he answered, she could hardly keep the quiver from her voice. "Dr. Bradshaw, this is Trish Evanston. Is Caesar all right?"

"Far as I know. He was so much stronger last night I planned to release him today, just like I told you. What's the matter?"

Trish shook her head. "I don't know. I—I just had this awful feeling." She stumbled over her words, all the while calling herself names inside her head. "Sorry I bothered you."

As Trish hung up the phone, Marge stepped out of the bathroom, pink towel wrapped around her head. "Trish, are you all right?"

Trish rubbed her aching temples. "I guess. I—I'm not sure." She took the aspirin bottle from the cupboard and poured two tablets into her palm. After downing the pills with a glass of water, she leaned on her arms over the sink.

Marge came up behind her and felt her daughter's forehead. "No temp. Any other symptoms?"

Trish shook her head, which only accelerated the beat of the bass drum echoing in her skull. "Patrick okay?"

Marge nodded.

"All the horses?"

"Far as I know. Trish, what in the world . . ."

Trish started to shake her head and caught herself just in time. "Where's Amy?"

"She had to meet with Officer Parks. She went early so she could be back in time for school. Tee, you're scaring me. What is this?"

"Wish I knew, Mom. Just bad dreams, I guess." She rubbed her forehead. "Think I'll lie down for a couple more minutes." She shrugged, her half-attempted smile more a grimace. "Don't worry. Everything'll be okay, right?"

All the way down the hall she placed each foot in front of the other with deliberate care, in order to keep the drum from deepening its beat. Lying down with the same degree of caution wasn't easy with the twisted covers, but she managed.

"Here." Marge laid a cold washcloth across Trish's forehead just after her head nestled into the pillow.

"Thanks."

"Remember, you have that appointment with what's-her-name from Chrysler."

Trish winced. She kept herself from shaking her head again. "I know."

Marge tucked the covers around her daughter's shoulders. "You want to skip first period or even stay home?"

"No, call me in fifteen minutes. I'll be better." And she was.

After taking a quick shower, she felt almost human again. What had gotten into her?

"I think you're psychic," Rhonda answered after Trish told her tale in the car on the way to school.

"Rhonda!" Trish clenched her fingers around the steering wheel. "Whatever made you think of something like that? I had a bad dream and woke up so tense I got a headache. No big deal!"

"I read about some guy who could, you know, pick up the vibes or something. They called it . . ." She paused. "Ummm . . ."

"Precognition?" Amy questioned from the second seat. "I've heard that many people have it but some only sporadically." She leaned forward. "But what I read said most people don't believe in such a thing. I agree with Trish—she had a bad night. There's enough stuff been going on around here to give anyone a bad night. Dreams sometimes just reflect what's going on inside of us . . . helps our psyche work it all out."

"Huh?" Rhonda turned in her seat. "Care to run that by me again?"

"It just means . . ."

"Let's drop it, okay? Talk about something upbeat."

"How's Caesar?"

"Better. We can pick him up this afternoon."

"And your meeting with the fancy car lady?"

"Thanks for nothing. Now my butterflies are trying to race each other out my throat." Trish swung the car into the parking lot at the high school. "Rhonda, sometimes I could . . ." She parked the car and set the brake. "If I don't get back to school, you'll need to get a ride home."

"No problema. Jason'll take me home any time I let him." Rhonda opened the car door at the same moment a certain tall exchange student reached for the handle. She turned and winked at Trish. "See? I told you."

Trish watched her friend laugh up at the blond giant. "They say he's a wizard with a basketball."

"Looks like he knows how to catch a girl too." Amy grinned at Trish in the rearview mirror. "We're going to be late if we don't hustle."

"Yeah." Trish swung open her door and stepped to the ground. Eleven o'clock wasn't very far away either.

Chapter
07

Sandra Cameron was late.

Trish glanced at the clock over the sink in the kitchen again. Here she'd rushed home to be on time and now they waited.

"Only ten minutes. You know how it can be renting a car."

"Even if you're a Chrysler executive?"

"Probably even if you were chairman of the board." Amy and Marge clutched matching coffee mugs and leaned against the kitchen counter. "Unless you get a limo, and those have been known to get lost too."

"Voice of experience?" Marge glanced over her shoulder to check the driveway.

"For sure. Cops get escort duty plenty in their beginning years." Amy breathed in the steam rising from her cup. "You sure make a good cup of coffee."

Trish eyed the platter of fresh cinnamon rolls sitting on the counter. "Wait till you taste her specialty." As if looking through a telescope, she watched her fingers drumming on the counter. The rhythm matched that of the butterflies fluttering in her midsection. Feeling the urge for the second time since arriving home, she headed down the hall to the bathroom. Did nerves affect everyone this way? She'd just flushed the toilet when Marge knocked on the door.

"She's here, Tee."

Trish dashed her hands under the water, made a face at the one she saw in the mirror, and finished drying her hands on her pants when she walked back down the hall. Through the front window she could see a tall, corporate-suit-clad woman retrieving her briefcase from the front seat of a black LeBaron. She tossed back her shoulder-length pageboy hair and strode up the walk.

Trish swallowed to wet her dry throat. Was this really about her being in an advertisement, or did they want to take her cars back? Maybe they thought three red convertibles were too many for one person. Her mother motioned toward the front door, obviously meaning for Trish to answer it. Having her feet glued to the floor made forward locomotion difficult.

When the knock sounded, Trish ripped her feet from their moorings and, pasting what she hoped looked like a smile on her face, answered the door.

"Tricia Evanston?" The woman extended her manicured hand. "I'm Sandra Cameron. How are you today?"

"F-fine." Trish swallowed again and gestured for the woman to enter. *You sound like an idiot, Evanston.* Thank God for mothers.

Marge greeted the woman, making the small talk that grown-ups did so well and that Trish felt tongue-tied over. Give her horses to talk about anytime and she did fine, but gosh, this woman was from . . .

Trish took herself sternly in hand. If she could talk easily over a microphone to thousands of fans at the track, surely she could handle this interview. After all, it didn't really mean anything—did it?

By this time Marge had them all sitting comfortably in the living room while she exited to the kitchen for the coffee.

"So now, how are things going with your racing?" Sandra leaned forward on the sofa and clasped her hands together on her knees.

"Good." Trish flashed her a grin. "We opened at Portland Meadows on Saturday."

"I hear you won the Hal Evanston Memorial Cup."

"You did?" Trish's voice squeaked on the "did."

"Trish, I don't think you know what a celebrity you are. Sunday's paper in Detroit carried a big article about all your efforts to keep the track open and then winning the cup in memory of your father."

Trish gritted her teeth against the flash of tears behind her eyelids. One sniff and she was fine again.

"No, I guess not."

"Curt Donovan is making quite a name for himself writing about the 'Comeback Kid.'" Sandra pulled a sheaf of articles, paper-clipped together, from her briefcase and handed them across the open space. "See?"

Trish glanced down at the picture of her accepting the trophy, then looked back up at her guest. "Wow—I mean, I knew this was in *our* papers, but clear back in Detroit?" She shrugged. "It wasn't like I was at Churchill Downs or something."

"But you will be soon, right?"

"Sure, we're running Firefly in the Oaks, and I'm riding for Bob Diego in the Breeder's Cup."

"But not Spitfire."

"I wish. But the syndicate would never let me. He's too valuable at stud now."

"How about if we make him a movie star too?"

"What?"

"Well at least a star model. We at Chrysler would like you and Spitfire to star in a series of ads we've designed for LeBaron convertibles. We'll shoot them at BlueMist Farms, since we already checked and they don't want to transport him off the farm if they can help it. I know this is tight timing, but we'd like to spend three days shooting—hopefully we can finish in that time—beginning on Monday next week. You'd fly to Lexington on Sunday, shoot Monday, Tuesday, and Wednesday, and have Thursday off before you race on Friday. What do you think?"

The shiver started at her toes and worked its way up. Star in an ad? Whoa!

"Don't you think that big black horse of yours would look great beside a bright red convertible? And the camera loves you. We know that from all the pictures we've seen, both TV and print."

Trish tried to find words. She really did. They just wouldn't come.

"We'll pay you, of course. And pay for the use of Spitfire also." She named an exorbitant figure. "And if this works like we think it will, you'd continue to be a spokesperson for Chrysler. Usually we'd make all the arrangements with your agent, but since you don't have one . . ."

Trish shot her mother a look of pure pleading.

"Trish has an agent." Marge set her tray down on the coffee table.

"I know she has one at the tracks, but this would be entirely different. All the big names in sports, film, or modeling have agents to help build their careers." Sandra accepted the coffee and cinnamon roll. "Thanks. This looks delicious."

Trish used the moment to shake her mind out of total shock and unlock her tongue. She looked over at Amy, sitting so quietly by the window, and caught a wink that helped bring her back to the mission at hand. *They want me and Spitfire to star in ads—for Chrysler. We can do that—can't we? Sure we can. No big deal—right?* She rolled her lips together to stifle the giggles that threatened to erupt. *Wait till Rhonda hears this. She'll freak. Totally freak!*

Ms. Cameron's voice brought Trish back to the living room with a thump. "I know I've been doing all the talking. Marge, these cinnamon rolls are simply scrumptious. So Trish, I'd like to hear what you think of all this. Are you interested?"

Am I interested? Do horses eat grass? Trish sucked in a deep breath and let it all out. This was supposed to help her relax. Could she count on her voice to work now?

"I g-guess." *Yeah, right. I sound like a total idiot.* She tried again. "I think this sounds exciting—like I never dreamed of such a thing."

"Then you're interested?" At Trish's nod, Sandra smiled and leaned back against the sofa. "Good. Then we can proceed."

They talked for another hour before Sandra asked, "How about if I take you all out for lunch? I need to call my boss and tell him this is a go, so if I could use your phone?" At Marge's nod, Sandra rose to her feet. "While I'm doing that, why don't you keep thinking of any questions you have. Also if you have an attorney you'd like to discuss this with, have him look over the contract."

Amy came over to sit on the stone hearth to be by Trish. "Wait till I tell 'em down at headquarters about sitting in at a meeting like this.

Trish, this is absolutely fantastic! I can't begin to tell you how thrilled I am for you."

"Pinch me to make sure I'm not dreaming." Trish held out her arm for Amy to pinch. "Ouch, guess I'm not." She leaned forward in her father's recliner. "Mom, what do you think? You've been awfully quiet."

"Just wishing your father were here to see all this. He'd be so proud." A tear meandered down her cheek till she swiped it away with the tips of her fingers.

"You'll go too?" Trish blinked against the moisture threatening to overspill.

"Of course. Just never thought I'd be a stage mother. 'Course I never planned on being the mother of a celebrity at all." She shook her head. "Life is strange all right."

"Couldn't happen to better people." Amy leaned back against the stone fireplace. "Just couldn't."

"You think God wants me to do this?" Trish turned again to her mother.

"If not, He'll close the doors. That's how I've been praying." Marge took her daughter's hand in hers. "I always pray for His perfect will and what is best for you."

"You two are something else." Amy leaned forward, hands on her knees.

"What do you mean?"

"I don't think I've ever seen real faith in action like I have here. Makes me want it too."

"Okay, that's all taken care of." Sandra walked back across the room. Her smile included them all. "We're really pleased with your agreement. Really pleased. The wheels are now in motion, not that they weren't before."

Trish clenched her hands together. *Wow! Is God working or is God working? Like Dad always said, "Walking the walk is a better witness than just talking the talk."* She shot an arrow prayer heavenward for Amy.

"Now, do you have a favorite restaurant?" Sandra stopped before the trio at the fireplace, as if aware she'd interrupted something. "You want me to go out and come back in a while?"

Marge shook her head. "No, this has nothing to do with our

discussions. Diamond Lil's is nice, has good food." She laid a hand on Trish's shoulder. "Unless you'd rather have Trish's favorite."

"Pizza."

"I *was* thinking of something a little fancier than that."

Within minutes they were all four piled into the minivan and heading down the driveway. They waved at Patrick returning from the track in the pickup.

By the time they were seated at the restaurant and had ordered, Trish had a multitude of questions bubbling over, like what lines to say, what she'd be wearing, what scenes they'd thought of, what a "shoot" was like, when the TV spots would air.

Sandra held up her hand. "Easy, I won't remember all the questions. How about if I just run through what a typical day might be like. Keep in mind, though, that Murphy's Law is nowhere more proved out than on a commercial shoot."

"Murphy's Law?" Trish wrinkled her eyebrows.

"You know, what can go wrong will go wrong." Sandra picked up a breadstick and smeared the tip in a pat of butter. She waved it in the air before crunching a bite. "Never fails."

"Oh." Trish reached for her own breadstick.

By the time they'd finished eating and Sandra finished talking, Trish had that becoming-familiar steamrollered feeling. What in the world possessed her to think she could pretend to be a model or an actress? While Amy and Sandra finished another cup of coffee, Trish and her mother read and reread the contract.

"What I'd like you to do is drop this off at your attorney's before we return to the farm for my car and he can go over it. You can sign it tomorrow in his office and fax me a copy, then send the real thing by overnight mail. Since you're a minor, Trish, your mother has to sign all of them too. I'll call you with a couple of names for agents if you'd like after I get back to the office."

"Do I really need one?"

"Depends on if you want to parley your popularity into more endorsements or not. They can give you good advice too."

"Why don't you see how you like this before we go any further,"

Marge advised. "It's not like you don't already have plenty to do. School has to come first."

"I know."

"We're required by law to have a tutor on the set for minors still in school."

"I can keep up. It's not like I'm going to be gone for months or anything." Trish could feel her old resentment flare. Her mother was showing her worryitis again. With her, school and good grades were most important, almost next to praying. What if her daughter decided *not* to attend college? Or at least postpone it? Trish tamped down the thoughts. They didn't need an argument right now.

By the time they arrived back at Runnin' On Farm, the sun was heading for its nest in the west. Trish felt herself getting impatient. She had planned to pick Caesar up right after school. Brad's metallic blue Mustang occupied its usual place in the turnaround in front of the house. He would be down doing chores. Patrick would be at the track again, feeding and putting the racing string to bed.

Even so, the entire place seemed empty without Caesar barking his welcome.

Sandra bid them all good-bye and left with a promise to talk with them the next day.

Trish heaved a sigh of relief. Right now she needed a bit of calm to recover from all the excitement.

"Kind of like a whirlwind, isn't she?" Amy joined Trish on her march to the house.

"I guess."

Trish opened the front door and turned left to the kitchen while Amy headed down the hall, stopping in the bathroom.

Brad had dropped the mail on the counter, so Trish began leafing through, hoping for a letter from Red. Instead a small brown package sported her name. She took a knife from the drawer and sliced the tape, surprised at how heavy it was.

What would anyone be sending her?

She undid the paper and pulled the top off the tan box. Inside lay a brick with a note taped to it.

Trish felt and heard her shriek at the same instant.

Chapter
08

"Trish!" Amy barreled across the living room.

Trish stared at the package as if it contained live rattlesnakes. "Bang! You're dead!" the letters on the note stated plainly.

Amy first checked out Trish to see if she'd been injured, then transferred her attention to the box on the counter. "It coulda been a bomb," she muttered under her breath. She spun around and pinned Trish to the refrigerator with a glare tipped in ice. "Why ever did you open it? I told you to let me check any letters—that's it!" She slammed her palm on the counter so hard the box jumped.

"It—it wasn't a letter and I was so—so happy I didn't even think about—about—you know. I just thought someone sent me a present, maybe Red—or—somebody." Trish couldn't keep from stammering. Or shaking either. She'd been having such fun and now this!

"Whatever is going on?" Marge charged through the door and skidded to a stop. "Oh, dear God, now what?"

"Let me set you both straight." Amy's voice slashed like a whip. "Let *me* open the mail, answer the phone, get the door. How can I get this through your heads? Some kook is out there trying to scare the daylights out of you . . ."

"He's doing a bang-up job of it." Trish wrapped her arms around her middle. She felt as if she'd stepped outside in the middle of an ice storm.

"Right. And maybe he has more than scaring you in mind." Amy's voice softened and she drew Trish into her arms. "Hey, buddy, I've come to care for you more than a little. You have to be careful—and let me do my job."

Trish bit her lip. She *would not* cry. But it was easier to keep the tears back when Amy was yelling at her.

"Would someone please tell me what is going on here?" Marge stared from Amy to Trish and back again.

"You tell her." Trish pulled away and jerked a tissue out of the box by the phone. She blew her nose and wiped her eyes. "I'm going after Caesar."

"No you're not. I'm calling Parks and he'll be right out to talk with us."

"He can wait. Caesar is more important right now. He's been waiting all day." She snatched her purse off the counter and headed for the door.

"Trish, you can't go alone." Marge snagged her purse, shot Amy a look of apology, and followed Trish to the van. "I'll drive home so you can stay in the back with Caesar. Otherwise he'll be all over the car, and he's still too weak for that."

Trish shoved the key into the ignition and waited for her mother to get in. "All I did was open a package addressed to me. And no, I didn't look to see who sent it—I was having too good a time. There must be a law somewhere against Trish Evanston having fun."

Trish drove the car down the drive and out on the road, and still her mother didn't reply. "Well? Aren't you going to yell at me too?"

"No. You're doing too good a job of that yourself." Marge fastened her seat belt. Trish looked over at her mother when she heard the snap of the belt. Her words sounded calm but the two lines between her eyebrows furrowed deeper. Trish could tell she was worried.

But then, who wouldn't be?

Most of the shaking had subsided by the time they pulled into the parking lot of the veterinary clinic. When Trish glanced at her mother, she received an almost smile in return. "At least we can thank God Caesar is getting better."

"And that you weren't hurt. When I think of that mail bomb that blew a man's hand off not too long ago . . . Tee, I'm just grateful you're only mad."

Trish shook her head. "Let's go get the dog."

Caesar struggled to his feet when he saw her and heard her voice. His tail feathered only a bit, but at least he was wagging it. When she opened his cage, he tottered a step forward and made sure her face got a requisite cleaning.

"You old silly, you." Trish tugged on his ruff and rumpled his ears. When just those actions made him waver, she turned to look at Dr. Bradshaw. "You sure he's okay to take home?"

"I'm sure. He'll get better faster there with those he loves. Just keep him in the house or a kennel."

"No kennel. We'll make him a bed by the back door."

"Make sure he has water all the time and if he quits voiding, bring him back in. That means his kidneys are in trouble. You might have to help him outside."

"That's fine, then." Marge shifted her purse to the other shoulder. "Trish, we need to get home."

Trish stepped back from the front of the cage so the vet could lift Caesar and carry him out to the car. She ran ahead to open the back door and climb in. When Dr. Bradshaw laid Caesar with his head in her lap, she smiled her thanks and buried her face in the dog's ruff. Caesar licked her nose once, then sighed. His tail thumped against the wheel well.

"Yeah, I'm glad to see you too, even if you do smell of disinfectant."

But she wasn't so glad to see the patrol car and Curt Donovan's white newspaper car parked in their yard when they got home. "More questions," she muttered. "If I never answer another policeman's questions, it'll be too soon." Caesar thumped his tail. When the door opened to the face of a strange man, the dog bared his teeth and rumbled low in his throat.

"Tell him it's okay." Officer Parks stepped back. "I just want to carry him in. He's too heavy for you."

"Hey, fella, it's okay. Parks is our friend." Trish's voice slipped into the croon she used on the horses with the same calming effect. Caesar allowed himself to be picked up in the officer's strong arms, and with Trish right by his side, her hand on his head, entered the house to a hero's welcome.

Brad, Patrick, Curt, and Amy gathered around while Trish grabbed a blanket from the closet and pulled a rug over to pad the bed for the weary dog. He lay down with a sigh, but as soon as Trish tried to move away, he scrabbled and lurched to his feet.

"Easy, fella, you stay there." But when her words had no effect, Trish sank down beside the dog. "Guess you'll have to question me right here."

They went over the events of the package-opening three times with nothing new coming up.

"I'll take the package in for fingerprinting and see if we can't determine which post office it came from—see if anyone remembers anything." Parks shook his head. "Whoever this is has to make a mistake pretty soon. Or he's a lot smarter than I think he is."

"All they have to do nowadays is watch TV," Patrick grumbled. "With all the crime and police shows, a body can learn to commit about any kind of crime. Don't take a genius."

"Could this be a copycat crime?" Curt asked. "Since Highstreet doesn't seem to have anything to do with it?"

"Could be. Highstreet would have a hard time. We've tapped his phone and have him under constant surveillance. He can't blow his nose without us knowing."

"Fat lot of good it seems to be doing." Trish continued stroking her sleeping dog's head.

"Yeah, cases like this don't get solved in one hour, like on TV. Welcome to the real world of police work—patience and persistence." Parks accepted the mug of coffee Marge offered. "Most cases are solved only through hours and weeks of digging out one detail after another."

"Amen to that." Amy joined Trish on the floor beside the collie. She ran a hand over the dog's side and shook her head. "Boy, he lost a lot of weight. Wait till I get my hands on that—"

"We're not sure if Caesar's poisoning is connected to this case or not," Parks reminded her. "He could have just picked up some bad meat."

Amy shook her head, sending her blond hair flying. "My women's intuition says guilty." She raised a hand, palm out. "No, don't you go shaking your head. How many times have I been right on?" She grinned at his pained expression. "Bugs you, doesn't it?"

"Well, I better get back to the track to feed. Brad—you coming with me or doing those here?" Patrick pushed back his chair.

"I'll stay here." Brad exchanged looks with Patrick. "Keep an eye out."

"Thanks for the coffee. Good as usual." Patrick picked his hat off the counter.

The phone rang and at Amy's glare, Trish didn't even begin to get to her feet. The police officer gave Caesar a farewell pat and stood. When she headed for the phone, Trish laid her cheek on Caesar's head. She could feel her pulse pounding, all at the ringing of the telephone. What a mess.

"Trish, it's Rhonda." Amy stuck her head around the corner of the refrigerator. "How about if you call her back?" Trish nodded. Rhonda would freak for sure when she heard this latest news.

After Parks and Curt left, Trish and Amy joined Brad down at the barns. While Marge worked the babies in the morning, Trish trained the two almost-two-year-olds in the afternoon. They were to be ready for the track sometime after the first of the year. Late as it was, all the horses, from broodmares and young stock to old Dan'l, lined the fences of their paddocks, waiting for their treats.

"That's some picture." Amy took several pieces of carrot from Trish's bucket. "Being here with you and the horses is going to make any other assignment stale by comparison."

"You're welcome to visit anytime." Trish whistled just for the pleasure of hearing the responding nickers. Old Dan'l let loose with a full-blown whinny, tossing his head enough to set his gray mane flying.

"You want to ride him?" Trish asked when she fed the babies their treats. "Easy now, Miss Tee." She grabbed the filly's halter. "You know better than to shove like that."

"Dan'l?" Amy sneaked Double Diamond a second carrot chunk. Trish nodded.

"You mean it?"

"You said you know how to ride."

"I do. Rode for years before I went away to college." She gave the youngster a last pat. "You be good now, you hear?" The colt nodded and rubbed his forehead against her shoulder, leaving white hairs on her navy sweat shirt. Amy pushed his head away with a chuckle. "What a lover."

Trish did the same with Miss Tee. "Yeah, these two ought to be really something about a year from now. Since Miss Tee was born last September, she'll be running a year late."

"This thing about all Thoroughbreds having their birthday on January first doesn't make a lot of sense to me."

"Me either, but they have to have some sort of guidelines. Would be pretty confusing otherwise." She gave the mares their treats and requisite pats. Dan'l nickered again and pawed the grass. "I'm coming. Hold on to your shorts." The gray only tossed his head and nickered louder.

"I think he likes you." Amy stuck her hands in her back pockets. "Talk about a peaceful scene."

"I know. My dad used to come out here in the evenings just to enjoy the horses and the quiet. Said it was his special time. Mornings were always too hectic what with works at the track and all."

"From what everyone tells me, he was a pretty special guy."

"Yep." Trish buried her face in Dan'l's mane. Would she ever be able to talk about her father without the tears burning her eyes? She gave the old gray another carrot and stroked his face from forelock to quivering nostrils. His munching filled the silence. A crow cawed from the top of a fir tree, joining the chorus of the peeper frogs from the creek.

Trish watched Amy scan the area, checking out the sounds and the silences, before returning her gaze to Trish with a smile.

Trish sighed. Amy was ever the police officer, keeping on top of her job. The thought of being the focus of that job made her stomach knot. Someone wouldn't invade her life here, would they? She snagged her thoughts back from the black well and concentrated on the warm, gray body beside her. "Well, old fellow, how would you like a turn or two around the track?" She snapped the lead onto his halter. "I'm sure Brad has those two ready to run . . . probably wondering what happened to us."

A shiver ran up her back. What if there really was someone out there watching them?

Trish couldn't shake the unease all through the gallops with the two horses in training. She forced herself to pay attention, working the colt through his paces, forcing herself not to look over her shoulder. Keeping her eyes on his ears rather than the trees across the track. Listening for changes in breathing that told of his fitness rather than listening for strange noises.

Bang! You're dead! The words of the note flew up before her eyes when she blinked. It would be so easy for someone to take a shot at them.

What if he hurt one of the horses? The thought clamped off her air.

By the time they finished, she couldn't keep her hands from shaking.

"What's wrong?" Brad took the brush from her hands. He turned her square to him so he could look right in her face.

Amy ducked under the colt's neck, leaving her brushing job. "You okay?"

Trish shook her head. "I can't get that note out of my mind. All of a sudden I realized how open we are here." She glanced over her shoulder. "Those trees and all. I've never been afraid in my own home before." She clenched and unclenched her fists. "I hate him. What kind of rotten person would do such a thing?"

Brad gathered her in his arms and, after taking off her helmet, stroked her hair. "Easy, Tee. Amy's here to watch for that. It'll be okay."

"No it won't." Trish clamped the front of his shirt in her fists. "Nothing'll ever be the same again."

That night in bed, she flipped from side to side trying to get comfortable. Knowing Caesar lay by the back door didn't really help. Up until now she hadn't realized how much she depended on him to warn them of people coming on the farm. *Of course, you idiot. You didn't worry about anything before. You always thought you were safe.* She called herself a few other names as she flipped over again. No dad, no dog—well, not quite, but out of commission for a time at least.

A knock sounded on her door. "Trish, are you all right?" Her mother poked her head in. "I could hear you tossing around."

"I'm just fine."

"Right. And I'm Mother Teresa." Marge sat down on the edge of the bed. "What's happening?"

Trish slammed her pillows in place behind her head and propped herself up. "I hate that man—person—whoever is doing this to us."

"I'm not surprised."

"Well, don't you?"

"I'm trying not to."

"I hate being scared. I've never been afraid like this in my entire life." Trish crossed her arms over her chest. "People shouldn't have to be scared in their own homes."

"Or anywhere else, for that matter." Marge brought one knee up on the bedspread, turning to face her daughter. "You know God has promised to watch over us. What's that song, 'His eye is on the sparrow . . . '?"

"Yeah, well, all I've felt this afternoon is eyes on me. Don't think I want anymore."

"You don't mean that." Marge reached over and smoothed back a lock of wavy black hair from her daughter's forehead.

"Maybe if I felt God's eyes, I'd feel better."

"Have you been praying for this person?"

Trish gave a snort that more than answered her mother's question.

"You want me to pray with you?"

This snort was even more descriptive.

Marge leaned forward and dropped a kiss on Trish's cheek. "I'll pray, but keep in mind that praying for those who hate us makes us feel better. Good night, Tee."

Pray for him. Right! "Okay, God, here's the deal—you get him before I do."

The nightmares struck with a vengeance.

Chapter
09

Trish sat straight up in bed, her heart pounding as if she'd run a mile. She stared into the corners of her room, half expecting the man who'd been chasing her to jump out of the darkness. Hand to her thundering heart, she sucked in air, sometimes catching on a sob. Who was he? Why was anyone chasing her? And even in her dreams!

She swung her feet to the floor and padded down the hall to the bathroom. When she heard Caesar whine, she continued on and sank down on the floor beside him. "What do you need, fella?"

His tongue flicked the tip of her nose. When he struggled to stand, she helped him with an arm around his back and rib cage, rising to her knees as he stood. "You need to go outside?" He whined and took a tottering step. The cold night air sent goose bumps racing up her arms when she opened the door. "Let me get a jacket."

Caesar whined again and wobbled toward the door opening. Trish grabbed a coat off the rack and shoved her feet into an old pair of boots her mother used. The dog was half out the door and falling before she caught him. "Silly, I said I'd help you if you could just hang on a minute."

"Everything okay?" Amy appeared at the doorway, belting her robe as she spoke.

Trish nearly dropped the dog. "Good grief, you scared me to bits."

"Sorry." Amy wrapped her arms around Caesar's hindquarters. "Okay, old man, Trish, let's get this potty break over with. My feet are freezing."

Back in the house with Caesar settled on his pad again, Trish led the way down the hall. "And to think a nightmare woke me up. I was just going to the bathroom." She shivered and rubbed her arms. "How come having Caesar helpless like that makes me feel so . . ."

"Helpless yourself?"

"I guess. Hey—don't you ever sleep?"

"Sure. Guess I'm like the scouts in the Old West—learned to sleep with one ear wide awake. Opening doors are a sure-fire signal to set me straight up and out before I even think."

"Sure glad I don't ever have to sneak up on you." Trish shut the bathroom door behind herself. Sometimes Amy helped her feel safer, but other times, like tonight, just brought the idea of danger even closer. "Couldn't have anything to do with my dream, could it?" The face in the mirror made the right moves but never responded. The sound of the flushing toilet seemed unnaturally loud in the nighttime stillness.

Or was it that anything sounded loud tonight?

"Trish, you're going to be late." Marge's voice sounded as if from a long distance.

At the same moment, Trish became aware of the buzzing from her alarm. No wonder she'd been dreaming about bees and being chased—again.

Her feet hit the floor at the same moment her eyes checked the clock. Seven-fifteen! "Why'd you let me sleep so long?" Barreling past her mother, she headed for the bathroom. "Now I'm going to be late." She scrubbed her teeth as if they'd never meet a toothbrush again. No time for a shower, no time for hair—her stomach growled—and no time for breakfast either.

"How's Caesar?" Her question floated behind her on her way back to her room. She grumbled her way through her closet, dressing and finding her tennies. So, she'd slept through her alarm. Wasn't that what mothers were for? Back in the bathroom, she jerked the brush through her hair, wincing at the pain.

Some day *this* was going to be—a bad hair day for sure. Ouch, she couldn't even braid it without snagging.

"Thanks, Mom." The tone said "thanks for nothing," and from the frown on her mother's face, Trish knew she'd read the tone. By the time she'd started the car, her nagger settled himself firmly on her shoulder. *Letting things get to you, aren't you?* Maybe he was half cat; he certainly purred like one. *Thought you were going to copy your dad and give God the glory for everything?*

Trish clamped her bottom lip between her teeth. Maybe if she clamped hard enough, she could drown out that infernal, internal voice. Were consciences supposed to snicker?

Even Amy shot her a raised-eyebrow look when Trish made a dig at Rhonda and her boyfriend. Rhonda's hurt look cut through Trish's bad mood like a chainsaw through cheese.

"Sorry." Trish reached out and caught her friend's arm before she leaped out of the van. "Guess all this is really getting to me."

"Yeah, it is. And your bad attitude is really getting to *me*. Don't bother to wait for me after school. Jason will take me home."

Now you've really blown it. Tsking away, her nagger only made her feel worse. It was all that jerk's fault, whoever he was. Hate was far too mild a word.

Rhonda didn't take her usual place at the lunch table, and when Trish tried to find her, she and Jason were sitting at a table clear across the room. For all their years in school, they'd always shared a table. Trish felt as if half herself was missing. All the football players, including Doug, flirted with Amy, leaving Trish to drown in her puddle of self-pity.

She finished what she could of her salad—a lump in her throat made swallowing difficult—and shoved herself to her feet. Needing to pick up the TBA letter from Mrs. Olson gave her a good excuse to bug out early.

Nothing had ever come between her and Rhonda before. The thought of "The Jerk," as she now called the person harassing her, made her want to slam her locker. And kick it! Guy trouble, that's what it was. Guys messing up her life. First Highstreet, now The Jerk, and Jason, Rhonda's boyfriend, coming between them. She smothered the thought of her father being a guy.

She also buried her nagger's next reminder: *It isn't guys, it's you—your temper*. Who needed to hear something like that anyway? She could feel him shaking his head, just as she was shaking her own. Why did life have to be so complicated?

Complications fled when she read the letter to the government class. Cheers, whistles, stomping feet, clapping hands—the response made her wish Bob Diego was there to enjoy it also.

"Now class." Ms. Wainwright let the excitement build and explode before stepping forward with hands raised for attention. "Okay, that's enough. They're going to send someone out from the office to find out what happened to the teacher here." The room settled down but the grins on student faces could have lit the school.

"More good news. The note I have from the office says this class gets to vote on how the money will be used." Cheers erupted again.

"You mean you didn't know about this either?" one of the kids asked.

"Nope. Best kept secret. Lets me know why Mrs. Olson kept grinning at me in the staff meeting this morning. Now, how should we go about deciding what to do with the money?"

"Throw a pizza party to end all parties." The suggestion came from one of the boys in the back of the room.

"Sorry, I asked for suggestions on how to proceed, not on what to do." She motioned to a girl toward the back.

"Form a committee?" Groans met her suggestion.

"That's one way. Stacy?"

"Each of us come up with one suggestion and we all vote."

"Good." Ms. Wainwright wrote them both on the board.

"How do we know what's really needed? Like, you know, projects the school board or some teacher has thought of?" another student asked.

"Good point."

"This democracy stuff is sure slow. I say let's just have a party." Snickers followed this observation.

"Just helping you understand why it takes so long to get a bill through Congress." Ms. Wainwright perched on the tall stool she kept at the front of the room. "Any other suggestions?"

"How about we make a list of people to talk to—for suggestions, you know—and all of us in the class volunteer to talk to one."

"Good idea."

"And then we could vote on the best idea."

"No, then committees could research the ideas we like best so we'd have all the information." Rhonda's red hair crackled from the excitement generated.

Ms. Wainwright finished writing all the ideas on the board. "Any more suggestions?" She waited, tossing her chalk from one hand to the other. "Good, then let's look for the process here. First, what is our ultimate goal?"

"To spend the money in the best way for Prairie High." Rhonda again, nearly bouncing in her seat.

"Well put. Anyone have any additions to her statement?"

"I still think a pizza party would be easier."

By the end of the class, they'd made a list of people to talk with, and all the students had volunteered to interview one and bring back a report by Friday.

Trish chewed her bottom lip. Most of the decisions would be made the next week, and she would be in Kentucky. Though she'd forgotten her anger during the discussion, it all came flooding back now. All the choices she had to make, and someone was out there trying to mess up her life even more.

"Good going, Rhonda." Rhonda and Trish stepped back to keep from bumping each other going out the door.

"Thanks." An icicle fell from the answer and crashed on the floor.

"Can I help?" Amy asked in the car going home.

Trish shook her head. "I don't know. We've never had a fight before. I said I was sorry." *What if Rhonda stays mad forever?* The thought sent Trish crashing even lower. "What would *you* do?"

"Guess I'd go over to her house after she gets home and tell her we need to talk. I've never felt waiting for something to blow over is the best way to handle it."

"Yeah, and my dad would say to pray about it first." A car horn blared behind them. Trish jumped. Her heart hit high gear before her foot could hit the gas pedal. "Same to you," she muttered. Her hands shook on the wheel.

"Pull over, Trish. Get your breath before we go on."

Trish couldn't summon enough spit in her desert throat to answer. Instead she did as ordered.

As soon as the van stopped, she dropped her head forward on her hands—hands that gripped the steering wheel as if it were a lifeline thrown in a raging sea.

A car passing broke the silence after she turned off the ignition.

Slowly but surely her heart resumed its normal pace. She could swallow around the sand and her fingers released their stranglehold on the wheel.

"Better?"

Trish nodded.

"Okay, then let's talk about how you're feeling. In our police training we are taught how to handle the kind of stress you've been experiencing. But even so, at the end of a rough time, we find someone to talk with. There are counselors for post traumatic stress for us. We can recognize the symptoms of a body on overload. Honey, you've got 'em all, and it's not your fault."

"I hate him."

"That's a normal emotion. Who wouldn't?"

"And I hate being mad at people and having them mad at me."

"You bet."

Trish sucked in a deep breath and leaned her head back against the headrest. When she let it out, she could feel her entire body sigh. "Why is he doing this to me?"

"I wish I knew." Amy shook her head. "I just wish I knew."

"I'm scared." Trish could barely force the confession past her trembling lips.

"Of course. Nut cases always scare me. Give me a good old-fashioned robbery any day. Then you can see who and what you're up against. Trish, there's no shame in being afraid or angry. If you ask me, you're doing a good job of coping."

Trish shot her a raised-eyebrow look.

"Well, most of the time. And even NBA players get time out once in a while."

"Yeah, well, I'm a far cry from an NBA star. . . ."

"But you are a star, a star athlete—only in another field—and stars, sad to say, are most often the focus of stalkers."

"So what do I do?"

"Keep talking. Don't try to stuff your feelings and don't think you can handle everything yourself. There's no crime in asking for help. That's one reason police always have buddies—we work in teams. Helps keep us sane. Besides safe."

Trish flexed her fingers and rotated her shoulders. "Thanks, Amy." She started the car and put it in gear. "You know, I almost hate going home, just in case there's something else."

"We'll get him, Trish. I promise."

Caesar wobbled to his feet and barked one yip from the front step when Trish got out of the van. "Hey, old man—no, you stay there. I'm comin'." Trish left her stuff in the van and trotted up the sidewalk. Caesar sat on his haunches, tail dusting the concrete, one yip telling her to hurry. When she hugged him, she could feel him sway. "Still mighty weak, aren't you?" She drew back from hugging him and studied his face. His pink tongue flicked out and caught her nose. "You could have stayed inside, you know." He shuffled forward, crowding as close to her as possible and resting his muzzle against her chest.

The door opened and Marge appeared, drying her hands on a dish towel. "Sandra called from Detroit. I told her you'd call as soon as you got home. How come you're late?"

Trish buried her face in Caesar's ruff. "Kinda fell apart there for a minute."

"Amy?" Marge shifted her attention to the young woman carrying Trish's gear as well as her own up the walk. "Did something else happen?"

"No, not to worry. She's a trooper. Just needed to clarify some things." Amy dropped a pat on Caesar's head and went on into the house.

Sure, nothing happened. Trish let the thoughts ramble. *My best friend isn't speaking to me, and I nearly flipped out when a car honked at me 'cause I forgot to pay attention at a stop sign. But . . .* The thoughts rambled onto a brighter road. *At least he didn't rear-end me or use obscene gestures.*

"I'm okay, Mom. How long ago did she call?" Trish gave Caesar a last pat and rose to her feet. "Man, am I thirsty! Did you get more Diet Coke? I drank the last one last night."

Marge nodded her head. "I went to the grocery store. How does fried chicken sound for dinner tonight? You don't have any mounts, do you?"

Trish shook her head before diving behind the fridge door. She popped the top on a Diet Coke can and chugged several swallows. Amazing how panic made one thirsty. But she surely wasn't going to tell her mother that bit of information.

Trish dialed the phone number in front of her, the phone tucked between shoulder and ear so she could sip from her drink at the same time. Hard to believe she was really going to be in an ad for one of the big three American car companies.

"I have some news I think you'll find exciting," Sandra said after the greetings. "Are you sitting down?"

"No, but I will." Trish pushed herself up on the counter. "Okay, what?" She listened intently. "Really! You're kidding."

Chapter
10

Red's going to be in the ads too? You're not just making this up?" Trish slapped her free hand on the counter. "I can't believe it. He doesn't know any more about acting than I do."

"The lines won't be difficult, we promise."

"Lines—I forgot about lines."

"Don't worry, Trish, you're going to have a ball with this."

Amy and Marge stood in front of Trish, hands on hips, waiting for some answers. Trish waved them back with her free hand. She didn't dare release her clutch on the phone. If she did, this crazy dream might just spin away.

She listened while Sandra gave her more instructions. Their tickets were all booked and would arrive by overnight express. All she needed for the shoot were several sets of silks, her helmet, and all the other gear she used every day. Trish nodded her understanding, then caught herself. These weren't video phones, not yet, so she added "uh-huh's" in all the right places. When she finally hung up the phone, she leaped to the floor.

Arms in the air, she danced first around Amy, then Marge. "You won't believe all that's happening."

"It would help if you'd tell us." Marge leaned back against the counter. "I'm sorry it's such bad news."

"Yeah, terrible. Trish." Amy grabbed the dancer's arm. "Tell me, now!"

"Red's going to be in the commercials with Spitfire and me."

"Got that part."

"We leave Sunday morning."

"Okay."

"They're sending three tickets. One for you." Trish tapped her finger on Amy's chest. "You ever been to Kentucky, m'dear?"

Amy looked as if someone had doused the sun. "No, and I'd love to go, but the department isn't planning on sending me."

Trish danced again. "They don't have to. Chrysler wants you along to protect me, and they'll pay you and your expenses. If Parks won't let—"

"It isn't his decision. It's the chief's."

"Don't worry. Sandra is taking care of that too. You have vacation time coming—use it for this, or else she said something about a loan. You know, like an interlibrary loan. Only you're not a book." Trish quit dancing to double over with laughter at her joke.

Amy and Marge laughed along with her. Who could resist?

"Maybe I'll really get to go?" Amy copied Trish's thumping dance step. "Who-ee."

"Just call Sandra a miracle worker. Come on, Mom, get in the act." She pulled her mother into the chorus line. "We're going to Kentucky on Sunday." She stopped so fast, Amy bumped into her. "We're flying first class." She whooped again. "I gotta call Rhonda. Wait till she hears this."

At the thought, her dancing feet planted themselves firmly on the floor. *What if Rhonda still won't talk to me?*

"What is it, Tee?" Marge leaned back against the counter. When Trish told her the sorry tale, she shook her head. "All these years you two got along so well, and now, wouldn't you know, a guy comes between you."

"It's all my fault."

"Well, I've learned through the years that it takes two to fight but only one to begin the making up. You've got a couple of horses who need training, and then I suggest you go see Rhonda. That way she can't hang up on you."

"You're right." Trish stared out the window. "Isn't Brad coming over?"

"Not today. He had something else he had to do. I'll help you."

"Me too. That way I can loosen up these aching muscles from riding yesterday. And I thought I was in good shape." Amy rubbed her inner thighs. "I better call the chief too—find out what he thinks about my trip to Kentucky. How long we gonna be there?" She chuckled, her voice carrying a sinister tone. "Wait till Parks hears about this."

As soon as the horses were all brushed and fed, Trish turned to leave Amy at the house and jog down the long drive.

"Where you going?" Amy stopped her with a hand on her arm.

"Over to Rhonda's. Why?"

"Not by yourself you're not."

"Amy, it's just down the road, not even half a mile away."

"We'll drive and I'll wait in the car." Amy snagged the van keys off the hook above the phone. "Come on."

Trish gave her a disgusted look but did as told. The phone rang just as they closed the front door behind them.

"Hang on." Amy tossed Trish the keys.

Trish felt the symptoms strike her body. Speeding heart, tight stomach, clenched fists. Even her hair seemed to lift from her neck. All because of the ringing phone. Sure, she was handling all of this just fine.

"It's for you. They're ready to release your car."

Trish took the offered receiver. "But I can't pick it up tomorrow. I have to be at the track right after school," she said after listening to the caller. "How about later in the evening?" She groaned at his answer. "Just a minute." She put her hand over the receiver so she could listen to Amy.

"You can have the repair shop pick your car up if you know who's going to do the bodywork."

Trish nodded her thanks and gave the instructions to the caller. When she hung up, she reached for the phone book. "You sure make my life easier," she told Amy. "You want to take on the job of big sister permanently?"

"Well, if I had my choice, I couldn't find a better baby sister anywhere." Amy gave Trish a quick one-arm hug.

Blurry eyes made it hard for Trish to decipher the phone number of the body shop. They'd be able to pick up her car, no problem, and a paint repair like that would take two weeks. Trish groaned. They'd call with the estimate as soon as they saw the damage. She hung up the phone, shaking her head. "Everything takes so long."

"You don't want them to rush a paint job like this. They gonna touch it up or repaint the entire vehicle?"

"They'll let me know when they see it." Trish shuddered at the memory. "I'm glad I don't have to see it again before it's finished." Together they headed for the van and Rhonda's house.

"Sorry, Trish, she's not home yet," Mrs. Seabolt answered when Trish stuck her head in the door. "Jason is taking her out to dinner and an early movie."

"On Wednesday?"

"I know, there go the rules, but you kids are seniors now. Guess you should be able to make your own decisions—right?"

"Yeah, I guess. Ummm—don't tell her I was here, okay?"

"Trish, is there a problem?" Tall and with hair several shades darker than Rhonda's carrot top, Mrs. Seabolt studied Trish through emerald eyes of love. "Okay, my other daughter, what's up?"

"Nothing much." Trish couldn't look her in the face. "I'll get back to her later." She turned and waved over her shoulder. "See ya."

"Kinda reminds me of a stakeout," Amy said when Jason's car had finally left the Seabolt home a bit after nine. This was her and Trish's third drive by. "As I said, I'll wait out here."

With her thumb cuticles chewed raw and her bottom lip feeling like it might begin to bleed any moment, Trish sucked in a life-giving breath when she mounted the stairs to the back door. All these years of running back and forth and nearly living at each other's houses, here she was having a terrible time going in.

"Please, God," she muttered the words she'd been praying all evening. "Please make Rhonda listen to me and forgive me. I can't stand having her mad at me." When she entered the Dutch blue kitchen, Mrs. Seabolt pointed upstairs. Trish heard Rhonda's voice on the phone.

"Thanks, Mom. Tell her I'll call later or she can call me when she gets home."

Trish felt her heart leap right up into her throat. Rhonda had been trying to call *her*.

"This soon enough?" Trish stepped through the door into Rhonda's teal and mauve room.

"Trish, I . . ."

Trish held up her hand, traffic-cop style. "Me first. I've been practicing all evening. Please forgive me for being such a downer and for my mean remarks about Jason. I'm really sorry."

"No, it was my fault. I know all the terrible stuff that's been going on. I shoulda been more understanding."

The two friends collided midway between the bed and the door. Between hugs and giggles, along with a bit of cheek wiping, they made their forgiveness definite. They both flopped backward on the bed.

"Man, let's don't ever do this again." Trish laid the back of her hand across her forehead. "I can't take it."

"Me neither." Silence but for their breathing rested gently on them.

"How was the movie?" Trish elbowed Rhonda in the ribs.

"Funny." Her voice settled into dreamy. "Trish, he's such a neat guy—not a kid like all the boys we know."

"Is he a good kisser?"

"Tricia Marie Evanston!" Rhonda picked up a pillow and bopped her friend in the face. "That's none of your business."

Trish rolled over on her stomach, feet in the air. "Well, is he?"

"How should I know? He's the first guy I've really kissed." Rhonda assumed the stomach position also and crammed the pillow under her chin. The silence draped comfortably around the room.

"So, what's gone on today in the saga of Trish Evanston, girl jockey?"

"Well, we haven't heard from what's-his-name."

"The Jerk!"

"But . . ." and Trish went on to tell Rhonda all about the phone calls. "So, Red and I'll be on national television." She finished her tale. "Awesome, huh?" She turned her head. "Oh my gosh, Amy's out in the van." She bounded to her feet. "What a creep I am!" The two girls pounded down the stairs to find Amy sitting in the kitchen sharing a cup of coffee with Mrs. Seabolt. "I forgot you."

"No foolin'. But don't worry, this bodyguard knows how to take care of herself. You ready to go home now?" She glanced at her watch. "It's after ten."

Once in the car, Amy asked, "How did it go?"

"She was calling *me*," Trish laughed.

"Good. I like happy endings."

Trish's last thought before dropping into the canyon of sleep was about Red. She'd forgotten to call him in all the uproar. *Tomorrow,* she promised herself. *I'll call him tomorrow.*

But Thursday passed in such a blur, Trish managed to forget several things, including calling Red. With a win and two places at the track, she felt pretty good, and when there'd been no contact from The Jerk, she felt even better.

She groaned when she heard the clock strike nine. Kentucky was two hours ahead, so Red was already sound asleep. She'd be seeing him before she'd have a chance to talk with him.

"You got a minute?" Amy paused in the door of Trish's bedroom.

"Sure."

"Want to hear some good news?" Amy settled down on the bed. At Trish's nod, she continued. "I talked with the chief."

"And?" Trish prodded her to hurry.

"And I get to go!" Amy pummeled the pillow she'd nestled in her lap. "I'm going to Kentucky! And it's on someone else's dime."

Trish applauded her friend's excitement. "What does Kevin think about it?"

"My loving and extremely understanding fiancé says to have a great time. Says he's pea green with jealousy, but I'm not to pay any attention to that, just go and take care of you." Amy grinned at Trish, leaning back in her chair with her hands locked behind her head. The blonde nodded and her eyes grew dreamy. "He's a pretty special guy, that man of mine."

"I'm glad. Both 'cause you're coming and 'cause he's so special. When do I get to meet him?"

"Probably when you—we—get home." Amy returned the pillow to its rightful place. "He's still in L.A. teaching at the Academy. These long-distance relationships are the pits."

"You're telling me," Trish agreed, thinking again of the phone call that never was.

Trish awoke feeling sure she'd run a hundred miles during the night-mare. Who was it that kept chasing her all night but managed to keep his face hidden? Or did he have a face? She lay in bed, trying to remember. You'd think by now she'd have recognized him anywhere, she'd looked over her shoulder so many times to see him about to grab her.

Just thinking about it set her heart to thundering again. She swung her feet to the floor and staggered down the hall. Feeling run over by a truck was getting to be a habit.

She jumped when her mother knocked on the door to remind her she'd better hurry. A car horn set her pulses to pounding. A slamming locker slammed her heart against her ribs. Even at the track, she kept wanting to look over her shoulder. She hurried from the women's dressing room out to the saddling paddock. Today for sure she didn't want to dwell on the sound of shots echoing in the cavernous building. But she'd heard them and she hadn't forgotten the sound.

"What's happenin', lass?" Patrick laid a hand on her knee after giving her a boost into the saddle.

Trish stared down into his faded blue eyes, surrounded by the crinkles of a man used to the out-of-doors. "Just more of the same—nightmares—can't forget what went on here."

"Well, now, you concentrate on that filly 'neath you and the race ahead. Let Amy worry about lookin' out for you. 'Tis her job, that's what." He patted her knee again. "And I'll be prayin' extra guardian angels round about you besides." He winked at her. "And ye'll be knowin' nothing gets through them."

"You're right." She stroked her hand down the filly's bright sorrel shoulder. "Come on, girl. Let's just give it the best we've got." When they trotted out beside the pony rider, Trish lifted her face to the breeze coming off the river. On around the track, she could see the sliding sun painting the cloud strata with a lavish brush of reds and oranges, tinged with purple and gold. The filly snorted and tossed her head, setting her mane to bouncing and Trish to chuckling.

"You're ready, you are." Her voice took on its cadence of comfort, gentling both herself and the filly she rode.

Since she'd come in fifth in the last race, Trish settled into the saddle, determined to win. The filly she rode had missed a win by only a nose her first time out, so winning wasn't a pipe dream. "Please, God, take good care of us." Her murmured prayer fit into the song she'd been crooning up till then.

The filly burst out of the gate and hit her stride as if she'd been running for years. Trish let two duelers take the lead coming out of the first turn and hung off the pace only a length. Down the backstretch she held her place, the filly seeming content to obey her rider. With two furlongs to go, Trish loosened the reins and commanded the filly to fly.

With powerful strides she did just that. They blew by the remaining leader as if the horse had quit, still picking up speed when they crossed the finish line.

"And that's number three, Money Ahead, owned by John Anderson and ridden by Trish Evanston, winner by two lengths." The announcement crackled over the speaker.

"Way to go." Genie Stokes cantered beside Trish as they rounded the turn back to the grandstand. "You have any idea she'd be that fast?"

"No, Anderson raced her in Minnesota because we weren't sure about opening here. Patrick took over a month ago." Trish brought her down to a trot. "She sure can run."

"Told you to just concentrate." Patrick beamed up at her when he took the rein to lead them into the winner's circle.

"Did you think she'd be that fast?" Trish leaned forward to speak for Patrick's ears only.

"I'd hoped so. John seems pretty set on her."

"Excellent ride, Trish." Anderson greeted her with a broad grin. "Pretty nice, isn't she?" He rubbed the filly's nose. "And look, I don't have to worry about being bitten."

They posed for the picture and Trish leaped lightly to the ground. "Not like our friend Gatesby, huh?"

"Friend, right." Anderson shook hands with a fan. "Thanks, yes, we're thinking of running her at a mile." He turned back to Trish. "If there were only some way of breaking that monster."

"We tried. Gatesby just thinks it's a game and he likes to win." Trish stepped back off the scale. "You bought yourself a winner there. See ya." She headed back toward the women's jockey room, Amy falling in beside her.

"Trish, could you sign my program?" The question came from both sides of the walk. Trish smiled, joked with her fans, and signed programs. She turned to leave when a deep voice drew her back.

"How about signing my program?"

Trish looked up into the bluest eyes she'd ever seen. Smiling, fringed with sooty black lashes, the kind of eyes girls die for and guys get—total unfairness in the distribution of features. His smile bordered on the punch-in-the-solar-plexus type.

"Sh-sure." Trish caught her lip between her teeth. Since when did smiles become so contagious? "There you go. Thanks for coming today."

"Oh, you'll see me again; you can count on it."

Trish felt a little shiver at his words. Who was he?

Chapter
11

W ho was that?" Amy sounded like Trish felt. Out of breath.

"Got me, but if Rhonda'd been here, she'd have fainted dead away. What a gorgeous guy!"

"That's putting it mildly. I wonder if the talent scouts from Holly-wood have seen him?"

"Amy, you're engaged, remember?"

"You bet I do, sweetie, but there's no law against lookin', and he's definitely worth looking at." She pushed open the door to the dressing room and held it for Trish. "You have any idea who he is?"

"Never saw him before in my life and probably won't again." Trish tossed her helmet down on the bench. "Did you see that filly take off? What I wouldn't give for three of her in my string." Trish shucked her silks and pulled off her boots. She had two races before she'd be up again. While yakking with the other jockeys was always fun, she pulled out her government textbook. The week she returned from Kentucky she'd have some big tests, and there wouldn't be much time to study once she got to Kentucky.

She finished the day with a place and headed out to the parking lot for her car. Most of the fans had gone home, leaving the cleaning crew to sweep up the debris. Sounds echoed in the concrete hall. Trish shivered. Sounds, including shots, still echoed in her head.

"You as hungry as I am?" Amy asked from right beside her shoulder. Trish flinched. "Okay, what's happening?" Amy could switch from friend to protector within the blink of an eye.

"Just remembering. I hate this feeling of wanting to look over my shoulder all the time and being afraid to."

"Don't blame you. All I can say is it will eventually go away. Just takes time." Amy scanned the parking lot. "Trish, anyone would feel the way you do with what you've been through. I know I sound like a broken record, but don't be so hard on yourself."

"Now you sound like my dad." Trish unlocked the van door and swung her bags in.

"I take that as a compliment. From all I hear and see, that man was one wise fellow. Makes me wish I'd had someone like him in my life." She fastened her seat belt. "Let's get outta here. I could eat a—whoops, guess I won't say that anymore. Cow—that's right. I could eat a cow."

"Burgers okay?"

"Nuh-uh. I want real food. Steak, baked potato, Caesar salad, the works. Or will your mom have dinner ready?"

"She always has something I can warm up, but she knows I usually stop on the way home. Too hungry to wait."

"Good then, we'll start with an appetizer that's quick. Lead me to it."

After a dinner that left them both stuffed to the gills, Trish felt only like falling into bed when they finally got home. She glared at the stack of books on her desk, promised them time the next day, and hit the sack. Her three praises—"Thank you for keeping me and all of us safe today, thank you for the win on the filly, thank you for Amy"—left her asleep before the amen.

Morning dawned cold, wet, and windy, but by the time silver cracked the eastern horizon, Trish had already taken two mounts on their designated trips around the track. While her slicker kept out the worst, both wet and cold slipped down the back of her neck. When she dismounted at the barns, she clapped her arms around her chest a couple of times and tucked her hands into her armpits.

"Man, I'm gonna race in California or Florida next year. This is the pits." She stamped her feet to get the circulation moving. "I think my nose is froze clear off."

"Can't be." Brad led up her next mount. "It's still running."

"Thank you so very much, Mr. Observant. You got any other words of wisdom for me?"

"No, but I'll buy breakfast soon as we're done. Having Amy here speeds things up, so we can get warmed up faster."

Trish waved to the blonde scraping down the last horse she'd ridden. "Don't you wish you'd stayed home in bed?"

Amy shot her a dirty look.

Trish waved again and raised her knee into Brad's waiting cupped hands. Once mounted, she pulled her neck down into her shoulders, turtle style. "See you guys. You might make me a cup of hot chocolate while I'm gone, Brad. Your coffee's strong enough to knock Gatesby here over."

The gelding tossed his head and jigged to the side at the sound of his name. "You don't like the miserable weather either, do you?" Trish patted his neck and smoothed a lock of mane to the right side. "Well, let's get it over with so we can both go back to the barn. You at least get a nice warm stall—I get more horses to ride."

By race time the clouds hung low, but the rain had ceased. Trish glared up at the glass-fronted stands. For sure there'd be no racing if the fans had to brave the weather like the entertainment did.

Everyone out took the first turn cautiously. No matter how hard the maintenance crew worked, today the track would be muddy. Trish thanked the Lord above that she rode a mudder. Her mount didn't care what the weather was like; in fact, the wetter the better. He didn't mind mud in his face, but he'd rather be in front slinging it.

Trish let him take the lead, holding him back so that he wouldn't wear out. "Think you're part mule, old man," she sang to his twitching ears. "You'd probably run straight up a mountain." He won by two lengths.

When Trish met Bob Diego in front of the grandstand, he nodded his approval from under a wide-brimmed western hat. "You rode that just right, mi amiga. Congratulations."

"Thanks." Trish smiled for the camera and baled off. "See you for the eighth." She picked up her sidekick and trotted back to the locker room. "Thank God for showers." She stood under the driving water for ten minutes before she felt warm enough to leave.

Back up in the third, the overcast had deteriorated to a mist. Patrick gave her a leg up, along with a reminder. "Be careful out there. Coming back in one piece is more important than winning."

"You're not telling me anything new. I hate weather like this." Her mount shook his head. "And he does too." The call of the bugle floated back into the dim, spoke-wheeled saddling paddock. "Pray us some angels. We may need them."

Trish wished more people would train their horses decently, or scratch those who hated the rain, when it took three tries to get one stubborn creature into the starting gates. His whinny of alarm set everyone's teeth on edge, not helped by the rain now drifting in sheets across the track.

She breathed a prayer of relief when everyone made it around the first turn with only a couple of minor slips. Down the backstretch, she kept her mount to the outside, off the pace by a length. Going into the turn, the two jockeys on either side of her made their moves. She heard the slap of the bats over the grunts of horses giving their best and the pounding hooves.

The horse on the inside slipped, caromed off the rail, and banged the animal beside Trish. Like dominoes, the force sent her mount staggering for footing, slipping and slopping in the treacherous mud.

Trish clung with all her might, her arms taut like steel bands, trying to keep her horse on his feet. Her heart thundered like the horses behind. An animal screamed. A jockey yelled.

But Trish had her horse straightened out again and running free. She shot a glance over her shoulder. Two down at least, other back runners pulling wide to keep from injuring either themselves or those down. By the time they reached the finish line, her mount was favoring his left foreleg.

"Thank God you kept him to the outside like you did or you'da been right there in the middle." Patrick took the gelding's reins and shook his head. "My heart was in me mouth, that it was."

"How bad was it?"

"I don't think too bad. Both horses got up again and the jockeys were up and walking." Brad bent down to check out the gelding's foreleg. "This guy's gonna need some ice."

"Looks like those guardian angels you prayed for had their hands full back there." Trish dismounted to ease the weight on her horse. "Do you know who went down?"

"Genie was one and a young apprentice the other. He shoulda knowed better than pushin' at that point." Patrick shook his head. "These young pups put too much on winnin' and not enough on giving their horse a good ride."

"That was too close." Amy fell in beside Trish after she stepped off the scale.

"You won't catch me arguing with that." Trish shivered. "I'm freezing."

Genie Stokes was already in the shower when Trish got back to the dressing room. "You okay?" Trish called above the water's rush.

"I will be. One good thing about mud—it helps cushion your fall." She turned off the taps and poked her head out the curtain. "I could smack that kid right up alongside the head though. What a stupid move."

"They gonna file a grievance?"

"Doubt it. 'Bout the time I calm down, I'm gonna give him a grievance or two."

"I'm just glad you're not hurt."

"Yeah, then you'd have to get your sorry butt over here in the mornings and work your own horses." She disappeared back behind the curtain.

"Right." Trish rejoined Amy on the bench and pulled off her boots. She felt like a major mud blob herself, and she'd stayed on top of her horse.

She only managed a show on Diego's horse in the feature race of the day. "Sorry."

"No problem. I almost scratched her myself. She doesn't like the mud too well."

"Horses around here should get used to it."

"They say mudpacks are good for the complexion, no?" Diego tipped the brim of his hat.

"Gracias, amigo. I'll keep that in mind." Trish turned to head for the showers. "See you in Kentucky."

Trish signed a couple of programs and thanked her fans for coming, all the while trying to keep a smile on her face and the shivers from ruining her signature. She'd just turned to leave when a deep voice stopped her.

"If you don't mind?" The gorgeous guy from the day before took up more than his share of space on the other side of the fence. In the gloom his shoulders looked broader than a football player's. And his eyes—those incredible eyes.

"Who should I make it to?" Trish couldn't resist smiling back.

"No matter, your autograph is enough." His voice—what could one call it but sexy?

Trish signed the program with a flourish and handed it back to him. "Thanks for coming, in spite of the weather."

He took the program back and touched it to his forehead before walking away.

"You care to put your police powers to work to find out who he is?" Trish stared after the cashmere-jacket-clad back.

"I thought you liked Red."

"I do, but . . ."

"I know, he's dynamite." The two headed for the locker room, laughing at themselves and each other.

Since Trish was finished for the day, she showered again and picked up her bag. "You know, I can get used to having a valet. Thanks for packing my stuff."

"At your service. Just means we can get home faster and crank up that fireplace. Your mom said she invited company for dinner."

"Who?"

Amy shrugged. "Got me."

Company included Brad, Rhonda, and Patrick.

"I decided we needed a send-off dinner." Marge set the platter of fried chicken on the table. "After all, it's not every day my daughter turns from jockey to model and then rides in the Breeder's Cup. And our Spitfire stars in the same commercial." She set the mashed potatoes and gravy in place.

Amy brought the broccoli and cheese and a basket of fluffy biscuits.

"Mrs. E, you sure know the way to this man's stomach." Brad took his place at the end of the table, where David usually sat.

"Man? What man?" Trish looked around the room and even under the table. "The only man I see here is Patrick." She turned to Amy. "What about you?"

Amy shook her head. "I'm staying out of this one." She took the chair next to Rhonda. "What about you?"

"Just feed me. I've been studying all day."

"Poor baby, in a nice warm room, dry, no wind. My heart bleeds for you."

"Yeah, and how much did you learn today?"

"Enough, children. Let's eat." Marge raised both hands, traffic-cop style. "Trish, you say the blessing."

The teasing continued on through dinner and into an evening in front of the fireplace. When Brad took out the black mesh popcorn popper, Amy flopped back on the floor with a groan.

"I didn't know people really did this anymore. In my book, popcorn is a microwave miracle."

"Wait till you taste it." Trish handed Brad a mitten-style hot pad. The fragrance of popping corn floated through the room, teasing nostrils and taste buds. "Shake harder, big B, so you don't burn it."

"You do it, smarty." He handed her the wooden handle. "I'll get a bowl." Bounding to his feet, Brad headed for the kitchen. As he went by, the phone rang, so he reached over and picked it up.

"No, Brad." Amy leaped to her feet.

"Runnin' On Farm. Hello? Hel—lo." He held the phone away from his ear. "Funny, I could have sworn someone was listening." He dropped the receiver back in the cradle just as Amy reached him. "Wrong number, I guess."

"Brad, I'm the one who answers all the calls here. Now, did the person say anything?"

Brad shook his head.

"Did you hear any background noise?"

Again, a head shake. "Sorry, Amy. It was just such a habit. Phone rings, whoever's closest picks it up."

"I know. Tell me exactly what you heard."

Brad scrunched his brows to think better. He shook his head again. "Nothing, no sound at all. I didn't wait for a click, so they might have already hung up."

Trish wrapped her arms around her raised knees. Maybe this was nothing at all—and then again—maybe not.

Chapter

12

Well, I for one am glad Amy's going with you." Rhonda sat cross-legged in the middle of Trish's bed.

"I can tell. I mean if Chrysler wants to pay her way that's fine with me, but me needing a bodyguard, that's a bit ridiculous."

Rhonda's eyebrows arched right into her flyaway bangs.

"I mean anywhere but here." Trish, mirroring Rhonda's pose, leaned forward and rested her forehead on the pillow she clutched in her somewhat lap. "Rhonda, this whole thing is absolutely insane." The pillow muffled her voice.

"I know. Tee, I keep praying all the time that God will keep you safe. You're my best friend—we're more like sisters, you know." Rhonda smoothed a hand down the back of Trish's head. "And if it takes a bodyguard to keep you safe until The Jerk is caught, I'd pay for one myself."

Trish could hear the tears hovering just behind Rhonda's words. She groped for Rhonda's hand. "Thanks, buddy." A moment of silence stretched to the end of the clock chiming midnight. Trish sat up straight. "Guess that tells us something."

"What?" Rhonda swiped a drop of moisture from one eye.

"Bedtime." Trish bonked her friend on the head with the pillow. "I have a plane to catch at seven-fifty, as in a.m."

"Tell me about it. I'm the designated driver, remember?"

"Thanks, buddy," Trish murmured after they were both snugged under their covers.

"For what?" Rhonda's voice said she was already half-asleep.

"For everything."

"You're welcome."

Two of Trish's many praises that night included Rhonda. Just think, by tomorrow evening she would be seeing Spitfire. She wrapped both arms around her pillow and hugged it. *I'm comin', fella, I'm comin'.*

They couldn't have asked for a better flight. Greeting the Shipsons felt like coming home to Trish. *How lucky I am,* she thought, waiting by the luggage carousel. *I have three homes. Washington, California, and Kentucky. And a mother at each one.* She glanced over at Bernice Shipson chatting away with Marge as if they'd been friends forever.

"Your friend is anxious to see you." Donald Shipson told her as he swung luggage up onto an airport cart. "Timmy says all he does is mention your name and Spitfire looks around to see where you are. He's one smart horse, that one."

"Have you talked with Adam yet?"

"Oh, sure. Saw him day before yesterday when I had a horse running at the Downs. He says your Firefly has a good chance if all goes well."

"Sounds like Adam all right. I can't wait to ride there again. There's just something about Churchill Downs."

"I agree. And while the Derby is tops, I'd rather race at Churchill Downs any time of the season, even more than Keeneland. By the way, you're not excited about the Chrysler deal or anything, are you?"

"Oh, not a bit. How about you?"

"Oh, I—we have commercials filmed at BlueMist every other week, didn't you know?" He winked at her as he beckoned to the women. "Bernice is heading for orbit any time now. And Sarah's been baking for a week. Red said to tell you he'll see you first thing in the morning."

"He's been doing real well, hasn't he?"

"You're talkin' about that fine young jockey who's been bringing our horses into the money nearly every time?" Bernice locked her arm through Trish's. "Mr. Shipson's had you to himself just long enough. Now it's my turn." She took Amy's arm on the other side. "Sarah—that's our cook—is so happy to have young people to fuss over . . . and the filming crew. . . . Why, she's in her glory."

"I think I've died and gone to heaven," Amy whispered when she followed Trish into the plush rear seat of the silver Cadillac.

"Wait till you see BlueMist. Just like Scarlett O'Hara could step out the front door herself."

"You a *Gone With the Wind* fan too?"

"Read the book even before I saw the movie."

Donald Shipson pointed the landmarks out to Amy while they drove around the city of Lexington and out to BlueMist Farms. Amy reminded Trish of herself the first time she'd been taken on this route—all eyes and ears.

Now with a different season, the views had changed again. All the oaks and maples had left their green dresses and now danced in hues of rust and gold and vermilion. Horses raced across the paddocks, trying to outrun the breeze and snorting when stopped by the wooden fences.

"I thought all the board fences were painted white back here, but I see equal numbers of black."

"Owners found it cheaper for upkeep, and they still looked mighty fine, so that's a trend. The purist who can afford it stays with the white, and I have to admit, I like white best."

"That's because he doesn't have to do the painting." Bernice turned to look over her shoulder. "You've never been to Kentucky before, Amy?" Bernice gave her a wink. "Well, we'll just have to make sure you see as much as you can. Just so's you'll want to come back. Our house is yours any time you can visit again."

"She means it too," Trish whispered near Amy's ear. "You'll leave here so spoiled you can't wait to get back."

Trish could hardly sit still any longer, when they finally turned into the long curving drive of BlueMist Farms. All the trees that lined the asphalt road had joined the fall finery parade. Trish sucked in her breath and exhaled pure delight. "Wow. I've never seen anything like this."

Marge sighed with pleasure. "It's been so long since I've seen Midwest fall color I'd almost forgotten how stunning it can be. But then I expect the vistas you have here are beautiful any season."

Trish could see the stallion barn over the creek and off to the left. Spitfire waited for her. She gave a bounce of excitement on the seat. It seemed like years instead of weeks since she'd hugged her big black colt.

Before the car finished moving, she had her door open and sent her whistle slicing through the air. A trumpet call answered her and then another. Other stallions answered the strident whinny until it sounded like an equestrian chorus in C major.

Trish started running before her feet touched the ground. Or maybe they never did. She whistled again—high, low, high—and jerked open the Dutch door to the cedar-paneled stallion barn.

She bit back the tears when she saw Spitfire, his chest tight against the webbing gate, straining to reach her with his muzzle extended to the limit.

"Hey, fella, looks like you missed me about as much as I did you." She threw her arms around his neck with a hug to end all hugs, then rubbed his ears and under the heavy mane. "I think you get more beautiful all the time. You look like a grown-up horse now, not just a colt." Spitfire snuffled her hair and lipped her cheek, all the while his nostrils quivering in a soundless nicker.

"Trish, he's incredible." Amy stopped a few feet back and shook her head. "I mean, I knew he was something from his pictures, but what a horse!"

"He is kinda special, isn't he?" Trish turned and Spitfire draped his head over her shoulder, just as if she'd never been away.

"He knew you were coming." Timmy O'Ryan, Spitfire's personal groom, joined the group. "All I have to do is mention your name and he looks all around for you."

"He's my buddy." Trish smoothed the long black forelock and down Spitfire's nose. "Aren'tcha, fella?" Spitfire closed his eyes and sighed, bliss evident in every muscle and bone of his body.

"Going to be interesting to see what kind of colts he throws. If they're anything like him, there'll be some mighty happy owners."

"Yeah, wish I had more mares to send to him." Trish motioned to Amy. "Come on over here and meet my friend. He likes blondes."

"Just be glad you aren't wearing a hat." Timmy touched the brim of his tan porkpie cap.

"Why, what would happen?" Amy stepped up beside Trish. "Gosh, he's huge."

"Yeah, they're letting you get fat, aren't they, fella? You couldn't race now if your life depended on it."

"There's a difference between breeding fitness and racing, all right. But his stamina's still right up there. He'll come back from galloping a couple of times around the track without even blowing." Timmy stopped just out of Spitfire's reach. "I warned all those photographer folks. I think they think I'm kidding."

Trish laid her cheek against Spitfire's. "You'll show them, won't you?" He nodded without lifting his head.

Amy stroked the opposite side of his neck. "So he not only understands English, he talks too?"

"Sarah has supper ready." Bernice returned from making a call at the wall phone by the door. "Think you can pull yourself away long enough to eat?"

"She'd bring him with her if you let her," Marge teased.

"I'll be back." Trish dropped a kiss on the black's nose and eased away. Immediately his whinny echoed and reechoed in the high-ceilinged room. "You be good." He leaned forward as if to go right through the gate.

"I'll stay with him." Timmy stepped forward and, with a hand on Spitfire's muzzle, eased him backward before the gate came off its hinges.

Trish followed the others out the door with a last long look over her shoulder. "I'll be back, I promise." She could hear his pleading whinnies long after the car pulled away, for when they faded from her ears she could still hear them with her heart.

"Oh my." Amy clutched Trish's arm. "Y'all weren't just a whistlin' Dixie were you, sugar?" Amy whispered her southern drawl in Trish's ear. She'd just had her first glimpse of the big house at BlueMist.

"Wait till Bernice takes you around. I learned more history in an hour with her than in a year at school." Trish slid out of the car. "And it was a whole lot more fun too." She tried to hide her giggles when Amy followed the Shipsons up the wide steps to the fan-lit front door. Three tall white pillars graced the edge of the veranda on either side of them. Three wicker rocking chairs with floral cushions visited in front of the parlor French doors.

Amy wore the same star-struck expression Trish knew she'd adopted the first time she visited. BlueMist did that to guests.

"Aren't you glad you got voted to be my bodyguard?" Trish asked.

They'd dropped Amy's bags off in her room and now stood in front of the tall casement windows of Trish's room, looking out over the rose garden.

"I know I was meant to have a lifestyle like this, but that bloomin' stork who delivered me went to the wrong address." Amy turned and looked around the room with its rose-patterned rugs and canopied four-poster bed. "I feel so young with all these old, old pieces being used like everyday furniture. This could all be in a museum."

"We better get downstairs. Sarah likes everyone there when she brings the food in. I'm warning you, she'll try to make sure you gain ten pounds. Says we're all too skinny."

Together they descended the walnut staircase. "And you know what?" Trish went on. "The Shipsons are such real people."

When they left the table they were all groaning, just as Trish had warned. After a jog down to the barn to say good-night to Spitfire, they joined the rest of the group in the parlor.

"Trish, Amy, I'd like you to meet Joseph Silverstein, Artistic Director for Merritt Advertising Agency. He'll be producing the commercials. You can say he runs the show."

"I'm pleased to meet you." Trish felt a quiver down in her middle, maybe because a whip-lean man who looked like he'd stepped out of the pages of *Gentleman's Quarterly,* a high-class fashion magazine, was studying her as if she were a bug under a microscope.

"Likewise." His concentration never wavered. "Unbraid your hair please."

"What?"

"Your hair. Let it loose." Trish raised trembling fingers and did as he asked. "There, that's better. Hair with riches like yours shouldn't be bound. We'll shoot you with it down."

"But I don't wear it that way when I have my helmet on."

"So, no helmet."

Trish felt the quiver turn to flame. Who did this guy think he was? Hadn't he done *any* research on horse racing?

"But when I'm riding I have to wear the helmet."

"We'll see." He walked around her, one finger tapping his chin.

The bug under the microscope began to squirm. Trish shot Donald a look of pleading, but all she got back was a shrug. She straightened her spine and returned look for look. *Shape up,* she ordered herself when she felt her teeth start to bite her bottom lip. She raised her chin a mite farther.

When he finally smiled, she caught herself just before letting out a whoosh of air. She smiled back, a right eyebrow slightly raised, in a barely-uncovering-her-teeth smile.

"That's it. Give me that look on camera tomorrow and we'll wind this up way ahead of schedule." A blow to the solar plexus wouldn't have winded Trish more.

It was as if no one else in the room had breathed before then either. A community whoosh made everyone smile, and when the conversation picked up, they all talked just a bit louder and brighter.

What kind of power does this guy have? Trish let herself study him now that he was talking with Donald. *I may be only seventeen, but even I recognize power when I see it. Is the whole shoot going to be this nerve-wracking?* But while she could come up with plenty of questions, she didn't dare ask them. Who wanted to be that bug under the scope anyway?

As they'd announced, Sarah started serving breakfast at five-thirty. The hubbub from the dining room made Trish hurry to get showered and dressed. She met Amy in the hall and they descended the stairs together.

"You'll keep them from eating me, won't you?" Trish asked halfway down.

"You made it through the inquisition last night. You don't need me." Amy, one step behind, laid a hand on Trish's shoulder. "But I'll be there. Count on it. Besides, I wouldn't miss this for anything."

The hand on Trish's shoulder spread comfort through her entire body.

"Okay, folks, we've got a bad weather report, so we'll get the running shots while it's still nice out. That early morning haze'll be in about an hour, so hustle."

A young woman with her straight hair pulled back in two clips stopped at Trish's chair. "Hi, I'm Meg. Here's your script for today's shoot." She checked her watch. "You need to be down at wardrobe in forty-five minutes."

"But I'm already wearing everything but my silks."

"Makeup's there too. You better move it."

Trish stuffed the last of her biscuit in her mouth and pushed back her chair. "Come on, Amy. Duty calls."

Shipson drove them down to a parking lot now full of trailers, cars, and trucks with people striding purposefully between them, all seeming to know exactly what they were doing. "That's wardrobe and makeup. Red won't be here till later since at this point the shoots with him are scheduled for tomorrow."

"Thanks, I was wondering." Trish beat back the urge to hide under the dash and instead nudged Amy to get out.

"Timmy will have Spitfire ready. You just do exactly as they say."

"What a pity! I have to ride Spitfire around the track a few times. This part is real hard to take." Trish reached back inside to grab her script off the seat. "*This* is the part I'm worried about." Worried didn't begin to cover it. The thought of saying lines already written and getting the right inflections turned her mouth to sawdust and her stomach to mush. Or tied it up in knots—whatever.

They crossed the gravel and stopped in front of a door on a tan trailer. The sign said Wardrobe/Makeup. Trish turned to look at Amy, who stepped forward and opened the door.

"After you."

"Hi, I'm Lennie." A young woman with skin the color of rich milk chocolate turned from the mirror where she'd been applying gloss to lips already lined with deep burgundy lipstick. "You must be Trish. Sit here and let's have a look at you." She gestured to the chair in front of the three-sided mirror bordered with lights that showed every pore and lash.

Trish did as she was told. "Guess I'm in your hands."

"Then you don't need to worry, honey. I've been doing this for ten years now." Lennie, rump perched on the edge of the makeup counter, studied her project carefully. "Hmmm." She tipped Trish's chin up and from side to side. "Joseph was right. The hair is glorious. With eyes like yours, no wonder the camera loves you. Good skin . . . those cheekbones will leap out with blusher . . . we'll narrow that nose a bit."

Trish now knew what dissection felt like. By the time Lennie was finished with her, she'd been pasted, powdered, and painted. Her hair had been braided loosely and her bangs fluffed to the side. But her eyes—they looked huge, and her lips—well, she grinned to see what she'd look like. Not bad. She glanced in the mirror to see Amy give her the thumbs-up sign.

"Ready in five." A knock sounded along with the voice.

"Now, you just go out there and wow 'em." Lennie handed Trish her helmet.

Spitfire nickered as soon as she stepped out the door. But when she tried to whistle, her mouth refused. Too dry to pucker. That along with the butterflies who awoke with the sun and now cavorted around her middle, and Trish thought of the rain and cold at Portland Meadows with longing.

"Easy, fella." She rubbed cold fingers up behind his ears. "At least you're warm." But when she stepped forward to hug him, Joseph appeared at her shoulder.

"Don't let him get your silks dirty." He pushed back his Detroit Tigers ball cap and checked something on his clipboard. "If you'll mount now, we'll get under way. All I'd like you to do is run him around the track."

"How fast?"

"Well, like you're racing. You know that butt-in-the-air, hunched-forward look. And fast enough so his mane blows. The camera crew will be shooting from different locations so you needn't think about them. But do look like you're having a good time."

"I'm always having a good time on my friend here." Just as she turned to mount, Spitfire raised his nose with lightning speed and tipped the cap off the man's head.

Trish bit her lip. Hard. "Spitfire, no! Sorry. He thinks hats are a game."

Joseph reached down and, after dusting off his cap, put it back on his head, at the same moment taking two steps backward. "Remind me to watch out for him. Does he bite too?"

"No, only Gatesby does that."

"Gatesby?" He stared at her over the tops of the half-glasses he wore far down on his nose.

Trish stroked Spitfire's nose and kept her face straight. "He's a horse we train. You gotta watch him."

"And him." Joseph pointed at Spitfire with the end of his pen. "Horses with a sense of humor." He shook his head. "You learn something new every day." He started to leave but turned back. "You didn't command him to do that, did you?"

"No. No way. I try to keep him honest."

"Just make sure you do."

Once on the track, thoughts of commercials and cameras left her mind completely. She drew in a breath of crisp fall air through her nose and let it out. "Well, Spitfire, old fella, this is your chance. Let's show 'em how beautiful you really are." She brought up her knees and found her stirrups. At the signal from Joseph she broke her mount into a canter and then a gallop. *Butt in the air, my foot.* She thought back to the producer's instructions. "Come on, fella, let's go."

Twice around the track and the signal came to stop. She pulled the colt down to a trot and then a walk. "Timmy was right. You're in good shape, old man." She stroked down the glistening hide. Barely warm.

"Okay, Trish, take a breather." Joseph gathered his camera people about him. Lennie came over to see if Trish needed any touch-ups but kept her distance from Spitfire.

"I never did trust anything bigger than me, honey. So don't you go taking offense. You look fine, anyway."

"Thanks. You seen Amy?"

"She's over talking to a good-looking redheaded young man."

"Red's here?"

"Guess that might be his name." She winked at Trish and marched back to her trailer.

"You want me to hold him?" Timmy asked, walking along at her right knee.

"No thanks, we're fine." She scanned the groups of people milling around. No blond Amy with a redheaded fellow. Then she saw an arm raised and waving.

"Trish!" Red broke away from the group and trotted across the gravel. "Sorry, I didn't realize you were on break." He walked the last few yards and, taking Spitfire's reins with one hand, reached the other up for Trish's hand. "You two look mighty fine out there." He squeezed her hand. "I am so glad to see you." His sky blue eyes said the rest.

"Can you believe we're doing this?" Her hand in his sent electric jolts clear to her toes. She leaned forward. "Can you believe they're paying me to ride my favorite horse in all the world?"

"I know. Rough life. Wish I could be out there with you."

"Okay, Trish, let's do the same again." This time Joseph stopped a few paces back. "We've clouds coming up from the west, so our sun might not last much longer."

Trish touched her gloved hand to her forehead. "Yes, sir," and nudged Spitfire forward. Red walked beside her knee. "I hear you've been having some trouble again."

"Amy blabbed." His comment snatched her thoughts of The Jerk from their hiding place and displayed them front and center. "Thanks for nothing."

"Sorry. I didn't realize it was so bad." He shook his head. "No wonder David was so worried."

"David? How'd you know?"

"You ever heard of the U.S. mail? Or maybe it doesn't go to Washington yet. Couldn't prove it by the amount I've received, that's for sure."

Trish patted him on the head. "Sorry. Been a lot on my mind."

"If I could get my hands on him . . ."

"You and about a million others. Amy said they'd get him. He has to make a mistake one of these days. And maybe with me gone, he'll forget all about it."

"What are you waiting for, Trish?" The voice came over a bullhorn.

"Sorry, gotta go." She glanced to the west. Black thunderheads rose behind the trees, darkening the sky and sending a cold wind to bite Trish's nose and cheeks. "Looks like we may get wet. That'll send 'em into a tizzy for sure." She nudged Spitfire to a trot and then a gallop. The sun had melted the ground mist and now sparkled through the flaming leaves on the elm trees along the track.

Trish sniffed the air. Perfume of horse and burning leaves somewhere. What a combination. But after two more laps, they signaled her in.

"We'll move into the barn for the interior shots next. You can put your horse away for a while. It'll take us some time to get set up." Joseph signaled someone else toward the stallion barn. "Oh, and, Trish. You'll do these next shots with your hair down, so get back to makeup."

"Guess his mother never taught him to say please or thank you," Trish muttered while she leaped to the ground and looked around for Timmy. Now she had to review her lines again. Her butterflies all fluttered at once—but not in rhythm.

An hour and a half later, the interior was finally set. Directly in front of Spitfire's stall sat a red LeBaron convertible, just like the one Trish drove at home. When it wasn't in the shop, that is.

All she had to do was hold Spitfire by the reins and stand with her hand on the car door. Besides saying her lines, of course.

After three dry runs, her mouth felt like the Sahara Desert. She hadn't said the words right any time.

Spitfire nudged her in the back as if to say, "Get with the program. I'm bored."

"Knock it off," she ordered under her breath.

"Okay, Lennie, get her some more mouth. And her forehead's getting shiny."

Timmy took Spitfire and walked him down the aisle while Trish stood still for more painting.

"You can do it, honey," Lennie murmured while dusting Trish's forehead. "Just relax."

Trish nodded. "Thanks."

Timmy brought Spitfire back and they started again. *Please, God, this is so new.* She took a deep breath. Spitfire snuffled her cheek. "Racing Spitfire is like riding the wind." She stepped forward. "So's driving my LeBaron."

Thunder crashed so hard the roof rattled.

Spitfire reared back, jerking the reins from her hands.

Chapter

13

"Cut!"

"Easy, fella." Trish focused all her attention on her quivering horse. "It was just thunder. You've heard it plenty of times living back here." Spitfire leaned his forehead against her chest, letting her rub his ears and down his cheeks. "You're okay, you really are."

"Easy, son." Red joined Trish, with one hand smoothing Spitfire's shoulder, the other locked on a rein. "You're doin' fine."

"Trish, are you all right?" Joseph stopped just beyond Spitfire's reach. "Looked like he jerked your arm right out of the socket."

"No, I'm fine. You kinda learn to go with a horse when he freaks like that. Besides, Spitfire wouldn't hurt me, would you, fella?" She kept up her stroking. "He's really just a big baby, you know."

"Not intentionally anyway," Red muttered, all the while keeping his hands busy calming the colt.

"Right." Joseph didn't look as if he believed her for one minute.

"Hang on to him, Trish. Here comes another one." Timmy appeared beside her and snapped a lead line onto the D ring of the bit. "That last one hit right above the barn."

Trish commanded her own body not to flinch with one side of her brain while comforting Spitfire with the other. She didn't like loud noises any better than he did.

Blue-white light flashed in the windows at the same moment as they heard a skull-vibrating crack. When the thunder kaboomed at the same instant, Trish kept a loose hold on the rein in case Spitfire reared again. She couldn't help the flinch. It sounded like something monstrous crashing into the barn roof.

Spitfire half reared again, one of his flailing front feet nicking the convertible door on his way back down. Feet back flat on the floor, he trembled from nose to tail.

But unlike thunder, the horrible sound kept on crashing. With metal screeching and booming, it sounded as if the entire world were falling and crumbling.

Spitfire stood with his head against Trish, his shiny black hide breaking out into darker patches of sweat. Timmy stood on the colt's offside, offering the same comfort as Trish.

"A tree fell on the wardrobe trailer!" one of the grips yelled from the doorway. "And two of the trucks. You won't believe the mess out here."

In spite of the pouring rain, everyone but the three with Spitfire dashed outside to see the damage. Trish looked down at her silks, now sprinkled with black hairs. "All the rest of my gear was in that trailer. This is the only set I have left."

"That's the least of our worries." Amy came to stand beside her after looking out the door. "Wait till you see the destruction out there." She joined Trish in stroking Spitfire. "I've never in my life seen rain like that. You can barely see the crashed tree and it's not a hundred feet away."

"Probably should just put him back." Lightning flashed again and Trish counted the seconds before the thunder boomed. "Two, three, four. It's passed us and going away."

"What were you doing?" Amy asked.

"Light travels faster than sound, so when you count between the light and the sound, you can tell how far away the lightning flashed."

"Remind me how grateful I am we hardly ever have thunder and lightning storms in Washington. I didn't want to know all this."

Trish led Spitfire away from the convertible and down the aisle between stallion boxes, Timmy and Red keeping pace. Other stallions hung their heads over the web gates and either nickered or laid their ears back. Spitfire ignored them all, whuffling in Trish's ear and nosing her pockets. Now that the rain no longer sounded like artillery fire on the roof, he barely twitched when more thunder rolled.

"He's been pretty good about the noises like that up to now," Timmy said, bringing the colt a handful of carrot pieces. "Just those two struck right here. I doubt they'll do any more shooting today."

"Great. And I never did get my lines right. This could take forever." Trish rubbed the side of her face against Spitfire's cheek. "I don't think I'm cut out to be a model, do you?"

By evening the crew had cut away the tree, brought in new trailers, and salvaged what they could from the damage. Trish's silks had only needed laundering, which she did up at the house. Lennie made a trip to Lexington to pick up new makeup to replace what was smashed, while one of the crew jury-rigged a makeup mirror and counter for her to work at. Fortunately the tree had fallen toward the end of the trailer, rather than in the middle.

"We'll start again right after supper," Joseph announced about five o'clock. "Trish, think you could have your lines down by then?"

"I have them now." She flashed a look of gratitude at Red. They'd been rehearsing for hours. "I never dreamed this could be such work. Three stupid lines and I keep flubbing 'em," she muttered for his ears alone.

"I'd rather take a fall on the track than this." Red spoke in the same low tone. The smile he sent her warmed her middle. How come when she was with him she felt all warm and fuzzy, but when she got home again, everything else took over and she only thought of him at night when she included him in her prayers or . . . She tried to think back. Nope, she didn't think of him every day during the day.

Someone else said something to him, so when he turned away, Trish studied his face. Intense blue eyes, a smile that warmed everyone in reach, square jaw, and wavy hair nearly the same carrot color as Rhonda's. In fact, the two of them could pass for brother and sister. He laughed and answered another question about racing.

His laugh brought a smile to her face. One couldn't be down when Red was around. Could they be more than friends? Did she really want a boyfriend? Maybe this long-distance, half-off, half-on sorta romance was the best kind. She fingered the filigreed gold cross she always wore on a slim gold chain around her neck. Red had given her the gift after she won the Kentucky Derby.

His attention shifted back to her, his gaze telling her she was special. Trish couldn't break away; it was like a steel cable bound them together.

"That's the look I want on film." Joseph stopped beside them. "When the two of you are arguing over red or black. That look—pure sex appeal."

Trish blinked and felt the red flare up her neck and over her face, painting her in sheets of heat. "Why did I ever agree to do this?" she muttered to herself. "Why in the world do athletes want to do endorsements anyway?"

"For the money, silly," Amy answered from Trish's other side. Her comment made Trish realize she'd spoken her question aloud.

"Think about it," Red joined in. "With what you make from this you could bid on a yearling or buy a new broodmare."

Trish nodded. "That's right. Help me keep this in perspective. Otherwise I'm afraid when I get in front of those cameras again, I'm going to melt right into a puddle and drain through the floor."

"Come on, you were having a good time up there." Amy poked Trish in the side.

"Right. And you like getting shot at."

"Well, the adrenaline does give one a high."

Trish chewed on her bottom lip. "Speaking of adrenaline, you talk to Parks lately?"

"Last night, and he said to tell you no news is good news."

"But no leads yet?"

Amy put on her official look. "Ma'am, as to that, I'm not at liberty to say." She grinned and shattered the image. "But at least The Jerk's not bugging you."

"How would he know where she is?" Red leaned forward so he could see Amy better.

"The press." Amy gave a sigh that spoke volumes. "You can bet Curt Donovan and his cohorts have let the entire world know Trish has this contract. Chrysler would have sent out press releases too. Trish, you just don't seem to understand. You are big news."

"I don't watch it or read it unless someone reminds me. Press doesn't really matter—it's doing your best that counts."

"I'll remind you of that the next time your agent has to turn away mounts." Red glanced up when someone called their names. "Let's go eat. We can continue this discussion later."

As if I want to. Trish rose to her feet.

By ten that night everyone's tempers danced like sparks from bare wires touching. Spitfire reacted to the tension and shifted from foot to foot, tossing his head and even laying his ears back. Trish felt she could do nothing right, and by now the car had a second ding in it from one of the colt's more determined protests.

Joseph finally threw up his hands and shut the entire process down. "Get some sleep and we'll start again at seven. Trish, it's coming, so don't tear yourself down. You learn really quickly for someone who's never done this before. Besides, working with animals is always difficult."

Trish stared at him, total disbelief mirrored on her face.

"Believe him, honey," Lennie whispered when she took the silks and helmet off to wardrobe. "He doesn't pass out compliments lightly."

Even so, Trish fell into bed wishing she were at any track in the world other than here. Freezing rain in Portland, or even taking a fall seemed preferable. Coming in last—well, not quite. She did hate to lose. She mumbled her three thank-yous and fell into the sleep of total exhaustion.

"Heavenly Father, please get me through this day." She whispered the plea before getting out of bed in the morning. "I can't do this without your help. I'm not a model or an actress. I'm a jockey." She rolled her head to the side. Outside the window was still pitch black. But she'd already shut off the alarm, so she had to get going. "I can do all things through Christ who strengthens me." She repeated the verse three times. Her "amen" was echoed by a rooster crowing.

"Rise and shine." Amy tapped on the door. "Meet you downstairs."

"All right." Trish threw back the covers. The rooster crowed again, sending his wake-up call echoing over the treetops. "All right, I said I was coming." Trish headed for the bathroom. She could get used to having her own private bath. She could get used to a lot of the things here at BlueMist.

Her heels clicking down the stairs, she caught herself humming the opening bars to her song. She needed some eagle's wings today for sure.

"We're all praying for you, Tee." Marge sat down at the breakfast table next to her daughter. "I watched for a while last night but I finally left. Joseph gives new meaning to the word *perfectionist*."

"At least he liked the clips of me riding Spitfire. That storm yesterday sent everything crazy."

"I just thank God no one was hurt. And a fire didn't start."

"A fire would have had a hard time of it with all that pouring rain." Trish drained her glass of milk and pushed back her chair. "See ya, Mom. Gotta go to work."

On the third take, she finally pulled everything together: lines, looks, and Spitfire's ears pointing in the right direction. "Cut. Good job, Trish, and give that black beast an extra carrot." Joseph pushed his hat farther back on his head and stretched his arms in front of him. "Okay, everyone, back after dinner. We'll be outside again."

They spent the afternoon rehearsing Trish and Red together without the horse. By dusk Trish felt if she had to say the lines one more time, smile one more time, or stroke that stupid car, she'd bust out screaming.

"No wonder models get paid a bunch of money. This is the worst job I've ever had." She glanced over at Red, who was shrugging his shoulders up to his ears to loosen the kinks.

"You ever washed dishes in a restaurant?" Amy asked. "Now *that's* bad. I put myself through college working in a restaurant, starting with dishwasher. Thought I'd died and gone to heaven when I finally made waitress, and that's no easy job either."

Trish shrugged off the twinge of guilt. "Does mucking out stalls count?" Then refocusing, Trish said, "We've gotta get this right tomorrow. I have four mounts on Thursday at Churchill Downs."

"And the weather has to cooperate." Amy raised her face to the evening breeze. "You sure can tell fall is in the air."

The three of them marched up the steps of the big house. Smells to tempt angels wafted out from the kitchen. Sarah had been hard at it, they could tell.

When morning came, it brought a fine mist.

"Weatherman says sun this afternoon, so you two keep at it." Joseph tapped his pen on his clipboard. "I want you back in the barn at ten, Trish. There's one spot we need to reshoot. Won't take long."

But it did. And the sun didn't come out till late afternoon, leaving too-long shadows and too little time with light. Joseph was counting on the sun glimmering through the trees.

Trish could feel Red's tension when they walked back up to the house. "I'm sorry." She didn't know what else to say.

"It's not your fault." He shoved his hands in his pockets. "Guess I better just call my agent and get it over with. Here I thought I could work it all in."

"I know. I hate letting owners and trainers down too and I haven't been winning consistently like you. Donald says you're going to be a force to reckon with in a couple of years if you keep going like you are."

"Thanks for trying, Trish. I'll see you later."

Bernice met Trish and Amy at the door. "Trish, there's some mail for you. It's on the table in the parlor."

Chapter
14

Trish felt her stomach bounce on her kneecaps.

"I'll get it." Amy shifted into police mode from one breath to another. "You stay here."

"Is there a problem?" Bernice stared from Trish to Amy, her hand to her mouth. "Oh no, that's why you're with Trish, isn't it—letters just like this."

"Just pray that's all it is." Amy said, her heels clicking out her concern as she crossed the hardwood floor.

Trish followed Amy into the antique-furnished parlor but stopped at the doorway. She didn't really want to see the thing. But then it could be from Rhonda or David or . . .

Amy muttered a word that told Trish her bodyguard's state of mind. For sure the letter wasn't an "I'm thinking of you" card.

"Let me see it." Trish stiffened her spine along with her knees and crossed the room. Amy held the plain white paper by the corner. "Good luck," the block letters read. "Did you think you could run away from me?"

Trish's stomach took another knee dive.

"You go eat. I have some phone calls to make."

"Since Red is on the line in Donald's office, you can use the home phone." Bernice pointed to one set on a carved-walnut whatnot table beside a deep leather chair. "We'll leave you alone." She put an arm around Trish's shoulders. "Come, dear. Let's join the others in the dining room."

Trish let herself be led out of the room. They met Red coming out of the office. He took one look at Trish's face.

"What happened now?"

"Another letter." Bernice locked her other arm through his and drew them both forward. "We can discuss this over Sarah's baked ham. Stewing about it won't make one whit of difference. That's a job for the police."

So will he show up at the track? Come here to BlueMist? Trish slapped a lid on her thoughts and took her place at the table. When Red held the chair for her, he laid a comforting hand on her shoulder, gave a gentle squeeze, and then seated Marge.

Trish flashed him a look of pure gratitude. "Guess I've been having too good a time. Seemed like I was safe here."

"Yeah, in between rearing horses, lightning, falling trees, and a director who can shoot daggers at ten paces, it's real safe here." Red sat down on Trish's other side.

"Better all that than a harassing letter."

"You just forget all your troubles and enjoy my ham and yams." Sarah set the platter of biscuits directly in front of Trish. "There ain't nothin' that a good Southern meal can't cure, child. You eat up and see."

Trish smiled up at the woman serving. One could never resist smiling with Sarah. "I suppose you baked pies again today."

"No, honey, I made apple cobbler. Wait till you try it." She bustled back out after giving Trish's shoulder a second pat.

Donald said grace and began serving the plates from the platters in front of him. As usual, there was enough to feed each of them three times and still have leftovers.

"I'm going to have to go on a diet when I get home, and I never have to diet." Trish bit into a piece of ham. She'd take Sarah's advice. Let the food do its work and Officer Parks do his.

"I do. And after a meal like this, I should run ten miles. But I'm always too full." Red forked another bite of ham into his mouth and closed his eyes in appreciation.

The next day's shooting took off from the first frame and stopped only for meals.

"You're doing it, kids," Joseph said at one point. "That's just the look I want."

Trish grinned at Red and hugged Spitfire, who acted like he'd been on camera all his life and what was all the fuss about? Maybe the modeling stuff wasn't so bad after all.

They took their places for the umpteenth time. They stood together between the two convertibles—one black, one red, front bumpers nearly touching.

"Okay, roll it."

"Red is best." Trish looked up at Red from under her eyelashes.

"Nope, black." His half-grin sent a shiver up her back.

"Either way, we'll take LeBarons." The words came out slowly, as if they'd been drenched in warm honey. Trish couldn't take her gaze from his mouth, his smiling, curved lips so near.

"Cut! That's it! Talk about sizzle."

Trish blinked. Spitfire nudged her for attention. The mood shattered.

"Okay, let's set up for the next shots."

No matter how well it went, it was still ten o'clock that night before they finished. Trish had heard a phrase once—"drug through a knothole backwards." Now she knew what it meant. And how it felt. They had to leave for Churchill Downs by seven in the morning.

Red dropped a kiss on the end of her tired nose and left as soon as they finished shooting. He had horses to ride for morning works. The thought of riding five or six mounts before seven and most likely freezing in the process made Trish shiver in sympathy.

She would enjoy her vacation just a little longer. If what she'd been doing could be called a vacation, that is.

She gave a halfhearted thought to her books, the ones she'd carted so faithfully across the country. She'd been studying all right, but lines, not textbooks. Maybe she could write a term paper on the joys of modeling. Trish groaned at the thought. Was there any chance her teachers would give her an extension?

One thought of The Jerk flitted through her mind, but there was a good side to exhaustion—she was too tired to care.

The sun didn't bother to get up early in the morning, and when it did, it dressed in gray clouds rather than golden beams. She'd slept right through her rooster alarm, so she had to hustle. She would take a shower at the track.

Trish gave a last longing look around her bedroom. Since Marge and Bernice were driving over later, they would pack and bring her clothes. She hefted her sports bag and tried not to clatter down the stairs.

Sarah met her with a food package at the door. "Land sakes, child! Y'all can't go off for a big day like this on an empty stomach."

A horn honked from the drive. "Gotta run." Trish took the gift and planted a kiss on the woman's dark cheek. "Anytime you want to move west, let us know. Thanks for everything."

"I'll see you at the track this afternoon. Wouldn't miss it for the world."

With the warmth of a last pat still on her cheek, Trish dashed out the door and down the steps.

"I was beginning to think I was going to have to come haul you out of bed." Amy opened the door to the shiny deep blue Cherokee. "As usual, we're going in style."

Trish munched her breakfast, letting the conversation flow around her. Traveling with either of the Shipsons was a touring lesson in history, done in a most entertaining style. She could tell Amy was as charmed as she was.

The first sight of the three cupolas on the rooftops of Churchill Downs always brought a lump to her throat. "Far cry from Portland Meadows, right?" She turned around when Amy failed to answer. If one's face could register shock, Amy's did. Mouth open, eyes wide. Yup, shock for sure. Trish felt a chuckle coming on. In spite of the low gray sky, this was going to be a super day. Wasn't it? But a niggle of fear set her butterflies a-fluttering.

"You all right?" Amy recovered enough to sense the change in Trish.

"Sure. Fine." But Trish caught herself carefully studying each person as they drove by, just in case they might be *the* one.

So much for trust and faith, her nagger whispered in her ear. *You claim God will take care of you, now let Him.* Trish breathed deeply to relax. And it helped, in spite of the fact that increased oxygen accelerated the butterfly acrobatics.

She was all right. Of course she was. Here at Churchill Downs she could be no other.

The first face she saw when they reached the Shipsons' barn belonged to her California trainer, Adam Finley. Trish leaped from the truck and flew into his arms.

"Hey, it's been worth the wait for a greeting like that. Let me look at you, now a world-class model no less. You have more talents than one person should know what to do with." A smile wreathed his face like the white fringe of hair circled his shiny bald crown.

"Right. You been kissing the Blarney stone or something?" Trish hooked her arm in his. "Come meet my friend Amy and then I get to inspect the string."

"Inspection, my foot. Firefly thought you were coming to take her out this morning. She's been pining for you."

"Sure she has. I bet she gave that redheaded friend of ours a good workout." Trish introduced Amy and Adam, then grabbed Amy's arm. "You met the humans—now come see the important ones around here."

Firefly had stretched her head so far out of the stall she looked as if she might topple over. Her nickers demanded attention, giving vent to a full-fledged whinny when Trish didn't respond quickly enough.

"You silly girl, I think you missed me." Trish handed Amy a piece of carrot. "Here, this sweetie will be your friend for life if you come with treats in hand. I should know."

"Right, you're the one who spoiled her rotten." Adam stood petting the gelding in the stall next to the filly so he wouldn't feel left out. "This is your other mount for today. He's looking mighty fine here—clocked out well."

Trish switched horses. "He does look good."

Amy stood next to Firefly's shoulder, stroking the red-gold hide and adopting Trish's habit of crooning sweet nothings into the filly's twitching ears.

"You're turning into a real horse person," Trish said.

"I think I've always been one. That side of me just got put on hold, that's all. You think Kevin would mind me having a horse?"

"How should I know? He's *your* fiancé. I haven't even met him yet." Trish left off with her filly and followed Donald Shipson down the line of curious horses.

"This is your mount for the second race. You've ridden him before, and he's improved a lot since then. By the way, you'll be riding against Red in all three races."

"That should make for more fun. I love beating out my friends."

"You better head up to the jockey room." Donald checked his watch. "You know how strict they are about check-in times."

Trish waved to Amy. "Come on, we gotta get going."

By the time they'd walked around the track, thunderheads reared above the skyline. Trish could see lightning flashing in the distance and hear the thunder muttering.

"Will they race even if it storms?"

"This track is so well maintained that it can handle a lot of water and still be dry enough to race. Sometimes they delay between squalls, though."

Trish tried to study while they waited for the program to begin, but she felt so restless she could hardly sit still. Up and down she paced, into the lounge between the men's and women's jockey rooms, where jockeys played cards or shot pool or just shot the breeze. She bought a Diet Coke and visited with Red. Then back to her books. What was wrong with her?

"Good luck." She gave Red a thumbs-up sign when he headed out for the first race. And when he won it, she went nuts along with the others. It was easy to tell he was a favorite in the women's dressing room, for sure.

When the call came for the second race, they took the escalator down and walked out the jockey passage together. While Trish heard her name cheered a couple of times, Red again seemed to be a special favorite of the crowd. She could tell why—his ready smile helped everyone enjoy their day.

Her butterflies lodged in a traffic jam, right in her throat. Donald Shipson gave her a leg up and an encouraging smile. "This is just a race, like any other. No big deal."

Trish's smile helped relax her entire body. "How come you always have just the right words to make people feel better?"

"It's a gift. Now, this old boy likes to set the pace, but he can't today because Red will run you right into the ground if you let him." At Trish's nod, he continued. "And he needs the whip to kick into the sprint, so don't hesitate to use it."

The bugle rose above the tall green roof of the stands and floated back down to the paddock. Donald handed her off to the pony rider, and out the tunnel under the stands they walked.

While the gelding strutted his stuff for the crowd, Trish glanced at the grandstand. This was nothing like Derby day, when every seat was taken and the infield was full. And now, spectators huddled in blankets.

Red saluted her with his whip from three horses over when the horses entered the starting gates. Trish nodded back.

At the gun they broke clear. Trish forgot all but the horse she rode and the finish line six furlongs away. "Easy, fella," she sang through the first turn. She looked to the right to see Red hanging even with her. Two horses ahead dueled for the lead. But out of the turn, she went to the whip just like Shipson said. Within strides she and Red had left the two front runners behind and drove nose to nose for the swiftly approaching tall white posts.

"Come on!" Trish swung her whip again, two right-handed slaps. The gelding leaped forward. Two strides and he crossed the line. A win by a nose. Trish grinned at Red and flashed him a victory sign. "Sorry about that," she called.

"Sure you are. My turn next."

"Good job, Trish. You rode that one perfectly." Shipson, Bernice, and Marge joined Trish in the winner's circle. "I'll bet Red wishes you'd stayed in Washington."

"Oh, I don't think so, dear," Bernice drawled, making them all laugh.

The next race could have been a rerun except for a different ending. Red gave the victory signal and Trish took the place.

"Sorry, Adam. I tried, I really did." Trish jumped to the ground.

"I'm happy with this. Winning would have been good, but this old boy did just fine." He let the groom lead the gray gelding away. "You be ready now. Firefly's waiting."

Trish nodded and headed back up the stairs to the jockey room. She had four races to wait out.

By the seventh race the rain still held off except for a sprinkle now and then. But when Trish followed the line of jockeys out to the saddling paddock, it looked like a mighty hand had painted the sky black.

"Sure hope this holds off a few more minutes. I don't like the look of those clouds at all." Adam rebuckled the girth and checked the fit on the bridle. "You know this girl better than anyone, Trish. You need to watch numbers four and eight. I think they're the real contenders."

Trish nodded her agreement. Her mouth had adopted the Sahara feel again. Thunder clapped and she flinched. *Knock it off*, she ordered herself. *You know how to relax, so just do it*. She smoothed her fingers down the bright white number one. She hated being on the rail. Firefly didn't care for it much either. Guess they'd just have to break faster than anyone.

Totally calm on the outside and fluttering on the inside, Trish waited for the gun. At the shot, the gates clanged open and Firefly leaped out in a perfect break.

"Easy, girl." Trish kept a firm hand on the reins but let the filly set her own pace. Going through the turn they pulled ahead enough to let Firefly run the way she liked. Down the backstretch they pounded, horses jockeying for position. Into the final turn. Lightning flashed just above the cantilevered roof of the grandstands, seeming to dance on the third cupola. The heavens opened like a dam sending water thundering down a river.

The riders and horses were drenched between one breath and the next. The horse who came up on the outside faltered and clipped Firefly's rear foot. Trish heard a crack. Firefly fell forward and Trish catapulted over the filly's head.

The force when she hit the ground came from both sides. She tried to roll as she'd been taught, but a weight crushed down on her chest. When Trish forced her eyes open to a slit, Firefly stood with one foreleg dangling. *Not Firefly!* Her silent scream followed her down the deep black pit of oblivion.

When she felt the medics putting her on a board, she came to enough to mumble, "Don't let them put her down."

"Easy, miss." A rich Southern voice tried to calm her.

"No!" Trish summoned every bit of strength she had. She heard Adam's voice somewhere near. "Promise! Adam! Don't put her down!"

"I'll try, Tee. As God is my witness, I'll try."

The blackness surged back.

Trish could hear her mother's voice, but no matter how hard she tried, no words made it out of her mind. Marge was praying; that much Trish knew. The medical people made several comments as they worked over her. *I must be hurt bad this time.* The thought floated through her mind. She didn't have any ability to stop it. But thoughts were all she could manage.

She heard doctors giving sharp commands and the words "surgery—stat!" along with "punctured lung." *Must be pretty serious.* The words "code blue" shocked her. What shocked her even more was her point of view. Trish felt as if she were floating up in the corner of the room, looking down on the table where the surgical team worked over a body. Was that *her* down there? And if so, what was she doing up here? *Am I dreaming? If I am, this is the strangest dream I've ever had.*

She felt herself drifting off when suddenly a long, dark tunnel beckoned, and with a mild sense of curiosity, she entered it. Far away at the end, it appeared as if a light were guiding her. Total peace surrounded her. In fact, she seemed to float on a current drawing her closer with love. She followed the light, her curiosity deepening. Just when she felt sure she would see someone she knew, she felt snapped backward like a ball on the end of a rubber band.

The doctor's voice sounded above her. "Okay, we got her. Let's get this stitched up and get outta here." Trish heard no more.

When she floated back up out of the gray swirling clouds, she could hear her mother talking with a gentle-sounding woman. Trish felt her eyelids flutter open, as if the action helped pull her mind back to the room.

"You're awake." Marge leaned over the bed so Trish could see her without moving her head. Trish blinked her eyes. Nodding took too much effort.

Why didn't you let me stay there? But with the tracheal tube in her throat so she could breath, she couldn't say anything even if she'd had the strength.

"You're in intensive care. The doctors repaired your lung."

The accident came screaming back. A shudder started at her feet and raced upward.

"Tee, it's okay. You're going to be fine." A tear trickled down Marge's cheek. "You're going to be fine."

What about Firefly? But Trish slipped back into fog, unable to ask her question.

When she swam to the surface the next time, David stood next to the bed, holding her hand. Maybe it was his voice that woke her up. "Hi, baby sister. Now don't panic, easy. Firefly is in about the same shape you are." As the tension eased out of Trish's jaw, he smiled again. "I knew that's what was worrying you. There's a plate and a bunch of screws in her leg, so if it heals right, we'll be able to use her for a broodmare, at least."

Trish felt ten-pound weights pulling her eyelids back down, and she was off to the swirls where there was no noise, no pain, nothing. If only she could stay awake long enough to tell them about the bright place.

Pain like nothing she'd known in her life brought her back to reality. *Leave me alone!* While the words screamed in her mind, only a groan escaped around the tube.

"Hey, welcome back." The nurse at Trish's head smiled down at her. "I know this is making you uncomfortable, but you're on your way to a regular room."

Uncomfortable! Lady . . . Trish clamped her teeth together, but all they hit was the tube.

"On three." They lifted her from one bed to another with a sheet, just like she'd moved Caesar on the tarp. Trish escaped back into the world of nothing.

"Water." Trish's eyes flew open. She'd actually said a word. No tube. Oxygen by nose prongs. Bed in a room with peach color on the walls.

"Here." Marge pressed a spoon against Trish's lips. "It's ice for you to suck on. It'll help the thirst."

Trish took the wonderful cold chips in her mouth and let them lie on her tongue. She'd never appreciated ice before. Better than—"Can I have a Diet Coke?" Her croak could only have been heard in a silent room.

David laughed from the foot of the bed. "She's getting better." He came up and took her hand. "That's my sister."

Trish accepted more ice chips. When she tried to move, pain shot through her from front to back and around. Maybe it was chickening out to sleep, but it didn't hurt there. When would she be able to tell them about her adventure?

"The doctors said we almost lost you." It was the next day, and with Trish able to talk better, Marge sat filling in some holes for her questioning daughter.

"I know. I heard them." Trish turned her head to be able to look right at her mother. "Mom, it was the neatest thing. Like I was watching what they were doing, watching from up in the corner of the ceiling. Then I saw this long tunnel with a light way at the other end and when I started down it, I wasn't afraid. It was full of peace. When I got to the end, there was the most glorious light. . . ."

Trish stopped, letting her mind remember and the rest of her feel.

"And then?" Marge whispered, tears streaming down her cheeks.

"I felt as if Dad was there but I didn't see him." Trish paused again. "I don't think he had a choice."

"A choice?"

"Uh-huh. I got to live. But I don't blame Dad for wanting to stay there. Such love. All around." Trish grasped her mother's hand. "It was beautiful!" She turned again to watch her mother's face. "Don't cry. I'm here." Trish's lips curved in a smile. "This world's a pretty special place, isn't it?"

Marge nodded. "Yes, it is."

"Mom, I just got the strangest feeling. Would you pray with me for Kendall Highstreet?"

"Of course." Marge blinked before leaning closer to the bed. "You're ready for that?"

Trish nodded. "It's like I have to." They clasped hands together and let the silence of the room surround them. "Heavenly Father, please come into Highstreet's life. Help him to know you as Lord and Savior." She paused. "Your turn."

Marge added some requests of her own and closed with, "Thank you for bringing Trish back to me."

"I'm not afraid anymore. Everything looks different, brighter, shinier. Like you. . . . Did you know your face glows when you look at me?"

"Must be love, huh?" Marge wiped the tears from her cheeks.

"I think I got a miracle." Trish's voice contained the wonder that lit her face.

"Having you right here is miracle enough for me." Marge laid her hand along Trish's cheek. "Why don't you sleep now so you can get better fast?"

"Wonder what I had to come back for?" Her eyelids fluttered on her cheekbones.

"I'm sure God will let you know—in time." Marge raised Trish's hand and held it against her cheek.

"He will, won't He?" Trish smiled again and drifted off into the healing sleep her body needed.

THE WINNER'S CIRCLE

BOOK TEN

To Wayne,
my best friend
and the love of my life.
We have plenty of adventures
yet to come.

Chapter

01

W*hat about Firefly?* Trish Evanston sluggishly swam away from the nightmare and back to consciousness. But it wasn't just a bad dream. The horrifying accident at the track had really happened.

"Trish, Tee, it's okay." The comforting sound of her mother's voice brought Trish instantly and totally awake.

"No, it's not. Have you been over to see Firefly?" Trish scrubbed the palms of her hands across her eyes and at the same moment ducked away from the pain. All the moving parts of her body were connected, in one way or another, to her broken ribs—and the incision to repair her punctured lung. The accident at the track hadn't been kind to either her or the filly.

"I've got to get over to the vet's to see her."

"Not until the doctor agrees." Marge folded her arms across her chest, a sure sign she didn't plan on changing her mind.

Hospitals were not Trish's favorite place to be, let alone hospital beds. Tricia Marie Evanston, as her mother called her when peeved beyond measure (which had happened with increasing frequency the last two days), begged the doctor for the third time to release her.

"Ah'm sorry, ma deah," he repeated for the third time in his smooth southern drawl. "Y'all just need some more healin' time here. Punctured lungs don't heal overnight."

By now Trish was fed up to her ears with soft-spoken southerners who smiled so winningly and did what they thought best anyway. All she wanted was out.

"But, Mother, what are they going to do about Firefly?" Trish clenched the blanket in her fists.

"They're doing what they can." Marge, slumped in the orange plastic chair beside the bed, studied her cuticles.

"How bad is it?"

Marge shook her head, obviously wishing she were anywhere but under Trish's grilling. "Infection has set in; she's not eating and drinking well. They've called in more equine specialists. Donald Shipson has been taking care of her so I could be here with you."

"I know and I'm sorry to be such a grouch." Trish ignored the pang of guilt. She tried to catch her mother's gaze, but Marge refused. *She's not telling me everything.* The thought clenched in her stomach. But rather than attacking, Trish continued her pleading. "But I'm fine now. Why won't they let me out of here?"

"Maybe the doctor figures you'll do something stupid."

Trish attempted an innocent look and failed miserably. "Me? What could I do? I can hardly even walk down the hall without puffing." She didn't add, *and hurting.* The doctor had told her that ribs smashed like hers would be painful, but pain didn't begin to cover it. She turned to stare out the window of her private room in Louisville Memorial Hospital. The Ohio River flowed serenely toward its distant rendezvous with the mighty Mississippi. "I've been cooped up in here nearly a week."

"The first three days you were too sick to care, but who's counting?"

Trish was. She couldn't let go of the terrifying feeling. "Mother?" She chose her words with great care. "Please answer me honestly. What more do you know about Firefly?"

"Nothing, nothing at all. You'll be able to see for yourself as soon as you're well enough."

Mother wouldn't lie to me, would she?

"Mail call." The bubbly day-nurse, Sue Morgan, interrupted their discussion. She hefted a shoe box full of letters and cards. "We're weighing the mail now rather than counting. This one's about two and a half pounds."

"Good grief." Marge and Trish just looked at each other and shook their heads.

"Where do you want this?" The nurse glanced around the room. Flowers and plants hid every inch of flat surface, and cards and posters covered half the walls. Balloons—square, round, and every color of the rainbow—bobbed in the air currents in the corner designated as "the balloon corral."

Trish shrugged. "Over by the wall, I guess. How am I ever gonna answer all these cards?"

"Ask some of your friends to help you when you get home." The nurse tossed a couple of extra-large envelopes—one hot pink, the other neon green—on the bed. "These didn't fit in the box. Guess you can start there." She headed for the door and turned to ask, "Can I get you anything? Ice, water, ice cream, tapioca, or chocolate pudding?" She ticked them off on her fingers, her eyes twinkling above cheeks always rounded by a grin. "A Diet Coke?"

"Oh, yes please. That sounds heavenly."

"Which?"

"All of the above. If I keep eating like this I'll be fat as a pig before they let me out of here."

"We don't intend to keep you forever, you know. Just seems like it." She flashed Trish another grin, the kind that did good things for anyone in sight. "Marge, you want something too?"

"No thanks." Marge checked her watch. "I should go back to the motel and get a shower."

"Shower . . . that's it. I get to wash my hair today. You promised." Trish ran her fingers through hair that felt as grimy as a horse's tail after a muddy race.

"I was hoping you'd forget. It doesn't look so bad when you keep it braided like that."

"Yeah right." Trish's look accused the young woman of lying through her teeth.

Sue leaned one hand against the doorjamb. "You feel up to bending over the sink? Doc says to keep that incision dry for a couple more days. Then we can plastic-tape you."

"Anything. Red's coming tonight."

"So what's new? I hear that good-lookin' redhead shows up here every night."

Trish raised her voice to talk over the nurse's comment. "And I want to look human again."

Sue winked at Marge. "Sure wish he'd come earlier so's I could meet him. Or maybe he could bring a friend."

"He's up in the eighth today. Sorry." Trish felt a grin sneak up from inside and blossom on her face. How come she could never think of or talk about this guy without a smile and the warm squigglies down in her middle that went along with it?

"Speaking of hair washing." Marge fluffed the gray-streaked sides of her hair with her fingertips. "Mine could do with some attention, so I'll let you two play beauty parlor while I do the same for me."

"There's a good beauty shop right around the corner if you like. I know getting my hair done makes me feel like a whole new woman." Sue headed for the door. "I'll call and make you an appointment right now."

"That sounds wonderful." Marge looked back to her daughter. "You're sure you don't need me?"

"Hey, I'm seventeen years old, remember? Time for me to stand on my own feet." Trish made a gesture that took in the hospital bed and her body in it. "Or at least, as soon as they let me."

"Good news." Sue returned in a rush. "They can take you in fifteen minutes. Turn right out the front entrance and left at the corner. You'll see it—Emma Lou's Emporium—two doors down." She handed Trish a cardboard container of orange and vanilla ice cream and set a can of Diet Coke next to a glass of ice. "Soon's you finish this, we'll get you to the bathroom."

Marge dropped a kiss on the top of Trish's head and made a face. "Yuk, you smell like . . ."

"Bye, Mom, and thanks a million. You really know how to make a sick daughter feel good." Trish dug into the ice cream and licked her spoon. She waved as Marge left.

Her mom really did need some time off. Ever since the surgery, her mother had been there every time Trish had opened her eyes—even during the long nights when the pain outlasted the medication. Last night had been the first time Marge had slept somewhere other than in a foldout chair by Trish's bedside.

Trish eyed the new box of mail waiting for her against the wall. So far there had been no cards or cutout notes from "The Jerk," as they all called whoever had been harassing her. The police had taken the threats seriously enough to assign her a bodyguard. Officer Amy Jones had accompanied Trish from Runnin' On Farm in Vancouver, Washington, and returned to Portland while Trish was still in intensive care.

Trish ate her ice cream on autopilot, her gaze focused on the box. *I should go over and see if there really are any envelopes with no return, a block-printed address, and a Portland cancellation.*

I really should. Instead she poured her drink into the glass and watched it foam. Just the thought of The Jerk brought back the dry throat and pounding heart she felt when she had opened the card that said "I'll get you." Letting that thought in was like opening a crate of snakes. Other thoughts slithered out.

What was happening with Firefly? What was her mother leaving out? Had they caught The Jerk yet? Who could it be? She poked the fears back in the box and slammed the lid. *Concentrate on the ice cream,* she told herself. *That's safer.*

She ate the remaining bites of ice cream before flipping back the covers and dangling her legs over the side of the bed. Maybe she should study for a while first. She glared at the stack of books on her bed stand. History, English, government. She shook her head. Later.

Once on her feet she crossed the room to the balloon corral and tapped the shocking pink one in front. That set all the others to bobbing. People she'd never heard of had sent her balloons, just to make her feel better.

One really pretty arrangement of pink rosebuds had arrived the day before—from Amy and Officer Parks. Trish sniffed the opening buds and reread the card. It didn't mention if they'd heard from The Jerk either. It just said they were praying for her to get well quick.

Trish felt a warm glow around her heart. Amy admitted that seeing the Evanstons' faith in action made her want the same. And now she wrote that she was praying for Trish. *Dad, you were right,* Trish thought. *It's walkin' the walk, not just talkin' the talk, that brings people to Jesus.*

Trish picked up a fluffy white teddy bear and cuddled it in both arms. "Hug this fellow and think of me," its name tag said, signed "Red." She rested her chin on top of the bear's head and eyed the box on the floor. Where had all her guts gone—to be so spooked by a box of cards?

"Must have left them on the operating table," she whispered into the bear's ear. She took in as deep a breath as her ribs would allow without making her flinch, set the bear back down on the end of the bed, and squatted down to pick up the box.

"What are you doing down there?" Sue crossed the room to stand by Trish's side.

"Going to look for ah—any . . ." Trish swallowed her words and changed directions. She rose to her feet, relief making her grin. "Can we do my hair now?" Why tell Sue about the messages she'd received? Maybe it was all over by now anyway.

By the time Sue had finished washing and towel-drying her patient's hair, Trish felt as if she'd run a marathon. Leaning over the sink made her woozy from the pain, but she toughed it out. Clean hair was worth whatever she had to go through to get it.

"Think you can dry it?" Sue handed Trish the blow-dryer and plugged it into the outlet at the head of the bed.

"Sure, why not?" Trish turned the machine on and raised her arms to begin the process. "Ow!" She let her arms fall back on the bed.

"That's why. An incision and broken ribs make for sore muscles. You just wait a bit. After I take care of the lady next door, I'll be back."

For once Trish didn't argue. Where would she go? She didn't dare draw a deep breath either for fear of another pain attack. She leaned her head back and concentrated on relaxing. The pain-caused wobblies left and she opened her eyes, eying the hair dryer as if it might bite her. She hated to admit the doctor might have been right. But if she didn't get going soon, Firefly could get worse.

"Father, what am I to do?" She listened for an answer to her whispered prayer, but nothing came. Really, what could she do? She could hear her mother's voice: *"Just behave yourself and do what the doctor says. Bad thoughts can't help you feel better faster but good thoughts can."* Sometimes her mother sounded just like her father had before he died from cancer a few months before.

Sue popped her head in the doorway. "Just one more sec." And popped it back out. Trish could hear the nurse's heels squeeching away down the hall.

You could study, you know, her nagger, as she called her resident inner critic, seemed to whisper in her ear. *It would make the time go faster.*

"There now," Sue said after blow drying Trish's hair, "you look stunning. And about ready for a nap." She patted Trish on the shoulder. "See you tomorrow unless they let you bust out of here before then."

"Thanks." Trish climbed back in bed. "You've been super."

Sue gave her patient a gentle hug. "So have you, kid. Take care of yourself."

Trish had finished her dinner and was watching television when she heard a familiar voice in the hall. Quickly she smoothed her hair back, tucking the right side behind her ear and fluffing her bangs. She should have put on some lip gloss. She started to raise the lid on her tray table to see the mirror, but it was too late.

Red's deep chuckle, the kind no one could resist, preceded him into the room.

"Don't make me laugh!" Trish warned him with a raised hand, as if she could stop him like cops halt traffic.

"Is that any way to greet a beat-up jockey?" Red paused in the door, the same height as Trish at five foot four and slender, but with powerful shoulders. His blue eyes sparkled like sun dancing on the Pacific and matched the blue sling holding his left arm against his body.

"What happened?"

"I did a Trish Evanston. You know, take a header and your horse down with you." He shrugged his shoulders and flinched at the motion. "But I roll better'n you do."

"Are you broken anywhere?"

"Naaa, just popped out the joint. Had to agree to the sling or the old battle-ax wouldn't let me out of the infirmary." Red stood by the side of the bed and touched Trish's cheek with a gentle finger. His voice softened. "You're looking much better."

Trish felt her insides melt and puddle in her middle. She swallowed. Her cheek still flamed from his touch.

"Ah . . ." She wanted to say something. Where was her brain? Down in the mush in her middle?

"Ah . . ." She cleared her throat. When he bent down to kiss her, words weren't necessary anyway. Her eyelids drifted shut as his lips feathered over hers. Things were definitely looking up.

He straightened. His Adam's apple bobbed. She swallowed a grin.

From the television set hanging on the wall above him, she caught a line about horse racing. "Just a minute." She picked up the remote and clicked the volume higher. Red turned to watch with her. A sportscaster's serious face filled the screen.

"Here's a late report on Trish Evanston, the Triple-Crown-winning female jockey who was injured at Churchill Downs on Saturday.

"While Trish is recovering at Louisville Memorial, her filly Firefly is being cared for at the Garden Grove Veterinary Hospital. According to the reports we have received from Doctor Grant, head of surgery there, they may have to put the horse down."

Chapter
02

Trish clamped her teeth on her bottom lip to keep from screaming. "No! They can't put her down. Not Firefly." Her gaze swung from the screen to Red's tortured face. "You knew! And you didn't tell me. Mom didn't either. If I can't trust you guys to tell me the truth, I'll have to go see for myself."

"No, Trish, listen!" Red shook his head, trying to interrupt her. "Your mother doesn't know any more about this than I do. Unless Firefly's failed in the last hour, the reporters are exaggerating, as usual. You know what they're like."

"I'm listening." Trish couldn't force her voice above a whisper. "So tell me, how is she? Really!"

Red shifted from one foot to the other. "Well, they have her on massive antibiotics to fight the infection." He stared into Trish's eyes, pleading for her to believe him.

"I know." Trish wanted to squeeze the words out of him but was afraid to. Next to Spitfire, Firefly was her favorite horse. And also her father's. Sired by Seattle Slew, the same stallion who sired Spitfire, Firefly would be valuable as a broodmare even if she could never race again. "She's too fine a horse to be put down. She's a fighter! I know she can make it." Trish wasn't sure who she was trying to convince, Red or herself. She slammed her fists into the bedcovers. "I've got to get out of here."

"You couldn't do any more than they're already doing."

The comment brought her up short. What *could* she do? "Is she eating?"

Red shook his head.

"Drinking?"

"A little." He studied the toe of his boots. "They have her on IVs."

"I could help. I know I could." Trish's runaway thoughts screamed so loud she was sure everyone in the hospital could hear them. "She's my horse. They can't put her down without my consent." Another thought caught her on the jaw. "Or could my mother give the okay?" *She wouldn't do that to me, would she?* The thought hurt as much as her ribs.

Red turned, relief evident in the smile he gave the entering doctor.

"Good evenin', y'all. Sorry ah'm so late, but ah have good news for you, Trish. You can be released in the mahnin', soon's we remove that drain and finish the paper work."

"In the morning? Why not tonight?" Trish knew her tone lacked any trace of gratitude, but she couldn't help it.

The doctor shook his head and peered at her over his half glasses. "Child, child, so impatient." His sparkling blue eyes and easy smile removed any sting from his words. "Now, where is your mother? She'll have to sign the forms."

"She went down for dinner." Trish grimaced when she crossed her arms over her chest, then tried to cover up the reflex.

"Those ribs will hurt for some time yet. You have to take it easy for a few weeks, you hear me?" He tapped his pencil on the edge of her chart holder.

Trish nodded. What did he think she was going to do—go out and ride in tomorrow's program?

You probably would if you had a mount. Her nagger seemed to be sitting on the pillow, right beside her ear. *And sulking never gets you anywhere. You aren't very good at it.*

Trish shot a look at Red and caught the glint of laughter in his eyes. What was he, another mind reader? She pulled her manners out from

12

wherever they'd been hiding and graciously thanked the doctor for his good news.

"Tell your mother I'll talk with her in the morning. I'll be here right around eight." He stopped at the door. "I sure hope to see you racing at Churchill Downs next year, young lady. From all I hear, you have a great future ahead of you."

"Funny he should say that," Trish said after he left.

"Not really. Everyone in Louisville keeps track of horse racing. It's our claim to fame. He probably watched you win the Derby last spring." Red stared around the room at all her gifts. "What are you going to do with all this stuff?"

"Pack it, I guess." Trish let her gaze wander from the flowers to the stuffed animals to the balloons bobbing in the corral. An idea exploded in her head. "I could take some of this to the children's cancer floor. Maybe the toys would make them feel better."

"Make who feel better?" Marge paused at the door in time to watch her daughter bail out of bed as fast as her bruised and broken body allowed.

"The kids who are here for chemotherapy treatments or whatever." Trish checked the stuffed gorilla in the corner. Sure enough, her organized mother had the card pinned to the animal's ribbon. The name of whoever had sent it was written on the card. She looked at her mother and shook her head. "You're something else, Mom."

"What did I do now?" Marge wore the familiar confused look that dealing with her daughter in full gallop caused. "You might bring me up to speed here."

"I get out of here in the morning, and we're taking some of this stuff up to the kids on the pediatric ward to cheer them up." Trish gathered all the balloon strings and tied them together with one string. "How about asking the nurse if we can have a cart or something?"

Trish moved at half speed. Bending over was *not* her best move. And lifting anything, even a floppy-eared bunny with blue print overalls, gave her pause. But when she reached up to take down a poster of Garfield scarfing down an entire chocolate cake, she couldn't stifle the groan.

"Okay, that's it." Marge took Trish's arm and eased her back to the bed. "You sit. We'll work."

For once in her life Trish didn't feel like arguing.

Later that night, Trish let the tears flow. The kids had loved the gifts. They'd laughed and thanked Trish, squeezing the stuffed animals as if someone might snatch them away. And that was the problem. Seeing the children hooked up to IVs—and one little boy barfing because of the chemotherapy—brought back the memories of her father's illness. Like those kids, he had smiled and made jokes when he could.

Trish hugged her ribs, stifling her sobs to sniffles and teary eyes.

"Can I get you anything, Trish?" Silent as a shadow, the evening nurse appeared at the edge of the bed.

Trish sniffed and wiped her eyes with a tissue. "No, those kids upstairs reminded me of my dad, that's all."

"Watching someone die is really rough, no matter what age they are." The nurse handed Trish another tissue. "That was something special, what you did. Your dad would be proud of you."

"I miss him so bad sometimes, it's like I have a hard time breathing." Trish was grateful for the darkness. Talking was easier when you couldn't see the other person very well. "I get my love of horses from him, you know."

"You're fortunate to have had a father like that. He must have been a pretty special man."

"Yep." Trish swallowed her tears, grateful for the compassionate woman holding her hand. "He was." When the silence stretched into comforting peace, the nurse squeezed Trish's hand one last time and left the room.

In the morning Trish felt as if everyone were deliberately working in slow motion. It was ten o'clock before the nurse wheeled her patient down to the hospital entrance, and she'd been ready since seven. Keeping a rein on her temper had been as hard as keeping Gatesby from nipping.

"Thanks, Sue. You've been a godsend." Marge hugged the young nurse before opening the car door.

"Y'all take care now." Sue set the locks on the wheelchair and flipped the footrests upright. "I don't want to see your face here again. I'd much rather come to the track and cheer you on."

Trish waved good-bye, not regretting her farewells in the least. If she never went to a hospital again, it would be too soon.

She closed her eyes and sent prayers for Firefly winging upward. Every time she'd awakened through the night, she'd done the same. Red had called back with reassurances after talking with the vet. As he'd said, leave it to the media to hype the situation.

"We could go to the motel first."

"Right." Trish didn't bother to open her eyes. Seeing Firefly in person would not be put on hold for anything.

Marge stopped the car in the space closest to the veterinarian clinic entrance. "You've got to take it easy, you know."

"Moth-er!" The one word said it all.

They entered the brick building and stopped at the receptionist's desk.

"We're here to see Firefly," Trish answered in response to the woman's greeting.

"Have a seat and I'll get Doctor Grant." The woman's smile was wasted on Trish.

"No, just take me back to see my horse." Trish started toward the door marked PRIVATE.

"Trish." Marge grabbed for her daughter's arm and missed.

The door opened just as Trish raised her hand to push against it. The man in a white thigh-length lab coat could have doubled as a pro-football linebacker.

"You must be Trish Evanston." He held out his hand. "I'm Doctor Grant."

Trish remembered her manners before her mother could deal out a poke-in-the-back reminder. "Glad to meet you."

"Come right this way." He gestured toward an office with chairs arranged in front of a polished teak desk.

"I want to see Firefly—now." Trish met him stare for stare, refusing to be intimidated by his size and soft southern drawl. *Just get out of my way*, she thought. *I've had about all I can take of interfering doctors.*

Dr. Grant shrugged and shifted his attention to Marge as she raised her eyebrows.

"Firefly *is* her horse," Marge said softly.

Trish debated pushing past him, but this wasn't an ordinary vet's office. This place was huge, with corridors running three ways and voices coming over intercoms—just like a regular hospital for humans. She tapped her foot instead. Besides, he looked big and tough enough to subdue a raging stallion, let alone a slightly damaged seventeen-year-old jockey.

"You catch more flies with honey than vinegar," Marge murmured right near Trish's ear. It was one of her mother's pet sayings. But right now Trish wasn't in the mood for flies.

"Right this way." Dr. Grant shrugged one shoulder before he turned and guided them through a labyrinth of white walls and tiled floors. The door he finally opened led into a dimly lit room with high ceilings and a rubberized floor. In the center, suspended in a sling from overhead pulleys, hung a terribly sick sorrel Thoroughbred.

"Firefly?" Except for the star on her forehead, Trish would have doubted the rough-coated animal was really her filly. "Firefly?" At the second call the horse pricked her ears and raised her drooping head an inch or so.

Trish crossed the room to stand by the horse's head. "Oh, my girl, what have they done to you?" She smoothed the filly's forelock and rubbed the slack ears. Firefly leaned her head into Trish's arms and sighed.

Trish wrinkled her nose at the odor of decay that rose like a miasma around her. The smell was only dimmed by the disinfectants used by the hospital. The filly's broken foreleg sported a cast from hoof to shoulder. She'd lost enough weight that even the cast gaped at the top and her ribs stuck out. The gallant spirit that usually beamed from her eyes had gone into hiding.

Trish murmured encouraging words into the filly's ears, all the while agonizing over the deterioration. Could they pull Firefly out of this? Or would it really be better to put her out of her misery?

She felt the doctor by her side before she heard him. "I had planned to prepare you. I know seeing her like this is a shock."

"Umm." Trish continued rubbing the filly's face. "How long since she's eaten or had anything to drink?"

"We keep offering but she refuses. I'd have to check the exact times." He retrieved a metal chart holder from its slot on the wall and returned to her side. He flipped the pages. "Hmm. Two days ago. And she hasn't urinated for eighteen hours, so her kidneys may be shutting down."

"Is that why you said on television last night that you might have to put her down?"

"That wasn't exactly what I said. However, you have to admit that's a strong possibility."

"I don't have to admit anything." Trish squared her shoulders but winced when she took a deep breath. *Why is it people are so ready to give up?* "She'll listen to me and do what I say. Can you get me some warm mash with molasses in it and a bucket of warm water?" She glanced around the room, looking for further inspiration.

"We've already—" The doctor cut off his sentence. "Of course." He and Marge left in deep discussion.

Trish winced when the filly rubbed against her chest. "Easy, girl. That hurts." A stool in the corner caught her attention. But when she moved away, Firefly flung her head in the air and started thrashing around. Trish halted in midstride and spun back to the filly's side. "Easy, easy. You know better than that." Her words and hands worked their magic, but not before the horse's sides heaved in an attempt to draw in sufficient air.

A medical assistant entered the room carrying two stainless steel buckets. "Doctor Grant said to bring you these." She set the buckets down with a clang and tucked a lock of blond hair behind her left ear. "Is there any way I can help you?"

Trish smiled in relief. "Sure. See that stool over there? If I could sit down, I'd be more comfortable. Firefly had a fit when I tried to leave."

"Of course. By the way, my name is Kim. You've been my idol ever since last spring when I watched you win the Derby on Spitfire. What a race!" She carried the stool to Trish while talking.

"Thanks." Trish sat down with a sigh she tried to stifle. "You have a shallow pan or dish anywhere, something I can hold on my lap?"

Kim studied her for a moment. "I'll find something."

While she waited, Trish dipped a handful of water out of the bucket and held it up to the filly's lips. After a second, Firefly lapped the water, slopping some on the floor and more on Trish. At least she was trying. Trish felt the thrill of it tingle clear out to her fingertips. Firefly *would* try for her.

She dipped into the warm mash and held that under the filly's nose. Firefly turned her head away, but when Trish coaxed her again, the horse finally nibbled at the feed.

17

Dr. Grant returned to stand off to the side. "Drinking is the most important," he said in a hushed tone. He handed her a nearly flat container. Trish poured water into it and drew Firefly's head over so her nose rested in it. Again the filly lapped the water, as if normal drinking were more effort than she could afford. After continued pats and murmurs from Trish, the pan gleamed empty.

"Thank you, God," Marge said softly.

Trish heard her. "Ditto." She dug out a handful of mash and offered it to Firefly. That too disappeared.

"Well, I'll be. Guess those rumors of your gift with horses are true after all." Dr. Grant rocked back on his heels. "Anytime you want to come on staff here, you're welcome. When we tried force-feeding that horse, she went nuts." He turned to his assistant. "Right, Kim?"

"Yeah. I was the one who took a whop on the nose." She rubbed the bridge of her ski-jump nose. "I bled like a stuck hog."

Trish offered the filly another pan of water. This time only half of the liquid disappeared. "She likes it better warm."

Kim left to heat the water.

"I left a message for Patrick. He's probably at the track." Marge came to stand by Trish's shoulder. "He'll call here with any suggestions he has."

By late afternoon, Trish felt as if she'd been run over by a herd of wild horses. Her ribs ached, her head pounded, and she could have fallen asleep on the stool. But she didn't dare move. Marge brought her a hamburger, fries, and Diet Coke when she complained of a growling stomach.

Every few minutes she offered the filly food and water. Sometimes Firefly took them, but more often she didn't. In between tries, the horse dozed, head down. The sound of her breathing paced Trish's own. When the filly coughed, Trish felt the spasm in her own chest.

When Kim wheeled in an office chair with padded back and arms, Trish smiled gratefully. "Can you take my place, Kim, while I go to the bathroom?" She stood and stretched carefully.

Firefly raised her head. She snorted when Kim sat down on the stool. When Trish backed away the filly nickered. Her hooves rapped a tattoo on the rubber mat, which set the sling to swinging from side to side.

"Stop her! She'll hurt herself!" Kim leaped to the filly's head just in time to take a slam on the chin.

Chapter
03

Kim blinked and shook her head to chase away the stars. She hung on to the horse's halter. "Easy, girl. Come on, you've been doing so well." The filly jerked back and flung her head from side to side.

Trish took Kim's place at the filly's head. "Come on, old girl. I gotta go." Firefly calmed, her head tight against Trish as if locking her into place.

Kim and Trish stared at each other. "What'll we do?" Kim pulled back the stool and sank down on it, rubbing her chin at the same time. "She'll hurt herself again, flailing like that."

"What's happening?" Dr. Grant rushed into the room. At the look of shock on Trish's face, he grinned at her. "No, I'm not omniscient. We have a monitoring system so we can keep track of the animals when we aren't in the room with them. Much like the ones parents use with babies."

"Oh." Trish tried to think if she'd said anything she didn't want overheard.

"So she has a temper tantrum when you try to leave, huh?"

Trish nodded. "Guess I'll have to spend the night with her too."

Marge groaned. "I knew it. You're not going to follow the doctor's orders one bit."

Trish continued stroking the filly. What could they do? At least she'd been able to leave Spitfire in the care of others, though he had tossed any rider besides Trish. Were these two opinionated horses related—or what?

The vet whispered in Kim's ear and, after nodding to the others, left the room. Kim followed him out.

Trish sank back down on the stool, wondering how they were going to handle this. In a few minutes Kim returned with a folding screen, which she set up near the chair. The filly never even flicked a whisker. A bit later another one of the helpers brought in a folding chair with a hole in the seat.

Kim whispered in Trish's ear. "Your rest room awaits—including a window for your friend here so she can see you at all times."

Trish heard a chuckle from behind her. Only her mother laughed like that.

Trish shot her giggling parent a severe look. "You better never tell *anyone* about this or I'll—I'll . . ." She couldn't say any more. Trying to keep from laughing when your ribs ache and you have to go made other actions downright impossible.

Sometime later the helper brought in another chair, one that folded out into a bed.

"That looks familiar," Marge said, "although that certainly wasn't what I'd planned for this night. I rented a perfectly good bed for you at the motel." She stopped Trish's sputter with a raised hand. "I know you can't leave—I don't expect it—but don't gripe when you need to wash your hair again."

Trish shot her mother an exasperated look. She was glad someone could find some humor in the situation.

Kim hung another bottle on the IV hook before leaving for the night. "I'll see you in the morning. John is on night duty this week, so if you need anything, he's the one who'll respond. Red Holloran called and said he'd be here about seven. Wish I could stay—he's about my favorite jockey—but I have class tonight." She looked around at the collection of bedding, the chairs, and the card table where Trish could study and eat.

At the moment Trish was encouraging Firefly to drink some more from the shallow basin.

"Thanks for all your help." Trish looked over her shoulder and smiled. "You gotta admit this hasn't been your usual case."

"Well, if you can just get her to pee, we'll all celebrate. She's got a good chance then—if we can clear up the infection and keep her away from pneumonia, that is."

By the time Red and Marge left that night, Trish felt like collapsing on the bed that was now ready for her weary body. Instead she held out the water pan one more time. "Come on, girl, you gotta drink. Patrick says we're doing all we can. Healthy horses need gallons of water a day, you know. And you're running a fever, so you need even more. How will you ever get to go home if you don't drink?"

But Firefly just turned her head, her eyes drooping shut.

Trish crawled between the sheets on the makeshift bed. Things certainly weren't going according to plan—her plan anyway. She watched the filly dozing in the dim light. "Please, God," she whispered, "you're the only one who can help her now. I don't know how many prayers you get to help a horse pee, but that's what we need most right now—that and making her all well again. That infection is really bad. My dad said you care about everything that concerns us, and this sure scares me." The filly snorted and coughed, a dry hacking sound that made Trish's throat hurt just listening. "Thanks for listening and for making me better too. Amen."

She knew she'd hear every sound the filly made. It looked to be a long night ahead.

About midnight, she gingerly sat up, her muscles warning her she'd had better ideas in her life. Moving slowly and stretching with great care, she scooted the stool back beside Firefly and, after filling the basin from the Thermos, she held it up for the filly to drink.

"Good girl." Trish set the nearly empty basin on the floor and rubbed the filly's ears. "You did great." Firefly rested her muzzle on Trish's knees and let her eyes close.

"You two all right?" John Adams, with skin as black as his lab coat shone white, crossed from the door on silent feet. He moved with the easy presence of one used to calming sick animals, and he spoke in the same soothing tone Trish's father had taught her to use.

Firefly didn't even open her eyes, just flicked one ear.

"She drank about a quart that time. That's the most so far."

"Ah'm glad for you, little lady. She wouldn't drink anything for me." He put his stethoscope in his ears and applied the round end to the filly's ribs and chest. "Thank God her lungs are still clear. That's a miracle in itself." He stroked the rough hair under the horse's limp mane. "She's gone through a lot. Last night I wouldn'ta given her half a chance, but now?" He shrugged. "Who knows? You call out if you need anything. The monitors are always on."

Trish crawled back in bed after he left the room. Part of her prayer was being answered. "Thanks, God. Please keep it up."

The sound of splattering water woke her the next time. John burst through the door as Trish catapulted from her bed. "She's peeing! Firefly, you beautiful doll, you. You peed!" Trish ignored the complaining from her rib cage and wrapped both arms around the horse's neck.

"Thank God for big blessings," John murmured while he checked the filly again. "Looks like her kidneys are back in production and we're on the right track. Hallelujah." He poured water in the basin and pointed to the stool so Trish could sit and hold it. Firefly drained it, then drank another half. When she raised her head, she snorted drops of water all over Trish.

"Yeah, I know I need a shower, but that wasn't the kind I had in mind." Trish handed the basin back to John and rubbed the star on Firefly's forehead. "Keep up the good work, girl, and we might get home before Christmas yet."

Everyone came by to cheer them on as the good news passed from person to person when they came to work in the morning. Firefly was on the mend. No one even mentioned the idea of her worsening again.

Trish fought back a lump in her throat at the caring the staff exhibited for both her and the filly. If any of her horses ever again needed surgery, she knew where she'd want it to be done.

Three days later Firefly's temperature was near normal, and she was eating and drinking as if to make up for lost time.

"I think you can take some time off now, Trish," Dr. Grant said on his late-afternoon check. "She's much calmer."

"I sure could do with a shower. . . ."

"I know—and wash your hair. I have a fifteen-year-old daughter at home. Our water bill doubled when she discovered showers and clean hair."

"Yeah, my dad said he was grateful we had well water when David and I turned teenagers." Trish continued stroking her filly. Firefly especially loved rubs all around her ears.

Kim took over the rubbing duty when Trish eased out the door. The filly snorted once and then leaned into Trish's substitute. Trish breathed a sigh of relief. She'd begun to feel as if she were being held captive—by a sick horse no less. One good thing—she'd gotten all her homework caught up, even the latest assignments her teachers had mailed.

Two days later, after a checkup with the surgeon, she and her mother drove east on the highway to Lexington and BlueMist Farms.

"Now, I hope you don't plan on riding Spitfire while we're there." Marge broke into Trish's half doze.

"Umm . . . ah . . ." What could Trish say? She'd just been dreaming about cantering Spitfire around the tree-rimmed track at BlueMist.

"You know what the doctor said."

"Umpfm." So much for being a heroine who saved her dying horse. Now she was back to being Trish, daughter of a mother who thought all doctors' orders were just that—orders. Trish liked to consider them more in the line of suggestions—to be followed if convenient.

"I'll take that as a yes."

"Spitfire'll think I don't love him anymore."

"Right."

Trish gazed out at the fields criss-crossed by black board fences. On the crest of the rise, a horse barn with three cupolas stood silhouetted against the blue sky. *What would it be like to own a farm here?* she thought. *Such a difference between my part of the country and this.* She closed her eyes to see Spitfire in one of the paddocks, one owned by her. Then she could ride whenever she wanted to—and see the great black colt every day.

"Just visiting is the pits."

"Sorry. Maybe you can come back over Christmas break." Marge eased up on the accelerator for the turn into BlueMist. "I know one thing, I need to get home. Bookwork is piling up, and leaving Patrick with all the work just isn't fair."

"I know." Trish dropped her pity cloak as if it were on fire. "But I can't leave until we get Firefly to BlueMist."

Now it was Marge's turn to agree. "I'll call for a flight—on the condition that you do what the doctor said."

Trish slapped down the thought that leaped into her mind. Yes, she'd act like a responsible grown-up and mind the doctor—no matter how much it hurt. But oh, to sneak off and ride just for a few minutes. To feel her horse surging beneath her, hear his snorts as he fought the bit, wanting to run full out as badly or worse than she did, the clean smell of fall overlaid with sweaty horse—that was what she wanted.

And what she couldn't have. She loosened her seat belt before the car had come to a full stop in the parking lot by the stallion barn. At the same moment as she opened the car door, her three-toned whistle lifted into the breeze.

A hesitant whinny, as if Spitfire didn't really believe he heard right, answered her. Trish whistled again. This time the colt whistled back, a full-throated stallion's call. He neighed again, the sound lifting and winging its way to Trish, a joyous song of welcome.

Trish took two steps into a trot and thought the better of it. Even whistling hurt her insides—along with the outside.

"Welcome back, lass." Timmy O'Ryan, Spitfire's personal groom and handler, held the door open for her with one hand, tipping his porkpie hat in greeting with the other. "Himself isn't being very patient, but I'm sure that's no surprise to ye."

"Thanks, Timmy, I couldn't wait to see him either." Trish crossed the wide-planked floor in a rush. "Hey, fella, it hasn't been that long since I saw you."

Spitfire leaned against the blue web gate, stretching his neck and muzzle out as far as possible to reach her. His nostrils quivered in a soundless nicker, his ears nearly touching at the tips.

Trish brushed his long, thick forelock to the side before wrapping both arms around his neck. Then she turned and let him drape his head over her shoulder, his favorite pose in all the world. Who knew which of their sighs was greater, or more heartfelt? Trish felt them both clear down to the tips of her tennies.

"Missed me, did you?" Her question right in his ear made his ear twitch. He tipped his head a bit so she could scritch up around his ears more easily.

"Now if that isn't a familiar picture." Marge crossed the room, her heels tapping against the wood. She glanced down the aisle to the other stallions, all with their heads hanging out of their stalls, watching the proceedings. "I'm surprised you haven't charmed the rest of them by now."

"Give her another day," Timmy said under his breath.

Trish looked at him and grinned. She'd made great strides in getting acquainted with the other studs the last time she was at BlueMist.

"I'm going on up to the house now," Marge said. "Why don't you call when you need a ride, but don't be too long. I'm sure dinner will be ready soon."

"Supper, you mean. Remember, we're in the Midwest now." Trish teased her mother, all the while continuing her stroking of the great black colt.

"I'll bring her up. I have to talk to Donald anyway." Timmy returned from the refrigerator with a handful of carrot pieces and gave them to Trish. "We shouldn't be much longer."

"See you later, then." Marge headed back for the door.

"Tell Patrick hi for me if you call him before I get there." Trish kept one carrot piece closed tightly in her fist so Spitfire had to plead for it. Instead of licking her hand, though, he nibbled with his teeth. "Ouch! You be careful."

"Don't tease him, then." Marge left on those words of wisdom.

"Here, lass." Timmy brought a blue canvas director's chair and set it beside her. "I been through smashed ribs enough times to know that you're still hurtin'. You sit here and let that big lug hold his own head up."

With a sigh of relief, Trish did as he suggested. She couldn't have stood much longer, and yet she didn't want her mother to know how badly it hurt or how tired she really was.

"I want you to know, lass, that the Shipsons, me, and some of the others have been praying for you all along. Ye cut ten years off my life, ye did, when you and the filly took that fall. I been there. I know what it's like. I thank my God every day that ye're up and about again." He leaned forward in the chair he'd set down beside Trish's. "Seein' ye here like this . . ."

Trish felt the tears well up and burn at the back of her eyes. *How good everyone is to me! How can I ever thank them enough?* She swallowed and leaned her cheek against Spitfire's forehead. "Thank you." The words seemed so inadequate.

"Well, we better get a move on or ye'll have me blubberin' like a baby." He rose to his feet and put his chair away. "And if I don't get you up there, Sarah'll have my hide for sure."

Trish gave Spitfire a last hug and pushed his nose away so she could get up. "I'll see you in the morning, okay?" Spitfire lipped her cheek, tickling her with his whiskery upper lip. "Oh, gosh, fella, it's so good to see you." She buried her face in his mane one last time before heading for the door.

When she looked back, Spitfire stood with his head up, looking every inch the champion he was. His nicker carried after her out the door.

The fragrance of burning leaves overlaid the clean aroma of fall as the truck wound up the incline to the house set on the hill. Trish caught her breath as she always did when the four white pillars gracing the front of the colonial mansion came into view. Stately trees lined the drive and a monstrous magnolia shaded a round bed of rust and gold chrysanthemums. To the right, wicker furniture invited all who entered to come "set a spell."

If she closed her eyes for even an instant, she could picture women in wide hooped skirts and parasols walking to and fro, laughing and chatting, just like in *Gone With the Wind*. She paused in the portico long enough to look up at the beveled glass and brass hanging light. Surely at one time those flame bulbs had been candles.

Timmy held the heavy walnut door open for her and signaled that she should enter before him. His actions made her feel just the tiniest like a young woman from long ago. She followed the voices she could hear coming from Donald Shipson's office, off to the right.

The sound of her mother's words stopped her as if she'd walked into a glass wall.

"I thought it was all over with, and here is another one." Marge's voice rose a notch. "Why would anyone treat Trish this way? Why?"

Why indeed? Trish felt that old familiar punch in the gut. It barely missed her ribs.

Chapter
04

The Jerk! He's at me again!

The low rumble of Donald Shipson's voice sounded as if he was trying to calm her mother, but his words were unintelligible.

"So it's only a letter. Next time it might be more than—" Marge cut off her cry before it became a shout.

Trish couldn't have moved if ordered by the president himself. Her feet might as well have been nailed to the burnished oak floor. When she raised her gaze from studying the cuticles on her right hand, she caught it on Timmy's compassionate eyes.

He took a step nearer and laid a hand on her shoulder. The warmth of it sank into one of the steel tendons keeping her from flying into a million minute fragments. The Jerk was still around, and he'd even gotten the address of BlueMist Farms. Had he sent one of his cheerful little notes to the hospital too? The thoughts sent shudders rocketing up and down her body.

"Just don't tell Trish, okay?" Her mother's voice had risen again.

Right! The look she got from Timmy clearly asked if she wanted to make their presence known. Trish shook her head. Timmy tiptoed back to the front door and opened it.

"They'll be in the office, I'm sure." He raised his voice as if they'd just come in.

Trish picked up the cue like a seasoned stage actress. "Thanks for the ride up. If you see my mom, tell her I'm going to my room to wash for di—supper." She caught the mistake as if it were something critical. She headed for the stairs and turned on the third riser. "See you in the morning, but probably not at the crack of dawn." Amazing how she could project her voice if needed. All the while her jaw felt as if it were clamped in a vise.

Timmy nodded and sent her a smile and a thumbs-up before walking to the half-closed office door and tapping with two fingers.

Trish trudged on up the wide walnut stairs, turning at the landing before she took hold of the railing with her left hand. She used it to help pull herself the remainder of the way up. Each step took an effort nearly beyond her strength. And this morning she had felt as if she could climb Mt. Hood. Right.

How would she bring up the questions about this person who insisted on intruding in her life? Who was he? Could it be a she? That thought hadn't entered her mind before. No girl would do something like this— would she?

Trish stumbled across the rose-patterned rug to the white canopied bed. Maybe if she would just lie down a couple of minutes she would feel like getting ready for dinner—supper—whatever. Knowing Sarah, the food would be terrific. But right now, the thought of food of any kind made her throat tighten. How could she possibly join the Shipsons and her mother and not let them know she knew?

She needn't have worried. By the time she opened her eyes, pitch black night had fallen, and she felt her mother carefully removing her shoes.

"What time is it?" Trish finally recovered her alertness enough to ask.

"A bit after nine. I came up to get you for supper and you were sleeping so soundly, I just covered you and left. But I thought you'd sleep better without all your clothes on."

"Thanks." Trish let her eyelids drift shut again, but immediately the conversation she'd overheard from the office rang in her ears. "Mom, I want you to tell me the truth about what's going on." Trish sat up, swung her legs over the edge of the bed, and snapped on the lamp next to the bed. She began unbuttoning her shirt so she could keep her hands busy.

Marge stood upright. "Of course."

"You—we've heard from The Jerk again, haven't we?"

Her mother sank to the edge of the bed and helped Trish remove her clothes. "Yes, we have."

"Why didn't you tell me?"

"Oh, Tee, we felt it was so important you get better without worrying that we decided to . . . to . . ."

"Lie to me?"

"Not exactly. We just didn't tell you."

"How many?"

"Two cards sent to the hospital and now this one here. Amy and Officer Parks are still working on the case on the Portland end. We send them anything we get." She retrieved Trish's pj's from the duffel bag and held the top so Trish could put her arms in without straining her sides. "How did you guess?"

"No guess. Timmy and I heard you when we came up to the house. I thought I'd try to let you keep the secret, but it was too hard. Besides, Dad always said the truth is easier to deal with than a lie." She leveled an accusing stare in her mother's direction. "I *am* an adult now, you know."

The smile that barely lifted the corners of Marge's mouth matched her wistful tone. "I keep trying to remember that, but to me, you're still my baby, my only daughter, and I want to protect you from all the evil things in this world. That's a mother's job, you know, to take care of her kids." She gave Trish a hug and followed it by a kiss on the cheek. "I love you, Tricia Marie Evanston, and too often you scare the livin' out of me."

What could Trish say? She leaned her head against her mother's shoulder. The light from the rose-painted Tiffany lamp glowed softly, feeling warm and loving like her mother's touch. Before she fell all the way back asleep, Trish pushed herself upright and crawled underneath the covers, shoving the white lace-edged pillows off to the side. "Night, Mom."

Marge rose and dropped a kiss on her daughter's forehead. "Good night, Tee. Just remember, God loves you and so do I." For a change, the words her father always said didn't bring a lump to Trish's throat. She drifted off thinking, *Thank you, God*, but too far gone to voice the words.

In the morning after visiting Spitfire, Trish joined the Shipsons and her mother at the dining table. Sarah, the longtime cook for BlueMist, brought in a platter of sliced ham with fluffy scrambled eggs. A basket of biscuits already graced the center of the white-linen-covered table. An icy glass of fresh-squeezed orange juice held the place of honor above Trish's plate.

"Any time you want to move to the West Coast, you just let us know." Trish grinned up at the woman serving them.

"Chile, y'all couldn't bribe me away from here. This been mah home far too long. But y'all know, you're welcome anytime." She plopped two slices of ham and a mound of scrambled eggs on Trish's plate. "Now eat up and get yo strength back. Y'all lookin' mighty puny."

Trish stared at all the food on her plate. "You want me to get so fat I can't ride anymore?" Her voice rose to a squeak. But all the time she was complaining and teasing, her hands were busy draping her snowy napkin across her lap and cutting up the ham. The biscuits appeared at her side, and she flipped two of them over to join the ham and eggs.

"And I have coffee cake comin' outta the oven for when you finish with this." Sarah handed the platter to Bernice Shipson and marched back out of the room.

"You better eat up. She's been known to pout for days when someone refuses her food." The twinkle in Donald Shipson's blue eyes belied his words. "And you wouldn't want to wish that on any of us."

"I'll try my best, sir." Trish saluted and dug in.

Stuffed to the tips of her ears, Trish turned away the second piece of cinnamon-and-sugar-topped coffee cake Sarah encouraged her to take. "I can't. You cut them like slabs for a football team."

"Half then." Sarah whacked the four-by-four square in two and slid one onto Trish's plate.

Trish groaned and shook her head at the laughter from around the table. "How come she doesn't pick on any of you?"

"You should have seen the way she mollycoddled Donald when he broke his leg one time." Bernice leaned forward, her silver-blond hair swinging forward on her cheek. "Nearly drove him nuts."

Marge glanced at her watch. "I better get myself on the road if I'm going to make that flight. Trish, you sure you won't come with me?"

Trish's "Mo-ther" conveyed all the nuances possible and then some.

"Before you go"—Donald laid his folded napkin back on the table— "I talked with Doctor Grant, and he thinks we can transport Firefly in another three or four days. That is, if Trish is up to it."

"Of course." Trish looked from him to her mother.

"You could get bumped around," Marge cautioned.

"Yeah, but probably not. She'll do just fine. You'll see." Trish got to her feet, being very careful not to flinch at the movement. She came around the table and gave her mother a hug. "Pass one of these on to Patrick for me, okay? And Miss Tee might like extra attention by now too." Trish referred to her nearly two-year-old filly who'd been born on her birthday last September. All Thoroughbreds' birthdays are officially counted as January first, so Miss Tee would be considered two in January.

The days passed quickly with Trish spending much of her time down in the stallion barn with Spitfire. Red came out to visit one evening, but he couldn't stay long since he had to be on the track again at five the next morning.

The next morning, Donald Shipson drove Trish and Timmy into Louisville to bring Firefly back. A taller-than-normal horse van was already backed in place by the veterinary hospital. Dr. Grant met them at the filly's room.

"As you can see, we've designed a walking cast that she can hobble, or rather, limp along with." He pointed to the contraption that went from under the filly's hoof to above her shoulder. "While we feel she would do well in the sling at least part time once you're at BlueMist, this makes her more portable. Since the infection is cleared up and the incision's healing well, the plates in her leg are really what protect her. The cast is just to keep her from banging it around."

Trish walked up to the nickering filly and rubbed her face and ears. "You old sweety, you. What a difference a couple of days make. You look almost like your old self—at least you would without that rig on your leg." Firefly scrubbed her forehead against Trish's shoulder. "Easy. You'll have us both on the ground if we're not careful." She dug in her pocket for a chunk of carrot. Firefly never hesitated for a second, just lipped it and crunched.

"Trish, I take it you are going to ride in the van with your horse?" the doctor asked.

Trish nodded.

"I've arranged for Kim to go along with you, sedative prepared, just in case Firefly becomes agitated again."

"She won't."

"Well, I live by my mother's oft-said 'better safe than sorry,' so I'm trying to cover all the bases." He turned to Donald, who'd been standing to the side. "I've already talked with your own Doctor Tyler this morning, and he'll be at the farm when you arrive. Your driver can call him from the truck."

"I have a cellular phone, so that's no problem," Donald answered. "And he'd already discussed this with me."

"Fine. Let's begin. Getting her in and out of the trailer will be the real trick."

Trish unbuckled the halter and handed it to Kim. With Timmy on one side and Trish on the other, they slipped a leather headstall in place and adjusted the two chain leads over Firefly's nose and under her chin so both of them would have a strap.

"I'm just back-up," Timmy sang to the filly, much like Trish did. The two of them made a fine duet.

"Okay, girl. Let's show them how smart you are." Trish took one step backward and then another. With one hand scratching the horse's cheek, she tugged on the lead with the other.

Firefly lurched forward, one ungainly step at a time. Dr. Grant, Kim, Donald, and another attendant acted like spotters for a gymnast, ready to lend their strength to keep the filly on her feet.

By the time they reached the wide-open double doors, Trish could feel the sweat trickling down her back. Dark wet spots were popping out on the filly's neck, evidence of the strain she was under.

"Come on, girl, you're doing fine." Trish let the hobbling horse pause in the open doorway and sniff the breeze. The bright sun made them all blink. "Feels like I've run five miles with a forty-pound pack."

"You've never really done that, have you?" Donald ran a comforting hand over the filly's rump.

"No, but . . ."

"Well, I have," Dr. Grant added. "In the army—and it nearly killed me. Wouldn't wish that on anyone." He walked around the filly, checking the cast and listening to her lungs and heart. "You're a game one, old girl." He patted the sorrel shoulder. "Never would have believed we'd be shipping you out on your own steam."

Trish swapped a look with Timmy that said what they thought of the good doctor's attitude. Trish bit her lower lip to keep from commenting. *He gave up on you, old girl. But you and me, we didn't.* She stroked the filly's sweaty neck. *And God didn't. Thank you, Father.*

"We better keep her moving or she'll stiffen up. I want to get a blanket on her soon's possible." Timmy motioned for Trish to step out again.

They worked their way the few feet to the ramp without any problems, but when Firefly put her front feet on the ramp, she shivered.

"Easy, girl, come on, you can do it." Trish kept her voice to the soothing singsong. "That ol' ramp's nearly flat. You'll make it fine."

Another step. Firefly threw her head in the air in spite of the chain over her nose.

At the upward jerk, Trish gasped at the pain in her side. She let the lead travel through her fingers and worked it back in place again. She swallowed and took a deep breath. Another mistake.

"You all right, lass?" Timmy kept his voice soothing and his hands busy stroking up around Firefly's ears.

"I will be."

Firefly dropped her head and sniffed the ramp. She sucked in a deep breath of air and, on the exhale, nuzzled Trish's arm.

"You ready for more?" Trish raised her gaze to the sky above, catching the flight of a flock of birds against the deep blue. "Sure wish we had some wings here about now."

Timmy grinned at her and nodded. "That would be good." He waited a moment. "You ready?"

Trish nodded. "Okay, girl, all the way." She stepped farther up the ramp and tugged gently on the lead.

Firefly planted her feet and leaned back on her haunches.

"Come on, Firefly, you know better than this." Trish tugged again. The filly's ears were laid back.

Trish released the tension on her lead.

Firefly leaped forward. She slammed into Trish in the rush.

No! Trish kept the scream in her head as she spun off the ramp.

Chapter
05

Trish grabbed for the rail, the door, anything. Her hands raked across metal.

She kept falling.

"Oof!" Even with a cushion of strong arms and a broad chest, Trish felt the jolt clear through her. She opened her eyes to see Dr. Grant grinning at her as he set her back on the ground. "Th-thanks. That was close."

"Glad I could be of service." The doctor's grin wobbled, looking about like Trish's legs felt. "Young lady, no wonder your mother is getting gray hair. If you'd have crushed those ribs again, she'd have strung me up."

"Hardly." Trish put a hand to her side and leaned forward to breathe more easily. At the same time she rubbed her stomach to get it back down where it belonged. If she looked as pale as she felt, she knew she was in trouble. "She's used to me. Besides, it wasn't my fault. Firefly just got tired of hobbling." Trish stepped up on the ramp and entered the van to find her filly rubbing against Timmy with her bony forehead.

"You okay, lass?" Timmy ducked under the filly's neck to check Trish out.

"I will be. Let's get this show on the road." *So I can lie down for a while* was the thought deliberately kept unspoken.

"Why don't you go sit in that chair and let us take care of your horse?" Kim joined Trish beside the filly.

"I will as soon as we get her settled." She turned to Dr. Grant. "Thanks for all you've done for her—and for being such a good catcher."

"Glad we could help." Dr. Grant gave Donald an assist with the quilted traveling sheet, smoothing a hand down Firefly's back after securing the last of the buckles. "Hope to see you at Churchill Downs again next year."

As soon as they were underway, Trish let herself sink into the canvas chair against the far wall. She closed her eyes, gently rubbing her side at the same time. That seemed to ease the pain. What she wouldn't give for some aspirin right then.

The trip to BlueMist passed without any further incident. At one point Timmy touched Trish's shoulder and pointed to a pile of horse blankets. She roused herself enough from the drowse she'd been hovering in and curled up on the pads. *How come pain can make you so sleepy?* The thought never had time for an answer because she sank beyond drowse like a stone falling into a pool.

Trish spent the next day alternating between Firefly's and Spitfire's stalls. During a thunderstorm in the afternoon she stayed with Spitfire. While he'd gotten somewhat used to the crashing storm, loud noises still spooked him.

"Easy, fella, it's just thunder," Trish crooned to him after a particularly close strike. Her eardrums still echoed from the boom. *If you were home, you wouldn't have to put up with such stuff.* The thought made her wince. Her mother had called last night wondering when Trish was flying in. They'd agreed on Saturday, only the day after next.

If only Spitfire could be brought back to Vancouver. Trish leaned her forehead against his neck. "Guess that's the price of fame," she whispered. "Only how come it has to hurt so much?"

Spitfire turned and nuzzled her shoulder. When that didn't get her attention, he lipped the braid hanging down her back.

"Ouch." She pushed his nose away. "You don't have to get so rough." He threw his head up and rolled his eyes, the whites gleaming bright in the gloom. "Sure, I know, you're scared to death." Another flash of lightning glinted through the windows. "Hang on, here we go again." She turned so he could rest his head over her shoulder and place a hand over the ridge of his nose.

Trish counted. But this time, the thunder took five seconds to boom after the lightning flash. The storm was quickly moving away from them. Spitfire only flinched, his hide rippling beneath her hand.

Once the rain let up, she crossed the gravel parking lot to the quarantine barn, where Firefly occupied a double stall so she could have plenty of room to move around. José, one of the grooms, stayed with her to make sure she didn't try to lie down.

"How ya doin'?" Trish asked the aging former jockey.

"Not bad. She's a good horse, that one. Shame she won't run again."

"At least she's alive." Trish stroked the filly's neck. "Much as I'd love to see her on the track, she'll make a good broodmare." She tickled the filly's whiskery upper lip. "Won't you, girl?" Firefly snuffled Trish's pockets looking for her treat. When she found the right one, she nosed harder. "Okay, okay, be patient, will you?" Trish drew the carrot out of her jacket pocket and let the horse munch away. The crunch of carrot coupled with the water dripping through the downspouts sang a kind of tune. One of peace and contentment.

Trish took her American government textbook out of her book bag and sank down in the corner of the stall to study. "You can take a break now if you'd like. I'll be here for an hour at least." She listened while José left the building. When his footsteps faded, she leaned her head back against the wall. Firefly snuffed Trish's hair and then rested her nose against Trish's shoulder, the horse's eyes drifting closed.

Trish let her book dangle between her bent knees. Vancouver, Portland Meadows, Prairie High School—they all seemed light-years away. What would it be like to stay in Kentucky? She'd be closer to major tracks, that's for sure. Probably even head down to Florida when Donald shipped his string down there. She could be at BlueMist when Spitfire serviced the mares that other breeders would bring in. Spend time in the foaling barns. Go to school.

She shook her head. No, her senior year took priority. She shut off the daydreams and reopened her book. Graduating with her friends *was* important. After all, she'd never be seventeen again. She had plenty of years to race.

Now she sounded like her mother. Trish's snort made Firefly jerk up her head. "Easy, girl. You can go back to sleep. I'll be careful."

She called Rhonda that evening to let her in on the latest plans.

"You mean you're *finally* coming home?" Trish could just picture Rhonda, flat on her bed with one knee cocked over the other.

"You mean you've missed me? What about that tall, handsome basketball player who takes all your spare time?"

"Jason *is* rather nice."

"Nice?" Trish choked on the word. "I'll tell him what you said."

"You know, he plays basketball every day after school, and he's even found a weekend league. So, it's like I never get to see him."

"Right!"

"Besides that, I've had shows nearly every weekend. Which reminds me—you haven't seen me jump once this fall."

Guilt dealt Trish a blow to the midsection. "Sorry."

"Not your fault, but I qualified for the Pan Pacific, so you better clear those days. That's my entry into the big time."

The two chatted a few more minutes before Trish hung up. Yeah, it was time to go home. She'd missed out on a lot.

Friday night Red arrived right on time to take her out to supper. "How does Barney's Ribs sound?" he asked on their way down the steps.

"Sounds good to me. We don't get real southern barbecued ribs in Vancouver."

"That's what I thought. Then maybe a movie—or just a drive?"

"Up to you." She wanted to add, *I just like being with you,* but the words stuck in her throat. She'd have thought with her being in Kentucky she would have seen more of him, but a popular jockey didn't have a lot of extra time. Now, if she'd been at the track . . .

Before their dinner was served, Red had signed three autographs, and when the fans realized Trish was with him, they kept both jockeys busy.

Trish smiled at a young girl who had braces glinting on her teeth and who swore she'd be a jockey someday just like Trish. "Spend all the time you can learning to ride and handle horses," Trish told her. "Any kind of horse. And keep up your schoolwork so you get good grades." Trish could hardly believe she'd said that. Must be her mother's coaching coming out.

By the time they left the restaurant, it was too late to do more than head back to BlueMist. The golden harvest moon sailed above the tops of the trees, gilding branches and rooftops and casting deep shadows.

"Wish you could stay here." Red took her hand in his.

"I've thought about it. The Shipsons invited me too." The warm fuzzies inched up her arm and around her heart. Was this what love felt like?

"And?"

"And I have to go home. Mom needs me, and so does Runnin' On Farm. Besides, I want to graduate with my class." She laid her head on his shoulder.

"But you'll come back?"

"Of course. But I've got a lot of races to run out there, you know." She smiled up at him. "You could come west and ride."

"It would have to be California."

"I know. Portland doesn't pay very well. But the Meadows has been good to me."

Red snorted.

Trish knew he was thinking about the mess at the track when she'd been shot at. "But that's all over now."

"Sure." He snorted again.

The thought of The Jerk snapped her head up from its resting place. "We're going to get him." She put all the confidence she could into her reply.

"It better be soon." Red kissed her good-night and hugged her close. "I gotta admit I worry about you. Please be careful, will you?"

Trish nodded against his shoulder. Why did saying good-bye always make her eyes water?

He dropped another kiss on her nose before opening the door to the mansion for her. "See ya."

She watched him jump down the steps and jog to his pickup. When the taillights disappeared down the drive, she entered the house and shut the door behind her. Major sniffing all the way up the stairs kept the tears at bay.

Trish stood in Spitfire's stall the next morning, fighting back the tears, glad Timmy had thought to leave them alone. Saying good-bye to him was never easy. "I know I'll see you again in a few months, so you just behave yourself, you hear?"

Spitfire nodded. He nosed her pocket for the carrot he smelled and blew carrot perfume in her face while he munched. It was when she left the stall that he kicked up a fuss. He snorted and stamped his front feet, then let out a piercing shriek.

Two other stallions answered him from inside the barn and another from his paddock outside.

"Knock it off, you goof." Trish returned to the web gate and shook her finger in front of his face. "You know better than that." Spitfire tried to rub his forehead against her chest, but Trish pushed him away.

"He'll settle down soon as you're out the door." Timmy unhooked the web and entered Spitfire's stall. "You take care of yourself now, lass."

"You suppose he knows I'm leaving for Vancouver?"

"I believe he understands a lot more than we give him credit for." Timmy smoothed the stallion's mane. "Have a good trip."

Saying good-bye to BlueMist was getting harder each time. Trish kept reminding herself she was lucky to have two—no, three, when you include California—places to call home.

"You'll come again—soon?" Bernice reached over the back of the seat of the Cadillac and patted Trish's knee. "Since you're now our daughter too, we'll just have to bribe Marge to let us have you more often."

"You could attend college here in Kentucky, you know." Donald caught her eye from his rearview mirror.

Trish grimaced at the thought. "I'm not sure about college. I know my mom plans for me to go next fall, but I'd rather ride. I can go back to college any time."

"Or part time. Some of the jockeys do that." Bernice turned in her seat so she could see Trish.

"It's hard to know what to do."

"Rest assured, God will let you know, if you ask." She rested one arm on the back of the burgundy leather seat. "And, my dear, you certainly have all kinds of options."

Trish nodded. "I know." She knew this discussion would be coming up at home and her mother would *not* be as understanding. To Marge, education was *the* most important thing, right up there next to faith. No matter how much her mother was now involved in the horses and managing Runnin' On Farm, changing her views on college would be like stopping the mighty Columbia River with one hand.

In fact, the college discussion came up the next evening. After attending church in the morning, Trish spent the afternoon at the track. Now she was sitting in her father's recliner in front of a blazing fire in the fieldstone fireplace that covered most of one wall in the living room. Brad Williams lay stretched out on the floor, studying for one of his college classes. Rhonda Seabolt, queen of the couch, was pushing her flyaway red hair back so she could wrap a band around it. Her government book lay open in her cross-legged lap.

Marge brought in cups of hot chocolate and a plate of chocolate chip cookies. "Now this is as pretty a picture as I've seen anywhere." She offered the tray to each of the kids.

"Been a long time, hasn't it?" Brad pushed himself upright and took a cup along with a handful of cookies. "Thanks, Mrs. E. You sure know the way to a man's heart."

"Sure. Give you cookies and you'll do anything." Trish snapped her book shut and set it on the end table. This was one of those times when she felt sure if she turned her head quick enough, she'd see her father standing right behind her chair—or rather *his* chair. She could almost feel his hand on her shoulder.

"You talked to David lately?" Brad asked around a mouthful of cookie.

Trish could tell that, as usual, they were all on the same wavelength.

The four teens—Trish, David, Brad, and Rhonda—had been inseparable for all their growing-up years. That's why Marge called them her "Four Musketeers."

"He'll be home for Thanksgiving. Says he loves college in Tucson." Marge took her place in her rocker.

"I'm thinking of going there next year." Brad dropped his bombshell into the peace and watched it explode.

"You are!" Trish and Rhonda could have been one person.

"The more I think about it, the more I'd like to become a vet too. David and I could build a practice together." He popped another cookie in his mouth.

Trish and Rhonda swapped startled looks. "But you never . . ." "I thought you . . ." Their comments overlapped. Trish set her mug down and leaned forward.

"All right, buddy. When did this all come about?"

"Just lately. I really like helping Patrick with the horses, like I always have, and yet I can't see myself as a trainer."

"So you decided on veterinary."

"With a specialty in horses." He wrapped both arms around his bent knees. "I'm sending off my application tomorrow."

"Speaking of applications . . ." Marge gave Trish one of those this-is-your-mother-reminding-you looks that Trish hated.

"I've filled out three," Rhonda said. "Cal-Poly in San Luis Obispo, Washington State University, and Cal State, Davis." Rhonda chose another cookie from the plate on the coffee table in front of her. "All have good jumping programs. I'll take my horse right with me."

All three of them looked at Trish.

"I don't think I'm going to go to college." Trish raised her chin slightly in her don't-mess-with-me look. But her eyes pleaded, *Please understand.*

Chapter
06

The log in the fire snapped like a rifle shot.

"I don't think so." Marge planted her elbows on the arms of the chair. She sucked in a deep breath.

Trish could tell her mother was fighting to keep her cool. Glancing over at Rhonda was a mistake. Her best friend's head shook back and forth and her eyebrows had disappeared into her hairline. Brad seemed to be counting the threads in the weave of his jeans.

"Anyone for more hot chocolate?" Trish had to clear her throat at the end of the sentence. Marge shot her a glance fit to fry eggs. Brad and Rhonda shook their heads.

"We better be headin' out." Brad set his cup on the raised rock hearth in front of the fire, then thought better of it and stood to cross the room, placing his mug carefully on the tray.

"Yeah, yeah, we better." Rhonda copied his moves.

Chickens! Getting while the getting's good. See if I ever bail you out of a family hassle again. But Trish didn't say it, she just nodded. She got to her feet and followed them to the door.

"Thanks for the treats," Rhonda called back.

Marge kind of grunted.

"In the morning?" Brad paused.

"Sure," Marge answered. The one word carried the edge of a newly sharpened knife.

"Thanks for nothing, guys." Trish muttered to her friends' retreating backs.

"See you in the morning, like usual?" Rhonda's question floated back, threading its way through the mist. Rainbows circled the mercury yard light that glinted off the droplets frosting Brad's metallic blue Mustang.

Trish took in a deep breath of the cold, wet air, wishing she could go anywhere but back to where her mother could be heard clanking cups. She shut the door and returned to the living room. What was that phrase she'd heard, something about a good offense being the only defense? That wasn't quite right but who cared? Right now she had to deal with a very unhappy mother.

"I know you're disappointed." Trish leaned against the cedar-paneled wall.

With the cups clanked into submission in the kitchen, Marge was now attacking the sofa cushions.

"But I know this is the right thing for me to do. And if you tried to see it from my point of view, you'd agree." Could looks really send daggers?

Marge strode over to the fire and poked until sparks flew up the chimney in fear.

"Mom, stop all this and talk to me."

She threw in a log, then another.

Trish sat down on the arm of the sofa. Marge now leaned against the mantel, her head resting on her arm. *Dad, where are you? I need you so. Right now.* Trish chewed on her bottom lip. It would be so much easier to just agree with her mother right now. Say, "Sure I'll go to college." But the thought made her heart stop.

Can't you see that I'm first and foremost a jockey? That's my gift, my calling. And after that I may want to be a trainer, like Dad. Or maybe I'll ride until I'm fifty. She stared at the rigid line of her mother's back. *Or maybe I'll just . . . just . . .*

Just what? Even her nagger didn't seem his usual naggy self. *You have to go with what's right for you, kid.*

Trish blinked her eyes. Had she heard right? What would her father do in a situation like this? She rubbed her sore ribs with one hand and her chin with the other, trying to remember.

Dad had always walked over, put his arms around his wife, and said, "No matter how we decide on this, just remember that I love you." Trish fought down the boulder that instantly clogged her throat. She ordered one foot to lead the way and the other to follow. One step at a time, as if she were just learning to walk, she crossed the room.

She put a hand on her mother's shoulder. "Mom, no matter how much we go round on this, just remember that I love you." The words started hard and got easier as they went. "I hate fighting and either one of us being angry."

The shoulder under her hand shuddered. Marge turned, tears caught on the tips of her eyelashes, and she wrapped Trish in a mighty hug.

"Would you consider sending out applications in case you change your mind?" Marge finally asked after they both snagged tissues from the box and blew their noses.

"It would be a waste of their time—and mine. Guess I made the final decision on the plane. I can always go to college later, but my career as a jockey is really building. I should be riding full time now, but I won't because I promised you I'd give my senior year priority. And that's what I want to do too." Trish sank down on the hearth. She watched her mother's emotions play hide-and-seek with the firelight flickering across her face.

"I can't say I'm happy about this."

"I don't expect you to."

"But I do honor your decision about what to do with your life. Your father and I always said we wouldn't force our career decisions on you kids. You do what you feel called for. Our job is to see that you have the most information possible to make a wise decision."

Trish breathed a sigh of relief.

Marge went on. "But you'll have to give me some time. I always dreamed of both you kids graduating from college and exploring new fields. Guess I thought that would make your life more secure. I need time to let go of that dream and tune in to yours. You know that racing is not the safest of sports."

"Mom, you're the best. I know you're angry. . . ."

"I'd prefer to say upset. . . ." A grin tugged at the corner of Marge's mouth. "And please remind Brad and Rhonda of that fact."

"Oh, I will." Trish glanced over at the picture-perfect-plumped sofa cushions. "And I'm glad you took out your 'upset' on those instead of me."

Marge laid an arm across Trish's shoulders. "Me too." She snapped off the lamp as they passed it. "But I won't promise not to try to change your mind once in a while."

Trish had no trouble coming up with three things to be thankful for that night. In fact, her list stretched beyond ten before she dropped off.

Since morning stiffness made dressing take longer, Trish bailed out of bed before her alarm went off. She checked the blazing pink scar three ribs down from her left armpit. Every day both it and raising her arm improved. If she really *had* to, she could probably ride all right next week. Maybe next Saturday she'd head for the track with Patrick and ride for morning works.

She brushed her teeth and opted for leaving her hair down. Raising her arms to braid it still hurt too bad.

Wearing the denim skirt, silk blouse, and boots she and Rhonda had bought in California always raised her self-confidence a notch, and getting back in her own red convertible added another. It seemed like years since she'd driven it, what with the time it spent in the shop for a new paint job. Thinking of the keyed scratches on her car brought back the thought of The Jerk. She shuddered. Where was he? Who was he? Why was he doing this?

When she got to Rhonda's she wrote in her notebook, "Call Amy." It was time they nailed this creature, whoever he was.

Rhonda talked nonstop all the way to school, which was nothing new, bringing Trish up-to-date on everything that had happened. Doug Ramstead, the star quarterback, had pulled a hamstring and missed the last game, but they won anyway.

"He's been asking about you." Rhonda raised her eyebrows suggestively.

"He sent me a couple of cards while I was in the hospital." Trish had her blinker on to turn into the Prairie High parking lot.

"I told you once and I'll tell you again: If you'd give that guy half a chance, he could really like you."

"Yes, Rhonda." Trish completed the turn. "But I like Red, remember?"

"But he's so far away." Rhonda threw up her hands. "We could double-date if you'd—"

"We'll see, okay?" Trish parked in what had become her usual place. "Right now I gotta set up a schedule for making up the midterms I missed. I promised my mom I'd keep my grades up, but I hadn't planned on being gone a whole month."

Trish waved and greeted all her friends as she made her way to the office to talk with Mrs. Olson.

"You sure do lead an exciting life," the smiling counselor said. "I've talked with all your teachers and we've made up a schedule: one test a day after school, starting tomorrow." She handed Trish a paper with the list. "You think you're ready for that?"

"Much as I'll ever be. Lying flat on your back gives you plenty of time to study."

"What a scare you gave us all. You aren't planning on racing yet?" Mrs. Olson reached for a pink slip and filled it out, since the warning bell had already rung.

"Probably next week but never during school." Trish got to her feet. "Thanks." She picked up the pink slip and headed for class. Back to normal. Now Kentucky seemed a world or two away.

When Trish and Rhonda entered the cafeteria for lunch, the guys at their table stood up and cheered. Trish felt the blush starting under her collar and blazing across her cheeks. A wolf whistle came from across the room. Trish could feel every eye in the place gazing at her as if she stood under a spotlight.

"I'm gonna murder those guys," she said through gritted teeth, trying to smile at the same time.

"I told you. Doug likes you." Rhonda nudged Trish from behind to get her moving forward in line.

By the end of lunch it was as if she'd never been away. Jason sat on the other side of Rhonda, laughing and teasing like he'd gone to Prairie all his life, not just the last few months as an exchange student. Doug, the dream of nearly every girl in school, sat on Trish's right, teasing her into laughing so hard she flinched.

"Ribs, huh?" He leaned closer and said softly, "I broke mine once; hurts like crazy."

"It's even worse when I laugh or cough, so cool it." Trish nibbled on a carrot stick. "When I'm gone, I forget how crazy you guys are."

He turned to look her in the eye. "Well, how about not being gone so much?" His deep blue eyes crinkled at the edges. "I'm glad you're back."

A shiver ran up Trish's spine. Maybe Rhonda was right after all. "Thanks. I'm glad to be here, and all in one piece."

Doug picked up her books and walked her back to her locker. He leaned one arm against the tan metal door next to hers. "You think while you're laid up, you might find time to see a movie or something with another laid-up jock?" His gaze met hers, then skipped away. Two books fell off the stack in the bottom of the locker and hit the floor. Doug dropped to his knees and picked them up, holding her gaze as he handed them back. "Please."

"But I . . ."

"Just as friends." He stuck his fingertips in the front pockets of his jeans. The warning bell rang.

"Sure, why not?" Trish grabbed her notebook and slammed the locker door closed. "I'm free Saturday night. What's playing?"

"Got me." He laid a well-muscled arm across her shoulders.

"No horror or gross stuff."

"Okay."

"And I have to be at the track at five-thirty. That's before sunrise, you know, so I can't stay out late."

Rhonda came up beside her and poked her arm. Trish knew it meant "I told you so." Trish poked her back.

Officer Amy Jones drove into the Runnin' On Farm driveway right behind Trish. She leaped from her sporty green car and threw her arms around Trish. "Hi, kid. I know, I'm hugging carefully." Her actions followed her words. "It's so good to have you home. I wanted to stay longer, but the powers that be thought you'd be safe enough in the ICU."

Trish just hugged her favorite police person back. She didn't try to break into the rushing river of words. She'd never heard Amy run on like this in all the time they'd spent together.

"Trish, you scared the life out of me." Amy gripped Trish's shoulders with both hands. "And there was nothing I could do for you. That's when I knew I had to let God in. Only He could take care of you, and I had to be able to ask."

Trish clasped Amy's hand and squeezed. "Thanks for the cards and flowers—and all the prayers too." She opened the door and motioned for Amy to go in first. "As you can see, they worked."

After greeting Marge and accepting her offer of freshly baked snickerdoodle cookies, Trish and Amy settled in the living room. Amy checked her watch. "Since I'm on a stakeout tonight, we better get busy."

"Not just a friendly call, huh?" Trish nibbled her cookie.

"Nope, I wish. But we need to nail this guy before he does any real damage." She handed Trish a list of names. "These are all the people we've investigated while you were gone."

Trish glanced down the list. "Doug Ramstead? Brad? You've got to be kidding!"

"Nope. In my business no one is exempt." Amy looked down at her list. "See name number sixteen? He's the jockey who whipped your horses during a couple of races last year."

"I know. Emanuel Ortega." Trish looked up from the list. "He went and raced at Yakima last summer. We're not friends, but he's never done anything like that again."

"At least, not that you know of."

"Right."

Trish felt a squiggle of doubt worm its way into her mind. Was everyone she knew a suspect? How could she live with that? "I bet it has something to do with Kendall Highstreet, the developer. Forget my friends and ask him."

"We have, let me assure you." Amy shook her head. "He's clean."

"What about his friends and family?" Trish set her Diet Coke down with a clink. "The people who work for him?"

Amy gave her what could only be called a police officer's patient-but-don't-be-dumb look.

"I'm sorry." Trish leaned back in the recliner. "You've already done that, and I should trust you to do your job."

"You got it." Amy leaned forward, her elbows on her knees. "Trish, please, keep your eyes and ears open and let me know if you see anything unusual. Immediately if not before."

Trish sighed. "I'd hoped it was all over."

"So did I. So did I."

After Amy left, Trish wandered down to the barns to visit with her four-legged friends. Caesar, the farm collie, danced by her side, yipping, then running ahead and yipping again. His feathered tail beat a cadence against her legs when he returned to her side. Trish bent over to get her quick tip-of-the-nose lick.

"Easy, fella. I did wash my face this morning." She buried her fingers in his snowy ruff and swung his head back and forth, the loose skin pushing wrinkles up to his ears and over his pointed head. The sable collie planted his front feet on her shoulders and tried for her nose again. Trish had always said he had the fastest tongue in the West, and in her absence he'd not lost his touch. After what could never be enough roughing, he dashed off and yipped again, running circles around her at lightning speed.

Trish planted her hands on her hips and laughed aloud at his antics. They had come so close to losing him. Had that poisoning been the stalker too? Or was it just an unfortunate accident? "Sure wish you could talk, fella."

Her three-tone whistle floated off on the evening breeze when she rounded the long, low barns and headed down the lane to the paddocks. White board fences lined both sides of the grassy lane, split by two wheel ruts cut through to the bare dirt. All the home stock lined the fence off to the left, as if spectators at a ball game. Whinnies and tossing heads greeted her next whistle.

Down at the far end, old gray Dan'l, the retired Thoroughbred who'd taught her much of her racing skills, stamped and whinnied repeatedly. He'd been her friend long before Spitfire was foaled. Dan'l was the first Thoroughbred her father had bought at a claiming race, back when he only trained for other owners. Right now Dan'l was letting the world know that he for one was glad she was home.

Trish gave out carrot treats down the line, taking an extra moment with Miss Tee and Double Diamond, the two yearlings. "Hey, that's enough." Trish grabbed Miss Tee's halter after the filly gave the young colt a nip on the shoulder. "I gave you both some, you know. You don't have to be piggy." The filly's nostrils flared and she tried to jerk her head away.

Double Diamond sidled right back up to the fence and reached over, sniffing Trish's shoulder and checking out her pockets.

"Think you're pretty smart, don't you?" Trish dug out a carrot for him with one hand, keeping the other on Miss Tee's halter. "Hope you remember your lessons as much as you do where the treats come from." She gave them each a last pat and worked her way down through the broodmares to Dan'l.

"How ya doin', old man?" He snuffled his way up her arm and checked out her hair, her shoulder, and her pocket. A silent nicker rippled his nostrils, then he dropped his head so she could reach his ears more easily. When she turned so he could rest his head over her shoulder, he sighed in contentment. Only he and Spitfire had adopted this position as their own. Trish gave him another hunk of carrot and rubbed his ear and down his cheek. Caesar sat at her feet, nose raised, sniffing the evening breeze. A pheasant rooster called from the brush at the edge of the woods.

Trish felt the peace of the evening seep into her heart and spirit. A narrow band of gold broke through and tinted the overcast on the western horizon. The pheasant called again. Dan'l stamped a front foot and bobbed his head, encouraging her to keep stroking him.

The sound of a car in the drive sent Caesar barking up the lane. "Gotta get you guys some feed." She stepped away from the fence and

51

horse and started to trot up the lane. Within two strides, she thought the better of it and walked fast. She had a lot to do, including studying for tomorrow's government exam. At least she was getting the hardest one out of the way first.

That evening Marge had left for a meeting at church. When the phone rang, Trish shoved back her desk chair and crossed the hall to her mother's bedroom extension to answer it.

"Runnin' On Farm."

A silence met her ear. "Hi, this is Trish."

A sinister chuckle sent shivers racing up and down her spine. A scratchy voice she'd hoped never to hear again said, "Welcome home. I'll be seeing you."

The line clicked dead.

Chapter
07

Trish didn't wait for the dial tone. The receiver clattered into the plastic stand. Her heart did triple time.

The phone rang again. She stared at it as if it were a rattler, buzzing its tail. Second ring, third. She reached out her hand, sure the thing would bite. She lifted the receiver to her ear. "Runnin' On Farm." She could barely get the words past the cotton filling her mouth.

"Trish, is that you?" Rhonda asked. "You sound awful."

Trish could hardly hear over the pounding of her heart. "He called," she croaked.

"Who ca—oh no, not The Jerk?"

Trish curled herself into a ball in the middle of her mother's bed. "I—I have to call Amy. C-c-can you come over?"

"Sure. I'll be right there."

As soon as she had the dial tone, Trish punched in the numbers for Amy's home. An answering machine suggested she leave a message. Trish stuttered and stammered her way through a message and hung up. Where was Amy? Where had that creep called from? Was he near? What if he had a car phone and was right down the road?

"God, I'm so scared!" She clutched her arms around her knees. "Help me, please." Trish huddled for a few more minutes, practicing her deep breathing to relax. For a change she was glad for the ache in her ribs. The pain made her think of something besides The Jerk lurking out there somewhere to get her. When her heart had settled back somewhere near its proper place, she let her hands, arms, and shoulders relax. "Thank you, Father. This feels much better."

She pushed herself to her feet and headed back for her room. One thing she could do—close all the drapes. If he *was* out there, at least he couldn't see in and she didn't have to feel as if eyes were staring in at her. When the drapes were closed, she crossed the room to the door. The soft light from the lamp on her desk shone like a laser on the three-by-five cards tacked to her wall. Bible verses, mostly handwritten by her father, lined the area. One in particular seemed to be lit by a flashing strobe: "Do not be afraid—I am with you!"

"Thanks, Dad, for the verses and thank our heavenly Father for me too. You seem to be a bit closer to Him right now than I am."

She chewed on her lip on the way down the hall. Was her father really closer? Physically maybe, but Jesus had promised to live right in her heart. "Huh! Can't get much closer than that." Without drawing the living room drapes, she went to the back door.

"Hey, fella," she said to the dog lying on his rug by the window. "You want to come in?"

Caesar never needed a second invitation. He leaped through the opening in one bound, his tail wagging his entire body. Caesar glued to her side, Trish crossed the kitchen to the phone and dialed Officer Parks' number. He picked it up on the first ring.

"What's wrong, Trish?" he interrupted her greeting.

"He—he called again."

"When?"

"Just a few minutes ago." Trish looked at the clock. "Maybe ten or so."

"Who's with you?"

"Caesar. Mom's at church and Patrick went somewhere. Rhonda's on her way over."

"Did you call Amy?"

"She—she had her answering machine on." Trish could see headlights coming up the drive. "Rhonda's here."

"I'll be right out. I'm bringing one of those new phones, the ones that show the number that last called on a screen. We may get him this way. Don't answer the phone again. Let your machine pick it up and then you can hear who's calling. That way you can screen your calls. I'm on my way."

She met Rhonda at the door. "Trish, you didn't even have the door locked."

"I—we never lock the doors. You know that. You don't either."

"Yeah, but no one's threatening me." She dumped her book bag on the sofa. "I got a paper to write by tomorrow. Is Amy coming out?"

"No, Parks, for whatever good it does." Trish left for the kitchen and returned with two cans of Diet Coke. "I don't think they have anything on this dude yet, and let me tell you . . ." She handed a can to Rhonda, who had flopped on the sofa. "I'm getting sick of it all. Real sick." She could feel that she was getting mad. It always started in her gut. But at least mad felt better than scared to death.

"What do you think he wants?"

"Got me. Make me crazy, I guess." Trish stopped her pacing to drop down on the raised hearth. Caesar sat down beside her and put one snowy front paw up on her knee. She rubbed behind his ears with one hand, leaving the other free to hold her Coke.

"They questioned all of us while you were gone." Rhonda dug in her backpack and pulled out a spiral notebook. "I just can't believe it's someone from Prairie. We've known each other all our lives."

"Me neither. I bet I don't even know this—this person, if you could give him such a compliment." Caesar got to his feet and crossed to the door, a low rumble in his throat. At the same time, they could see light beams from an approaching car. Caesar set up a crescendo of barks.

"Must be Parks. Caesar doesn't bark more than once for Mom or Patrick." Trish crossed the room and let him out. The collie bounded down the walk, barking all the while. He stopped. His tail began wagging as soon as Parks stepped from his car and greeted him.

Trish held open the door.

"Trish, for crying out loud, get out of the doorway," Parks said after only a perfunctory greeting. "You make a perfect target that way."

"But—but I knew it was you." She stepped back to let the tall, tired-looking detective in.

"No you didn't. Not at first. You should have let Caesar out the back door so no one would see you in the light like that. The creep knows you're home. He just called."

"Oh." Trish felt like a little kid who'd just been scolded for playing in the street. She hugged herself with both arms.

Parks turned toward the kitchen and placed a caller ID phone on the counter. He plugged it in and showed her how to use it. "Now, tell me everything that happened." He took his worn black notebook out of his inside jacket pocket.

While Trish detailed the call, Parks sat on the hearth, long legs bent to form a desk. He tapped the end of his pen against his teeth when she was finished. "Did you hear any background noises, music, loud voices, some such?"

Trish shook her head. "He always sounds raspy, like he's trying to disguise his voice."

"Are you sure it's a male voice?"

Trish shook her head again. "But I *think* so. Besides, girls don't do this kind of thing."

"Don't kid yourself. They do, but it's not as common." He wrote himself another note. "Now remember, screen your calls and call me with the number if he calls again. Maybe this time we'll get lucky."

By Friday Trish felt as if she'd been to the moon and back—on foot. She dragged herself into the house after making up her last midterm exam and collapsed on the sofa.

"Bad, huh?" Marge hung up the phone and joined her daughter in the living room.

"Worse than that." Trish closed her eyes. "And to think that quarter finals are only two weeks away. I have a term paper to write and another short paper, besides one Haiku. You ever write poetry?"

"Sure, but not since college." Marge leaned a shoulder against the edge of the wall. "You want something to eat? I baked brownies."

"Do horses whinny?"

"I think that's 'Do ducks have lips?' but I've never understood that particular phrase. Brad's down at the barn. I just came up to make some calls. You want to call him? I'm sure he could use a goody break."

"Have you ever heard of Brad turning down brownies?" Trish shook her head at the absurdity of the idea. "Or any other cookie for that matter?" She shoved herself vertical. "We should send David another goody box."

"I know. I thought maybe Sunday afternoon Rhonda would help us. Go call Brad now."

"Let's send one to Red too. He's always giving me presents and I never get one for him." Trish could feel her energy coming back. She stepped out the front door and yelled, "Brad!"

She heard her mother from inside. "I could have done that. Go down to the barn and get him. They got in a load of hay today."

Well, at least four days since Jerk Face called. She'd made up a new name for him during the wait. Each day Marge had shaken her head at Trish's question and each night she'd gone to bed using "no call" as one of her *thank-you*'s during her prayers.

She whistled once just to set the lineup to whinnying. "Hey, Brad. Brownies are ready."

"Back here." She found him in the hayloft, moving hay that had been stacked on the straw side of the barn. When she stuck her head up through the entrance, she watched him dump the last bale in place. "You'd think they could figure out what went where, wouldn't you?" He wiped the sweat from his brow and stuck his leather gloves in a rear pocket. "We're about due for a load of straw too. Patrick said we should start keeping the broodmares inside at night pretty soon."

"We'll have to keep Firefly in too as soon as she arrives." Trish backed down the ladder so he could come down. "Sorry I can't help."

"Yeah, right." He snagged his jacket off the gate of a stall. "I know how much you love tossing bales, even when you're all in one piece." He patted her on the head, then jerked her braid. "There *are* advantages in staying small, not having to sling hay being one of them."

Arm in arm they sauntered out of the barn and up the rise. "I seem to remember Rhonda and me moving our share, even though we did it as a team."

"You're right." Brad ushered her in the door in front of him. "And as the football team knows, there's no better way to get in shape than tossing those suckers around."

Trish felt a tide of confusion wash over her. Since when had Brad started treating her like a girl? They'd always raced to see who hit the door and then the cookie plate first. She shrugged. Maybe this growing up wasn't so bad after all.

The phone rang while they sat around the big oak kitchen table. Trish rose to get it but slowed at her mother's reminding look. First they had to wait to see who it was.

A familiar voice came on. She clapped her hands over her ears so she couldn't hear—but then let them drift down to her side in morbid fascination. She felt the cold begin at her toes and work its way up.

"I'm sorry you can't come to the phone right now, Trish, but I'll call back later. You can count on it."

Trish dashed to the phone. Sure enough, there was a number right across the screen. Beginning with the 503 area code made it Oregon.

Trish grabbed a pencil out of the cup. She dropped it. Got another. Her hand was shaking so badly she broke the lead. After a deep breath, she picked up a pen and wrote the number down, then dialed Officer Parks. A ripple ran from her head to her fingertips. Would this be the breakthrough they needed? It *had* to be.

Chapter
08

Trish waited by the phone for Parks to call back.

Brad hovered beside her, nibbling on the brownie clenched in his hand. "It'll probably take a while." He too jumped when the phone rang.

Trish left it until she heard the detective's voice on the machine, then picked up the receiver. "What'd you find out?"

"Bad news, or rather no news, Trish. He called from a pay phone located over by Lloyd's Center. We had a squad car out in that sector so they swung by. No one around."

Trish felt as if someone had just let out all her air, leaving her flat and wobbly, a balloon lying inert on the floor. "Oh." She'd had such high hopes. Now they were back to square one. When would they catch him?

"What is it?" Marge cupped her coffee mug in her hands.

Trish shook her head and covered the mouthpiece. "Pay phone." She took up her conversation with Parks again. "So we just keep on like before?"

"Don't panic, Trish. We're going to find him. He'll get cocky and make a mistake. I know he will."

As Trish hung up she wondered if Parks had been trying to convince her—or himself.

The next morning at the track, Trish was greeted like returning royalty by everyone, from the bug boys and the jockeys giving their morning charges a good workout to the kids cleaning stalls. Trainers shouted greetings, and every time she returned to the barn, more people came by to shake hands and welcome her back.

"Can't get nothin' done this way." Patrick went about checking the horses, all the while grumbling around the half-smile on his rounded face.

Trish figured that today he looked more like a leprechaun than ever. "Would you rather I stayed home?" she asked, a grin tugging at the corners of her mouth no matter how hard she tried to sound serious. "Maybe Genie Stokes is a better rider."

"Leastways she don't have half the track hanging around, swapping lies and such." He gave her a boost up on her waiting mount.

Trish grinned down at the old trainer her father had hired after he'd become so sick he couldn't do it himself. "Patrick O'Hern, if someone didn't know you and heard you talking like that, they'd think you're an old grouch."

"I heard him and I know he's an old grouch." Genie Stokes, who always rode for Runnin' On Farm when Trish wasn't available, came striding up the walkway, sidestepping buckets and blankets as she came. "Welcome home, Trish. You're looking good for scaring us all half to death."

Trish leaned over and grabbed her friend's hand. "Feeling plenty better, let me tell you. But then you know what busted ribs are like."

"At least I didn't try dying on the doctors while they patched me up." She patted the horse's shoulder and looked up at Trish with a wobbly smile. "I'll tell you, there were a lot of prayers sent up from around here." She squeezed Trish's hand another time. "You take good care of my horses, you hear?" She turned to Patrick. "See she stays out of trouble now."

Patrick shook his head. "Takes the Almighty himself to do that, or leastways He bails her out again."

"Well, while you two figure out my life for me, think I'll take this old boy out on the track." Trish touched a finger to her helmet. "See ya."

Trish huddled into her down jacket, grateful she'd worn her long johns. Even when it wasn't raining, the wind blowing off the Columbia River managed to penetrate down to the bones. The gray overcast hung low enough to blur the top of the glass-enclosed grandstands. The thought of winter racing in Florida was sounding better and better.

During the change of mounts she took a moment to blow her dripping nose and drink half a cup of hot chocolate. Feeling somewhat warmer, she left the office to find Patrick holding Gatesby's head while Brad finished the saddling.

"I see you haven't broken him of his favorite habit." Trish stayed just out of mouth range.

Brad glared at her from under the bill of his baseball hat. "Anytime you want to try. . . ."

Trish copied Patrick's hold on the steel D-ring bit and rubbed Gatesby's black ears. "Stubborn old boy, aren'tcha?" The gelding leaned into her ministering fingers. "Who's his latest victim?"

Brad cupped his hands to give her a knee up. "Need you ask?"

Trish buckled the chin strap of her helmet and gathered her reins. One never took a chance with Gatesby. He'd dumped her more than once. "Okay, joker, let's go see what we can do." As usual, he wanted to go at his own pace—fast. However, Patrick had scheduled him for a slow gallop—two times around the track, after a warming-up half-lap. By the time they returned to the barn, Trish's side had set up a complaint department.

"I'm ready for breakfast any time you are—and since this is my first day back, I'll even buy." Trish stripped her saddle off the now-docile gelding and walked past him to put it away, but Gatesby got a nip in anyway. "Owww." She dumped her saddle on the trunk in the office and rubbed her shoulder. "You let him do that on purpose." She glared at Brad, who wore the same sheepish "gotcha" expression as Gatesby. "See if I buy *your* breakfast." She grabbed Gatesby's halter. "And you know there's always the glue factory for horses like you." Gatesby rubbed his head against her chest. "No, I know you're not sorry, not one bit."

While she scolded the horse, Brad started washing the gelding down. Within a few minutes they had him washed, blanketed, and snapped to the hot walker, where Gatesby followed the other three horses around the circle.

Trish hardly found time to eat with so many people coming by. Bob Diego, head of the Thoroughbred Breeders Association and one for whom Trish frequently rode, slung an arm about her shoulders.

"Welcome home, mi amiga." He dropped a kiss on the top of her head. "Good to see your shining face." He took the chair across the table from her. "What a scare you gave us! Have they found the man who has been troubling you yet?"

"You coulda gone all year without bringing that up." Trish's heart took a sudden belly flop. "The answer is no. He called again on Friday."

Diego mumbled a few unmentionable names for the stalker.

"I call him The Jerk." Trish forked the last bit of ham into her mouth and gathered up her dishes. "Gotta run or I won't get back in time for the afternoon program. I've a term paper to research first."

"Will you be riding soon?" Diego rose to his feet when she did.

"Saturday." She glanced at Patrick. "We have one then, right?" Patrick nodded around a mouthful of pancake.

"For your amigo too?"

"Sure 'nough. See you guys." Trish crossed the noisy room, shaking hands and answering greetings as she tried to get to the door. She'd just reached for the door handle when Emanuel Ortega stepped to her side.

"Excuse me, please," the young jockey asked, his dark eyes flashing, "but could we talk for a moment?"

"Of course, what is it?" Trish stepped out of the doorway and next to the wall.

"You know for when I hit your horses last year, I was very sorry. . . ."

"I know."

"Well, the police have been questioning me about the person who is, what they say, horsing. . . ."

"Harassing?"

"Yes, that is the word. I do not do that. I tell them but I think they do not believe me." He stepped closer, waving a hand to make the point. "I do not call you and send you bad letters. I want to be great jockey here in America."

Trish nodded. "I understand, but, Emanuel, the police are talking to everyone, not just you. Don't worry about it. But if you have any idea who it might be, please tell them."

"I know nothing." He shook his head again. "All I know is I do not do such a thing." He turned to leave but swung back, a smile now lighting his thin face. "Gracias, señorita. Buenos días."

"You too, hombre." She watched him cut his way across the crowded room without looking back. Had he talked with her because he really wasn't guilty or because he was? She shook her head once to clear it. *You can't think things like that!* she ordered herself. *It'll drive you nutsy.*

Curt Donovan, the sports reporter from the Portland *Oregonian*, met her at the door. "Trish, I was hoping you'd be here today, or else I was coming out to see you." He gave her a hug that left no doubt about his concern. "Did you see that article by the reporter in San Mateo?"

Trish shook her head. "The one who dubbed me the Comeback Kid?"

"That's the one." Curt kept pace with her. "He says there's some company thinking of making a movie about you. Called it a 'real heart-warming story.'"

"You're kidding. He predicted the endorsement with Chrysler long before it happened too." She raised one eyebrow. "You think he's serious?"

"I'd bet on it. He seems to have better sources than I do." Curt waved to the guard at the gate, who gave Trish a thumbs-up sign. "You got a quote for me?"

"Sure. I'm glad to be home, will be riding Saturday, and don't believe everything you read in the newspapers." Trish slid into her car and grinned up at him. "And if anyone knows who's harassing me, they can call Officer Parks. He'd love to hear from them and so would I. See ya." She watched him walk back across the road to the back entrance to Portland Meadows. Rhonda was right. Curt Donovan *was* one good-looking guy.

Trish spent the morning researching her term paper at the Fort Van-couver Library, then after grabbing a burger, she headed back for Portland Meadows. Since—wonder of wonders—the sky had cleared, she pushed the button to lower the top of her convertible. What a treat, to enjoy the sun, feel the wind in her hair—except her teeth clacked together like drummer's sticks by the time she drove into the parking lot. Sun and blue sky or not, November in Oregon definitely wasn't convertible weather.

"Bet David doesn't have to worry about freezing to death down in Tucson," she muttered as she punched the button to raise the top. "Bet he's wearing shorts instead of long johns too." With the other hand she shoved the heater to high. She clamped both hands over her frozen ears and waited for the temperature to get somewhere near warm in the car. Her face and hands felt the blast of hot air long before her feet did.

"Well, my girl, you learned a good lesson there. No convertible tops down until summer, no matter how cool you want to look." She snapped down the sun visor to look in the mirror while applying lipstick. Her hair stood out all over, in spite of the braid, her cheeks looked as if someone had painted them red—bright red—and her mouth wouldn't stop jiggling long enough to put on the proper "paint," as her father had called it.

She flipped the visor back up. "And if cool was what you wanted, you sure did get that." She shoved the heater controls off and climbed from the car.

"Welcome back," called the woman at the side gate.

"Thanks. Good to be back." And it was. The sun still shone, and without the draft from a moving vehicle, Trish even thought about taking off her red jacket. The tan down vest and green wool turtleneck sweater would be warm enough.

You've been known to lose jackets that way. Sometimes her nagger could be real helpful.

So instead of veering into the women's jockey room, she headed for the track side fence where most of the trainers and many of the owners watched the races. Since it was her father's favorite place, she liked it best too.

"Hi, guys." She slipped into place between Bob Diego and his trainer. "You got one running soon?"

"Couldn't stay away, huh?" Bob moved down a bit for her to have more room. "I have one in the third. Wish you were up on her."

"Me too. But I promised Mom another week off. She gets the worries, you know."

"How is your mother?"

Trish liked the way he said his *s* softer than American-born people.

"Fine, I guess." She looked up at the tall, broad-shouldered Hispanic gentleman. "Gentle man" was a good way to describe Bob Diego. And honorable. She felt proud to be his friend. "Why?"

"I just think about her sometimes. She has been through much."

"You too, my friend." The sound of the bugle floated across the track and rose above the snapping flags in the infield. The sound of it caught in her throat, as usual. That was one of the things she remembered from the day they buried her father, the bugle singing the parade to post. She lifted her chin and rubbed her lips together.

The roar of the crowd at the sight of the horses dancing onto the track drove back the pending tears.

Bob Diego laid a hand on her shoulder. "You so rarely see from this angle anymore. It is different, no?"

Trish smiled up at him. "Sure is." She glanced down at her program to see who was running and who was riding. Genie Stokes had the number one slot. Trish waved as they trotted past. "Go for it, Genie." The jockey in black-and-white silks touched her whip to her helmet.

A voice calling her name behind her caught Trish's attention. She turned around to drown in the most gorgeous hot fudge eyes she'd ever seen. The smiling mouth below them wasn't so bad either. "H-hi."

"Hi, yourself. Welcome back to Portland." His voice made her think of warm maple syrup.

"Do I know you?" Trish left off staring into his eyes long enough to catch a fleeting glimpse of jacket, sweater, and shirt with the look of Italy, probably by way of Nordstrom's.

"You've signed my programs a couple of times." His smile showed teeth an orthodontist would hire for an advertisement. That same smile crinkled a dimple to the left side. Wait till Rhonda heard about *this* fan. "My name is Taylor Winthrop."

"Good." Trish tried to think of something clever to say. Where was her brain when she needed it?

"I'm glad you're better."

"Thanks." Her brain finally kicked in. "Do you come to the track often?" *Wow, some conversationalist!*

"Usually on the weekends. My classes take up too much time during the week."

Classes? You're too old for high school. Trish could feel her mind working, so why didn't it give her something clever, cute, or funny to say?

"I'm a junior at the University of Portland."

College, not high school, you idiot. "That's nice." She felt like smacking herself in the forehead like they did in the movies.

"And they're off." The announcer took over and the shouting crowd made conversation impossible. Trish wished for her father's binoculars. She never needed them when she was riding and so never thought to bring them.

"Come on, Genie!"

"And it's number one by one length coming out of the turn, followed by three on the outside. . . ."

Trish gripped the top rail of the fence as if she could transfer her strength to Genie. Down the backstretch and into the turn, Genie still held the lead. Out of the turn, two horses challenged her. "Go, Stokes. What're you waiting for?"

Three abreast, but Genie went to the whip and her horse stretched out, taking the lead again, stride by stride. She won by two lengths.

"She almost waited too long on that one." Bob Diego let his binoculars fall back on their cord. "You think so, Trish?"

"Yep."

"She's a friend of yours?" Taylor asked from her other side.

Trish had forgotten all about him during the excitement of the race. "Yeah, good friend. She rides for us when I can't."

"I know." He rolled his program and stuffed it into his pocket. "Would you care to go for a drink or something? We could talk better in the clubhouse."

"Um—I—thanks anyway, but I don't think so. I—umm."

"I know. You don't know me and your mother told you never to talk to strangers. Right?" His smile crinkled his eyes. "But how can we get beyond being strangers if we don't talk?"

"He has you there." Diego turned and gave Adam an assessing look. "I need to head for the barn. See you later?"

"No, I'm going with you. Thanks for the invitation, Taylor. See you around." Trish walked off between Bob and his trainer.

"Another time, then?" Taylor called after them.

Trish turned to answer. "Maybe."

"He seems like a very nice young man. Much wealth too, I suspect." Diego held the gate open for her.

"I guess."

"Why didn't you go with him?"

Trish shrugged. "I don't know. Rhonda'll kill me for not." She thought a moment. "Guess I just don't need another man in my life about now."

Bob Diego laughed and tugged on the end of her braid. "You have much wisdom for one so young."

When Trish drove into the yard at home later that afternoon, a plain white car waited in the drive. The *E* on the license plate told Trish it was a county car even if she hadn't known Officer Parks drove one like it.

"Now what?" She grabbed her book bag and, after greeting Caesar, headed for the house.

Parks stood up when she entered. Amy occupied the other end of the sofa. Trish stared from face to face.

"All right, what's going on?"

They both looked at a vase filled with a dozen creamy peach rosebuds in the middle of the coffee table.

"Awesome. Those are beautiful." Trish crossed the room and bent over to sniff for a fragrance. "They even smell good." She stood up again. "What's the catch?"

Amy handed her the card.

Trish opened the envelope. "I'll be seeing you—soon!"

"Well, you gotta admit he has good taste." Her comment fell as flat as the silence in the room—and as her stomach felt.

Chapter
09

"So the phantom strikes again." Trish collapsed on the hearth.

"Regrettably so." Parks removed his notebook from his side pocket and flipped the pages. "We called the florist. A woman ordered the flowers, paid—"

"Wait a minute," Trish interrupted, "you said a woman?"

Amy and Parks both nodded. Parks continued. "I know, it doesn't make sense. She had on a stocking hat, dark glasses, and a tan wool coat. Paid cash. At least that's what the girl at the florist shop thought she remembered. It had been busy about then."

Trish looked up at her mother leaning against the corner of the wall.

"The flowers were delivered about one o'clock," Marge answered the unspoken question.

Trish stared at the arrangement. How could something so lovely bear such a cruel message? She got up and sniffed the buds again. "Well, I can throw them out or enjoy them. It's not the flowers' fault for all this, so guess I'll just love the fragrance and appreciate how beautiful they are."

She rubbed her chin with her forefinger. "Shame I can't tell whoever sent them what great taste he has."

She could feel the tension lighten up by about a hundred pounds or so. "You guys need me for anything else?" At the shaking of all three heads, she grinned. "Good, 'cause I got a date to get ready for." She stopped and turned at the hall entrance. "I'm not gonna let this creep mess up my life. He can send me flowers any time he wants." She thought she heard a "Let's hope that's all he sends" as she turned into the bathroom, but she chose to ignore it.

Trish reminded herself later that going to dinner and a movie with Doug Ramstead was not to be confused with a *real* date. He had said they were "just friends," and she believed him—almost. But when he held her hand during the movie, the warm tingles swam right up her arm. And his shoulder next to hers felt good and solid and kinda—well, nice would do until a better word came along. When he turned his head to whisper something in her ear, the warm air set up tingles up her spine too. Maybe Rhonda was right after all.

She shut off the thoughts and concentrated on the action on the screen. Could one be "in like" with two guys at once? She really shut that one down. Doug was her friend and Red was—Red was—clear across the country in Kentucky, even though she liked him a whole lot.

She was just about asleep that night, in the totally relaxed state where good ideas come from, when she heard her nagger clear his throat. *You could try praying for The Jerk like you did for the developer Kendall Highstreet.*

Trish startled instantly awake and sat totally upright in bed. "No way." She flopped back down. What an idea. One of her verses floated through her mind: "Pray for those who spitefully use you. . . ." This was spiteful all right. Her teeth snapped together as if her body didn't want to say these prayers any more than her mind did.

Pray for The Jerk. "Yuk!"

Your father would have. "Double yuk!" Trish crossed her arms over her chest. God sure didn't ask for easy things. She flipped over on her left side. Then her right. Looked at the clock. Nearly one.

She shut her eyes and took deep breaths. Nothing. She felt the urge and headed for the bathroom. But that didn't help either. When she crawled back in bed, she was *really* awake. Eyes wide and mind running like Thoroughbreds driving for the finish line.

"All right." She threw back the covers and thumped her feet on the floor. By the time she was on her knees, hands clasped and eyes closed, she could only grumble. "Father, please bless the idiot who's sending me stuff, whoever he is." Her voice softened. "I can tell he needs you, and I know that you'll take care of him." She rested her forehead on her hands. "Please help me not hate him, and keep us all safe. Amen."

She climbed back in bed and pulled up the covers. Was it her nagger she heard clapping?

Thursday in government class they were discussing—again—how ordinary people could make a difference.

"What are some things you've heard about that other people are doing?" Ms. Wainwright asked from her perch on the tall stool in front of the chalkboard.

"Our church does things like give out food baskets and stuff."

"The Salvation Army always has people ringing the bells for money. I did it once."

"People can get food at FISH, the food bank in town. I helped collect canned goods for them one time."

"The football team cleaned up an old lady's yard one year." Doug Ramstead's voice came from right behind Trish.

"And we collected petitions for the racetrack." The answers kept coming from different parts of the room. "Helped keep it open too."

Trish nodded. Thanks to all their efforts, the Portland City Council had voted not to close Portland Meadows.

"The cub *sprouts* had a food drive not too long ago." Chuckles floated around the room at that.

"Now that it's cold outside again, I think about the homeless people who don't have warm coats or blankets." The speaker, a girl two rows over from Trish, tucked her hair back around her ear.

"Aw, they can go to shelters," a male voice answered. "They want to live on the streets."

"Right!" Trish could feel her anger starting to bubble. "What if there aren't enough shelters? You slept out in the cold and rain lately without stuff to keep you warm?"

"Naa, he doesn't even like going camping with a tent." Snickers rippled over the group.

"We could bring in food or something. If all of Prairie got together we could do a lot."

Ms. Wainwright nodded her approval.

"What if we had a coat and blanket drive?" The suggestion came from right behind Trish. Good old Doug.

"We could hand them out ourselves so we would know who got them."

"Call it 'B and C'—you know, like Blanket and Coat. If everyone in the school brought just one, we'd have . . ."

Trish heard a buzz going on—"How many kids go here?" "Would everyone bring something?" "Who cares?"

She and Rhonda grinned at each other. "This could be fun," Trish whispered. Just then the bell rang.

"To be continued tomorrow. Please come with ideas to contribute to make this work." Ms. Wainwright got to her feet. "Class dismissed. Trish, can I see you for a moment?"

Trish waited beside the teacher's desk while the woman fumbled through a stack of papers.

"Here's your test. Good job, and I'm sure glad you're back safe and sound."

"Thanks." Trish looked at her grade. A bright red *A* decorated the top of the paper. "Thank you."

"Don't thank me. You earned it."

Trish had a hard time keeping her feet on the floor. It looked as if she might have between a *B* and an *A* average in spite of being gone. Now to just get ready for finals.

By Friday afternoon the entire school was buzzing about the new project of fifth-period American government. The B&C drive was underway with students painting signs, calling social agencies to see if their contributions were needed, and printing handouts to get the community involved.

Rhonda stayed overnight at Trish's that Friday since she didn't have a jumping event until Sunday. After devouring two large, thick-crust supreme pizzas with the help of Brad, Marge, and Patrick, the two girls lay across Trish's bed.

"I think I'm going to explode," Rhonda groaned.

"I was fine until we made hot fudge sundaes. Somehow pepperoni and hot fudge don't mix too well." Trish propped one hand under the side of her face. "We're supposed to like, you know, study?"

Rhonda groaned again—louder.

Trish reached down and snagged Rhonda's blue book bag off the floor. "Here." She dumped it on Rhonda's stomach. "Go to it. I have to work on my term paper." The rustle of papers and the scratch of pencils were the only sounds for a while, except for the occasional groan.

"I've had it." Rhonda stuffed her notebook back in her bag an hour and a half later. "You want something to drink?" Trish shook her head. "Care if I get one?" Trish shook her head again. She nibbled on the end of her pencil, trying to think of just the right word.

When Rhonda ambled back, Diet Coke in hand, Trish looked up from her scribblings. "Where's mine?"

Rhonda stopped in midstride and gave her a you-gotta-be-kidding look. "You said you didn't want one."

Trish flipped her pencil at her friend. "You know me better than that. Would I ever turn down a Diet Coke?" Rhonda started to hand her the can. Trish pushed herself to her feet. "No, I wouldn't want to deprive my best friend of the drink she's been dying for. I'll get my own." In the best tradition of old-time actress Sarah Bernhardt, Trish laid the back of her hand to her forehead and limped out of the room.

The pillow Rhonda threw just missed Trish's back.

In bed a bit later, the room dark except for the reflection of the mercury yard light, the two lay talking.

"I have a question, O mighty man killer." Trish turned on her side so she could look over the edge of the bed at her friend lying on the blow-up mattress on the floor.

"What?"

"Can you—I—be in love with two guys at the same time?"

"What makes you think you're in love?"

"Okay, in 'like,' then?"

"Of course, you nut. That's what we're supposed to be doing now—liking all kinds of different guys, trying new things."

"But at the same time? I mean I like Red, I *really* like him. When I'm with him, I think there's nobody else. But when I'm home again and he's off on another continent . . ."

"So?"

"I felt sorta the same way the other night with Doug." Trish mumbled the words in a rush.

"Told ya he likes you."

"But does that make me a—a cheater or something?"

"I don't think so. It's not like you're going with Red or anything."

Trish flopped over on her back. "Life sure is complicated."

But it didn't feel complicated the next afternoon when she rode Diego's five-year-old into the winner's circle of the McLoughlin one-mile stakes race. Handshakes, cameras flashing, reporters asking questions—she felt fantastic. Curt Donovan gave her a thumbs-up sign and tapped his notebook.

"After the program?"

She nodded and turned to sign an extended program. Halfway to the jockey room, she heard her name being called again. When she looked past the program offered her, her gaze traveled up a leather-jacketed arm, to broad shoulders, a square jaw, and those to-die-for fudge eyes. The smile that stretched those perfectly sculpted male lips made her grin back.

"Congratulations. That was some race." Taylor Winthrop spoke in a way that made it seem as if they were the only people around, in spite of the hundreds of spectators passing by.

"Thanks. Good to see you again." Trish finished signing her name and handed the program back. Her hand touched his in the transfer. Whoa, another tingle. She snatched it back as if she'd been burned.

"I hope you mean that." His voice felt as warm as his eyes looked.

"I—ah, gotta get ready for the next race. Bye." She refused to let herself look over her shoulder to see if he was still there. Her back, however, felt branded by his gaze.

"Who was that?" Genie Stokes waited for her on the other side of the gate. "What a—there aren't words good enough to describe him."

"I know. Name's Taylor Winthrop. A student at University of Portland. Says he loves racing."

"Well, I'll sign his program any time." Genie held the door to the women's jockey room open for Trish. "He sure had the eyes for you."

"Just 'cause I won, that's all." Trish dumped her helmet on the bench and pulled off the rubber bands that kept the sleeves on her silks the right length and too snug for drafts to creep up her arms. "You up in this last one?"

Just before Trish leaped to the ground in the winner's circle again, she caught a glimpse of fudge eyes, a sexy smile, and a waving hand. She waved back and concentrated on the festivities. When she walked off afterward, talking with Curt Donovan, Taylor was nowhere in sight.

Was she glad or disappointed? Trish didn't take time to puzzle it out.

What with morning works, church, riding twice in the afternoon, and trying to study, Trish found herself with her head on her desk by nine o'clock. A glance at the clock informed her, if her neck hadn't already, that she'd been sleeping for half an hour. With eyes half closed she undressed and hit the bed. Remembering the touch of Taylor's hand made her smile. Could she like three guys? *Rhonda'll have a cow.*

Tuesday after school, she returned to the teen grief group at the Methodist church. She'd attended off and on before her trip to Kentucky to get help with all the feelings caused by her father's death.

The welcome she received made her more than glad she'd taken the time. By the questions they asked, she knew the group had kept up on what was happening to her.

"Okay, let's get started." The advisor waved everyone to the chairs formed in a slipshod circle. When all were seated, she smiled at each person—a warm, welcoming smile that made Trish feel as if she hadn't really been gone at all. "Trish, how would you like to start?"

"Things have been pretty good—about thinking of my dad, I mean. Sometimes it's like, if I turn my head real quick, I'll see him standing there, smiling at me." She could feel the burning start behind her eyes. "But he's never there." She paused. And sighed. "I guess, I'm kinda thinking about Thanksgiving—and then Christmas." Again a pause.

The advisor handed Trish a tissue. "The first holidays are the hardest. But you get through. Each day is still only twenty-four hours long."

"Yeah, but you can cry an awful lot of tears in twenty-four hours." A member across the circle leaned forward. "It's been two years since my mother died, and still I cry sometimes."

"It helps if you do something totally different than what you used to do," someone else added.

"Yeah, like don't try to keep everything the same as before—'cause it ain't." A younger boy with owly glasses tried to smile at her, but his mouth quivered.

Trish could feel her chin wobble. "Like what?"

After they tossed out a list of suggestions, she wiped her eyes again. "Thanks. I'll let you know how it goes."

"Being here every week will help, and you have my number if you feel like calling." The advisor nodded to the girl next to Trish. "Melissa, how're you doing?"

Trish left with ideas climbing on top of each other to be first. She and her mother were due for a long talk.

Trish approached Ms. Wainwright before class the next day. "You have a few minutes to talk after school?"

"Sure. See you then."

Trish dragged herself out of weight-training class. This was the first time she'd tried arm weights since the accident. Now she hurt—everywhere.

"How come it's so easy to get out of shape and so hard to get back in?" She leaned her forehead against the cool of the metal locker door.

"Like it's not fair, I know." Rhonda dug through her stack of books. "Jason's taking me home, okay?"

Trish nodded. "See you in the morning."

Her face still felt flushed by the time she took a chair in front of Ms. Wainwright's desk. "I have something I'd like to add to the B&C project." She caught her bottom lip between her teeth. "If you don't mind and won't tell anyone where it came from."

Ms. Wainwright stuck her hands in the pockets of her denim skirt and leaned against the back of her chair. "What's up?"

"I was thinking—and I checked with my mother first—what if we cook and serve Thanksgiving dinner for the homeless?"

"We?"

"All of us. Mom and I—we'd like to buy the turkeys and fixings—then if all of us cooked—at a church or something over in Portland—and served it. We could give away the blankets and coats at the same time." Trish leaned forward, her elbows on her desk top. "What do you think? Would it work?"

"I don't see why not. We'll have to ask the class."

"But I don't want anyone to know we bought the groceries."

"No problem. I'll just say it's been donated." Mrs. Wainwright tipped her pencil from one end to the other. "You sure this is what you'd like to do?"

"Uh-huh. I—we need to do something different this year at our house, and maybe this way we could do some good for a lot of people."

"No maybe about it, Trish. This is a fine idea. I'll bring it up tomorrow and we'll go from there."

The next afternoon the government class voted their overwhelming approval. Rhonda gave Trish a questioning look and then an I-know-what-you're-doing grin.

"That means all of you have to check with your parents to see if you can help. If your folks would like to join us, they could do that too. We won't just cook and serve, we'll celebrate Thanksgiving with a huge family." The teacher posted a clipboard on the cork wallboard. "Here's the sign-up sheet. If we don't get enough from this class, we'll open it up to the rest of the school."

Trish tried to act like she always did, but still Doug and Rhonda grabbed her arms after class and marched her to a quiet corner.

"All right, when do we go shopping?" Rhonda's grin made the Cheshire cat look like a failure in the smiling department.

"You mean . . ." Doug looked from Rhonda's grin to Trish's shrug. "Awesome. We can use my truck to haul stuff."

"Don't tell anyone, please?" Trish looked from one to the other. She checked her watch. "We're going to be late." The three charged off to their separate classes.

But that night at home, things weren't quite so smooth. David called, and as ordered, Trish didn't pick up the phone until she heard his voice on the recorder.

"What took you so long?" David sounded pushed.

"Um . . ." Trish knew she'd better tell the truth. "Officer Parks said not to answer until we knew who was calling."

"You mean that . . ." David used a name that made Trish glad her mother wasn't on the other line yet.

"Jerk?" Trish added with a smile.

"Whatever. He's called again?"

"Yep. And sent the most gorgeous roses. At least he has good taste."

"Trish, this isn't a joke."

"Yeah, but—"

"And you guys didn't tell me what was going on. I thought maybe it was all over."

Marge had picked up the phone. "If we were more concerned, we would have told you."

Trish held the phone away from her ear while David went off on a tirade. When he calmed down again, she rejoined the conversation. "I got other news for you," she said after catching him up on what happened at the track. "We're donating the food to serve the homeless for Thanksgiving. Isn't that super?"

"We're *what*?"

She could tell by the tone of his voice that David didn't think the idea was super at all.

Chapter

10

So he's not coming home for Thanksgiving?"

"I was just as shocked as you. Maybe we should have asked him before we talked with Ms. Wainwright." Marge curled her feet up under her on the sofa. "I just never dreamed he wouldn't be as excited as we are."

"I think—no, I *know* Dad would think this is a great idea." Trish snuggled back in her father's recliner.

"Yep, that's one of the hard things for me. All those years we gave what we could when we didn't have much, and now that we have plenty of money, he's not here to enjoy giving it away." Marge leaned her head back on the cushions. "I'm not looking forward to the holidays at all. Every time I think of mailing Christmas cards or putting up the tree, I see a big hole where your dad should be." She reached over and snagged a tissue out of the box by her rocking chair.

Trish huddled deeper into the recliner. Her mother's thoughts matched her own. "At least Thanksgiving will be fun. Even if David bugged out." Her words sounded brave, but inside, she could feel the yawning chasm. Would their family never be whole again?

When she woke up the next morning, an idea flashed into her mind.

Trish threw back the covers and leaped from the bed. "Mom!" She charged down the hall, nearly crashing into her mother.

"What's wrong?"

"Nothing. I just had a great idea."

"Yeah, well, you scared me half to death."

Trish couldn't stop jumping up and down. "Mom, listen. What if we go to visit Gram and Gramps for Christmas? That would sure be different—Christmas in Florida. We've never been there for Christmas. What do you think?" Her words tripped over each other and came out with a whoosh.

"But who would take care of everything here?"

"Patrick and Brad. We could hire more help if they need it. We wouldn't have to be gone long, a couple of days. Beaches, warm sun, and if Gram doesn't want to cook, we'll buy dinner. You think David will like the idea?"

"We'd better check with him before I call Mother." Marge gave Trish a hug. "I think you came up with a winner this time, Tee."

Within two days, all the arrangements were made, with David agreeing it was a great idea. Marge's parents were totally floored but thrilled.

Trish went into finals week feeling as if someone had turned her treadmill up to racing speed when she wasn't looking. On Friday night she and Doug went out for pizza to celebrate with Rhonda and Jason.

"I have something else to cheer about." Trish held up her tall glass of Diet Coke. "The Jerk hasn't called or anything since he sent the roses. Maybe he fell off the face of the earth or something." They all clanked their glasses together.

Or maybe God is answering your prayers for him, her nagger whispered in her ear. He sure liked to say "I told you so." Trish ignored the voice and teased Jason about the basketball team. The Prairie High boys' team had never gone to the state tournament, while the girls had gone nearly every year.

"This season will be different," Jason promised. "You wait and see. With Doug guarding and me at center, we will show them all." The two guys slapped high fives. "After all, that is why I come to your school, to win at basketball."

"And here I thought you came to meet me." Rhonda pulled a sad face.

"That is how you say 'the frosting on the cookie.' " He reached over and draped a long arm across her shoulders.

"On the cake." Trish sucked on her straw.

"What?" Jason looked around. "Do they serve cake here?"

"No, Wollensvaldt. You messed up the saying again. It's 'frosting on the cake,' not a cookie." Rhonda shook her head, her red hair flying and her grin making them all laugh.

"Oh. I will learn." He wagged a long, bony finger at all of them. "But you watch. Prairie will go to state."

How will I find time to go to the games? Trish thought, stirring her drink with her straw. *Doug's already talking about me being there, like it's important to him. Men sure can complicate your life.*

She thought of that again on Saturday when Rob Garcia, one of the apprentice jockeys, cut her off in the third race, nearly causing an accident.

"Dumb punk kid," she muttered to Genie Stokes when they walked back to the jockey room, neither one of them making it into the money.

"Trish, he's older than you are," Genie leaned close to say, "and been racing longer. He just wants out of apprenticeship so bad he'll do anything to win."

"Well, it didn't do him any good. He got called for recklessness. I'd hate to be near him with my car if he drives like he rides." Trish dumped her stuff on top of her bag. "I think I'll let Dr. Dan over there work on my back. I have two races to sit out." She left Genie and crossed the room to where the resident chiropractor was working over one of the other jockeys on his table.

"Sure, give me fifteen minutes," the gray-haired man replied. "Why don't you go take a hot shower to soften those muscles while you wait."

Trish did as he suggested and let the water wash away her resentment of the offending jockey.

By the time Dr. Dan was finished with her, she felt both relaxed and recharged.

She met Brad and Patrick in the spoke-wheel-shaped saddling paddock. Crowds lined the railings to watch the preparations. Gatesby wasn't happy. His laid-back ears when Trish entered the stall said it all.

"What's the matter with him?" Trish stayed out of nip range.

"Got up on the wrong side of the stall, I think." Brad held the gelding's head while Patrick adjusted the throat strap.

"Glad you've got him and not me," Genie said from the stall next to them.

"Thanks." Trish took a solid hold on the bit shank and rubbed Gatesby up around the ears and down his cheek. "You ready to run, you silly horse?" Instead of pricking his ears forward as he usually did when Trish talked to him, Gatesby laid them back again.

"I been thinkin' mayhap I should scratch him." Patrick checked the girth and the wide white band that went over the saddle.

"It's up to you," Trish said, all the while her hands keeping up their soothing rhythm.

"Riders up." The call crackled over the sound system.

"Just watch 'im, lass." Patrick tossed her into the saddle. "And watch out for Garcia. He's riding again in this one." He smoothed a hand down the gelding's shoulder. "Don't be afraid to use the whip on Gatesby here. You got to keep his attention."

Brad and Patrick both walked her out to the pony riders, one on each side of the fractious gelding. "Watch 'im." Patrick cautioned the young woman riding a palomino. The bugle called the field of eight out onto the track, gray in the drizzle and fog.

"Have a good one, Trish," a voice called from the sidelines.

Trish looked up in time to catch a flashing smile from Taylor Winthrop. She waved back. She hadn't seen him lately. Would he ask her to go for drinks again? Would she go?

Gatesby snorted and crow-hopped, reminding her to pay attention to one thing—him.

"Watch out for him," one of the handlers reminded the others at the starting gate. "He bit me bad last time." It took three tries to get Gatesby into the starting gate. Finally two handlers got behind him and literally pushed him in.

Trish could feel the heat rising up her neck. Today even a blush felt good. "You—you—" Trish couldn't think of a name bad enough to call the horse without cussing him out. Instead, she switched from scolding him to soothing him with the singsong croon that usually worked.

Gatesby stamped his feet and switched his tail. With the gates all shut, Trish settled in for the start. Finally, Gatesby's ears pricked forward. She could feel him settle on his haunches.

The gun! The clang of the gates and they were off.

Gatesby decided he wanted the lead. He drove past the other horses as if they were still in the starting gates. With a three-length lead coming out of the first turn, Trish tightened her reins. But it was like trying to stop a freight train with a leash.

Down the backstretch and into the turn. She checked over her shoulder to see the field a furlong behind. Down the stretch she let him go. Gatesby was still picking up speed when he crossed the wire.

It was into the turn again before Gatesby paid much attention. "Fella, you can get up on the wrong side of the bed any race day if this is what you can run like. Wait till Anderson hears about this. Sure sorry he's away on a business trip."

"Just went along for the ride, didja?" Patrick's blue eyes twinkled up at her.

"And to think you almost scratched him." Trish stroked Gatesby's arched neck. "He coulda gone for another quarter or maybe a half mile. And I felt like using the whip was getting him in the gate. What a brat!"

Taylor was waiting for her. "Good race."

"Thanks." Trish signed a program for a man next to Taylor.

"You feel like a cup of hot chocolate?"

"I wish. I'm up in the next two. Sorry. Maybe another time?"

"You're on."

Now why did I say that? Trish shook her head. *Do I really want to get to know him? Do I need another man in my life?* She shook her head again. "Men!"

But Taylor wasn't around when she finally exited the jockey room after the last race of the day. Trish wasn't sure if she was happy or sad. Actually, all she wanted was home and a long hot bath.

Thanksgiving Day turned out to be all that Trish could hope for and more. They fed over three hundred people and sent leftovers home with their guests. The students handed out 398 coats and 602 blankets, besides another fifty-some sleeping bags.

"I've never seen so many turkeys in my life." Marge joined Trish with her friends all crashed at one of the tables.

"If I never peel a potato again it will be far too soon." Rhonda studied the bandage on one finger. "Do you realize that ten of us peeled potatoes for three hours?"

"Be glad you weren't carving the birds." Doug was stretched out flat on one of the benches. "And I thought hoisting hay bales was hard work." He laid a hand across his forehead. "Someone want to carry me out to the truck?"

"So much for big, strong basketball players." Rhonda pointed at Jason, sacked out on another bench. "What a bunch of wimps." She got to her feet and took only two steps before flinching. "Let's go home before I crash too."

Christmas bore down on them like a runaway team. Finding presents for the men in Trish's life wasn't easy. All David really wanted were more shorts and T-shirts. One did *not* find shorts, tanks, and tees in Vancouver or Portland in December, so she gave him a gift certificate. She finally decided on a coffee-table book on the history of Thoroughbred horse racing for Red. The pictures were stunning, so Trish bought one for Patrick, then went back for another for her and her mom. She wanted one on their coffee table too.

It took two shopping trips before she found the perfect sweater for Doug. Since they weren't really going together—only all the kids at Prairie thought so—she debated on buying him a gift at all, but then he *was* one of her good friends. Rhonda bought a similar one for Jason.

Trish and Marge spent one evening buying gifts for the family they'd adopted off the Christmas tree at church. With seven kids and the father out of work, this family was hurting badly. After buying the groceries on the list, they included another ham and a fifty-dollar gift certificate for the grocery store. Trish made stockings for each of the kids and tucked a twenty-dollar bill in the toe of each furry red gift.

When they dropped their stack off at church, the entryway was nearly full of gifts. The youth group had volunteered to deliver all the presents on Saturday.

"Wish I could help." Trish stood beside Pastor Ron, their youth minister.

"I think you already did your share." He looked over his shoulder at the monstrous pile in the corner. "Did you leave anything at the toy store?"

Trish grinned up at him. "A little. But it sure was fun. Now I know how parents must feel when they're buying dolls and stuff for their kids."

"I hate to ask this, but we have one family that wasn't adopted."

"No sweat." Trish took the slip of paper from him. "We'll take care of it." She glanced down at the paper. What did you buy for a grandfather in a wheelchair? The two grandkids he was raising would be easy.

By the time she'd finished her shopping and wrapping, Trish could hardly get into her room. Since they'd decided on no tree, she mounded the presents all up in front of the living room window. They called the UPS truck to pick up all the ones to be shipped, including those to Florida. By the time the truck left, the mound had sunk to manageable proportions.

Even though they were leaving on Sunday, Trish agreed to ride in three races on Saturday. The cold, windy day made her question her better judgment. After the second race, Taylor waved to her, greeting her like a long-lost friend.

"Hey, Trish, I've missed you." His smile lit up like the sun parting the clouds.

"Thanks." Why could she never think of anything brilliant to say to this guy?

"Since it's almost Christmas, how about joining me for a hot chocolate after you're finished? The fifth's your last, right?"

Trish nodded. "All right. Meet you here after I change clothes." His smile warmed her clear to her frozen toes. Whyever had she waited so long to take him up on the invitation?

Winning three races that day made her float six inches above the ground anyway. And the look of envy Genie gave her made her giggle. She *was* meeting about the best-looking guy she'd ever seen.

She was still floating when she got home. Taylor was nice, she'd finally gotten over her lazy tongue, and he hadn't pressured her for a date . . . even though she could tell he wanted to.

"He's kind of old for you, isn't he?" her mother asked that evening.

"He's twenty-one. It isn't like I'm planning on marrying him or anything." Trish grinned at her mother. "I just had a cup of hot chocolate with him. No big deal."

Christmas carols on the stereo and a crackling fire filled the silence of the pine-scented room. *Will I go out with him if he asks? He won't ask. Sure he will. He had that look in his eye. Speaking of eyes, his are gorgeous!*

Trish sighed. "Mom, did you ever like more than one guy at a time?"

"Sure." Marge looked up from her knitting. "Lots of times."

"Was Dad one of them?"

"Nope. When I met him I knew it was the real thing and I never looked at another man again."

"How did you know?"

"When you meet the right man, there'll be no question in your mind." Marge laid her knitting in her lap. "Trust me, you'll know."

Trish sat back into the peace of the room with peace in her heart. She started counting the things she could be thankful for. Her mother—they'd come a long way. Friends—both guys and girls. Her horses—soon she'd see Spitfire. Miss Tee, a beautiful home, money to do what she wanted. Even her father feeling closer than usual. She closed her eyes. And The Jerk hadn't been heard from in weeks.

The next day she came home to two dozen roses—one dozen red and the other white. The card said, "Did you think I'd forgotten you? Merry Christmas."

So much for being thankful about not hearing from him. She tossed his card into the fire. As she'd said before, he had good taste. But who was he? While she tried to joke about it, a little worm of fear dug into her mind and stayed there.

Chapter
11

And you didn't call the police?"

Trish held the phone away from her ear so David's yell didn't break her eardrum. "Well, I did eventually. Listen, big brother, I will not . . . cannot—whatever—keep getting scared every time I get something from him. I called Parks and they did the usual and still nothing. At least I love roses. I don't care who sends them to me." She winced at his groan.

"We're not being careless, son." Marge's voice held all the calm of the ages. "But I guess you get immune after a while."

"And careless." David refused to back down.

Trish flinched again. That's exactly what Parks and Amy had said. "So, we'll see you tomorrow?"

"No, on Tuesday, late."

Trish wound the cord around her finger. "I thought you got done early."

"I do, but one of the professors wants me to help finish this research project. I can't turn down an opportunity like that."

"Congratulations. You must be pleased to be asked," Marge said.

Trish wished she could have said that, but all she could think of was how much longer till they were all together.

"I was already working with him, we just thought this phase would be finished sooner."

When they hung up, Trish pasted a smile on her face and joined her mother back in the living room. She was happy for David—really she was.

"So, how'd it go?" Rhonda and Trish were sitting cross-legged in the middle of Trish's bed, knees touching, with a big bowl of popcorn in the middle. It was the night after Trish had returned from Florida.

"Super. But let me tell you, even with a tree and presents, Christmas doesn't seem like Christmas in eighty-five-degree sunny weather." Trish pulled down the neck of her T-shirt. "See, I even got a tan line." She dug out a handful of buttery corn and nibbled one piece at a time. "You'da thought our coming gave Gram and Gramps the best present ever, but their condo is so small, I wouldn't want to live there." She scrunched her eyes in thought. "Except for the pool and beaches—maybe it's worth it."

"Did you go snorkeling?"

"Yeah, but the water right there isn't real clear. We needed to drive down to the Keys for good water." She tipped her head to one side. "Or at least that's what they told us. I coulda stayed in the water all day. I loved snorkeling. The fish, the light—you'd love it. It's a whole new world."

By the time they'd caught up on all their news, the numbers on the clock clicked over to one. Trish groaned. "And I told Patrick I'd ride in the morning. What an idiot."

"Do you have any mounts in the afternoon?"

"Of course. Four of them. Wouldn't it be awesome to win a hundred percent like I did before I left? Three up and three in the winner's circle. I liked that."

"Maybe tomorrow night the Four Musketeers can go out for pizza." Rhonda's voice kind of floated, as if she were nearly asleep.

"Sure."

"Maybe you'll see ole hot-fudge eyes." A wisp of a giggle said Rhonda still inhabited the land of the awake.

Answering took too much effort.

The remainder of Christmas vacation flew by at breakneck speed. Trish both won and lost at the track; Taylor never showed. She figured he must have gone home for Christmas. The four musketeers, together with Doug and Jason, attended the New Year's Eve lock-in for the teens at church. Having been up all night, Trish slept most of the next day. Football had never been her thing, though Brad and David could be heard hollering in front of the television.

When Trish finally wandered out of her room, she found her mother with her head in the closet and stuff flying out.

"What are you doing?"

"Cleaning closets. What does it look like?" A pair of half-worn shoes landed in the box marked "Goodwill."

"David, you ever going to wear this again?" Marge held out a leather jacket.

"Nope, too small." The jacket hit the Goodwill box too.

"Mom, is this some New Year's resolution or something?" Trish caught a tube of tennis balls. They hadn't played tennis in years, so the balls were flat. Another addition to the box.

Marge wiped her hair off her forehead with a sweep of her forearm. "No. I decided I had to do something really busy or today would drive me nuts, so . . ." She waved her arm at the accumulation. "A woman in my group said this helped her, so I thought I'd try it." At the question on Trish's face, Marge nodded. "And yes, it has. I cleaned out some boxes of your father's clothes that were still in the closet. Somebody should be using his things." Marge picked up one box and put it back on the shelf. "And when I'm all done with this, I'm going to fill the bathtub and soak while I cry it all out." She handed Trish another box. "Put that one in the hall, please."

Marge scooped up a mound and stuffed it into the washing machine. "So if you kids want dinner, you either make whatever you want or order pizza." She nudged another mound with her foot. "David, you need to come sort this."

"Brad and I were just going down to do chores."

"Fine, this will take only a minute."

Trish and David swapped looks of pure astonishment. Was *this* their real mother or had some alien taken over her body during the night?

Trish joined the guys on their way down to the barn, after David had finished sorting. That seemed the safest of all her options. She had to admit, this New Year's Day was different than any other.

Having David with them at the track the next day made Trish feel as if old times hadn't disappeared forever. But when she pulled only one win out of four mounts, she accused him of jinxing her.

"Sure, blame it all on me." David tugged on her braid. "Was it my fault you let them box you in like that? And when that nag stumbled coming out of the gate—I tripped him? Come on, Tee, you can do better than that."

She did; she punched him in the shoulder. David grabbed her and rubbed the top of her head with his knuckles.

Trish wrapped both her arms around his waist and laid her cheek on his chest. "I've missed you so much."

David propped his chin on the top of her head. "Hey, it's only six months till your graduation. I'll be home again before the middle of May—that is, if I don't go work for Adam Finley."

Trish jerked free and studied his face. "You're kidding—right?"

"Margaret Finley bakes mighty good pies."

"Mom's cinnamon rolls are better."

"You better come home and chase away all the guys who are after her." Brad kept step with them on their way to the parking lot.

"Brad Williams, you—you." Trish gave him a dig in the ribs with her elbow. The three of them locked arms and marched out the gate. "Why? Who else likes me?" Trish stopped in the act of stepping up into the truck. Brad gave her a boost and climbed in beside her.

"That's for me to know and you to find out."

She elbowed him again. "Rat." She watched the smug look on his face. Was there *really* someone else who had a crush on her?

Trish had barely settled back into the school-track-study routine when Donald Shipson called to say he felt Firefly was ready to be shipped home.

"Unless you just want to leave her here and see if she is ready for breeding later in the season."

"You think she'll be well enough?" Marge, Trish, and Patrick were all on the line.

"I'd rather wait, give her a year. Let her get strong and grow some more." Patrick gave his opinion.

"Is she limping still?" Trish had a hard time getting the picture of Firefly in a cast out of her mind.

"Somewhat. Actually, yes. She could stay here that long, you know."

"Thanks, Donald, but all things given, maybe we should ship her back here. She may never do for a broodmare; we all know that."

Trish felt her heart hit the bottom of her belly. Please let her mother be worrying for nothing. Surely the filly would recover enough. She had the fight to get well, but everyone even doubted that. "Would another surgery help?"

"I've thought of that too. How about if we have her X-rayed again and then make a decision based on what Doctor Grant says?"

The three on the Runnin' On Farm line agreed.

"Okay, then. I'll make the arrangements and let you know."

When they hung up, Trish meandered into the living room. "Sure wish she could run again. First Spitfire and now Firefly. We lost our two best entries this year."

"Hard to say you lost Spitfire, my dear. He ran himself right out of contention." Marge tapped her chin with the end of her pen. "But I know you miss them. One thing I've been trying to learn is to go ahead and grieve for the losses—that it's okay to feel sad for the things that go out of our lives."

"I know one thing that I won't feel sad about when it goes out of my life." Trish propped a hip on her mother's desk.

90

"The Jerk." They said it together and then slapped hands. As Trish left the room, she threw a grin over her shoulder. "You know what, Mom? You're pretty cool—for an old lady, that is." She ducked around the corner before the throw pillow could hit her.

Saturday at the track, Trish heard a familiar voice after her win in the first race of the day.

"That's the way to start the new year." Taylor leaned his elbows on the fence rail.

"Sure is. How ya doin'?" Trish realized she was happy to see his smiling face.

"Did you miss me?"

His question caught her by surprise. "Ah—umm." There went her brain, checking out again.

"I had to go home for Christmas." He leaned closer. "I have something I want to show you."

Trish waved to Genie, who was waving her toward the jockey room. "I have to go. See you later."

"I'll be waiting."

When he waited for her at the end of her last race, Trish knew she'd go up to the clubhouse where they could sit in comfortable chairs and get to know each other without all the noise around them.

"Let me go change," she said in a rush. "And then I need to talk to Curt Donovan also."

"Not bad." Curt checked his notes for the day. "Two wins, two places, and a show. Should have been three wins."

"I know. But he just didn't have any kick left there at the finish."

"And the other one did. But a nose-to-nose duel like that—the specta-tors loved it." Curt scratched his forehead with the end of his pen. "You heard any more from San Mateo?"

Trish shook her head. "I'll let you know if I do."

"*When*, Trish, when—not if. You gotta think positive." Curt tucked his notebook in his pocket. "You better get going. Lover boy awaits."

Trish could feel the heat dye her cheeks. "Curt! You—" But her brain couldn't find words fast enough.

"Hi." Taylor fell into step with her as soon as Curt trotted off to talk to someone else.

"Sorry I took so long."

"You hungry?"

"Starved. How'd you know?"

"I always was after a game. You want to eat first or can I show you my surprise?"

Trish ignored her rumbling stomach. Agreeing to see whatever it was that made him so excited was much more polite. "Your surprise." She had to jog to keep up with his long strides.

They headed out the front entrance and across the parking lot. Off on the horizon, a line of gold still reflected up on the gray clouds. The encroaching darkness set some of the parking-lot lights flickering on. At the far northwest corner, a black Corvette was parked across two parking spaces.

"Whoa, what a set of wheels!" Trish reached to smooth a hand down the gleaming hard top.

"No, don't touch it."

She jerked back as if she'd been stung by a bee. She looked up at the man grinning at her.

"You'll set off the alarm." Taylor punched in a code on the remote in his hand. "Now you can open the door."

When Trish did as he said, the aroma of new car and leather interior met her like a fine perfume. She sniffed and grinned back at him. Now that she was close enough, she could see the Corvette wasn't really black, but a deep Bing cherry hue. The leather interior matched.

"Want to go for a spin?" He saw her hesitation. "We could eat at Janzen Beach. I'd bring you right back."

Trish glanced at her watch. "I need to call my mom first. She thinks I'm at the track."

"No problema." He pointed to the cellular phone. "The car's a Christmas present from my folks, the phone from Grandpa. Get in. I'll show you how to use it." Taylor walked around the car to open the door for Trish.

When she sat down, the seat wrapped around her, inviting her to sit back and relax. The dashboard looked like the cockpit of a jet airliner. Tape deck, CD player, car phone, the works.

"Did it take you two weeks to learn how to work everything?" Trish snapped her seat belt after puzzling the contraption out. She inhaled. "They ought to bottle the smell of a new car. I love it."

When Taylor turned the ignition, the engine roared to life and settled into a lion-sized purr. "Call your mom. Just punch the numbers here and you'll have her."

Trish did as he showed her. "Maybe I'll put one of these in my car someday. Talk about handy." She waited through the message before Marge picked up the phone.

Trish explained what she was doing and waited for her mother to say "Fine," but instead Marge hesitated. "Trish, I've never met Taylor, and you know that's our agreement before you go out with someone."

"But we're not going out." Trish bit her lip. How embarrassing! Taylor could hear every word. "Once we eat, I'll be right home."

The doubt hovered in Marge's voice. "You be careful."

Trish agreed and hung up the phone. "Sorry. I didn't think before I agreed to come with you. How about if we just go to McDonald's?"

"We can't eat in the car." Taylor put the machine into gear and eased forward. "Knowing me, I'd spill my Coke and—"

"Would be a shame to mess up anything this pretty." She smoothed a hand down the side of the seat. "What a car."

"That's why I couldn't wait to show it to you. Now, maybe you'll go out with me sometime soon. I promise to come and meet your mother first."

By the time Taylor had run through the gears on the freeway on-ramp and eased into traffic, Trish was wondering if maybe she should trade in her LeBaron. There was something magical about a Corvette.

When she told Rhonda all about it on the phone later, she could hear her friend flop back on her bed.

"Ol' fudge eyes has a Corvette and wants to take you out—and you didn't say, 'Yes, yes, yes!'?"

"He *is* nice."

"Nice! Nice! You say he's nice? Compadre, you're missing something upstairs."

"Hey, remember, I like Red. . . ."

"And Doug. . . ."

"And I don't need another man in my life."

"You don't have to be in love with him to go out with him—and his Corvette."

"Rhonda, do you ever think of anything besides guys—and new cars?"

"Sure. But this is more fun. I been thinking about term papers and calculus equations and filling out scholarship forms. And I've been doing 'em—not just thinking about it. Some of us have to go to college next year."

Trish felt a twinge of guilt, but only for an instant. "Speaking of books, I better get busy. See you tomorrow in church." Trish hung up and ambled out to the kitchen to fill a plate for studying fodder. Sometimes she wished she could call Red, but the time difference, and never knowing where he was racing, kept her from it. She could write him a letter.

An hour later she stuffed the four folded sheets of paper into an envelope. She hadn't mentioned the Corvette—and Taylor. Should she have?

"I don't know." She addressed the envelope and propped it against the lamp base. Talking on the phone was certainly much easier.

But when the phone rang a bit later, she didn't run for it. Her mother would wait until the caller's voice came on the machine before picking it up. What a hassle that was. Trish kept on reading her literature book. They were due for a quiz any time, and she was behind.

"Trish, it's for you. Officer Parks."

Trish leaped from her bed. Maybe they had finally found out something about The Jerk.

Chapter

12

"So, Trish, I hear you're seeing someone new," Parks continued after the greetings.

"How'd you hear that?"

"Curt Donovan. He wondered if we'd checked into the background of Taylor Winthrop. Why didn't you mention this person?"

"But I only had a hot chocolate with him one time and dinner tonight. What's this 'Am I seeing him'? He wanted to show me his Christmas present, that's all."

"So what do you know about him?" Parks' voice sounded thoroughly entrenched in his official mode.

Trish took in a deep breath, willing herself to be patient. The man was only doing his job after all. "Taylor's a junior at the University of Portland, he's from southern Oregon someplace, he likes horse racing, is a frequent fan, and . . ." Trish couldn't think of anything else to say. Surely Parks didn't want to hear about deep brown laughing eyes, a dream of a Corvette, and a smile that could break a woman's heart.

"When did you first meet him?"

Trish scrunched her eyes shut to remember. "September, I guess. At

Portland Meadows. At first he just asked me to sign his program. Lots of people do that."

"Is he ever with a group of friends?"

"Not that I know of."

"Do you know where he lives?"

"On campus, I guess. I think he mentioned roommates. . . ." Trish tried to think back. Funny, but he didn't usually talk about himself. "Mostly we talk about the races, you know, like the horses and jockeys and what's going on."

After they hung up, Trish stayed by the phone, leaning on the counter and doodling on a piece of paper. She didn't like the thought that she didn't know more about Taylor. The next time she saw him, she was determined to remedy that situation.

If Trish thought she was on a treadmill before, by February, it was more like being caught in a hurricane. Only she couldn't seem to find the eye of it for a few days' respite. Her government class voted to buy new books for the library with the money from the Thoroughbred Association. She was on the committee to decide what the senior class should give the school for the annual senior present. Racing took up the weekends. Studying seemed to take more time, not less, as she'd hoped for her last semester.

True to Jason's predictions, the basketball team had only one loss so far and was being touted as a state contender. Basketball fever swept Prairie with both the girls' and the guys' teams doing so well. Trish hated to miss any game, let alone a home game.

Taylor kept asking Trish for a date, and she kept putting him off. He didn't discourage easily, that was for sure.

Nothing had happened lately with The Jerk either.

"I think he just gave up," Trish said one night when Rhonda was sleeping over.

"I sure hope so. You talked to Amy lately?" Rhonda lay on her stomach on Trish's bed, feet in the air, keeping time to the Amy Grant tape in the tape deck.

"As in Grant or Jones?" Trish ducked her friend's fake clobber and hugged her knees to her chest. "She says the file is officially closed for lack of evidence, but that in her mind there's more to come."

"That gives you confidence, right?"

"I don't care. Just so I don't hear from him ever again." She propped her chin on her knees. "You think I should go out with Taylor? He keeps asking and I keep putting him off."

"If you don't want to, just tell him no."

"But he's so nice, and I think he's lonesome. I gave him my phone number, so he calls once in a while."

"Invite him out so your mom can meet him, and if she likes him, we'll all go to a show or something." Rhonda pulled her gum to a long thread and then folded it back into her mouth.

"Yuck, don't do that." Trish pushed her toe against Rhonda's elbow. "*We* usually means you and Jason and Doug and me."

"You know what I meant. Maybe we should make it me and Brad. Jason would blab to Doug, and his feelings might get hurt."

"Good idea. But you know, Doug and I aren't like really going together or anything."

Rhonda gave her that have-you-lost-your-marbles look. "Right."

"Well, we almost never go out alone, so I only see him at school and when we're all together."

"And at the games."

"He's playing."

"Whatever."

Trish thought about their conversation the next afternoon while down at the barns checking on the mare that was due to foal. Did she want to go out with Taylor? Was she 'going with' Doug? How come she hadn't heard from Red for quite a while? How come her life was a whole series of questions? And none of them had easy answers?

When she offered Double Diamond a carrot piece, he nipped her hand. "Ouch! What'd you do that for?" The colt jumped back. "Men! You're nothing but trouble."

Miss Tee, in the adjoining stall, stretched her muzzle as far as possible, her silent nicker making her nostrils quiver. "Now see? She's getting sweeter every day, and you're a pain." Trish rubbed her hand on her pant leg. "That stung, you rotten horse." Miss Tee rubbed her white star against Trish's shoulder and sniffed her pockets for another treat. Gone was the stubby mane and baby fur. Miss Tee now stood at 14.2 hands and looked as gangly as any teenager. Her long winter coat showed the bright red that would sparkle in the spring, and her lighter mane laid smoothly to the right.

"You're a real beauty, you know that?" Trish stroked the filly's forelock. "You and me, we're going to be spending lots of time together, starting pretty soon. Mom's done a good job with your training, and now it's my turn."

Would Miss Tee have the speed and heart of Spitfire? She looked good according to Patrick. Trish knew she couldn't give an objective opinion, but she had high hopes for her namesake. She was foaled on Trish's sixteenth birthday and was the first Thoroughbred with Tricia Marie Evanston listed on the registration papers as the owner. Trish gave the filly a last pat. "Gotta run. You be good."

Trish jogged up the rise to the house. She'd invite Taylor out for a tour tomorrow afternoon, but mainly to meet her mother. If all went well, maybe they'd go out for pizza.

Trish left a message on Taylor's answering machine and hit her books. When he called back later, she cleared her throat. She wasn't used to inviting boys—men—to things. But he agreed to the invitation, sounding pleased.

She got a big thumbs-up signal from Rhonda the next afternoon after school. "Way to go, compadre. Call me when it's all over."

"You make it sound like I'm going to jump off a cliff or something."

"More like sky diving. See ya." Rhonda dashed up the steps to her house.

Chocolate-chip-cookie perfume beckoned Trish up the walk and through the door. "Smells heavenly." She followed her nose into the kitchen where Marge was just taking another pan from the oven. Trish took a still-warm cookie from the cooling rack. "You sure know how to impress a guy. I shoulda thought of this."

"You want me to tell him you baked them?" Marge raised one eyebrow.

"Nope, but thanks."

Trish had just checked the clock to make sure it was working when she heard Caesar announcing company. Trish leaned over the counter to peer out the window. Sure enough, a sleek, dark Corvette rumbled up the drive.

Should she open the door and meet him outside? Or wait and let him knock?

Caesar's welcome yippy bark stopped. The tone deepened to a dark woof along with a growl.

Trish jerked open the front door. The sable-colored collie stood at the front end of the Corvette, growling softly.

Taylor stood still, one hand filled with flowers and the other a square box. "Hey, Trish, call off your dog."

"Caesar! Come here! What's the matter, fella?" Calling to her dog, Trish leaped down the steps and hit the walk running.

Caesar looked at her over his shoulder but kept his place. He whimpered as Trish reached for his collar.

"I'm sorry, he's never done this before. He's usually very friendly." Trish grabbed the dog by the collar and led him back to the house. "Come on in. He must not like your car. Too fancy for an old farm dog," Trish laughed.

Caesar rumbled deep in his throat. He eased his way to the front of Trish and pushed against her knee with his shoulder, as if to shove her back.

"Easy, boy. Sit." Caesar did. "Now stay."

But that he didn't do. He kept his place right by her knee as the three of them walked up to the house. He growled again when they went in the door. And woofed one more time when the door closed.

"I can't believe him, Mom. Caesar's never done anything like that before."

"I know. Sorry for the greeting." Marge took the huge bouquet of daffodils that Taylor handed her. "Why, thank you, Taylor. It's a long time since anyone brought me flowers. And daffodils, my favorites. Makes me think spring is really coming again."

"My mom likes them too." He handed her the square box.

"Godiva chocolates! Oh my. You certainly have good taste." Marge set the box on the counter and rummaged in the cupboard for a vase.

Trish watched the two like a spectator at a performance. It didn't seem real somehow. None of her friends ever bought presents for a parent. But she had to admit her mother looked pleased.

"You want some chocolate chip cookies? Mom's been baking. And a Coke? Hot chocolate?"

"Or coffee?" Marge turned from filling the vase. "And thank you, Taylor, for the flowers and candy. We'll both enjoy them."

"Coffee, if you already have it made." He took the plate of cookies while Trish dug a Diet Coke out of the refrigerator. "If these taste as good as they smell, you have a friend for life."

"You want to see the home stock?" Trish asked after they'd demolished the plate of cookies.

"Sure. See where the great Spitfire grew up?" He pushed his chair back and picked up his mug. "Thanks for the goodies."

"Come back soon." Marge walked them to the door. "Trish, make sure you check on the mare. I think it's only a matter of hours."

"You want to go out for hamburgers or something—when you're done with chores, that is?" Taylor flashed her his heart-stopping smile as they neared the foaling barn. "I think I passed inspection."

"Yeah, I guess." She bit her lip. Was it that obvious?

A chorus of nickers greeted them as Trish whistled.

"They sure know who you are."

"They'd better. I'm the carrot lady as far as they're concerned." Trish went down the line, introducing Taylor to each of her friends. "The young stock are over in the big barn down from the foaling stall. Come on." She flicked on the overhead light when they entered the dim interior. Miss Tee and Double Diamond set up a nickering contest, but the mare didn't show her head. Trish walked swiftly to the double-sized foaling stall. The mare lay on her side, head flat against the straw. Two small hooves peeked out from beneath her tail and withdrew only to come out farther on the next contraction.

Trish laid her arms on the top of the half-door and her chin on her crossed hands. "You ever seen a foal born before?"

"No." Taylor's voice was as soft as hers.

"Well, it won't be long." Together they watched as a slick black bundle slid into the world and separated the sack that had kept it safe for eleven months. Trish opened the stall door and slipped inside. "Easy, girl, let me give you a hand." She picked up some clean straw from the corner and wiped the mucus out of the foal's nostrils. He snorted and raised his head, a perfect star visible on his forehead and a dot of white between his nostrils.

"Meet Spitfire's baby brother." Trish continued to clean the colt with the straw. "See that bucket by the wall? Would you hand it to me?" She kept her voice gentle, much like the song she used to calm her mounts in the starting gate.

"Here." Taylor handed the bucket across the gate.

Trish set the stainless steel bucket down beside her, took out some string, and tied off the foal's umbilical cord. Then with scissors that had been dipped in disinfectant, she snipped the cord. "There you go, little fella. You're on your own now."

The mare raised her head, curling her neck around to sniff the foal. With one last contraction, she expelled the afterbirth and heaved herself to her feet. Head down, she nuzzled the foal and began licking him.

Trish pushed herself back against the wall and glanced up at Taylor. He stood with his chin on his hands, never taking his eyes from the spectacle before him.

"I've never seen anything born before." His hushed voice would do honor to a cathedral.

"Something, isn't it?" Trish crossed her wrists on her bent knees. "Makes me almost cry every time. Sometimes we have trouble, but this old girl has been at it so long, she could write the script."

The foal pushed his spindly front legs out in front of him. His head bobbed, but still he tried to stand upright.

"He's a strong one, all right." Trish checked her watch. "Not even half an hour old and he's already trying to stand." The mare continued licking her baby, making snuffling noises. "She's telling him how wonderful he is and that he's going to be the fastest horse in the world."

"Sure. You understand horse talk too?"

"That's what my dad used to say. Every baby needs to hear he's the greatest, and who better to tell him than his mother?"

"I bet that would be good."

Trish looked up at him. "You mean you never heard that?"

"I doubt it. My mother didn't think talking to her kids was important. In fact, she didn't think taking care of them was either, so she split." The words dropped like rocks into a calm pool, sending waves to shatter the reflection and crash on the shore.

"I—I'm sorry."

"No big deal. I better get going. You need anything else?"

Trish shook her head. "No, I'll take care of her. See you." She got to her feet and watched him stride out of the barn, shoulders stiff but head bowed. *What was that all about?*

Chapter

13

"But why? Why won't you go out with me?"

"Taylor, I'm sorry. I just don't have time. Finals are next week and I wish I could even cancel racing for the weekend."

"But you're going to the state tournament, aren't you? I could drive you up there."

"I told you, there's a bunch of us going. We're going to share one motel room." Trish curled the cord around her finger. Right now she'd like to curl her fingers around his neck—and shake him. He just wouldn't quit.

"Look, Trish, if you don't want to go out with me, just say so. Don't make up excuses."

"All right. I don't want to go out with you." The phone clicked in her ear. "He hung up on me." She stared at the receiver as if it were to blame. "I don't believe it. He hung up on me." She dropped the receiver in the cradle and glared at it. "Of all the nerve."

When the phone rang later, Trish waited for the voice on the answering machine. As soon as she recognized Taylor's baritone, she turned to her mother. "Tell him I don't want to talk to him." At Marge's frown, Trish pleaded, "It wouldn't be a lie."

"Just don't answer. You can return the call later."

"Not on your life. *He* hung up on me." Trish headed for her bedroom and three more hours of studying—that is, *if* she got done fast. She ignored three more calls, each one sounding more contrite than the last.

The next day a bouquet of balloons, anchored by round jingle bells, waited for her just inside the front door. The card said, "Please forgive me. I didn't mean to be such an idiot. Please answer when I call." The balloons all bobbed when she socked the one that said "Sorry."

Trish picked up the phone when it rang a few minutes later. "Yes, you're forgiven," she said after the greetings. "And thanks for the balloons. You didn't have to do that."

"I know, but I don't want bad feelings between my friend and me. See you at the races."

Trish breathed a sigh of relief. Those hadn't been just excuses she'd given him. She felt like a piece of bubble gum blown to the max and about to burst any second.

Trish and Rhonda didn't stay overnight in the capital after all for the state basketball tournament. They drove up early in the morning, watched Prairie lose their first and therefore *only* game, and drove home that night.

"I didn't say we'd win state," Jason shrugged.

"I know, just that we'd go." Trish could tell both he and Doug were taking it hard. They'd had such high hopes. "But you drew the toughest team of all. What can you say?"

"See you tomorrow at Prairie," Doug grumbled.

In March the ads she and Red had made for Chrysler hit prime-time television. Trish sat studying on the living room couch when the phone rang.

"Trish, it's Rhonda," Marge called from the kitchen. "Really, right now?"

Trish could hear the change in her mother's voice.

"Tee, turn on the TV, quick!"

Trish did as she was told and stepped back. Red's smiling face greeted her, and then the camera zoomed out to show both of them standing behind the hoods of a black and a red LeBaron. Trish had seen the rushes at the end of the shooting, but somehow it was different standing in her own living room watching herself on TV. And not on a sportscast.

Marge joined her. "Looks pretty good to me."

"I guess."

The phone rang again—Doug this time. And again, Brad. Trish didn't get any more studying done that night. The calls came in back to back with some of her friends complaining they'd been dialing for hours, but her line was always busy.

When Curt Donovan finally got through, he accused her of leaving the phone off the hook.

"I did not, but right now that sounds like a pretty good idea. I have a paper due tomorrow and I'm not getting it done."

"So, when are you going to let me start on your biography?"

"Curt, that's a dumb idea. No one would buy a book about me."

"Trish, my love, one of the things I like about you is your humility. You *are* famous, whether you want to believe it nor not."

Trish let her snort give him her opinion.

"You watch—there's a movie in this yet, whether for TV or the big screen I don't know."

"Curt, are you taking crazy pills or something? Because this is crazy."

"I'm going to love saying 'I told you so.' Talk to you later."

Trish hung up the phone, shaking her head.

She got lots more phone calls, but only Taylor sent her flowers, this time red and white carnations in an arrangement with a balloon that said "Congratulations." When she called to thank him, he wasn't there.

The next night Red called from Florida, where he was racing at Hialeah. Trish felt the usual bump of excitement when she heard his voice.

"Hi, yourself," she said. "I sent you a card to your mother's house. You look mighty good on TV."

"Look who's talking. You stole the show. Bet every guy in America goes out to buy a LeBaron hoping you'll come with it."

"Red, that's crazy. One of my friends said she'd buy one if *you* came with it." She could feel her cheeks flaming. "So, how's the racing in Florida? Bet it beats freezing to death here."

"You could come on down."

"Maybe next year." They talked for half an hour, and by the end of the time, Marge was making pointed glances at her watch and the clock. Trish checked their new phone message service and sure enough, there were three calls. David was one of them.

"So, why didn't you call and tell me about my television star sister?" David sounded put out again.

Marge and Trish were both on the phone. "I left you a message," Marge answered. "Don't you ever check your machine?"

David muttered something about clobbering his roommate.

By the time they'd finished *that* conversation, Trish glared at her watch. Burning the midnight oil was getting to be a habit, one her eyes didn't think too much of.

"Anybody else calls, tell 'em I'm not home."

On Monday the prosecutor for the upcoming Kendall Highstreet trial called with the date. They were set to begin in two weeks if another postponement didn't happen.

Trish felt her stomach do a series of flip-flops. "Do I have to be one of the witnesses?"

"You're the one he's accused of shooting at. Attempted bodily harm with a deadly weapon makes this a stronger case than just extortion. We have five counts against him, and that's just on the criminal side. I'm sure there will be civil lawsuits also."

How am I gonna fit all this in? was the question dogging Trish's mind whenever she had a free moment to think—usually in the shower or driving her car.

"Look at this." Marge handed Trish the paper at breakfast the next morning. Pictures of both a man and a woman graced the middle of the page with the headline, "Developer's Wife Sues for Divorce." She was quoted as saying she didn't want any part of his criminal activities. She was taking their children somewhere safe, away from all the negative publicity.

Trish finished reading. "Serves him right."

"I thought you were praying for him."

"I am. Isn't praying for justice okay too?" Trish folded the newspaper and finished her toast. "I'll be home late. I have a committee meeting after school."

"Patrick's not feeling well. Brad may have to take care of things at the track, so that'll leave you and me here. Pray that he gets better or you'll have to be at the track in the morning."

"What's wrong?"

"I think that cold he's been nursing has gone into his chest. Sounds like he's coughing up his guts when he starts in."

"How come you didn't tell me earlier?" The thought of coughing flashed her back to the days when her father was so ill. Fear clenched her stomach and dried her throat. "He's going to be all right, isn't he?"

"He's not as young as he likes to think he is. That's why I've ordered him to bed."

By the time Patrick was on his feet again four days later, Trish felt as if her bubble had burst and she was the gum splattered all over a face. Stringy bits and pieces everywhere and no one gathering her back together. When her quarter finals were finished, she hit the sack and slept the clock around.

"How many mounts this afternoon?" Marge asked when Trish finally staggered out to the kitchen that Saturday morning.

Trish groaned and looked at the clock. "Only two and they're late in the program. Otherwise I'da set my alarm." She sank down on a chair and rested her head in her hands. "I'd give anything to just go back to bed."

"So call your agent and have him get someone else to ride."

"Because I'm tired?"

Marge raised a hand to stop Trish before she got going. "Just a thought. You haven't only been burning the candle at both ends, you've had a fire going in the middle." Marge took Trish's hot chocolate out of the microwave. "I think we'd better hire some more help."

"Well, when you do, hire them to do my homework."

Between races, when Taylor pushed her for a date, Trish just shook her head. "Not now. Maybe next weekend. A movie with Rhonda and Brad maybe?" She watched as he switched from pleading to pleased.

"Really?"

"We'll celebrate the end of the quarter and one more to go."

"So you finally gave in." Genie Stokes waited for her.

"Yep. He's nice and I like being with him, but I've just been too busy. This school year can't get over too soon for me."

"I was like that too."

"Some of the kids are already moaning about leaving dear old Prairie. Not me." Trish held open the door to the jockey room for Genie. "Graduation can't come soon enough, far as I'm concerned."

"So we're to be your bodyguards," Brad teased when Trish told him about their coming night out.

"You know how my mom feels about me dating an older man."

"I know, us college men are—"

Trish interrupted him with a sock on the shoulder. "Not the hot stuff you think you are." She stroked Gatesby's nose, all the while keeping the other hand on his halter. "If you don't behave, I'll sic my horse on you."

Brad rolled his eyes. "Can't do any worse than he did this morning. When am I gonna learn to watch him at *all* times?"

Trish looked at the horse, his eyes drooping in contentment at her scritching his favorite places. "Hard to believe this guy's the one you're referring to."

"Right." Brad rubbed his shoulder. "And I've got the green and purple marks to prove it."

Trish wasn't quite ready when she heard the Corvette in the driveway the next Friday night. But when Caesar's tone changed from welcome to cautious, Trish threw her lipstick on the bathroom counter and headed for the door.

"Caesar, you know he's a friend. Knock it off." When the dog didn't quit barking, Trish ordered, "Caesar, down! Quiet!"

"Guess he just doesn't like me." Taylor came around the front of the car while Caesar glued his haunches to Trish's foot.

"I don't understand it. Usually only his tongue and tail are the dangerous parts. He'll either lick you to pieces or beat you with his tail." She kept a hand on the dog's head. She could feel the tension quivering in the dog's body. *What's with him lately?*

"How about if we take my car? Your backseat is pretty small."

Taylor gave her a look of pure astonishment. "We can all fit if you girls ride in the back. Otherwise, we'll meet them there."

Trish rolled her eyes. This wasn't starting out well at all. "Fine." *Men!*

No wonder they called it the battle of the sexes. "Brad is over at Rhonda's. It's just up the road."

"Make sure you kick any mud off your feet before you get in back," Taylor ordered when they picked up the others.

Trish and Rhonda swapped "Oh, well" looks. They wouldn't dare mess up his fancy new car.

While Brad raved about the beauty, the sound, the smell, the power of the Corvette, Trish and Rhonda swapped scrunched-up looks and mouthed sarcastic words. Two people crunched in the backseat of a Corvette ranked right up near the top on a list of torture techniques. At least they weren't going far.

Their dinner arrived late and cold, and the movie had enough blood in it to restock the Red Cross. When it was time to climb back in the Corvette, Trish just prayed for the evening to get over.

"But the entire mess wasn't Taylor's fault," Rhonda said the next day on the phone. "Other than insisting we take his car—and you know how thrilled Brad was."

"Don't even mention cars. How can anyone be so picky about a bit of mud on the floor?"

"It's a guy thing, for sure," Rhonda giggled.

There's something else." Trish doodled on the pad beside her. "Caesar seems uneasy around him."

"So?"

"So, why? Caesar's usually so friendly. You know that."

"Probably it's just the car. Too fancy for your farm dog's taste."

"Rhonda, be serious."

"Are you going out with him again?"

"He wants me to. Asked again at the track today, but I don't have time, so there's no worry." Trish hung up the phone and stuck her head in the refrigerator. Where, oh where was a Diet Coke when she wanted it?

The Highstreet trial happened right on schedule. With all the media hoopla, Trish wondered if the trial was necessary. The man had already been tried, convicted, and hung by the press.

But the morning she was to be a witness for the prosecution, she dressed with care. Breakfast was beyond possibility since her resident troupe of stomach butterflies seemed bent on wearing themselves out before noon.

As soon as they entered the courtroom, Trish looked for the man who was accused of trying to shoot her down. All she remembered seeing was the barrel of a gun pointing at her. The man behind it had been huge, but other than that, she couldn't identify him.

At the table on the left, a man sat hunched over by his attorney. While Trish recognized him from pictures she'd seen in the paper, she could still hardly equate this beaten human being with the arrogant man she remembered.

When they called her name, Trish started to rise. Marge squeezed her daughter's hand. "You can do it, honey. I'll be praying for you."

All you need to do is tell the truth. Even her nagger was a comfort at this point.

And that's what Trish did. She told what she remembered and refused to be swayed by the attorney for the defense. When she stepped down, she again caught the gaze of the man on trial. Was he trying to say he was sorry? A flash of pity ripped through Trish's mind. *Please, God, care for him.*

Amazed at what had just happened to her, Trish pushed open the gate to return to her seat. Sitting in the back row—she looked again to be sure—it *was* Taylor. What in the world was he doing at the trial of a real estate developer?

But when she asked him that the next time they talked on the phone, he said he'd gone to watch her "do her stuff."

"Why?" Trish shook her head.

"Maybe I'll go into law. I thought this was a good chance to see our legal system in action—and you too." He chuckled. "You looked really good up there."

"Thanks, I think." Trish hung up the phone a bit later with something niggling at her.

With the Kentucky Derby only three weeks away, Trish caught herself remembering the year before. By this time they were worried if Spitfire would fly all right, if his leg could stand the strain. How she wished to have another horse to take to the Derby!

One sunny afternoon, she led the mare outside, her foal dancing beside her.

"He's just a doll." Marge stopped to chuckle when the shiny black colt leaped away from a shadow. "He's about the most curious baby I've ever seen."

"Dad would say that shows great intelligence. He's nothing if he's not gutsy." Trish led the pair through the open gate and unsnapped the lead strap. The mare immediately found a dirt patch and collapsed to the ground, rolling and scratching her back. The colt charged away, ran in a circle, and came back to watch what he obviously thought was crazy behavior.

"We need to name him, Mom." Trish propped her elbows on the fence behind her.

"I know. Nothing either Patrick or I've thought of seems to fit. We tried something with Seattle or Slew in it, but all those seem to be taken. Since he's Spitfire's full brother, I thought something along that line might work, but again nothing."

"Dad was usually the namer here." Trish sighed, wishing for about the millionth time that he were with them. "Did you ask David?"

"Uh-huh. No help."

"What about Hal's Angel?"

"For a colt? Sounds more like a filly." Marge rested her chin on her hands on the fence. "If you say it wrong, you get Hell's Angel. You want people to think he's a biker?"

"Well, they have a lot of speed."

"Right, of every kind. Hal's Angel. I don't know."

"I'd like to name him after Dad. Let's think about it."

The last day of racing at Portland Meadows dawned cloudy but turned clear and sunny. The fans came out in force, and with a list of six mounts, Trish felt as up as Gatesby. Only *she* didn't try to bite, or rather, nip everyone in sight.

John Anderson threatened to sell his gelding, even though Gatesby had won his last three times out, including today.

And when she won five of her six starts, Trish didn't think she'd come down for a month.

"Sure wish David had been here for this," she said to her mother when they stood in the winner's circle for Sarah's Pride, the claimer they had bought the year before. "And Dad."

"Oh, I think your father knows what's going on, and he's busting his buttons with pride." Marge shook hands with the presenter and they all smiled for the flash.

"You want to invite a bunch over to celebrate?"

Trish shook her head. "I just want to crash."

"Is *this* the Trish we all know and love?" Marge stepped back as if to make sure.

"Mother!"

"Well, don't wait up for me, then. Bob Diego and I are going out to dinner."

"You're what!" Trish nearly dropped her saddle.

"You heard me. He's invited me out for dinner to celebrate the end of the racing season here, and I accepted."

"Maybe I better invite Rhonda over. I'm not so sure I like the idea of my mother and Bob Diego."

"Trish, he's just a friend."

"Where have I heard those words before?" Trish tried to put a smile on her face. "Oh, yeah, they were mine."

On the way to school the next day, Rhonda was yakking on about Jason when she suddenly asked, "Has Doug invited you to the prom yet?"

"Well, he mentioned it but not really asked me. Why?"

" 'Cause I think you've got a problem."

Trish waited for the light to change. "Now what?" She turned to check out Rhonda's expression. Her friend wore that cat-and-canary look that meant something was cooking.

"Well, what if Taylor asks you and Doug asks you? Who will you go with?"

"I think I'll just stay home." Trish pulled into the Prairie High parking lot. "Besides, why would Taylor ask me?"

" 'Cause he said he would." Rhonda raised both her eyebrows and her shoulders. Her silly grin left Trish certain that Rhonda knew more than she was letting on.

Now what'll I do?

Chapter
14

True to Rhonda's prediction, both guys asked her to the prom.

"But what am I gonna do?" Trish wailed at her mother as soon as Marge could be found. She sat in her bedroom at Hal's desk, paying bills.

"What do you want to do?"

"Go see Spitfire?" Trish perched on the edge of the bed.

"Be serious." Marge leaned back in the swivel chair.

"Well, Doug and I've gone to school together since kindergarten. He knows everyone and so do I. While Taylor won't know anyone and half the girls will love me for making Doug ask someone else. But I hate to hurt Taylor's feelings."

"Would you rather hurt Doug?"

"No-o."

"Enough said."

"Sometimes growing up isn't all fun."

"You're right there, honey. Much of the time, it's downright difficult." Marge turned back to her bookwork.

"One more problem—what am I going to wear, and when do I have time to go shopping? Next Saturday is the Kentucky Derby. I fly back there on Wednesday, returning Sunday night. The next Saturday is the prom."

"First things first. We'll find time. We always do."

Trish left the room and headed for the kitchen. Much easier to deal with a mess of this magnitude on a full stomach. Finally, sandwich finished, she dialed Taylor's number. Maybe he wouldn't be there and she could just leave the message on his answering machine. She could hear her nagger making scolding noises. Not a good idea.

The answering machine clicked in.

Rats. She waited and asked him to call her back later in the evening after chores were finished. And Doug was at baseball practice. She'd tell him tomorrow.

When Taylor called back, Trish wished she were in another country. "So, you're going to let me take you to the prom, right?"

"Sorry, but Doug had already asked me. . . . Well he'd sorta mentioned it, so I . . ." She stuttered to a halt and took a deep breath. "But thanks for asking." Silence filled the receiver and echoed in her ear. "Taylor?"

"I'm here. This just takes some getting used to." His voice sounded brittle, harsh—not like the smooth, warm way he usually spoke. He paused. Like a mask falling into place, his normal voice took over. "I was really looking forward to seeing you all dressed up. You'll be so beautiful."

Trish felt shivers chase each other up and down her spine.

"Well, may the better man win," Taylor went on. "How about if I get to take you out to dinner the night before? You know, a loser's consolation?"

"Okay, but . . ."

"We'll go somewhere really nice and maybe dancing so I'll get to see you in evening clothes after all."

"But . . ." *Now I'm going to have to buy two dresses.* "I'll see you later, then. I gotta get to work here." When he hung up, she slumped to the floor. *What have I gotten myself into?*

"So what's buggin' you?" Rhonda asked a few minutes later when Trish called to tell what had happened. "Here you get to go to the prom with the dream of Prairie High and out to some fancy restaurant with the most gorgeous guy on the planet the night before." Rhonda groaned. "I should have such problems."

"Now I have to buy two dresses, and I don't have time to go shopping for one."

"Never fear, your friend is here. I'll go shopping and bring home some for you to try on. I know your taste better than you do."

"Shoes too?"

"And accessories. You want your diamond drops for the prom, madame?"

Trish chuckled at Rhonda's idea of what a maid would sound like. "Thanks, buddy."

"No problema. I'll just get yours when I look for mine."

After a red-eye flight east, accompanied by her mother, Trish slipped back into all the ceremony of Kentucky Derby week as if she belonged there. Having been through it all once made the second time around even more fun and exciting. If only she were riding one of her own horses rather than a colt for Adam Finley.

Red was riding for BlueMist.

With whirlwind speed, the weekend disappeared in a puff. Trish, on a filly for BlueMist, took a place in the Oaks, the filly race on Friday. She won with a mount for Adam earlier in the day.

"So, you think you can beat me?" Red rode beside her in the early morning mist at Churchill Downs. They were both walking their Derby entries to loosen them up.

"Of course. I did it once; I can do it again."

"Nothing like confidence. Just think, another month and you'll be graduating."

"I'll be free. I can't wait."

That afternoon they gave each other the thumbs-up sign when their horses were filing into the starting gates. Trish stroked Sunday Delight's dark neck. While the BlueMist colt was considered the favorite, you never knew what would happen on the track. At least the sun was shining, not a downpour like the year before.

Trish jerked her thoughts back to the present. The handlers had just gated the last of the fourteen entries. Her position as number three was ideal. Red had drawn number twelve.

At the shot, the gates flew open.

Trish held her horse firm when he bobbled in the first steps. Adam had told her to hold him back, a few lengths off the pace, so he could handle the mile and a quarter. Coming out of the first turn, she and two others seemed to have the same idea. Two ran neck and neck about three lengths ahead.

Sunday ran easily, ears flicking forward and back, listening to Trish sing him around the track. Going into the turn, a rider came up on the inside and bore down on the leaders. The pace quickened. Out of the turn and into the stretch. The tall white posts with golden knobs gleamed ahead.

Trish loosened her reins. With a surge, Sunday drove for the leaders. On the outside, the horse they'd been pacing, BlueMist's Rival, kept his place. Past the three who were slowing, having run themselves out too early, and down for the wire.

The horse beside her lengthened his stride. Trish went to the whip— one crack, as Adam had instructed her. Nose to nose. Whisker to whisker. "Come on, fella." Trish sang her song. Under the line—a photo finish. Had Red's horse stretched his nose out farther—been one step ahead— or had hers?

"Good race." Red raised his whip and touched the visor of his helmet.

"You too." Trish brought her mount back down to a canter and then a trot. Winning the Kentucky Derby two years in a row would be another kind of record, let alone being a woman winning it twice.

"We have the results." The announcer's voice sent a hush over the crowd. "And the winner of this year's Kentucky Derby is BlueMist's Rival, ridden by Red Holloran and . . ."

Trish could barely hear the rest over the screams of the crowd, but it didn't matter. She blew Red a kiss and walked the colt over to where Adam and José waited for her.

"Nothing to be sorry about," Adam said before she could apologize. "I've never had one that close before, so this feels mighty good. Maybe you'll take him at the Preakness."

Trish leaped to the ground. "Thanks for asking me to ride for you. It sure feels good to be here."

"There's lots more to come, lass. Now that you're finished for the year in Portland, bring your horses south and we'll keep you busy."

Trish watched the award ceremonies with a lump in her throat. That was Red up there, and if it couldn't be her, he was certainly her next choice. The Shipsons looked like waving royalty.

By the time Trish said good-bye to Spitfire and Firefly and got on her plane the next morning, having spent the night celebrating with her friends, she was ready for the time-and-space warp back to Portland.

"You think we should leave Firefly there after all?" Marge asked after they had changed planes in Chicago.

"She sure looks good—hardly a limp at all—but when I asked about racing her again, Donald shook his head. He thinks she'll be ready for breeding next winter. Now we have to decide on what stallion."

"Patrick's been mulling that around. So we leave her there?"

"Guess so." Trish settled in for a sleep. "Tell them I don't want any food."

Rhonda had found one dress but not the other. "Don't worry. I said I'd take care of it and I will. Your personal shopper will not fail you."

Trish held the bodice of the glimmery gold dress up to her chest and swirled the black bouffant skirt. "Is this really me?"

"You can't wear racing silks every day, you know." Rhonda gathered Trish's hair on top of her head. "A few curls, some extra makeup, and you'll be a knockout. Doug Ramstead will positively drool when he sees you."

"You sure?" Trish felt a thrill of excitement in her middle. This reminded her of their day shopping in California. Maybe this dance would be fun after all.

The next day Marge showed Trish an article in the paper. Kendall Highstreet had tried to commit suicide. "Pray for him." Marge shook her head. "I wondered about him that day we saw him in court. Now that he's facing prison, he must feel he has nothing left."

"I will."

On Wednesday, Taylor called. "Hope you're looking forward to Friday as much as I am. I decided to rent a dinner jacket. How about that?"

Trish felt her heart ricochet off her ribs. And she didn't even have a dress yet. Could she wear the prom dress for both dates? Wasn't it too dressy for dinner? Why had she ever agreed to go out the night before anyway? Falling off a horse was easier any time. At least she'd been trained how to do that.

Trish heard the Corvette enter the driveway at the same moment Caesar started barking. His welcome woofs deepened to a warning.

Trish called the dog inside and scolded him, but let him out the sliding-glass door when Taylor knocked on the front door.

"Wow! Look at you." Taylor handed Trish a box with three perfect creamy rosebuds in a corsage. "You're more beautiful than I even imagined you'd be."

Trish caught her breath at the sight of his dark good looks set off by the white dinner jacket. A red tie made his smile sparkle even more than usual. "Wow, yourself." Her voice squeaked. "See you later, Mom." Trish turned so Taylor could drape her cape around her shoulders. She ran a hand down the side of her black velvet sheath. If this was what a million dollars felt like, she'd dress up more often.

She slipped her hand in Taylor's proffered arm on their walk to the car.

"That blasted dog." Taylor's tone said more than his words.

"What?" Trish followed his gaze. "Taylor, for goodness' sake, he just peed on your tire. All male dogs do that. It washes right off."

Taylor closed the door for her and stomped around the front end of the car. Although he closed his door gently, it felt as if he had slammed it.

A shiver ran up Trish's arms, setting the fine hairs on end. *What's his problem?* "I'll wash it off when we get home if you like."

Taylor sucked in a deep breath. Trish could see him order his face to smile, and then he turned to her. "That's okay. I overreacted. Sorry."

"Sure." But Trish still wondered: his hands were shaking.

The Top of the Towers restaurant lived up to all the rumors Trish had heard. The piano playing through dinner, their table next to the huge floor-to-ceiling windows, Portland in her nighttime finery spread out at their feet, candlelight that deepened the dimple in Taylor's cheek. He did know how to make her feel special, that's for sure. Trish wiped her mouth with her napkin and laid the snowy square in her lap.

She looked up to catch Taylor staring at her, his eyes flat and vacant.

She looked away, shivering as if an icy draft had kissed the nape of her neck. What was wrong? But when she looked back, Taylor smiled, his eyes lit again with the warm look that thrilled her. *Silly*, she scolded herself. *It must have been the light.*

"May I have this dance?" Taylor took her hand. "Or would you rather have dessert first?"

Trish looked up to where several couples swayed to the dreamy music.

Their waiter stopped at the table with a tray of goodies, most of which Trish had never seen before. "Can I tempt you with one of these tonight?" He went on to list them all, half of them made of chocolate in one delicious form or another.

Trish pointed to one called Chocolate Decadence. "I'll take that one. Even the name sounds tempting."

"What are you going to do this summer?" she asked when the silence seemed to stretch.

"Oh, probably work for my father again. He and my uncle—"

The waiter interrupted him by placing their desserts in front of them.

When Trish looked up after sampling her wedge of sinfully rich dessert, his eyes had that strange look again. She glanced at her watch. Ten-thirty. Where had the time gone?

"Taylor, I had no idea it was so late. I have to be at the track at five-thirty." She took another bite of her dessert. It was so rich it made her teeth ache. "I'm so stuffed I can't eat another bite."

Taylor pushed his plate away, his dessert only half-eaten. He waved for their check and, as soon as it came, stuffed some bills into the dark leather folder. "Shall we go, then?"

"I—I'm sorry." Trish suddenly felt like a little kid being reprimanded by an adult. It was his voice that did it. They walked out to the parking garage and waited for the valet to bring the Corvette around. Neither spoke a word.

"Thank you for a wonderful dinner." Trish leaned back against the cushy seat while Taylor navigated the streets of downtown Portland.

He didn't answer.

Trish looked at his profile, lit by the array of colors from the dash panel. A muscle jumped in his cheek. Was he so mad he was clenching his jaw? What had she done to make this happen?

They crossed the towering Fremont Bridge over the Willamette River and roared onto I-5. Trish couldn't see the speedometer, but she knew he was driving way over the speed limit.

"Taylor, is something wrong?"

He shot her a look that made her skin crawl. With one finger, he flipped the electric door locks.

Where had her charming dinner companion disappeared to?

Trish bit the inside of her cheek. The commercial "Never let 'em see you sweat" jangled through her mind.

After crossing the I-5 bridge over the Columbia River, Taylor turned left into Vancouver instead of right onto Highway 14 heading home.

"Where are we going?"

"You thought you'd get away with it, didn't you?" Venom dripped from his tone.

Trish closed her eyes. *What is going on?*

Chapter
15

"What in the world are you talking about?" Her heart thundered in her ears. "Where are we going?"

"You don't need to worry. You won't be coming back."

God, help! Trish felt the bitter taste of panic coat her tongue. "Taylor!" Her voice squeaked. *Never let 'em see you sweat. What a crazy thing—crazy, that's right. Taylor's gone round the bend. God, how do I deal with a crazy man?*

Knock it off, Trish ordered her mind. *Calm down. You can't think in a panic.* "Taylor?" Good, her voice sounded somewhere around normal. "This isn't making any sense. You're joking, right?"

"No joke, Miss Perfect. You remember Kendall Highstreet? The man you ruined?"

"I did n—"

He slammed his hand against the steering wheel. "You did!" The words cracked like a rifle shot. "You destroyed him, and he's my uncle. I swore I'd get you for it and now I am."

"Taylor, he's the one who—"

"You! You did it. If you'd have left well enough alone—now his life is over. No wife, no kids, no money, no business, and he's in jail. For two years."

Each word pounded into her as if he were hitting her instead of the steering wheel. The Corvette lurched to the side. Taylor put both hands back on the wheel.

"Taylor, I didn't mean—"

"Yes, you did." The words ricocheted off the windows of the speeding car.

Don't make him madder, her nagger whispered gently in her ear. *Be calm. You can calm him down.* Words came back to her from a PE class they'd had on self-protection. *Talk gently. Agree with him. But keep him talking.*

"I'm sorry your uncle is in such trouble."

"It's all your fault." Taylor turned and smiled at her, a grimace so full of hate that Trish shivered and wished she could melt into the seat. "But I'm taking care of you. When I'm finished, you won't hurt anyone ever again."

"You—you must love your uncle very much."

"I was going to wait till after the prom, but when you decided to go with that baby Doug, I had to find another time. You almost wrecked my plans." His voice rose again. "Like you wrecked my uncle."

The Corvette swerved on the curving river road. "You'll just disappear. Maybe someday your body will be found in the river by a fisherman. Wouldn't that be nice?"

Nice? Nice! Trish stifled the urge to laugh. If she started, she might never stop. *God, where are you?*

"You know when your stupid dog got so sick?"

Trish gasped. "You? It was poison."

"Right you are. He should have died, but I only wanted to scare you some more."

"The letters? Flowers?"

"And the phone calls. It was all so easy." His face in the shadow looked like an evil mask. "And you didn't have time for me—hah!"

The headlights cut the darkness, lighting first the trees on her side of the road, and then the grass bank between them and the river on the other. If he didn't slow down, they might both end up in the drink.

The thought of the dark waters closing over the car sent Trish into another burst of panic. Her hand crept to the door handle. But she couldn't jump out at this speed. She'd get killed in the fall.

The car lurched again and so did her stomach. Trish felt a sheet of warmth drive the icy fear away. It was as if her mind suddenly tuned to laser-beam frequency. The dashboard, each tree—everything stood out in perfect clarity, as if lit by a super spotlight.

The smell of sweat filled her nostrils, not her own but that of the man beside her. Dank and heavy. She raised her hand to her nose to shield it. Her light perfume, smelling of apple blossoms, filled her senses. A song filtered through the fragrance of spring. . . . *I will raise you up on eagle's wings, bear you on the breath of God.* . . . Her song. Her verses. . . . *Hold you in the palm of His hand.*

The car lurched again.

"Taylor, please slow down. I'm going to be sick," she pleaded, both hands over her mouth.

"No, you can't be. Don't you dare throw up! Not in my car." Taylor hit the brakes.

Trish flipped the lock on the door with one hand. She gagged into the other. She slipped her high heels off, ready to run.

The car slid from side to side, tires screeching like an animal in agony.

Trish made a retching sound. She leaned forward, pretending she was about to heave all over his leather interior.

Taylor swore, each word more vicious than the last. The Corvette skidded toward a stop.

Before the complete stop, Trish unsnapped her seat belt and threw the door open. With a mighty heave she rolled out, tight in a ball so he couldn't grab her. One bounce on the pavement and she rolled to her knees. Like a distance runner exploding from the marks, she was on her feet and running. Down the asphalt. Back the way they'd come.

She could hear the car behind her, engine roaring, tires screaming, as Taylor turned the Corvette around. The horn blared.

Trish threw a look over her shoulder. He'd turned. He was coming after her. Trish dove for the edge of the road. The rush of air from the fender, the heat of the engine, told her how close he'd come.

Trish rolled again. All her years of training in how to fall stood her guard.

The taillights of the Corvette fishtailed in the dark. Headlights cut out across the river and back around.

Behind her—a canal filled with water. Across the road—the river . . . and a steep bank with trees to hide in before the river itself. Trish ran through the alternatives while the car turned. Could she make it across the road? How deep was the waterway behind her? Crushed rock bit into the bottoms of her feet.

Above the thundering of her heart she heard a new sound. Police sirens wailing in the distance.

The Corvette roared toward her again. Too late to cross the road. The car hit the gravel on the shoulder and screeched to a stop.

Trish thought she heard "I've got a gun" from Taylor, but she wasn't sure. She swung around and hit the canal in a racing dive.

When she surfaced, red and blue flashing lights turned the scene into a carnival.

"Trish! Trish!" Amy's voice rose to a scream.

"I'm here." Trish tried to find the bottom with her feet, and when she couldn't, she swam to the bank. Feet down, she stood, water streaming down her body. Her teeth had already begun to chatter. A flashlight beam struck her full in the face.

Trish threw up her hand to protect her eyes.

"Are you all right?" Officer Parks' deep voice had never sounded so welcome.

"I'm fine." Her teeth clacked together again. The breeze sent a shiver clear through her.

Amy and Parks reached her at the same moment. He wrapped his jacket around her, turning the action into a hug.

"Did he hurt you?" Amy wrapped her arm around Trish's other side.

"N-n-no." Trish could hardly talk around her chattering teeth.

"Can you walk?" Parks' voice felt as warm as his jacket.

"I—I left my shoes in the car." Trish could feel the sting of her bleeding feet.

Parks swung her up in his arms and carried her to the squad car.

"Get a blanket out of the trunk." He set her on the seat and crouched in front of her. "Thank God you're all right."

"Wh-where's T-Taylor?"

"He took off. They'll catch him."

"H-how'd you find us?" Trish let Amy wrap the blanket around her. Now that everything was all right, her mind seemed to go into reverse.

"The cellular phone in his car. It has a device that lets the area cell know his location. We tracked you by coordinates using that system."

"How'd you get him to stop?" Amy asked, her hand on Trish's knee.

"Said I was going to throw up. He has a thing about his new car."

Amy's laughter pealed forth like joyful church bells. Parks started to chuckle and Trish, never one to be left out, joined in.

"Throw up on his fancy upholstery—what an idea!" Amy could hardly talk for laughing.

On the way back to Vancouver, Trish thought to ask, "But how did you know to look for us?"

"Your mother called. Kendall Highstreet called her."

"Highstreet called my mom?"

"That's right. Seems Taylor bragged to him about how he was going to get even with you." Amy, sitting in the backseat with Trish, tucked the blanket more securely around the shivering girl.

"Highstreet called my mom?" Trish felt like a parrot.

"You know all the praying you've been doing?" Trish nodded at Amy's question. "Well, it worked. Highstreet, being brought low—"

"Very low," Parks added.

"Decided to turn his life around—you know, like ask Jesus in—and when he realized what Taylor was planning, he just couldn't let that happen."

"So he called your mother, who called us, who called the restaurant, and you'd already left," explained Officer Parks.

"I'm glad you came."

"Seems like you had things pretty well under control."

"That water is awful cold." Trish could feel the warmth of the blanket, Amy's arm around her, and the full-blast heater doing its work. The shivers only ran up her muscles now, instead of shaking her entire body.

"All I can say is 'Thank you, heavenly Father.' " Amy hugged Trish again. "And thank you, my friend, for leading me to Him."

By the time they arrived at Runnin' On Farm, they'd heard from headquarters that Taylor had been arrested. He'd wrapped his Corvette around a tree in the high-speed chase, and though he was injured, it wasn't life threatening. His car was totaled.

"Guess there's some justice in this world after all," Trish mumbled as she tried to disentangle her blankets.

"You wait. I'll carry you," Parks ordered. "Silly kid. You should have gone to emergency for a once-over."

"Mom can bandage my feet. Besides, they only sting now."

By the time she was bathed, bandaged, and tucked into bed, Trish could hardly keep her eyes open—until she saw the prom dress hanging on the closet door.

"How am I gonna be able to dance tonight?" she wailed.

"We'll worry about that tomorrow—or rather, later." Marge hugged her daughter one more time and whispered their old words, "God loves you and so do I."

Trish nodded. "Me too." Her eyes fluttered open. "Tell Amy and Parks thanks for me." A pause. A whisper this time. "And please call my agent. I don't think I'll make it to the track this afternoon."

"You're right, you won't. I'll call."

Trish, in a crimson robe and mortarboard with a gold tassel, stood with her partner in the line. The band struck up "Pomp and Circumstance," and the march into the Prairie High gym began. Graduation night.

Trish turned and waved at Rhonda, two couples behind Doug. Both of them waved back. Doug winked and gave her the round-fingered seal of approval.

Trish looked forward again. She and Doug had had fun at the prom after all, even though her feet were too sore to dance. She couldn't even wear the sexy heels Rhonda had bought to go with the dress, so she wore some sandals and limped a lot.

Her turn came. She and her partner each started out with their left foot as they were supposed to. The line paraded forward and she turned into the row of seats saved for them.

She kept her mind on the program only through sheer willpower. Her brain kept wanting to play back the last few weeks. Taylor had been released from the hospital into custody at the county jail. His father had refused to pay his bail and his uncle had no money left, so Taylor awaited arraignment.

Trish had learned more legal terms than she needed for a lifetime. The funny thing was, she could even pray for Taylor. She felt a grin tug at the corners of her mouth. Her song had sure helped—eagle's wings. She could use some right now. Without God's help, that night would surely have turned out differently. A shudder ran up her spine.

The speeches done, the principal began calling names. One by one, all the seniors took their turn up the steps, shook hands with the principal, Mr. Patterson, crossed the flower-decorated stage, took their diploma, shook hands with the superintendent, smiled for the camera, started down the steps, and at the bottom flipped their tassel to the other side.

She could do that. They were on the Ds now.

Dry mouth attacked her. What if she stumbled?

Their row stood and walked in a line to the side of the stage. The person in front of her moved forward one step. Trish turned to look at the audience in the bleachers. Her rooting section included David, her mom, Brad, and Patrick. Four tickets—that's all they'd been allowed. If only her father were here to see her. Trish bit her lip against the *if only*'s. Her father *was* here. He wouldn't miss it.

"Tricia Marie Evanston." Head high, Trish took in a deep breath. She mounted the steps, shook hands and smiled at Mr. Patterson, and crossed the stage.

"Congratulations, Trish." The superintendent handed her the crimson folder.

"Thank you." She smiled at the camera, stepped forward, and down the stairs. *My own winner's circle.* She clenched her fist and gave a triumphant pump at her side. Then head held high, she flipped the gold tassel to the other side.

She felt like dancing. Shouting. "Look out world! Here I come!" The ovation echoed off the rafters.